One Hell of a Year

Beverley White

authorHOUSE®

AuthorHouse™ UK Ltd.
500 Avebury Boulevard
Central Milton Keynes, MK9 2BE
www.authorhouse.co.uk
Phone: 08001974150

First published by AuthorHouse 10/28/2009

ISBN: 978-1-4490-3469-6 (sc)

This book is printed on acid-free paper.

"Wake up woman!"

If you had seen me that is what you would have screamed too. The blur of the last few days had made my mind swirl. The confusion, making me dizzy. The pain, unimaginable. The heartache, making me feel sick. The truth, being ignored.

I stood staring out of the window. I couldn't sleep. I had tried but had just laid there uncomfortably. Tears ran down my face making sticky tracks and leaving bright red marks as they went. My eyes were sore and swollen from the last few hours.

I turned and sat on the edge of the bed to face him. I just stared at him. The man I was crying for. My husband. He was sleeping soundly, despite the events of the last few days. He was not troubled. As far as he could see he had done nothing wrong. He was out with a friend, enjoying himself on the night before his 30th birthday and I was blowing this out of proportion. Those words in my head made me cry more. The realisation that it meant nothing to him made the pain worsen.

I didn't know him anymore. This man in front of me. The man I loved had changed. He had become someone else, looking for something different to what I was looking for. A stranger in my bed.

The last two weeks I had spent treading on eggshells, arguing with him as soon as the children had gone to bed, trying to put my point across, you know, make him understand what I was going through. Had it been noted? No. Of course not. I bowed my head with that thought, the sorrow taking me over completely. My shoulders drooped and my limbs hung lifeless.

Facing him again, the tears stopped. Watching him sleep made me want to wake him. I wanted him to be troubled like me. I wanted him to see me in this mess. To talk to me. Reassure me that I was wrong in thinking he had someone else. I pictured myself shaking him awake. What good would that do though? None. He probably would have just told me to go to sleep and stop the drama.

It was hours before I went downstairs. I walked cautiously into the front room, where his presents from his birthday evening were still on the table and the cards stood proudly on the shelf over the fireplace. Tears fell again.

In the pitch black, I sat on the settee staring at the blank television screen. There on it a sequence of pictures seemed to be playing. Showing me what I had hated seeing last night. The two of them walking along the road. The two of them going through the doors to watch the concert. Her in a pink scarf and jeans, him in his black jacket. Those pictures made my face screw up tight as the tears burnt my eyes and then my cheeks. It didn't stop the images playing though, they repeated over and over again. The two of them. The two of them. Laughing and smiling. I hadn't made him smile for a long time.

The voice in my head echoed what he had said to me in the car on the way home this evening, "We met people inside.....she is a friend.....I really like her......you have to accept this or we have a big problem."

A big problem was an understatement. She was Sue. She was his work colleague. She had been out with him the other night. She was *amazing* according to him. She had been mentioned so many times in his conversations, merely saying her name lit up his face. She had been on my mind for the past few weeks. She had haunted me terribly for the last few days.

It was like watching history repeat itself. The history with Tess.

Tess had been his work colleague in his previous job three years ago. She had been as "wonderful" as Sue was right now. Tess and my husband had exchanged flirtatious emails and text messages. Tess knew the ins and outs of our marriage and how unhappy he was which had been something I had not known. Tess had helped him break my heart three years ago.

Sue was not like that though. I met her at Christmas last year. She was young, pretty and full of life. So easy to talk to. Sweet Scottish accent. Laughed and smiled lots which made her eyes sparkle. She would not do what Tess had done. Would she?

I soon realised I was talking myself round again. I knew that it was irrelevant what she was like. I had to see it as what he was like. Him upstairs. Sleeping in my bed. The real criminal in all this. The person that had hurt me again.

I went back upstairs and looked into each of the children's rooms in turn. The three of them curled up in their beds, tight under the covers, breathing deeply, oblivious to the pain and heartache that was to come. I felt guilt wash over me. I could never do something to hurt them. I have to accept this like he said. I have to ignore my thoughts and feelings and believe him. I have to trust him in this. There is no affair - I am being stupid as he said. He has no feelings for her - they are a figment of my imagination. I have to keep plodding on. She will go away soon. He will get bored and come back to me again. He doesn't want the single free life. He will see sense. He will look at me and the children and everything will be fine.

I climbed back into bed beside my husband. The man I was in love with. The man I took care of. The man that was my whole life. I smiled as he turned over in his sleep to face me. He was right, wasn't he? I have to trust him, right? I have to ignore these nagging feelings and my intuition that is telling me something is going on and close my eyes to it. I have created this mess in my head. I have changed and become obsessed with him leaving me. I need to stop it now.

The thoughts continued swirling round inside my head for what seemed like hours. I stroked his face and kissed his forehead. I lay in the same position, still, watching him sleep,

until I gave in and let the tiredness sweep over me. As I let sleep engulf me, I knew life was going to change.

Look at yourself.

I threw him out. I sat there and made the conscious decision to throw out the man I love. The man I need. But is that just what I think rather than what is real.

I could see myself, you know. Sitting at the computer staring at an email he had sent his female friend, Sue, thinking I can't handle this. I can't accept his friendship with her and I could see myself crying. I could see this pathetic woman that I had become and I hated her. I hated her for being so weak. I hated her for being so hurt by him. I hated her for not hating him. Most of all I hated her for loving him. He used to be everything I needed and everything my life revolved round.

I'm sure he has not done this on purpose. Maybe it's just living with a pathetic, dependent person that was the problem. *When did I become this?* This is not who I really am.

Oh my god, what happened today?

I found the email this afternoon. They were going out again tonight. Yes there was a group of them. There were only two tickets in that envelope for Monday night, but I had bought the 4 tickets for this gig for his birthday. And he had given one to *her*. Reading that email made the realisation that he didn't care what I'm feeling so real, the pain shooting across my chest, making it hard to breathe.

"How stupid are you?" my mum had said. She had a point I suppose. I could see what was going on. It was so obvious. But, I couldn't face this though, not again. He said they are friends. I needed to believe him.

I sat in the chair in the conservatory with my mum and his mum holding my hands while I cried. They were talking to each other about my marriage and my husband and yet I couldn't hear a word they were saying. It was muffled. I wasn't really there.

I just cried.

"Marcus only thinks of Marcus"

"He needs to know how bad you are feeling"

"Pack his bags"

I heard those sentences alright.

I nodded pathetically and then just cried. I remember the hugs and the cups of tea and the pitiful smiles. I remember Pheobe wanting me. She didn't know why her mum was so upset. She cried with me.

I heard his voice on the telephone.

"I can't take this anymore. I can't handle this. I don't know what else to do. Your clothes will be at your mums," I squeaked.

Nothing. Silence on the phone. No apologies. No promises to sort it out. No ideas of coming home. Nothing! Nothing! 14 years together and I get nothing!

The wave of pain hit me again as I hung up. I curled up in the chair trying to squeeze the pain away. Trying to justify my actions to myself. Telling myself I was doing the right thing. The tears streamed down my face. When will they stop?

I straightened myself out. I drank tea and talked to my mum. I sat curled up on the settee, feeling lost. I waited for him to come through the door and hold me telling me it was ok. I waited for the phone to ring. I waited to hear his voice again. Nothing.

Upstairs I joined my mum who was now packing his bags. Watching her fold his clothes and place them in the bag, I felt like a child who was losing her favourite toy. I was in my own little world. Not settling in one place. Not sitting down. The wave of pain that had become so familiar to me these days washed over me again. The nausea followed.

Then I was alone. I held the phone in my hand and sank into my settee. I brought my knees to my chest and lowered my head between them, feeling my trousers getting wet with tears even though I was unaware I was crying. I waited, staring at the phone. Call me I pleaded.

The silence was eerie. Only the sound of the kitchen clock ticking in the background. The emptiness of the house so apparent. The lost feeling once again.

He will come home. Just like he had done when I kicked him out over Tess. He will walk through that door any second. He won't go out with her. He will come home to sort it out. He loves me. He will be here.

He never came.

The next couple of days were exactly the same. The school run, the cuddles with the children. The silence and emptiness engulfing the days and the darkness even when it was sunny. The memories of our life together and the pictures of him and her mixing together in my head. I had to be stronger. I had to test him and see if I was right.

I spent the hours just sitting in his study. His jacket hung on the side wall where he had always left it. The computer stayed off. It was quiet.

Mum fixed dinner in the kitchen each night. She was looking after me. She was here helping. Why did I need help? I had been doing everything by myself for months now. He was hardly ever here and when he was he sat in the study. He never helped, never even sat with us. And yet, there was still the empty space next to me. There was still the gap, the hole where he had sat and dictated my television programmes for the night. Where he had talked to me about his day in the office. Where he had mentioned her name so many times. The tears kept falling. I couldn't eat. I couldn't sleep. The hours blurred into one long one.

My body numb, I plodded on. Things have to get done. There are plenty of things to occupy me. Life has to go on.

Saturday 31ˢᵗ March

Big interview today. Well, training day. Marking English tests for year 5. I was so scared it was unreal. Did not want to be there as you can imagine. It was so hard. My mind kept trailing and I was always awarding 1 mark too less, I must be a hard marker. Some laughs though and a huge sense of achievement when I walked out that door. Got in the car and picked up the phone and realised that I didn't have Marc to share it with. I couldn't phone him. *Would he have wanted me to?* Its always been him I shared everything with. *Would he have been proud?*

It was like there was a huge gap. Something missing and my heart sank. I'd heard that expression before but that was the first time I had really felt it. I miss him.

He came round after the interview. There we stood in the kitchen. We argued a little and the tension was fierce. I stared at him while he was talking. Just listening. All I was thinking was: how are these words coming out of his mouth? How can he be saying this to me?

"I think we have made the right decision."

We....decision....what decision?

"This is what we needed. A temporary split. A few weeks break. "

Split? What? Really? That's not what I need.

"We haven't been happy for ages."

Haven't we? Perhaps not. I didn't know anymore. So confused.

I sat on the kitchen bench swinging my legs like a child that was being told off. That was exactly me at the moment. Reduced to the feelings of a child. Not understanding, not knowing what was going on and trying to discover the reasons why I was in trouble.

I watched him as he paced the floor and talked to me. My eyes wide and staring sadly, the tears silently falling. He placed his hands on my thighs, moving his thumbs gently up and down as if that would soothe me in some way. He looked into my eyes,

"You understand, don't you?"

I shook my head pathetically. I didn't understand no. No.

Was he saying he needed something else? Was he saying that I hadn't loved him enough? Was he saying I wasn't enough for him anymore? Was he saying that our whole marriage had fallen apart because he did not get enough sex? Was he saying that because I had not slept with him as often as he wanted I was the one who had wrecked our marriage? Was he saying this was entirely my fault?

When he speaks it is like he is telling me rather than explaining. I listened, taking everything in. I reached the conclusion that to agree with him was the easier option. The better option. He was right and I was wrong. That's how well he can twist your mind, making you believe what he is saying is the truth. It is my fault, I could hear myself saying. This is all my fault.

He left and the house returned to the dark emptiness. The night engulfed each room except where the moon shone through the conservatory roof. I still sat on the kitchen bench, staring out of the window. Tears slowly streamed down my cheeks. I could feel my legs shaking and my heart racing.

I had just been told what an unloving wife I was and it was all true. I should have showed how much I loved him. I should have told him. I should have spoilt him. If I had done all of those things he said I hadn't done, then this woman would not have come along and stole him from me.

But that's not true either according to him. There is nothing going on. There is no relationship. She is just a friend and she means nothing to him.

Those words had been said before though. Tess had been nothing but a friend, Tess had meant nothing to him either. There was no affair there either. Was I wrong a second time? Was I wrong the first time? After Tess he had said he loved me. He had promised my Grandad as he lay dying in the hospice that he would look after me, care for me and that we would get through the mess. My Grandad would be looking down on him now frowning. My Grandad would have told me to fight for him and forgive him because he was just a man. That's what he had told me the first time. He was just a man. And men needed forgiving for their stupid mistakes. That they needed guidance.

My thoughts then turned to my Nan. She would not have agreed and they were probably arguing right now. She would have said to punish him and to move on and find happiness. Had I been truly happy?

On the realisation that I was straying from the life that I had right now and dwelling on the past, I climbed down from my seat. I had achieved something today that I needed to be proud of. I lit a cigarette and stood by the sink. It was then that I realised I was still crying. There was no sound coming from anywhere in this house except the occasional sniffing from me.

Then it was like I was no longer there. My mind drifted and I stood still. Motionless and hardly breathing. Taking in the silent emptiness.

All of a sudden I could see the pathetic outline of a woman I hated. I could see her tear stained cheeks glowing in the darkness that surrounded her and the throbbing of her chest as her heart lay broken underneath. I could feel her rejected soul clambering for air as it was being suffocated by the misery. The soul that was left damaged and cold by the man that she had loved after he had stripped her of the self that she had once been. The feisty, independent girl that had thrown tantrums and wrapped him round her finger to get her own way. The one that had stood up to him in the beginning. The one that had always been in control, had become so weak. So worthless. So unwanted. So alone.

The image before me was me. The person I was seeing was me. The person I hated was me. The air rattled as I gasped for breath as if I had been held under water. My lungs ached from the acceleration of cold air that hit them and I fell to the floor. I sat, huddled up in a ball and sobbed. Loud, childlike sobs of pure agony as every inch of my body was rendered helpless.

Were you really happy?

Sunday 1st April 2007

So here I am. A single mum. Life can be quite scary.

It's hard to see the positive things in life when you feel so low.

Marc's feelings were not the same though I don't know quite what that means. He does not say exactly. I knew something was wrong. That feeling when you look at them and there seems to be nothing. They don't look back, they don't hear what you are saying really though they nod and humph in agreement without looking up from what they are doing. You just know.

They say the heart or the head rules all of your feelings. The problem comes when they don't agree with a solution.

I threw him out. I was the one who ended it. That responsibility is just too much. *What if I had held on a little longer? What if I closed my eyes and kept going for a little longer? What if... what if... what if? How the hell does that help?*

Dwelling on it. Marcus said that maybe we were in love with the people we used to be and not the ones we have become. Sounds plausible. Perhaps we were holding on. Perhaps we held on too long.

Looking back over the last few years I could see the faults in my marriage. I could see the lack of contentment and happiness that had made us change. The slow demise of love and trust that had severed our closeness.

I could not cope with the Tess situation. That was the beginning of the unhappiness I was sure. The true unhappiness anyway.

I can still remember the day, three years ago now, when I found the messages between him and Tess. Something from her about the love tokens she had given him. A message from him asking for a picture of her in the shower. There were so many on that phone. I had placed it back down behind the settee where I had found it. I had covered it back up too as if that would shield it from me, out of sight and out of mind. I had tried to ignore it. I didn't know what to do or what to think. It had hurt so much.

That night I had sat there staring at the wall when the children had gone to bed. Marcus had been abroad for two weeks with his new job and he wasn't there to talk to. Over that fortnight I read the messages over and over again. I hadn't cried. I switched off from emotion and decided I needed more proof. For the next eight months I followed his every move, I discovered his password to his email account and collected all the emails between them. I searched his phone when I could and I hid away from everything and ignored everybody telling me to confront him. I couldn't. I didn't want to hear it. I didn't want to hear him say he was going to leave me.

Eventually I had showed him the messages. I had printed them all out and handed them to him. He cried and said he was sorry. There was nothing in it. It was just plain flirting, over the top flirting. Someone was paying him attention when I didn't have the time for him. I had listened to it all and just cried and cried for the eight months I had suffered.

I had not really talked to him about the feelings I had. About how much the pain had eaten me away. About how when I looked at him it was different. About how the trust had been severed and I needed more from him. About how hearing that name, Tess, made the tears burn at my eyes. About how I read the messages over and over again. About how I had waited for him to prove he was happy with me and had not needed anyone else. I just didn't tell him, I couldn't put it all into words; I couldn't begin to describe the sorrow.

I knew I was a difficult person to live with - but then everybody is really. I had not been able to accept that the fling with Tess had been down to him and his failings. I had blamed myself. I had questioned what I had done wrong and how I had deserved it. I had had two children within two years and had neglected him. How could I have done that?

A father was supposed to feel the same though wasn't they? They were supposed to feel that overwhelming rush of love and place their children above anything else that was in their life prior to them. They were supposed to rush in from work to see their children and relieve their wives. Marcus had never done that. He had never done even the simple, basic things. He had never put Pheobe to bed and she was almost 4 now. He had not helped out when Fiona woke up not being able to breathe because her asthma was bad. He had never held Pheobe while she screamed all night and then all day. He had never done the sleepless nights, seldom given me a lay in at the weekends. Always needed them for himself. He was the one working - not me.

The doorbell rang. Within seconds the thinking had stopped, the sorrow dispersed a little and the silence was gone. My babies hugged me as if they had not seen me in weeks. They chatted about what they had done with Daddy and Nanny. They told me everything in such speed it made my mind rattle. My mood lifted and I felt happier. It was my babies that made me happy. Not him.

I watched them play, listening to them laughing and making such a noise. They had not asked why they had been away for the weekend. They did not ask why Daddy had left them again. They were not questioning my tear stained cheeks and my faint smile. They were happy to be home. Happy to be with me. That must mean I am good at being a mum, just like my Grandad had told me so many times before.

The evening blurred into bath time and bedtime and then I was alone again. I watched whatever I wanted on TV. I watched all the programmes that he had hated like I was rebelling against him. It was a good feeling.

I fell into bed really late. I had a sense of attitude hovering within. A sense of 'I can do this, so watch this space.'

I was scared though. Scared of sleeping alone. Scared of tomorrow coming and the pain kicking in. Scared of the moment you wake up and realise that it wasn't a dream. Scared of the dark and its ability to play images in front of you, the ones you spent all day trying to avoid.

I got out of bed regularly to check on my children. I checked they were breathing, I checked they were sleeping. I watched them protectively. I felt the pride oozing out of me and every now and then, though not too often, I allowed myself to smile.

2nd April 2007

Felt more positive today when I got up but I soon realised that was because he would not have been here anyway. 'Away days' for work. No phone call as yet - it's now 6pm. He is busy at work, with her, too occupied to think of us, though that is probably a mean thing to say. Wandering round the house. The chores seem such a big deal. Occupying the children seems a big deal. Lonely.

Shut myself in the office playing a stupid game for hours on end so I didn't have to face the state of my house or the emptiness. Can hear the children playing and then arguing but all I feel is guilt as I have sent their daddy away.

Who is here now? Who is picking up the pieces? This is just how I felt when my Nan and Granddad died, except Marc was there for me to hold as I grieved. No one is here now. Don't even have a friend who will run to be with me. I know my mum would come but I can't keep her here with me while I sort my life out. Wanted to stay in bed but it was uncomfortable. Everything is uncomfortable. Sitting, eating, walking, thinking, sleeping, talking, listening - all uncomfortable.

Run through things in my head as if I am doubting my decision now. *Why can't I be angry? Why can't I hate him?* He has made so many stupid choices and I have to keep reminding myself of these when I miss him. And I do miss him. I want my husband back - except he isn't my husband anymore. He became somebody I just didn't know.

It is that feeling of rejection that I cannot handle. The rejected soul of mine has returned and taken over for today. Reminding me I just wasn't good enough. The depressed feeling kicked in this afternoon. The sadness took over and the helplessness followed. The positive outlook and the attitude that had showed its face a little last night had become lost in the hours of daylight.

It's funny how my thoughts are always of him on his pedestal where I had placed him. I was seeing him as the best husband in the world and the pain that causes is made worse by the fact that I had lost him. I still hope he comes back. I still wait for him to come back. I keep expecting him to walk back through the door telling me he has made a huge mistake and he wants me back. Telling me he is sorry and doesn't know why he thought we needed a break. That's not happening though. I have to convince myself it will never happen, just in case.

I occupy my mind with all the mundane things I can think of, just so I wouldn't think of him. It doesn't work. I wonder what he is doing now. Who he is with. Why he hasn't called. Why did he not want me? Again my feelings sink to a low. I could feel my eyes burning as I tried to stop the tears. The confusion ate at me. The questions piled up on the unanswered list and I had tried so hard today.

Still 2nd April 2007

Second instalment of today. As the evening draws near when you know he would be coming home from work, loneliness has a way of reminding you. You are not thinking about it in particular but this feeling is there tugging at you waiting for you to sit up and take notice.

He said yesterday that one of his mates at the office party had his fiancée there. She turned up after work and they went off together. Once upon a time he would have done that for me. He would have said to meet him after I sorted the kid's dinner and dropped them at his mums. I would have gone and then we would have had the evening together as a couple. He would have done that once. That realisation hurts like hell. I wonder where he stayed that night - I didn't ask. Too scared of the answer I suppose. One of his new mates. One of the new crowd he hangs about with now. His new girlfriend even. *Does she have him now? Is she Sue?* A person in his new life that doesn't involve me, his wife, the one he left behind.

I had watched the bus that would have brought him home to me pull away from the bus stop opposite our house. I don't know why I tortured myself really but I did. I watched the bus hoping that when it moved he would be standing there waiting to cross the road to home. I felt that tinge of sadness when he was not there.

I had fed the children and put them to bed. That was all I had done all day. I had done a measly amount of housework but the rest of the time I just sat there, holding the phone and waiting.

Now I was alone again. Alone. I hated being alone.

The darkness of the night swept in on me again. The silence surrounded me and it hurt my ears as they strained to hear something. I sat on the settee in the front room. No lights on and the TV off. I curled up in a ball and lay there. I felt so lost. Abandoned. An unwanted puppy left to survive on my own. I hate this feeling. I wish there was a fast forward button on life that you could hit so you do not have to face all the negative crap that life chucks at you. But when would I forward it to? When will I reach the point that these feelings are no more? That I feel happy again. Will I ever be?

I looked at myself from the outside. Would I ever be loved again? By him or any other man? Did I want to be? Who in their right mind would take on a woman with 3 children? What man would be strong enough to cope with a needy, dependent woman who hates herself? Do I really care?

When you have time alone you think about all the events, anniversaries and happy times you have been through and you question it all. If I look deep down inside myself and if I am brutally honest I can say I was not happy. I was not happy with my life. I was not happy with my marriage. I was not happy with the man he had become. I was not happy with the things he did, or the things he said. I was not happy with the father that he was. I was not happy with the lack of support he gave to me. I was not happy with the way he had made me need him so much to live my life. I was not happy with the way he had treated me or the children.

So why the hell am I grieving like this? Why am I crying all the time? Why am I so upset that he has gone? Why am I missing him so much?

Still 2ⁿᵈ April 2007 - the longest day ever.

Sitting here thinking how things have changed. Knowing my ears should be burning. *How is he discussing this with his friends? What is he saying about me? Is he pulling me to pieces or is he blaming himself or both of us?* I will not be able to face his friends again and will definitely never be able to face anyone from his workplace which is lucky I will never have to. Had a friend on the phone offering me advice about what to do when they turn sour. About how to organise a divorce and what benefits are available to me. *Has my life really come to that?* Marc asked "are you worried now - dreading going through that?" I replied I wasn't thinking that we would be doing that yet. He said he saw that as a positive sign. He said he didn't want that, not now or ever. I had smiled then.

I thought about what she had said and how her son has changed and become less confident and unable to see his dad and I wondered what it would be like if Marc went and I never saw him again. If he never turned up to be a dad to his children. And I found myself crying again as if I have not done enough of that already. I seem to be able to cry without realising or thinking I am. It's a shock when you suddenly come back from the daydream and realise you are worse than you were ten minutes before. It's a shock when you come back from the daydream and realise you are still trapped in this life that you don't want but that there is still nowhere left to go. Even your daydreams are places where you cry. It all feels like it's over. Everything is over. My life. Love. Companionship. Comfort. Security. Family. Happiness (what there was of it). Sanity. Normality. Over.

I curled up on his side of the bed. I hugged his pillow. The smell of him still there to taunt me. I opened the drawers beside the bed. Some of his things were still there; though there were more tags from the clothes he had bought and then hidden. I snuggled into the pillow once more. I closed my eyes and I could picture him walking round the bed, banging his knees on the ottoman like he did so often. I could picture him climbing into bed beside me. The heat radiating off him. The smell of his hair gel as he snuggled up to me. I felt the warmth of his breath on my neck as he laid his head on mine and the tugging of his arms as he used to turn me round to kiss me goodnight.

I clung to that pillow all night. I clung to the memories of the bedtime routine as if I knew it would never be that way again. I clung to the thought of him coming home. I clung to the thought of him. I miss him. I want him here with me.

Aaarrgghh! - So angry!

3rd April 2007 5.30pm.

Took the children out today and felt for a little while that this was not what I was going through, that I was a normal person taking out her three children. Then I came home.

Marcus phoned and we spoke ok for a while. There was a difference in his tone as if he is losing patience. He said he did not want any of this. Said it was not in his *plan*. It was hardly mine either. And anyway he started this. He said he was confused, wanted something else from life, wanted the free life with no responsibility. *How did he think I was going to react? Did he think I was just going to forget it was ever said?*

He is out. He still has his life, his friends, and his night down the pub, his ordinary life, his escape from responsibility. I have the other life, the one with the children 24 hours a day. The one with no friends, no nights out, no sanity. The one where you sit and think about everything that is stressful in your life, about the finances, about the kid's schools, about the fact that your life consists of a list of mundane activities and each day repeats itself because nothing ever changes. You think about the things you want to do but can't for one reason or another, about the fact that you are watching your children grow older and then realising you are too and it's all shit. It's so shit and he can't see what my problem is. I don't care about his female friend, I don't care about the freedom he craves. I care about the life I lost and the fact that he has not bothered to include me in his. He has not bothered to keep us special. He has not bothered to care. He has forgotten to need me in his life. He has forgotten to talk to me. He has forgotten who I am and what I am supposed to mean to him. I'm the good little wife who has the children while his life continues down the 'responsibility free' path. *Did he consider me in all this? Did he think of me while he was out? Did he wonder what I was doing? Did he miss me?* No.

I want to go out. I want to escape this hell I am living in. I want to run somewhere where no-one will find me. Somewhere I can be seen as an ordinary woman living an ordinary life. I want to be free. I want to stand in the middle of a large field and scream without being heard. I want to stay in bed all day. I want to change my name, my life, me. I want to smile and laugh and not be dragged down by a sense of guilt. I want to feel as if it is ok to be happy.

God where has this anger with myself come from? When did the frustration kick in?

My emotions are all over the place. I cannot seem to get hold of them and settle them down. I cannot focus on just one of them. They seem mixed in a tangle never to be unwoven. I am up and down like a flaming yo-yo. All I can see at the moment is red. He tells me one thing on the phone and he spouts off about how this was not what he wanted and that it was my decision. For crying out loud. It was not my decision to have you all over her was it. It was not my decision for you to fancy some other woman instead of me. It was not my decision to hear her name mentioned a hundred times in one sentence. God I am so angry I can't settle.

The feelings are keeping me on a bit of a high though. I am wound up like a clockwork toy that keeps going and going, round and round in circles. I am running around the house getting things done like I need to work this anger off. Like I need time to calm down. I feel as if I need to walk out of the house and run wherever my legs take me. Just run to work off the steam that seems to be pouring out of my ears. I am breathing so fast and my heart is racing.

I can still hear his voice and the words he said whirl round and round. He didn't want this - so why not come home?

The split was not his plan - what was then? More flaming questions. All unanswered - again!

I have this urge to do something and yet I cannot place what that something is. My head continues to whirl around making me feel so nauseous I want to throw up. I am on a huge roundabout and there is no way off it. There is no let up of speed and I am being flung around like a rag doll. I need some help to stabilise. I need someone to jump in and stop the rotation that is making me ill. I need someone. Anyone. Please.

Throughout the day the anger comes and goes. It subsides for a while and then rolls back in. I feel in turmoil about everything. My mum has listened to me moan and groan about it all over and over again. She is probably as confused as I am. She is going through this with me. I can feel it. I know she is and I feel bad for making her listen. I have no one else to do this with. She is my rock and without her I would be even worse. But the feeling of guilt is there. She has her life and I am imposing on it.

I look at my children and I pray that no one ever puts them through anything like this. I know I would be there every step of the way for them and that reassures me a little about my feelings towards my mum's involvement.

I laugh at them as they play. That piece of happiness is tinged with the sad feeling that he is missing this. That he no longer wanted this. When we sat in his parents house two weeks before the split, he confessed to me that he could not take the responsibility anymore. He had walked out on me that day. He said that he could not cope with the stress of being the man we were all dependent on. He did not want to do the journey from Essex to London every day. He pushed for the move out of London as much as I did. He wanted to bring the children up with better schooling than London could provide just like me. We only moved here last July and he was already complaining.

I remember him sitting on that bed just repeating the words "I don't know" over and over, no matter what my question was. I got the feeling then that it was the lifestyle of the group of singles that had moved to the London office that appealed to him. He said he had lost his twenties because of having children so young. I understood of course. I had lost out too, but I was not sitting there moaning about it like he was. I was not trying to run. We decided to have these wonderful children and I would not change that decision for the world despite knowing it all had a tremendous effect on our young lives.

I watched them playing, smiling up at me lovingly. It melted my heart and for those few minutes I felt happiness run through me. I wish it would never leave. Their faces lifted my mood and lit up the darkness that was hovering over me, just like they light up my life every day. Their play was so imaginative and innocent - it's hard to imagine myself being like that ever. They skipped and ran with such energy it wore me out watching them. The love I felt for them overwhelmed me and the tears bit at my eyes. A lump formed in my throat and I had to swallow hard and breathe deep to make sure I didn't cry.

I wandered round the house aimlessly. There is no reality to life in some ways. I look for something to do and yet I can't find it. I look for something to occupy me and yet my brain stirs up thoughts of him and her again. There is no escape from these feelings. There is no escape from the swirl of images in my head. There is no escape from the grief of losing someone.

As I continued with the list of mundane activities around the house and watched the children tire out ready for bed, my mood softened a little too much. The depression hovered as if it was stalking me, ready to pounce. I could feel it following me everywhere I went.

I took my time tucking the children into bed. I was avoiding leaving them. The walk down the stairs into the front room after saying goodnight is becoming longer and longer. It's like I don't want to reach the bottom and meet the empty loneliness that awaits me. The darkness is in sight once more and the whole atmosphere of the house changes without the children's voices to brighten it.

I stood at the top of the staircase and looked down, one foot held out in the air trying to step downwards. At the foot of these stairs stand many people with black cloaks and no faces. No feelings, no voices. They are ready to crowd me as I set foot in the room, to smother me as I walk deeper into them. To suffocate any positivity I was feeling and turn me back to the negative, depressive side. To return to black. To return me to the darkness within myself.

Entering the living room I realised that once again, I had allowed them to win. Within seconds I was crying, thinking of my husband and how he is not here.

5th April 2007

Yesterday was a bit of a turning point. The depressive mood lifted for a while and I suddenly felt anger. It was in an instant - no build up, no trigger, just there. I'm not really angry with myself anymore either. It's now all towards him. It's like I can finally see what he has been doing. Everybody else felt like this when I was telling them but to feel it myself was pretty weird. I don't understand why I did not get angry. I would have done before. I was always in control. I wore the trousers and now I see that somehow I allowed him to take over.

I'm getting a bit fed up with his phone calls now to be honest. There are the ones like last night when he phones and says something positive and then there are the ones which just feel as if he is rubbing my face in it. '*Oh, I'm just going out for dinner darling...I'm just down the pub....I'm out with a few friends ...*' Well, lucky you. *Where am I?* Stuck in with the children again for the hundredth night in a row. I know part of it is my fault because I have let myself become stuck in this rut and I haven't built up a circle of friends to go out and about with etc etc. But I have sacrificed all that in order to bring up my babies even if it does piss me off at times. *Does he?* No. *Has he given anything up for them?* No. *Has he lost his life because he is a parent?* No.

I'm going to have to sort this out. He can't have them this weekend because he has nowhere to stay with them. That is great. I'll just wait and care for them full time by myself and he can do what the fuck he wants. I sat with my friend Jemma today. Didn't discuss a great deal but she said she admired me for having the courage to just try and split for a while. It doesn't feel like courage at the moment. It doesn't feel like anything because there is nothing to feel. Losing Marc has made me realise how totally alone I am. I had no one else but him and that surely is not right. It would be easier to just let him come back if he wanted to and plod along with life as we were but my life would just be exactly the same. I'm going to take the holiday next week to think about what action I can take in order to change this. I need to feel like a normal person again. I need to feel as if I have a life outside these four walls. I need to feel like I am not just a mum. It's going to take one hell of an action to change that.

Life has a funny way of making you face up to what you are scared of even if you don't want to. I am scared of being alone. Always have been. Yet here I am not only alone but a mum too. The two of them don't seem to mix. I can't be alone because I have them. The meaning of alone has changed for me. Alone used to mean without anybody - just me. Now it seems to hold a different meaning. Alone, to me, is without a partner. Without someone to live through life with. Without that someone asking you how your day has been. Without that someone to hug you when you have had a rough day. Without that someone to make you feel warm and safe after you have felt so scared and unsure.

There was never anything strong and manly about my husband. A 6 ft tall man who weighed less than his wife. Yet, his love made me feel safe in a way that I needed. I always had faith in his love for me. I thought that no matter what I looked like, no matter what I was, no matter what I did or how I viewed life, he would always love me. When I packed his bags that day, I had enough faith in his love for me to believe that he would come home.

My dreams are filled with him coming back to me. I dream of him holding me. I dream of him telling me he loves me and wants to be a family again. I dream of being husband and wife. I think about all of the things I would do for him when he comes home. I think about how I would spoil him and take care of him. My hours alone are spent dreaming. I sit in the peace and quiet and imagine the happiness I have to come. It usually involves him.

The children are asking questions and I have no answers to them. I do not know why Daddy is not home. I do not know if Daddy is coming back. I listen to them talk between them and it provides an insight into their little minds and how they are working. Pheobe talks about how Daddy is at work in the office and is very busy. Fiona seems less certain. She is too intelligent to believe something so simple. She needs an explanation. They all do. Seb needs to know what has happened. That is one thing I am not doing alone. That is one job he has to do. He has decided to stay away.

He has hurt us all and he needs to explain why. I am intrigued to hear what he will say. I am curious to see how he makes them understand when he has not succeeded to make me understand.

6th April 2007

Today was a hard day. Marcus was late picking the children up. He was supposed to be here in the morning but ended up not arriving until half one, which meant the children were driving me crazy about going to the zoo and were so hyped up that I was worried it was going to be a let down for them.

I watched them skip off across to the entrance and my heart broke because I was not part of that family. Another first in the wake of the split.

The chat after the zoo was quite hard. I made him discuss his feelings rather than him dictating the conversation. He admitted to me that if I asked him to come back now, in a couple of months or even in five years time and he still felt like he does today he wouldn't come back. His feelings towards me have changed. He doesn't love me like he used to. It hurt like hell. It was a mixture of *how dare you say that to me* and *oh my god how could you?* I didn't want to listen to his answer and yet I needed to know. I wanted to throw everything of his and him out onto the street and slam the door and yet I wanted to lock him in so he couldn't leave. I wanted to shake him and scream at him and yet I wanted to beg him to reconsider. I wanted to hit him and hurt him back and yet at the same time, I just wanted to kiss him one last time. *Is this confusion normal in these circumstances?*

It seems so weird. I hear him talking about finding a flat and moving out. About finances and sharing the money and the bills. About his furniture for the flat and where he is going to find the funds for his new life. It was like the words were coming out of his mouth and floating above my head rather than being listened to and taken in. It's like I still can't believe he is saying it. I just sat on the settee staring. He kept asking me what I was thinking but my mind was honestly blank. There was nothing. Every now and then I can hear myself saying I will wake up soon and this bad dream will be over. I will turn over and he will be there next to me and I'll lie in his arms and everything will be ok. *But that's not true is it?*

That's what I need to face.

Talking to my mum and sister, I believe I will sort myself out, although I wish I could skip the next few months or so and fast forward to the bit where everything is working out. I know they will be there helping me out and supporting me and picking up the pieces as I fall apart every now and then. It still does not make it any easier though. It does when you can hear their voices but when you put the phone down, it all goes quiet again. Silence comes back to haunt you and that's when the pain jumps out and crushes you once more - just for the fun of it.

I sat there crying again. He actually said those words.
"I don't love you anymore"
They stopped me breathing. I was not ready for that. I never thought he was going to say that. I had sat here expecting him to come home. I was waiting for him to get his head straight. Waiting for him to figure out what he wanted. I never once thought it would be this.

There must be someone else. There must be another factor in this and she must be Sue. It must be down to her. She has fluttered her eyelashes and moved in on him, ready to take my place. And he has let her. He wants to replace me.

Of course he says this is not the case. He says there is no one else. He says he cannot live without me totally. He says he still needs me in his life and that he wants us to be friends because he cannot be enemies with me. He says in a way he still loves me but not like he should.

"I don't love you anymore"
The words echo all around me.
"I don't love you anymore"
In that split second I felt my heart crumble. I can look back and see the pain on my face. The feeling went from

every part of my body, like it had been sucked out. I managed to stand still and just stared at him. He carried on talking trying to justify what he had said. All I could hear was "I don't love you anymore."

My thoughts turned to her. I thought back to Christmas where she stood in her dress, with that sparkle in her eyes talking to me about him. Not a lot was said between us. But I remembered those few minutes now. She had said how she enjoyed working with him. She had talked about our children. I remember thinking how she seemed like a fun person to be around. I even spoke to Marc about her the day after. I said how it would be nice if we could meet up with some of them as Nancy, one of the other consultant's wives, does. He shrugged.

There was this uneasy feeling about her now. The kind of feeling that causes your stomach to turn over and over. The sickening feeling that maybe, just maybe, she was with him now. This feeling of has she got my husband? I was not sure what to think. I tossed the scene over in my mind trying to force the images into some sort of clarity. I tried to focus on her as I realised that it was pushing my anger to the surface and I was so much stronger when I was angry.

I sat on the bench in the kitchen by the sink and smoked a cigarette out of the window. I opened my bottle of vodka and had two on the trot. Those depressive feelings were back. I could feel their prickly hands all over my skin and the claws digging into my head where they passed on the sad thoughts and the feelings of loneliness. The weight of them tugging me down and making it difficult to move, like my whole body weighed a ton.

The empty house sat around me and I felt lost in it. This no longer felt like my home. It was strange to me and I felt uncomfortable. Again, I wandered round aimlessly. I never know what to do when I feel like this. I never know how to settle. I can't do anything. It becomes so frustrating and I start to lash out at myself. I call myself names and tell myself how stupid I am, how ridiculous I was to believe in him. How pathetic I had become and how I had driven him away.

There she was again. Her pink scarf with my husband beside her. Going to a concert that my money, my overdraft, paid for. Her hair long, her figure small and toned. I beat myself up as I walked round and round not knowing what to do.

I collapsed into the settee and burst into tears so violently, I thought my chest would explode. The pain seared up into me as if it came from the floor and it felt like I was on fire. The tears streamed and the urge to scream became so fierce I had to. I fell onto my side and brought my knees to my chest. The sobs became quieter and I became calmer. I sobbed silently into the cushion, allowing the darkness of the room to swallow me and tiredness ravage my body. I lay motionless, unable to move. I closed my eyes and let sleep take me to a place I never wanted to return from. I prayed I would not awaken.

The hard days are here for good.

8th April 2007

Couldn't write yesterday. Too strange a day. Up and down the whole time wondering how I was feeling. Marc came over and asked too many questions. *Do you regret your decision? Do you feel like we have made the wrong decision? Do you know if this is right for both of us?* The problem is my feelings are kind of irrelevant now as he said he didn't love me anymore. He said those awful, heartbreaking words and my world as I know it fell apart. *Does he really think that I can sit and discuss the right or wrong in this now?* It doesn't matter to me anymore.

Today is another horrible day. I'm shattered from lack of sleep as my children don't seem to need any. I'm worn out from all the stress and my body is close to collapse because I haven't managed to eat in days. Feel sick constantly and my head feels as if it is too heavy for my shoulders to carry. I always knew today would be hard. Fourteen years today. I met him and wandered round the park holding his hand and feeling pleased that I had found him before any other girl. If you told me then he would tear me apart I would have laughed for I was much stronger then. More independent and backed away from emotions and feelings. I would never have pictured myself being this dependent woman. Being so wrapped up in his life and his friends that I felt excluded when I was not there. Being so empty and feeling so lonely it would lead to feeling despair.

Seeing him today was hard. He took the children to the park and I cried my eyes out. I feel as if I should be so strong and yet I can't be for some reason. I suppose love doesn't just disappear when you wish it would. Comparing the days today is the worst. I have had to face up to the fact that this date will no longer be significant. No longer be an anniversary. There will be so many of those days though won't there. The kid's birthdays will be difficult. The wedding anniversary. The day we moved here. All irrelevant, ordinary days now in terms of me and him. A chapter of the book is now over. It can be erased from the diaries. I just wish they could be erased from memories as well.

The meaning of this life has changed so much. It feels like this has been going on for much longer than the 11 days I have been through. He didn't remember the significance of today. He is too wrapped up in his new world and I have been shut out of it. I am no longer needed, surplus to requirements. Just a person in his past. In his old life.

I think back to the day all those years ago when we walked through my local park in London. He was visiting relatives and my sister and his cousin had organised a meeting for us. We talked about what we were doing. Me in my first year of A - Levels, him at grammar school doing his GCSEs. He spoke so well, pronouncing each letter. I wondered what he thought of my terrible speech. We walked round and round and then at the top of my road, before he went back home, we kissed. One of those weird fumbling kisses that you have as a teenager. I walked home, knowing that I would make sure I saw him again. I liked him and that made me walk round with that silly smile on my face.

Fourteen years later, the smile is gone. The feelings are still there. I was always proud to introduce him to people. Always proud of being his wife. I suppose I never gave him a reason for being proud of me. I had become such a mess after the girls were born. Looking in the mirror I focused on myself. I had put on weight and could not get rid of it before now. I had awful skin, still suffering from spots at 31 years old! My hair was always left to dry without styling and my clothes were drab and mumsy. I had become one of those mums that let themselves go once they had children.

Looking in my wardrobe at the new clothes I had bought where some weight had fallen off with the stress of the last few weeks, I realised it was time for a new me. If this life is going to be new then I needed to be new. It would take time to build it up. I sat down and began a list of things I wanted to do in my new life. New clothes were the only thing on that list.

The thoughts of my babies and their Daddy were swirling round and round my head. I did not know which was hurting more. The fact that I was no longer with him or the fact that I was not with them.

How could he hurt me like this? Did I deserve this in some way? I want today to end now please. Let's finish it here.

9th-13th April 2007

Holiday in Hastings.

Tough start to the week. children crying because they wanted their daddy. They knew he was supposed to be coming with us and they knew he was now not because nanny was there. It was so hard to listen to them crying. I wanted to kill him for upsetting my babies.

The holiday was ok but all the way through I kept thinking what Marc and I would have been doing. Taking them swimming, watching them play outside, having time to sit and talk as there was nothing else to do. It was such a pull away from my 'old' life. It hurt.

The children were great. They had a smashing time, ran off some energy and made friends with the children in nearby caravans. If only making friends was that easy when you are older.

He phoned me a couple of times to nag me about money. Like I care where he is going to get the money to pay for his 'new' life. Nice new flat, nice new friends, nice new girlfriend, nice single lifestyle. Mine continues as it was. Still a mum, still wondering how to pay for things the children need, still stuck. He wanted to borrow 5 grand on the mortgage and we are struggling to pay what we have got. I just couldn't do it. I nearly did give in just to make him go away. Mum was there though. She was my strength in saying no. Each time he phoned it brought me down again. It's a weird feeling - too hard to describe as it is neither anger nor heartache. It's kind of numb.

Even smoked in front of my mum which is something I have never done. Stress is killing me, literally.

I had asked him to come. I had asked him to spend the week together as a family.

"We could talk in the evenings," I said.

Some time alone I thought. But he had made his mind up. Said it was not wise for him to go. I walked around the caravan site. I knew which bits he would have moaned about. I smiled as I walked up this huge hill, picturing him moaning about his knees. His weak knees. He would have moaned and groaned all the way up. That made me laugh. The noise from the neighbouring caravans would have made him moan. He would have gone on and on about it. That made me smile. I don't know whether the smile was from picturing him moaning or from the fact that I did not have to listen to it.

There were parts of the holiday where I smiled a lot. Pheobe and a golf club. That should never be allowed. She swung it so hard and she whacked that ball so far. The golf club was taller than she was and yet still she swung it with all her might. I took a picture and sent it to him.

The children ran round the caravan in the evenings and their belly laughing was contagious. Their happiness spread to me and I was calmer as long as I did not talk to him too much. He expected me to solve his problems and there was absolutely no way. You got yourself into this, Marc, you sort it out. Like I would finance his new plans.

Mum and I chatted into the nights and we worked through the thoughts and feelings that hung around in the air. Life was being sorted; I just had to be patient. I could see the light at the end of this darkness. I could see myself getting through these hard times. The difficulty was accepting how long it would take. How I had to wait. How I had to move on slowly. There were obstacles to remove out of the way first. There were events to get through. There was hardship to sustain. I knew all of that. Just needed the courage to face it.

13th April 2007

What a day. Had this sinking feeling all day. Stomach gurgling away as the stress set in. I knew I would have to face him and that's when it hurts loads. It's like I'm expecting him to say we should try again and he is now coming home and then when he doesn't the reality sinks in again. I don't think I really want him back so if he did say that I don't know what I would do but I would like to think he wants me again. I want him to want me again. It's the rejection that is hard. It feels like I have failed somehow though I don't know what I feel I failed to do. Maybe that is the real problem.

Confrontation time. Mum was so mad and then the row and the shouting and people saw his true colours. So hard to say no to him. He still has that way of making me feel that he knows best and that he will get his own way whatever the cost. I just wanted him to go away and to do that I had to give him that money. In that split second I saw this manipulative man and I thought of the stress he has put me through and I knew I would be bailing him out again and I found myself telling him exactly what I was thinking. He didn't like it, but how could he expect me to pay for his new life because that is how I feel. I know he is paying it but that mortgage was for our life together not for adding money on to, to kick start his flat payments. To kick start his life without me and the children.

He finally left with the children and this sense of relief washed over me. He was gone. It might have been easier if he had gone and never come back. Easier for me but not for the children.

The holiday over we had returned home. I had survived the first holiday without him. I had made it as special for the children as I possibly could. They had enjoyed themselves and were so excited to see him and tell him all about it. I could see by his face it hurt him that he had not been part of their good times. That he had not been there to watch them. That he would not be part of their memories. For the first time I wondered whether I had been wrong to think he was finding this easier than I was. I had thought where this was what he wanted, he was getting on with the new life he had created without ever thinking of us, but that look on his face seemed to suggest I was wrong. I felt mean to have had those thoughts. I felt like I had let him down and my opinion of him was lower than it should have been. How could I have thought that about him? For a moment I was disgusted with myself.

We sat in the office talking about finances and how he was going to struggle with his new flat if he was supporting us and this house at the same time and that I would have to help him.

I could hear the voices of my parents and my in-laws outside. A blur of sound and my head spun. I was so ready to agree with what he wanted in order for the noise to shut up and go away. I walked out of the room for some breathing space. The phone rang and my aunt's voice was added to the mix of noise in my head and I made a break for the peace of the garden.

My mum was talking to him. I had heard the names Sue, Tess and Sarah. Sarah, our brief lodger. The one my mum believes he was in bed with the day she walked round to my house unannounced while I was away at a friends wedding for the weekend.

Then, shouting. Door slammed. I followed the sounds. My mum furious. My dad on edge. My in-laws with bowed heads. He had yelled at my mum. She had touched a nerve. I followed him into the street. He was so angry. He was steaming. His temper flared. The shouts in the street. The storming off.

I had not known what to say or do. I had not known what had happened. The confusion made me feel sick and I was glad when he left with the children.

These days are filled with nothing but stress and anger and emotions rising and diving. The rollercoaster that life had become was roaring at full speed, not braking at the twists and turns, forcing everyone's stomach to flip over and over with every movement. The waves of nausea rose up and crashed down. The hard days were plentiful. The challenges, the obstacles placed at regular intervals throughout them. The hard days were here and I knew then that they were here to stay for a while.

Time to get organised.

The days being so hard made me realise that I had things to organise. The conversation about finances made me scared.

I sat alone in the house and wondered what we would have been doing now. A Saturday was never the most exciting day in our family life but I still missed them. The shopping, the time indoors together. I thought back to the weekends of the past. I thought about the trips to the supermarket. The moaning of the children as they were forced to trapse round the store, the expensive items appearing in the trolley, the tense atmosphere in the car on the way home as he started telling the children off for their behaviour. Next would have been me putting away the shopping with the children tugging at the bags and eating what I had bought, while he switched on his laptop and hid away from us again.

Why was I missing that?

A calmer feeling had washed over me. The tension had faded a little and there were other things on my mind. I felt this urge to understand my position now I was separated, in case he never came back. I felt this urge to see if I could get my life organised in some way so it might help me to move on. I felt this urge to get up and move like I was testing to see if I still could. I had these weird urges these days. The pain was still there but seemed to have been numbed. I had overcome the raw feelings that appeared at first. They were still there but more pressing issues had to be dealt with and sense seemed to have taken over. The need to organise and move forward had become stronger. Whether this was for me or for my children I could not tell.

14th April 2007

Visited the bank and found out it is going to be harder to organise than first thought. Finances are shit but I am on the lowest risk band for credit which is a plus. It felt so weird saying to some stranger that we had split. Every time I say it, it doesn't sound right. It still feels like we will sort the mess out and end up plodding along again. I don't want to plod but I do want to protect my children from the pain they are going through. It just gets so hard and then I crumble again.

It's getting harder to write this as the feelings are not as raw as they were and I don't understand what is going on in my head. I listen to him talking about his flat and how nice it is and how he will be in London and have the life he would have had if he were single through his twenties and it hurts that he has that. Maybe it's jealousy. Maybe it's feeling rejected and unwanted. Maybe it's just because it is the unknown.

People ask me how I am and I just say fine. *What do they expect me to say?* I don't feel any anger towards him. I don't feel that he has ruined my life. I feel nothing. I try so hard to feel something but it is just nothing. I want to hate him and move on. I want to be angry with him. I want to hurt him.

He tells people that *'this has been on the cards for a while.'* That is something that doesn't ring true with me. I can't get my head around what he is saying. I can't believe that that was the case. I just accepted his behaviour. I let him go out and enjoy himself because it was me he came back to in the end. I had his children. I looked after him. Alright, he annoyed me incredibly and he wasn't the daddy I wanted for my children. But I never felt as if I wanted this. I didn't want it all to end. I wanted him to stop and see how good his life was. How good we were. He never did though. *Could I have carried on like that? Could I have continued to be the little wife who didn't have a life of her own? Could I have accepted that my life was on hold so he could live his separate one?* I don't know.

Maybe the feeling is fear. Maybe I'm just afraid of the future. I depended on him a lot and I don't have that now. Maybe he is right and we just existed. *But what if he was wrong? What will he do if he ever thinks that he was wrong? Will I have changed too much by then? Will I be strong enough to tell him where to go? Will I ever feel like I don't need him? Will whatever I felt for him still disappear and become non-existent? Will I ever accept this feeling of abandonment? Will I ever move on from Marc? Will life ever be good again? Will I ever know happiness again?* Wallowing in it like this does not help. Trying to understand what is going on doesn't help. Reminiscing doesn't help. And yet these are all the things I do time after time. I get angry with myself. Don't know what for but I hate myself. *What on earth is going on?*

This evening was another one that was spent thinking. Thinking a little too much in ways.

I have this feeling right now that I cannot describe. I try to explain to people but it doesn't come across how I want it to. I suppose it is like I am watching someone else's life unfold before my eyes. It is like these feelings are not mine and somebody has forced them into my body without explaining why I need to carry them around for a while. Like I am having a dream and I am waiting to wake up. Does that make sense? No, probably not.

I have not spent hours crying. I have not walked around as if I am carrying weights on my head and shoulders that are pushing me into the ground. I am not happy, don't get me wrong here. Happiness with the situation - god no. How could I be?

I still feel emotionally drained all the time. I still long for the time of day when I can curl up in bed knowing another day is finished. I still cannot sleep. I still cannot eat. I still wish I could stay in bed forever. I still hope that he will come home; he still says this is temporary. I question everything I do a dozen times. Maybe I am trying too hard to understand. Maybe I believe he will come back soon. Maybe I am living each day thinking that tomorrow he will be home. Maybe I am not facing up to the situation as I should be. There are lots of maybes.

I think about him all the time. This long lonely evening has probably been the worst for that. I cannot watch the TV. I found that the TV was on but I was looking at the space where he would have sat instead of at the screen. I looked back to the TV and realised I had missed the whole programme I was originally watching and probably most of the one that had followed. I had spent hours just staring at that empty space.

The feelings are so strange at the moment. I talked to him on the phone a lot today. He called to speak to me and throughout the whole conversation I wished he would hang up. He spoke about how he was thinking three months apart would be best for us to know what we were feeling. What he was feeling. I just wanted him to stop talking. Then, when he hung up, I wanted him to call back again.

It has been a struggle to keep up with my emotions the last couple of days. Anger tumbles in and out of my days and each wave that hits me is stronger than the last one. The sadness still tinged my day and the darkness hasn't left. The emptiness still surrounds me and the loneliness is still so suffocating. The children have filled my day with pleasure and I hate it that they have gone to bed even though I was longing for it all day. The confusion is endless.

15th April 2007

He promises to take the children swimming, originally telling them he will spend the whole day with them arriving early morning.

I met him at the station at 1.45pm. That is not the whole day. He took them off swimming and I went shopping at Asdas - lucky me!

There were not as many tugs at the heart strings really. It was a different feeling, like I did not want him to have them as they are my children. I don't see him as being entitled to spend time with them as he never did before really so why should he now he has left.

He phoned while he was out and I could hear my baby crying. He was shouting at Seb and I just thought - *what is the point?* Why try and do something like that if all you are going to do is moan. He even said *"if this is how they are going to behave, I don't think I'll bother having them!"* That's one way to get my back up. I could feel the rage inside me brewing and I had to bite back from saying something that I might regret. It was so hard.

He made it back and came in with an attitude problem as he usually did. He muttered something about Seb not doing his homework and again I just felt angry as they are my children and if I don't get time for homework I sort it out later. I think Seb deserved to be let off during all of this.

The feelings were such a change. I was angry. Angry at him for interfering. I bring up the children now and I do it my way as to me he lost the right to have any say the day he decided to be the selfish pig that he is. The day he walked out of here and said he did not love me anymore and said how he no longer could cope with this life anymore, was the day he forgoed all rights in my house, in my life and in the life of my children. I will do everything by myself from now on.

They say that feelings during the first few weeks/months of a split are up and down but this is an incredibly bumpy rollercoaster.

I am crying again. I am alone again. I am lost again. I wander round the house wondering what to do. I walk in and out of the children's rooms. I stand by their doors and watch them sleep. They had such an emotional day today. They had been so happy to go swimming with him and he spoilt it by shouting at them. As Fiona's chest moves up and down gently, I wonder whether she is ok. I worry about them all, but my Fiona is the one who takes everything in. She watches my every move and seems to be aware of my every emotion. The hug she said she needed tonight was as much for my benefit as it was hers I am sure.

Pheobe never sleeps soundly. She thrashes about in her bed and by the time I look in her room she is upside down with her feet under her pillow. She made me laugh today. Her recount of swimming and putting her face under the water was in so much detail. Her eyes were wide and twinkling. Her smile took over her whole face lighting it up as it went.

Then there is my Seb. My little man. I sit on the edge of his bed and watch him. He snores like his dad. He has an air of his dad about him even when he is asleep. Tears well in my eyes as I think back to the day I had him. I was so amazed by the love I had for him when he was born. I remember looking in his cot watching him sleep as I was doing now. I laughed as I realised he was sleeping in the same position he was that first night in the hospital. His arms above his head, fists clenched as if ready to fight. I kissed his forehead and went back downstairs.

I still had tears running down my cheeks. I sat by the sink and had a cigarette and a glass of vodka. This was becoming a regular thing I thought as I sipped my drink.

The realisation of the huge responsibility I faced hit me. I had just checked on my 3 babies. My 3 babies who were now totally reliant on me to give them everything. Yes he would still be in their life but not every day. I was the one that would be here for them day in and day out. I would take them to school, help them with their homework and care for them, healthy and sick. I would feed them, clothe them, and look after them constantly. It is strange because as a mum you do all of that anyway but it had just hit me that I was now doing it all alone.

Fear swooped down and grabbed me. It didn't let go and the tears fell faster. Tears for what I would do if I brought them up wrong. Tears for the mistakes I would make and tears for the hope that they would not damage their lives in any way.

In swooped the guilt. The guilt that it was my fault that they were confused and hurting at the moment. The guilt that I had made their daddy leave. The guilt that I had been such a bad wife that he had felt he had to leave. The more I thought how it was all my fault, the more I cried. I cried and cried. I was crying for my children not for myself.

I switched off the light in the kitchen and the house was black again. Wandering through the darkness I shivered. The images of Sue hit me again as I walked up the stairs and I was beginning to think that it was turning into an obsession.

I pulled back the bedcovers and the smell of him hit me again. I ripped the covers off and I turned the mattress over, struggling with the weight of it but determination pushing me on. No energy left I lay on the bare mattress and pulled the bare duvet over me. I spent the majority of the night awake with images of my children, Marcus and Sue hovering in front of me. Sleep did not help me out tonight.

16th April 2007

The more I spoke today of what he had done and said over the weekend, the more angry I got. It's weird to think that I am actually beginning to look forward to a life without him as that is something I never dreamt I would do.

The part I missed out yesterday was the bit when he said that there will be weekends when he has *stuff to do* so will not be able to have the children. Bollocks to that. If he thinks I am going to play mum all week, sitting indoors and concentrating on my babies and then let him have weekends to himself too, he is very much mistaken. I want my life too. He did not do a good job of giving me a life when he was here but he will be giving me one now he is not.

I wonder whether he will continue to see his children or whether they will become too much of a burden to him. That he won't be able to cope with them so will end up leaving seeing them. Maybe they won't fit into his new lifestyle which he tells me is not what he wanted. *How come everyone else can see it except him?* This is how it happens for others. This is how so many children end up without a father because they get to walk away and create new lives and the children get left behind. If that happens then he better watch out. They say there is nothing like the temper of a woman scorned but when that woman is a mother as well it is tenfold!

I spoke to Marc on the phone again. His voice is becoming cold towards me. I am beginning to get sick of the tone he uses. I hate the way he speaks to me sometimes. The constant mention of how he didn't want this new life is really making me angry. How can he say that? For a life he doesn't want, he seems to be getting on with it ok. He seems to be enjoying it to me. The words that he says roll round and round my head. What I don't understand is if this is not what he wanted where the fight to save it was? Where was the determination that appeared after Tess?

I thought back to that February in 2005, when I finally confronted him about Tess. I had found the text messages and emails between them back in the May of the previous year. I had told a few people and had spoken to them about what I should do. I had chosen not to confront him straight away. I was scared that he would choose her over me and leave.

I remember the shouting in the kitchen that Friday night when I told him what I had found. I had been reading his emails for months, saving them in a different account and I had printed them off and handed them to him. He swore blind that nothing had happened. He had asked her to go to Paris with him. He had asked her to send him a picture of her in the shower. Said he would be waiting in bed for her to get home from work. He had told her he was unhappy with me and had lied about the things I had said. I was heartbroken.

He said it was nothing but over the top flirting. That he needed the attention from her in some way. I had felt guilty then. I had flipped it round to blame myself then. I had decided that it was my fault, just like I have done this time.

"This is not what I wanted."

His words were echoing again. I sat there in my dark house with those words going over and over all the questions again. Why did you not try to change it then? Why did you stay away? Why did you not come home?

It must have been what he wanted. I let myself be dragged into the spiral of blaming myself and questioning whether I should have reacted differently. I thought about what he was doing now and where he was and who he was with.

Once again the dark emptiness swallowed me whole and gulped. There was only one difference. This time I did not cry.

17th April 2007

What a good day today. It was the first day back at work for me after Easter and I thought it was going to be awful. I told a few people and they were all quite supportive. I can have extra hours when I need them; I can run after school clubs if I want. It was nice knowing I was needed and wanted somewhere in my life.

Then, once I got home, and after I got the hero's welcome from my babies, I couldn't get off the phone. I have arranged nights out over the next few weekends and actually have a social life again, which is something I have not had in years.

47

Every now and then a voice in my head would say *'and you thought you would be alone.'* I walked around with a smile on my face even though there was no one here to see it. It still felt good.

It's strange how you can pick yourself up after so long. I thought it was the end of my world when me and Marc split but I am already realising the relief from the strain that surrounded us. From the stress that was there between us and I can kind of understand how he was dragged into the life he had with the people from work where that was no longer. I don't think I would ever have made the choice to just end everything, as I still feel we have been through so much hardship and the good stuff was only just out of reach, but in a way I can understand just a little more. I don't believe he was right about what he said about us. I don't think we were any less in love as I never felt that way - that was just his feelings. I never felt like I could end a relationship that had lasted for so long. I was never unhappy enough to put the children through what they are going through right now. And I suppose all that is because I do still love him. The question that is hovering in my mind is *do I love him like I should? Was it more the dependent love that comes with such a long relationship?* I still feel as if I need him in my life at the moment but *is that just because I am not ready to let go? Is it just because I am used to him being here?* Is it just because I became a nothing - no life, no career, no spirit. My aunt Alice told me that he dragged me down and knocked the spark out of me. Maybe she was right. I was in too deep to realise it. *Or did I just associate that loss of spark with having the children?*

It's good to be free of the tears. It's good to be free of the persistent heartache that never went away. It's good to be feeling just a little like me again. As they say, a little can go a long way.

Work helped me forget about it all. It gave me a focus and I realised that that was what was missing from my life the past few weeks. I had a focus here. My children. I had not used it to help me properly. I had not focused on them properly. I know what I have to do now.

I felt this unfamiliar feeling wash over me. It was one I had not felt properly since he had left. Tiredness. This is what true tiredness feels like. The kind of tiredness that is physical and mental. Natural tiredness.

I decided to take advantage of the feeling and to avoid the loneliness that awaited me in the evenings and I went to bed early. I snuggled under the covers and despite the usual images that appeared before me, I slept.

Have I reached a turning point?

18th April 2007

I have thought of nothing but the time I feel it all went wrong. Pheobe being born, his redundancy and then that woman. All of those happened one after the other. I wonder whether that was the trigger of his unhappiness.

Another fairly positive day really. I didn't get too down about anything. I marked the papers I was sent, I did a little housework as my mother in law had done most of it the day before which I am amazingly grateful for. I never really thought about all of this, not even when he rang. Not even hearing his voice made me sigh that sigh I heave when I'm thinking of him.

I'm not sure whether that is good or whether I am blocking feelings out again. I always do that you see. I always have done. If something hurts too much, I block it out until it is less painful to deal with. It's not a great way of dealing with things but you are what you are.

I kind of plodded through today. Had mum and dad over this evening and wondered how I could have ever lived with a man and amazed at how they must be all the same. *Can I ever imagine living with another one?* No.

My dad moaned about the noise level, took over the TV and huffed constantly at what I'm not too sure. He sat while mum cooked the dinner and he sat while mum and I cleared up. I don't know if I could take that again. From him it's ok in a way as he is my dad and I adore him, but seeing how he was just made me think *I don't want another man in my life again.*

I laughed with the children, I watched them play and smiled and I did not miss the fact that Marc was not here to share it with. I don't even remember thinking about him too much. I am amazed at myself. I do think that this has come a little too soon and I do worry about bottling it up unintentionally but maybe the days are just different.

I sat having my cigarette and my glass of vodka in my usual place by the window. I was pleased with myself for having another positive day. I was proud that I was letting myself feel positive. It was only little things that I had achieved today but if I look at the way I was a few weeks ago I have to be pleased at the little things.

I stared into the dark garden and listened to the silence. It was still tinged a little with emptiness and loneliness but those feelings were a part of my life now and I have begun to accept them. I daydreamed again about the two of them together. It still seems to me that they are. He has said over and over that I am wrong but this nagging doubt is still hanging around my neck. I felt the tears biting and I switched my thoughts back to my children. Sue was not going to ruin my positive day. Not today.

I climbed the stairs to check on them. Watched them sleeping. This was becoming a ritual, like I couldn't settle until I had done this. Again, I sat on each of their beds in turn and kissed their foreheads. My little man, my sweet angel and my upside down girl. A smile crept on my face and I wore it back downstairs.

I sat back on the bench. I knew there was no point in trying to watch TV or play the computer. Those are fruitless. The programmes remind me of him and the study is still exactly how he left it. His coat hanging on the side and his CD's in their cupboard.

I looked at the door to his study and slid off the bench. I opened the door and slowly walked into the room like I was expecting something to jump out at me. Looking at the computer it occurred to me that I did not know what he had been doing on there for the hours he was transfixed to the screen. Probably emailing her. "Stop it!" that little voice shouted at me in my head.

I turned to see the CD's. He had been so particular about keeping them in order. They were alphabetical and when there was more than one from a group they were in order of release. There were at least 300 sitting in that cupboard. He used to go mad when the children were younger and they used to pull them all out to make towers. I could never put them back in the correct order so he had always known they had played with them. I found myself giggling at the memories.

I placed my vodka on the top of the cupboard and knelt down in front of the CD's. I smiled with the thoughts of my babies pulling them out and piling them up running through my head. I smiled as I remembered how he huffed as he rearranged them back into the correct order, moaning and groaning at the children as they hid behind me. I began to pull random CD's out. From different places. From different groups and I piled them up in front of me. I kept going placing them on the tower one after the other in any angle until eventually they crashed. I laughed out loud. "If you could see me now Marc," I said loudly.

I giggled as I built another one, again watching them crash. I took great pleasure in placing them back anywhere I wanted to. A smile on my face the whole time. The children's faces smiling with me in my head.

I finished putting the CD's back in their new non-alphabetical, non-chronological positions. Finishing my vodka, I switched off the light and closed the door. Still wearing my smile and giggling, I climbed the stairs for the evening.

The tide turns back again.

19th April 2007

Another good day. Opened own bank account, spent the afternoon filling in tax forms with mum and being happy.

Then, I came down with a thud.

I went to Seb's school and spoke to his teacher. Thought it was necessary for her to know what was going on. She knew. Seb had told her. My heart pounded as she said he had talked for three quarters of an hour about how he was feeling and what he was thinking. It hurt in a way. Seb does not talk to me. I know sometimes a stranger helps you because they're detached but that reasoning did not stop the pain I was feeling. It was not a huge pain just this ache that stayed there for ages. I was listening to her voice but I was not really taking in everything she was saying at the time. What hurt more was when I was told he had said *'I've got the best dad.'* That was really strange. It kind of feels like you have been stabbed. It's burning and sharp and it feels like if anyone comes near you, you will shatter like glass in a heap as you see on cartoons.

It was a horrible feeling. A mix of pain really. Some from the fact that he has been so horrible to Seb and yet he still thinks he is wonderful and some from the fact that he does not have that 'best dad' anymore. I couldn't make out which one I hated Marcus more for achieving. I know children love their parents through times like these and I know that Seb does have some sort of bond with his father that Marc could never see but still I could have punched Marc if he was standing before me.

I don't understand what is going on in my own child's head, I have no idea and I never will. I want to hold Seb and never let go. I want to grab him and tell him to tell me what he is feeling and I want to protect him from the future he has with his dad just in case he is let down. I don't want him to lose his dad. I don't want him to lose that respect he has for him. I want to understand how he can love him so much. I want to know if he has the same amount for me. The tears stung my eyes. They never fell but every time I looked at Seb tonight, they were there. Welling up over and over and threatening to come but never bothering. A half hearted attempt at emotion.

Two steps forward and three steps back is the phrase that springs to mind. Just when I thought I was doing well and positive thinking was working, here I am crushed to the core again.

Here, in this house, are a wife and three children that love that man and he has chosen to walk away. He needed something more. How could he? What was missing? How did he think we didn't love him? He thought we would not miss him. He thought we did not need him. He thought he was unloved.

Tears streamed as I sat in the dark. The thoughts of my Seb sitting with his teacher talking about his wonderful dad. The dad that had shouted at him so often. The dad that had said so many awful things to him. The dad that had pushed him away. The dad that had left him. I squeezed my eyes shut in an effort to stop the tears.

Here I was again. Suffocating under the strain of emptiness and feeling so lost in this house, so lost in my life. I had been trying so hard to move forward and thought about taking the tentative steps to plan the few months ahead. Now all I can think of is why he left.

I am back to the bottom. All the effort seems to have been a total waste of time. I am riding that rollercoaster again. Holding on tight until my knuckles turn white. Up and down. Nausea. Stomach flipping over, confusion.

If I allow myself to think about this too much, I will go mad I am sure. I have come to the conclusion that it was the thought that he will come back once he has had his space that allowed me to be positive. If that happens we would have been through this for nothing. We would have gone through all this suffering for nothing. It dawned on me that I really have to focus on the likelihood that he will not come back.

Again my thoughts turn to Seb. Seb talking to somebody else. He must have needed to say all those things. What did he say? I wanted to grab hold of Marc and shake him. I would scream at him and force him to look at Seb and see what he has done to his son. How upset he has made him. Would he care? Would that make him change his mind and come home?

Where do I go from here? I have to think about the future life before me if Marc is not coming back to us. I have to help Seb and the girls to come to terms with the fact that Daddy has gone. How do I do that if I have not come to terms with it myself? How can I make them see that we will be ok, if I do not believe it?

I cried well into the night. I just let the tears fall. I want all this to go away. I want to rewind time and change my decision to throw him out. I gave him what he wanted. I gave him his freedom. I gave him the life he craved instead of fighting to save the one we had. How could I have done that? It's entirely my fault for making that one stupid decision.

Come home Marc. Please come home.

20th April 2007

Boy have I crashed today.

Not in a dreadful way.

The weight of my head is back. The wanting to cry is back. The constant thinking of him is back. *How can every day be so bloody different?* I know two days are never the same but the ups and downs are making me feel dizzy.

It's amazing how much you talk to yourself while you are doing other things. I stood their washing up and then again while I was on the computer, just talking to myself. This little voice inside my head sending my crying probability levels soaring and then crashing. It was different things too. Each time. Sometimes, I was reliving meetings with Marc over the last few weeks. Getting angry again. Sometimes I was saying what I should have said to him at a certain time, you know if you could go back to that same point you would have done or said things differently. Sometimes I was talking to myself about what I was going to do with myself in the future. Thinking about nights out and dancing with men I've never met in my head and accidentally running into Marc and his new mates. I would realise I was doing it and then snap out of it like you do with a nightmare. Body rigid, hands sweaty, pulse racing. Hearing his voice made my chest hurt. Speaking to him on the phone I had to remind myself that *we* were no longer. *Why does your brain do that?* Having a conversation and saying to yourself you are no longer together. Multi-tasking at its finest.

Did not want to do anything. Snapped a little at the children, though they just came and hugged me or kissed me like they knew what was going on. They are so cool, I am so lucky.

Marcus was talking about losing his flat and I was saying in my head *don't care, don't care, don't care* over and over again. *How childish?*

Felt very alone this evening too. I needed company tonight. I needed to be with someone. I would not have wanted to talk to anyone, but I just wanted to have someone else on the settee instead of the empty space that looked at me.

Every now and then I look around the room just to check there is no one there. I watch the phone hoping it will ring. I watch my mobile hoping for a text. I turn the TV on to hear another voice and then I turn it straight back off so I can just sit again. It's like the emptiness hovers and the silence rings out at you. The homeliness is gone. The comfort is gone. You want to have something but you don't know what. You need something but there is no point in looking as you don't know what it is and it probably wouldn't be there anyway. You wait for something to happen. You wait for a noise. You wait for all those feelings to go. You just wait and listen to the nothing. The nothing that has replaced the something. Haunting you.

This was definitely one of those days you can't wait to be over. I have walked around all day with this dragging feeling that has taken over my whole body. I have done the usual mundane chores of the day. I could not settle on anything so there are so many things half done. A bit like my life feels at the moment. Half there. Half gone.

The warm feelings are there because of the children. The loving feeling surrounded me when I was with them. I had felt the tingle of happiness at the sounds of their laughter and their chatter; even their arguing made me smile. Pheobe and Fiona had played 'mummies' today. I think they were making a point at leaving out the 'daddy' from the game in a very unsubtle way. The play of children can give so much information.

Every movement of my body was an effort. It seemed to take twice as much energy to move and as I haven't eaten properly for days, I don't have any of that required energy. So I didn't move too much. I just sat.

I stared into space. There were images in the black air around me that I watched. My eyes were forced to stay open and watch them like I was under some sort of torturous spell. Him again. Him and her. Me and him together. Me alone. Her again. I struggled to see her face as if I had forgotten what she looked like. Why am I so obsessed with this woman? I squinted as if that would help me see her. I need to let go of all this. But, I need answers to the questions first. Something is making my husband stay away. He cannot be on his own. He never has been able to be alone. Is it her making him stay away or am I seeing things that are not there?

I tortured myself over and over with these thoughts, not moving from my seat, not changing position. All the discussions I had had with him over the last few weeks, all the dreams I had had, all replayed right there before me. I was missing something. There was information in there somewhere that I had not picked up on. What was it? Where was it? Give me that sign. Someone show me.

21st April 2007

Okay so I am emotional. I don't feel too depressed or anything. He came and took the children and it did not hurt as much as it used to. Listening to him saying how he wants them alternate Saturdays was more painful. Those children need their dad in their life as much as possible and even if he has got plans he should put his children first. Selfish to the core.

The real problem with today is the party. It's the first family gathering without him. He has not got to face everybody and their smiles and winks towards you, as if silently saying, *you will be ok*. People asking how you are and how you have been. People asking awkward questions. People watching you and what you are doing. I was never one to enjoy a party but this one is going to be so hard. People want to know all the details. They want to understand what happened even if it is just for gossip.

Don't get me wrong, my family are great. Whenever something like this happens everyone pulls together. If I needed someone, one of them would be available. It's reassuring in a way. I'm not a talker though. I don't like to sit and pour my heart out to anyone who will listen. I'm not sure exactly how much my mum knows about my feelings and she is the one I am closest to.

You can see it and feel it in their body language too. You can see they keep checking on you. Out of the corner of their eye. The way they rub your knee or hold your hand. Just that *I feel sorry for you* smile will start me off. They will tell me I will meet someone else. They will tell me their stories that end with *...and look at me now.* They will say if ever I need anything just ring. All of those things come hand in hand with a family like mine. It's not a bad thing at all but I know that already. It's just hanging silently. It doesn't need to be said. When it does get said it breaks through the protective shield. It tugs in the emotions and the feelings that are around the room and they clump together in one big ball and your body sucks them all in. You become an emotional fireball, feeling what everybody else is and getting overwhelmed by it all.

Maybe I will turn up and no one will say anything about it. Maybe nobody will care and they will all act as if it hasn't happened. *Would that be worse though?*

I was just sitting at the computer writing this and I realised I was crying. *How am I going to be when someone in my family comes and gives me a hug?* I suppose the key is to cry my heart out this afternoon so I will not be on the edge of tears before I even get there. I don't want them to see me as this pathetic woman who can't cope without her husband. He couldn't stand it so why should anybody else be able to. I can't let anyone know or see what I am really like at the moment. Next week I will be stronger. Next week I will be ok again. I just need to lapse into the pitiful, weepy girl inside every now and then. But I need to do it alone.

I felt lost in that room. I was surrounded by the family and I felt lost. I sat in the corner on a settee with people that care all around me. Every now and then I would catch somebody's eye as they looked over and I would look away. I had to keep checking to see if my mum was there, like a child playing in the park, looking over their shoulder to make sure mum is still sitting on the bench chatting to her friends.

I sat with Danny, my sister's boyfriend. Conversation had never been a strong thing between us but tonight was different. He had many caring words to say. A few carefully chosen words of encouragement. I felt kind of safe, tucked in the corner talking to him. He had known about Tess and the pain I had gone through afterwards. I had talked to my sister about it and she had relayed his little snippets of thoughts and feelings to me. When I said I thought it was happening again he was there to help. He had come with me to watch

Marc that night. I had explained to my sister about the two tickets in the envelope that Marc had hidden and not told me about and he had agreed to take me to the place and stay with me. It must have been hard for him to see my reaction to finding my husband with another woman. To be part of the moment that would destroy my marriage. I felt indebted to him. Like I owed him something.

My sister stood there chatting to everyone around her and laughing loudly. Every now and then she turned to look at me. It was a checking look. Is she ok? I would ruin the life of anyone who hurt her like this and I wondered whether she was feeling the same. It must be hard to watch someone you love go through something that tears their life apart. She has been great. Listened to me moan and groan, listened to me cry over the phone. Just like my mum has done. I watched the two of them chatting together and realised how lucky I was to have them in my life. They are truly amazing people and the love I felt for them in that instant overwhelmed me and the tears bit furiously at my eyes. The familiar burning sensation I had felt so often these days.

My girls danced the night away. They were twirling around trying to make their dresses go up around them. They ran in and out of the people, skipping up and down the room, weaving in and out of the bodies that were around with such skill. Their belly laughs rang out over the music. My Seb stood by my dad. He was with his Grandad, where he felt safe. He looked so grown up in some ways. Wanting to be part of the conversation, but not sustaining the concentration to take part in it. I could see him look up at my dad with such love and respect. I'm glad he has that connection.

I sat and watched. I half expected Marc to walk over and join me. I had to remind myself that he was not there. I sat, feeling lost for most of the night. Silence still had a way of approaching me. The music was playing but I couldn't hear it properly. People were talking, their mouths moving but I couldn't hear them either. I let myself bathe in the pain that was within. I let the loneliness take over and drive home that I was alone. I was loved by all these that stood round me, but I was alone.

22nd April 2007 01.15am

See what this does to you is play on your mind influencing everything, even down to your sleep. Have had a few vodkas and feeling very low. I was right about the party. It was the hardest thing I have done so far. I was a mess. I did not expect it to hit me that hard. I think it was seeing everyone in their lives and realising that it was mine that was not the same. Everybody was smiling.

It was seeing my Aunt Violet that was hard. She knows me too well and I knew, as she has been there, she would know what I was feeling. It was just the way she looked at me that made me hurt. That smile. It was not a pitiful one, it was a reassuring one. As if she had just said, *I know - it's ok.*

I bit back the tears and then someone asked me if I was ok and I had to run. I cried a little. Mum was there. Had a fag with my sister. Felt a little better.

My cousins hugged me later, full of words of encouragement and positivity. Trouble is I am not as positive as they are. I wish I was like them but I'm not. I'm not tall and slim and pretty and outgoing. I don't ooze confidence like they do. I can't go out and let my hair down because that is not me. I can't break the mould - I am not strong enough to do that yet. Maybe I will be one day.

I don't feel able to consider the future with or without another man. I don't want that. I don't want to go back either. What do I want? Too complicated. Don't know.

The day has been the longest one ever. The night seemed to go on for hours. The hugs and the smiles. The looks asking if I was ok without voices being heard.

My cousins gave words of advice and sympathy. They were smiling and positive and Rene held me so tight as if she was trying to pass some strength from her to me. It boosted me while they were talking. I forced a smile and tried to say something that suggested I was ok which, for a split second, made me feel like I was. They lifted my mood. They made me feel like I could survive this. They made me feel sure that I would get there in the end and maybe even be a little happier than I had been with him. But when they were gone, they took it all with them. I was alone again. Alone, with my feelings and sorrow smothering me. Alone with the longing for him. Alone with the wanting. Missing him.

22nd April 2007.

Marcus text me this morning to find out if I was ok. I don't know what he wanted me to say. He put me through hell and then wants to make sure it wasn't too painful. *Is he here? Is he facing everyone? Does he have to be cheery for the sake of the children?* He is off in a new scene, with new people that do not care what he has done and do not know what he has left behind. I don't expect them to care and I don't particularly want them to know. He is out of it though. He is not going through this.

Feel better than I did this morning. The feeling of dread has lifted a little. I try to smile through it all and think about what I have got now. It does not seem a great deal because I don't have him. But I didn't really have him anyway. There was no real difference. I got the children ready, I organised the gifts, I watched the children dance and run around. As I always did. No difference. It's just he was not there. That was all it was really. *Why is it such a big deal?*

Why is it such a big deal?
Why have I made that man the be all and end all of my life? He was never part of it really. He was never around

much. He was never part of the family. His life was work. His wonderful job that he loves. He can have it. I'd have my children any day instead of a career. He will miss out. He won't have the bond, the memories that I will have.

He was being nosey. He wanted to know if anybody was running him down or speaking of him badly, that's what he wanted to know. He hates the fact that people might think badly of him. He always has to be the one in the right. He hates being seen as the bad guy. Can't bear to think that people might have a low opinion of him now. Shouldn't have left then.

To be honest, I don't know what they think. They were checking on me more than speaking about him and what has happened. He can't see that though. Everything has to be about him. To him, he would be the topic of discussion. He would be the one they were concerned with. Even if they had asked, they wouldn't have asked me, knowing I was ready to burst into tears at any moment. Stupid man!

He is still the main thing on my mind. I think about him all the time, like he is all I have. Aside from my babies he was I suppose. I never really had a lot of friends. I never really went out. Even when I did, I had to have the children in bed first. I used to go to the pub with my best friend Anna and as soon as I had bought a drink, my phone would ring telling me one of the children had woken up and I had to come home. It's good when I think of those sorts of things. It is something else to add to the things I disliked about him. You know the reasons why it is good to have him out of my life. Like therapy.

There were many things about Marc that made me cross. I always switched them around though. I always found a reason for his behaviour that reflected on me in some way.

When he would phone because Pheobe was crying and he couldn't settle her, I would say that I had not given him enough opportunity to spend time with her. When he couldn't cope with Fiona because of her asthma, it was because I had not told him what to do. I made excuses constantly. I am a fool really.

I sat in my usual place in the kitchen and made a vow to my reflection in the window. I swore that I would not make any excuses for his behaviour anymore and that I would no longer let him convince me that anything that went wrong in our marriage, with our friendship and in our future was my fault in any way.

With a sigh and a giggle at myself, I wondered how long it would be until I broke that vow. Not long, I bet.

Is it still only April?

23rd April 2007

Had a very busy day today which meant I was not really wallowing in it too much. If you sit on your own for too long you find your mind straying and going over things that should just be forgotten. Had friends over all day. Full of advice and it is amazing how everyone has a story to tell. They all know somebody who is going through the same or worse. They all moan about their husbands and discuss how or if they could survive without them.

As a relationship progresses, it is incredible how you become more and more dependent on the other person. It does not seem to matter how independent you are in the first place or whether you have the intention of staying your own person. children come along or circumstances change and you find yourself living your life through them. The effect of the man is to change the woman, not always for the better. Everybody is the same. Women are full of *I used to* and not *I am* or *I do*. I wonder how many women are not in this kind of relationship. *How many can actually say they are not dependent on them for anything? How many can say they are truly and honestly happy?*

The last few days have gone so slowly. It feels like I have lived a week in every day. It seems like forever ago that he left. It seems longer still when the problems all started on that Sunday back in March. Why is it that time passes slowly when you are down?

I thought back to some of the discussions I had had with friends today. There do seem to be so many women in the same boat as me. There are women who are separated that are happy to be and that instigated it and therefore are moving on, I know that. The trouble is all you hear about are the ones who are just like me. The affairs, the neglect, the loss, the heartbreak, the lack of contact with the children. It is all so common.

I listened to tales today that make me feel grateful for the contact I still have with Marc. He still phones and listens to me and the children. He still asks what they have been up to. He asks them how their days have been. He comes down to see them even if it is not for as long as they need him to be here. He is making an effort.

There are so many men that walk away from their families and act like they don't exist. A few problems hit their relationship or their life and that is it, they are gone. They don't contact the person that they had once loved and they neglect their children. They seem to need to forget it all and I cannot understand how they can do that. They walk out and it is as though that life had never existed. Do they not realise the damage they can do? Do they not care?

Is there a gene in some men that make them naturally selfish? Women devote their lives to their children from the start. They sacrifice their own lives in order for their children to know that they love them, to take care of them and to bring them up in a loving, family life. They are the ones who are left behind and who continue to raise the children when their father wanders off. I know there are women out there who do the same. There are women who do not sacrifice their lives in the way that other mums do. There are women who walk out on their children to start a new life but they are the minority aren't they? So many children come from broken homes. So many children come from families without their dad. I never thought my children would become some of them.

It also dawned on me through my discussions the amount of times women talk in the past. They use words like 'I used to.....before I got married I was.....before I had children....I was.' I'd never thought about it before but you don't hear men talk like that as often. Is that because men's lives do not change as much as a woman's when they marry or have children. Or have I just become bitter at men here? Am I reading too much into it? I wonder how much of the past tense in a woman's conversation is used with sadness?

I resumed my position for the evening on the kitchen bench, as always, and thought back to what I was like when I was without children. I couldn't really remember. I had my son at 20, so there were not a lot of years without children really. I was never one for partying the night away. I didn't frequent the club scene. I didn't go out and get drunk. It was not my thing, I didn't particularly like it. I was happy to be with someone special instead of out drinking and dancing. Once upon a time Marc had been like me too. Happy to be at home. Never really wanted to go out - or so he said.

Maybe it was me he changed for. Maybe it was me who changed him. That vow lasted 24 hours didn't it. I giggled. I knew I could never do it. I am clearly one of those people who have the tendency to blame themselves for other people's misgivings. Get used to it girl. You are what you are.

I sat staring into the darkness outside and I wondered how many other women were sitting there feeling like me. There must be some out there who can relate to my feelings. There must be some out there in a worse position than me. At least, in a way, I still have Marcus. I hope he never leaves me completely. I'm not sure whether I could manage. I still need him so much. I felt the familiar sunken feeling in my chest and that ache was back.

I wanted to hear his voice. I wanted to hold him. I wanted him to tell me about his day at work. About the people he had been with, the people he had met.

Sadness is an awful feeling. It's heavy. A weight on you, pressing down and with gravity's help drags you to rock bottom. My legs ached from hanging over the bench and I slid off, down the washing machine and onto the floor. I stared at the radiator in front of me. My eyes felt so dry. That was probably the reason I wasn't crying as much, the tears had finally dried up.

The longing made me ache all over. The tiredness from lack of sleep turned into feelings of exhaustion. Drained. The silence around me made me shiver. Drawing my knees into my chest, I rested my weary head on them and closed my puffy eyes. Immediately, they were there again. The two of them. The happy couple. They were there in Marc's nice new flat, in his nice new life with their nice new relationship. It's not true though. I am making this up. This is not the case at all. You are blowing it out of proportion. Still, they were there. Walking down the road, hand in hand, laughing and smiling. I sighed heavily and raised my eyes to the ceiling; as if not looking down would make the visions stop. True or not, those visions are not going to stop are they? Those visions are never going to leave me. They will taunt me for as long as it hurts. And that could be a very long time.

24th April 2007

He phoned this evening. The day was fine until then. He talked to Fiona and then because she could not hear him, she could not really have a conversation, so he shouted at her and hung up. Tears welled in her eyes and I felt so sorry for her. When he phoned back she refused to talk to him. It's so hard to not bad mouth him in front of the children. They should not hear all the things you say about him. One thing I am not going to do though is make excuses for him. I did not comment on him shouting. I didn't give a reason; I just shrugged my shoulders and smiled at her. She smiled back and did not cry. She seemed to cope ok.

The problem I have now is not the situation with me. It's seeing my children struggle to come to terms with and understand what has happened. They don't know why he is not coming over, though in a way I don't either. These are his babies as much as mine and yet he seems to be unable to make time for them. He seems unable to show them that he still cares for them and will still be there. He says it to them but it's the actions that are missing. He does not realise that all these things will be remembered by them and they will make up their own minds and eventually speak it too. I feel sorry for him in a way. Sorry that he has this inability to see past himself and his own life. I look at my children and I feel a happiness that cannot be explained. The warm feeling that builds up and takes over and I know that if anybody tried to separate us for any reason I would fight my hardest to change that. Sorry that he is so self centred and feels that life will just revolve around him. He is selfish beyond belief. Everything has to be about him and what he is doing and he expects me to care. He expects everybody to care and also understand. Sorry that he cannot take responsibility for his actions. There is something about being strong enough to stand up and say yeah I did that wrong and I'm sorry. It gains respect from others as well as yourself. And I feel sorry for him that he has not grown up yet. He is still so childish and has not discovered the positive side of adult life. The satisfaction of achieving the goals you set as an adult. Of seeing your children blossom. Of enjoying the simple things.

I feel he is searching for something that can't be found. I don't know what it is he needs or wants but I don't believe he will ever stop searching. I'm just pleased that I don't feel like that. Even without him, I'm not searching for anything. I have everything I need right here in my children. It's a great feeling.

A more positive day today. I had one of those experiences where I think; thank goodness I don't have to cope with that anymore.

The shouting at Fiona for nothing, well because he was stressed, was a regular thing. We all used to suffer. He would be snappy and his temper would flare. He could be so vicious with his words and the children and I hated it. We still hate it. There was something about that incident tonight that made me feel glad. Glad I was out of that I suppose.

I love the man dearly, but I don't like him. He could be so nasty. There were times when members of his family and mine, had said that they did not know how I lived with him. They did not know how I put up with him. There are elements to that that are true. His temper and his lack of stress management were two of them.

I pictured my little girls face at the table. She had done nothing wrong and her daddy, the one she missed, had shouted at her. Her face was puzzled and she had looked to me for reassurance. I had seen that look from the two oldest so many times. Pheobe had never cared. He could shout and scream and she never batted an eyelid. Pheobe was too defiant to care what daddy thought. She is sometimes too defiant to care what anyone thinks. That's just Pheobe. The other two cared. Seb had bore the brunt of his anger a few times. He had been told off for nothing much and called various names by his dad. In a sad way, it was almost natural to him. He had always looked to me for help and usually I did not agree with Marc. We had arguments over these situations so many times. Marc would never listen. He would just storm off. It was so hard.

The problem was I was not always contradicting what he was saying. Sometimes Seb had done something wrong.

Sometimes he had misbehaved. Sometimes he had an attitude problem as all boys do. What I was always angry at was the way that Marc dealt with these situations. He had always stormed in there and gone over the top. He never saw it like that though. He saw it as me taking Seb's side in everything and Seb getting away with things and it seemed to blow a huge rift between father and son.

I just didn't understand why Marc could not just listen to me.

I was beginning to see more of the advantages to living without Marc than I had done before. I had not made a list or anything but I knew that there were parts of living with him that I was not going to miss. I am not saying I am pleased to be without him. If I had a choice perhaps I would prefer to have a husband. The confusion is where my real husband had gone to. The man that had left was not him. He was his replacement. He was the one that had grown in the body of my husband.

The stress in my life was different. I had the confusion of missing Marc, loving him but not liking him. I had the wonder of what made him change. I had the heartache of losing the man I loved. The sadness of the broken marriage. I have the worry of raising three children alone. The financial worry. All of these were everyday worries and anxieties. But the stress was still different. Living with Marc had produced a different type of stress. An unhealthy, heavy, burden really. Like I was carrying him in some ways. I can't really explain.

The unhappiness was different too. I was sad now, but I had been unhappy before. Just in a different way. I seemed able to handle this sadness better than the previous unhappiness. Confusing huh?

I stopped trying to understand what I was meaning and shrugged at the thought of acceptance that there were some things I didn't miss and that was the end of it.

I watched the faces of my children as they became engrossed in the TV. They sat huddled up together on the settee, crammed into two spaces instead of having one space each. The third seat was where Daddy used to sit. None of them sat there. Their eyes were flickering with the light emitted from the screen. They were transfixed, not taking their eyes off it, as if they were too frightened they were going to miss something. They were submerged in it, like they were part of the programme. Every now and then one of them would laugh at the cartoon and then check round to see if the others were laughing too. Every now and then Pheobe would feel the need to explain to me what was happening as if I was not watching it. Every now and then one would poke and prod at one of the other two to provoke a moan or a groan. They were all invading each other's space but not one of them would move. It was like they needed to be that close to each other.

After a while of watching I became aware of the smile on my face. That is what watching them does to me. I stood up and waded in between them. Pheobe on my lap, Fiona curled up under my right arm and Seb resting his head on my left shoulder. My family. They are mine. These amazing, beautiful children are mine. I made them. How did I do something so great? There we sat. Huddled on top of each other, squashed together, laughing and smiling and poking and prodding and tickling. There we sat. Me and my children. My children.

A lighter mood to life.

25th April 2007

Another busy day. Feeling shattered today from working yesterday as well as lack of sleep.

Life is getting a bit mundane at the moment. It's like living groundhog days and they are all merging into one. I know I am a mum every minute of every day. I know I have the school run to do two or three times a day. I know I will have an incredibly little amount of time to do all the things I want to do. I know I will have trouble getting the children to bed. I know I will not be able to sleep. It becomes this circle of the same chores and duties that make life dull and predictable. It's not really that it is getting me down as such; it's just that I'm waiting for something to change and nothing is. The days are running away and, looking back, the weeks seem to have gone so fast and I don't want to wake up one day and regret the fact that I have put my life on hold because he left.

He came round this evening to see the children. It was awful because he did not know what to do with them. He has never played with them or got them ready for bed. He has never had the time to devote to them and the couple of hours he gave them he did not know how to please them. He could not bring himself to just sit and watch them play in the garden. He couldn't listen to them read or read to them. He even asked what to do when I said to take them up and get them ready for bed. He spoke to me about how difficult finding a flat was. About how hard it was to manage his money. About the grief he was getting at work because he was spending time on the phone talking to estate agents. He is realising how hard life can be and hopefully he will soon realise that it was me that took over on a lot of the hard stuff. That it was me who organised most of our life together and that he cannot manage himself because of that.

He probably would never say that to me though. It did not hurt as much to see him as it has done previously. It made me very tense and feel a little stressed but that was all. It was a nice feeling to know that I did not have to listen to his pessimistic moans and groans every day. At the same time it is hard to look at the father of your children, the man you love, and know that it is not the same anymore. That he does not want you as he did. That he does not want to be the man you want him to be. It's harder in some ways when looking at him and thinking those things does not make you cry.

It is funny how I see him so differently now he is no longer mine. It is weird when I look at him and I know he will leave again and go to stay somewhere else. When he is here, I have to keep reminding myself that we have split. Temporary as first planned or otherwise. We talked a lot tonight.

We chatted about many different things. They were all conversations that I had never ever pictured having. It was quite surreal. I listened to him talk about what it was like to be in his position and it occurred to me that not once did we talk about my position. He was too absorbed in his new life. He seemed happy and I hated that.

I watched his mouth move as he talked. He has such womanly lips. They are shaped and full. He never sat still for long. He was up and down, unsettled. He checked himself in the mirror a dozen times. So vain. That used to irritate me. Still does.

I watched his skinny frame pace up and down. The whole time he was talking. The whole time I was listening. I wondered if his unsettled behaviour was due to him feeling uncomfortable. It must be strange for him being in a house that used to be his home. It must be strange for him seeing his children for these few hours only. It is what he wanted though.

He left. We said our awkward goodbyes on the doorstep. We hugged each other tightly. I didn't want to let go. I didn't want him to leave. I watched him walk across the driveway. Shutting the front door, I turned and looked into the front room. There was that silence again. There was that loneliness. It was hovering there in front of me, I could almost see it.

I enjoyed my cigarette. Sat on the bench with my vodka in the other hand. Thinking again. I seem to think without realising sometimes. The house was cold. Dark and cold. I felt so uncomfortable. I felt like I should be crying. I looked at my reflection in the window. How unhappy was that face? How down was I? Not as down as I had been. Accepting the situation had been the first step.

I wondered whether he would ever say he wanted to come home. I didn't want to ask if he still saw this as a temporary split. Whether we were still going to review the situation at some point in the future like we had discussed in the first few days after he left. I was too scared of the answer I suppose.

He text me to see how I was. He was still thinking of me. I text back goodnight and then stared at the phone. I don't know what more I wanted but I did want more. Was he still thinking of me? Was he thinking about the children at all?

I lowered my head and hugged myself. The feeling of being a child was here again.

The child who didn't understand what was happening. The child who didn't understand her own feelings. The child that was confused. Confused by life as it had become so hard. I let myself become one with the darkness and faded into the background of the kitchen with just my thoughts for company.

26th April 2007

A feeling of 'life is good' washed over me today. Nothing bothered me too much. Even seeing myself in the mirror at the changing room and thinking *god you are still a fat cow* didn't bother me as it would have done so before. Pheobe's temper tantrums didn't bother me as they did a few days ago. Life was kind of calm. Shopping trip, spending time with mum and helping Seb with homework was all good too.

His phone call was hard to listen to. He phoned whining about how hard life is and I just listened. I listened to him moaning about the hardship he was going through and I did not even get angry. I did not get upset. I did not get frustrated or feel the urge to yell and scream. I just listened. There was not a part of me that cared that much. It was a satisfying feeling of his life getting worse and mine not. I could tell he did not like the fact I was going out tomorrow. He used that jealous tone he has when I'm going out and this time there was no effect. It seemed as though his life was not going as smoothly as he thought it would, so he was focusing on how mine was going. His way of doing this was to try and make me feel sorry for him. To try and make me say sympathetic words. It did not work. I just listened. No comments, no replies, no sharp retorts. Nothing. He hated it. Said he was going to go and get wrecked by himself if I didn't mind. I didn't mind, no. Do what you like. I have no say in what you do and I'm certainly not going to be pleading with you to not feel so bad, to not get drunk, to not be so pessimistic etc.

A strange indescribable feeling fills me tonight. A lack of concern. A lack of worry. A lack of fear. No dread. No love. It's like I've switched off but I haven't. Like a television would be on standby!

The silence is grumbling away around the house. The emptiness hovers in the background and the cold night air creeps in where it can. I don't feel any of it. It isn't weighing me down tonight. It can't get me tonight. I'm in a different place with a protective wrapping swaddling me and I'm ok. I'm ok. And I'm smiling.

I hate the way your own emotions seem to play a game with you. They gang up against you and see which one will be the strongest one and win you over for the day. Then they have days like this one. The kind of day where there are no real emotions taking over. There is just life. There is just plodding on.

Days like these are harder in some ways. I wandered round the kitchen, feeling low as if I should be crying. I think I preferred the rawness as at least then I knew what to expect. Wait till the children go to bed and cry my eyes out. On days like today that is not there and it makes me feel lost.

The determination and the strength are not prevalent enough to take over either. They are there, just hovering in the background. The phone call with him proved that. A feeling of indifference was present. Maybe that is the way to describe it, indifferent. I had neither love nor hate for him at that point. Neither sadness nor happiness. Neither anger nor bitterness. Strange. A little game within yourself.

I looked around and shrugged to myself. Why am I thinking again? Am I trying to make myself feel crap? I watched the garden become darker as night set in outside. It crept through the air and tinged it with a coldness. I sat just staring at it, as if I could see it moving. It wasn't getting at me. It tried to. It tried to come in to the house and smother me as it had done so many times before. I watched its invisible, bony fingers, scraping at the window, almost hearing the ear piercing screech it would have given out if it was real.

It couldn't reach me in here. I was safe, hidden under my protective cloak of indifference. Beneath my wrapping I was safe. I was secure. My bubble wrap was not going to pop tonight. There I sat watching the night and I smiled at it. A tentative, uncertain smile. But a smile nonetheless.

Are you ready to crash and burn?

27th - 28th April 2007

Spent the day itching for the escape time to come. A night without children. A night to myself. A night with Jemma. Drinking down the pub in Hornchurch I was technically happy. I wasn't getting too upset talking to her about everything. I didn't mind all the personal questions. But, despite all this, there was something hovering over me. I couldn't relax. I couldn't totally enjoy myself. I couldn't let go. Images of him came and went and as the drink took over me people started looking like him. I drank more to overcome this feeling and then the sadness came. That washed over me with such force it nearly bowled me over. The blues. What I had been suppressing all this time had finally bubbled violently to the top. I didn't need to cry or anything like that. I carried on drinking and talking to Jemma and slowly I managed to push it back down. This time I hope the hole it is in is covered so it doesn't resurface.

The more I talked away about everything the more uplifted I felt in a way. I admitted that things were not right and I admitted that I wasn't sure if I loved him the way I should have been. I still can't gauge what it is I'm missing. There is a hole. Some days it's just a little one and other days it feels as if it goes right through me, engulfing my entire torso. It's not enough to make me want to run back. It's not enough to make me want to withdraw myself as I felt I had to do early on in the split. It's like a taunting sensation.

I can't face or cope with the rejection. I know that and I freely admit to that. The feeling of being unwanted by someone who had wanted you for so long. It spills over into the fear of being rejected again. I don't want to be close to another man again. I don't want to feel this insecure again. You wonder if there would ever be someone who wants you anyway. I get scared because I know I don't want to be alone forever, as much as I am enjoying it for now. Yet I worry that I will never be attractive to somebody else. I look at myself in the mirror and I cannot see someone that would be attractive. I know it is only human to concentrate on the pieces that you are not happy with, the faults you see in yourself, the marks you know are there. But even if I try and look objectively, I still can't see anyone wanting this. I am nothing.

The feelings I had this weekend were a little unsettling. The indifference from the other night had disappeared and I was left mourning him a little. Jemma was great. She is an amazing friend. She seems to question the right things and gives advice that you have to listen to. She and I have been good friends for years now. We were at college together. She has been with me throughout all the ups and downs with Marc.

We both have three children, close in age too. We are alike in a lot of ways. We have moaned together about everything. We have withstood the trials of coping with two children within two years; we have drank endless cups of tea and put the world to rights. We have moaned and groaned about our men.

Jemma was there for me when I talked about Tess. She was there for me when I needed someone to listen to me, when I needed to cry. She was here for me now. I appreciated her support. She had put me up for the night, gone out of her way to come out with me. She was a good friend and I knew I could trust her.

I sat in my usual space and thought back over my night out. It had felt weird to be out in a pub. I had looked about and felt like I did not belong. It was not right to be out. The drink had helped me to relax, but at the same time it had brought me down. It had made those familiar feelings of missing him return to knock me down.

I did miss him. I missed him a lot. I can accept that. I can't accept the new single life. I have to hope that he realises the error he has made and comes back. He acts like he misses me but then you never know what someone else is feeling do you.

I turned all the usual images over and over in my head. I thought about whether this was still temporary, I thought about his new flat and the new life he was making for himself. Yet again, my thoughts turned to her. I really believed she was with him. I believed they had been having an affair, that he had feelings for her for the last few weeks of our marriage at the least. There had been too many mentions of her name. Too many talks about what she had said or done. There had to be more to them than he was admitting.

I got angry with myself for trawling it all up again and wondered whether it was a normal thing to do after a split. I hated myself for dwelling on everything and I hated the up and down motion of the last few days and weeks. I don't know where I am at the moment. I don't know how I am feeling or why I am feeling that way, whatever it is. It makes me so confused. The more I try to understand it, the more upset I become that I can't make sense of any of it.

The confusion made me feel sick. The whirling of the images made me tired. I was tired of trying to find answers to questions that did not want to be answered. I was tired of waiting for him to call, to speak to me and ultimately come home. I was tired of waiting to feel better and for the acceptance of the split to hit me. I was just tired.

The darkness and its cold claws broke my protective shield tonight. The emptiness and the loneliness won again. They took over and I could feel them choking me as I tried to breathe. I sat there wondering what I would become. The woman who willed her life to be back the way it had been even if something better was hiding round the corner. The woman who was not good enough for the man she loved. The unwanted woman.

29th April 2007

Today was a bad day in some ways.

I woke up feeling ok. I spoke to him ok. I saw him and then I crumbled. Once you crumble, whether they sense it or not, you cannot rebuild yourself. You cannot become the happier, stronger you that you are some days. It's too hard to climb back up.

Driving along in the car to get the shopping, that little voice was back in my head. It was telling me to pick myself back up and get back into the more positive shape I was a couple of days ago. *Come on, you can do it - up you get.* Didn't work.

I walked round the supermarket like a zombie. The only thing that made me smile was *Chelsea Dagger* being played on the radio. That is the only thing that picks me up a little - not enough - but a little. I was standing by the shelves and suddenly realised that I had been there for ages. That sudden jolt you get. I must have been daydreaming and I could tell it was for a while as the song playing was different to before and also some man asked me if I was ok. I nodded pathetically and smiled. He gave me that look of pity. Great, I'm receiving that look off strangers now too.

It does not matter what you do on a day like this. You always have this cloud that hovers over you and everything you do causes more problems. The bags not fitting back in the trolley even though the food came out of the bloody thing, hitting every red light on the way home so your frozen food turns to mush before you get it home, having to stop suddenly because of a ridiculous driver in front of you, which results in you hearing the bags fly off of the chairs so the shopping spills out in the car and then the heavy bags splitting as you carry them in so the food falls out on your feet causing yet more pain. It's like someone notices you are having a hard time and sets you up to make it harder. You half expect Jeremy Beadle to jump out and laugh at you with the stupid halfwit of your friend that thought that type of show was funny.

Speaking and listening to Marcus brought me down. I got really fed up with him talking to me about what he was doing, what the people in his group were doing, his nights down the pub, his busy week etc. I wanted to just scream at him to piss off. I looked at him and I could see his mouth moving but I couldn't hear anything. No words came out. I don't really care what he is up to. I don't really care what he is doing, where he is going or how hard he is working. I just care about him going away again. Part of me just wants him to go. Part of me wants him to stop being so bloody nice so I can hate him. I'd like the boot to be on the other foot. I'd like him to feel the pain. I'd like him to have the children crying because mummy has gone. I'd like to watch him suffer and cope with the difficult bits.

You can't describe the feeling though. It just feels weird. A mixture of feelings. Some you can understand. Some you can't. Some incredibly strong one day and then the weakest the next. Some don't ever change. Some don't go away. Some hover over you ready to pounce as soon as you hit a low point in your day. Some you recognise and deal with and some you ignore, pushing back inside you. There are the feelings of disgust, hatred, loneliness, grief and loss. There are the feelings of determination, anger, courage and sensibility. But it's the one of love that causes the most upset and confusion, maybe because it cannot be understood.

Love is complicated crap. Love is different to each of us and yet can still be manipulated by another person. It's hard to believe the impact it has on our lives. Right now, analysing it, I feel that the need for it, the desire to find it and the importance of holding on to it, is far greater than the feeling itself.

What a day. A day that is nearly over thank goodness. I just want to escape from this life and disappear somewhere. It is that 'lets run away' feeling.

I don't really know why it was so hard today. He dropped the children off at 2.30 this afternoon. He needed to get back to London he said. Why? What did he have there that meant his children were not that important right now? Why does that make me feel so bad?

The crumbling was the worst part. He hovers when he visits. He seems to want to stay. He wants to talk. He has to ask me if I am ok and again say things like "I think this split will be good for us." He waits for me to contest it. He seems to want to hear how bad I am feeling, like that makes him feel good. I think, in a sad way, every time he comes over I am expecting him to stay. I am expecting to hear the words, "I want to come back home now." Every time those words are not said, I crumble.

He spoke about the people that he had been with like I actually cared what they were all doing or saying. He wants me to be happy for him. He wants to treat us as if we are friends. He cannot seem to understand that while he is obviously happy with this situation, I am not. Has he even spared a thought about whether I am happy? Probably not.

I listened to him tell me about his nights down the pub. He did not seem to ever mention her name. it stood out as it was said so much in the past. She hadn't suddenly disappeared I was sure. I wondered if he was not mentioning her deliberately or whether she was just not around. Deliberate I decided. He was avoiding talking about her which made alarm bells ring loudly in my head as I began to piece his behaviour together.

I remembered when I had said to him a couple of weeks ago that I could not handle the thought of "Marcus and ....," whoever it was. He had given me this look that suggested that there was an "and ..." somebody. The look seemed to say it all. I pictured that face in my head now and married it up with the lack of Sue in conversation and for a minute I paused. I paused to think. I decided to test it again. I repeated the sentence "Marcus and..." There was that look again. This sorrowful, uneasy look. I didn't question it any further as I felt sick to the stomach. I just churned the thoughts over and over.

There I was again, convincing myself that they were together. There they were in my head together. I needed to stop obsessing over this. Cross that bridge if it ever comes. It won't come though, I love him and he knows it. He said this was a temporary split, he said three months apart would be good for us. He was still talking about an 'us'. He said he still cared for me. He wouldn't replace me just yet. He wouldn't replace me ever.

Pushing the thought of a "Marcus and Sue" to the very dark depths of my mind, I focused on those last few sentences as if I had to do that to convince myself they were true. The hopeful thoughts turned my mood slightly sweeter. It didn't bring me out of it completely but it changed it a little.

The children broke my train of thought with their noise outside. They were jumping on the trampoline and making such a racket. It was a wonder the neighbours didn't complain. They were so loud. They were having so much fun. The girls' hair was flowing in the air as they bounced away without a care in the world. How wonderful to be like that. They began singing.

Any songs that came into their little heads. Pheobe nagging Fiona to watch her and Fiona bossing Pheobe about, trying to get her to sit still. They carried on playing their little games, oblivious to me watching them. Seb was kicking the football against the wall. Back and forth. No smiles really, except every now and then when the girls made him laugh. I wondered what was going on in his head. He had not spoken to me. He seemed to play it cool when Marc had explained that he was living in London for now. He told them it wouldn't be forever and said that he hoped we would work things out soon and he would be able to return home one day. Seb had just nodded. What was he really thinking? He asked if it meant we were getting a divorce and Marc replied that things were not that bad yet and hopefully would never be. He said he never intended to let things go that far. Seb and the girls had then left the table to go and play.

I sat in the conservatory with some of the shopping still on the benches. I couldn't be bothered to put it away. I would rather sit here and watch them. I took great pleasure in sitting back and watching. Hours passed by and then the evening routine was started. Dinner, bath time, bedtime. All completed as if on autopilot. All done without remembering the processes. Sitting down I was glad the day had ended and another was beginning. I hoped the next would be better. I hoped the next would be more positive.

29th April 2007

Ok now I am so low I wish I could cry and be done with it. Nothing has really happened since this afternoon to make me this way but I have just hit the lowest point I have been at for a long time. I have phoned a few friends but they were not in. That adds to the loneliness. All you want is to hear another voice at the end of the phone but it's just the bloody answer machine. My Pheobe is still awake. She is sitting watching television and drinking hot chocolate. I will go and cuddle her soon. That usually makes me feel better.

For the first time I have felt that I need someone. I really need someone. Just here sitting with me. I'm sick of this empty feeling I constantly have and I'm sick of not knowing what to do with myself to make it go away. I'm sick of the loneliness. All this has probably come from the night out. Being back on that scene is no fun. I should not be there. I'm too old. I'm too down. I'm too not single. I don't feel single. I feel as if I still have somebody as this is just a temporary split. I felt guilty that I was out and not spending the time with my children. I always felt like that before, when Marc and I used to go out, but I feel it even more so now. Like I have to make up to them for not having their father around. I'm trying to be two people. Two parents. Give two lots of love and attention. I know it does not work like that but you can't help yourself. Maybe it's not just for them I am doing it. Maybe it's more for me.

Fingers crossed for a better tomorrow.

The better tomorrow is not here yet. Tomorrow is not here yet. I have tried to sleep but I can't. At this rate I will be able to watch the sun rise.

The days have been so hard. They have been so cold. They have been so dark. They have drowned me in sorrow and grief so deep I am sure there is no way out. I don't understand this depressive side. It seems to go away for a little while and then all of a sudden it has kicked back into me. It hits me so hard and viciously too. I hate this feeling. I want to be positive, I really do. I want to pick myself up off the floor and fight back. I want to feel as if I can cope without him, just in case this is no longer temporary in his eyes. But I can't. I just can't and I don't know why.

The feelings of desperation are here again. A huge, dark cloud has rested over me and there is no gust of wind to move it on. The will to move is gone and I wouldn't know what to do if I did move. I am lost and lonely. I wish there was someone here. Someone to sit with me. There in the corner. They would not have to say a word. They would not have to listen to me. They would just have to be there.

I miss him.

The dark windows radiated the cold air and I shivered as it touched my skin. I really miss him, where was he?

My cigarette smoke clouded my sight. As the smoke cleared, there were two figures. I closed my eyes to try and stop myself from seeing this. I closed them tight. I couldn't cry now. I screwed up my face. I could still see those two figures. I could still see them. Tormenting myself again. Torturing myself again. It's the not knowing. These last few weeks have been like a suspense thriller that will never end because I can't get to the truth.

I huddle deeper into the corner, knees up at my chest, arms hugging them tight, my whole body tense and rigid. I could feel the heat from the kettle burning into my hip as I sat so close to the wall. I concentrated hard on these images before me. The couple walking along, laughing and smiling. Snuggling up to each other. Is that what was really happening right now? Maybe this was a premonition of some kind. Maybe I am just going insane. Madness has set in.

I felt the tears run silently down my cheeks. Through teary eyes I saw Marcus. His face. And I heard his words. The words that had made my world freeze and then shatter into thousands of tiny pieces the size of grains of sand, that I had to somehow pick up one by one and put back together. I felt my body relax and I let go of my arms and legs and let them hang. My head fell to the side and my back slouched. As if in slow motion, my tears flowed down my cheeks, round my chin and dripped onto my chest. My chest seemed to be crushed under their weight, the ache from that crushing feeling spreading throughout me, causing a tingling sensation along my arms and fingers.

I hated myself for being like this. I hated feeling like this and I wanted it all to go away. I wanted it all to be over. I didn't care how. All I knew is that when I hit this low, there is no point in fighting it. There is no point in trying to stop it. I just have to give in to it. I just have to let it take me. I just have to let it win. I have to cry it out. Even when it takes all night.

30th April 2007

Hooray - the morning routine is back. The packed lunches, the children to get moving, the school run. Bloody morning routine. One day I won't have it and then I will miss it - hmmm!

Felt down again today. So low.

Visited my friend Michelle this afternoon and met another woman who has been treated like shit by her husband. Amazing. What did I say about everyone having stories to tell? Men really need to sort this out. They need to look at what they are doing and realise what they are. But then again, maybe its women who should sort this out. I'm sure if we all put our heads together we could eradicate them. There's a thought for the future.

A little dazed today. Lots of daydreaming. Lots of sudden jolts into the real world. Some simple pleasures. Smiling away as I watched the children playing, wondering why he could not get the same level of pleasure as I can from them. Don't understand. I am now at the point where I am trying even harder to get answers to the questions I have. I don't necessarily have to ask him. I am looking at it from his point of view. I know he has always been a quitter. If he couldn't do something first time he would not have another go. Maybe this was just too hard and it was easier to quit. Feeling very rejected again. Wondering what I did wrong though logic tells me it was nothing on my part exactly. Strange how you blame yourself. Missing him. So much. Longing for his company, his voice and his hugs. Going to bed now - hurts to think now. Just want to sleep.

Tried sleeping and although the desire was so strong, I couldn't do it. I lay awake in the bedroom, just like I had done so many nights before this. Lying awake was the worst thing I could do, I knew that. Normally I would go downstairs, have a drink, maybe a cigarette or just walk around, but, the energy had been zapped from me tonight and my legs could not have carried me down the stairs no matter how nicely I asked.

I laid there staring at the ceiling. The light from the lamppost outside shone through the blinds making it light enough to see the room. I had not drawn the curtains again as that was something I still couldn't do. I hadn't closed them since he left, unless I had company. I just couldn't do it. Couldn't add to the darkness. Turning my head to the space where he would have slept I swept my arm up it, almost stroking it. Pheobe was not in the bed yet to take that empty space away. To stop it taunting me the way it does. I rolled onto my stomach and held my legs up in the air with my feet crossed. I leaned a little further forward so my face was closer to the pillow. The smell of him was almost gone. I missed it. I had tried so hard to not smell it all those nights and now I wanted to, it wasn't there. Typical.

Laying my head back on the pillow I could see his wardrobe. I dragged my body across the bed diagonally and stretched to open the doors. His clothes were still there. He had so many. I had sent a large bag to his mums and he had collected some and there was still a wardrobe full. And the drawers beside his bed, the two drawers in the chest and the built in cupboard in the corner, I said to myself, nodding to each one of them as if I was talking to someone.

"And I wondered why I had an overdraft!" I said out loud, sighing with disbelief.

My attention back on the clothes in the wardrobe, I realised how there was no order to this. That was strange. Most of his important, material possessions had an order or a place. His CD's were in order and his DVD's were in the same alphabetical, chronological fashion. His hair gel was always placed on the second shelf of the tall cupboard in the kitchen, while his deodorant and aftershave were always on the first. His jacket was always hung on a hanger on the side wall of the study and when he took his shoes off he placed them side by side exactly next to him on the floor. Shoes he wore often were in the wardrobe, the occasional shoes and trainers were under the bed. Each pair sat separately. They were not allowed to be placed on top of another pair as they would be creased. Laces were placed inside the shoes and they were wiped down after wearing so as to remove any trace of dirt. Any CD's or even papers from work were placed on the desk in perfectly straight piles. He even fussed about the position of the TV, regularly adjusting it as it had apparently moved.

His wardrobe however was a complete mess. For someone who worships clothes so much, using them as a tool for trying to cope with his insecurities about his body, he didn't treat them in the same fanatical way he did his other possessions.

Trousers were slung over the top of the rail; you couldn't see the shelf for the erratic piles of jeans. He had another 10 pairs up there and we had just sold or thrown out a further 11 pairs about six weeks ago. Work shirts were crushed between casual shirts and t - shirts, long or short sleeved, there was clearly no order to this. Mind you, there had been no room left in there. The items were hung up so close together, nothing more could fit in. I hated putting his clothes away as there were never any free hangers. You couldn't see what he had in there without taking each item out and that was a fight.

Still lying on my stomach, I glanced up and over to the left hand side of the wardrobe. The side furthest away. I noticed the sleeve of a red and white shirt. It was rolled up so it was three quarter length and fastened with one of those straps that come from inside the sleeve and attaches to the button on the outside of the sleeve. I loved him in that shirt.

Tears stinging my eyes, I hauled myself up slowly and stood up next to the wardrobe. I was almost too scared to touch it, as if it might bite me. I lifted it and the smell of him wafted upwards.

"It still smells of him," I whispered to myself, quite taken aback by its strength.

It must have been one of those he bothered to spend 20 minutes ironing, put on and then took off again a few minutes later as it hadn't looked right or was still too creased or some other reason just as ridiculous. He would then have ironed another one.

I stroked it, letting it run through my fingers. I smiled through the tears that were now burning down my cheeks again as I remembered him in it. He had worn it a lot compared to some of his other shirts. I thought he looked great in it. I let the sleeve go, watching it fall back to where it was. The lost feeling bit at me, the empty hole where my heart had once been burnt, the pain moving through me in waves crashing up and down.

I stood still for a minute just about keeping my balance with the sea of emotions tugging back and forth inside me. I slowly pushed one strap of my night dress off my shoulder and then the other, letting it fall to the ground. Standing in just my knickers, I reached out and took the shirt off the hanger. I unbuttoned it and slowly put the first arm through the sleeve, breathing in the smell of his aftershave as it went. I placed my other arm in its sleeve and pulled the sides of the shirt in and up to my face. I sobbed into it for a few seconds before letting it fall back down. I fastened the buttons carefully, making sure they were right through the button hole so as not to undo again.

In slow motion, I turned and crawled back onto the bed. I pulled myself into a ball and brought my knees up to my chest, under the shirt. I let my neck sink inside the collar and bowed my head further forward, pushing my shoulders up so I could take in the smell of him more. I didn't want to pull the duvet over me in case it clouded it in some way.

There I lay, in that position. The light from the lamppost outside shining across the bed. My sobs making my whole body shake. That's where I stayed, wallowing in him, breathing in the last little bit that I had left.

1st May 2007.

Woke up feeling quite happy today. Maybe because I was escaping and heading out to work. Maybe the down days are finished again.

Day started brilliantly. A lovely young man in a big blue van smiled and waved at me across the traffic lights. He made my day. A big smile on my face and my head held high as I walked into work. Great feeling.

Work went quick and then the journey home. Arrived and realised that I had not thought about all this for the entire two hours of the trip. Smug smile to self!

Spoke to mum a fair bit tonight. The little bits I miss. I miss having someone here. I miss the last cup of tea before bed. I miss the heat from him at night. The little bits. Dawned on me that I never actually said I miss Marc. I could have been talking about anyone.

Still, the need to sleep tugs at me. The amount I have had over this week is impressive compared to my usual small total. And yet still I want to sleep. The dreams have stopped. The ones where you wake up in the middle of the night crying and yet you can't remember what you were dreaming about. The awful heavy feeling in the morning has stopped too. At first you wake up fine, like it is a normal day and then suddenly you remember what has happened and that it was not a bad dream and that this empty life is your reality and the world crashes on top of you. That is gone now. Maybe that was the shock. Get more fed up with things. Mum said I'm snapping at the children more. Very irritable. Just because life is not going my way.

I was surprised at my mood today, considering how awful I felt last night. The sleeping in his shirt thing freaked me out a little when I woke up in it. I threw it in the wash. I'll wash it one last time for him. The fact that he has not picked up the rest of his clothes must be a good sign right? Maybe it is because he is considering coming home after all. Maybe he does not really want to go completely.

The day was an ok one. Mum had a moan at me for snapping at the children. I know she is right but I just can't help it. I don't even know I am doing it sometimes. I just want to be left alone really. They are the ones keeping me going at the moment, they are my reason for getting out of bed every day and yet their needs and wants are weighing me down. I know that if they were not here, I would have been curled up in bed for this whole time, I am grateful to them for their help but I am tired and just want to sit and be left alone.

The mood was deep tonight. That is the only way to describe it really. Deep. Not sure whether that is a type of mood but all I was doing was sitting around thinking. Not dwelling on everything, just thinking. The thoughts that you are trying to get your head around are constantly there, churning around in your head, mixing together and making your brain work overtime. Maybe that's why I am so tired.

The children's energy is endless. They have run around all evening and made so much noise. Yet, I can't stand the emptiness they leave when they go to bed. I long for them to wake up and chat away to me, though I am sure if they did I wouldn't be that happy about it.

I think a lot about them. I think about how I will afford to buy them all the things they need. I think about their unhappiness should Marc never come back. I worry about their education and whether it is suffering because of all that has happened. I stress over their behaviour, not allowing for the effects of the break up, and worry that it will reflect on what kind of parent I am. Most of all, I worry that if he does not come home soon, whether he will have enough time for them, whether he will show enough love to reassure them and whether he will devote his time and energy to making them happy. He has always struggled with the little things that make them smile. Sometimes I wonder if he knows them enough to know what makes them tick. What their favourite cereal is for the mornings he has them. What their favourite game is. What they like to talk about. What friends they have made in school. Whether there are any clubs they take part in.

With all these thoughts whirling I feel the overwhelming need to be with them. I take my glass of vodka upstairs and sit on the landing. Mum is in Pheobe's bed tonight as she is staying over. I couldn't sleep as usual so came down. I listen to my babies tossing and turning in their beds. I get up and check on each one.

Pheobe has taken over my whole bed. Feet on my bedside cabinet and head over where her dad used to sleep. She seems to need her comforts more and more lately. She needs her dummy all the time. One in her mouth and one in her hand, though right now both of them are scattered across the bed. She has her teddy too. He is crushed beneath her. And her blanket. Always there with her wherever she goes.

Fiona is coughing a little. Her asthma must be flaring up. Poor thing. She looks so peaceful in her sleep. She moves slightly and slowly and goes further and further down the bed. Never sleeps on that pillow.

Seb is snoring again. Sprawled out over the bed. He is still not talking to me about all of this much. He has told me he thinks Daddy will come home soon. He is missing him more than he lets on I am sure. He has his SATs coming up soon. Next week. He will not revise and I am hoping this situation has not had too much effect on him.

Anger wells up inside me as I go back to my landing. Anger for what he is putting us all through. For the pain and suffering he is making my children endure. I breathe deep and calm down. No anger tonight. I won't let it take over tonight.

Leaning against the wall, I watch the light pour in through the porch. It lights up the bottom stairs. I just sit there and watch it shining, making a peaceful setting as it spreads.

2nd May 2007

Mum hit the nail on the head today when she said I had never been good at being alone. She is so right. Even when I was younger I was never without a boyfriend/date for long. I walked from one to another quite quickly. Some may have only lasted one or two dates but they were still there. Oh, how easy it is when you are young.

Don't feel I could do that now. Can't stand being on my own. Don't want anyone else either. Even if he never comes home and I have been waiting for him for nothing, I still wouldn't want anyone else. I probably never will. With him too long and I just can't picture being with some other man. I have looked and smiled and flirted but I think if somebody actually approached me I would run like the wind.

It's scary. 31 and scared. Not right. As a teenager I would picture myself grown up. Taller, pretty, long hair, responsible, happy, more confident. Didn't reach any of those. You don't realise that it is only your life that changes and not actually you. In your head you don't grow up really. *I still feel 21* you hear 80 year old women say. You hear women of all ages saying that. The problem is life. Its expectations of you. You will get married. You will have children. You will have responsibilities. Those expectations are put out there as the norm. It's what we strive for. Some don't achieve it but *are they really less happy than those who do? Are those that do achieve it really happy anyway?* Expectations should be individual and not be influenced by the world around us.

I expected so much of myself that I have not appreciated what I have. What I am. I know that I look down on myself. I know that I am insecure with myself. I know that Marc, before and after leaving, has not helped me feel better about myself, but it's all down to you and who you are. I'm realising that life is going to be what I make it become. I realise I need to turn this around to suit me. I need to believe in myself, get out there and achieve what I want. Get what I want. It's hard to do when you have no confidence left. I feel so low with everything but maybe I feel low purely because of me. I automatically fixated on what I thought Marc did not like about me. I automatically assumed it was the way I had gained weight, not wanted to go out, cared for the children every hour of every day. Instead of saying I did all that because I wanted to, I questioned my decisions and I blamed them and me for losing Marc. *It's not like that though is it?* Not really. Whether I am strong enough now to change this is another story. I need to appreciate that the strength will come gradually. It's not a quick overnight fix. I need to understand myself. I need to appreciate myself. I need to believe in myself. Something I've never been able to do. Splitting up with the one you have loved for so long goes deeper than you think. It goes deeper than anyone can understand. It makes you question yourself on so many different levels that you cannot be prepared enough to cope with it. I am certainly not prepared. I know I need to stop being so down with life. I know I need to pick myself up. I also know I won't feel this or use this acknowledgement every day. But each day that I do I need to utilise it to its full capacity.

Being alone is something I need to do for a while. I have to stop this constant need to feel wanted by somebody. The need to be loved is not one you can live with. I need to try and understand why I feel that urge to be desired. *What is it making me feel? What is it about it that I crave?* My need for a relationship goes deeper than the human desire for love. I need to stop it from controlling my drive. I need to be comfortable with living my life for me. *How do you begin to change yourself? Where should I start? Will Marc come back or somebody else come along before I do this so I don't face my lack of confidence and I don't change it again?* This will be one hard journey, one I intend to take slowly, but one I intend to complete.

The acknowledgements in my thoughts of today are all doing me good. It means that I know what I have to do. In some ways though, they make it harder. It is hard to know what you need to do when you know you can't quite do it. I am rubbish at believing in myself. As a child I always compared myself with other children. I did it all the time, with friends and family. I always looked at them and believed they were better than me in some way.

I don't think I have ever looked in the mirror and thought I looked ok. Even on my wedding day I didn't and the dread I felt at seeing the photographs was amazing. I don't understand what it is about myself that makes me act in this way.

My achievements so far are probably more than some people. I have a degree and a post graduate certificate. I am a primary teacher so I have a good career that could develop well. I have 3 children, who are all healthy and amazingly beautiful. I own 50% of my house and can pay the bills and mortgage without too much stress, although with his help. All of this and I am only just 31. So what is my problem? Why can't I be proud of myself?

The problem is that I don't see these as major achievements. I see them as something that other people have too. Lots of people go to university and get a degree. Lots of those get a higher degree than what I got. Lots of people achieved higher grades than I did in their exams. Lots of people are teachers and have a better career in education than I do. So many people have children and they too think they are beautiful. There are quite a few home owners too, some with less mortgage or none.

I view my life so negatively. I have not achieved anything that has not been done before or that is not being achieved by lots of people out in this world right now. There are people everywhere that are better than me in lots of ways, so I just can't look at myself and my life positively.

My confidence in the person I am has always been a big downfall. I always compared myself to my cousins as a child. I used to look at them (and still do) and know that they have more than I do. I always saw them as prettier than me. Like I was the one in the family that stood out because she was the ugly one. They were tall and I was shorter. They were slim and I was not. They were chatty and I was not. They were confident and I was not. I still see it like that except that I have accepted it now and don't question it as much.

Sitting on the bench I ventured further into this. I was pleased in some way that I did not see myself as this better than everyone else kind of person but I was not pleased with how it was affecting me now.

With Marc leaving and the constant belief he was with someone else, I had questioned my part in this. I was not good enough for him. I did not look good enough to him, I was not outgoing enough for him and I did not mean enough to him. I could not love him as much as he needed. I could go on and on. This is the problem I'm facing, I can't change the way I feel about myself. Therefore I cannot change the path my life leads down.

I began to cry on this realisation. These tears were not for the loss of Marc, these were for me. I knew then that I did not have a hope of achieving all those things that I wanted to. It hurt. I want to change my opinion of myself. Just once I want to look in the mirror and believe that I look good. Just once, I want to go out and walk down the road with confidence instead of with my head bowed looking at the floor. I want to go out and be the person I want to be without worrying what people are thinking of me or how they perceive me. This is not going to happen because that isn't me.

I got off my bench and looked into the mirror hanging on my chimney breast. I lifted myself up so I was sitting on the dining table looking at my reflection. Look at yourself Stephanie. Look at yourself and see what is there that makes you feel so unhappy to be you.

There was not one positive thing running through my head. Your eyes are puffy, your face is round and fat, your skin is scarred and you are still getting spots which will give you more. Looking down I continued, you are overweight, you are out of shape, and your thighs are huge. The list went on.

When I had finished, the tears were running thick and fast. My cheeks and all around my eyes had turned bright red and puffy from crying so fiercely, something else I hated. I am pathetic. I am so low in confidence and so low in opinion of myself that there is no way to clamber out no matter how hard I try.

I lay down on the settee and cried. I cried for the person I was. I cried for the person I had become. I cried for not believing in myself. I cried for my lack of positive thoughts. I cried for my lack of achievement. I cried for the way I looked. I cried for the way I felt about myself. But most of all, I cried for the person that I really wanted to be. I cried for the real person that is within somewhere, hidden away where no one will see her. The person I am in my dreams. The person that has been locked up inside for fear of anyone seeing her and not liking her. For fear of disapproval. For fear of doing something that nobody agrees with. I cried for her. I cried for hours.

Oh No - I was right!

3rd May 2007

Just found out he has started seeing Sue. It's official. Someone from work has been told and I found the email. Was having a good night until this. Don't quite know what to feel. Want to run to a solicitor and file for divorce tomorrow. I still can't believe he has done this to me. *What the hell have I done to make me so bad that he needs her?* I knew that she was a possibility but to find out he is seeing her now hurts like hell. I wish I could hurt him that bad. I wish he could feel the pain. *He has not had the guts to tell me though has he?* He has not actually admitted the fact that he was having an affair and yes there is scandal involved darling. I hate her now. Now I am angry. Now I can feel it welling up in me and I feel as if I can explode at any minute. Will never sleep tonight now. The bitch. I will ruin her. I swear. Now he can shove amicable. Now he can shove everything. Now I will take him to the cleaners. I'll show them both what a bitter woman I can be. You just wait and see.

The anger running through me was intense. The pain was like I had never felt before. I had been snooping I know. I had had a bottle of wine with a friend and I was thinking about him. I was wondering whether to call him. I was wondering whether to text him. It then led to emailing him and that's when I did it. I switched on the internet, saw his work address and entered the password. It was like a calling. I hadn't snooped since he'd left. I hadn't bothered. Now though, now look what has happened.

I was steaming. The anger made me breathe so fast and yet I couldn't catch my breath. My chest was being crushed so violently and I was sobbing loudly. I sat in the office chair just staring at the computer screen. I was right. I was bloody right and this was one time I didn't want to be.

I stormed out of the office not quite knowing what to do. Pacing up and down the kitchen my head swirled with all sorts of images and thoughts and they all mixed into one. There was no sense in them. There was no path to follow. Why had he done this?

Her. The utter cow. She had swooped in. How long ago? Since when? Why?

The confusion made me feel so sick. I kept running my hands through my hair, as if pushing it back would help me to see more clearly. I picked up the phone and put it down again. The tears stung my face and my temperature soared. My heart was thumping at my chest as if it were going to explode. Still I was pacing. My mind rattled.

"No!" I cried. "No!" and I just fell to the floor in the kitchen. I crumbled up into a heap like an old teddy bear that had just had the stuffing ripped from inside him.

A few minutes later, the shock over, I picked myself up off the floor. My arms hugged me. Wrapped around me so tight. I walked slowly into the office. I stood just beside the screen and peeked round cautiously so I could just about see it again. Sue had emailed her friend in work.

Friend: so how are things with you and the lovely Marcus?

Sue: what exactly do you mean by that? :-)

Friend: I dunno I thought you guys get on pretty well and now that you are both single??

Sue: we do, very well I guess

Friend: I was wondering if anything to announce?

Sue: Hmmmm

Friend: it's all good

Sue: shall talk to you later... but yes (embarrassed face)

Friend: lovely I am delighted for you both

Sue: kinda started seeing each other, very recently...

Friend: you both deserve it :-)

Sue: feels like people might think there's scandal involved... I'm nervous about it

Friend: no don't be silly everyone will be happy for you both............I certainly am x

Sue: thanks, that really means a lot

What? Deserve it? No scandal?

My heart broke again. I couldn't believe what I was reading. This conversation can't be real. This cannot be happening. What was I going to do? He said this was temporary. He said it was just for a while. He is supposed to be coming home. I wanted him to come home.

I turned to make an exit again but I was stopped in my tracks by the sight of his coat. I walked over to it, still crying, and took it off the hanger. I scrunched it up in my hands and walked back through to the kitchen. I stood next to the fridge and leaned against the bench. I began sobbing again. Those big loud sobs that are noisy and mean you can't catch your breath. With the pain running through me so intensely, I slid down the bench and sat in a heap, with my knees up to my chest, covered by his coat. I held onto it so tightly as if I was holding on to him. I cried for what seemed like hours. I had lost him. I had lost everything. She had won. I hated her. So much.

As the sobs slowed down and the thoughts of her and then the two of them together came and went, the pain subsided. All of a sudden I was angry again. The bitterness took hold and the shouting at myself began.

"Get up off that floor woman! You knew this already! Get up!"

I pulled myself to my feet, looked at the jacket in my hands and I knew what I had to do. I dragged out the bin bags from the cupboard, causing everything on top of them to crash to the floor and marched up the stairs. I ripped off black bag after black bag and I filled them with his stuff. I pulled out his clothes from the wardrobe and stuffed them into the bag. The jeans off the shelf. I pulled the shirt I had slept in the other night out of the washing basket - no way was I washing that now - I threw the socks and underwear from his drawers into the broken case from the cupboard. The chest of drawers were emptied and the built in cupboard too. I stood there exhausted and panting and looked down. Six black bags and a huge case. How much stuff does he have?

The anger had become stronger than the pain. The whole time, the email was running through my head. "Scandal involved...just recently..." The hatred I had for her now was so overwhelming. I ran down the stairs. It was almost midnight. I text him: 'I have packed all your stuff away...' He replied, 'What have you done? What's going on?' Another text from me, 'haven't even got the guts to phone and find out.'

The phone rang. I picked it up but everything that was in my head would not straighten itself out into sentences. Nothing would come out. I heard his voice asking what had happened. What was wrong? The email was mentioned. Me knowing. He said he never wanted me to find out like this. Nothing was going on before.

How could I ever believe him now?

"How long?" I screamed.

"A few weeks"

A few weeks. A few weeks. We had only been apart for five weeks. Two weeks it had taken him. Two weeks to replace me. That's what the last fourteen years had meant to him. That's what he had thought of me waiting for him to come back. Two weeks and I am already gone for good. Two weeks.

I wanted to scream. I wanted to shout. Nothing would come out. Nothing but sobs of pure agony. He listened to me cry.

"This was supposed to be a temporary split," I sobbed.

"I know. It was going to be," he muttered.

"How could you do this to me?" I cried. He was just quiet.

"I'm sorry," he said.

Sorry. Sorry. Does he think that will make it all ok? Does he think that will heal my pain? All this time I had been sitting here wanting him to come home. All this time I had been waiting for him. All this time he had me believing we were splitting for just a little while. All this time he had been telling me how this split was not what he wanted. All lies. More lies. They were together before. They were developing their relationship. He probably did cheat on me. I was probably right all along. Oh no! I had so longed to be wrong.

The tears came in another huge wave. I hung up the phone.

What kind of woman does that? What kind of woman steals a husband? What kind of woman steals a daddy away from his children? Does she know what she has done? Or has he been feeding her a load of lies too? The tears quietened as my thoughts turned to Tess, the first relationship he had with another woman. He had told her lies about us. He had told her he was unhappy and that we were on the verge of ending it all. He must have told Sue the same thing. I couldn't blame her.

Within seconds I decided that I could blame her actually and I will. They are both to blame. They are cheats and liars and I intend to ruin what they have. I intend to make life difficult. I don't know how. I will take my time and work it out.

I stood in the silence and the emptiness hit me. Not from the house this time, it was the emptiness within me. The emptiness from realising he was not coming back. He was not coming back to me. But I loved him. I did. Not her. Me. This is his home. His children are here. His life is with us. I need him. We need him.

The tears seemed to dry up. I couldn't cry anymore. I just stood staring at the floor with all the thoughts and feelings racing around inside of me tearing up my insides as they went. Ripping me apart from within.

The anger and the tears had had such an effect on my body that I suddenly felt so drained. I felt even more tired when I heard Pheobe calling out. I let out a sigh. A 'not now' sigh. I carried her into my bed and looked at her confused face looking at me. I tried to force a smile for her. She looked at me, almost knowingly. She brushed the tears off my cheek. "Don't cry mummy," she whispered and yawned. I lay beside her still in my clothes. I had my head on her shoulder and she turned onto her side and wrapped her arms round my head tight. She didn't let go, not even when her body had become limp with sleep. She didn't let go.

4th May 2007

A good day at first. Blocked everything out. Had company all day and felt positive, like I knew what I wanted to do. Pack the rest of his stuff up. Contact solicitors.

Went into London for evening out with my uni friend Frances and her friend. Had a few laughs. Danced and drank a fair bit. No pleasure came of it though. It wasn't like I did not want to be there. I was ok. The club thing just is not my scene. Maybe mum is right and it is just too early. Maybe that club was just not the right one for me. Maybe it was bad timing considering I have just found out about them.

I don't know what it was but all the way back on the train I just wanted to burst into tears. My life was with Marc for so long and I never thought I would lose him. I thought he would always love me and want me and the rejection and the realisation that he wants somebody else now is too much for me to handle. I don't know if I would have ever left him if I had carried on with him for longer. Part of me thinks I would have and part of me thinks I would not have been able to, despite disliking the person he had become. I do love him still. I do need him still. Ok so we were not happy, not entirely, but I did not want this. I miss him. *Or do I miss being in a relationship?* I never thought I would feel so down about everything. I want the pain to end and for me to accept that this is my life now. I can't seem to carry on without him. I can't seem to let go. I don't think if he ever came back to me now I could take him back. I just can't get him out of my head. He is all I have known for so long. He is everything I had. He was my life because I never had one of my own. I don't want one of my own. Everything I do I think of him. Everywhere I go I wonder what he is doing. I can't carry on like this for my own sanity but I can't seem to want to move on. I just want my safe, secure life back.

I want him back. I want this nightmare to end. I want to wake up and be back in his arms and be happy. I am so fed up.

I wander round aimlessly. I let myself be swallowed by the emptiness and the loneliness. I am starting back at the beginning again. I am back at the bottom and this time I know how far it is to the more positive bit. I never reached the top. I never reached the sign that read 'happiness straight ahead.' That was too far away then. So who knows how far away it is now.

All those days I sat there wondering whether he was coming back. All those days I believed this to be a temporary split. All those days I believed in him and his love for me. All those days I listened to what he was saying and believed him. How stupid?

I believed him when he said he hadn't meant for this to happen. I believed him when he said he never wanted to split. I believed him when he said that we would work it out. I feel so foolish. All the time he was dating her. He was seeing her. I should have listened to myself. I should have listened to my intuition.

I wandered up and down the stairs trying to gain some comfort from the children, from my bed, from a bath, from my cigarettes and alcohol. Nothing helped.

I gave in and just sat. I just sat in the front room. The TV off. The lights off. The house silent. There was nothing here. There was no one here. I listened to the sound of my heart beating. It sounded like it was struggling a little. I listened to the nothing. The eerie nothing that had swept into my home and made it its own. The quiet, the peace, the sadness all so apparent in my little world here.

I just sat and stared into the space in front of me. The house was dark and yet the images were still there dancing in front of me, taunting me and teasing out the pain from within. The tears started to fall gently onto my lap and yet I just sat. I was motionless. Not able to move. Not able to fight back. I was swallowed whole by the nothing. And it wouldn't let me go.

5th May 2007

Feeling so low today. I saw the children off with Marcus after speaking to him. He wanted to talk to me he said. All he spoke about was how I should blame him and not her. How I should be ok with this because it was what we both wanted. The truth is I don't know what I wanted anymore. I don't know what to say, what to think, what to do. All I am doing is sitting drinking vodka. *How is that good for me?*

Since when has he known what I wanted? Since when has he known what I was feeling, thinking, doing. He had never paid any attention to what I said so how would he know.

"I need to talk to you," he had said.

All he talked about was her. Like I wanted to hear that. Like that was going to help.

"It's not her fault. Don't blame her," he had said.

Well I do. And him saying not to was not going to change that.

If I had met a man who was married with three children, split from his wife or not, I would have walked away. Two weeks we were split, two weeks and she was waltzing in on my husband, taking my place beside him. And, that's only if he was telling the truth. I was sure it was longer than the time he had said. I was sure it had started back in March, before we split. Of course I blame her.

I could hardly look at him. I didn't want to face him. He tried to hug me lots of times, like that was going to make me feel better. Kept pulling me close. Why?

He didn't love me as he had said. He needed her now. What did it matter what I was feeling? Why did it matter to him that I was hurting? I didn't understand.

I shut the door after watching the children walk away with him and my knees buckled. They just crumbled and I sat in the porch and cried.

"I hate you!" I screamed as loud as I could.

"How could you do this?" I yelled. "How could you do this? How could you do this?"

Each question got quieter and I fell to the side and hit my head on the box. The box with all the children's stuff in it. Their little scarves and hats and gloves. Their reading folders. I took each one out and stroked them and then put them back in neatly.

Hauling myself up to my feet, I walked into the kitchen and poured myself yet another vodka. And then another. I lit a cigarette and inhaled deeply like it would make the pain go away.

I wandered round the house talking to myself. Giggling to myself. Having a conversation with myself. They say the first sign of madness is talking to yourself, well I'm answering my own questions here so what does that make me?

Jason had said that quite a few times. Jason. One of my best friends. He would know what to do. I had to call him. I didn't care that he was in America; Marc was still paying the bill.

Jason had always been there for me. He was amazing. We had met at secondary school and quickly became inseparable. Everyone had thought it was more than friendship but it wasn't. It could have been. I adored him. Always will. He knows what to say to brighten my day. He knows when to listen to me ramble on. He knows when to shout at me to buck my ideas up. No one treats me like that, except him. We have a close relationship. I love him lots. It was him that I always ran to when I had a problem and it was him I was running to now.

I needed to hear his voice. I needed to feel his closeness. I needed to know he was there. The phone rang. Answer phone. I hated him being so far away. I wanted him here with me. I cried for him. I cried again.

The more I drank, the longer I went without crying. The more conversations I had with myself, the less they made any sense. To an outsider I must have looked like I was a little crazy. I felt it.

The day blurred past me. I don't know how but all of a sudden it was the evening. I had done nothing. Hadn't even switched on the TV or the computer. Hadn't done a thing.

Seb was on the phone. "I want to come home."

Waiting for him was awful. I knew I would have to face Marc again. Seb was fine and went off to bed. Marc stood in the kitchen with me. I had on a pair of shorts and an old jumper. He commented on how it was too big. It was the first time he had commented on how much weight I had lost. He said I looked good. I frowned at him.

I put the computer on and turned up the music. I tried to drown out what he was saying. He carried on talking. We discussed what had happened. He still swore nothing was going on before the split - couldn't believe him. He said that he would always love me - couldn't believe him. He said he would always be there whenever I needed him - couldn't believe him.

I looked at him. I looked up at this tall, thin man and thought to myself. Why do I love him? He has given me nothing but heartache over the last few years. Nothing but stress. Nothing but anger and frustration. And yet here I am broken hearted over him. What?

I watched him talking. Not hearing a word except the one I really didn't want to hear. Sue. Sue this. Sue that. He had stuck the knife in and now he was giving it a few short, sharp twists, just to make sure it hurt.

He left me at half 10 and I sank. Down to my bottomless pit of hell. Down to the dungeon of pain and sorrow. Down to the tears. Down to the loneliness. Down to the lowest point I could get to.

6th May 2007

He came round with the girls this morning. Again he asked me if I was ok. *Does he really think that one day will make a difference?* It's amazing how I have crashed over this. The thought of him and Sue together makes me feel so ill it's untrue. I feel sick all the time and I blame myself. I'm angry that I have made such a mess of myself that he needed her. Been traded in for a new model. My heart is broken. I just want to cry all the time. I just want to curl up and do nothing. I want someone to take this pain away. To mend everything. There is no one who can do that though. No one at all. All I had was him and even with everyone telling me to find something to fill my time, to go out and see people, to go and follow an interest, I can't see the point. I can't see the point in anything.

He insisted that I had not been replaced. Of course I had. And quickly.

I listened to him asking repeatedly what was wrong. I don't understand how he can expect me to be ok with this and just accept it. I can't. There is no way I can accept it.

Looking at him I could feel the hatred for him welling up inside me. I wanted to scream at him but I just did not have the energy to do that. I couldn't be bothered. It would be a waste of my time. Falling on deaf ears.

He irritated me the whole time he was here. His voice. The pacing up and down. The checking of his phone every five minutes.

"Waiting for her?" I had asked viciously.

The look he gave me. As if I was not supposed to be angry. He kept hugging me and trying to pull me towards him. It drove me mad. But then when he said he had to go, the anger disappeared and I did not want to let him leave. I did not want him to walk away from me and go to her. The hatred twisted itself round to be directed at her.

"That's enough time with the children is it?" I yelled.

"That's their daddy's contribution over."

"Need to run to her now - she is more important!"

I screamed at him as he got ready to leave.

The children were so confused. They looked at me and then to him. He hugged them, telling them he would be back soon.

"Don't lie to them Marc," I shouted.

"Why are you being like this?" he replied.

My mouth dropped open and I just stared at him. He has got the nerve to ask me that question. Why does he think I am being like this? Why would I react this way? Is he stupid or what? Has he not been listening to a single word I had said over the last few weeks?

I slammed the door after pushing him through it. I saw his reflection stand there for a few seconds as if he expected me to re-open it. Tears streamed down my face again.

I huffed at myself and walked back through into the kitchen. I straightened myself out and got on with the usual things. I played with the children as much as I could. I read to them. I bathed them, fed them and put them to bed. The whole time I was not really there. On auto-pilot again. Felt so numb. So tired. So let down.

He tried to call me a few times. I couldn't bear to hear his voice again. I didn't want to hear the stupid questions all over again.

The thoughts of her filled my head again. What was she that I wasn't? Why was she so bloody great? What was so special about her that made him want to leave his wife and children behind? That made him want to move 60 miles away? Change his life so drastically?

I hated her I thought as I wiped a solitary tear from my cheek. My movements were all so slow. Walked around slowly. Sat on nearly every chair in the house. No settling. I moved on every time the pain welled up again as if I was walking away from it. If only it was that easy.

Sleep never came. I watched the night turn to day. I saw the sun come up at the back of my house, through the conservatory windows. I tortured myself with thoughts of them waking up together. Getting ready for work together.

I tortured myself until I heard the children wake up. Another day - another day and I am still here.

7th May 2007.

Think I've cried all I can possibly cry. I still picture the two of them together. Sat up all night crying my eyes out. God knows whether this is all I will do from now on. Can't see the end. Marc phoned again asking if I was ok and if I was alright. *What's wrong?* He said as if he didn't know. I don't understand what he expected when he did this to me. When he walked out that door to rebuild his life happy because he was finally free, what did he expect me to do, throw a party perhaps, *rejoice in my shitty life without him?*

Talking to his family was hard. Answering the questions about him and what he was doing was even harder. Both said when I meet someone new things will be different for him. *How is that ever going to happen? Why would that ever happen?* I don't go out, I hate going out. I hate meeting people so will not put myself in that position. I can't go back to work, partly because I haven't got the guts and partly because of the complications of childminding. I have 3 children who need me constantly. One child that does not sleep so I'm always exhausted and just want to curl up in bed, although I can't sleep myself at the moment so that is not really an issue right now. I can't see a way out of this life. Well, I can see one way but that is for cowards and besides I would never do that to my children.

I sat in the dark and thought about what his family had said. I had listened but I had not agreed with everything. I was relieved that they had not seen it as my failing. They said he had always been so difficult and had made life hard for me in many ways. They had seen it too then.

The discussion on meeting someone else was weird. I can't see that happening. There are all the complications regarding getting out, talking to people which I hate doing, meeting a man again but there is one further one. I don't want anybody else. I just want him. I just want him.

Feeling stupid I poured another vodka and began the conversations with myself. It was such a torment.

"He was so hard to live with."

"I know but I love him."

"You were not entirely happy."

"I know but I love him."

"He cheated on you."

"I know but I love him."

"He was no help with the house or the children."

"I know but I love him."

"He has walked away and left you."

"I know but I love him."

See the pattern. See the torment. See the frustration.

Every reason I had to not be with him was valid. Every reason I had was dismissed by the other side of me. This tugging sensation at my heart appeared every time I tried to reason with myself. I made a mistake. I packed his bags. I need to suffer the consequences. I need to get on with it. But how do you do that?

8th May 2007

Anna turned up to save me. She is always there. She listened to me moan and didn't really comment. She packed up the odds and ends of his stuff that I had found lying around the house. Found a couple of entries he had wrote in my diary when we were young saying how much he loved me. Tore them out and put them in his sacks too. Don't know why. I am still thinking about him every minute. Its killing me now and I feel as if I can't do anything else. Just sit. Had this urge to go out to the shop and buy another bottle of vodka. Drinking again. I need to get this out of my system. Just wish it would all hurry up and go. It's not going fast enough. Wish I could hurt him as much as he has done me. Want to rip his heart out. *Can't carry on like this though can I?* Need to be careful as the children will be coming home soon. Need to get up and sort myself out. Come on girl, move.

The piles of stuff in the garage were significant to his life with us. No family photos apart from the wedding ones I had included. I had kept all the family ones but the ones of me and him together I had put with his things. The daddy mugs had been dusty as they had hardly ever been used.

Anna had left. She was such a good friend. We had been a little distant since the move to Essex but that had not stopped her from jumping in the car and driving for an hour and a half, with her little boy, just to support me. She always listened. She never judged. She never preached. Mind you she had never really approved of him anyway. Never uttered bad words against him. Questioned his actions, yes, run him down, no. She was as shocked as most people. She had not thought he would do this to me anymore than anyone else did. Anna was so calm about everything; it had rubbed off on me. I felt calmer.

Watching her pull off the drive and wave goodbye, the calm feeling was gone with her. The loneliness had hit me again and I hated it. I drank more to try and get rid of that load on my shoulders. It hadn't worked so I gave up.

Putting the empty glass on the bench, I sobbed and hunched over it, as if I was trying to refill it with my tears. I just felt so ....so....empty.

Empty.

There was a feeling inside of nothing. Like there was nothing left. He had taken it all. He had removed every part of me. I was just the shell of the body I had once been. The shell that had been cast aside because it was no longer wanted. No longer needed.

No more tears.

13th May 2007

This week has been an incredible journey for me. I have been so up and down in myself that I have felt sick for the majority of the time. Each evening I had to fight the thoughts of what he was doing and where he was and who he was with. Fight the urge to call him. Dealing with feelings of rejection and sadness over losing my family unit. You long for what has been and think constantly about what has happened. It's like it never leaves you. Over the last few days I have felt my emotions change. The self pity is still bubbling under the surface. The pain is lying silently there too. Both waiting for the opportunity to grab hold of me and take over again. The only emotions keeping them under control and laying low are the ones of bitterness and anger. They are the alpha feelings at the moment. They are on top. The anger I feel is not directed in any one direction. It is aimed at different people, different events and even different conversations and on occasions, all of the above.

I am angry at him for what he has done. Really angry. Not like the anger I felt before. It's stronger. So strong I am wondering whether it will turn into hatred for good. I can't believe he is putting the children through hell like this and does not seem to have a solution to making them feel better. I know it's not a quick fix but I am tired of fighting alone to keep them from feeling too bad. They don't want to stay with him and he upsets them by shouting at them when he has not seen them for days and should be spoiling them and playing with them. But then he never did that before so why I think he would change I don't know.

I'm angry with her but at the same time the hatred is already there. I can't believe she moved in so quick on a married man. Only a couple of weeks apparently and she was there. She obviously likes them vulnerable and weak. Maybe that's the only way she can get a man at all! No. She wouldn't have any trouble. In some ways I can see the attraction. She is lovely. She is outgoing, easy to talk to, likes the same things as him, smart, independent, confident, slim etc. Everything I am not.

At the same time and some days more than any one else I hate myself. I hate the fact that I could not be what he wanted. I could not be enough for him to stay. Not even having his children was enough to make him work at it. I could not give him what he required and sometimes wonder if I would be able to keep any man. I wouldn't want another one, I'd like to feel I could have one, but I don't want another. I will never let myself get that close to somebody again. I will never let myself be in the position where I could have my heart ripped out again.

All these ups and downs in a week. At the end of it, sitting here now is a very lonely, very scared woman. One who does not believe in herself. One who has no confidence. One who has a heart in tatters. One who plans revenge. But she is also one who is getting stronger. She does not burst into tears all the time. She does not cry after speaking to him on the phone. She is pulling away from him and beginning to branch out on her own. She is making friends. She is going out and smiling a little. She is making a few small plans for the future even if they are only for the next week or the next month. She is seeing the old woman shine every now and then. A glimpse of who she was before she let herself slip too far into him and his life. And now and again, maybe for a passing second, she thinks that there is a chance that she will be ok. She is daring to believe, to hope, to dream, that she will reach that better place and be happy. I hope she stays and takes over the woman who never dared venture into those thoughts. I hope she becomes the permanent one.

The tears have stopped falling. The change is apparent. Apparent enough for me to notice. This is just a slight adjustment to myself I know, but it is one in the right direction. There are still going to be down days I'm sure, but they are becoming a little more bearable at the moment so I decide to sit back and enjoy the change while it is here.

Sitting alone in the conservatory, the emotions tugged back and forth. There is so much anger boiling away under here that it could be used to destroy whatever is in its reach. I just don't know what to do with it. I don't know how to channel it into doing something that would benefit me.

The confusion of how to tackle these feelings now was quite overwhelming. So much so that it is those thoughts that cause the pain and anguish rather than the feelings over Marc and what he has done. It's hard to explain, so I give up trying to.

The darkness sweeps into the house again but it doesn't quite seep through my skin and into me. I watch the stars twinkle and the moon shine. I watch the movements in the garden and the plants swaying. I sat there with all the thoughts pouring through my head, daydreaming my life away.

This life is so strange to me at the moment. I try to focus in on one thing that I can do to make me feel better. Would telling everyone the truth help? Would going to see her help? Would attempting to destroy the life Marc has now help? Would I feel better if I filed for divorce?

The questions lay there in the list inside my mind unanswered. There was no way to know what to do. How can you? One wrong move and things could get worse in some way. The confusion is endless.

Creeping upstairs to check on my babies, I started to think how well I was coping. Not with what happened as such but more with being a single mum. It's strange how his absence has had little effect on the amount I do. Peeking round Seb's door, I see all three of them huddled on the bed. They looked so comfortable I didn't want to disturb them.

They caught sight of me and smiled. Their faces alight with happiness just because they saw mine. How great is that? A wonderful warm feeling arose inside of me.

They had spent a few hours with him today. He had taken them to his mums and to the shops. They had come home with a bagful of goodies, which were now scattered across the bedroom floor. They were watching high school musical on DVD, again!

"There is room for you here mum," Fiona said.

How could I refuse? I snuggled in beside them and cuddled up close, feeling their body heat radiate onto me with such force it warmed me right through. I listened to their little snippets about their day, to their moans and groans and to their version of what was happening in the film. I didn't need to watch it myself. I was too busy watching them. They sung along to the songs. Seb shook his head as the girls got up to dance like the characters they adored.

That safe, secure feeling that I thought was missing actually wasn't. It was right here all the time. With my babies. That warm love that shone out of each of them. The priceless moments I was sharing with them. Their giggles and smiles that I was watching. All of this was my life now. How could I have possibly thought any different? He might have taken away his love and destroyed the faith and respect I had for him. But he will never take this away from me.

I sat between them smiling and my thoughts turned to him.

'You will never have this Marc,' I found myself thinking. 'You will never have these moments. I feel sorry for you.'

The peace inside was there again and I owed it all to them. I wallowed in my pride, in my love for them and in that 'happy to be a mum' feeling. My babies were amazing and the bond we have will never be broken. This is one love that will last a lifetime. I am so lucky to have it.

14th May

Went to work as the science tests were today and I was asked to invigilate. Felt so tired from the weekend. Realising how bitter I am over the whole thing. Spent the day going up and down in my moods. Weird and hard to control. All I keep thinking about is how he needed someone else. He needed her. It hurts so much. I think it was made worse by the fact that at first he was talking as if this split was a temporary one. That this would be just a taster. Now he has her he sees things differently and it rips me apart. It's strange though as I don't cry as I used to. I just feel awful and go into a helpless daydream about life as it was.

If I'm really honest, there are times I am glad he is not here. Times when I think that the stress is over and done with and that I should be grateful to him for helping me achieve this. There are times when I realise that he was never the husband or father to my children that I needed him to be. That I was just as unhappy at times in the last few months as I am now. The trouble is, then I was unhappy but I knew I still had a husband. I still had Marc and I believed he loved me. Now that has been taken away from me and it is that feeling of not being needed anymore that eats you up inside. I feel low with myself. I feel unattractive and desperately lonely in some ways though I could never be totally alone as I do have friends and family around.

I hate him for the life he has. He does not need to worry about the children not sleeping, the children's schooling, going out when he wants to etc. I need to organise everything in my life around the 3 children. I can't go and sit down the pub if I want to. I can't go and eat out one night or on the spur of the moment see a friend. It makes me angry to think that he chose to have these children as much as I did and now they are solely my responsibility. Everything is down to me. He has decided to change his life and walk away. As a mum you don't get that option. You don't get to just turn and run. I know there are some mums that do, but the majority of the time it is the father that feels they can abandon their family in the search for something new.

I know a lot of my trouble at the moment is feeling sorry for myself. I know I am wallowing in self pity and feeling the pain more because of this. I think it is the only thing you can do in times like this. If you don't get it out of your system, you can't really move on. The pain is annoying me now and I long to reach the point where I can say I'm happier and am feeling content with the way my life is going. I still can't do that at the moment as I am still mourning for him. I have just got to ride these difficult times. Cry when I need to. Curl up and sit alone when I need to. Feel sorry for myself and drink when I need to. I will be a stronger person because of this one day.

My mood today was a strange one. I did not really want to be in work. It was a hard start to the week. Not used to Mondays at school. Thought about how Seb would be doing with the tests and whether he was ok.

I put the whole mood down to the journey to work. There was a lot of traffic on the roads and the two hours in the car alone gave me too much time to think. It has a habit of doing that. The drive down was brought down by the images of her, the woman who has my husband, in front of me. It was like I was trying to run her over but the car just wouldn't reach her. How awful is that?

Yet again though I had not shed a tear at these thoughts. They just made me a little sombre. A little down. A little fed up. I was proud that I hadn't cried for a while. I did not hold too much significance to it but I was proud all the same.

I did not know what to do with myself tonight. Tiredness hung over me like a dead weight and yet the stress of everything stopped me from sleeping. The conversations I had had with his parents today, my mum and then my sister repeated in my head as I was checking what had been said. Nothing new. No happy topics really. Life was a little mundane at the moment. Probably spend too much time dwelling on everything but I just don't know what else to do with myself. This is such a big change in my life it is only to be expected it takes over completely I suppose.

I sighed at myself for feeling this way after the days before were so much better. I shrugged it off quickly, convincing myself it was normal. I sat on the settee and turned the TV on for the first time in weeks. It seemed so loud and so bright. I flicked through all the channels. That's funny; Marcus and Sue seemed to be on every one of them. Nothing to watch then. I turned it off.

The ticking of the clock was almost calming. The still of the night almost refreshing. Weird how the emptiness is not so apparent now. Still there hovering ready to pounce but locked up for a bit almost in an attempt to control it.

The bed still seemed so empty though. There was no escaping that. I had hated sharing my bed. All those nights I had spent squashed up so close to the bedside cabinet because me, Marc and the two girls were all crammed in the same bed. The nights I had pushed his leg off me because I wanted my space. The nights I had moved closer and closer to the end of the mattress just to escape the heat and the touch of him. Now it's just me and it does not feel right. I miss the closeness. There are too many cold patches in here.

With the emptiness and the coldness of the bed that seemed too large for just me hitting me so hard, I climbed out to escape. Standing on the landing I saw Pheobe stir. She was thrashing around in the bed and looked up at me.

"Mummy," she cried pathetically.

I climbed into bed beside her. We snuggled under the duvet together both comforting each other in our time of loneliness. We clung to each other as close as we could as we both drifted off to sleep.

15th May 2007

Didn't do a lot today though I was not sitting around feeling sorry for myself as I have been doing. There was no real reason; it was just a good day. I can't see a pattern in these up and down days. You don't know when it's going to hit you. You don't know that going to bed in a good mood will result in you getting up in a good one too. The minute you open your eyes in the morning you know what mood you are in and how the rest of your day will pan out.

Sat in all day but had company for the morning. Nicky has 6 children and her boyfriend left her just before Christmas, so she is a little further down the line than me. It's nice to see where I can get to in just a few more months. I hope it hurries up.

Sat watching crap TV all afternoon but it was nice to not move. With the children nagging for things from morning to evening it is nice to sit down and enjoy a hot cup of tea and watch rubbish that you don't have to think about, follow a story or even understand what is happening.

Feel a little more positive. Have thought about him a fair bit at intervals throughout the day. Wonder why he has done this still and wish I could understand how he thinks this is going to be better for everyone in the long term. Thought about her too. No tears this time, just anger. Watching my babies in the garden this evening I cannot believe they are going through this. They are playing and laughing and they are happy. Maybe I should take a leaf out of their books. They say that you can learn a lot from your children and when it comes to changes in life they certainly are capable of accepting things and getting on with it. You spend your life as a parent trying to protect them from alterations in their life, their school, themselves. You worry about them and whether they will be scarred by your actions. Yet if you watch them after something like this, you realise that they can actually teach you so much about handling life and seeing it for what it is. Life is for enjoying. It should be happy and about having fun. As an adult you lose this outlook due to pressures of life. I intend to find mine again.

My children were there again to brighten my day. Playing, giggling and laughing. It was great to see them and it made me smile on both the inside and the outside.

Life is so carefree when you are a child. The simple things like playing with your toys and tucking into a chocolate bar bring so much pleasure. There is no need to worry about things. Life is fun. I wish you could keep that as you get older.

I sat back and wondered if it was possible. To not worry about life. There are so many things that you want to achieve in life. So many things you want to have. I have never been that materialistic but there is still the presence of "wouldn't it be nice if..." syndrome. Never satisfied with what I do have. The wonder of whether there is something better to be found. That I am missing out on something.

Maybe that was Marc's way of thinking. He had always gone on about how I was his only girlfriend. How his friends had their freedom and he didn't. He used to talk about what everybody else was doing with such jealousy. Maybe he just thought there was something else to be found. I wonder whether he has truly discovered it or whether it will just be a case of the grass is always greener on the other side.

I remember talking to Paul about the way Marc was thinking when he had first gone to work for this company. He had gone on a training fortnight in America and I was feeling like I had lost him then. I had said that I felt Marc was looking for something else and was not that happy with having a family so young. Paul had said that it was strange to him, because Marc had what they were all searching for.

Paul has always been a part of our life. He has been there for varied amounts of time. Sometimes a lot, sometimes hardly at all. But he was always there. He is a great guy and one that I respect highly. Intelligent, good looking, patient, calm. Seemed to know what to say to help you out. Nothing ever seems like too much trouble. Marc had been to school with him and they had shared a one bedroom flat together in their early twenties. I had stayed there at weekends when Seb was a baby and he had never moaned about the noise he made or the mess we made. I was sad when we moved out. When that chapter of our life was over.

I was close to Paul. I confided a fair bit in him. I knew I could trust him. Nothing romantic as Marc had feared, just a close friendship. He was Fiona's godfather and had been pleased that we had asked him. He spent time playing with the children. Came round to see us when he could.

I had told him about Tess when I found out. I went round to his and spent the evening talking about everything and crying on his shoulder. I had told him about Sue too. I make sure I never run Marc down in front of him. He makes sure of the same. He asks about me and how I am coping. He seems to care about how I am getting on rather than the why and how of it all. It makes a nice change. Women go for the reasons and the bad mouthing. Men ask simple questions and expect simple answers.

The night drew in again and I felt lonely again. I hate the evenings. They last too long. The quietness surrounded me and the inability to focus on anything but Marc was there. Time alone gives you time to think. That's not good in situations like this.

16th May 2007

Positive day today. Made sure I smiled as much as I could. Had Nicky for support again this morning and then ran around in the afternoon trying to get rid of the things I had accumulated and did not need anymore.

I think the urge to tidy and change comes from needing a new start. I need a fresh new outlook on life and I think changing my house and getting rid of the things that have been hanging about is going to be a big part of it. I have the urge to decorate, to change furniture around, to sort the children's bedrooms out etc. I have not got the money for any big changes but the little ones will suffice. The children are not too impressed, checking what I am throwing. It does not help that his stuff is still sitting in the garage. It's like I can't move on as he is still here. I can look at his stuff now without crying or becoming down. There are still little bits that I find but again I just put them in the bags and walk away. No tears.

I even looked through the wedding photographs today. Showed Nicky. It was weird looking at them knowing they just don't mean anything anymore. They were of something I used to have. Someone I used to be. Felt like I was looking at somebody else's life.

Had a bit of a row with him on the phone. He wants to change the mortgage so he can save money. I intend to become financially independent from him from July so if he just copes for the next month or so, he will be ok. He tells me it is the better idea but I'm not convinced. Of course the emotions ran high and the calm talking soon stopped.

Feels like a battle that will never end at the moment. We are both shouting about how difficult our lives are but neither is listening. There is no point in telling him that he is being selfish and by changing more things, it will be harder to continue on amicably. It's like he needs to eradicate everything from his life with me. Can't hold on to anything. Needs his new woman. *Is he doing these things just so he has more for her?* I can't believe how much she is being dragged into it, though I fully admit it is me doing the dragging. She is on my mind constantly. I can picture her face. I can see her smile. A ball of hatred is always there afterwards and this weird feeling in my head as if I'm going to explode. I am tormented by thoughts of confronting her. I compare myself to her and usually decide that she is better and that's why he left. It's hard to believe that I have been deserted for someone else.

Fighting is not going to sort this out. Talking doesn't help either. Revenge is all that will make you feel better and you get enough of it in your dreams to help you through each day. Not the same I agree, but helpful in some ways.

Change this. Change that. Enough with the changes, there have been too many as it is and I don't think I can cope with anymore.

I thought back to the phone call with him. I have had enough of him telling me what is best for us, just because he is having trouble with piecing his new life together. I don't care about his problems; I have enough to cope with thanks.

I sat there wondering how I can make him see beyond himself. How I can make him be empathetic to my needs and wishes at the moment. It's all about him and what he wants and needs me to do. The anger is there again. Taking hold again. Moods like this are a little dangerous. I had to keep myself calm so I didn't do anything stupid like email her with exactly what I was thinking. It's so hard to remain sensible at times like this.

I collected my evening comforts and placed them by the sink. The vodka bottle, the coke can, my cigarettes and my lighter. That way I didn't have to move tonight. Sad woman, I thought to myself. Still, whatever you got to do right?

I sat there on my kitchen bench, wasting the evening by talking to myself. It seemed a little crazy at first but then it began to help a little and so I carried on. I talked to myself about everything, from the pain of losing him to the pleasures of my children. I made a list of things to do in my head and compiled a 'where do I want to be this time next year' statement too. Simple things were in it. Lose more weight and tone up. Be happier with myself. Fiona settled into school and happy to be going again. Seb settled in secondary school. Pheobe happy in her reception class. All this seemed so far away though. How quick does a year seem to have gone when you look back?

Looking back I realised that it was this time last year when we had found this house. We had sold ours and I had viewed this place on the 11th of May 2006. It had seemed so large to us. I thought I was going to be happy here. I am happy here in some ways. It has just been blighted by this unforeseen change of circumstances. This had not been on my agenda. This house was not going to be our last move, which it has clearly become. This house was going to see me give up work until Pheobe went to school, which will not happen. This house was going to be a fresh new start, an idea Marc had taken to the extreme.

That last year had flown by. So much had happened. Would I look back on the 28th March 2008 and think the same? Would I look back and say that is where I was last year but now I am happy and doing this, that and the other. Or will I still be crying? Will I still be missing him? Will I still be alone and standing there empty inside? Only time will tell I guess. It just seems a long time to wait when you look ahead.

17th May 2007

Feel more in control today. You never know how long the positive feelings are going to last so I decided to make the most of them when they are here. Went into town with Pheobe - spoilt her and myself. Watching her in Mcdonalds smiling across the table I felt so guilty about putting her through so much. It must be so bewildering for her and the other two. They are trying to understand why mummy is down and why daddy is never around. You can't put yourself in their shoes really.

It's weird how your whole beliefs of marriage can be so different as a child. Life is so cut and dry. You have your parents and that is it. You don't think that things can change so dramatically. I remember growing up and listening to my mum and dad fighting and shouting at each other. I remember feeling so lost as they were arguing. I also remember promising myself that I would never put my children through anything like that. Yet there I was doing exactly that. I was prepared to hang onto him despite the unhappy cloud that hovered. It's horrible to think that I may have put my children through what I swore I would never do. To me marriage should be forever. I think that is why I never really wanted to do it. I never really wanted to get married. He did. He wanted the security. It was always him that thought I would run off with somebody else. He hated the way I behaved around men and the fact that most of my mates were men. I was never any good at being mates with women. I was too bitchy about myself and them to remain good friends and I did not believe in the same things they did. I would never have worried if I stole one of their boyfriends or just the guy they liked - sorry Terri - as I just believed that it was just a guy and they would come and go as they please.

Yet thinking about it, I'm penalising Sue for doing what I did when I was younger. Alright I was a lot younger than her and the commitments were not there at all and there were no wedding rings and no children but still I question whether I am being hypocritical.

Looking at Pheobe made all this run through my head and I realised how sad they must be. How sad my parents fighting made me. I feel awful and vow to not do this to them. I need to get on with Marc no matter how difficult it is for me purely so I don't add to their sadness.

This made me lift my head and smile like I found the strength to be happy with her even if sometimes it is forced. *How will I raise my children properly without that happiness together?*

That question was the drag of my evening. It dragged me down as I searched for the answer. I didn't know. I didn't know how I would make them happy. I didn't know if I ever would. I worried about it the whole time.

I sat on the landing as they slept. I talked to them. I promised I would do my best but that they had to help me. They had to tell me if or when I went wrong. They had to keep me in touch with their feelings so I could help them.

I apologised to them for making the choice that I had made and I tried to explain it to them. I tried to explain to my sleeping babies why I had sent their daddy away and that hopefully it would benefit us eventually.

I sat there after my speech and stared down the stairs at the porch door, aglow with the lights from outside. I sat there wondering whether there was a higher being looking over me right now. Whether they had heard what I had said and would help me in my quest to be the best parent I could be. I hoped that there would be one hovering above me. I hoped that I could believe in my guardian angel like some do. I wish I could feel their presence now. The soothing peace. Something to take my fears and quash them.

18th May

Such a turn around. The rollercoaster lifted me up so high yesterday and today was time to plummet down the loop fast enough for my stomach to flip over. Fiona cried her eyes out at school today. Somebody's dad brought them to school and she watched them with these sad longing eyes. She cried so much and looked at me with a look that ripped me apart. I wanted to pick her up and carry her home and hold her. I cried silent tears as I went home. I thought about her all day. Wanted to ring and ask how she was but she seemed so far out of reach.

Pheobe did the same thing at nursery. She cried and said she did not want me to go. She did not want to leave me. The insecurity is so difficult to endure and to see them suffer is killing me. The feeling of utter helplessness. I'm supposed to be protecting them and anybody else that had hurt them would have had a mouthful but it's me. I can't punish myself any more than this.

When they came home I just kissed them loads. I held them so tightly and did not want to let go. I have to make their lives better somehow. I have to focus on what they need from me and see if I can make them smile once again. It's going to be one of the biggest challenges in my life so far.

I did not know how to soothe their pain tonight. I did not know how to soothe mine either. The guilt I felt was so intense it washed me away in its waves. I felt so helpless and weak. Yet, technically none of it was my fault.

I felt so low and this ugly, black cloud loomed over me as I realised I had failed to protect them. I could not protect them from the pain from this and I was powerless in watching them go through it. My poor babies. They are so mixed up.

I spoilt them all evening. Not with material things but with love and cuddles and staying up a bit later for more time together. I ran around the house playing hide and seek and pretending to be the cuddle monster. I caught them and hugged them so tight, not wanting to let them go.

The evening was tough but I did not want it to end. I did not want to stop the time I was spending with them. I did not want to put them to bed. I did not want the same thing happening tomorrow morning. I wanted a protective shield to surround them.

After they went to bed and they were asleep, I sat in my spot in the kitchen. I shed a few tears. The ones that escape while you are thinking and trickle down your cheeks slowly. No sobbing. Just internal sadness. External silence.

The vodka numbed the pain and hatred came in to say hello once more. I felt that pure hate that you feel for your enemy. Except it was not my enemy, it was my love. Their dad. The one who had let them down and hurt them.

I felt sick with the feelings. I was upset that I could love and hate one person with such intensity. This is not what life should be like. I prayed for guidance. I prayed for help. I prayed my pleas would not go unnoticed. That somebody, someone, something would listen and come to the rescue.

Rocky road ahead.

19th May 2007

A better day. Walking on air tonight. Shopped all day with Lucy at the shopping centre and bought myself a few new bits for my wardrobe. Mostly size 8 which pleased me so much. Went out, danced, got drunk and pulled! Brad was amazing. He seemed so manly compared to my scrawny ex. The type of man I should be looking for. The type I could care for. He seems to need love as much as I do. He is unhappy he said. I feel as if I could try to make him happy. I could try to make him smile.

The shopping trip was great. I thought all about the new clothes and took so much time deciding what to wear before I had gone out. I had never been like that. Hardly ever had a cause to dress up. Hardly ever had a choice of what to wear.

Lucy, Marc's sister, had met me at the shopping centre. Marc had been an hour late to pick the children up and she had been just as disappointed as I had. He strolled across the grounds and apologised lazily. The children went off with him and the familiar tug at my heart was there as I watched them walk away. Would that ever go?

Lucy took me in all the shops. She pulled the clothes off the rack like a true professional. She loved shopping. Especially clothes shopping. Had done for as long as I could remember. When they had visited her Nan on Saturdays they had spent many hours walking up and down the local high street shopping for clothes, shoes and accessories. Coming back with many bags, mainly hers. That would be another memory. Never done again the same way.

I had watched Lucy grow up. Grown up with her like I had grown up with Marc. She was 6 years younger than me. Engaged to my cousin. Had a figure to die for. Tall, pretty, always dressed immaculately since she was out of school uniform. Walking round these shops with her I realised that we had never really spent enough time together. We had been sisters in law for all these years and yet had never spent days shopping or doing lunch as often as we could have. It was something that had never appealed to me because I never believed I was good enough to have all those nice clothes that some people had. I was frumpy. I was a mum. I was fat and nothing ever looked right anyway. I had let those feelings influence my time with her. That was quite a sad thought really. Now, though, a size 8-10 figure. Thanks to the stress from Marc the weight was falling off. Just over 9 stone now and a size 8-10 instead of a 14. It had not hit home before. Never really took in the change.

Enjoying the day with her I realised my concerns. How did his family view me now we had split? Would they split from me and just see the children? Would I become a redundant person with no real role to play in the family? I was concerned that I was going to lose Lucy and her family too. I had thought about it a couple of times since the split but standing round with Lucy now it seemed to be more prominent in my mind. What if they shunned me eventually? What if she took my place in their lives as she had taken mine in his? Maybe I was worrying too much but maybe not. No one could predict the future feelings of themselves or others.

After shopping we had a drink and a quick chat. I wanted to know how they felt about Sue and Marc getting together. She said she was not surprised. After all the speculation she had kind of expected it really. Did that mean they had doubted him and his protests of innocence? I wanted to explain how worried I was about losing her and her family but I couldn't seem to organise the questions in a way that did not sound pathetic. So I gave up trying.

The black low cut t-shirt was obviously a good choice for this evening. I had felt a little uncomfortable with the situation when Michelle had arrived, purely because I wasn't used to doing this. We drank some red wine and chatted. She was so bubbly and confident. Did not believe in mincing her words clearly. I liked that. Upfront and honest - it makes a change to meet someone like that. Talking to her about everything that had been going on, you would have thought I had known her for a long time. We had only met a few weeks back at nursery when our girls had become good friends. Yet, I now felt so comfortable with her. I could say anything, no matter how stupid or strange and she would just answer me in this straight forward manner. By the time we had left I was walking with my head held high, knowing that I had found a good friend.

3 o clock in the morning. It was 3 o clock in the morning and I was standing at the sink after just saying goodbye to the man I had met. He had come back with me to talk. Nothing else. Just talk. We kissed and we talked. We exchanged numbers. He wanted to see me again. He wanted to replace

my brand new jeans he had accidentally ripped in the door of the cab. They were the ones I had just bought today and I was suitably devastated.

I looked down at the huge tear and shrugged. At least they had only cost 12 pounds! I started to think about Brad more. I recalled the face, the muscles, the conversation and the way he had swept me up in his arms and kissed me. It had me so weak. It was a little odd though, there he was a complete stranger and yet he had had such an effect on me in that short space of time. I know I had been drinking but I had been so happy to be chatting to him.

He had said he was not happy. He said he was separated too. No children. His wife had cheated on him with another woman. He seemed genuine and was naturally upset by it. We listened to each other and realised that we were both aware of the others feelings and were going through the same thing. It seemed to settle us. We both admitted that we did not normally pick up strangers in a bar. I certainly never thought I would have a stranger sitting in my front room. As we talked and told each other our stories, the strangers disappeared. Then it was just us.

I rested my head on his shoulder as he told me he was unsure of his future and that there was a lot to sort out. I was the same. I listened to him and then he listened to the same forlorn story from me. We were a right pair. Staring into his eyes, I knew I really liked him. He was the kind of man I was attracted to and yet never seemed to get attention from. Out of my league. Not this one though clearly. He asked about everything in my life. The children, Marc, my job, my house, my background. I didn't hide my feelings as he understood them and I think he felt the same way with me. There was an understanding. There was a connection. Nothing major. I hadn't fallen in love at first sight. I wanted to see him again though. I really wanted to see him again. I really liked him.

Before we knew it, it was incredibly late and he said he should be going. I had watched him walk down my driveway. I watched him as he turned and looked at me, smiled and waved.

For a few seconds I kept that smile on my face. Then for no known reason, I let my mind wander back to Marc. The guilt had washed over me now. I had started to feel bad about being happy without him for those few hours I was with another man. Why did I feel like I had cheated on him? So confusing.

I quickly altered the image of Marc in my head to one of Brad instead. It made me feel happier. I could attract another man. Maybe nothing would come of this. Maybe I would never see him again. It didn't seem to matter too much. My confidence was boosted a little and for the first time in ages I thought I might be attractive. I might have the ability to attract another man after all. A smile crept on my face. Just a little one. I could feel this warm glow within me, perhaps still from the alcohol, perhaps from the way Brad had kissed me, perhaps from both of these. Again, that did not matter. I had to enjoy it, whatever the cause, while it lasted.

20th May 2007

Really worried about how I acted last night. I was a bit of a fool. I drunk way too much and behaved so badly. I am ashamed of myself in some ways and I have made a vow to have a couple of weeks off the going out thing. I am a mother of 3 and I did not act like it. It is really playing on my mind. I can't settle today. I have an upset stomach from all the booze and I feel tired out and not ready to be a mum tonight. Obviously I will be ok but it's not fair on the children to do this. I must not go out and get drunk anymore.

I was so happy at first this morning. Brad had turned up in his flash car and the smile had made me weak at the knees. He smelt so good and was clean and fresh. We chatted for a little while. He apologised for his behaviour last night though I told him he had done nothing to apologise for. He said he was just making sure. He said he wanted to see me again and that he still had my number and would it be ok to call or text me this week. Of course I said. He said he really liked me and I told him I felt the same. He gave me a hug and said I smelt so good. I had just thought the same about him. He left again and I watched him drive off. I wore my stupid teenage girl smile the whole time I talked to my mum on the phone, filling her in on last night's events.

Then I started thinking. That was not a good move.

Sitting alone in the house, waiting for the children to return, my mind wandered too much. I should not allow myself to get to that point. Should not allow myself to think for too long. But I had done. I knew then that I would spend the rest of the day questioning my actions.

I had only kissed a man in a bar. That was all. Women do that all the time and more. To me though it was wrong. I never behaved like that when I was young so as I was older and also a mum, I should not start doing it now. I began to feel guilty again, like I had done for those few seconds last night. Like I had cheated on Marc.

Just because he had done that with Sue, did not mean I should do the same in return. It was wrong. It was cheating. It was not the correct way to behave.

I began to listen to myself talking. The things I was saying did not seem to make sense to a part of me. It was as if there were two of me inside that were battling it out to see which one of them would win the argument. I heard conversations happening inside my head, listened to them going round and round in circles. One telling me I should never do it again and the other demanding me to ignore that voice and remember I was now single so enjoy the freedom.

I was single. I was single. I had not looked at it like that before and now those three words were echoing around my head, bouncing from one side to the next over and over. It was such a daunting realisation. I was single. I had no one. I was no longer married except for the legal side of it. It was just in name now, a piece of paper, not in practice.

I could do what the hell I wanted. I could see whichever man I wanted to. I could date who I liked and I did not have to answer to anyone but me. This made me feel so alone. This feeling of dread and despair, of freedom and loneliness, of heartache and excitement all mixed together in one huge mess. One huge knot. I cringed as I felt that huge mass sink to the very pit of my stomach and settle there, wiggling around as if it were trying to untangle itself.

The weight of this mass dragged me down as I could not work out which voice to listen to. Which view was the right one? Which should I believe? Which opinion should I grab onto with both hands and live according to?

A huge sigh escaped from me and I knew it was time to give up trying to understand my thoughts and feelings. I just gave up. Sunk into a chair and closed my eyes. Ignoring may bring complications later but for now at least, ignoring brings peace.

21st May 2007

Feeling ill still. Don't know whether it is the drink or the fact that I am thinking constantly about the man I kissed. I feel so bad about it. I should be feeling happy and excited but I don't. I told a friend about him and what I did and she said there was nothing wrong in it and that I should use it purely as a confidence boost. Don't get me wrong I do see it that way. It's nice to know that somebody out there fancied me enough to kiss me in a pub full of people.

The problem is the struggle between the message saying hey its ok and the one saying what the hell do you think you are playing at. The conscience is nagging at me as if I cheated. The feeling of guilt is hanging in the air and is ready to attack if I leave my defences down. The sense in me is trying to be proud and use the experience to the better degree in order to make myself feel good.

There is something though that I can't explain. I can't figure out what it might be but whatever it is, it is weighing me down. I can feel it pressing on me like I need to explain myself. It's hugging round me so tightly and it feels horrible.

Sitting in the dark tonight was eerie. I could not watch TV. I could not listen to my music. I could not settle in bed or downstairs. There was just this silence and silence makes your mind wander and think too deeply about your actions and the things you say or have said.

What's weird though is that I bet he doesn't feel like this when he is kissing her.

Aha! So that's my problem.

Him. Of course it had to come back to him didn't it? It isn't my actions that are eating me up inside really, it's his.

If I think about the man in the bar and only him I am happy. I get a tingling of excitement run through me. I wonder whether he will call. I smile smugly to myself as if to say at least you had those feelings even if for one night only. I am pleased that I can feel happy about being with another man. I am glad that he found me attractive because I truly believed no other man would. All the positive things.

However, Marcus creeps into my thoughts and I feel down again. I saw the connection. Sitting here in the pitch black, with no sounds from anywhere to be heard, I analysed it deeper. I allowed myself to fall into the images, the thoughts and the conversations inside my head. The real thing had just hit me. The real problem.

It was the knowledge that when Marc had started this relationship with Sue, he had not felt an ounce of what I am feeling now. Their first kiss. I bet he didn't go back to wherever he was staying at the time and feel guilty about his actions. He didn't feel like he had cheated on me. He didn't feel like it was wrong. He had just been happy.

God, how can I be like this?

I began to get really cross with myself, telling myself off on the inside, shaking my head on the outside. How am I supposed to move on with my life if I let myself get so wrapped up in his? I was feeling bad because he hadn't felt bad. How stupid is that? How pathetic?

I made myself get up off the settee and walk out into the garden. Let the air breeze through you and clear your head I thought to myself. Standing just outside the back door, I closed my eyes and listened to the wind. I heard the movement of it through the leaves and trees. I felt the coldness touch my skin and the goose bumps appear. I took slow, deep breaths, inhaling and exhaling rhythmically and steadily.

I returned inside the house and felt the warm air wrap itself around me. The anger had calmed and I felt soothed. No more thinking about Marc and his feelings. Let them go. Let him go. One more positive breath in and the last negative one out.

22nd May

Work today.

Two and a half hours to get there. Music blaring but it never seemed loud enough to drown out the thoughts going through my head. The thoughts were a mixture of things. They were of Saturday night. Brad. Marc and his tart. My children. Everything.

Didn't care that I was not getting to work. Just had to sit. Did not want to get out of the car when I arrived at work. Did not want to talk to anyone or do anything. Just sat and thought. It was one of those days where you cannot get on with anything because of this stream of images and conversations you have in your mind, going over and over the same thing like you are lost on the ring road.

Nothing seemed to move. Hours went by so slowly and I began to have a headache from all the frowning and arguing with myself.

At home I could not concentrate on any tasks around the house. Asked the children the same questions because the answers were not being received.

Could not sleep.

I hate these days. These horrible days that make me so tired and fed up. These days when I wish there was an on/off switch to my thoughts. I would definitely have turned it off.

I can't sleep. Everything has been rolling round my head. Images I conjure up and believe I have seen them for real, conversations in my head getting louder and louder and then of course there were the feelings of the future. The future of Marc's life together with Sue. Why am I thinking of his? Do I not have one?

I have tormented myself right into the night. I have driven myself crazy with the ups and downs of today. Now I sit here, feeling down and upset and fed up. What am I doing?

23rd May 2007

Still have a headache. Mood lifted slightly but still not great. Something feels severely wrong. Not physically. But wrong all the same.

Had Nicky over for the morning and had periods of silence. Strange topics of conversation. She remains so positive all the time and I can just about manage a day.

Decided life is most unfair. Thinking about Marc, again, and although I have probably said this before, I shall say it again. The man gets bored and stressed with his life so leaves. *Who is left to pick up the pieces?* The woman. The man decides being a dad is too hard. *Who is left to be a parent on their own?* The woman. I was getting wound up about it all and I realised that this is what is hanging over me. I knew that Saturday night would be the last night out for a couple of weeks. I was determined to enjoy it and I did. If I had been asked to see that man again, I would not have been able to as Marc is out this weekend. His social life is really kicking off now. He gets to sit down the pub any week day he chooses and then he gets his weekends to take the skank out. He does not need to worry about a childminder because I am his childminder. He does not need to worry if he gets in a bit late as he does not need to get up with the children as I do that. He does not need to worry if he has a hangover as he can stay in bed all day until he feels better, unlike me. Basically, he gets his life and every now and then he gets to play with his children for a little while and then send them back. *How is this a fair deal?* We chose to have the children. We chose to be a family and then the bastard runs away, leaving me alone and caring for our 3 children. Don't get me wrong, it's not that I don't want them. I love them to bits. I just wish he would realise how hard he has made life for us. He thinks about how easy his life is now. He says how he is happier and more relaxed and less stressed. Well, bully for you darling, you selfish bastard - don't worry about anyone else will you.

I hate him for switching off from us like that. It should have been us getting to know the local night life together. It should have been us going out for meals and sitting down the pub in the evening, not him and her. It hurts so much. I should stop thinking about it but if I do that I will just be burying it and then one day when I least expect it, it will jump back at me and bite me hard. I need to face him and his tart head on and take them down. Deal with the hurt and upset and move on.

Can't though. It hurts so badly.

There have been so many things running through my head this week. I have not been making sense of them all and I feel such a mess.

I sat in my place, on the bench, and tried so hard to switch my brain off. I tried to find that happy place that people talk about where you can visit in your head to take your mind off the problems and stresses you have. I could not find it. I don't think I have a happy place. That made me feel so sad.

I didn't cry. There was a part of me that wanted to but I didn't. I felt low. I felt down and fed up. I know I have to do something to try and make things better, but I don't know where to start. Mixed up emotions are hard to un-weave.

Looking at the darkness outside, I tried to organise my thoughts. I thought about the love I have for my husband. I thought about what we had been through over the last few years. I thought about the two of them together. I thought about how unfair life seemed. I thought about being a single parent.

I tried to organise these separate thoughts into priority. Maybe if they were in that sort of order I could try and deal with them one at a time. What would I put first? My children of course. They had to come first. I had to ensure they still had their dad in their lives and he would never leave them. I had to make sure they were happy and realised that our love for them had not changed. I had to make sure I raised them properly and their needs were catered for correctly. I had to be a good mum. But, how could I do all that when I am not strong enough? When I am not able to fight my own troubles? Is it possible to be a good parent if you are not sure of your own life?

I questioned myself further. I could not make myself a priority here as being a mum has to come first. At the same time I realised that if I did not sort my own feelings and worries out then I would not be able to be a good parent. Putting me first is not a possibility, that would be too selfish. And probably almost impossible too. My problems consist of loving Marcus. I cannot switch that off and just stop loving him. Therefore, I will remain sad and upset.

The unfairness of life will make me bitter and twisted. I cannot make that change. I cannot give up my children to him, I wouldn't want to. I cannot force him to be there for them whenever they need him. I cannot make him come and see them or make him become the perfect absent father. I cannot change the fact that we chose to have a family together and that had gone wrong. I cannot change the amount that I had done for him because those are the things you do when you are a couple and they are not going to be influenced by the possibility of a split when you never expect to.

The questions and the thoughts went round and round in circles. I could see the tangle right before my eyes and I sighed as the thoughts of giving up came into my head. The swirling of the problems and the questions with no answers going back and forth, linking together and coming back to the beginning, made me feel a little nauseous. I realised they were so interlinked and there was no way to distinguish between them in terms of importance and priority. They were all welded together like a chain. One would influence the other. One could not be solved without the other being solved too. I could not break that chain.

I brought my legs up on the bench, huddled myself into a ball with my arms pulling myself closer and laid my head on my knees. I stared blankly at the wall in front of me as if I was waiting for the answers to appear before me. I just held myself tightly and there, in that dark, empty, silent place, I waited. For what I don't know, but I waited all the same.

24th May 2007.

Thoughts of his weekend are really beginning to piss me off. I cannot take this. I know he will be taking her to meet his best mate, Robert and the rest of our old group of friends and I know that she is so much better than me at the mixing thing. It is hard to accept that you have been completely replaced. She is such a nice girl and Robert and his girlfriend will be happy in her company and they can have lovely dates together. Something I could never do because of the organisation of the children. *She doesn't have that though does she?* She can have conversations. She is an extrovert, outgoing and chatty. She is confident and everybody likes her.

Except me. God I hate her.

Why do I compare myself to her? Why do I believe that she is so much better than me? I know my confidence is low but I can really see how low when I start to listen to myself thinking. I am always thinking, as every human being is, I just don't think I listen to myself enough.

Sitting eating dinner with the children, I listened to their highs and lows of the day. Their time at school, their friends, their stories and their fights over whose turn it was to watch their TV. We snuggled up on the settee afterwards and I listened to Fiona read which is always a pleasure. I spoke to Marc and listened to his moans and groans for the day and I listened to my mums advice and opinions on the events of the day.

I never really listened to myself.

I wrote in my diary when the children went to bed. I sat at the computer and just let my fingers do the talking. I looked up and read it. The hatred for her is so evident in there. I was blown away by what that extract was saying. The lack of confidence and the belief that she is so much better than me. Why? Is that the case really?

I leant back in the chair and I began to beat myself up about it. I thought and thought and I could not understand the reasoning behind the words I was saying. I pictured her in my head. Well what I could remember anyway and I wondered how much of it was accurate. I see her as my replacement. I see her as this amazing woman who is perfect. How much of that is really the truth and how much of it was the pain making me feel this?

I pictured her again and I thought back to the night I met her. The Christmas party. I couldn't remember too much detail. I remembered a green dress. I remembered a friendly smile and a warmth about her. Does that sound strange? Probably. The lack of detail, in terms of that night was evident. The gaps had been filled in by Marc. His constant talking about her was the basis of my opinion, the fuel to my hatred.

I began to question whether I should be hating her and then realised I was straying off the original reason for thinking of her. Was I using her as a scapegoat for the hatred I had for myself?

I closed my eyes and tried to picture myself. I couldn't. Not properly. It was really hard to do. I could not form an image of myself in my head without it being distorted. Surely that means I don't see myself for what I am. I concentrated harder, trying to force myself to picture my face. I couldn't. It was like my brain refused. I couldn't describe myself properly either. I concentrated solely on the negatives. The bad skin, the fat face, the large out of shape body.

I tried to focus on my personality instead of my looks. That was hard too. I don't see myself as having a personality.

I don't know who I am. I don't have the confidence to build myself a picture of me in my own head.

The thoughts of her and how great she is filled my mind. They danced around almost teasing. She had to be better than me to have stolen Marc from me. She was probably more intelligent. She works for the same company so she knows what he is talking about. She has the same taste in music. She is independent and confident. She is able to hold down a conversation with anybody. She is outgoing. She is everything I am not.

I was right in the beginning. I hate her.

25th May 2007

Feel so alone. So fed up and pissed off, thinking of him out enjoying himself while I look after his children. It's really hard to split up anyway and dealing with the children and their tantrums over everything and anything, knowing that the man that is supposed to be here and support you is out bedding some skank is awful. It rips you apart. It doesn't matter if you feel like you don't want him or know him anymore and it doesn't matter if you hate him. It still hurts. You still want to destroy them as the bitterness takes hold.

There is a silver lining though. Last night when I was down and depressed and did not think I could cope with life, Brad text. The man I met in the pub last week. He made me smile when he text and asked if I was out. Unfortunately not. *Whose fault is that?* Still, back to Brad. He asked me lots more questions. About my marriage, my children. It gave me a warm feeling inside. One I have not felt in ages. A real pick me up. It broke the silence and I could not sleep. I could not stop smiling either.

A real down day today. I had felt so fed up and trapped. I hate feeling this way. It's so hard to snap out of these moods. I started to talk myself round a couple of times. It's ok. It doesn't really matter. I enjoy being with the children. There was nothing else to do anyway. Suddenly the bitterness that was swimming inside me flowed through my body and attacked that reasoning. It muffled that voice, taking away the uplifting effect it was having and crushed it. It then spread its talons and sank them deep inside every bit of me and took hold firmly.

There are so many monsters living inside me at the moment. Each one has its own effect on my emotions and my logical reasoning. Each one has the ability to take over my thoughts and feelings and change the way I feel at any point in the day. Each one has the ability to override the other and take complete control and they fight all the time. I'm sure that is what makes me feel so sick.

I dwelt on everything today. I don't know why. A weekend in maybe? That shouldn't be so I know but I can't help it. I sat in the conservatory after running around after the children on auto pilot again. Didn't remember what I had done. Wanted the day to end.

I sat there, watching the world outside as if it was a place I would never dare to venture. The memories were washing in and out of my mind. They were there all the time. The children when they were young. My nans. My granddad. The times we were happy. The wedding. Everything whirled around. No one memory was thought about for more than a few seconds. Like they were trying to organise themselves in my head. I could feel myself frowning as they came and went. I could feel the tears welling, ready to overspill.

The thoughts turned to my husband again. The minute his image came into my head, the pain shot to my chest. I gasped with its severity. When is that going to stop?

I decided to change the thoughts. I closed my eyes. I pictured myself out last week. I pictured that man. The frown began to ease. I curled myself up tighter on the chair. I pictured him again. I let his image flow into my head and it helped. It didn't matter that he hadn't contacted me. He had helped me still. In some way. I could feel myself smiling and tried to open my eyes. I couldn't. Tired. So tired.

I dragged myself upstairs and checked on my beautiful babies. I watched each of them sleep. That proud feeling was there again. They are mine, I thought to myself.

Pheobe tossed and turned and became unsettled. I watched her hoping she would calm down but she didn't. Again I lifted her and placed her in my bed. I curled up beside her and felt her soft, warm skin smother over me, her nestling her head under mine, her legs across my stomach, her arms across my chest with her fingers closed in a fist with my nightdress between them. She held on so tight as if I was going to leave her.

It was when I was absorbed in her love that I felt safe just like she did right now. I held her tightly, staring out at the lamppost shining. The curtains, open as normal, hung useless beside the window. The house was quiet. I lay there, with my eyes closed, sucking in the emptiness and the uselessness of the room around me. This was where there used to be so much love. Marc and I used to chat before we slept. Talked through our problems, which were never the problems we should have been talking about. Talked through the plans for the following day, week and beyond. Too much useless talking. Idol chat. No real point to it. This was where the children used to snuggle between us. Both girls sometimes. Always Pheobe. This is where we cuddled up in the winter. This is where we slept so far apart when we were angry. This is where we used to make love. Rarely.

I could feel the tears running over my earlobes as I thought about how busy our bedroom used to be. Now it was all gone.

My phone clicked to say I had a message. I reached for it without any urgency, wondering who on earth would be texting me at this time of night. It was Brad. The tears stopped. They just dried up and a smile appeared.

"Are you out tonight?"

"No - my weekend with the children - are you?" I replied.

"I'm stuck out with people I don't want to be with."

Each time he replied the messages got longer.

"I'm fed up with being miserable in marriage..." he had said. " I want to be happy..."

I felt so sorry for him. I knew what that was like. We texted each other every five minutes until gone midnight. I wished I had been out tonight even more than I had before. I would have been with him again and it would have been great. I hope I hadn't missed the boat.   The warmth was back. The emptiness lifted. Not a lot, but it lifted. I fell asleep awash with a tiny splash of happiness.

26th May 2007

Felt a rush of excitement this morning. Shopping in Asdas with the children was no picnic and I came down again. Spoke to the arse and felt like shit. The evening was so long and boring. The silence became deafening. I was waiting for the phone to ring. For my mobile to beep. Anything.

Could not get my mind off the evening out that Marc was having. Sue meeting Robert hurt like hell. She is taking over my whole life and will probably live it better than I did.

I do wonder if she will wake up one day in the future and realise what an arse he is. The problem is without the stress of the children he will be just how he was when we first got together. I think he got in over his head having the three children and could not cope. I hope he realises that the children are not going to see him in the same way as they would have done if he had been around. In some ways I can see it already. I can see their angry little faces when I say daddy will not be back today. I can see the hurt in their eyes when they hear his voice on the phone. I just hope the hurt and anger extends to her too as I feel she is just as bad as him. I don't care whether they say it happened after we split. The problem is it happened.

It's weird how I can talk about all this. The hurt and pain is still there. The missing him is still there. But the tears are gone. I can't cry over him anymore. I get the sad feeling in the pit of my stomach. I get the anger in my head and I get the need to scream out loud. Then nothing. The point at which I was bursting into tears has gone. I don't understand why there is no connection really. *If I am still upset, why does it not come out?*

I look forward to the days where there is a pang of sadness and then it disappears. You know where you can say oh isn't that sad but then it's over. The day I have fully moved on I suppose.

The pain of her meeting Robert was something I had not expected. It really affected me. I imagined them all sitting around chatting. Her and her lovely Scottish accent, talking away about anything, joining in their conversations as I had rarely managed. They had forgotten about me. Not one single piece of communication between Marc's friends and me. Not one text or call. It hurt. They were a part of my life for 14 years too. I had lost them too.

I thought back to when we had got together as a group. I had always enjoyed it. Marc had hated it. That was the reason why we never did it often. Him. I never stood up to him when it came to things like that. I know the organisation of the children was a nightmare. I should have picked up the phone myself I guess. But I never did. I left it to him so nothing was ever arranged. And he used to blame me. He used to say he was not able to get out because I wouldn't let him. That was never true. I didn't always want to leave my children but I never dictated to him as to what he could do. In some ways, he dictated to me.

My thoughts returned to the night they were having. It was horrible sitting here torturing myself but I just couldn't stop myself.

I felt as if I had lost everything. My whole life was crumbling in front of me and there was nothing I could do to stop it. I was in the middle of a nightmare and there was no chance of ever waking up.

I know it's difficult when people split up but surely when you have been together this long, the friends have some consideration for you.

I sat in my usual place, in the quiet darkness and let the tears fall. They streamed down my cheeks and fell into my lap. I had never felt so alone. Well, not even alone. More..... forgotten.

27th May 2007

Oh what a day!

Started badly. Daddy did not turn up when he was supposed to. Delays on the train. Raining so the children were cooped up waiting for him. They were driving me mad. Excited, anxious, hyperactive... His sister Lucy and my cousin Jack saved the day by picking them up early afternoon. They were happier and so was I. I had planned to do lots of marking in the time I had without them, in the peace and quiet, but it did not work out as planned.

When they left, I texted B. He responded by saying he was coming over at 8pm. From then on, my day was a shambles. I could not concentrate. I could not watch telly. My heart was beating so hard. Teenager again! It was amazing to see the effect on me this man has. I did not care that my work was not being done. I did not care that the children were not here with me. I did not care that Marc was going to be round the corner. I just wanted to fast forward the time and be snuggled up in his arms.

The evening was amazing and I am still awake at 1am. Again I can't sleep. I just smile. I feel so good. No thoughts of Marc at all. No worries. No cares. Just a hot flush and lots of sighing.

The evening went way too fast. It was a blur when I looked back on it. I tried to hold onto it. I tried to just grab every bit and make it all slow down. I wanted the happiness to stay. I wanted the warm feeling to last and last. I clung on for dear life to every piece of my time with him.

He took me to a restaurant. So much food. Such a high bill. Thoroughly spoilt. Amazing. Two bottles of wine. Whatever I wanted. Smiles and laughter galore. A whole different world to what I am used to. I lived a dream. Money was no object. The company was fantastic.

We had talked so much tonight. Snuggled up on the sofa in the pub. Just sitting there watching the people who came in and out. Both of us content with the silence as much as we were with the chat.

We ended up back at mine again. We cuddled up close on the settee in front of the TV and I was so happy to just lay in his arms. He held me tight, stroking my arm and talking to me gently. He asked about my break up and how it was going. We chatted about his. We talked about nothing in particular and then we sat in silence just holding each other. We lay on the settee. My head on his chest, I listened to him breathing. Every now and then he kissed the top of my head and pulled me closer. I was happy to be with him once again.

We stayed in that position for ages. We kissed and cuddled the rest of the evening away until eventually he said he had to go.

Reluctantly, I walked him to the door and stood there to say goodbye. He started to walk away and then turned and came back to kiss me one last time. He held my hand as far as our arms would stretch and then let it go. Then he was gone.

The smile on my face was not gone though. It could not be wiped off. It could not be changed or altered. Such an amazing feeling. It stayed with me all evening and well into the night. This cosy warm shrug that surrounded me for the time being was a welcome change and I wanted it to stay forever. So secure. So safe. So wanted.

The night was so long. I lay there awake thinking of Brad and how he had been so happy to be with me. The way he had looked at me. The smiles. The way he listened. The way he watched me walk round the place. The way he kissed me at the end of the evening.

I closed my eyes and breathed deeply. I allowed myself to dream that I was there again. With him. I snuggled down deeper into the duvet and hugged it tighter, as if it would take me back if I held it tight enough. My breathing slowed. I could feel tiredness creeping over me and for the first time in a long while, I felt relaxed. And very happy.

28th May 2007

Woke up eventually with this stupid grin on my face. I was glowing. Just beaming. Feeling very strange. A good sort of strange. I never thought I was going to feel this way about somebody, the excitement rush, and the thoughts drifting all of the time. Done as much work as I could. No concentration. Just wondering whether I am doing the right thing. *Am I being stupid seeing someone so soon after the break up?* It's nothing major. There is no certainty I will ever see him again. I am just thankful that he has helped me to realise that there may well be someone after Marc. It probably won't be him. I just know that I am capable of attracting another man. The feelings of rejection by Marc were so strong that I had blamed so much of it on me. I thought it was because I was unattractive. That I was overweight. That I was not confident enough or chatty enough. I was not worthy of being included in his life. It's weird because I do sometimes still feel that way, but then every now and then I listen to myself thinking these thoughts as if I was an outsider listening. I can't help but tell myself that I am wrong. There is still the other side of me telling me I am right and it will be at the point when that other side is too weak to answer back that I will truly be able to believe it.

I sat indoors all day today with a strange feeling all around me. It was not horrible, just strange. I felt like I was trapped inside a bubble for the whole day. There was no way out of it. I floated around the house doing odds and ends of jobs. I tried marking some papers but I was daydreaming, allowing that bubble to carry me off on a tangent and place me somewhere else. I would suddenly jolt myself back to the real world and try to carry on but I found I read the same bit of the paper over and over again.

I sighed a lot too. I stared into nothing and sighed. Deep breaths and deep thoughts. Everything was something that I didn't want to concentrate on. I wanted to sit in a chair and dream I was somewhere else. Somewhere with him. Somewhere with friends. Somewhere I was laughing and smiling and happy.

No concentration. No work getting completed. No attention being paid to anything but my dreams. I gave up and sat in the conservatory watching the plants sway and the leaves blow across the garden. I didn't move. I curled up and hugged a cup of tea tightly. And I let myself be captured by that dream. I dreamt about the happy feeling I had found. I dreamt about the next time I would see Brad. I dreamt about not questioning whether it was ok.

The negative feelings had crept in again and I could feel myself frowning. Suddenly it was no longer a happy place. The questions had begun flying through my mind at top speed and had smashed the image of contentment into a thousand small fragments. There were voices talking to me inside my head.

'Don't get too excited.'

'You may never hear from him again.'

'He might not want you now.'

'He has probably changed his mind.'

All of these seemed so hurtful. They should have been heard alongside cackling and giggling as they taunted me. Then, along came the answers. My answers. My rejected soul was back.

'You are not good enough for him.'

'You should think again if he is going to want you.'

'Look at yourself. You are in no fit state to keep a man.'

'You are way too unattractive.'

'Your husband didn't want you so what makes you think this stranger will.'

Suddenly I could hear someone shouting. It was me.

"For crying out loud," I yelled at myself. "Why do you do this every time?"

The tears pricked at my eyes, hot and fiery. I tried to breathe deeply and avoid crying on a day that had been so good. I closed my eyes tightly, to stop the tears escaping at first and then to try to bring back that dream I was having. I tried and tried to envisage that place where I had been. I even tried to picture his face and the pub. I couldn't do any of it. No matter how hard I tried.

I threw my cup on the floor as I stood up so quickly and hurried up the stairs. I ran into my room and threw myself onto the bed. I sobbed so heavily and loudly into my pillow. I curled under the duvet where I was safe and I cried. The tears made the pillow wet and the sobs made me so hot I felt uncomfortable. Still I cried.

Silence came as the sobbing stopped. I closed my eyes, tired from the last half hours events. I pulled my duvet tighter as if it was my protection. I felt wounded. My bubble had burst and let me trample all over myself.

Work, work, work!

2nd June 2007

Ok. Life is busy. No time for this diary really. Half term with the children. Loads of marking to do. No time for anything at all.

Have organised the last of the car payments and paid a chunk off the gas bill. That is all I have managed to achieve since I last wrote.

The children are driving me crazy. I feel so guilty about the way I keep wishing they were not here. I don't do it because I don't want them; I do it because I am tired and have this pressure of marking these scripts constantly on my mind.

In terms of the children and the housework, today has not been such a hard day. I finally finished one of the schools of marking and inputted all of the results. Mum took the children to the beach after having them overnight which was an amazing help. I had until 4 to sort out all the little bits around the house and work in peace. It was heaven. Hard mentally, but heaven all the same.

The children came back. Mum left. I crashed again. I can't understand my emotions at the moment. I just sit and feel sorry for myself. I am beginning to annoy myself at the way I am behaving. I was drinking again and smoking, both of which need to be stopped. There are days like today where the pull of escape and relief is just too much and I succumb to the temptation.

I knew where Marc was this weekend. The thoughts of those two together are tormenting my every move. The daydreams of their lives being so simple and carefree destroy the happiness of my own life. There was only a little left anyway so for that to be ruined is a shame.

The anger and the bitterness are back and they are so strong. *Where does the man get off telling me he loves her and he is meeting her parents?* If I am honest, I am worried about him. I don't know why. *Why should I care if he gets hurt? Why should I care if his life crashes?* He is obsessed with her and I am worried that she is going to break his heart.

The problem is I do care for him. I don't know if I love him still or whether I think I do because I feel so alone. I know that when you have been with someone for so long you are not going to switch off suddenly and stop wondering what they are doing. You can't stop wanting to know if they are happy. And yet all of this hurts so much. Knowing he is happy with her hurts. Knowing he wants her hurts. Knowing they are doing what we used to hurts. When he calls, it hurts. Hearing his voice, hurts.

I just wish the hurt would stop and I could switch off.

Before I start with the moaning and groaning of the day and its crapness, I have to say that I have spent the last few days texting Brad. We have texted throughout each day and flirted like crazy. I cannot wait to see him. I enjoy the days now, I can get through them. I can survive them, purely because I have a little of his attention. There is someone out there thinking of me that much. The evenings are still a little hard - not as much contact. But each text brings a smile and a giggle.

Then.

Oh what a crap day.

The children in bed I sat in my spot on the bench and still felt uncomfortable. So much going round my head. Meeting the parents. What on earth is all that about?

Why did I care? Why did it hurt so much? Why was I so bitter?

I longed to hear his voice and yet when the phone rings my heart goes into overdrive and paces at an unforgiving beat as if preparing itself for the pain.

I hate this rollercoaster I am stuck on. It is endless with so many loops that start when you are not looking. One minute you are sailing along on a straight track and then the next you are upside down with your whole body twisted in convulsions.

I felt like screaming. I felt like shouting. I felt like crying. Just couldn't decide which one to do first. There were no reactions to these desires and I sat in the deafening silence once more. I thought these evenings were gone. I thought I had survived all of them and they would never return to darken my thoughts and encourage the depression again. So wrong.

The sound of the clock ticking was back. The unsettled sitting was back. The memories were back. They entwined with their new life. Those happy memories of our life together were blighted by the appearance of her and my husband together.

The hatred ran through me again and the bitterness twisted my thoughts. I can understand why people do strange things out of character when they feel like this. Those crimes of passion. The anger driving the person to hurt the other. I can understand now.

I walked round my kitchen trying to focus on something else to remove the low mood of tonight. Trying to take my mind off it. But still the pictures twirled around in front of me.

The vodka bottle was being poured once more. I drank more and waited for it to numb the pain inside. Waited for it to bring on tiredness so I could sleep the hours away. Nothing. So I drank another glass.

I checked on my babies a dozen times. Up and down the stairs every few minutes. Listened to them sleeping. Watched them settled in bed. I was jealous. That was where I wanted to be. My bed wasn't the escape anymore. It's still 'our' room. It's still 'our' bed. Can't settle there either. The pain is still in it. The emptiness of it so apparent it rips through me as soon as I lay down. Its talons sinking into my skin keeping me awake as they go deeper and deeper.

I sit in his space on the settee. I curl up pushing my weight down as if I can crush the image of him sitting there that I still have in my head. Looking up I see Sue. She dances on the black television screen for me, twirling and spinning round as if she is entrancing him towards her.

I look away trying to focus on something else. Trying to steer myself away from the painful sight of her. But still she dances. I close my eyes, yet still she dances. I laid down on the settee and sank into a deep sleep.

Yet still she dances.

4th June 2007

Feeling low but not as low as I did yesterday. I feel shattered. Could not sleep properly last night - again. Still awake at 1am. Could not settle. Everything was uncomfortable again. Don't feel as bad as I have done in the past. Don't feel as washed out. But still feel crap.

There is the sinking feeling in my chest again. That numbness all over. The sitting hunched up and the lack of smiling. All back but not as bad as I said before.

I had a nightmare last night. I dreamt that I was ill. That I was in hospital. That I was dying. And I saw the scene in Marc's office where my mum burst in and told him. He didn't care. He even said she could have the children and that I would probably be better off dead. It was harsh. Woke up at 4.30 with a start, crying my eyes out. They say dreams reveal your inner feelings. Maybe I should look at that more closely. Not in terms of me killing myself or anything, just in case anybody is worried, but more in terms of how I believe Marc to be feeling.

I know I care for him greatly. I just wish I felt he did the same. I'm scared of meaning nothing. Nothing to anyone. That's how I will end up. That's perhaps how I am already.

The last couple of days have been so hard. They have been tough to get through and still I am struggling. I struggle to smile. It takes all of my effort. The weight of my tired body is so heavy that walking anywhere, even a short distance, wears me out even more. My legs don't feel as if they are mine. My head feels at least twice the size and my eyes keep closing whenever they feel like it.

Walking round in a trance the children have to repeat themselves several times before I understand what they are saying to me. I feel so guilty. I am not a good mum at the moment. I am letting my own feelings get in the way of looking after them properly. That is not good. I am constantly thinking of them and wishing I could be stronger but no matter how hard I try, I fail.

Watching them play together helps. Listening to their sweet voices and their conversations make me laugh. Snippets of how it should be. The guilt kicks in again and I feel sad.

I cannot understand how the lack of routine makes me feel so low. No school runs, no packed lunches, no time keeping should be appreciated more. Having the children around me makes me feel so tired all of the time. The extra work I am doing has come along at the wrong time. Maybe I shouldn't have tried to continue with it. Maybe I should have given up on the idea.

I sit on the settee and let the children run around doing whatever they want to do. They seem happy enough. They seem to be willing to occupy themselves and when I ask if they are ok, they look at me wondering why they wouldn't be. They are coping so well with this. I suppose daddy would not have been here anyway and they only miss him in the evenings when they know he should be here. I wish it was the same for me. Evenings are worse, but I miss him all the time.

The day passes so slowly when you are willing it to end. I want the night time to be here. I hate the lonely evenings but I look forward to each new day as I hope that one will see me feeling better. That if enough of these new days come and go the end to the pain is closer.

The hours drag. The children tire out. The TV goes off. The silence returns.

His voice on the phone rips me apart. The tales of their time together makes the hole in my heart bigger. The excitement of him as he tells me what he has been doing makes the tears well up. Then the silence returns.

Come on tomorrow. Where are you?

6th June

I finally got a reply from Brad. I had texted him quite a few times and I had heard nothing. It was strange as we were in touch every day until the last few. I didn't understand his silence. *Had I done something wrong? Said something wrong?* I wanted him so much and then I was wishing I hadn't because I was confused and unsure. Maybe he had met someone better too.

I was at work today and mid morning my phone clicked and there popped his name. A huge smile and a sigh of relief came out. I stared at it for a while. When I read it, it was a little disappointing. He was in America. But he wanted me to wait for him.

Brad had had me so worried I had lost him before I truly had him. I had felt sick the last few days wondering if that was it and whether it was all over before it had really begun. I kept talking to myself. I drove past his house on the way to work. He only lived round the corner to me. I saw the car was gone but then that meant nothing to me. I had never driven past it before. Didn't know if it was usually there. The entire journey to work was taken up with thoughts of him. The evenings we had been together.

When I received that message I was still happy even though it was not quite what I had wanted to hear. Sitting on my kitchen bench again, I re-read it. "I am in America," it said. "I'm not sure how long I will be here. Wait for me... please. Xx"

I inhaled the smoke from my cigarette and breathed deeply. I stared through the window to the outside and wondered what he was doing out there. It seemed a strange place to go. Was he there for work? Was he there for time alone? Was he there with his wife?

I felt quite unsettled at that thought and decided to dismiss its possibility in favour of one of the other two options. I felt a little low at the prospect of losing Brad. I hadn't known him for long I know and perhaps I was being stupid but I really liked being with him and felt we needed a little longer together before something like this happened.

I closed my phone and placed it beside my vodka bottle on the bench. I poured myself a glass and sipped it slowly. I was worn out from work but I knew with all this I would never sleep. I tried to think about something else, but the alternative was the weekend ahead and that was no better so I went back to it.

Two men in my life. Both causing me grief in one way or another. Were they worth it?

She has them too.

10th June 2007

She met them.
My children were with her.
Marc's sister was there.
God this is hard.

Today has to have been one of the worst days so far. I waved my children off with tears in my eyes. I knew exactly where they were going. I watched them walk off. Fiona cried as she got in the cab. Pheobe followed her lead but probably didn't know why. I closed the door and fell to my knees, right there in the porch.

They were going to have a lovely day. They were going on a picnic on Clapham common with their dad and his friends from work. The problem was Sue would be there. And that was the fact that I just could not handle.

She had wanted to meet them, he told me about it this week. Said how it would be good for them to see her and talk to her so she would be a real person to them instead of just a name. Instead of just Sue. I had spent the last few days going over and over it in my head. Could I go through with this? Could I stop this from happening? Could I cope?

The whole day was spent thinking of them. I couldn't sit down and do anything. I didn't want to go out. I couldn't even write in my diary. I wandered round the place, listening to the echoes of my footsteps in this big, empty house. I had no aim to my roaming, just needed to keep moving.

Felt so lost. Neglected and abandoned. She had stolen my husband and now she wanted my babies too. I pictured them all together. I sat there and made up scenes in my head about what they would be doing and how happy they would be. I tortured myself continuously.

I imagined them playing together. Talking together. Laughing together. One happy family. My family. She had taken them. She had them with her and I was alone. She had come into my life and taken what is precious to me as her own. How could she?

I settled in the kitchen and suddenly realised it was dark. I moved the vodka bottle off the side and onto the floor. I placed the glass and the coke next to it. I collected my cigarettes, lighter and an ashtray and slid down the wall until I was sitting amongst it with my back to the radiator, right in the corner where I was swallowed by the room around me.

Pouring my vodka and lighting my cigarette I noticed I was crying. The tears were silent too. They just ran down my cheeks following the tracks of the ones before them. I looked up at the window and could just make out the moonlight outside. I could see the stars in the sky. I was glad they couldn't see me right now. I was glad no one could see me right now. Sitting on the kitchen floor, drinking and smoking again, I would have looked so pathetic.

I did look pathetic. Even to myself.

Still I sat and still the tears streamed.

The thoughts returned to my babies. I tried to hear the sound of their laughter in my head, but it never sounded right. I wished they were with me. I brought my knees up to my chest and rested my elbows on them. My hands covered my face, still with the burnt out cigarette sticking out between my fingers and I sobbed into them. The tears were now accompanied by gasps of air. I couldn't stop once I'd started. I just couldn't stop.

When I eventually calmed down, I left everything there on the floor and stood up. Upstairs, I felt closer to my children. I wandered into each of their rooms and soaked in the empty beds and the untouched toys. I straightened their beds as I always did when I said goodnight. I stroked their pillows, where their little heads would have been and made sure their curtains were not letting any light through, as they never liked it when they did. I stood in each room for a few minutes. Just stood there.

What if I lost them to her too? What if they preferred to be with her too? If Marc had chosen her over me, would they?

I sat on the top of the stairs and looked down into the front room. I didn't want to leave their rooms. I didn't want to go down to where I was alone. To where I was lost. To where I was lonely. Shivers rippled through me. I felt so cold.

I made my way to Pheobe's room and pulled her blanket down off her bed. It had Fifi and the flower tots on the front of it. She always slept with it. It smelt of her and I smiled as I breathed it in. A mixture of her and chocolate. That was about right for Pheobe.

I went back downstairs, wrapping the blanket over my shoulders. I curled up on the settee so my whole body could fit under the blanket. I closed my eyes, which were still a little wet from the sobbing earlier on. I could feel the tears welling up again and I knew there was no point in trying to fight them. I pulled the cushion under my head and felt the tears running down the sticky tracks. I just laid there. I had yielded to the pain and suffering. I had no strength in me to hold back. I had surrendered. I let my emotions take over completely and render the rest of me useless. No movement. No strength. Motionless. Lifeless even.

11th June 2007

I knew that she would meet them yesterday. My babies came home so happy. I listened to Seb's football story. His 3 goals. He was so proud. Fiona looked at me meekly and said I'm sorry mummy. I knew what she was saying sorry for. I knew it was because she liked her. I was pleased in one way. Imagine how awful it would have been if they hated her as much as I did. I didn't really want that. I felt this immense pain in my chest as if somebody was crushing it. I hugged Fiona and said it was ok. She told me all about her. She said she was really pretty. She said she talked nicely even though she said words in a funny way. She said she was really nice to her.

I listened to as much as I could and then left it there. Seb and Fiona went up to bed and Pheobe fell asleep on the settee. I walked into the kitchen, lit a cigarette and slid down the kitchen cupboards sobbing like a child. It was like something you had seen in the films. I sat on the kitchen floor, gasping for breath. My heart was broken all over again.

I don't know what I expect to feel anymore. Me being in touch with my feelings has gone right out of the window and I cannot believe how low I am all over again.

Sitting on the kitchen floor I felt like I was in pieces. I had been cut to the core. I didn't know what I had expected to hear when they came back. It is something that can't be prepared for. I suppose I just wanted it to be forgotten. I wanted it never to have happened.

It was such a weird feeling. They had been chatting away about their day. The words were being heard and each one

171

cut through me. A stabbing each time. This burning sensation was inside me. Like I was on fire. I swallowed hard as they spoke. Her name grated on me every time it was mentioned. The smiles on their faces causing pain and sorrow for me.

Fiona knew. She is so in touch with other people's feelings. She knew it was hurting me. She apologised. I told her it was ok and that it was a good thing she liked her. Those words hurt as I said them. I had focused so much on them seeing her as being the worst bit that I had not accounted for the talking about her afterwards. That was actually the worst bit.

I sat there staring at the washing machine and feeling so numb. The pain had become so immense that I had stopped feeling it. I knew it was still there, that was why I was still crying, but the pain itself had been numbed. Just the crushing feeling left. So crushing I found it hard to catch my breath.

I couldn't move. I couldn't stand. I just sat there with tears streaming down my face as I gasped for air. The weight of my whole body was huge. I felt suffocated. I knew at that point, I couldn't withstand much more.

12th June 2007

Went to work. My car broke down. It was like the end of the world. Could not even appreciate the fact it had got me out of work early. Sat in the back of the smelly, dirty, greasy breakdown truck and could have cried. Looked out of the window and all that was there were couples. Pushing buggies, walking with toddlers. Began to think. Those spare moments in the day when you are not occupied are terrible for allowing the brain to think. I knew I had a long journey so tried to think about something else.

The driver turned the radio up and what came on? Doctors, psychiatrists, the public talking about the effects of divorce and separation on the children. *Wouldn't be anything else would it?* No.

Not politics, cars, schools. No, bloody divorce and separation. Thanks a bunch talk radio. Cheers!

By the time I got home I was ready to cry. Another shit day and an even worse one in some ways tomorrow.

The children were on top form tonight. They had so much energy; they were bouncing off the walls. They ran around and played for hours. They didn't even comment on me being home early.

I thought back to my ride home and the talk radio that had made the journey even more unbearable. One of the women had said that it was important that the parents did not bad mouth each other in front of the children. I knew I had blown that one already.

I had bad mouthed Marc in front of the children quite a lot. I felt bad about it but it is so difficult when you are venting your anger to remember all the little details like *can the children hear what I am saying about their dad?* I know it's wrong to do it but it just happens sometimes. Always without thinking. The words come tumbling out of your mouth before you realise.

They said it scarred the children. I would have thought that their dad leaving them would have scarred them anyway and probably worse than hearing their daddy get put down.

I looked at the children and realised that the whole thing was being made worse by the fact that it was Pheobe's birthday tomorrow. I had bought the present and the card. It felt weird knowing he wasn't going to be here. I had hard enough trouble wondering how I will cope with the day without having the car break down on me and listening to the separation and your children lecture this afternoon.

Slumping in the chair, I threw my head back and sighed. The sigh of 'what did I do to deserve all this crap!'

Here I was again, feeling sorry for myself. I had a right to though really. Life had been dealing me an awful lot lately. They say that god only gives you as much as he knows you can handle. I was beginning to question that theory. At this moment he seemed to be dealing me a whole lot more.

The children ran around me and I smiled. The only scene in this world right now that could have done that. Making dinner, they weaved in and out of my legs, talked endlessly about Pheobe's birthday, the presents and the cake and ran around the garden singing various versions of happy birthday. Pheobe's belly laugh rang out loud on many occasions and I'm sure was heard for miles. My mood lifted slightly.

Seb and Fiona wrote their cards and couldn't sleep for the excitement. Pheobe crashed out like a light. Mum came and stayed so I wasn't alone. I was so appreciative of that. I feel I can cope with anything when she is here. We wrapped the presents and talked about Pheobe's birthday last year and the day she was born. I could have cried. I would have cried. But I didn't need to because mum was here.

Last year, we were in the old house. In London. A family. I would never have thought that a year down the line I would be in this situation. I wrote Pheobe's card and at the end put the words...I love you baby girl, love Mummy xx. I felt my heart break. It just snapped. The pain seared through me like a burning rocket. The first time I had to write that.

Closing the envelope quickly to beat the tears, I slouched on the settee and me and mum chatted well into the night. All topics. All events. The future. The past. The present. In a way the talking was my way of stalling. I was stalling bedtime in a stupid, vain attempt to stall the dawning of tomorrow.

first happy birthday.

13th June 2007

Pheobe's birthday.

Her little face was a picture when she opened her bike from me. She opened her card and it hurt when I read '...love mummy.' at the end. Just like it hurt when I wrote it.

It was a hard day, I thought about the day I had her and it was tinged with sadness. The memories of what Marc and I were like then. Before the stress, the pressure, the other woman that caused most of my problems in the first place.

It hurt that we had been through all of that and then he walked out. We had got through the redundancy, the financial difficulties, the stress of having 2 children so close together, the difficulties in finding a job and the Tess scenario. For what. I should have given up then.

Getting the children all together at the end of school cheered me up. Watching Pheobe smile and laugh with her presents made me smile. She is infectious in that way. Some of my family came over. The support felt good. The comments about how I looked were great. They didn't seem to be enough though. Marcus sat miserable in the garden. He could not settle. I felt sorry for him in a way. I can't seem to say ... *it serves him right* ... like everybody else seems to be able to do. It's hard for me.

He hugged me when he took Pheobe's present to her room. I hugged him back. I miss that so much.

Laying Pheobe in bed when she had finally gone to sleep, I watched her lay still, slowly breathing. A little smile crept on her face. I wish I was happy like her. I wish I could smile for no reason like she can. I wish life was as fun as it was when you were a kid. The trouble free existence.

The tears regularly came to my eyes as I watched her. I know my babies are all I really need. I know I need to fill my life with them now. Happy birthday baby girl.

My baby is 4. Four whole years that have gone so fast. I watched her among her presents. I watched her play with her friend Harvey and smile and laugh. This huge grin sat on her face all night. My Aunt Violet and my cousins Sophia and Cathe came. So did Marc's mum and dad. That was enough for her and enough to support me. I had had Nicky here since after school. I was pleased as I needed her here too. She had become almost part of my family now. I was upset Charlie hadn't come. My sister. I tried to understand why, but it was hard. I really needed my sister here. I needed her boldness and her chat to pick me up. I felt the hole where she should have been.

They all commented on how much weight I had lost and how I was looking good and it made me feel so much better. I chatted and laughed a little and even managed a smile or two. I watched Marc sit outside on his own and my heart sank. It annoys me when I feel bad for him. Why the hell should I? What is going on with me?

The sadness lifted later though and so I felt better. I had survived today. My family were here for me. Cathe took me aside and said, "If I can do it, so can you." Her life was turned upside down, in some ways worse than mine. She got through it and came out happier. She probably didn't realise, but she is one of the people I use for inspiration. When I'm feeling low, I think of the women who have been there and passed the test. I had a lot of admiration for her before, but now even more so.

Taking the TV up to Pheobe's room and rearranging her fish tank, Marc grabbed hold of me and hugged me. It seemed to last for ages. It was a tight hug and I didn't want it to end. I held on back. The warmth of his arms. The smell of him. The sound of his breathing. I had missed it all. I had missed him. He bent down so his head rested on mine. He kissed the top of my head a couple of times and then squeezed me tighter. I squeezed back. My breathing quickened as I realised that it was weird. Suddenly, the tears pricked and I knew I had to let go. I pulled away and left the room for a bit to regain myself. Hated the feelings I was having. Hated myself for feeling them. Became so angry.

Downstairs, the time passed, the candles were blown out and the gathering dwindled. Eventually, everyone was gone. The house resumed its silence. It returned to the emptiness. Loneliness was back too. They couldn't get me though. I was protected from them and their despair.

It was the strength in myself that kept them at bay. The pride I felt glowed brightly within. I had given Pheobe a birthday that was happy and I hadn't thought that possible. Some of the time, I had felt happy myself and I hadn't thought that possible either. With a smug smile I waded through those faceless monsters with ease and climbed the dark stairs. I snuggled up close to the birthday girl. My baby girl. I held her tight and watched her chest rise and fall so gently. Her smile coming and going. Her fingers twitching. I listened to the sound of her deep breathing. Her sucking on her dummy. Her occasional whimpering as she dreamt. I looked at her, aware that the tears were falling slowly and silently.

"You are my baby girl," I whispered gently in her ear, "You are all mine and I love you so much. Happy birthday."

14th June 2007

It's not my fault I love her now! That's what he said.

How dare he. *How dare he make me feel so low? How dare he be so callous with his words?*

I sat on that kitchen bench and listened to his poor me routine again. *Nobody talked to me. What was the point? I'm not coming to Fiona's if they are going to treat me like that.* I just wanted to slap him but I was too tired after the last stressful day or two.

I sat and cried. He kept asking me what was wrong and I just said you.

He is worried about me. He still wants me to be his friend. He still needs me in his life. He thinks he still loves me but he doesn't know what type of love. Piss off man. Don't play games with my head.

The emotions from yesterday stayed with me all day today. This morning he had arrived before going to work as he said he needed to see me, to talk to me. Having him ironing his clothes in my kitchen was really hard to see. It reminded me of what used to happen.

He stood there and was so vicious with his words. Last night he had been hugging me and looking so miserable and I had felt sorry for him. He had said he felt lost. Overnight, he had changed. He had become so nasty again.

"It's not my fault, I love her now!"

The tears were too difficult to hold back. I sat on the kitchen bench and just sobbed. I did not care that he was there in front of me. I did not care that he was seeing how much of a mess I was in. I just cried. Everything came out in my tears.

I told him how much I loved him. I told him how much I hated him. I told him how much I hated her and how much I hated the fact that she was with my children and would be more and more. I told him how unfair it was that I was left behind with the children but without a life. He basically accused me of being melodramatic. He said I was pathetic.

His mood softened a little and he said he didn't think it would hurt me so much. He hadn't thought I loved him. Would you stay with someone for 14 years, have 3 children with them and forgive them for cheating on you because you were too scared to lose them, if you didn't love them? No answer.

I looked at him and saw there was an element of pain in his eyes, but it didn't seem enough. He said he still loved me somehow and didn't want to see me so upset. He didn't like to see me in this much pain.

"I hope she hurts you the way you have hurt me," I spat.

Harsh I know, but true. I was not one for lying. I was an honest person. Emotional also. The anger was surfacing and I could feel myself harden to his words of pity. I asked him to get ready as quickly as he possibly could, as I wanted him out of what I now classed as my house. His reply that it was half his house fell on my deaf ears.

The first hour or so after he left, the words tore me apart.

"It's not my fault I love her now."

"It's not my fault I love her now."

That flaming echo was back.

The darkness grabbed hold of me tonight and flung me into the arms of the loneliness that was looming over me wherever I went. It threw me with such force that I was bowled over breathless with the impact.

The gasp for air was back. The weights I had carried before were back. The slow passing of time was back. The pain was so raw, it hurt to touch anything. Open wounds.

I walked round the house all night. Up and down the stairs. In and out of the children's rooms. In and out of the study and kitchen. I walked the circle of my house almost continuously like I was stuck in a time trap and did not have the power to do anything else. That lost in my own home feeling.

Looking in the mirror, I became aware there was no expression on my face. It was blank. There was no feeling there. I looked awful. Pale and washed out. Red stains on my cheeks. I could almost see the throbbing motion on the sides of my head as it pounded inside. I sat on the table and glared at myself.

"You let yourself get like this over a man that did not make you happy. What kind of a woman are you?"

A weak one - clearly.

16th June 2007

I apologised for the way I behaved on Thursday. I said sorry. I looked him straight in the eye and told him I loved him. I missed him. I also said I would get over it one day. Which I will.

It seemed to cause him distress. He looked really fed up. Good. Have some mind games back darling, two can play that game.

We hugged again. This time I pushed him away and told him I didn't want his hands on me after he had been touching her. Images of the two of them touching then haunted me for hours.

How can we behave like that if we are no longer together. He said he would have wanted to come home if he didn't have her. *How can he say that? How would that make her feel? Why do I care?*

Feeling like I have done something wrong again. Like it was my fault. I am doing that a lot lately. I must have behaved in a way that was not good enough for him. I must have looked bad. I didn't take care of myself. I drove him away.

It's amazing how I do that so much. I look at him and I know deep down, I would not want him back. My life is easier in some ways without him. But I miss him. I miss his security. I had the hard bits. I never seemed to have the laughs, the fun, the closeness that she has with him now. It's unfair. I gave him 3 children. I saw him through the bad times. I devoted myself to him. I forgave him his mistakes. *What did he do in return?* Leave me for her. Bloody cheek.

There is no anger around at the moment. There is a lot of hate. A lot of bitterness and an awful lot of jealousy.

I am jealous of her. I am jealous of the life she has with him. I am jealous of the life he has now. I am jealous that he has walked away and has the freedom to start again and I don't. I am jealous he does not have the responsibilities that I have.

I don't think for one minute I would be happy if we swapped over. I could not be without my children for anything. But, I need a break from them. I need some time for me, even if all I do is go to bed early. I just need a little bit of time to learn to love myself again and to love my life. I don't do either of those at the moment.

Feeling a little confused right now. There seems to be too many thoughts and feelings rattling around to separate out and attempt to understand. Sometimes the thoughts make me upset and I wonder how I could think them. Sometimes they make me frustrated and bitter. Sometimes the jealousy strikes out.

Throughout the day I have been riding that rollercoaster again. This time there have been the occasional pit stops where I have regained my thoughts and felt almost normal. All of a sudden though, the ride is raring to go dragging me along kicking and screaming.

I drifted off into my daydreams many times. I pictured myself laughing at him with his broken heart. I pictured myself shouting the truth in his office. I pictured myself meeting her. Each time I came back to reality, the jolt was electric, powering through my body sending my muscles into spasm and my face grimacing with startled pain.

Most of the evening was spent in self pity. Feeling sorry for myself. For what I had lost and yet didn't want to fight to get it back. For what my children had lost and how that affected me as well. For what I had to look forward to, which I feared was nothing. For what I had to go through to get to a better place. It was all too much.

Sitting in my spot by the window with my glass of vodka, I thought of what I would say to her. Maybe if I talked it through with myself I might feel better. They say to conquer the things that you are scared of, or those that upset you, you have to face them. Maybe I should face her. What would I do? What would I say?

Leaning back against the cold tiles on the wall I shivered. Was that from touching them or the thought of her? I wasn't sure. I closed my eyes and pictured her in my head. I could feel my heart beating faster and a faint feeling of nausea washed over me. The effect of her.

I opened my eyes and it was like I was standing right in front of her. The image as clear as anything. How would I start?

"Why?"

Why what? Why did she want him? Why did she choose him? Why did he make her feel there was a chance for them? Why did she think I no longer mattered? Why did she think it was ok to steal a man from his wife and 3 children?

"What?"

What did she think was wrong with our marriage to make him unhappy? What did she expect to happen between them? What were her thoughts knowing he was married?

What had he said about me and the children and why he wanted to leave? What were her plans for the future?

"How?"

How could she even think about being with a married man? How had it not affected her? How did she see her part in the break up, if at all? How does she view me? How does she think I am coping? How will she support the children through it all? How can she live with herself? How much of the truth does she really know?

The blank expression on her face made me think. Did she even know the truth? I had been blaming and hating her this whole time and yet maybe he had spun her a web of lies too. That thought actually made me feel better. Sounds stupid. But it did.

I flicked the kettle on and waited for the heat from it to reach me before I moved out of the way. I was so cold. Jumping off the bench, my legs gave way and I fell to the floor. I knelt beside the washing machine and did not need to move. My thoughts rambled on incoherently in my head. The questions I asked myself whirled around too. The lies he might have told echoed round and round. The jealous rage rumbled in the pit of my stomach. The uncertainty making me nauseous. The frustration making me breathless. The gasps of air getting louder. The beating of my heart getting faster. The pain becoming unbearable.

The effect of her.

17th June 2007

Father's day. Such a joke. Bought a couple of gifts for the children to give him. They had stayed at his parents for the night and his sister met them there about midday. She would bring them back. He cannot even give them the day today. The one day a year when they really should be with their dad and he has booked to go to a concert with the skank. I am fuming. I spent the afternoon at my mum and dads and they enjoyed running up and down their garden. At least they had a good day. I can't believe he could not devote his day to them. *How awful can you get?*

That man has to be the most selfish git I have ever known. The children knew it was Father's day. They had made and written their cards and they had wrapped the gifts and that bastard had left them halfway through the day to go to a concert with his little skank. He claimed he hadn't realised it was Father's day when he had booked the tickets. That make it ok does it? Err...No!

They looked a little deflated from the morning when they returned. His sister Lucy brought them back and then I had taken them to my mum and dads for the rest of the afternoon. I was so angry with him. I sent him a few text messages with a few choice words involved in them but he didn't seem to understand why I was so mad.

"Why are you being like this?" he had said.

Why? Why? How can he ask me why?

Does he not see how he has upset the children? Does he not see that he should be devoting his time to them instead of her? Does he really not see my point? Clearly not.

I didn't understand why he could not have cancelled his plans when he had realised it was Father's day. But that would mean putting someone else first as opposed to himself or his girlfriend. His skank.

I sat back and thought about it. Was I being too hard on him? As quickly as that question finished running through my mind, I had answered no. I didn't really need time to think about it. I was upset with him for not wanting to be with his children on Father's day. I was upset with him for not making them his world when I had done so. I just didn't understand him.

I sat there in my dark, empty house that was silent with sleep and I wondered whether he would ever put them first. Make them his main priority now. He didn't see them that much really. Not enough really. I thought he should see them more. There always seemed to be something in the way. Mainly to do with her.

"We are going to the pub."

"We are going out to dinner."

"We are going to a concert."

"We are having a picnic on Clapham common."

"We are going to Glasgow."

I could feel my face moving in strange ways as I was mimicking him in my head. I giggled at the sight I must have looked doing that.

I stared out at the black room ahead of me and sighed. Another evening alone. Another day done. Another not so good one.

Come on tomorrow. I'm ready for you.

19th June 2007

My car broke down again. Again, I had it towed from London.

I got the train home. Spare time again I hate it. I drowned myself in loud music. I watched the people on the train, wondering if they were happier than me. I looked at the figures of all the women and wondered if I looked as good as some of them did.

Text Brad again. Asked him if I was waiting for nothing and whether he was actually coming back ever. Don't expect a reply.

I tried to remain occupied so I did not think too much but every now and then an image of Marc popped into my head. Then an image of her. I wanted to scream.

He called me this evening. Did not ask to speak to the children. He is coming down tomorrow. Will spend the evening with the children to make up for not being there on Father's day. I'm impressed. I know though the line, '*I can't have them Friday though*' will be said at some point. Then it will be ruined and I will be pissed off again.

Walked home from the station. Did it to burn calories. Hope I lose more weight this week. I've been stuck at this weight for two weeks now and I'm not happy. Becoming obsessed. Even thinking about joining the gym. *What is happening?*

Tired now. Will write again tomorrow night hopefully.

With the thoughts of Marc and her and the rough time I was having, I was thinking more and more about Brad. I was missing the man even though it hadn't been that long a relationship. Well not even a relationship. Just a couple of dates. I was so happy though. To have him made me feel special again and I liked that. I liked being in his arms and snuggling up together. I liked the thrill of going out with him, of having someone. He was exactly what I wanted too. The muscles, the humour, the conversation, the personality.

I looked around the train. I had just text him and asked if I was waiting for nothing and decided to answer my own question and yes I was. Why did he not have the courtesy to say so though? Could he not have dumped me properly? Even by text? At least it would stop this weird feeling of uncertainty.

Walking through my front door finally, I had never been so glad to see this place and I sat for at least an hour hugging my babies. We squashed onto the small settee and sat watching rubbish American teenage comedy.

Dinner and baths finished and bedtime routine done, loneliness and emptiness afflicted their faceless misery on me once again, though to be honest I was expecting their company. The low points of the day coming back to haunt me. The low point of my life now taunting me. The dreaded feeling of utter despair flowing through me, causing the chills as it went.

Once again, I reached for the vodka and cigarettes. Every time I did that I hated myself and yet I couldn't keep away from them. They were my crutches as I limped about pathetically, usually round and round in circles.

The tears rolled freely, I knew they had to. The question of what did I do to deserve such a hard time was raised again, and again, went unanswered. I felt pathetic and yet I was at ease with it. Used to it. Sad, huh.

For hours I just sat and wept. There on the kitchen bench again, with no one listening. I just sat and wept. It all seemed too much to handle at the moment. Losing Marc, Brad disappearing, the children crying for their daddy, the car breaking down, finding the money when the bill came in. Everything I had to do just to get through one day seemed such a battle. Every day was a battle. I had to fight it. I had to keep going and keep wading through the turmoil, but I didn't want to. I didn't want to fight my way through anymore. I didn't want the hard times anymore. Maybe I didn't deserve anything else. Maybe this was all I was entitled to. Maybe it will never change.

I just sat and wept.

23rd June 2007

Couldn't write the last few days. Had no will to do anything.

Had a free weekend this week. Marc had them Friday and Saturday night. It feels like he is doing me a favour. Sometimes I wish he had them all the time.

Feeling incredibly low today. I don't seem to be getting over this split at all. In some ways I know I have come a long way. I know I am better than I was, but in other ways I know I am worse. It doesn't make sense.

I'm not sure what it is that I am so pissed off about. I mean, Marc came round Wednesday night. We ended up kissing in the kitchen. Although not mentioned before, this wasn't the first time this had happened. I feel good when it does even though I know it is totally the wrong thing to be happening. I look at him and to be truthful I'm not sure I fancy him anymore. *So is it the rejection that hurts the most? Is it just because I can't have him that I want him?*

I think back to the day I packed his bags. I thought he would beg me to come back after a short while. I thought a week or two at the most and he would want to come home. I thought he loved me enough to miss me. I hate it that I was wrong. I hate it that I made a fool of myself in this way. The pain is immense. I never realised how much he meant to me until he said he was not coming home. *Is that my problem?*

I believe she got in the way - he had said similar in the past. If she wasn't there then he would have come home because he cannot be alone any more than I can. We are alike in that way. I hate her for getting in the way, for nipping in and stealing my husband. She is my enemy forever.

The children were with him all weekend. They stayed at hers both nights and spent a lot of time with her during the day. They were really happy there. Even writing that makes me cry. She has come into my life and has moved in on my family. For those few days she has what I lost. She has my babies, my husband. They do things together as a unit and I can't stand the pain that brings.

People say he will get his comeuppance for what he has done. I don't think he ever will. He will never live to regret it. It will always be my regret that I am who I am.

I look at myself and I hate me. I hate the way I look, the way I act, the things I do and don't do. I hate the fact that I am not as good as she is. I hate the way other people will think that too. Everybody will be patting him on the back and saying well done. He has someone better now and I can't live with that. It hurts too much. I can't see the keys anymore because of the tears.

Wallowing in it really doesn't help. It has to be done though. Thinking it through has to be done. Analysing what you are feeling has to be done. There is no point in trying to ignore it. There is no point in trying to stop it. Do what you have to do.

Wandering round the house alone makes it rattle. Your footsteps echo through the rooms, acting as a reminder that there are no others to be heard. Strange noises ring out of the house. Creaks and bangs not noticed before are now heard. I walked in and out of the rooms. Sat on the settee. Turned the TV on. Turned it off. Sat in the conservatory. Picked up a newspaper. Put it down. Sat in the study. Turned the computer on. Turned it off. Went to lie down. Got up again. Started the cycle again. And then again. And then again. So unsettled. I hate being alone. I long for Marc to have the children and give me a break and when they are gone, I hate it. I hate being alone. I miss them so much.

Lost. Confused. Sad. Angry. Empty. Lonely.

So emotional.

Thoughts of them as a family unit hurt like crazy. Every now and then there was a tugging in my chest, followed by a vice like grip of suffocating pain. A gasp for air and a huge sigh. My babies and my husband. She had them again. The tears welled in the corner of my eyes. But I refused to let them fall.

Tired too. So tired. And yet can't sleep.

Laid on the settee with Pheobe's blanket wrapped round me. Laid there. Didn't move. Stared at the blank television screen before me. Just stared. Lifeless once again.

I pictured the scene from last Wednesday evening. Marc had visited the children. He hadn't played with them or bathed them or read them a bedtime story. He had talked to me. On the TV screen, I could see us in the kitchen. I sat on the bench and he stood in front of me.

"How are you?" he asked.

"How do you think?" I replied.

He looked upset. He looked sad for me. Like he pitied me. I didn't want his pity. He asked if I still loved him. He asked if I still missed him. I was honest and said yes. He said he couldn't understand why I was so upset as we were not happy. I wanted to change things as much as he did, except my version of change had not involved him building a new life without me and our children. He didn't understand that either.

We looked at each other and then we kissed. We held each other so tightly. The warmth almost made us glow. I don't understand that. Why does he do that? Why does he still want to kiss me when he wants her? It confuses me. I'm not going to push him away. I know I should but I can't. I don't know why. I just can't.

The kissing lasted a while. The hugging lasted longer. Then he was gone.

I watched the scene unfold in front of me like I was watching a soap opera. I was screaming at them inside my head. I was screaming at the woman on the TV. Why are you being so stupid? Why are you letting him do that to you? I was an outsider watching the replay of something I had done and I was screaming at myself. So bizarre.

Sometimes it feels like there are two people inside me. The one who loves and needs him, mourning the loss of him. And the one who is so angry with him, hates him and wants to destroy him. They fight all the time. One day one of them wins and takes control and the next day it is the other ones turn. Jekyll and Hyde.

4th July 2007

The last 10 days have been an uphill struggle. They have been up and down with me sometimes being happy and ok and ready to face the world alone and other days crying and fed up, feeling like shit.

I hate Marc for so many things and yet I can't hate him enough to ruin his life like some women seem to be able to do.

I have not felt so alone at times. I sat here Saturday night and I had no one to turn to. I had no one to go out and forget my troubles with, I had no one to phone, no one to talk me through the worst times. The feeling of emptiness and solitude grabs hold and pulls your mood down so low you can't even get up off the settee.

I drank whatever came out of the cupboard first and I cried on and off for hours.

All I could think about was how unfair life is. How he gets to start again completely and remove himself from the family, while I pick up the pieces of the mess and try to carry on with life as it was. He doesn't realise how I have not just lost him. I have lost friends that I will never see again because he was such a bastard and walked out of my life like it was the easiest thing for him to do. He is ok. He has his time taken up with new love, new friends and new job. I have the children but they are the only thing to stay the same in my life. Everything else is gone.

Looking forward to my weekend out this week. It should be busy and fun.

The rollercoaster just keeps having more twists and turns added to it. It's beginning to make me feel so ill now and I just want to get off. I have rattled around this house for so long. I have sat for hours and thought about my future. I have wallowed in my own self pity. I have talked on the phone for hours on end to my mum and friends. I have gathered their opinions, their advice and their suggestions as to what to do next. I have whirled them round in my head until now they are tangled in a huge knot and there is no way they will be separated. They are mixed together and they don't make sense and they have added to the bumps on the rollercoaster track.

None of that will probably make any sense. None of my own thoughts seem to make sense. I am fed up with feeling like there is nothing there for me anymore. I am fed up with battling my own feelings, thoughts and opinions. I am fed up with the constant changes. I am fed up of waking up one day feeling fine and coping with everything and then the next dragging the ten tonne weight of uncertainty and sadness round with me by my neck.

My body is heavy and seems to weigh loads. My muscles ache and I want to go to bed and sleep all day until bedtime and then I can't sleep. My head is pounding with the constant questions I am asking myself. My stomach is swirling from lack of food and too much drink.

The unfairness really hits me when I spend the weekend alone. I was grateful to him having the children. But it felt like he was a babysitter who had found a space in his diary rather than their father who was supposed to want to see them. Waving them off feeling like that is worse.

I thought a lot about what I have lost. I thought a lot about Marc's friends and the fact that I won't see them again now we have split despite knowing them for so long. I try to look at it from their point of view and no matter how many ideas I come up with; it still doesn't stop the confusion as to why they stay away. The effort of sending a text or a five minute phone call is obviously way too much for them to make.

I have drunk an awful lot over the last few days. This became even more apparent looking at my glass of whisky and realising I was now able to drink it neat. This isn't me either. I am not acting like me at all. I don't recognise me in some of the things I say and do. It feels so weird. Like I am someone else at the moment.

I sat there on my bench hugging the whisky glass and staring out of the window. Thoughts of Marc crossed my mind. Thoughts of her followed. Thoughts of the children came next. There were no thoughts of me really. There were no plans to look forward to. There were no exciting events coming up. There was no positive trend to them. There were none.

Tears fell silently down my cheeks and dripped off my chin into my whisky. Maybe this is all I will have. Maybe this is it. Maybe this is life as I will know it for years to come. The heavy sigh and the sloping shoulders were back. Cry your heart out girl I said to myself. You deserve to. Cry your heart out. Then somehow find the strength to fight back. It's hidden in there somewhere. I just have to find it.

12th July 2007

Ok this has been a weird kind of few days. Haven't had the time to write and keep this up to date. I never seem to have the time to do anything now. *Or is it that I don't need to at the moment?* Writing is a way of letting out what is going through your head so maybe I am settling into having these strange thoughts running around up there.

I have these days where all I think about is those two together. It's weird as it doesn't make me cry any more, and yet it makes me feel shit and still I do it. I talk to myself a lot more too. I talk to her in my head. I probably would never be able to say it all to her face. I bet if ever I ran into her I would not know what to do or say. In my head I do though and it helps in a way even if it feels really stupid.

A couple of things have happened since I spoke to you last. My mum had a car accident. She was ok, her car wasn't, but she was very shaken up. I hate seeing my mum like that. She is not weak at all and I find it very unnerving to see her upset and almost helpless. God knows what I would have done if it was worse - could never be without her. It also made me question whether my feelings were significant to the rest of my life. Whether I needed to pine for Marc or whether I should just move on. I decided I didn't know which wasn't too helpful. I was distracted by looking after her which cannot be a bad thing at all. I didn't really think of him, what he was doing and where he was. It was a nice break. I needed him still to get me through those couple of days and he said he wished he could be here for me.

Marc visited for the day. He spent the whole day with me and the children. We went shopping, had lunch together and took Pheobe to nursery. We spent the afternoon in an awkward silence at times. He kissed me too. I let him again. I must be mad and I don't know what we are doing. I don't think it means anything at all to either of us. It's weird how we just can't let go. There is a need to be together. Maybe it's just where we were together so long. It's confusing both of us.

Had an awful dream. It freaked me out and meant that I could not close my eyes for the rest of that night. I know it is said that your unconscious thoughts and dreams are those that reveal your inner feelings. If that is the case I am one angry person. The dream consisted of me having to live with Marcus and Sue. The children were there too. It was a really difficult time. The children went to her instead of me. She was so horrible to me. She criticised everything, almost like she was the boss. She was laughing at me for the person I am. I did as I was told by both of them. Anyway, it ended up with me telling her all the things that I have been thinking lately. As if she was right there in front of me. I called her all the names I do, I was very forthcoming with exactly what I thought of her. She went off to bed and sulked and Marc had a go at me as he would have done. I then walked into the bedroom and stabbed her to death while she slept on the bed. The children were then not there anymore. Me and Marc then made love beside her dead body and disposed of her together. I woke up in a start and crying. It was dreadful and I was physically sick. I was sweating, my heart was going mad and I was quite disturbed by what I had just dreamt. I know I can lash out at times but I hope I would never become someone like that. Kept telling myself it was just a dream and to chill out and not think about it at all. But it's still there at the back of my mind and still makes me shiver when I think about it.

The children had a stressful weekend with him again. They were walked around the shops and Seb was shouted at regularly. It will get to the point where he will not want to see him anymore. He then dropped them off early on Sunday so he could go back to London to see her.

She had been away and chose to go out on the Saturday night instead of being with him. It really upset him. I think he was hurt and thinks that she does not see their relationship as he does. He is such a needy person and so insecure that he is worried he will lose her. She does not seem to be as wrapped up in him as he is with her. Maybe she is not in it for anything too serious or maybe he is suffocating her like he did me in the beginning. Don't know why I care.

Feel quite indifferent about everything now. They have gone away this weekend to Barcelona. It hurts in some ways but in others I'm fine with it. It's a numb kind of feeling. I feel as if I am convincing myself to be upset about it. Telling myself how I should be feeling and what I should be thinking when that is not necessarily the case. *Weird huh?*

The days seem to be going quicker than they did before. I sat on my bench this evening after seeing to the children's every demand and was quite relieved to be alone. I thought a lot about the dream and realised how my feelings were predominantly of anger lately. I hadn't cried as much as I had been. I was still weeping every now and then but not as much. I just felt let down and angry at the pair of them.

I keep questioning myself and the reason I kicked him out in the first place. I ask myself why I did it as if I am trying to find fault with my decision or even try to justify it so I feel better. Neither of those is happening. I know why I did it. I just didn't count on it being so hard to live with.

I felt quite numb this evening. I had checked on my babies so many times my legs ached from going up and down the stairs. I had wandered round the house so much that I knew where there were toys, washing and general kid stuff that wasn't in the right place even before I got to it. I didn't pick it up though, I didn't have the energy.

There was something missing from me. It always used to feel like there was something missing from my life since he had left, but recently its felt more like there was a part of me missing. There was a piece of me that he had taken with him. I needed it back and yet I couldn't place what it was that I had lost.

I spent my evening as I had done the last few. I stared out of the window into the garden. I had conversations in my head with Sue and Marc. I pictured them together, torturing myself as I often did. I worried about my future and where I was going to end up. I thought of my children and whether they were strong enough to get through this.

All the questions, thoughts and feelings danced around inside me making me feel like I was going nowhere. There was no way of answering my concerns, there was no reassurance that things would be ok and there was a no entry sign on my future life. I was blocked in many directions. Everything that would change my life had a not yet ending. Maybe I will concentrate on my career - not yet. Maybe I will meet someone else - not yet. Maybe the children will get through it - not yet. As the children grow things will get easier - not yet. Maybe I will get over the heartache - not yet.

Blocked in every direction.

There were numerous stumbling blocks to get past and the strength to tackle them and climb over victorious was fading a little. As I sat there I realised that it was the anger in me that gave me the strength and that if I focused my attention on getting angry maybe I would get stronger. Maybe then I would rise above all this and see the benefits. The lack of stress, the lack of fighting a losing battle with Marc. The lack of strained atmosphere in the house. The lack of getting upset every time he shouted at my babies for a reason I couldn't understand. The lack of worrying whether he was cheating on me once again. The lack of worrying about the lies he told. The lack of finding he had spent all of our money and we had a huge overdraft still. Those are the positives I should concentrate on. Those are the things I needed to think about. The anger came bubbling up. The stress he had put me through was quite amazing.

I thought some more about how he was doing what he wanted to do. How he was able to walk away from the children and start again. How she had come along into our lives and ruined mine. How she had my husband now. It was working. The anger was festering. The hatred was fuelling it even more.

There were no tears tonight. There was anger and bitterness and hatred. And from all of that came strength. The strength to battle on. The strength to keep going. I wish I could bottle it. I wish I could grab hold of it so it couldn't leave.

I climbed the stairs to bed with an air of determination. An air of courage even. I let tiredness take over and for the first time in a while, I slept soundly through the night.

Friday the 13th July.

Friday the 13th. Due to have a nice quiet evening to myself. Mum was having all 3 of them overnight so I could rest. But no! It was not to be. Pheobe was so sick. She threw up in mum's new car. Picked her up and brought her home. Staying quite positive though. Only a 24 hour thing hopefully. She will be ok by tomorrow and then I can enjoy the rest of my weekend.

Sitting here makes me think of him and what he is doing. I try not to because that brings me down. I have been more or less ok for the last few days but knowing she is with him enjoying herself in Barcelona makes me bitter. She has got more out of him in this short time than I did in the fourteen years I was with him. He hardly ever took me out to dinner let alone took me away for the weekend. Knowing he is out there while I was coping with his sick child depresses me and makes me almost twisted with rage. I want to shout and scream at him for ruining my family and taking away the little support I had. I am beginning to hate him so much.

The emotions ran riot tonight. I was fuming with him. My poor baby was so ill. She was throwing up everywhere and so much my house stank of it. It was so horrible to see her suffering.

The fact that my night was ruined was not really the problem. My baby was ill and I was needed by her. I didn't have any plans. I was a mum and this is what mums are needed for. What made me angry was the thought that he does not have to cope with this sort of thing. The fact that Pheobe is ill has not affected his life. It is not him that has to drop everything and run. It is not him that will have to spend the night nursing her and trying to make her feel better. It is not him that will have to watch her suffer. He no longer has to do all of this.

It is so unfair. We both chose to be parents and yet he can run away from his responsibilities and forget them. He can carry on with a life without them. How can he possibly do that?

All the thoughts merged as I cared for Pheobe. I didn't mind doing it. But every time she threw up I couldn't help the 'and where is he?' question popping into my mind. I was just so angry that these things will never affect his life, and yet he was their dad.

At 4 o clock in the morning I was trying to turn a king size mattress by myself. Pheobe had thrown up on it yet again and the smell was so disgusting. It was wet on my side and she had managed to get me covered too. Struggling with the mattress, feeling so tired, I could have cried. I didn't. I was more concerned with my baby who was crying behind me, desperate to get back in bed. The mattress was so wet we couldn't get back in my bed. Instead I took her into her small, single bed and squashed up beside her.

She settled back down but my thoughts didn't. They were still swimming around my head sending the bitterness swirling into a mini tornado inside me. The anger was immense and took over me. Suddenly the tiredness was irrelevant to my body. It didn't seem to care that I was utterly exhausted. My mind was determined to keep me awake. I crept downstairs and had a cigarette to de-stress. It didn't really help and the smoke accompanied with the smell of Pheobe's sick that had stayed inside my nostrils made me heave.

I sat myself on the bottom stair. I could hear Pheobe moaning in her sleep and I felt so sorry for her and so helpless that I could not make her feel better. I sat there and just stared ahead. In front of me was the fireplace. As I looked up at it I caught sight of the figurine that he had bought me for Christmas. It was of a couple holding each other. The ticket said 'for those that have found their true partner in life.'

I could feel myself glaring at it, like I was willing it to fall and smash. What a load of crap. How dare he buy me something like that when according to him he hadn't loved me for months? Years even. How could he?

I got up and walked over to it. It was so beautiful and yet I felt like it didn't belong with the collection. I held it in my hands. We were like that once. We were content with being with each other. We were always up and down and there were things that came along to knock us back every now and then but isn't that what relationships are about? Isn't that why they are so much hard work?

I held it tightly as if it was a voodoo doll. I could feel my nails digging into the palms of my hands. The pain ran through me and I let it go. It fell to the floor hitting the hard hearth. I closed my eyes as if I didn't want to see it break. Opening them and looking down, a look of shock came onto my face. It was not broken. It had not even chipped. I was amazed.

Picking it up, I turned it to every angle looking for a fault in it. How could it withstand that fall? Why did it not smash? Seb had smashed one of my others twice by kicking a football at it and yet this one was still in one piece. How?

I placed it back on the shelf and felt a little confused. I couldn't bring myself to part with it. I couldn't bring myself to smash it intently. I didn't really want it anymore. It was a symbol of lies. He had bought it for me. Maybe I should post it to her.

I went back to my bottom stair and listened for Pheobe. She was still sleeping. Maybe that was the last time she would be sick. I sighed a huge sigh and closed my eyes. I felt so tired and yet my mind was racing so fast I knew I would not be able to sleep.

I made myself some warm milk and sat back down. I realised that I had not turned on any of the lights while sitting down here. I seemed to be so used to the darkness now. I didn't need the light. I held my head in my hands and hugged myself tight. There was no one else here to do it so my arms would have to do.

I sat there for the rest of the night, moving to see to Pheobe being sick once more before she got up at 7. The poor thing.

"Mummy is here for you darling," I whispered. "Daddy might have gone. Mummy never will. Ever."

It will always be me and my babies, through thick and thin.

14th July 2007.

Pheobe was better today after an incredibly rough night. Really noticed being on my own. She was sick in the bed and I had to cope with cleaning her up and calming her down and then was scrubbing the mattress regularly throughout the night. Then had to sleep with her in her bed. So cramped. Thoughts of *he hasn't got to cope with this has he? He does not deal with this; he left me to do this alone*, had then kept me awake. Once you start thinking those things you change mood and can't sleep.

Part of the time I'm ok. I know I will get through this because I'm strong enough to. But then there are times where I don't see how I will come through the other side. Like I'm stuck here. Can't see the point where life will get better.

Dwelt on everything today. Spoke to him and told him how ill Pheobe was.

"If I could be there I would," he said.

"Yeah, what would you do?" I asked.

Nothing. Silence. That was the answer.

I was fully aware that had he been there last night the most his contribution would have been was a hand in turning the mattress. I was the one seeing to the children when they were ill. He had hardly ever got up. It was me that saw to Fiona when she was sick two to three times a night from coughing due to her asthma. It was me that changed beds; it was me that fetched medicine and drinks. It was me that saw to Pheobe when she screamed. It was me that got up time after time and saw to them when they took it in turns night after night. So why did I miss him?

I came to the conclusion that I hadn't actually missed him last night. I missed an extra person to tell me she was ok and that she would just get better. I missed the extra person to help me when she was covered in sick, and so was I and so was the mattress. What do you do first? She wanted a cuddle and I needed to clean.

Most of all though I think it was the fact that he did not have to deal with it. Illness did not interfere with his life. He was not affected by it; he could carry on regardless doing exactly what he wanted.

I began to imagine what Barcelona was like. The last time I went abroad for a holiday was when Marc and I went to Lanzarote in 1995. I didn't particularly like holidays. The thought of packing and flying with the children did not appeal to me in the slightest. The washing and ironing when we got back even less so. I still envied them though. I envied him for the freedom he has to go away for the weekend. For the thought of taking her there when he never considered it for me. I know why. I would have said we didn't have the money and that was true. I know he has put this weekend trip on the credit card and I couldn't stand the thought of debt.

I also envied her. Even if I met someone, I probably wouldn't be able to up and go away with them. I had children. I envied her for not having them.

Most of all, I envied their relationship. They had each other. They had things in common which they could share. We never really had that. It didn't mean anything to us really but it still wasn't there. I envied their closeness, their happiness and just the time they spent together. He never devoted his time to me. He devoted it to work, but never to me. He couldn't even bring himself to spend an entire evening sitting beside me on the settee. He would never have given me a whole weekend.

Life was cruel really. Life was tough. The people you meet and spend it with can sometimes make it even tougher. I never dreamt my life would turn out like this. I held on to Marc hoping that he would change back to the original man I fell in love with. Kept making excuses, hoping they would be the reason for the misery he was. Kept holding on because I didn't want to give up on him. Instead he gave up on me.

A cruel twist.

Back for good?

15th July 2007

Managed to get out last night after all. *Who did I meet?* Brad. He was standing there as bold as brass asking me to text him again. We ended up spending the evening together in and out of clubs and spending money like it was going out of fashion. I'd just given up on him and convinced myself that he was too much work anyway when this happens. My knees went weak and my heart was racing as he kissed me good night. That all left as soon as we went further. His hands on my body were not what I expected. I closed my eyes and all I could see was Marc and her doing what we were doing and the mood was gone. I freaked out inside and stopped myself before I went too far.

Lying in bed with him the guilt washed over me. When he left it was worse. It was awful. I could not have felt more messed up. When I'm with Brad in general everything is fine, when I'm not I fall apart again. I feel like I am betraying Marc. *Why?* He is sleeping with somebody else now, he is settled in a new life, he is happy and here I am trying to stop myself moving on. Maybe it's me wanting to get back with him someday.

The effect of that man is amazing. He is everything I ever wanted. He has the brains, the personality, the body, the money etc. I just went weak. At first I looked at the napkin he had given me with his new phone number on and I knew I should have thrown it away. If Michelle had been with me she would have made me see sense. But no. I have a few drinks and have this stupid smile on my face and that was it.

I watched him walk about the bars and I couldn't take my eyes off him. I watched him everywhere he went. That was it then I had to text him. We met up at the bar and talked. I wanted to be with him so much and yet I knew I was being a fool. Just have a great night I told myself. He bought me drinks and paid for the entrance into the clubs. He gave me his cash card and let me buy drinks in one of the bars. I had a fantastic time. I got so drunk it was unreal.

I listened to him saying how he had seen me so many times. How I looked sad when I did the school run in the mornings. He described my Pheobe perfectly and said how beautiful my children were. It felt a little weird. Had he been watching me? Where was he when he had seen me? At the same time I was pleased that he had noticed me. He had seen me. He was looking for me.

Sitting back in my house it dawned on me as I was sobering up what had just happened. I had been taken out and now he was in my house probably expecting more from me. I would gladly have done so if he hadn't disappeared before. Go missing for weeks after asking me to wait for him. He explained how he had lost his phone in Mexico. He had not had my number. He knew where I lived though didn't he? He could have popped a note through my door if he didn't want to knock.

I looked at him and none of it seemed to matter. I didn't seem to care.

We kissed and hugged and fooled around like teenagers on the settee. We then went upstairs. We fell into bed and it was at that moment that I felt uneasy. It felt too weird. Like it suddenly wasn't right. I felt his hands on my skin and I shivered. I tensed up and made some excuse that I don't even remember. He just held me. We laid there in each others arms both wondering what the hell we were doing.

In the quiet of the darkness and the warmth of his arms, words came out of his mouth that shattered me.

"I'm married."

The thing is I knew that. I knew he was married. He had told me that when we had first met. He was unhappy.

I looked up at him. "You are not separated like you said are you?"

"No."

I had this sinking feeling. This disgust feeling. I felt the sadness wash over me.

He had said his wife had had an affair with his mate's wife. Was that true? How would I tell? Whatever he said would be a lie.

"I want to have an affair with you," he said.

I looked up at him. With every inch of me straining to say yes, I knew I couldn't. How could I do to another woman what had been done to me? How could I be responsible for such pain that it would cause? I just lowered my head onto his chest. We lay there a little while longer. We just held each other. How could something that feels so right be so wrong?

I looked at the clock. It was 6 o'clock in the morning.

"You should go back to your wife," I said.

He got up and got dressed. We went downstairs and hugged again. He gathered his things and left. I closed the door knowing it would be the last time I was with him. The tears fell. Again I was the unlucky one. Again.

I went back to bed and cried myself to sleep. I was so upset. I didn't want to get up again.

16th July 2007

Pheobe was sick again last night. Everywhere. My bedroom stinks.

Feeling very tired and very low tonight. Want to kill Marc for doing this, for not being here, for not offering to be here, for seeing her, for living even!

Fiona was sent home from school after being sick over herself. Another one. At least it's before the holidays I suppose.

So fed up. I'm trying to stay ok for the children but really I just want to feel like I have my life back. Everything is so hard. I can't get anything done. I can't move without it hurting. Whatever job I try and do, I create three others first. I walk round in circles half the time and I can feel my stress levels rising. I'm reaching for the fags more and more and any of the alcohol in my cupboard is so tempting right now.

I just want Brad to turn up and whisk me away somewhere where I can relax and unwind. *That will never happen though will it?* It probably wouldn't make me happy anyway.

I need to take my anger out on someone - preferably Marc - so hurry up and call, boy!

My head was a whirl again. Thoughts of the two men that had let me down swirled round and round. Thoughts of how stupid I was to have fallen for two men so similar in ways mixed with them. I didn't know which one I was most upset about.

Brad text me. His wife had found out. Tough. Deal with it. She had found the texts we sent on Saturday night and of course was incredibly suspicious as he never came back that night. I felt sorry for her. I know what she is feeling.

I became angry with everything and walked round the house looking for something to occupy me but finding nothing. I had so many feelings writhing inside me and there was no outlet for them. There was nothing I could do with them. Felt a little helpless in ways.

I needed to let them out. I couldn't phone Brad and have a go so it had to be Marc. I spoke to him calmly at first when he called. Then I let rip. The feelings came out. What I was thinking about him and his skank came out. How I felt so low and tired from Pheobe's illness came out. The fact I hated him for not being there for her came out. He got the lot.

I put down the phone and in a way I felt better. It had helped.

I was much calmer through the bedtime routine and the chores of the evening. I was calmer dealing with the sickness and the crying from Pheobe feeling so rough. I could feel the sadness tingeing my evening. I could feel the dark emptiness looming. I knew I was low. But I fought it. I put up a good fight and battled on through.

The children asleep, I sat in my sad, lonely state and held myself tightly. I felt weird. I could not cry because I was not that upset. I could not think about it too much because I did not know which to think about first. I couldn't settle down to anything because I was waiting for Pheobe to be ill again.

My chest felt crushed and my head ached. My breathing was deep and painful in ways. My body felt useless. Nothing was working properly.

I trod wearily up the stairs and fell into bed. I pulled the covers up so tight and snuggled under them looking for comfort but not finding it. I closed my eyes to shut out the darkness but not succeeding. I listened to music to drown out my thoughts.

I lay there, just staring out in front of me waiting for sleep. I laid there and waited. For what seemed like hours.

Another twist of the knife.

17th July

Was down anyway but tonight was the worst.

He came round tonight. He tells me about his holiday and about the fact that his family will be meeting her on Saturday. The feeling of sheer pain plummeted through my heart at such speed it bowled me over. The anger took over and I didn't know what to do with myself. The feeling is so intense. I kind of expected this to happen. But I just thought that maybe his parents would be more considerate of me and what he has done. They know what I am feeling. They know I am unstable. They know I love him still. It feels like the ultimate betrayal. The feeling of loneliness swamps over. The feeling of bitterness takes hold like it's never going to let go.

How is he in touch with me all the time? Why does he call every day? How can he hurt me so many times? If he cared he wouldn't do these things. He is contradicting himself.

I can't explain the feeling now I'm settling down. I feel numb. It's too much effort to even breathe. I'm almost as low as I was at the beginning. It was hard enough coping with the holiday and the fact they are well and truly a couple. It's hard enough coping with him leaving me and the children in search of something new. It's hard enough keeping going. Now this. I can't stand the pain - I just want this life to be over.

Oh the anger ran through me so much I didn't know what to do. I couldn't stand being in the same house as him. I couldn't bear to look at him. I thought I was going to hit him.

Maybe I should have done. I drank glass after glass of vodka and spat my words at him, lips tight and voice low.

My heart was pounding away in my chest and his words were not heard. I could see his mouth moving but I blocked out the sound. His parents were having her over for a nice family barbecue. How nice. How lovely.

The stabbing in the back was felt. I couldn't understand it. If that was my son and she was the reason for the break up, she would not be welcome in my house. I had to sit round the corner to where she was with my in laws and my cousin. My cousin. My family. My cousin.

I screamed at the top of my voice.

"Haven't you hurt me enough? Why do you want to twist the knife some more?"

I collapsed in a heap as my legs buckled from the pain. He knelt down beside me.

"I'm sorry," he said.

Did he think that that 5 letter word was going to make it all alright? What did he want me to do with that?

I stormed out of the house and just walked. I had nowhere to go. Marilyn wasn't in. I turned the wrong way to go to Nicky's and I didn't know where Michelle was. I felt so alone. I was standing in the middle of this long street and there were buses and people driving and walking up and down it and yet I was alone. There was just me.

I sat on the corner of one of the roads and I could see Marc hovering outside the house. The tears streamed down my face so hard I couldn't see. I sobbed so loudly I'm surprised no one heard me. No one did. No one was there.

I stayed sitting there for a few minutes while I calmed my crying down. I staggered slowly along the street feeling like all the hard work I had done up to just then was over. All the anger. All the hatred. It had all been replaced by the sadness again. I was devastated.

I kept picturing the family unit. My face scratched out of the photos and replaced with hers. I was so hurt. She would be there. What more did this woman want from me? She had my husband. She had the love of my children too. Now she wanted the rest including my cousin. It hurt so much and my eyes became so hot from the tears. I could make excuses for them. I could say why they were doing it. I knew the reasons. But I still couldn't cope with it.

I thought my cousin Jack would have snubbed that. I hoped he would have said no, like I wanted him to. He had to stand by Lucy though. They were his family too and I had to accept that. But it hurt.

I stumbled back through the door. Marc tried to put his arms around me to comfort me. I pushed him away. I went into the kitchen and poured myself another drink. I went through to the garden. He just followed me. He wouldn't leave me alone.

"Why are you doing this to me?" I pleaded.

"What did I do that was so wrong you had to rip me to pieces?"

He just looked at me. He didn't think it would hurt. He didn't think I would feel like this. I could see it in his eyes. I could see the way he looked, like he was surprised. I started to feel angry. Did he really think I hadn't loved him at all? That this wouldn't have affected me. Could he not see that this was going to hurt me? Could he not see what it would do to me?

No of course not. He was getting on with his life. It was all so easy for him. New woman. The last 14 years with me didn't affect him. New family. He was determined to introduce her so quickly. He had forgotten me in all this. Not one thought of how it might upset me. The bastard. I looked him straight in the eye.

"I will never forgive you for what you have done. I will never forgive you for what you are doing to me now. I will never forgive you for what you will put me through for the next few months. I will repay you. I will repay you with pain back. I don't care how long it takes me. I won't rest until you know exactly what it feels like."

With that I pushed my chair under the table and walked inside slamming the door on him. I threw his coat at him and said, "You can leave now. And please don't come back." I poured myself a larger glass of vodka and went upstairs to be alone with my heartbreak.

18th July

A diary entry to be ashamed of coming up here.

He didn't leave me last night. He didn't want to leave me. He hated seeing me in that mess - I could tell. He was unsure what to do. He didn't know which way to turn. Whether to comfort me or just leave. He was as confused as I was.

That's why it happened. I sat on the bench. He stood close. Neither of us said a word. I laid my head on his shoulder. I don't know what I needed - just something. I had drunk an awful lot but I knew that things were getting too close. He wrapped his arms around me. I felt so warm and safe. Like it was just an argument and nothing else. Like we used to have.

Then the kiss. Soft, warm and loving. Almost as it was when we first met. We stared into each others eyes, both of us seeming to know what we were doing was wrong. We couldn't help it. We just fell into each other and before we knew it we were in bed. We made love like we hadn't done for so long. The love was still there. The warmth, the passion red hot. It was amazing. We held each other tight for a while afterwards. We fell asleep holding on to each other. Neither wanting to let go. *How were those feelings right? What was going on here?*

I sat on my bench and felt so confused. I had been so stupid though regret was not what I was feeling really. Last night. Last night I slept with my husband. What?

Those words echoed round and round my head as I went over and over what happened. I replayed it in my head until I knew the details of each minute. I don't know what I was looking for, but I wouldn't have found it anyway. Last night was my problem tonight. Tonight I stared out of the window wondering what the hell happened, but it was the night before and the events that had taken place that ran through my head.

I had come down the stairs last night not long after I went up. I was stumbling after drinking so much and I felt knocked for six by the news. It was a shock.

He looked at me. "Do you really hate me that much?" he asked.

"Yes."

Walking into the kitchen I knew he was following me. I lit a cigarette and went over to the spot by the sink. He walked over too. The house was deadly quiet and the tension was fierce. I smoked my cigarette while listening to his drivel and then threw it into the sink.

I looked at him. I could see the hurt in his eyes. What was that from? Hurting me? He was shocked I could see that. He was shocked by my reaction and the viciousness of it. I was shocked at it too. I had felt out of control and I hadn't liked it.

He was looking at me in a way I knew. That look in his eyes of love. I thought I was seeing things. I leant forward and rested my head on his shoulder. I needed to be held and at that point I didn't care who by. He began to breathe deeply and swallowed hard. He lifted his hand and stroked my hair.

"I didn't want to leave you like this," he said.

I nodded in silence. I didn't care really. I wasn't going to say thank you.

"Do you want me to stay?" he asked quietly.

I knew what he meant. I looked up at him surprised. He rubbed his fingers on my thigh and wrapped his arms around me. I moved myself forward and put my arms round him. I wanted him so much. I had not felt like this with him for so long it was almost shocking to me. But it did feel right. But it was wrong. What do I do?

I lifted my head and looked at him. I didn't know what to do. I knew what I wanted to do but that was somehow different. We both bowed our heads until our foreheads touched. We looked into each others eyes. Then the kiss so tender. So warm. So like before. I could hear a voice in my head shouting at me. It was telling me to stop and asking what the hell I was doing. I blocked it out. I fell into his arms like I had used to do so long ago.

He led me to bed. The children were asleep as we tiptoed through to my room. Our room. The bedroom. We undressed each other and fell into bed. For the next couple of hours we were married again. A couple again. In love again. I snuggled up close to him and fell asleep. I was aglow. Until this morning.

I woke up to him in my bed and I can't explain what I thought. He got ready for work. The children were running round him. He was ironing in my kitchen and then he was gone.

As he closed the door I breathed a huge sigh of relief. Then I shivered. "Add to the confusion why don't you, you stupid cow," I shouted to myself.

I looked out the window and became aware that I was daydreaming. I had pressed stop. Now it was time to erase the tape. Erase the scene and pretend it didn't happen. Ignore it. Forget it. Just let it go.

Second happy birthday.

20th July

Fiona's birthday. It went ok. I could not talk to his mum as I felt so upset that she was accepting her into her family. It hurt. They would be round the corner to me playing happy families. Can't handle it. Maybe that makes me a bad person. Maybe that makes me weak. Still I don't care. Marc held my hand during the evening. He kept looking at me as if I should worry about what he is going through. It bugs me to think that he still has this "poor me" attitude. He is so irritating.

Still I got through another first. Fiona's first birthday without her daddy at home. It's a big deal for a little girl. I try to put myself in her position. I know she is a child but in my eyes it just makes it more difficult to understand.

I need to get through this weekend in one piece.

Seeing my little girl opening her birthday presents on her own hurt quite a lot. It had hurt on Pheobe's birthday but there were more to remember for Fiona. I remembered bringing her home. I remembered how we were so happy. Our little girl.

I concentrated on Fiona. Took her to school. Her last day at this school. She finally had a place at the same one her sister would be going to. I was so pleased. No more dropping children off at three separate schools. The school run took half an hour in the mornings and I was always exhausted by the time I got home. At least now they would be together. One thing had gone right.

The day passed quickly and the girls from Fiona's class came home for a party. It was a lovely time. She smiled and skipped about. I painted their faces. She laughed and played with them all. She didn't settle totally though. She kept asking when her daddy would be here. Not yet was the only answer I could give.

The family arrived in the evening and she was spoilt with all the presents she received. Spoilt rotten. She had a great time unwrapping everything and testing each new toy and each new piece of clothing. It was lovely to see.

In some ways the evening wasn't as hard as Pheobe's. I suppose Pheobe's was the very first and that made it harder. It was still tough. It was good to see people here though. It was good to see them supporting me and spoiling her. I felt quite warm inside.

One by one, they all left. The children went to bed and I was alone again. The darkness, the emptiness, the loneliness all hovered. The only feeling left was confusion. He had held my hand. He had talked to me for ages in the kitchen. He had said I would never take him back now. He said if he asked to come home, he thought I would say no. I didn't know what to say, I just looked at him. I was still confused from the other night. Why was he saying that? What was he doing? What did he mean?

I felt a little lost by this but I also felt quite smug. I could have Marc if I wanted. I knew it now. I felt ok. Confused as to why, but ok. I felt I had had some revenge on her by sleeping with her boyfriend. I felt like I was a bad person for feeling that, but that didn't stop it.

I wanted to tell everyone. I wanted everybody I knew to know what had happened that night. I wanted to tell her too.

But I would save that for now. Get rid of the confusion bit first. Feel happier about it first.

I wanted to tell his mum most of all. I couldn't bring myself to talk to her for what she had decided to do. Thanks for the support was all I could think. She could have told me that it was happening. If she had explained things from her point of view maybe I would have understood more. I suppose that neither of us are like that though. I pictured myself walking up to her and saying Marc spent the night here the other night. That would have wiped the evil look off her face. She could sense that something was up. That there was a problem. She didn't try to put it right though did she? She didn't come and talk to me did she?

Still never mind. This is life and we have to get on with it. Whatever happens. I won't understand what Marc is playing at and I won't understand what he hopes to achieve. There is no point in trying to. So I won't.

21st July

He arrived to pick the children up. It was hard to let them go knowing they were going to be with her. It always is, but knowing they would be with her round the corner to me was worse. I felt sick. I was angry and wanted to see them all together. I wanted to go round and face her, but I knew I couldn't. Not just because none of them would have let me close to her but because I was not strong enough just now. I was too weak and if I saw her I would probably just cry. Not too sure why.

I had my interview at the dating agency. It went well. I felt better afterwards. Came out with a smile on my face, feeling as if my life wasn't quite over yet and things would look up. I crashed quite quickly but then once out with Marilyn, I was fine again.

Coming back to an empty house was horrible again. All I can think about lately is getting my children back. I never know what to do to amuse them anymore but I still want them here with me instead of there with him.

God I hate her. I hate her so much. All I thought about was how she had my family round her, how she didn't seem to care what she had done. I was angry and hurt and those two emotions are a vicious combination to yourself. It made me feel awful. I couldn't stand it. I wanted to be strong enough to storm round there. I wanted to go and shout outside their house until someone came out to face me. I wanted her to know that I was angry with her and that he had lied and that four nights ago he was in bed with me. Not her, me.

I couldn't do anything I wanted to though. I knew I would never go round there and that was just a dream. I knew I would never tell anyone about the other night for I was too ashamed. I knew I would never be able to confront her. I didn't want to see her face. Just was not strong enough. I was alone with my hatred and if it ate me up then so be it.

That is what it was doing right now. On the way to the interview I nearly turned round. I was desperately trying to stop crying. The tears kept coming and I was fighting a losing battle against them. The hatred and the anger were eating me alive. They were gnawing at every inch of me and there was no way of releasing them. I didn't want to arrive at this place. I didn't want the journey to end. I would then have to talk to people and be pleasant and normal when I felt nowhere near normal.

After the interview I felt a little high. It was a good feeling and I was pleased I had managed to accomplish it without bursting into tears. Maybe this dating agency thing will work. Having doubts that I am ready though.

I returned home and the knowledge of her being so close hit me. It made me remember that she was with them round there and that was it my emotions went crazy again. I thought of them all sitting round chatting away to her and the children playing with her. It affected me so much and I crumbled into the chair and sobbed, holding myself for comfort. It was horrible. I thought the pain would never ease.

It didn't help with it being today. This time 6 years ago we were arriving home with our new baby daughter. We were so happy to have our little girl, our little family. I pictured Seb's face as he had held Fiona in his arms beaming his proud big brother smile. That memory was stamped on by Sue. Sue had our little family now. She had taken them from me. I hated her.

The powerful feelings of hurt, anger and hatred made me storm out. I sat in the car and placed the key in the ignition. I stared straight ahead, tears streaming down my face. I willed myself to start the car, to drive round there, to knock on the door and drag her out by her hair. I wanted to have her there in front of me; I wanted her to see what she had done by stealing my husband. No matter how much I willed myself, I couldn't do it. I knew I couldn't. How could I face her? How could I see her? It would hurt even more to be standing there with his skank. My head bowed down looking at the floor, I made my way back inside ever so slowly.

I straightened myself up and met Marilyn to go into town. We drank and danced. Came back to the dark, empty house once again. It made me shiver. That horrible feeling of loneliness loomed over me, taunting me with its dark sadness. The thoughts of my children not being here and then them two together snuggled up in bed caused the tears to prick at my eyes yet again and I climbed the stairs to the safety of my bed. The room spun as I lay there holding the covers over my head tightly as if they would keep out the feelings. I was locked into the duvet and there was no way loneliness could get at me in here. I screwed my eyes up tight and waited for sleep to come.

22nd July

Went to lunch.

Had 16 missed calls from Marc about bringing them back. It seemed as if he could not wait to get rid of them. As if he had had enough of them. It brings me down. I hate him for that.

Went to lunch with mum and dad. A lovely little pub with nice food and lots of families sitting round happily chatting. Children playing, running in and out of the garden. Couples sitting next to each other engrossed in conversation. Babies crying. It was not the best idea I had had. It hurt. It's amazing the things that hurt.

16 missed calls. That has got to be a record. He needed to bring them back so they could return to London. Return to their nice little lives where the children were not around. I couldn't even have an extra few hours to relax and get over the trauma of yesterday. Thanks.

He arranged for his mum and dad to bring them round. She glared at me and said something about me not talking to her on Friday. I could see she was angry. My heart raced as the anger swelled up inside of me. I glared back at her.

I said I was stressed at the moment and that her being there had affected me badly. She said that everyone was stressed and I shouldn't think I was the only one. I said her son was to blame for the mess - she disagreed. She said it was both of us. I made him cheat on me twice then did I? I had put up with so much crap from him and that drove him away did it? She let rip at me on my driveway and I shouted back at her too. She then turned and walked away. I watched her go and could not believe what she had just said. I phoned Marc and told him what a bitch his mother was. I said what she had said. He apologised on her behalf - get stuffed with that.

The phone rang and it was her. She apologised and seemed calmer. I listened to what she said and accepted her apology. I put the phone down and thought about it. How dare she? Can she not see her son has run off with another woman? Could she not see that he has done this to the family? I couldn't understand why she couldn't. I became more and more angry. I decided that if she could not see that then I did not want to see her anymore.

The children's excitement had returned to the house. In all the arguing I had not noticed them itching to tell me what they had been up to. I forgot about her for the time being and listened to them. They chatted on and on about their weekend and I just smiled and nodded and made pleasant remarks even though I was dying inside. Each word of happiness said about the skank stabbed into me. Ripping through the skin and attacking my heart. Each one made me want to beg and plead with them to stop and each one brought a tear to my eye which I had to force back in. Still I smiled.

I snuggled up on the settee with my precious babies and held onto them tightly. Watching their rubbish programmes knowing there was no need to rush them to bed as there was no school. A nice feeling.

I took the girls in with me when we went to bed. They had been watching telly in Seb's room and had not wanted to sleep. I needed some comfort. I needed a cuddle. I needed to feel there was someone there. So I used them. They were here, they were my comfort.

I lay in the bed with them watching them sleep. I took in their every move and their every twitch. I watched their chests rise and fall and I watched them fight each other with the covers, one pushing them off with the other pulling them up. I studied the features of their faces. How beautiful they were. I watched their eyes flicker and their lips move as if they were going to say something.

I enjoyed my time awake for the first time in ages. I laid there for hours with the lamppost flickering outside allowing me to see them. I felt calmer than I had done. I felt more relaxed than before. For the first time in weeks, I drifted off to sleep without realising. Without watching the clock. Without getting up and down. I just drifted off.

Give me back my family.

Holiday weekend - 2nd - 7th August 2007

The hardest weekend of my life. There she is on holiday with my husband and my children doing what I should be doing with them. I hate her for moving in on my family. No matter how much they say it's not like that, that's exactly how it feels.

Had to keep busy. Had to be occupied. Had to work all day - painting the house. Had to not think about anything. Had to go out. Had to have a drink. Had to cry.

What a difficult time. So hard watching them go off with daddy. It was hard because I knew I would not see them for a few days and it was even harder knowing that she would have them. My little family. Oh how I wished these feelings would end.

I painted the kitchen. It looked so much better and it felt like mine at last. Brighter. More cheery. I did it. Well, mum and I. It was easier with company. She knew these few days were killing me and were so hard. She was there as support. It was never said like that. It went unmentioned. But she was there.

We talked about this time next year. How things would be better by then. Will they? We talked about the future and all the what ifs. What if he chose not to come anymore? What if he stopped the financial support? What if he chose her over the children? What if I never saw him again? What if? What if? It really didn't help but it needed to be discussed.

Mum made sure I ate even if I didn't want to. I had lost a lot of weight up to now and I was happy for it to continue, but I knew mum was making sure I was healthy. It was hard. All the food seemed hard to swallow and my stomach felt full with just a few mouthfuls. I had gone off food so much lately.

I kept busy as much as I could. It was hard to stay occupied and I felt exhausted. I slept easier knowing my mum was in the house and for the first time since he had left, I pulled the curtains. I let the darkness swarm the bedroom and laid there in it wearily. I felt a little uneasy but knew it was a stepping stone.

Holiday weekend continued - 2nd - 7th August 2007

Heard her laughing with one of my children while I was on the phone to them. It turned my stomach.

Talking to my babies was hard enough without having to hear her in the middle of it. Fiona had cried when she heard my voice. I cried too. I couldn't help it. It was so hard. Talking to Seb, I heard Sue in the background. I heard her laughing with the girls. I stopped breathing when I heard her. It hurt whenever I tried to inhale like something was stopping the air reaching my lungs.

My eyes stung like crazy and I longed for that memory to be erased. I wanted to put the phone down but I couldn't. Marcus came on the phone and sensed there was something wrong. He kept asking me if I was ok. I didn't understand why he was asking. Surely he would know. Surely he could put himself in my position and realise my pain. No. Obviously not.

3rd August 2007

Met John. Went out with mum into Essex. Had a great time. Got so drunk - needed to. Forgot him. Stared at this tall man looming over me. He was so sweet. Mum chatted him up on my behalf. He was so calm and caring. I had wanted someone to protect me from all of this and I bet he could. He took me home. We drove around by my house and he told me where he used to live. Where he went to school. I felt like a teenager again. The fear was there too. The fear of being in a car with a stranger. We kissed goodnight.

He dropped me off and before I got in the house he had text me already.

It was the Friday night of their holiday and we had finished painting for the day. Dad had joined us in painting the living room. He had come for extra support in the workload and also for me, though it was all unmentioned again. We had got so much done it was pretty amazing. Mum and I made this last minute decision to go out into town, so I could show her where I went when I was out with Marilyn. I think she sensed she had to get me out for a while, away from the house.

We went to a couple of the places and we met Gary in one of them. He was the man Brad had been with the first and last time I had met up with him. We chatted for a bit and then he left. I remembered wishing Brad was with him then.

In the last place we visited we were enjoying the atmosphere. I was slightly worse for wear, rather drunk but needed to be for obvious reasons. All of a sudden, this figure was standing next to me and mum. Mum was chatting away to him and I heard my name mentioned a few times. His name was John. He seemed quite nice - incredibly tall. He took my number and rang it there and then to check it was mine.

We went out into the night and dad came to pick up mum. I stayed with John. We walked and chatted down the street. We got in his car. He told me how he grew up round here, his schools, where he used to live and what he was doing now. He seemed such a caring guy. He talked soft and calmly. He made me feel calm. We drove to a secluded spot near to my home and we kissed. It really made me feel like a teenager. That is the type of thing you do at that age. Kissing in the car at 31 years old is not really the done thing. I wasn't complaining though.

I got out the car and he had text me before I had set foot in the house. There was a warm glow again. I felt good and it made me smile. He wasn't Brad but I couldn't have him could I?

Mum was going mad when I walked in and dad was angry that I had been left to come home with some stranger. They were stressed and worried and seemed angry with themselves. It didn't bother me. I was ok. I hadn't really given it much thought. I was home now too so they didn't need to be stressed anymore.

Falling into bed I felt much happier. I was nearly at the end of my weekend without children and now I had met someone that maybe will take me out and spoil me again. Another day was over and this time it had ended well.

4th August

John text me all day. He was nagging in the evening about me going to his friend's house. I was tempted but I was with Marilyn and I was safer with her. I didn't know this guy - I couldn't go.

Oh such a good feeling. That little bit of attention goes a long way. Felt happy all day as I finished the painting and got ready to hit the town again with Marilyn. John had text me all day. Each one made me smile. I replied and kept the texting sequence going as I didn't want it to end.

The town was good tonight. I had received texts from John right up to 2.30am. I sat on the settee in my dark empty house wishing I had gone to his friends like he had asked me to. I couldn't do it though. I knew I would have been putting myself in a situation that I did not want to be in with a man I did not know. The head rules decisions like that, it has to.

It was the loneliness that made me dwell on my decision. Marilyn had gone, the children were not here and so I was alone. Again. It made me feel sad inside. It always did. I hated coming home on a Saturday night knowing that the weekend was over and I was back to my lonely life again. I wanted the children to be there when I returned. I wanted a reason to get up in the morning. I wanted somebody to check on when I came through that front door.

I climbed into bed, already knowing that I was not going to be able to sleep, pulling the covers up to my chest as I sat hunched up against the headboard. I was so uncomfortable but I didn't see the point in lying down if I wasn't going to sleep. Now was the time I needed the texts. This time of night when everything is still and silent, is the time that you needed to think that someone was thinking of you at least.

I sat there staring at my window. My curtains were open. I thought about shutting them but my body was not going to follow through with those thoughts. The light from the lamppost streamed into the bedroom through the slats in the blind. The pattern of it flickered onto the wall, moving with the breeze outside.

I sat there in silence feeling a little lost. I wished mum and dad had stayed. They would be here and then I could sleep.

That feeling of someone else in the house was settling. I snuggled down under the covers, lying down on the pillow at an angle, admitting to myself that I actually felt tired. I looked up at the ceiling and soon became aware that my thoughts were of them again. I wondered what they were doing. I wondered how my children were. I wanted my babies back now.

The thoughts of my children and the fact they were not here triggered the tears. The silent ones. The ones that drizzle slowly down your cheeks as if you really couldn't be bothered. They fell onto my pillow as I turned to face the door, pulling the covers up tight under my chin. I pictured my babies with her and felt that searing pain across my chest like someone was burning my flesh with hot iron. I pictured them all asleep in their beds. I pictured their little faces as they slept. There was that searing pain again. I wondered what beds they had. Were they all together?

Then, for some stupid reason I thought of Sue. I pictured her asleep with my husband. Her head on his chest and her arms across him. His arms wrapped round her shoulders and his chin resting on the top of her head. There was that pain again. Straight through the chest. I gasped for air this time. I wondered what happened when the girls woke up. They were always up and down during the night when they were at home. They always came into bed with me. Always had come into bed with us. There was that pain again.

Would they take them into bed with them? I screwed my eyes up tight to try and stop the mental images of my girls in between their dad and her. I tried so hard to think of something else. I really tried. I knew I had failed when I heard a loud cry of pain and I could almost smell the burning flesh too. I sobbed loudly into my pillow. The tears came thick and fast. She has my family. She has my husband. She has my children.

I want them back. Please bring them back. I need them with me. Now.

5th August

Met John for a drink. He took me to a pub in town. We talked and laughed and had a good time. He came back to mine for a drink before going to work. No furniture as I was decorating. I curled up on his lap on the one chair I had in my front room. He was strong and comforting. We kissed and he held me so close. For those few minutes I was happy.

The texts came thick and fast all day. He was spending time with his daughter, which made me smile. We finished the painting. I didn't tell mum how my day of happiness and great time out last night turned so sour at the end. So quickly.

I painted and chatted all day and then got asked for a drink before he went to work. The nerves kicked in and I could feel my heart racing with excitement. The smile on my face seemed to stay.

I spoke briefly to the children. No tears. Talks of coming home.

"Won't be long now will it mum?" Fiona said quietly.

I could hear the sadness in her voice. Her little quiet voice. It just tinged it slightly.

"We are having a good time mum," said Seb.

I could hear the guilt in his. He needed the reassurance that it was ok to be enjoying his holiday. It was ok to be happy with the two of them. He needed to be happy.

"I'm glad babe," I replied.

"I'm missing you mummy," my little Pheobe stated when she came to the phone.

"I'm missing you all too," I squeaked through my tears.

I need them home now, I thought to myself. I let myself cry. I let myself feel a little sad. I picked myself up though as I got ready for my date.

The doorbell rang and I could feel myself shaking. I locked everything up and we drove into town. We sat and drank in a pub I had never been in before. It was quiet. He was sarcastic to those that were not as quiet. I liked that. We talked about children, our break ups, our jobs. We talked for ages.

We ended up back at mine for tea before he went to his nightshift. I only had one chair and he took up the whole space in that being so tall and fairly well built. I felt safe having him in my house. I was not worried at all. He seemed a caring, sensitive person and I wondered whether he could be that way or whether it was a front. After a while he joined me on the floor and we kissed goodnight. He held me close and tight. It was lovely. Not quite knee trembling, but soft and warm. We spent the last ten minutes just hugging and talking about his nightshift and plans for the following day.

He said he would call me as I waved him goodbye. I watched him drive off and came back to my empty house. I sat there in my one lonely chair looking at the bare room and remembered it looking this way when we first moved in.

A text from John made me snap out of the memories and move back into happier mode. I called mum and told her how it went. After putting the phone down I realised how the silence is what made the brain think and promptly switched the TV on to drown out the quiet.

Crawling into bed I felt so tired and pulling the covers up tight I made myself think of my night with John instead of anything else. Sweet dreams tonight please Mr Sandman.

Another one bites the dust.

6th August

Absolutely nothing. Haven't heard a thing. I know it was only a few minutes. I know it was only one date. No weirdness like I was cheating on Marc. No feeling of wrong waiting behind me ready to pounce. The chance of happiness gone. The hope of seeing him again dashed. *Why?* I don't get it. I don't understand. No text message today. No reply to mine. *How come these men just want to play silly games?* I'm so confused, so frustrated and a little hurt.

How frustrating. No word. No contact. No explanation. Why?

Why can't people pick up the bloody phone and say what has happened? He changed his mind. Ok fine. Say so. Ignoring is so rude. It makes you feel awful. Did he decide last night? Why respond to my text last night then? Did he change his mind this morning? What was the reason behind his change of decision? Why?

All day I had picked up my phone to check if he had contacted me. All day. I hate the not knowing. All the questions. Straight away my question was, what did I do wrong? Why did I blame myself?

Unwanted again. Not quite what he was looking for. Not right. Not good enough.

Negative feelings about myself came creeping out of the woodwork again and no matter how many times I pushed them back inside, they still crept back up to resurface. It was a joke to think that I had done it again. Unless all men are the same. Is that it? I just haven't had to deal with this before. Having Marcus for so long, I had never experienced this.

How difficult was it to pick up the phone, man?

Returned from shopping to find a bee's nest in my chimney breast. Packed up the fireplace. Phoned the pest control places. Wait 3 days to see if they go away? No chance. Tomorrow. Great. Watching them creep out through the packed up grate at the bottom of the fireplace I packed my bags, locked the cats outside and ran to my mums. Excellent day today. Thanks!

Sleeping at my mums was weird. Strange bed. Strange noises. Unsettling. Felt uneasy and my head hurt from all the things that had been running through it all day. All I seemed to be doing was collecting unanswered questions. Lists of them. Marc, Brad and now John. Each one of them had created questions to add to the ever expanding list. Where were the answers? Who was going to give them to me? Anyone?

The frustration took over a lot. It made me tense and stressed but at least I wasn't crying. The questions rattled around and I asked myself them over and over again. Still leaving them without an answer. They echoed round for most of the night.

I concentrated hard on the events of tomorrow. Picking the children up. Getting them away from her. The excitement kicked in. The rush of love as I pictured holding them again and telling them how much I missed them. I longed for tomorrow to come. Hours seemed to pass and yet it was really just minutes. The long nights were so draining.

I laid there still thinking about my babies and getting them home. Listening to their voices. Listening to their stories though hearing her name in them all would be hard. I felt myself frowning. Stop it I told myself. I went back to the happier thoughts. She will be away from them and that's what matters. They will be back with their mum again. They will be back home again. They will be where they belong. With me. Safe. Loved. Hugged and kissed. Missed so much.

11th August 2007

I have not sat and wrote in this diary for ages. Don't really know why, just really busy I suppose. Had a few days that felt like an uphill struggle. You know those times when you feel like you are actually taking a couple of steps forwards and then something comes along and whacks you back down a dozen paces.

It's hard to keep your chin up and stay positive when there are always obstacles in your way.

The other thing that is happening to me at the moment is the acceptance of being single. When I first split one of the things on my mind was that I was not part of a couple anymore. After so long that was something difficult to accept. It seemed really important to me. The devastation of failing at a relationship was huge and had serious effects. I couldn't see myself as a single person because I had never been one. I had wanted to jump straight back into being a couple again. Now I just want to be spoilt. I wouldn't mind a little attention, a drink down the pub but that is all I desire now. It feels better.

I have my children during the week and yes I look forward to having the time to go out and socialise at the weekend, but I am not always looking around to see who is out and about. I want to have fun. I want to have a drink and dance the night away. It's a good feeling.

Joined a singles website though. Spur of the moment decision! There are some very strange people out there. They sit at the computer at all times of the day and night and email strangers all over the country. It's nice in some ways. There are some nice people turning to the internet dating scene. I still felt it had a stigma and it probably won't be something I will tell my friends quite readily.

Been talking to a guy online. He sounds the most amazing father I have ever known. He is a single dad and adores them. Obviously, there is that doubt of whether the guy is for real but it's nice to think there are these great men out there somewhere.

Also have a date with a man from the dating agency I joined. Really nervous. Really happy. Going with the attitude of just getting spoilt for the evening.

The shift in my attitude is pleasing to me. I sit back and think of how far I have come in the last 5 months and I am becoming quite proud of myself. I know there is a long way to go. There are still obstacles that will jump up at me from time to time and slap me down for a while. I also know that I will bounce back up at some point and slap them back.

Life can keep chucking it at me if it wants to. I'm ready for the battle to continue; only now I have the determination to win. Happiness will be here soon - for good.

I got my children back and spent some time listening to their stories and what they did, said and how they enjoyed it. At first it hurt like mad. I heard her name lots and the thought of her and my family doing all the holiday things together like we should have been doing made me feel sick. I knew we had never done those things because of me. I would never get into debt for the sake of a holiday and as Marc spent the money like it was going out of fashion, I never had a chance to save up for one either. It was sad really.

Then I listened properly to them. At the end of each story which was told fast through excitement, the tone of their little voices lowered. Then the words "but you were not there mum," were said. Or the words "I cried because I was missing you," or "we wanted to phone and tell you straight away."

They were missing me. The whole time they were with her doing all these exciting things and being spoilt and yet they were still missing me. They wanted me. There was a smile alongside the tears that had welled up in the corner of my eyes. They were not tears of sadness, they were tears of relief. I held them close and whispered, "mummy missed you too - so much." My girls had a smile much the same as mine on their faces. A smile of relief. They had felt the same way as me. Unsure whether the other was missing them. Thinking of what they were doing. I had assumed that they would be having such a great time away with her and daddy that I would have been forgotten. They had thought I would forget them. The bond was there and the way we looked at each other, we all knew we were stronger than before. Closer too.

It seems strange to walk around with a smile on my face. It made me realise that I had been without one for so long. I was still hurting inside but the acceptance that it was a normal pain, and it would go away soon was there, and it made it seem more bearable. I fussed over my babies lots. They had lots to do. Out and about. The beach, the zoo, the park, I took them everywhere I could within financial restraints of course.

My sister came to stay with us for a couple of days. We chatted the night away and spoke endlessly about the trouble with men. How we are never satisfied. For once I spoke about the things that I didn't miss. I didn't miss the constant fighting. The moaning about the state of the house or the noise of the children. The way he took my TV over and never helped with the bedtime routine or the housework. I didn't miss the stress of him and Seb fighting and shouting at each other. I didn't miss the worry about what mood he was going to walk through the door in and how much he would then moan at me.

I realised that the only things I missed was his love, when it was ever on show, and his company. We had had evenings where we had talked and laughed. We laughed at what our girls had done or said or the way our Seb reacted when he had scored a goal on the football game on the X - box. He had enjoyed those few games with his dad. It was always nice to watch. We had nice evenings where we snuggled up on the settee watching crap TV. I used to love watching Marc watch the Simpsons. He used to laugh out loud, throwing his head back and looking at me and then back at the TV. I always wondered what he had found so funny. It used to make me smile.

The things I missed did not outweigh the things I didn't miss. The things he used to shout and get stressed about. I didn't understand them and it used to make me sad and long for the morning to come so he would go to work again. I couldn't understand where my husband had gone for he was no longer there when he was in moods like those.

I think it was talking to my sister that night that had provoked me to analyse those things over the next few days. I felt like I was in deep thought the whole time and it was on my mind constantly. Once I had those things straight in my head, I felt like a different person. I felt like I was a little stronger. I was not back to how I was before and I was not happy that the split had happened, but I was coping with it. I had a long way to go.

The run of firsts were not finished yet. All of the things you do alone for the first time. All of mine were in the space of twelve weeks. I had got through the girls' birthday but I still had to get through Seb's and the big one, our wedding anniversary.

I put that day to the back of my mind and began planning Seb's birthday. The present I was going to buy him, the people coming over and the problems with Marc and his family. So much to think about.

I had spent some time sitting thinking about the singles website. I had been speaking to men on there and enjoyed the light hearted conversation. I enjoyed the attention but that was all I needed. Just the attention. It gave me the boost I needed and that was it. When the man online spoke about meeting up I got scared and called it all off. He was quite persistent but not threatening. I did not want to meet anyone from there; it was all too scary and too quick.

I spent my nights sitting in the usual place. I had not felt so alone. More frustrated at the things that had to be done and the planning I was doing alone. I was getting more annoyed, angrier and more bitter at everything. Things were so complicated sometimes. Marc phoned regularly. He talked to me as well as the children and I listened when he moaned about finances with annoyance. How could he moan about his? I work part time and have to feed and clothe three children as well as pay some of the bills. I keep a tight budget. I know he pays out more, but he earns more. All my money goes.

I became frustrated at the silence too. I began playing games on the computer with the music on when the children were in bed or watched the TV even if I wasn't giving the programme my full attention. I had to have some noise around me and I was beginning to settle in the evenings. I had my moments of sadness. I had my moments of reminiscing and

I had my moments of feeling sorry for myself, but they were gone as quickly as they had begun.

Life was beginning to look up for me. I was beginning to let the positive feelings stay around for longer and felt that was a good thing. I was aware that I would have my hard days but I also knew that I could feel this way now, so I would fight myself back to these feelings when I needed to. It felt good.

Third happy birthday.

18th August 2007

Seb's birthday.

Marc arrived about 11am. He spent some time with me reminiscing. He then took him out to his mums for the day. He gave Seb his old phone and plugged it in to charge.

When I got back from shopping something made me check the phone. *Why did I do that?* I only found things I didn't really want to see. There was no shock though. I knew he would have left something to do with her on there. I knew he would play mind games whether on purpose or accidentally. I wonder whether he is getting a kick out of hurting me like this. *Why is he playing this game? What does he want me to do?*

Spent the whole night wondering what to say to him. *Should I bother?*

Drank a bottle of wine and then had an idea. I gave Seb her mobile number. I let him text her and ask her to phone him. Marcus phoned me panicking. I could hear the stress in his voice. I could hear the trembling. He thought it was me. She wouldn't phone straight away as my family were here and they thought it was me or one of them. Cool. Paranoia for them.

By the time everyone left I was so drunk. Seb left with mum and Fiona left with Lucy. Pheobe went to sleep. I finished the second bottle of wine - no point wasting it. I then decided in my drunken wisdom to text him and then John too to tell them what I thought of them. I was nicer to John. He replied with some shit about how he was sorry but could not be with somebody else right now - he wasn't in the right place. Oh well.

Marc was feeling worried. I told him how I hated both of them. I told him how I was going to tell her how we slept together when

240

he came to see me. That we kiss in the kitchen every time. That we still need each other.

Don't remember much else apart from climbing into bed with a pounding headache and feeling less than unhappy.

Seb's birthday - another first to be done. He was a little upset when he woke this morning. His dad had travelled down from London last night to be with him. We had had a nice evening together as a family. He treated the children to McDonalds and they had thoroughly enjoyed it. We talked for a while when the children had gone to bed and then he left. He was coming back for him this morning.

Seb was pleased with his present from me and this time writing ...love Mummy xx...on his card did not make me as upset as before. I watched him open his cards and presents and smiled.

As most parents did, I remembered the day I had him. I had a long labour with Seb and still don't know how I got through it. I remember it being a hot day. I remember being so shocked when he was a boy; I had expected a little girl. I remember him lying in his sleep suit that was already a tight fit. He had been a big boy - 8lbs 6 and a half ounces. A little bruiser. Lying there with his fists clenched.

I pictured that baby lying in the crib beside my hospital bed and I looked at Seb standing there now. How is it possible that the time has flown by so quickly? 11 now. 11 years old. He seemed so grown up it brought tears to my eyes.

He wandered round the house, waiting for his dad to arrive. I spoiled him with his favourite breakfast and let him watch what he wanted on TV. Those were the birthday rules in this house. You were thoroughly spoilt and Seb knew them so well, he milked them for all they were worth.

We sat together for most of the morning. His dad turned up. We chatted for a while but I was keen for him to concentrate on Seb. He gave Seb his old mobile phone which meant he had an extra present. He was really chuffed. I could see the excitement on his face at having his own phone.

Marc took him out for a while. Visited his mum and dad. I went off and bought some food for tonight. Mum was buying most of it as it was my dad's birthday tomorrow and we were having a joint birthday, as always. I bought Seb's cake and his candles. I phoned him while I stood in front of the shelves of cakes. I didn't seem to know which my son would want. They all seemed too babyish. He seemed too grown up.

I wandered round the store with a blank expression on my face. It was weird. I didn't like him not being with me. I didn't like sharing him on his birthday. He was my son and he should be with me choosing his birthday treats. I rushed around filling the trolley with goodies and then loading them into bags. Shopping was so mundane. Even birthday shopping.

Back at the house, something made me check Seb's phone while it was charging. Knowing Marc as I did, I had this feeling that he wouldn't have thought to ensure it was empty. I twirled it around in my fingers and I knew there would be something on there to do with her. I just knew it. Question was did I really want to find it?

I slid up the screen and the phone lit up. I slid it down again. Do you want to see whatever it is on there Stephanie? I slid the phone back up again and looked at the menu. What would he leave on there I thought to myself. Pictures? I scrolled down and searched through the file. No, not in the pictures folder. What about in messages then? I scrolled down again and went to Inbox. No, nothing there either. Sent messages? No nothing there either.

I can't be wrong I thought. Then I saw it. Saved messages. It has to be I thought. I opened the folder and...bingo! I found them. A pile of lovey dovey shit. I read through each one. One was saved from Pheobe's birthday.

"Don't worry. Ignore them all. Remember you have done nothing wrong xx"

Excuse me Sue. Nothing wrong? My family were not ignoring him for nothing. He was with you, in your bed, while married to me. Nothing wrong, you stupid cow.

"You make me feel so amazing xxx"

Bleurgh! How crap. He makes you feel amazing does he? Ok, love if you say so. I looked down at the date on that message. It was the 7th April. Oh my god! That was only 10 days after I chucked him out! Well, that proves he is a bloody liar. He had said that they had just started to think about being together two weeks after.

I knew I had been right. I couldn't believe a word he was saying. They say the truth has a way of coming out in the end. Well, there is part of it. What had he done to make her feel so amazing ten days after leaving his wife temporarily? I can just imagine what she was referring to. Didn't take her long did it? Would she jump in my grave that quickly?

There were other messages about wanting to kiss him in front of people. Telling the others in their group. It was all wet and sloppy messages but I still read each one of them.

I slung the phone on the bench. I believed he had left them there on purpose. He had wanted me to read them. I was sure that was all part of some stupid mind game he was playing. Stupid git.

I carried on preparing everything and then stopped mid flow. I had suddenly realised that it had not made me sad. Wow. I was not a mess. I was not crying. I stared straight ahead as I was telling myself all this. A smile crept on my face. It hadn't bothered me because I had known it already. It hadn't bothered me because I was expecting to find something. It hadn't bothered me because....because...did it matter why? It hadn't made me cry. He hadn't made me cry. I smiled. I walked to the other side of the kitchen and turned on the radio. The music blaring, I sung along to it and prepared the house for my birthday boy's return.

His dad left him early evening. He had stayed for the girls birthday evening but not his son's. I wondered if Seb was bothered by that. He didn't seem to be. People started arriving earlier than first thought and mum helped me to rush the last of the preparations. Family were here again and once again I was appreciative.

I poured myself a glass of wine. People noticed I was drinking again. I hadn't drunk at family parties before. Of course they were going to notice. After a couple of glasses I had an idea. I called Seb over and took his phone. I inputted Sue's number into his phone and showed him.

"Text her," I said. "Tell her it's your birthday and she can ring you if she likes."

Seb looked at me smiling. "Can I really mum?" he asked excitedly.

Of course, I replied with a smile. Marc didn't know I had her number. I had taken it off his phone when he had been round here one day. I had saved it under a different name too so he wouldn't find it when he checked my phone as he did so often. They will both know I have it now won't they?

She wouldn't phone straight away. Sure enough after a few seconds of it being sent, my phone rang.

"What is going on?" his voice said. "Who sent that message?"

"Seb, who else would it be? Who else could it be?" I said with a snigger.

"How did you get the number?"

"I'm a clever girl," I replied with a giggle.

"Are you sure it is ok to phone? No one else will pick it up will they?"

"Doubt it," I said. "She should phone him or he will be upset."

I put the phone down and smiled. He was stressed and according to him, so was she. He had thought it was perhaps a member of my family that had sent the message. That they were perhaps laying in wait for her to ring. What an idiot. Why were they concerned if there was no scandal? I smiled smugly as she phoned Seb, though his beaming smile in response to her voice did hurt a little. I drank more wine and ignored it. Talked to everybody else. Spent time laughing in the kitchen with my sister and Nicky.

Eventually, it was the end and people were gone. Seb had gone back to my mum and dads to be spoilt a little more and Fiona had gone back to Marc's parents house with his sister. I had talked a bit to his sister Lucy tonight. I had been honest when she asked if I missed him or just missed having someone. I missed him of course. I really missed him. I had got a little upset. She kept telling me I will be happier one day and there would be something better out there. I don't see how they can say that. Something better than the man I love. Something better than the father of my children.

Something better than the man I chose to be with for 14 years. Whatever.

I closed the door, comforted Pheobe as she was crying because she was left behind and got her to sleep.

I came downstairs, pushing past the faceless creatures that had permanent places at the foot of them and went through to the kitchen. I poured the rest of the wine into my glass - no point in wasting it. I didn't even like wine - why was I drinking it? I grimaced at the taste of the last mouthful in my glass. I certainly didn't like that one. I saw another half filled bottle. No room in the fridge for that either I told myself, and poured that in my glass too. There was still some left in the bottom of the bottle, so I drank that bit first.

I perched up on my bench with my knees huddled up towards my chest. My wine glass balanced on the top of them with a shaky hand trying to steady it. I didn't want to spill any of it. My mind started to wander. It was only 10pm and here I was alone. Family gone. Support gone. Company gone. I thought about what they were doing. They were not alone were they? They had each other.

My thoughts then turned to John. The one who had just disappeared. The one who thought ignoring people was ok. Both of these men were frustrating me. I should tell them what I thought of them I decided, pointing my finger in the air as if there was a light bulb above my head like in the cartoons. I should tell them.

I jumped off the bench and rummaged round the kitchen to find my phone. Marc first. I needed him to know that it was early on a Saturday night, his son's birthday and I was pissed off, why did I need him to know? I don't know really. I just did. The message was a little rambled but it was nasty and to the point. I said how I was annoyed that he hadn't wiped the messages. I was annoyed that he hadn't been here for his son tonight. I was annoyed that he treated his son and daughters differently and when they grow up they will be annoyed too. I also told him I hated him. I hated both of them. I said I hoped that one day they too would feel the amount of pain I am feeling and they too would be made to suffer. Vicious I know.

The next one was to John. It took me a lot longer to phrase this one and then when I had almost finished, Marc text me back and wiped it off. That annoyed me again and I sent another awful message saying how I would tell her we had slept together a few nights ago and that she needed to know he was a liar and a cheat. I searched for John's message. I said I was drunk enough to not care I was texting him. I said it was rude of him to ignore me. I also said thank you for making me smile and feel happy even if it was so short lived.

I staggered upstairs to bed deciding that I had done enough for tonight. I had finished embarrassing myself for the time being. I had drank too much and needed to sleep it off. I fell into bed, literally, and snuggled next to Pheobe. Did I put her to bed in here? I didn't remember doing that. My phone clicked. It was John. He apologised. He said he was not in the right place to be with someone else right now. I had made him realise that. He also said that I had been through so much there would be too many complications.

I replied saying there were no complications on my part and that it was a shame that he was not honest and couldn't have talked it through before making his decision. I also said it was a shame that he was clearly that type of man that couldn't be friends with a woman.

That was a shame. We had got on well. Men and women are not meant to be friends though are they?

I don't remember anything else. I don't remember the tiredness sweeping over me. I don't remember checking the clock. I don't remember the waiting for sleep. I don't remember anything.

What a mess.

24th August

The lowest feeling in the world could not describe the feeling today. The mood was awful. Arguments with Marc brought me down further. He did not want to have the children. He had things planned.

In my eyes it was his duty to have them. He left me. He has somebody to help him through this difficult time. He can curl up on the sofa with her and forget all about the fact it is our wedding anniversary. He can be comforted. There was no way I was sitting indoors alone with the children submerging myself in the feelings of pitiful sorrow.

He turned up. I gave him a card to signify the memories of the wedding day 5 years ago. I watched him cry. I held him.

I went out with Michelle and her friend. They were great. Made sure I had plenty to drink and that I danced and would not allow me to feel sorry for myself.

The problem came when I walked through the door. I turned the key in the lock and the tears fell. They cascaded down my cheeks turning them bright red within seconds. They were uncontrollable.

I felt so lost. I feel so lost. I feel empty and unloved and alone. The negativity just oozes out of every pore of my skin. I can't pick myself up. I had a good night with them but then they left. They went back to their husbands and family. I went back to my dark, empty house. It signifies my life quite well. The pain is overwhelming and uncontrollable. I need him back. I want him here with me. I'm sure he is not thinking of me.

I had spent the whole week getting ready for this day. Each day I had spoken to Marc about having the children and each day we had had an argument about it. He didn't see why he should have them as he had made plans to get him out for the night. What? He had a girlfriend to help him through. It shouldn't affect him anyway. He was the one who wanted to split. He expected me to have them for the night didn't he? He expected me to sit indoors with them so he could go out. I was furious. How selfish?

For the entire week I made his life hell until he organised someone to have the children for him. He expected my mum and dad to have them. It was their wedding anniversary too. How could he expect that? He couldn't ask his mum and dad because we were still not talking. He finally got his sister and my cousin to have them. They were staying at the flat. Bet he doesn't go back there.

I gave him a card when he arrived. A plain one. I just said that we should think of the significance of the day and the memories it holds for us despite it not meaning the same. I signed it with love always. It blew him away. He cried a little too. I was glad. There was still some feeling in the cold, selfish man he had become.

The children left and I started to get ready straight away even though I was unsure what I was doing. It was a Friday night and Marilyn was never around. Michelle had said a little while ago she would come out with me but she had people staying and I really didn't want to disturb her from that. I got low again and phoned. I couldn't stay in. Maybe she would let me go round hers and sit in her corner for a bit if nothing else.

She was fine about it. Said her and her friend Shirley were going to take me out. They arrived. Immediately my mood lifted and I felt better. I showed them a picture of Sue before we left. Marc had left the holiday pictures of the children on the camera for me. He hadn't thought to erase the ones of her first. He had showed me them too on his laptop a few nights ago. He had sat with me and the children and ran through the pictures he had downloaded. I was crying my eyes out and still he kept showing them. He even included the ones of them together as a couple and the ones of my children and her together. Inconsiderate sod. I wondered what Sue would think of that if she knew. I put up the picture of the happy couple.

"Blimey, she even looks Scottish!" said Michelle in her Scottish accent.

What did that mean? How could you look Scottish? I just laughed. They didn't really comment. Never said too much. Screwed their noses up at the sight of her.

The night passed in a blur. Once again I was so drunk by the end of it. They drank so much so quickly. They kept plying me with alcohol. So I drank it. They made me laugh. They were so full of life and both had a great sense of humour. I couldn't help but smile when I was with them. They ran through the bars so quickly. Dancing wherever they felt like dancing. We watched the people that were out and about, making comments about their appearance.

We danced the night away in a nightclub and then made our way home. I thanked them for a great night and they waited in the cab until I had shut the door. I saw the cab pull away through the glass, walked inside and locked the porch door. Before I had turned around to see my house I was crying. The tears came so fast like a waterfall and by the time I had walked over to the mirror, my cheeks were bright red and amazingly hot.

I fell to the floor beside my kitchen door and just sobbed. Inside my dark and empty house and on my wedding anniversary, I was alone. The faceless creatures, the ones that usually stayed at the foot of my stairs, that bore such pain and misery came over to be with me. It was almost like they felt sorry for me. They crowded round me and I could hear their moans and groans as they circled my pathetic figure. They swarmed in for the kill and I felt their sharp talons sliding into every inch of me as the pain got more and more intense.

The darkness surrounded me and them and the figures of loneliness and depression circled above me like vultures circle their next meal. With great velocity, they flew into me through my open mouth as I tried so desperately to breathe. I inhaled short, sharp, agonising gasps of pity and my lungs ached. The pain blew me over and I lay on the floor next to my dining table and chairs. I curled up in a ball and held myself tightly. I sobbed and sobbed, gasping for air as I choked on my own self pity, my sorrow and despair.

I laid there staring at nothing as the sobs calmed down and my breathing became more regular. This time 5 years ago we were in our suite at the hotel. Our wedding night and we were in bed together. Holding each other. We were making love for the first time as husband and wife. Now my husband was in bed with her. Making love to her. And his wife was alone on the floor of their house crying like a baby.

The tears carried on streaming down my face as I made my way upstairs to my bedroom. I lay on the bed and closed my eyes. I could feel myself rocking trying to find some comfort. I thought this was supposed to get easier. I thought time was the healer. I thought I would get better.

The reason why it's not? I love him. I miss him. I need him. My husband. My world. My love. My life. Come home. Please.

Now bloody angry?

4th Sept

That bastard did not call his son before he left for school. His first day at secondary school and he cannot pick up the phone and wish him luck. I could kill him.

Seb left crying. I spent the whole day worrying about him and what he was doing. I felt ill. The stress was amazing and engulfed everything I did today. Mum was here for support as always.

I hate Marc even more now. I feel so helpless. He has let his son down and what can I do to make it better - nothing! Nothing! *What kind of useless mother is that?*

I sat and cried. I smoked whenever I could. I was so nervous and the day was so slow I thought it would never end.

I had spent the last 11 days organising the back to school necessities. I don't know how many times I had to ask Marc to buy some of the uniform for the start of the new schools. I had dreaded this week for the last few days and now it was here. The first day was over.

My mum was sitting with me again tonight. She wanted to be here to support the children as well as me. She was sitting in the front room watching TV while I had a cigarette in the kitchen. I had been smoking more and more in front of her and I knew she was not impressed at all with the habit. She also knew how I turned to it more when I was stressed.

She had helped me through the mood of today. Through the hard bits. Through the long slow hours.

I sat on my bench and flicked the ash from my cigarette down the sink. I was so angry with him still. I couldn't switch the feelings off. Seb was settled into his bed after his stress filled day and Fiona was tossing and turning with nerves of her big day tomorrow. I was struggling with the guilt from her fears. It was my fault she was starting another new school this term. The school she would be going to was so much better than the one she had been at. I was doing it to give her the best start in life. I was making her change because I knew it would be better for her in the long run. Better education. She was so clever and I wanted to make sure she had the best. Pheobe would be starting there too in January, so they would be together then instead of in two different places.

I knew there was no need to justify it. I knew I was doing the right thing for my babies but it didn't stop me feeling guilty for putting her through it.

I was also sad. I felt like I was doing this as a lone parent. That feeling was kicking in a lot lately. I know I have my mum here but it shouldn't be her doing it. Their father should be here for them too. He should be here giving them the support of their dad. New life of his was far too demanding for that. Or was it that he just didn't think of it? Had he not thought to book some time off to be with them? Had he thought there was no need? Did it not mean anything to him?

The anger was there still from this morning. Seb had gone off with his friends on his first day at secondary school, crying his eyes out. He was so scared. I thought back to my first day at secondary and I remembered what that felt like. I had to walk in alone. My best friend at that time, Caroline, had moved and there was no one for me to walk in with. No one for me to meet up with. I hadn't cried. I had felt awful, but I hadn't cried.

Seb was probably crying because of everything. He probably felt that his life would never settle down. He had moved away from his friends in London to live here. He had started a new primary school without his sister. He had had his first holiday with the school and away from his parents. He had had to get used to not being round the corner to my mum and dad. Then he had lost his dad and seen his mum in a mess. He had to try and understand why dad had Sue and get used to her too. He had changes to cope with financially and had to get used to them. Now he was starting yet another school.

Again, an element of guilt hung around me. I had put him through all of that. I was doing it for him but he wouldn't see it like that would he. He still had to cope with it all. And I knew he found it all so hard.

The anger built up in me again. Why am I putting these changes solely at my feet? They were Marc's decisions too. He had chosen to move here. He had chosen to start again. He had chosen the schools with me. He had fought for a place in them with me. Most of all he had chosen to move back to London and to be with Sue instead of us. The worst decision was choosing not to support his children through all of it. How could he just leave them to get on with it? How could he think he was not needed?

I hadn't cried so much for him lately. The wedding anniversary had been a big changing point for me. I had cried as much as I could and I had also realised that I needed to buck my ideas up. I had accepted he would never come back to me. It didn't mean I didn't want him to, but I had accepted he wouldn't.

The hatred and the anger I felt towards him at the moment was immense. I find it hard to forgive people who upset me and I was finding it hard to forgive him right now. No one hurts my babies like this - no one. And my Seb was hurt. He was hurt that his dad didn't call him this morning. He didn't call him to wish him luck. He had said he would call last night, so why didn't he? How could I answer that question for him?

I could see Seb felt lost this morning. He panicked and said he wasn't going. I had to literally push him out of the door. Both mum and I had cried when he left and had spent the day trying to keep busy so not to think about him too much. It had been so hard.

I had spoken to Marc on the phone. As normal he didn't see what he had done wrong. I gave up trying to make him see. I couldn't make him see any of it at all.

I climbed down from my bench as my cigarette had burnt out with all my thinking and made a cup of tea. I went back into my mum and curled up beside her on the settee. I lay on her lap and she stroked my head. I was 31 years old and still needed a cuddle from mum. I smiled as I thought that. It was strange that even as a grown up, your mum could still make you feel safe. I felt better just having her here. Secure. Comforted.

We watched crap TV. I could have the TV on now. A little progress. I could watch what I wanted and turn it off when I felt like it. That was a nice feeling.

We chatted into the night. We analysed Marc and his actions and came up with so many maybes. Maybe he had just forgotten. Maybe we were expecting too much of him. Maybe he was too wrapped up in his life now. Maybe the children were not that important to him, not at the forefront of his mind as they should be.

Too many maybes. Not enough definite answers. I was used to that now though. I was used to not knowing what was going on. I was used to the uncertainty. My life was filled to the brim with it.

I checked on each of my babies. Pheobe was now a permanent fixture in my bed. At least it was never empty anymore. Fiona had slipped down the bed again and I pulled her back up so her head was on her pillow. Before I had left the room, she was back down again. I just shrugged and laughed to myself.

Seb was sleeping soundly. I perched on the edge of his bed and watched him sleep for a while. His eyes were twitching. He was dreaming. He turned over in his sleep so he was fully facing me. He was so handsome. Had I really made him? Maybe he was switched at birth. I smiled again. I brushed my hand over his head and gave him a kiss. When he was asleep was the only time I got away with giving him a kiss now. That was forbidden now he was older. It was not allowed.

I watched him for a little longer and I heard Pheobe and her pathetic cry for Mummy. I waited a little while before going in there. I wanted to be with Seb. I couldn't be there during his school day and I wanted to be with him now. I hovered on the bed waiting for Pheobe's next cry. It didn't come so I stayed there. He was so grown up now. My first baby at secondary school. Where did the years go? If the next 11 go as quick I will be 42 with children of 22, 17 and 15. Oh my! What a thought. I discarded that quickly. I didn't want to think about being in my forties at all.

I crept back into my bed and snuggled alongside Pheobe. She opened her eyes and looked at me sleepily, her eyes trying to shut again. "Mummy" she whispered and moved closer to me. We cuddled as we always did. I kissed her forehead and held her tight. I felt our breathing synchronise and our bodies relax together.

5th Sept.

He phoned Fiona this morning before her first day at school. I was pleased for her but Seb's little face when I looked at him. It was a 'he didn't bother with me' look. My heart shattered. He needs protecting from his father and that's not right.

Fiona cried her heart out. The school phoned and said she had settled down and she was ok. I still wanted her home.

Why was he not here for us? Why could he not have wanted to be here? Arranged to be here? I needed him as much as they did. I needed his support. He was always the one who said the right thing, who calmed me down in times like this. He never really empathised with the children. He seems to be quite cold when it comes to things like this. I would have liked to think he cared though.

A mixture of emotions tonight. Another hard day. Mum had gone home. I didn't have the comfort tonight. My cigarettes were my only comfort and I was trying to avoid that temptation right now. Alcohol had worked its way out of my evenings a while ago. I didn't need it and I longed for the day I didn't need the cigarettes either.

I was a little upset tonight. The stress was pretty high and intense and I felt angry that I was coping alone again. The silence of the house echoed out at me a little and tiredness weighed me down. I had so much to think about. It felt like the weight of the world was on my shoulders.

The children starting school had knocked me for six. I thought back to this time last year. We were going through the same thing with Seb. He cried for two weeks at the primary school. He had found that so hard. I hoped that it would not take him as long to get used to this one.

The phone call had been hard to watch this morning. Fiona had smiled the biggest smile going and had been so happy that her daddy had called and said how proud of her he was. She had enjoyed the photos being taken and had loved the attention. She had told him all about it. Seb was eating his breakfast at the time and I looked up to see his sad, forlorn face. He had been upset that daddy hadn't called for him yesterday and now he had phoned for his sister. He sniffed and fought the tears. I felt so sorry for him. His stupid dad and his inconsiderate ways. I had to protect him from this. How? Why should a child need protecting from his father's actions?

I thought back to what I had just said. We were going through it. We. Were we? What had Marc done last year to support me and Seb? Nothing much really. I remembered him taking him to school once or twice but that was it. It was always me. I was the one who had done the school run and I was the one who watched him walk in crying and had to walk away from him. It's hard enough to do that when they first start school at 5 years old, let alone when they are 10 years old. I remembered Marc moaning at Seb for crying. Said he had to toughen up. He had said all the children would laugh at him and tease him. They hadn't though. They had supported him.

So that was the 'we' element wasn't it. That was his contribution. I sighed and shook my head and got up out of my seat as if I had a purpose for doing so. I stood in the middle of the room trying to work out what I had stood up for. I faced the stairs and listened for the children. No sound. Still I stood there. Why did I get up?

Walking into the kitchen I made myself a drink and lit a cigarette as I just couldn't avoid it any longer. I stood next to the bench and blew smoke at the black window. I thought back to Fiona and how I had had to leave her crying. I hated doing that. Especially her. She really affected me. I don't know why, maybe the guilt I felt at making her start yet again.

I breathed a deep sigh when I thought about doing it all again tomorrow. I just wanted to fast forward two weeks and hope that it would be better then. They seemed so happy when they came home. They didn't want to go again tomorrow though. I knew I would relive these mornings for a while yet, like bloody Groundhog Day.

What was a groundhog? I don't know. What did they look like? I don't know. Why was it called Groundhog Day? I'm not sure. Why was I asking myself that question?

I laughed at myself for having a conversation in my own head yet again and I was sure I was going insane. I was also sure that I knew the answers but I couldn't remember them at that moment. No one else to talk to though is there? I shook my head and finished my cigarette. At least there were a few smiles around these evenings. I picked up my mug of hot tea and held it close to my chest so I could feel the steam rising under my chin. I stood there listening to the nothing that used to bother me so much. That used to upset me so much. It was so peaceful. I quite liked it now. It's amazing what you get used to in time.

I settled on the settee and looked at the space where he once sat. I smiled and shrugged and turned the TV over. I sat back in my chair with my tea on my lap and thought of nothing. Just relax, I thought. Just relax. Another hard day tomorrow so relax now while you can.

9th Sept

I did it. I faced her. I had to hype myself up all day but I did it.

Marc had told me she was driving down here. He had said she was coming with him. He has found another person to call on to run him around now. The fool that she is.

He thought I was going to let her come and sit outside my house and collect my children. No chance.

I stayed calm. I put on my make up and wore clothes that made me feel good. I tried to walk out. He grabbed me gasping for breath, asking me what I was doing over and over again. I told him it was between me and her and that I wasn't angry and wasn't going to do anything stupid. There are things I need to know about her. There are questions I have and I would have thought she has some too. She is a bit like me in some of the descriptions that he had given me and so she would understand. She is made of strong stuff and faces confrontation well, so I gather.

As I walked towards her I had to calm my breathing. In my head, I was dragging her out of the car by her hair. In real life, I would talk to her calmly.

The doors were locked when I got to her. She unlocked them and I sat beside her. I knew then that my opinion of her was right. I knew then she was willing to be approached. I told her there were things that I needed to know about her. That there were questions I had to ask. That my children were being left with a stranger to me and I was uncomfortable with that. She seemed to appreciate what I was saying. She seemed to understand. I asked her to contact me when she felt ready to talk. She said she would. We will see.

I felt on such a high when I returned to the comfort of my house. I felt so positive. I am proud of myself for making the first step. Sounds stupid but I am. Dead proud.

I can't stop smiling. I go over and over it and I feel my request was justified. I know that whatever the outcome, I will feel like the better person. If she contacts me and we meet, I am better as I approached her. If she does not contact me, I approached her and I tried to close the rift. It's in her hands now. It's all down to her.

It was late at night and yet I still had the smile on my face. I was still so proud that I had done it. I confronted that woman, his skank. I had been thinking about it the last couple of days. He had made me angry with his plans for the weekend. He said as he had had the children two weekends on the trot he was taking this one off. All he did was sit and watch football. A great reason for not seeing them. To make up for it he was taking them out today.

I knew she was driving him down here so she could see them as well. Or rather so he didn't have to use the train. They were late which had made me more nervous. I still couldn't work out why I was nervous about seeing her. I suppose it was just the thought of facing the woman who stole my husband.

He arrived at 2.30 and came in to get the children. I knew what I had to do. I had gone over and over it in my head. I walked towards the door. He ran back to it and stood in front of it blocking my path.

"Move please," I asked calmly.

"Why? What are you doing?" he asked, squirming. I could see the panic building up in his face. His breathing began to get faster and he clutched his chest as if it was hurting. Like I was going to care.

"I am going to see her," I stated clearly.

""No you are not. You can't. Why?"

"This is between me and her Marcus. She is a big girl now and can look after herself. I am not going to do anything stupid. I am not angry. I just want to talk to her."

"Why are you doing this?"

"You can't block the door forever," I replied. I fixed my stare straight at him. He knew I was not budging on this one and he helplessly moved away from the door.

I walked out into the fresh air and turned round the hedge. I saw her sitting in the car and I walked towards her. I could feel my breathing getting faster now as I got closer to the car. I took slow deep breaths in an effort to calm it down. I got to the door and asked her to unlock it. She looked at me a little puzzled but opened it all the same.

I sat in the passenger seat and looked forward through the windscreen. I could see Marc panicking and my children looking down the street wondering what was going on. I smiled and commented on how he was panicking now his wife and girlfriend were together. She smiled too.

I turned to look at her. I explained that I was only there for the children.

"I think it's about time me and you met up for a chat," I said.

"I never leave my babies with a stranger and right now you are a stranger," I continued.

"I just want to get to know you a little, so I don't feel as uncomfortable with the situation. I hope you appreciate that."

She smiled and said she did and that she understood.

I got out of the car and walked towards my family. I kissed each of the children goodbye and then looked him straight in the eye.

"See. It wasn't that bad. She is still breathing"

I knew what he had been panicking about. He thought I was going to tell her we had slept together and we still were. What a fool. I needed to prove that. She would never believe me otherwise would she?

I smiled as I walked back to my front door. I stayed there so I could wave them off. I wondered what the conversation in the car would have been on their way to their outing. I smiled again. I called a few people and told them what I had done. Some said she would never get in touch, some said she would. I didn't care. Either way I felt great and like I was the better person. It was in her hands now. If she doesn't get in touch then the rift will get bigger. If she does we might be able to be civil for family events, such as Christmas.

The fact that I didn't want to be civil entered my head. Tough I said to myself. The children need you to be so get on with it.

I thought back to her face. She had been just how I remembered her. I had a good memory clearly. She was not as perfect as I had first made her out to be in my head. But I could understand why my husband was attracted to her. That was hard to say.

I enjoyed my peace and quiet that afternoon. I basked in it. I smiled constantly. He brought the children back to me at 6.30pm. That was a day out was it? Well done. That was a joke. He asked again why I had done it. I told him the same thing. Things between me and her need to get straightened out. I knew he would never allow it. I knew he would persuade her not to if she decided she did want to.

This evening was a quiet one. I had been so angry the last couple of days and my body relaxed with its absence for once. Anger was a horrible thing. It was eating me up and making me bitter and I could be so horrible when I was like that.

I sat on my bench and looked out the window just like I did every night. The smile was still there. I swung my legs and looked down at the floor. I wonder whether she will. Could I do it again? Could I see her again? I would make myself.

What would I ask her? I knew by what Marc had said about her that she would be happy if I took her a bottle of wine. She liked her wine. She was a bit of a drinker to say the least liked a bottle, or two, every night. Maybe I could add a little arsenic too. I smiled and shook my head. Nasty.

I thought about my babies. They hadn't batted an eyelid at mummy going down to her. They hadn't mentioned it. Seb had said that daddy kept apologising to her and saying he didn't know it would happen. I giggled at the prospect of dealing with his panicked mood. He was a pain when he got started on something. Never let it drop. I'm sure he will moan at me lots more over the next couple of days.

I smiled and jumped down off the bench. I could feel how tired my body was. Time to sleep. On a high so not sure how much I will get. I stretched and yawned and walked up the stairs. Halfway up, I stopped and turned.

Looking down I realised something.

Those creatures were smaller now. Much smaller.

"Well done Stephanie," I said out loud. "Well done," I grinned.

Why do I do this?

21st September

    I made him dinner. We had a family dinner altogether sat round the table like it used to be. It was hard going but it was worth it. After dinner we stood in the kitchen in our usual spot. He was breathing deeper, slower. I knew he was going to kiss me. He leant forward and I brushed his lips. He accused me of teasing - cheek of the man!

    I leant forward and kissed him. Slowly and lovingly. He responded well. He put his arms around me and pulled me in close. The warmth was there once more. The spark between us had not gone completely. We kissed and his hands ran under my shirt. My knees went weak and I sank forward into him.

    We were there kissing and touching each other until he was satisfied.

    Shortly after he left with the children. He asked to see me tomorrow if possible. I know what that is for. He has complained before that she does not give him enough.

    Felt a little weird after he left. I was smiling. I was a little confused. I don't quite know why I am doing this. I know it is complicating matters. I know he is not going to come back and I know he is having his cake and eating it. But I love him. Still.

For gods sake what is wrong with me?

Why do I do this? This is just stupid and I am so angry with myself. I know it has been hard over the last few days, weeks, months even, but that is no excuse.

I feel pathetic once he leaves. I am happy. But I'm not. That doesn't even make sense.

He walks in here and he just takes over. I let him I know I do. I stand back and let him take me over and I just can't fight it. What I can't work out though is why. Is it because I still love him? Or is it because I want to be wanted? Both of them are stupid reasons anyway so what does it matter.

We had such a nice time together tonight. We were a family eating dinner together. We did the high - low points and discussed our days. We talked about the children, their friends and their school. It was a nice atmosphere for once.

The children went upstairs to play after dinner and he followed me into the kitchen. We had often been kissing and cuddling by the sink, in the corner out of sight, so it didn't mean too much. I sipped the last of my wine and put my glass down as he slipped his hands round my waist and turned me round to face him.

"This shouldn't keep happening," he said.

"No, it shouldn't," I replied. "So don't do it."

"I don't want to stop though," he said with a smile.

He leaned forward just a little and our lips brushed together. He breathed faster and slower and I felt his hands close in a fist around my top. I pulled back a little and he looked me in the eyes.

"Teasing me now are we?"

I smiled and put my arms round his neck. I pressed up against him and kissed him. We kissed for ages. It became more and more passionate and we were touching each other all over. We knew the children were now in the other room but it didn't seem to matter. I wanted him and he wanted me.

Once it was over, we cooled off and I went and organised the bags for the children as if nothing had happened.

"Can I come and see you tomorrow?" he asked with a grin.

I know he had often complained about the lack of sex between the two of them but I didn't realise it was that lacking. He moaned that she fell asleep on him quite regularly which I found funny. Rather sleep than have sex with him, I can actually understand that, I laughed to myself. I nodded. We held each other for a little longer and both of us seemed happy to be in each others arms. He spoke about his plans for tomorrow with the children. Staying at his mums tonight. Taking them into town to shop and treating them to McDonalds.

He left before it got too late to walk the children round there. He walked them to the end of the driveway and then walked back to me at the door. Checking they were not looking he gave me a quick kiss. Then he was gone.

When he has gone, the realisation of what I am doing hits. The feeling of stupidity hits first followed closely by the feeling of being ashamed that hits me second. I just can't believe I am doing this. We always end up doing this and of course it is my fault. I am the one that should be saying no. I am the one who should be pushing him away and asking him to leave. But then again he is the one that is playing on the fact that I still love him to get what he wants. He is the one who left me, the one who has the girlfriend.

I always feel guilty then. I feel bad that I am doing this to her. Did she think of me though? No. I suppose I know how much it hurts when you find out. And she will find out. And then she will probably kill me. Or him. Or both.

Why am I so stupid?

I beat myself up about it all night. I got more and more angry throughout the evening too. I slammed cupboards. I stormed up and down stairs and I threw things around. None of it helped. None of it took away the feelings. None of it took away the shame.

I stood at the kitchen sink and smoked and drank. I stood there and stared out of the window. I can have him whenever I want though, I said to myself. That in itself was quite a good feeling. I was still wanted. Wasn't I? Or is it just a game? Maybe he is merely having his cake and eating it.

What am I gaining from it? What am I getting from this? Nothing much really. Just a whole load of guilt and shame.

It has to stop. I am not going to let him do that to me anymore. I am going to put a stop to it. I will not let him use me. I will not let him win me over and make me weak again. No more.

2nd Oct

I am severely down tonight. I am at a low point again and I can feel the pain and the anger and the bitterness rising in me. I try not to give it the satisfaction. I am not giving him the satisfaction of knowing I am low. I am not contacting him.

He didn't need me. He spoke to the children and I was left alone. He did not want to talk to me. He did not want to make sure I was ok. He is too busy with her. When she is not giving him the attention he needs he runs to me. I suppose I am the fool for letting him but I just can't help it. I wish I was stronger. I wish I could tell him where to go, but I can't.

He has hurt me again and I have let him. I feel rejected and neglected all over again. I cried into my pillow. I am upset. The thoughts of the two of them reel around my head and I can't sleep. I am so upset again. I want him to want me still. I want him to need me. I need to accept that he doesn't. I need to let him go fully. I'm just too scared.

I don't want to lose him completely. Not yet. I can't cope without him in my life at all. I can't do without him. I need help with this - I know I do.

Such a bad day today. So low and fed up. I can't get the other night out of my head. It was the most passionate we had been in a long time and it had played on my mind constantly.

I hadn't really seen him since. Not me and him to see each other anyway. He gives that little bit of him and then he snatches it away and then wonders why I crumble into a big mess again. I let him though so what do I expect.

I'm not sure why else I am down. I don't think there is any particular reason for it; I suppose I have just had enough. Every now and then the loneliness and the enormity of the situation hit home and it brings me down. I need him in my life and he is not there because she is giving him the attention he needs. She will stop again soon and say she needs space and then he will be back. He will come running back to me again and knowing weak little me, I will be stupid enough to let him have his fun for the night.

I watch the blank TV screen again. I am unsettled again. I rattle around in this empty house and the nothing swallows me whole again. The faceless creatures are full size at the foot of my stairs again. The wanting to cry is back. The depression is back. I am having a hard time again. I try to remember how I shook the feelings off last time. The periods where I am ok with everything are getting longer and longer. The days that are good days are getting more and more. But these days are still here. They still come back to haunt me and I torture myself once more. I think of the two of them together. I think of them as they are free to go out, to be together and to hold each other.

Maybe it's just jealousy on my part. Maybe I am jealous of the time he devotes to her and not me. I am just here every now and then. I am not seen as anything in particular. He loves her and it has broken my heart. He needs her and I can't handle it. This is so hard.

I wandered round the house aimlessly. My arms hung limp by my side, too heavy to lift up and my feet dragged from the weight of the rest of my body. I didn't know what to do with myself tonight. There were no comforts tonight.

I smoked a cigarette and blew the smoke towards the window. I sat on the bench with my arm resting on the handle of the kettle and I looked around the place. So quiet. The ticking of the clock was all I could hear and it was beginning to irritate me as it invaded my thoughts. They were only of them two together so why the problem I didn't know. I should have been grateful for the interruption.

I sat there, my eyes glued to the window as if it was the most interesting film I had ever seen. I could see them drinking down the pub with their mates from work. I could see some of their faces from the previous Christmas parties. I pictured myself bursting in and telling her how he was with me too. How he was playing the pair of us. She would never believe me though. She wouldn't. She would think I was the psycho ex wife who wanted to split them up. She just wouldn't take it as the truth.

There was absolutely nothing I could do apart from succumb to the feelings of heartache and sorrow once again. I heaved a huge sigh and opened the door of my mind to them. There, inside me, they danced around with glee. There, inside me, they teased and kicked and punched me until I was black and blue. There, inside me, they laughed and taunted and brought me down once more.

They were pleased to be back. They were pleased to have got to me after so long. They were pleased to be part of me once more.

I was not pleased. The tears came on slowly. They trickled down my cheeks, each one taking a different path, each one shed for a different reason. I let them fall. I didn't fight it; I just let it all take over. I closed my eyes and hoped for a better tomorrow. A stronger tomorrow. A tomorrow where I didn't hurt as much. I didn't cry as much. I didn't miss him as much. One of those tomorrows where life seems better. Happier. Brighter. I prayed for that sort of tomorrow.

3rd October

The hurt turned to anger today. I was at work and all I could think about was him. I was angry when he text me and I was angry when he didn't. I wanted to scream and shout at him, but I didn't want to talk to him. I was so confused.

I never really faced how much I still need him. I'm sure he doesn't realise either. I can't accept not being part of him anymore. I can't accept that she is all he needs now.

Then the anger about being left as a single mum starts again. The anger at being the one left behind again. I want to tell her about everything. I want to say all these things that are rattling around my head. I want to know what she has been told about me.

He is right. One day I will get angry enough to tell her. It won't be pretty. When you feel like this the urge to wreck the other ones life is so huge and overpowering. I write a text to her but I don't send it. I feel better.

The problem I am facing is no matter how much I want him, love him, need him in my life, I don't actually want him back. Otherwise I would fight for him. So let him go? I can't.

Why do I have days like these? Feeling like I am just not normal.

Sat here in my empty house and did nothing but think. I don't understand what my problem is now. Am I still coming to terms with all of this? Is that my problem? Or is it that I have realised that I don't want him back?

I try to analyse my thoughts and feelings way too much I think. It is just too hard to say well this is what I am feeling and leave it at that.

I sat on my own in my quiet house and I stared at the TV screen. There was a programme on it but I was unaware of what it was. I could feel the tears trickling down my cheeks. I could feel the sticky wet patches they left. Yet I didn't know why I was crying. I don't understand why I am feeling like this.

I have been riding this rollercoaster for months now. I have been negotiating the twists and turns and the upside down loops that make me feel so sick the whole time, so surely I should be used to them now. I thought that by now I would be better than I am. I thought that by now I would be able to say that yes, this is a terribly sad situation, but I just have to live with it. Is it because I am still involved with him that makes it so hard?

I shrugged at myself and looked down at the soggy wet tissue I was squeezing between my fingers. I hated myself for feeling like this. I wasn't directing my sadness towards either Marc or Sue. I couldn't figure out whether they were the reason I was feeling so low or whether it was my own actions that were bringing me down.

I sighed and threw my head back to look up at the ceiling. My eyes were searching for something as if I expected the answers to everything to be written up there. I lowered my head again and dragged my hands down my face, pulling the tears away with them.

I had been so angry today at work. I had been furious and had taken it all out on him. I had searched and waited for texts or a phone call from him, and then when I got one I ignored it. I had watched my phone vibrate with his number flashing at me wanting to answer it but shaking too much to pick it up. Then when he rang off and didn't leave a message, I got even angrier. Why phone me? If there was a reason for phoning you leave a message right?

I kicked myself at the thought of him still having this little bit of control over me. I was angry with myself and yet I couldn't pinpoint why, which means I couldn't find my way out of it. I couldn't shrug it off. I couldn't talk myself round. It was so frustrating.

I thought about sending her a text message. But what would I say? What did I need to say to her? Too much to text that's for sure. I thought about her and the fact that she has this life with him now. It's not fair. It's not fair that I am sitting here alone listening to the silence that deafens me and waiting for my children to wake up and need me so I can go to bed for a reason and he is out and about and free to do whatever he wants with her. Where are his ties? Where are the limits to his freedom? When does he care for our children?

The frustration became worse as I realised that there is absolutely nothing I can do about it. Absolutely nothing. I have to get on with it and I have to accept this but I can't. I just can't.

Squeezing the soggy tissue against my face I realised that I actually wasn't crying anymore. I wasn't sobbing my heart out. I hadn't noticed when the tears had dried up but they had. I sighed and forced myself upstairs to check on my babies. Maybe I would find some comfort from them. Their snoring became louder and clearer as I climbed the stairs. I could hear the moving of covers as they tossed and turned and these sounds made me smile.

Coming back downstairs I could feel my mood lift a little. I talked to myself as I walked into the kitchen. I stood in the middle of it and asked myself whether I wanted him back. Truly. Honestly. Deeply.

"Do you want him back?"

A question my mum had asked me so many times before.

"Do you want him back?"

If you do fight for him she had said.

"Do you want him back?"

No. No I didn't. I truly didn't. I sighed again. This is what is so hard. I don't want to step backwards. I don't want to fight for the man I love. So something isn't right then. So why do I feel so low. I felt a little calmer as I lit a cigarette and stood by the sink. I breathed deeply as if the extra breaths would bring answers to my sorry state of mind.

I stared into the blank window in front of me and watched the smoke curl upwards from the end of the cigarette. I wished I could float away up into the air becoming invisible as I went. Float like this free flowing wisp of smoke. Just disappear and be gone. That carefree.

That wouldn't make me happy either though. To give up what I have now and go off and live for just me isn't what I want either. To be happy is what I want. The problem is I still haven't figured out what it is I need to happen for me to be happy. What would make me truly happy?

What is truly happy? Will I ever know?

Are they his world?

4th October

A phone call this morning was all it took to bring me down a little. It's a weird sort of feeling, one that can't be described. I don't feel like crying. I don't feel like screaming and shouting. I just want to sit and talk to him and tell him how he is making me feel. I don't bother though as he wouldn't care. He wouldn't listen.

He said about the weekends in October. He has to go away one Saturday. It means he cannot see the children that weekend though he is not too sure which one.

When I asked what he was doing he replied he was going to Glasgow with Sue to pick up her dog. He will be staying up there for the night. Again it feels like she comes first. What he wants to do is be with her all the fucking time. Even above his children. They are going through hell at the moment. They are probably feeling like me. We have lost him a second time. If he had made the clean break in the beginning, we probably wouldn't have felt so bad now.

When he left he phoned all the time, for hours sometimes. Some days it was 2 or 3 times or more. He was coming down during the week and seeing them at weekends. Now we are lucky if we get a 10 minute phone call in the evening. He doesn't come every weekend. He is taking more and more time off. He never comes midweek anymore. We have lost him again.

It feels as raw as it did when he originally left. I have to get used to it. I have to adjust to not being in his life anymore. But my babies shouldn't have to. My babies should always be the most important thing to him and he is not showing them that. Maybe that is because they are not. He clearly does not think like I do.

I'm hurting again. And seeing my children hurting makes me hurt even more.

My children are everything to me. I know I feel sometimes that they are too much hard work. That they are the reason I can't move on. They are the reason I can't get out. They are the reason for all the difficulties in my life. I know really that that is not the case. They are my world. I love them so much and I would travel miles to see them for a short time.

I think about them all the time whatever I am doing. I think about them when they are at school, when they are with him, when they are with my mum, when I am at work. I think about them when I am washing up, preparing their dinner. I care for their every need and nothing would ever come between us. Nothing would ever come before them. No one would ever come before them.

Why doesn't he feel that way? Why does he keep booking weekends away when he should be with them? Why does he not want to see them every weekend? How can he be away from them as long as he is?

I can't understand what she has, what his new life has, that keeps him away from them. All I ever hear now is sorry I can't have them on this weekend because I am going out, because I am going away, because I am in Glasgow, because I am taking her out to dinner, because I want some time with her, because we haven't seen much of each other this week etc etc.

The reasons usually involve her. They are usually something to do with her. They are usually because she wants to do something and he wants to join her. That's what makes me so angry. She took precedence over me, she barged me out of his head and now she is doing the same with our children. That is so wrong.

I looked at the calendar with the dates for October on them. November was even worse with weekends booked off already. Over the next two months the children would be lucky to see their dad four times. Four days. That is a joke.

I slammed the page down and walked off. If it was quality time I wouldn't mind I mumbled to myself as I picked up toys that had been thrown across the room. I was so bored of doing this. I had had enough. One day is all they get with him and most of that is travelling and sleeping, I whispered. Talking to no one again, that helped.

I laughed to myself as I thought about it. I can't keep letting him get to me like this. He doesn't want to see his children, fine. Let him go and bring them up yourself. But then shouldn't I fight for them? Shouldn't I try to give them a dad? Shouldn't I try to teach him to be a good father that sees his children regularly?

I sighed as I knew that yet again I didn't have the answers and yet again I was stumped and could do nothing. I can't make him do these things. I can't make him turn up. I can't make him want to be part of their life. How can I?

I stomped around the house finishing housework and hanging up clothes. There seemed to be so much mess everywhere and I just couldn't get on top of it. With this all going round in my head I seemed drained of energy.

The evening came really quickly. I sat there thinking about him and whether he is actually missing them. I sat on my bench in my favourite spot and watched the night garden. The peace. The still. The darkness.

Is he missing them? Is he missing their little voices? Their hugs? Their kisses? Their belly laughter? Is he missing picking them up and cuddling them? Is he missing watching them sleep? Their stories about school that go on and on forever?

It was then while sitting there thinking about all the little things that he should be missing, that I realised the reason for the sadness that I was feeling. It was not so much that he wasn't here, that he wasn't coming. The sadness was from not being sure that he was missing them. I was sad because I didn't believe that he missed my babies as much as they missed him. I had lost that much faith in the love of the father of my children that I could not be certain that he loved our children enough.

I had never doubted Marc's love before this. I never doubted his love for me but I was wrong. Now I was sitting here doubting the strength of his love for his own children. I sat bolt upright as it dawned on me that I didn't think he loved them enough. He didn't want them. He didn't miss them. He didn't need them. That meant he could walk away from them like he did me.

The tears started slowly falling. Just one or two trickled down to my chin. A few solitary tears as I realised that I was unsure of the man I had had three children with. I doubted the man I had loved so dearly. I doubted the father of my children. I doubted the man I thought would be the one who protected them from pain, who loved them unconditionally, who was there whenever and wherever they needed him and who needed them in his life more than he needed to live.

I had lost faith in him. It had gone. It really had gone.

6th October

Went out last night and had a really good time. I had a fair bit to drink and met two really nice guys. Nothing romantic in the slightest - just intelligent and interesting conversation. One of the men was really spiritual and lifted my inner self in a way that is hard to explain. He made me actually talk about things that I would not normally do with a stranger. I held the conversation for hours which is something I cannot normally manage. It was amazing. They say there are people you meet in life that can change your outlook or that touch you in some way other people can't. He was definitely one of those people. It is unlikely I will ever see him again, but he will be somebody I was glad to meet and will probably never forget.

I have logged on to the singles website and finally I have some men worth the effort of messaging and possibly meeting. I realised I am missing the other side of life with Marc. I am not missing him as a lover or a husband. I am missing his conversation, his intelligence and his friendship. I reached the point where I knew I could not take him back a while ago. I know it would never work now and that he has a new life. I am still upset that he felt the need to run off and start again without me and I'm sure if we had not made that break we would probably still be plodding along. I'm not too sure whether I have accepted losing him yet even though I am getting there. I feel more positive today about moving forward with my life and trying to find the happiness I seek with more of a gutsy motion. I enjoy my freedom more than I give it credit and I have to remind myself of that when I am down. I have to let go of my frustrations of Marc not having the children as often as I would like him to and I have to let go of the sadness that I have a failed marriage.

I need to focus on the lack of stress in my life. On the fact that I no longer have to deal with the issues that made me so unhappy when I was with him. His insecurities, his eating problem, his debts etc are no longer a problem in my life. They are for her to deal with now and good luck to her because I never want to have that job again.

I love him and I always will. I don't know whether it is the true soul mate kind of love or whether it is the friend love. But I know I can never be his partner again. I would lose the happiness and carefree life I have now. I would lose the relaxed optimism that is working its way into me. I would lose the warmth and the strong bond I have with my children. I would lose the lightness of life I have now and I would feel weighed down again.

I am happier without him. I know that now. I just have to get used to it. And I will.

One man and he made such a difference. I was captured by his spirituality. His whole aura. I have never been like that with a stranger before. We talked and talked for hours and he made me feel so good about myself and my life. I wished I had been able to bottle it somehow.

He was a great man. He was bringing up his boys as his wife had left. His eyes welled up when talking about them, his pride shining through. His concern for their welfare and their education was his top priority. His love for them was overwhelming and bowled me over. He adored them. It was so obvious. He talked about his love for them as if it was normal and he couldn't understand why I stared at him in wonder. So many things he said made me want to cry. Why wasn't Marcus like him?

He was a great believer in destiny. He said he could read people, though he couldn't explain how he did it. He said Marc had hampered my spirit and my soul and that it had lost me. I needed to regain its trust and welcome it back with open arms. He said my true self was there somewhere and I had to grant her her freedom. Her freedom to come to the surface and achieve the great things we had been put on this earth to achieve. He said to remember that the reason for living was life itself. Life was a white knuckle ride and we had to hold on with all our might until the ride quietens and calms and we can smile. He said the ride would end one day and we shouldn't get to the end without being proud of what we had to look back on.

He said all of this before he asked me about anything to do with my life. He didn't know my situation. He didn't know my background. He knew nothing about me. He has touched my life in a way I can't explain. If I had him as a friend, life would be uplifted. I am too scared to have that at the moment.

If I could meet him again in a few months when my white knuckle ride is calmer, my life would be enriched even more.

Right now, tomorrow and for the rest of this particularly bumpy part of my life I will use his words. I will think of him and his spiritual wisdom. And I will use it wisely.

Sitting in my spot tonight my inner mood was so different. I felt so positive and uplifted. I felt cleansed almost. Like I was free. I had realised what it was that I needed. I had realised that I needed me and I needed my children and that it was this life that would make me happy. I feel as if I am ready to begin letting Marc go completely. This is the start of it. This is the beginning. I still have to undergo the process of letting go and I know there will be weak times and lapses in my determination. But there will also be days of confidence and forward motion.

I smiled to myself as I thought about myself. I could feel the difference. I could feel the strength inside which is something I haven't felt in ages. I need to find it again and make sure that it stays permanently. That is who I used to be and she is lost. I will search for her and I will find her again.

Climbing the stairs I walked into the bedroom. I walked over to the curtains and pulled them tightly shut. No holes, no gaps, no light. I stood there in front of the window and smiled. I breathed in deep, soaking up the new aura that surrounded me. Even if it disappeared again in the future months, I had found it this time. It won't be buried so deep. This is a turning point. I can really feel it. This is it. I am finally starting my journey properly. My journey to my new life. This is the beginning.

7th October

Got very drunk last night. Went out with Marilyn and her friend. It was a fun night. I was only thinking of Marc though. Not in a sad forlorn way, just a missing him way. It's hard to explain.

I text him to make sure he was ok, quite a few times. I had him on the phone crying earlier on in the night and it upsets me to hear him that way. He was upset because Sue had gone out again for the third night with her friends. He can't handle that kind of independence. He needs her world to revolve around him and she isn't like that. We have had that kind of conversation before and it just used to make me angry. Last night it hurt. It hurt to hear him so down as it would if it was any one of my friends. I didn't really know what to say. I wanted to tell her to give him some of her attention. I wanted to call her and ask her if she knew how she was making him feel but I don't have that kind of relationship with her and probably never will.

I have begun writing in this diary a lot more again and I think this is because I am trying to understand the shift in feelings. I am still flirting with him. Flirting like mad. It's not a good thing either.

He phoned again this afternoon, talking about his conference and how busy he is going to be. It made me a little down to think he has his life so sorted and there is me with a fight on my hands to get mine back on track. Feeling a little bitter again. Bitter at not being free enough to just begin again. Too much organisation.

Something he said on the phone upset me a bit. It was one of those times when it is after you put the phone down that you churn what was said over in your head and work yourself up over it. Basically, we were talking about my change of figure - which he has said he likes on a number of occasions. I said it had improved my happiness a little as well as my confidence. He asked if it had improved my sex drive too laughing. I told him that actually it had and I could feel the frustration kicking in. He then said "If you had been like this a year ago, who knows what would have been different."

After thinking about it I decided that that was a shallow thing to say. He is insinuating that our relationship fell apart because he did not get enough sex from me. Sex does not equal love. He is associating the two too strongly. If he left me because of that, that makes him so shallow.

Ok, so I did not fancy sex that regularly. He was too skinny for me for one thing - I wanted a man for crying out loud. I was so tired for another thing. The sleepless nights and the depression causing some insomnia over the last few years had taken its toll.

Mainly though I think it was the extra weight I was carrying. I did not see myself as attractive and therefore should not be loved in any way especially not that way. Sounds stupid now, but it was real to me then. None of that meant I did not love him.

Mood lifted once my babies were home.

I had a strange day today. The feelings were a little marred. They were strained a little. I was trying to feel something I wasn't and it felt weird.

I spoke to Marc and listened to him going on about Sue and the way she is not there for him. She was out again and he was down about it. He hates being alone. I could hear the pain in his voice as he spoke to me and it hurt me too. Not in the way I expected it to though. It wasn't the familiar pain I had felt talking to him before. It was a numbed down pain. I felt the urge to help him. As if I could do something.

I did text him a number of times while I was out. I had wanted to hear that he was feeling better about things. That he wasn't hurting as much as he was before. I never really felt that though. I could relate to his pain, I suppose that was my issue. I knew what it felt like and my empathy levels went through the roof. I should have been revelling in it really. Well that's what I thought. I should have been happy that he was hurting but I wasn't. That felt weird too.

I went out with a bigger smile on my face even though I was hurting a little from him. I still smiled and I still felt the urge to pull away from him in the emotional dependency sense of course. I remembered what the man I met last night had said to me and remembered the sense of determination that had engulfed me the night before. It was still there and that pleased me.

I returned home, worse for wear at 2 in the morning. I sat having my last cigarette for the evening in the peace and quiet and enjoyed the silence. I thought of him and what he had said in our phone call. Yet again I had tried to analyse it and that had made me angry at what he had said. If only I left the analysing and thinking alone, I am sure I would be further down the line than I am at the moment.

I shrugged at myself. You can't change what you need to do can you. You can't change who you are and how you deal with things. Analysing to understand was my way in life and I had to accept it even if it frustrated me.

We had been talking about my figure. How I was a size 8 now whereas I was a size 14. He had commented a few times in the past and had said regularly how I looked great. For me I was still fat but I also had a lot more confidence and was enjoying buying clothes and changing my style from mumsy to more what it was before I had the children.

After changing I had begun to realise that a lot of my problems had revolved around the fact that I hated my body. I hated the way I looked from an early age but I had seen the toll having three children had taken on me and I hated it even more. I remembered how I used to look before the pregnancies and I wanted that back even though I had hated it when I had had it.

I also realised that my hatred for myself was why I never bothered. I had retreated into the comfortable mode. I wore clothes that I didn't like because I thought that was all I deserved. I hated trying on new clothes. I hated trying to find something I liked when I had to go somewhere special. I wore the same few outfits over and over again.

I hated going out because I never thought I looked good enough. In some ways I never thought I looked good enough for Marc. I always believed he should have a decent looking woman on his arm and that I wasn't worthy of being that decent woman. I also hated going out because I never had anything to wear, which meant shopping and as I had just mentioned to myself, I hated that.

The crucial part for Marc was that that was a reason why I hated sex. I didn't think that a body like mine was attractive. That I shouldn't be loved in that way because I wasn't good enough. It seems really stupid to say that but it's the truth and you can't help how you feel. Marc had said that he loved me and he had said that he found me attractive but I always felt that he was trying to have sex with me out of his duty as my husband. I'm sure now it was an underlying cause of my pathetic sex drive.

There were other reasons of course. The constant tiredness you experience when you are a mum. The sleepless nights that had gone on for years and were still going on. The depression weighing me down. I know that but I believe the main one was my body.

To say to me that things would have been different if my sex drive was higher was so shallow. I thought about it and got more and more annoyed as I repeated his words over and over again.

"If you had been like this a year ago, then who knows what would have been different."

What exactly did he mean by that? How could he mean that?

I was beginning to believe that the split was due to his lack of sex. How awful was that? I am not saying that there were no other factors in the breakdown of our marriage but as this type of thing had been said before, I believed now that it was a fairly significant part to him. He had said before that he had thought that I didn't love him anymore. When I asked him why, his immediate reaction was 'because you kept rejecting me' or 'you didn't want me.'

To me that does not constitute love. Love is so different. At the end of the day you can go out and have sex with anybody and it doesn't mean anything. Love is deeper and the sex adds to that love. Am I wrong?

I pushed my already burnt out cigarette onto the side of the sink and climbed down from the bench. I was a little bewildered by all these thoughts and feelings and a little scared by them too as I needed to get to know them to feel comfortable with them. Those thoughts needed to stop now.

I walked into each of the children's empty rooms and whispered goodnight. I took in the smell of each one and looked at their things scattered around. I straightened the bedclothes and pulled their curtains. I missed them so much.

I climbed into bed and then realised I had left the curtains open. I made a point of getting up to shut them. It was very significant to me now. I lay down and stared up at the ceiling in the darkness. I just stared and wondered where my journey would be taking me next and whether I would have the strength to finish it. I just laid there listening to the silence and staring up at the ceiling waiting for the answers to appear.

They never came.

9th October

At work today. Tuesdays come round so fast. I feel like I am always there. Lots of work on the computer and text Bill most of the day. He is a little too sexual really but I decided to enjoy the attention. I quite like him. Something about him that appeals to me. Maybe it's his honesty and confidence that comes through. He is very much a 'this is what I am so take it or leave it' man. He isn't threatening in any way. Not really distasteful or overbearing. We haven't met yet, just photos and chatting. I am happy with it all so far.

So tired tonight. The weekend has caught up with me. Two nights out in a row and I collapse. Must be getting old!

Becoming very frustrated with Marc and his 'I need a weekend' routine. It is amazing how he has changed towards the children. I figured he would from the things he had said in the past and I told his mum so too. He says he wants them alternate weekends. That would be ok with me I suppose. The children will not be impressed. They are really missing him at the moment. He has already cut them down in stages.

First he left, then he stopped coming mid week and now he wants to stop seeing them every weekend.

When he does have them for a full weekend he picks them up around 6.30 on a Friday. He drops them off or leaves them with his mum around 4 on Sunday. Sometimes earlier. That is not quite 2 days a week. That means he sees them 4 days a month. That equates to 48 days out of 365. That is awful. *How can he call himself a father?* I appreciate that he wants to go out till late at the weekends. I do too. I understand. He can sit down the pub or sit indoors with Sue on 5 days of the week. He is seeing her more than his own children.

From a selfish point of view I will only have 48 days a year to rebuild my life. If some guy wants to get to know me more then I will have to say he will have to wait a fortnight in between dates. *How is that fair? Is that too selfish of me? Wanting a life?*

I would never place any man above my children. I would like to know I can go out on a date if the chance arises though.

I get so frustrated and then I can't sleep. He wanted these children as much as I did and now he has walked away. It is ok for him. He has his life and what he wants all sorted out. Me and the children cannot get straight, cannot get a new life without Daddy as he is not allowing that. They don't feel secure in his love for them as he cannot devote enough time to them.

He mucked up our lives by not coming back and now he is mucking them up further by staying away. *How much damage does he want to do?*

The frustration weighed me down a little all day. Tonight was no different.

I had tried to keep occupied and I had company with mum being here but I still felt so stressed and annoyed that life is turning out this way and there is nothing I can do about it.

The problem is I don't understand. I know there have been many things about this whole split that I haven't understood. But this seems much harder to get my head around than all the other things. Mainly because it involves my babies. I talked to Marc today about the fact that I feel he is putting the children last in his life. He had said he wanted them every other weekend from now on so that he can have a life at weekends too.

Lots of partners do that don't they? Lots of fathers and mothers who do not have custody of their children pick them up on alternate weekends. I appreciate that. I also appreciate that when they have them alternate weekends, they have them during the holidays and some even one evening after school. Marc will not be doing either of those. He chose to move too far away and he works too hard for another thing.

From my point of view that is wrong. Alternate weekends are not enough to be a father figure to your children. Marc would only turn up on a Saturday and bring them back on a Sunday as Fridays are too difficult for him. When you choose to have children, there are two of you making that decision. There should be two of you bringing them up. It should be a 50-50 share. How are alternate weekends a fair share? How do alternate weekends give that parent who is no longer directly involved in their life the chance to be a proper parent?

I churn all of these thoughts over and over in my head. I go over and over it and the frustration becomes unbearable. So unbearable I thought I would end up crying again. I talk to mum about it. She sees my point of view and agrees with him in some ways too. She too thinks the reasons he is giving are too selfish.

Maybe it is me being selfish? I have the children 5 days a week. I care for them, feed them, take them to school and do any additional things needed. Why can he not take over at weekends? He can't be there during the week as he is working so he should be with them at weekends. He says he needs a social life at weekends - what about mine? Where is my time?

Is that too selfish?

I felt confused again and also let down by him again. He had become this man that I did not recognise anymore. The things he was saying to me now were not things I had ever foreseen him saying. I never thought for one minute he wouldn't want his children. Did he not miss them?

Realising I was dwelling on this again I knew I had to stop. I thought of something else instead, desperately searching for something in my mind to distract me. Nothing could. I thought of Bill, who I had been texting, I thought of people who I hadn't been in contact with for weeks. I even tried to distract myself by watching the television. None of them worked. I still had this hanging over me.

I wallowed in it to be honest. I sank my head into my hands and wallowed in it. What had he become?

Laying in bed in the darkness, I couldn't sleep. I just couldn't. I tossed and turned but my mind raced and I still couldn't answer the unanswered questions sitting in that list that had become so long now. I still couldn't understand. I turned and watched Pheobe sleeping. Her little lips pursed as if she had eaten something so sour. I smiled as she sighed and rubbed her nose with her fist. She was so beautiful.

The tears stung at my eyes. How could he not want to see them at the end of a busy 5 days without them? How could he not want to travel for however long it takes to feel their little hands in his? How did he not miss their sweet little voices? How?

I cried myself to sleep.

What next?

10th October

I text Alexander today. I really like him too. He is kind and romantic. He comes across as sensitive and sweet. I'm hoping to meet him. God knows when though. I'll make the time somehow.

Work again today. It went quite quickly which was good. Got lots done and managed to team teach a lesson in year 3. I enjoyed it.

The journey home was ok too thankfully. The music blaring and this time my thoughts were of Bill and Alex rather than Marc which made a nice change.

The evening went incredibly quickly. It was nice to sit and chill out for a few hours when the children went to bed early.

Overall, a fairly good day. Just exhausted and can't wait for bed.

A new perspective today. Don't get stressed over something you can't change. And I didn't. Not once all day.

I sat on the bench. I treated myself to a glass of white wine, which was most unlike me but I enjoyed it. I smoked my cigarette and smiled as I blew the smoke against the window, watching it swirl around and then slowly disappear. I felt ok tonight.

I text Alexander. I didn't know quite what to say. We had been emailing each other on the website I had joined practically every day for the last few weeks. He had given me his mobile number to contact him when I was ready. I finally made the move.

I stared out of the window and thought about my life now. The new friends I had made. The people I had met. I never really had many in London. I knew people. I knew the ones I had grown up with but most of them had moved away. I didn't have many friends at school so there were no real friends around for me there. Here I had so many and I was still making more.

I closed my eyes and thought about my future. Ok it was a little scary, being alone and bringing up children with no one to share the pressures, stresses and strains with except my mum who had already done this once. At the same time though, I felt a little confident about it. Not a lot, just a little. Maybe I would meet someone eventually. Pheobe will be at school next year and I will be free to lunch during the day with friends and family. Maybe I will develop my career when the children are older. There would be more people to meet then.

I listened to the peace and quiet and sipped my wine, holding the glass close to my chest after each one. I felt so chilled out tonight. And I felt tired. I liked feeling tired as I didn't get much sleep these days.

I climbed down from my seat and curled up on the settee, turning all the lights off except my fairy lights wrapped round the twigs in the corner. The soft glow made me mellow even more. I laid my head on the cushion on the arm of the chair. I breathed deeply and relaxed into the soft settee.

Today was a good day. I was pleased to have had one again. A good day. I will have more of these please.

12th October

Oh what a bad day today. I have plummeted again and the anger and bitterness has finally taken over and reached a boiling point. I wanted to scream at him when he finally called the children tonight. I was not too bad all day - just a little down. I was texting Alexander and was fairly happy.

Tonight, it all changed. I became tired and worn out. I didn't want to get up and cook dinner. I didn't want to have to deal with the children. I wanted to shut myself away and be left alone. The days like this are always hard and I am grateful that they are getting less and less as time goes on. Writing the book has not helped. Yesterday I stayed up till 11pm writing about the night I found out about him and the skank - sorry, Sue. It made me relive everything and it was harrowing enough the first time I went through it. To relive it was even more difficult. I was surprised at how well I was remembering the feelings I went through. I suppose you never forget.

Anyway after dinner I sat and had a drink. That was not the best idea I have had. It brought me down and made me wish I was drinking it out on the town. I want to be dancing and drinking the night away tonight so I can forget everything.

Then the phone rang. His voice and my drunkenness did not mix well. Then it got worse. The girls had it on speaker phone. Her voice. That was the first time they had asked to speak to her. Her voice on the end of my phone. Talk about pain. I tried to occupy myself by hanging out the washing. Tried to ignore it. I managed to ignore the words but I could still hear her voice. I wanted to switch the speaker phone off but I couldn't bring myself to get close enough to the phone. I didn't want the voice to get any louder. Thankfully it was over fairly quickly. At least the girls never have much to say!

I spoke to him for a while but it just made me angry. I listened to him and his *we are just chilling out. We are just sitting indoors.* It hurts still to think of him and her together. He said yesterday that she didn't know we were supposed to be on a temporary break. That hurt. He had lied to her. It made me feel slightly better about her but it made me angry all the same.

I am sick of feeling so upset and bitter all of the time. I know the period between these bad days and the better ones are getting longer so will, hopefully, be wiped out altogether eventually. I just wish I hadn't loved him. I wish I had fought harder. I wish I had said something earlier. I never spoke up. Now it is all too late.

I sat on my bench feeling relieved the day was over at last. The children had all gone to bed and were settled and the peace had installed itself around the house once more. I listened to the ticking of the clock and found myself breathing more calmly almost in time with it. I soaked up the relaxation that had begun to weave through my body.

For those few minutes I was fine and then it started. The voice in my head again. I wish that could be switched off. This time it wasn't my voice talking to me, it was hers. Her bloody Scottish accent. The few giggles she had shared with my babies, on my phone, were now in my head echoing round seeming louder because of the peace and quiet around me. I jumped off the bench and turned the radio on. Some crappy love song - excellent timing.

I walked around the kitchen for a while and then settled back in my corner. I drank another glass of vodka and lit a cigarette that I knew I didn't really want or need. I just stared at the smoke as it billowed out of it and placed it in the ashtray. I watched it burn out slowly, mesmerised by the patterns the smoke made as it travelled upwards.

I took a deep breath and listened to the voice again. I knew I had to address and deal with it otherwise it would just eat at me more. I talked myself through the feelings. Maybe it was her voice that made her even more real. Maybe it was the fact that she was talking to my babies. Maybe it was the fact that my girls had asked to talk to her and were enjoying it. Whatever it was, I didn't like it.

I had also got angry with his 'we are just chilling out' comment. He hadn't seen why that bothered me. He doesn't seem to understand that it is hard to hear my husband talking about sitting around watching TV with this skank, sorry with another woman. Didn't seem to understand why it would be a problem for me. Here I am on a Friday night sitting indoors alone because he didn't want to have his children this weekend again and he doesn't see the problem. He has somebody to sit with. He has company. When the children are in bed, I just have four walls and a telephone, that never rings.

I huffed at this point and got up walking in the direction of the study. Whether I was huffing with them, just with him or whether I was actually huffing at listening to myself moaning yet again, I wasn't sure. I am becoming more and more frustrated with myself and my intolerance of being alone lately. I am struggling with it and I'm not sure why as most of the time I am ok with it. Silly cow.

I sat at the computer and stared at the screen. I recalled the date I had written about in my book last night. It had been so hard. I had written about the night I found out about them. It was horrible. I think I smoked at least 10 cigarettes while I did that. The feelings were still so real and raw. It was like I was watching a replay. I could see each step I had gone through as a moving picture in my head and I described it in writing.

I opened the pages and read it back to myself. I had come so far really. I wasn't as much of a mess as I was then. I had had all this unknown territory to cover. I had accomplished a lot really. It seemed to make me feel better.

I picked myself up, made some hot chocolate and lit a cigarette. Yes I was angry and bitter. Yes I had been hurt by her again today. Yes I had had a good day turn sour. Today was still better than some I had been through though wasn't it.

13th October

Did not want to get out of bed this morning. So I didn't. The children played happily downstairs while I stayed in bed. They checked on me every now and then and then when they had had enough Seb brought me breakfast in bed.

It felt weird to have my mum's birthday and no Marc around. I hadn't thought of it affecting me but it did in a way. I suppose being so down over the last couple of days it would have done. It was also a year ago today that my Nan died. That day Marc had rushed home to be with me. To help me. To hold me. I don't have that now and the memories of last year made me realise again that I miss him.

I try to shut those feelings off but I can't. It's too hard to bury them all of the time. Nancy, the wife of somebody he worked with, said to me once that I had to go with the flow. Cry when I need to. Feel down when I need to. And enjoy those times when I am strong and happy. She is right and I need to feel down at the moment, so I have to accept it and wait for a better time to come.

The day has gone quite quickly which I am pleased about. It's nice to think that the hard part of the week is nearly over.

I wish he would call though. Just pretending he is interested in how the day went would be enough. Nothing though. Too busy for the children as usual. See, hurting again!

I woke up with mixed thoughts going round my head this morning. They made me feel quite sick and dizzy. I thought of Marc. I thought of my mum and her birthday. I thought of Nan. I had huffed at them all and knew I couldn't face the daylight just yet and so pulled the covers over my head and buried myself for a little longer.

From that moment, I knew I didn't want to face today at all. There were things I had to do. I had to go to mums and I knew that would make me feel better. I knew I had to shop for the last few things for her birthday and I knew that would make me feel better too. I still didn't want to face it though. So I didn't.

The afternoon and evening went quite quickly in the end. I walked through town in autopilot and drove to mums in much the same state. Dangerous I am sure. Saw my aunts Violet and Alice as well as cousin Sophia at mums. Spoke about Alex which cheered me up. Still felt as though I had the weight of the world on my shoulders though. All that kept going through my mind was that Marc hadn't phoned us yet. Us. I still said us. He didn't necessarily phone me but I still said us. I tried to focus on something else. I didn't want to seem down on mum's birthday.

Last year had been awful with Nan dying and my thoughts turned to her. I was so close to her and losing her had been so hard for me. I had cried myself to sleep in Marc's arms many times and he had supported me so much over those difficult weeks. He had come home to be with me the day it happened and had just held me while I wept. I couldn't believe my Nan had died. I had no grandparents left now; I had lost all three of them inside three years. It was a sad feeling. I could feel the tears sting my eyes as they had done before and I swallowed hard.

The drive back home was a solemn one. The children had asked why Daddy hadn't called and I had no answers and I was on my way home to an empty house once more. I just couldn't work out why some days were worse than others. Was it that first syndrome again? The first anniversary of Nan's death and the first birthday of my mums without Marc. Was it just that I was down and blamed that instead? Was it that he hadn't called?

I put my babies to bed and checked them so many times I should have just stayed upstairs. I felt so needy and wanted to be with them all of the time. I watched them sleep. I watched them dream. I listened to their calls for daddy and their whimpers. After a while I managed to keep myself downstairs.

There I sat again looking out of the window at nothing but darkness. I became aware that I was thinking of him again and that was when the tears started to fall. I cried for what seemed like ages although I was unsure of the real reason why. I just wanted to be held tonight. I needed someone to come and hold me for the night. I hugged my knees to my chest and pulled them in tight trying to gain some comfort from that pose.

Eventually the tears stopped and I gave up trying to understand myself. I was unhappy. Let it be. There is no comfort from anything. It will change one day.

17th October

His Nan's birthday today. I stopped there after work and gave in a card from the children and flowers. She was staying at his mums but still phoned happy that I had remembered.

Keith, his cousin, was there when I arrived. He asked how I was doing to which I replied not too bad. Can never think of anything else to say when people ask me that question. Have come to the conclusion that they are only asking out of politeness rather than wanting me to waffle on and on about the upset in my life. Talked to Keith for a while. He seemed to be coping ok with his illness and is heading back to hospital to talk about his operation on Monday. He said that he and his family did not approve of Marc's behaviour and they looked down on him. He actually said 'he doesn't realise his family hate him for it.' He said that every dog will have its day and that is what I am holding on to right now. It was horrible to listen to him saying those things about a member of his own family, but at the same time it was quite reassuring really. They didn't blame me and have not shut me out even though he has.

Marc annoyed me again this evening. He called about 7.20 but the children were still in the bath so I told him to call back as Fiona wanted to tell him about her day at school. He forgot to call back until 8.40. And then the children were all tired and ratty with him.

It upsets me how he uses us. He needs me when he is lonely or she has upset him. He phones and talks to me about all of his problems when no one else will listen. He will show his children off to her and the others sometimes. He will spoil them when he is with her so he will score brownie points for being a good dad when he isn't really. And yet when she is with him and he is happy and doing what he wants to do and he is not upset, we never hear from him. Feeling very low again.

Sitting on my own I began to think about my conversation with his cousin. I had found it quite reassuring that they hated him for the way he had behaved with his children, and possibly me, but at the same time I was disturbed by it. I had wanted somebody to say things like that for so long and now they had I still wasn't happy. I was disturbed that I felt ok with them thinking badly of him. I still had this urge in me to protect him from the pain that that would cause him. Why?

On the realisation that I was analysing too much again I gave up and gave myself a stern talking to. Earlier this week I had had a conversation with myself stating clearly that I was not to analyse too much anymore as I was convinced that it was trying to understand everything that was bringing me down time and time again. I tutted at myself for doing it yet again.

"How are you?" Keith had asked. I had begun to hate that question. It is a question that is asked almost automatically when you talk to someone. How are you? Or, how have you been? I just look at people who ask me that question now. I feel like I am stuck for an answer like when I used to get an exam question I didn't know. You scour the pages ahead of you as if the answer lies there somewhere. I scour the faces of the people who ask me now. Do you really want the truth? If in doubt I just say fine. 'I'm fine.' That answer hides a multitude of sins.

I remembered when my uncle Michael had asked me that very question at Rosie's birthday party in April. It was that question that made me burst into tears and run to the toilets. At least I didn't cry anymore. I just didn't know what to say. It's quite a choice. You either ramble on about everything, probably boring them to tears in the process, or you stand there and say 'I'm fine' so they immediately know you are lying and don't want to talk about it.

It was a nice feeling to know that his Aunt Sally and family had not blamed me at all. They had stated they felt he was wrong and I felt welcome there anytime. I was really pleased to have that. They have been in our lives for so long, since we moved to that house when I was just 5, and so to have them against me would be awful. I then started to think about the 'for and against' syndrome.

A split of any kind shouldn't really come as for and against should it. It is not necessarily so either. I wouldn't say that the reason that his friends have not contacted me at all is because they were on Marc's side in all of this. That's how it is perceived though isn't it. They haven't contacted me because they cannot be my friends now he isn't my husband. How bizarre?

I realised I was analysing again and tutted at myself once more. I lit another cigarette and pulled myself up onto the bench. I curled my hands round the hot cup of tea. I lifted the cup closer to my face so the steam warmed my chin and looked out into the darkness.

After a few minutes my thoughts turned to him again. He hadn't called when he said he would. He is probably out. He was with her having fun and we are never given a second thought when he is with her. Even the children get pushed away. The feeling of hatred for her raised its ugly head again seeming to grow from the pit of my stomach and I could feel my face screw up to accommodate it. Hatred was becoming quite an overwhelming emotion lately. It took over every part of me and oozed out of my pores.

I took a deep breath in an attempt to control it.

Again the image of the two of them together taunted me on the window. The hurt was still there. It tugged at my heart like it was never going to let go. I will just have to learn to live with this. Why should I though? How could I?

The combination of the analysing, the thoughts and the feelings of hatred and betrayal defeated me into tiredness. I yawned and fell back against the tiles on the kitchen wall. I climbed down and shut everything off. For a minute or two I just stood in the front room in the pitch black listening to the silence. It didn't scare me anymore. Silence doesn't make you question things more or think about things more. Silence just makes your voice in your head louder.

19th October

Had a busy day preparing for my evening out. Packed up the children's things for their weekend with daddy. Got myself ready while Pheobe was at nursery.

The cab was late due to traffic so I missed the early trains. They were then trying to fix a carriage to the back of the train which delayed its departure. Became very stressed. Finally arrived at rush hour and shouted at 2 people for barging into my baby. Met him at 6.15. Both girls began crying because they did not want to leave me. He moaned about being tired so he was unsure about whether he could stay up for me. I promised to leave fairly early.

Had a good time with my friend Frances and drank lots considering I was not there for that long. Went back to Marc's flat around 11pm. Within just a few minutes I was naked and we were making love on the settee. Afterwards I could not settle. It felt so strange to be in the same bed as they sleep together in. Marc did not settle. He was up and down all night. He is clearly very stressed and I felt sorry for him. I don't like seeing him in such distress.

Spent the night up and down too. Slept for little periods throughout the night but kept waking up with the cold as well as Marc getting up every now and then.

I was so relieved when I had finally reached Marc at Oxford Circus. The preparations for the weekend had consumed my whole afternoon and then the early evening was taken up with the journey. I was stressed by the time we arrived and became even more so when he said he wasn't sure I should go back to his. I was so angry. He had suggested this not me and now when I was there in front of him he was trying to back out of it.

I gave him my overnight bag and said I would call him when I was on my way back and we would take it from there.

I met Frances and had a great time. The place was lovely and the company was good. Her friend was there and her brother and a couple of others too. I watched the rugby and chatted with everyone for a bit and then managed to dance a little. I drank lots considering I was only there a few hours. The whole time the nagging doubt that he wouldn't let me stay hovered over me no matter how hard I tried to block it out. By 10.30 I knew I couldn't take it anymore and left.

Dialling his number I was unsure what I was going to hear. Either he was going to be fine about me going there or he was going to back out at the last minute and I would be picking my bag up and going. I wanted to stay. I wanted to be with him. I knew he wanted that too. He said he was just scared of her finding out or turning up. She was in the way again. It was my night with him and she was still ruining it.

I arrived at his flat and his eyes met mine as he opened the door.

"Do you want me to go?" I asked as I walked through into the living room.

The children were all asleep. Seb in his flatmates bed and the girls in his bed. I looked at him. He walked towards me and without a word from either of us we were kissing. He pulled me in close and held me so tightly. Before I knew it we were on the settee making love. Again the passion was red hot and the fire between us was burning so brightly.

We laid there for a while afterwards cuddling each other. I could have fallen asleep there but he couldn't settle. He kept getting up afraid that she was going to walk in unannounced any second. I climbed in bed with the girls and he got in beside me. He had originally said he would sleep on the settee just in case she did come in and also so the children didn't see us together, now though he said he needed to be with me.

Getting to sleep was too hard. I was too hot with the covers on and too cold with them off. The girls being in the bed made us all so squashed and it became unbearable. I didn't know how I had done this every night since the girls were young.

My main problem though was the images that lying in their bed was conjuring up. My mind was filled with them and it drove me crazy keeping me awake. I didn't want to close my eyes as they would be there as soon as I did so. The images were of Marc and Sue. He had told me some stories about their bedroom activities and now lying in this room I was picturing them. Each time I blinked I saw something different. Him kissing her, her kissing him. The two of them holding each other, the two of them making love. At that image I was quite disturbed and I got up and went into the front room. I stood by the window and breathed deeply.

Those were pictures I did not want to have in my head. I closed my eyes again and the image of the bed and the duvet moving made me open them quick. Oh my god, this is crazy. I smiled a small, confused smile noting how ridiculous this situation was. I turned so I faced the door. Looking through the opening I could just see the bedroom door. I continued to look at it. Suddenly, there were the figures of two people in front of it. As clear as anything. I pushed myself forward a little taking a few tentative steps. There was Marc holding her hand leading her into the bedroom, pulling her close and leaning down to kiss her. I walked a little closer, waves of nausea running through me, horrified at the image before me.

Now standing in the hallway, I saw his hands move around her waist, grasp the ends of her top and lift it up, throwing it on the floor once he had taken it off. He started to kiss her neck and then her shoulders, moving downwards, his hands running over her hips and down her thighs. At that point I looked at her, her head bowed down watching my husband kissing her body. As I went to step closer, as if I needed to check it wasn't real, she turned to face me. Her bright eyes twinkled as she seemed to look straight at me and then she smiled. She smiled at me. This knowing, smug smile that I wanted to wipe right off her face. The tears were hot in the corners of my eyes and my face contorted with the sheer disgust of the vivid picture before me. My breathing quickened and my pulse was racing making me feel quite faint.

"You ok?"

I jumped when I heard that voice. It was Marc, walking towards me looking really worried.

"What's wrong?" he said concerned and wrapped his arms round me.

"N-N-Nothing," I stammered through heaving breaths. I glanced over his shoulder. The image had gone. Thank goodness my mind had finished its mean and cruel trick.

Neither of us could settle after that. We sat on the settee together in silence. He kept checking his phone in case she contacted him. He got up and down so many times he made me feel sick. He paced the floor. At about 3am we became too tired to sit up and clambered back in bed. We didn't quite know what to do to settle either of us and the more we tried to sleep the less we slept. The girls fidgeted and took up most of the bed so we literally laid on top of each other for the rest of the evening.

Insomnia - don't you just love it?

Oh my word - such a bastard!

20th October.

It is now 11.20pm. I am furious. I am so irate that I don't know how to calm down. This is it I think. I have finally reached the point where I can no longer control this anger. Up until now I have always suppressed this anger that rages. I hate it. I hate the feeling of not being in control that it gives me and so I fight it with reasoning inside my head. I make excuses that will allow me to see it from his point of view and make myself the last person to consider. But then again those times tend to have been about me and not my children. This time my anger is uncontrollable and he knows he has pushed me to the limit I am sure.

Today has been a rollercoaster for me from the beginning. I tried to enjoy a family morning with him. I tried to relax and not get too down.

First I got angry because he mentioned how he is earning a large sum of money this month. Well done I thought. Part of me was proud of him for achieving this as I had listened to the struggle he had had meeting his targets. That feeling soon turned to bitterness as I hit the shower with thoughts of *that should have been us, I am on a budget, I am worrying about getting through Christmas and you are buying yourself a new ipod and guitar.* The bitterness ate into me in the shower and the tears fell because I did not know what else to do. He spotted this when I came out and kept asking me what was wrong etc. That wound me up more.

I then had to get ready with her stuff all around me. He held a pair of jeans of hers up against me to see whether they would fit me. Comparing us. It made me a little uneasy. He kept telling the children to be quiet and calm down when they were really not making that much noise. That made me annoyed and I remembered that this side of him was the bit I did not like.

He rushed us out of the door as he was coming to Essex with us. Pheobe spilt her drink all over his stuff as he sat on his laptop booking a car for her. *He can spend his money on that alright can't he?* He flipped at Pheobe and demanded to get on the train. Left me clearing it up while he finished what he was doing. The children's faces showed their feelings. They were unsure of the way daddy was shouting. They had not seen him for two weeks and all he had done was moan at them. That made me worse.

On the train Sue phoned and said she was on her way to his. She was going to surprise him and take them all out for a couple of hours. He got upset and she became frustrated. He threw a tantrum like a child. I was so shocked by this display in public that I had to look away. He paced up and down the train texting her and worrying that she had not responded. It drove me mad. He then decided to get off at Shenfield despite me telling him she would not want him to be so obsessed.

At the station he walks off and leaves the children with me while he phones her again. She gets angry with him checking up on her and tells him what she thinks. He gets upset, comes back to us clutching his chest saying that he can't breathe. He falls to the floor in a heap sitting on the platform. I get embarrassed and the children became upset and worried. He behaves like a teenager throwing a strop because he did not get his own way.

We get to Essex and me and the children get a cab and go home. He gets the bus. He phones her again and gets an ear bashing for it. *Why can he not leave her alone?* She had plans with her friends today. Just leave her be. He comes to me crying and I feel bad for him. He calms down and goes to meet his mum with the children. He picks up their stuff on the way back from town and takes it round to hers.

About 6, I get a phone call from Seb to say he has left them to go to the walk in centre. He texts me to say that he has high blood pressure and they were making him see someone else. I just knew he had gone to her. I don't know why. I was so angry with him. He had deserted his children for her again. The anger started to set in but sitting with Marilyn she managed to get me to text him asking him questions to let him dig himself a deeper hole. And boy did he dig.

Eventually, once I said I was coming to meet him as I was so worried about him he told me the truth. He was with her. I was right all along.

The anger just spilled up in me. I shouted at him down the phone. I told him what I was really thinking. That I had now lost all respect for him. That I had idolised him once and that he had destroyed it all. That he did not deserve to be my babies' father. I could have killed him. I told him that I would text her and tell her to ask him about what he had done today if he did not tell her. That that was a promise and not an idol threat. He seemed to tell by how angry I was that I was not bluffing. He kept apologising. I told him I did not care. That he had become obsessed with her. That he had her on a pedestal and was blinded by this. That he put his children second to her and that I was not happy.

The anger I am feeling is immense. No one does this to my children and gets away unscarred. This time I am going to make my point heard and I intend to make him stand up and listen!

In general, I am a calm person. I like to try and keep myself that way as my displays of anger are ones I cannot control. I end up lashing out and there have been a few people, including Marc, that have been on the end of my fist when this happens. I have spent most of my life controlling my rages, but every now and then one bubbles to the surface and that is it then. I let go. I fly into a rage and I don't really realise I am doing it.

To say I was pushed into anger today was an understatement. He started pushing me towards it from the time we got up to the time I went crazy on the phone at him.

The morning was so hard and I ended up in tears. I listened to the way he was telling me about his wages. He was going to earn just under £8,000 this month. Well done. I was proud at first. When I mentioned that he could treat the children, they needed new trainers or a few new clothes, his face changed. His answer then sparked the flame of bitterness inside me that had been just a glowing ember.

"I will see. There are a few treats I want to buy myself first. And I have bills to pay don't forget."

I stormed off into the shower. The thoughts swam through my head with each drop of water that hit it. I was struggling financially. I was grateful to him for paying what he is as I know that some men pay nothing. But to receive that kind of money. To treat himself so often. To have been on holiday with his girlfriend. And yet the children get nothing. How could he do that? Don't give me any. That's fine. Why should he give me some, but the children are his. Surely he would want to make their lives a little brighter.

The thoughts were integrated with the ones that said this should have been us. He always said that our finances stressed him. We would have been fine now. I would have bumped up the savings, cleared the credit card which was only a few hundred and treated us to something. Instead I will watch him throw it all down the drain or on her, whichever comes first.

There was no fighting the tears. I couldn't stop them. No point in trying. On my return to the bedroom he noticed I was upset and yet again he couldn't figure out what was wrong. How dumb is he?

I began to get ready and slowly the tears faded. He came over with a pair of jeans of hers and held them up against me. They would probably be too big for you he said. My mouth just fell open and my skin crawled with the thought of him comparing us in such a way. Whether he meant it or not. This sharing a man thing is weird enough. My situation in sharing this man is weird enough without him doing things like that.

I finished getting ready and put the children in the bath. I lit a cigarette and smoked it out of the window. He kept asking if I was ok and whether we would be ready to go soon. He was so agitated that I was there and at that point I was pleased to see him so uncomfortable.

In no time, we were ready to leave. We walked to the tube station. I was holding the children's bags as well as my own and he was holding just his. Typical. Another thing I hated about him.

The first were the moans and groans at the children and now the second was his inability to consider someone else other than himself. Keep going I thought, I will be glad to see you go when you do.

We stopped at Liverpool Street station to have coffee and snacks before boarding the train. Sue rang him and asked him to book her a car. He got out his laptop and sat down while I helped the children with their drinks and snacks. Pheobe passed me her crisps to open and as she did so, she knocked over her hot chocolate. It went everywhere. She looked at me scared stiff. I caught sight of her and as I said it was ok and it was just an accident, I watched his face contort with anger.

He threw down his laptop and grabbed his bag. The drink had gone inside it all over his things for tomorrow. He was furious. He shouted at her and while I reached for the napkins and began clearing up he continued his tirade watching me. The children sat in silence, the hurt showing on their faces. They hadn't seen him for so long and had so looked forward to it and now all he had done was shout at them and tell them off.

We were rushed to the train with Marc still in a rage and eventually found seats. The train pulled away and within a few minutes his phone had rung. She was on her way to his flat to pick them up. I obviously found this quite funny, but the tantrum he threw was amazing. I don't think Pheobe could have done any better and she is the queen of tantrums.

It was as if it was the end of the world. Sue had told him she wouldn't be seeing them today as she was meeting friends at lunchtime to watch football and sit down the pub. Now she had changed her mind and he was supposed to be there. She went mad at him on the phone, he sucked up to her. The whole thing made me feel quite queasy.

He got off the train at Shenfield and I followed with the children. He phoned her again and again she had a go at him. He then phoned her again and she went mad. He threw himself on the floor in front of the children and every one else on the platform. They all stared at him. He sat on the floor clutching his chest. My mouth just fell open for the second time today and I cannot possibly explain what was going through my head.

A man who worked there shouted across the railway lines. "Is he ok love?" I looked over at him and the anger and the embarrassment came over as I shouted back - "I actually don't give a shit!" He looked shocked while those nearby who had seen his behaviour sniggered and giggled quietly.

Eventually he got back on the train and we sat in silence the whole way back. He phoned her again while making his way to mine and again gets a mouthful, and ends up on my doorstep crying. I did feel sorry for him. I'm not sure whether it was because of what had happened or that he was so pathetic.

He took the children to his mums and I basked in the peace and quiet of my house and my life. I had not really realised the difference in my life that him leaving had made.

When someone goes you only see the positive side of them. You miss them. You want them home. You remember the good times you shared and the laughs you had. In some ways you put them on a pedestal that they are not worthy of.

Today had made me realise that there were so many things that I did not miss. There were so many sides to Marc that I had forgotten about and that he was so difficult to live with at times. I smiled a little smile as I listed the few I had seen today that had made me thankful I did not have to put up with him every day. My smile faded as I realised that while that was true and while I probably couldn't have him back because I couldn't live like that again, I missed him still and those things didn't stop me loving him. The smile returned as I thought of my freedom for a whole night.

I sank back into my settee with a hot cup of tea and began the long, hard process of trying to relax.

Speaking to Marilyn we realised that we were both sitting alone and decided we may as well sit together. Just before I left a phone call from Seb revealed his dad was no longer with them. Apparently he was sitting in the walk in centre with an irregular heartbeat and high blood pressure. As I walked to Marilyn's, I thought back over the day. The way he acted with Sue. If I knew my husband at all I would have expected him to run to her to make sure she was not angry with him.

I could suddenly feel the disbelief coming over me. This feeling tugged away at me and I just knew that he was with her. He had deserted his children to be with her. The anger rose. How would I prove it? How would I know?

Texting him he told me how he was waiting to see another doctor because they were not happy with him. How his blood pressure was so high. How his chest pains were worsening. He was there for hours. Something told me this was all lies.

The feeling made me nauseous and I could feel myself becoming more and more agitated. I was getting edgy and couldn't quite sit still. I asked what his pressure reading was and he couldn't tell me. I became frustrated as I was not getting to the bottom of this and I was also a little confused how I knew that he was lying. It baffled me completely.

What if it was true though? What if he was sitting alone in that place for all this time?

I left Marilyn's to the text of 'I am in A&E,' in a frenzy. Either the git was lying or I am being an utter cow for sitting indoors while he was suffering. Anger fuelled my obsession. The possibility of it all being lies was now too much and I needed to know. I held the phone in my hands as I stood outside my house unsure of what to do next. Should I call him? Should I phone the hospital?

A text from Seb came through.

'Dad is still not back. Is he ok?'

That was it then I saw red. My boy was sitting there worrying about his dad and I was sure it was all lies. I went inside and phoned him only to hear the answer machine kick in. I left a message saying I was on my way. I was going down to A&E to be with him. I grabbed my car keys and ran out of the house. Before I had even reached the car my phone rang. It was him.

"Don't come down - I'll be here ages. Go out and enjoy yourself."

"I can't do that knowing you are ill," I replied, faking concern. "Seb is worried about you. I'm worried about you. I'm coming."

I knew by the tone and the panic in his voice that he was lying. You know him so well I thought to myself.

"You can't come down. Sue is coming."

She would never do that I thought. There is no way when she has been out drinking all day and is still sitting down the pub watching the rugby game she would leave and travel down to Essex just to sit in the hospital with him. I knew it, he was lying.

That is when the anger raged even more.

"I don't care. I don't care if she will be there. I will face her. I'm coming. I'm your wife and I am here. I will be there sooner than she will," I said through gritted teeth trying to hide my anger.

My breathing was getting quicker. I turned the key and started the engine. He was going to believe I was on my way.

"You can't come," he cried. The panic in his voice was very prominent now and that in turn made my anger even fiercer.

"Why not Marcus? Why? Is it because she is coming? Or is it really because you are not there. You are in London with her aren't you?" I blurted out angrily almost spitting my words.

My heart rate was insanely high and I could hear my head throbbing as I was waiting for his response.

"Look. Don't get angry babe. I came down to London. I had to..."

"You bastard!" I screamed down the phone and hung up.

I knew he would phone me back straight away and I didn't want to be shouting and screaming on the driveway. I went back inside and walked into the kitchen, slamming every door behind me and cursing him the whole time. I didn't know what I was going to do now. My anger was so high and I knew the rage was there and visible.

I tried the deep breathing technique, but that didn't work. I was furious.

The phone rang and I let him have everything. I flew at him in a rage and I am not even sure whether I made any sense. I screamed at him for lying. I shouted at him for making my son worry about his dad. For treating his mum so badly and taking advantage.

I laid into him over the fact he had deserted his children for that skank again. How he had ran off to make sure she was ok, leaving his children who he hadn't seen for two weeks with his mum.

My words came tumbling out so fast, I spat them at him down the phone in an attempt to get over my anger with him. I called him all the names I thought of and they just flowed naturally out of me. Pure anger and hatred for him came with it.

He said sorry so many times but I still didn't let up. He tried to explain why he had done it but he couldn't possibly make me understand. The whole time I was walking the circle of my kitchen, dining room and conservatory, weaving through the doors and behind the chairs.

He had lived with me all this time and he knew he had pushed me too far. At one point, I heard her voice asking what was going on.

"Does she know what you have done?" I screamed.

"No," he said quietly.

I could tell he had walked away from her at that point. She was calling him but he carried on trying to calm me down with his empty promises and lies.

I just kept pacing up and down and round and round. My feet pounded the floor and my heart pounded at my chest. If he was closer I would have gone to him just to hit him and be rid of this feeling that raged inside of me. My body was rigid and I was breathless from it all.

I hung up knowing that there was nothing I could do. Nothing I could say would ever get through to this man who had deserted his children. My babies. I wished he had brought them to me. I wished I could go and collect them now.

The anger boiled and I knew there was no way I would settle if I didn't let it out. I need a punch bag in my garage I thought to myself then I would be fine.

I grabbed my Ipod and ran out the front door. I turned it on full blast and began to run. It was pitch black and freezing cold but I didn't even notice. I just ran and ran. I pounded the streets pushing all of my anger through my feet and into the floor.

I paid no attention to where I was going. I had no planned route and I was wearing boots rather than trainers. I just kept running. I could feel the hot tears stinging my cheeks as they met with the cold air. I just kept running. I could hear all the excuses in my head and I discounted every one. I just kept running. I could feel the pain in my chest worsen and the tightness made it hard to breathe. I just kept running.

I knew that I couldn't stop. I couldn't stop until I had outrun the rage that burned inside of me. Until calm was restored. Until I could face it again. I bowed my head, crying furiously and listened to the music. I just kept running.

22nd October

Took the children to the zoo today. I was freezing cold! They loved it. It amazes me how every time they visit it, they act as if it is the first time they have been. They ran around the 'familiar friends' part, feeding the animals with such delight it was warming to watch. Pheobe was simply terrified by the goats that ran to greet her. She held the food out to them and then snatched it away quickly before they got it. She was so funny to watch. She wanted to be like her big brother and sister but she was too afraid.

Seb was really good with her at this and when it came to the play area too. He rescued her quite a few times when she yelled for him. He played the role of big brother perfectly.

Had spoken to Marc on the phone before we left and got angry again. He didn't seem to understand that the fact he was taking a day off work to go to Glasgow to be with Sue and yet he would not take a day or two off to be with his children this half term was upsetting for me to hear. He is a joke. He just doesn't get it at all. I'm bored with trying to explain.

Still feeling very angry today. The feeling is there bubbling away like hot lava ready to spill out of any crevice it can find. It's good in a way as it means I am not being brought down by his inconsiderate actions. I just get mad with him. Sitting here this evening I still feel like I can fight this. It is nice to know I can finally say I never want him back. He has done too much damage. All I have to do now is make sure I am over the love I have for him and to move on with my life. I think I can give it a very good try now.

The more time I spend with my babies the happier I become. I had no time for him today. He is still being over nice on the phone after the other night. I seem to have switched off to it now. The rage still hasn't gone. It was still there. It was just bubbling away almost like a simmer.

I had sat and spoke to mum for hours on end and came to the conclusion that there was no point to this anymore. There seemed to be no point to fighting him to be with the children. I had come so close to giving up.

He isn't having them this half term at all. He didn't want to book time off to see them on their holidays. He has booked time off to go to Glasgow with Sue though. That was ok. I could feel the simmering get knocked up a notch and I knew I had to stop thinking.

There is no point being at the zoo with your babies if all you are going to do is talk to yourself about that man I had thought to myself.

I laughed at myself for that.

I stared out my kitchen window and watched the smoke from my cigarette ease over to the cold pane of glass. I breathed deeply and thought about my babies today. They seem so much more together lately. They look after each other more.

I pictured Pheobe at the top of this climbing frame. She was stuck in the rope net part and was too scared to move. She didn't even look up. She just yelled for Seb. She knew he would be there. She only had to call him once and he was there. He picked her up and put her feet firmly on the rope lines. He held her hands and pointed to each place she needed to put her feet with his knee. I could see his hands going white where she gripped them so tightly.

My heart warmed as I replayed the images from today in my head. A smile crept across my face. My babies made me so proud.

I feel a great deal stronger now. I think between him pushing me that far this weekend and the feeling I got when out with my babies today, I have succumbed to not wanting him here. I have accepted he will never be here again. I really thought that I wanted him back. He is not the man I married and he certainly isn't the best father in the world. Why would I have someone who would only cause me and my babies stress? He can't even put them first.

I jumped down from the bench and wandered into the front room. The house was still and quiet. The darkness was surrounding me as I sat on the settee. I sank into the cushion and hugged another in front of me. I pulled my knees up and hugged my tea closely trying to draw in its warmth.

There I sat tonight. Not angry. Just calm. Happy in a way. I sat there in the peace and quiet for at least an hour before I curled up in bed beside my little one. I kissed her forehead as I had just done to the other two and covered her over with the duvet snuggling up close to her. Sleep washed over me easily tonight. There was no fight against it from any part of my body. As sleep engulfed me, I realised I was still smiling.

24th October

Phoned me at about 1.30 to say that he would not be turning up this evening. The children were really upset again. They have had enough of him and his empty promises. Fiona was very down. She referred to herself as daddyless. She is adamant that she does not have a daddy anymore. She told me she was hurt and upset at the fact he is never there. He never takes her to school, he never picks her up, and he never answers the phone when she calls. All these things are noticeable to a little girl and they mean so much to her. I had another go at him. I said how I was not disappointed as I never expected him to come as there is always something that gets priority over the children. I said everybody knows it. His reply was merely - 'I love being Mr. Popular.' *How dare he react like that?* That just fuelled the anger again. He cannot stand anyone thinking badly of him so to him the family's opinion is important. *Does he attempt to change it though?* No, of course not. Stupid man.

I cuddled the children, watched their TV and spent some time just sitting with them. Making sure they knew they had one parent who loved and cared for them.

I feel so sorry for them and I am angry that he cannot see what he is doing. I am angry that I cannot make him see sense. I am angry that I cannot help my babies. I'm angry with him like I never thought I could be and it is quickly turning into an intense hatred.

The feeling of helplessness surrounded me tonight. I felt so frustrated and so let down and the hurt for the children was so intense it made me feel worse. Their little faces frowned when I said Daddy wasn't coming. Seb wasn't surprised to be honest. He just said, 'I knew he wouldn't mum.' In some ways that hurt more. He wasn't supposed to feel like that about his own father.

The anger is something that eats into you. It takes over everything you say and do. Watching TV with the children was great and we all enjoyed it, despite the rubbishness of American comedy for children. The thoughts were there still though. Things were still churning through my mind at such speed I could hear the echoes of each sentence. The conversation I had with myself made things worse.

You want to shout and scream but you know there is no point. I told him about the children missing him and needing their daddy but he just wants to do something else. There is always an excuse, always a reason, genuine or not, that gets in the way of him seeing his children. It is so upsetting for all of us here.

The stress of it finally got to me when the children went off to bed. The silence, as I have said before, made the conversation and the repeat of the words he said louder and I began to tense up. The frustration comes with each part of it. The fact he didn't come was the first brick to be laid. The fact that he is busy doing something else is the second brick. The next one came with the children being upset. The next was Seb's remark and the next was Fiona's tears. The rest of the wall is laid with bricks of past let downs and excuses, but most of them are from the realisation that there is absolutely nothing I can do about it. I can't change it. I can't make him see what he is doing.

I sat in the kitchen laying the wall of frustration in my head wondering whether there is something that could act as a bulldozer and knock it down. Something that would make that wall, and him, crash to the floor as much as he makes me and my babies do so. I would love to have this wall as a heap of dust and cement lying on the floor and meaning nothing. There is no way of doing that though. Not yet anyway.

I breathed a huge sigh of tension and almost let out a scream at the same time. My baby thinks she is daddyless. She was talking with her friends in school and there are a few of them that refer to themselves as this. It just sounds so awful. I remember my dad as a little girl. The way you look up to them is amazing. They are the greatest man in the world to a little girl. The dad is the one that protects. I believed my dad could fix all problems. He was stronger than the strongest man in the world and I still believe now that with my dad beside me I can do anything. My dad is now seen with all his faults. I now have a proper picture of my dad but throughout my childhood he was the perfect man to me. If that had been destroyed before I had grown up enough to understand why, I don't know how I would have coped. My little girl was facing that battle now. She shouldn't be.

I hated him for this.

"How can you destroy her illusions? You stupid bastard!" I yelled into the silence.

My next thought was that yes I am going crazy, but I shook that off quickly. I had that horrible need to do something without knowing what the something is. I had begun to dread these feelings. They were awful. The aimless wandering round the house was fruitless and nothing whatsoever was achieved.

I decided to write everything down as that usually made me feel better. I started a letter to him. I got as far as Dear Marc, when I had writers block. Excellent idea brain, well done. Putting pen to paper was not going to work here clearly. I screwed up the paper and threw it into the bin as if I was playing basketball.

I lit a cigarette and stood by the sink. I couldn't keep still. I was itching to do something. I picked up my phone and started to type out a text message. This time the words tumbled out easily. I told him what I thought of him letting his children down again, said he didn't deserve to be a father, and told him I hated him right now.

"Feed that to your self pity," I said as I pressed send.

I breathed another huge sigh and turned off the phone. I didn't want the reply even though I was sure I wouldn't get one anyway.

I slung the phone on the bench and sat on the floor. Stretching out my legs I let the rest of me slump in a heap. I looked up at the ceiling and around the room as if the solution was hiding here somewhere. Absolutely nothing.

I pulled my knees up to my chest and let my arms hang loose between them, tapping my nails on the floor. I listened to the conversation in my head again and just shrugged my shoulders. The wall was firmly there now and the tense feeling of frustration that was turning into anger and hatred once more was settled deep within.

On the wall, I hung a picture. A picture of the man that caused the wall to be built. The man who caused the stress, the frustration, the anger and the hatred. The man who made my children upset with his continuous let downs. The one who made my babies cry. I made a promise. I made it to myself and to my babies. The day I knock down this wall. The day I leave it in a heap of rubble. The day it falls to the floor and lies reduced to nothing but a heap of useless dirt and dust, you, Marc, you will lie there amongst it.

26th October

No mention of seeing them tonight. He told me he was just sitting in the flat for the night and I immediately did not understand why he could not come down and see them. They need him and he is still not putting their needs first. He never will though, he is not like that.

Mum and Dad came over to baby-sit tonight. I had cleaned the whole house, except the windows, from top to bottom. That was seen as a good sign.

Went out with Marilyn and had a very strange night. I spent the first bit thinking about Marc and wishing I was drunk. The next couple of hours I spent texting Alexander and sitting outside while Marilyn chatted to her male friends. Then I spent an hour wishing I had not drunk so much. I then met and chatted to two men, boys, whatever!

The first was really sweet though a little smarmy. Harmless. 27yrs old, looking more like 21. Had a great smile though. It lit up his whole face. Nice eyes too. He took my number. The second guy I spoke to that evening was Lee. He was a friend of Davy, who Marilyn was talking to. He was quite good looking, friendly. We went outside for a cigarette and a chat. We stood and talked for a while. He is an Arsenal supporter and plans to convert me, a stonemason, lives near me. Didn't care I had 3 children. Just after a little fun I suppose. So am I really. No need for anything other than that. He was warm, polite, kind and a gentleman. He waited for me to get a cab after I had waited about 30 mins for Marilyn. He waved me off and text me about 4.20 am to ask if he could see me again. That's more like it.

Throughout today I was running around occupying the children and doing so much housework. I had the urge to blitz the place and it carried right through the day. The urge was fuelled by the need to forget everything that had been dragging me down over the course of the last few days and I used it to escape the reality and fill the time up at the same time.

The children watched me run around and clean up. They helped a little but mainly watched. They could see something was pushing me into doing this. Fiona's eyes followed me everywhere I went and every now and then she would smile and say 'love you mummy.' It always warmed my heart.

Sitting here now in the calm and still of the night, I could feel the tiredness swarming through me. I had been out on the town again and had a great time. My confidence boosted by two guys that had been so nice to me and asked for my number. I could feel the alcohol still swimming round too and the mixture of the emotions, alcohol and cigarette smoke had started to make me feel quite nauseous. It had been an eventful evening after such a busy day.

Mum and dad came round to look after the children while I went out with Marilyn. They were giving me a break that I was so grateful for. I needed to escape from these four walls which seemed to hem me in, the space growing smaller and smaller by the day.

Marc had annoyed me again today and the anger had risen itself inside me hence the housework and the attack on dirt, grime and children's toys. It was hard trying to understand another person. It is even harder when they don't have the same values and opinions as you. He was not seeing the children again tonight. He had let them down in the week and now a Friday night was out of the question too. He was just sitting indoors alone. Sitting in the flat, waiting for her to come round after her night out and yet he couldn't bring himself to come down and sit with them. Even if that was all he had done. Come down here and sat in with them. At least they would have been with their dad instead of wondering where he was.

I decided I had tortured and confused myself enough recently over the actions of this man and changed my thought pattern to accommodate something much nicer. My night out.

Marilyn was talking to an old friend of hers and her new one at the same time. I spoke to them for a bit but quickly became a little bored and went outside. I sat on the rail outside the bar and smoked a cigarette while texting Alexander. He was cheering me up saying such nice things and also making me smile with his cheekiness as usual.

I kept looking up waiting for something to change. Waiting for Marilyn to come outside or some gorgeous man to come and talk to me. Neither of those happened and I sat outside for what seemed like ages. I watched all the people inside and outside. They all seemed so happy, though whether it was with life or drunkenness I couldn't really tell. I watched them laughing and chatting, and loneliness and solitude bit into me quite hard. I didn't seem to have that. I didn't seem to have people to laugh and smile with and the tears stung a little.

A guy came up and started talking to me. He said I had a great smile, after I smiled at him of course, and said he had been watching me. He chatted away for a little, asked me a few questions and took my phone number. I was a little bowled over by his words but chuffed that someone, even a young someone, thought that way. He left and I carried on standing alone. Thoughts of making the effort to go and talk to someone crossed my mind but I quickly dismissed them when I realised there wasn't actually anyone that I would want to talk to anyway, so why make myself do something I hated doing.

I spotted a guy going into the bar and he stopped and talked to the man Marilyn had been talking to. I decided to get a closer look just in case and went back inside. I stood next to Marilyn while she chatted to her friend at the bar. I watched her and him seemingly deep in conversation, but I still kept an eye on this guy who was squatting next to the table chatting.

I can't quite remember what happened next but I was then outside with the guy I had been watching. One of us went out for a cigarette and the other followed. We stood outside talking but I still can't remember what the topics of conversation were about. I remembered him saying he was 26 and he asked about my children. Not once did I feel like he was chatting me up. He held my gaze during the conversation and seemed interested in what I had to say. I must admit I found all of this quite attractive.

We were outside for what seemed like ages. Lee's friend came out and went on to a bar while Lee stayed chatting to me. I smiled at this and began to feel happy to be in his company. The bar shut and Marilyn and her friend came outside. They stopped on the way to get a cab and wouldn't stop talking. I called and called her but she stayed with him. Lee waited with me. He didn't leave.

I was shivering and I stood closer to him. He offered me to phone home as my battery had just died but I declined. I carried on calling her. Eventually she wandered over to us and waited for a cab on the corner. Lee stayed with us again and saw us into the cab. He said he would get in touch and went to join his friend.

On my arrival home mum and dad were worried sick. They had been trying to contact me as it was getting late and they were frantic. I hated seeing my mum get so upset and wished I had taken Lee up on his offer. They left and I burst into tears with Marilyn there to comfort me. I felt a little like a teenager all over again. It had been such a good night.

I sat there now alone after Marilyn had gone home and my thoughts of Lee were making me smile. I didn't hold out much hope of him contacting me again but he had made me smile for tonight at least. He had given me a little glimpse of that warm feeling again and I was thankful for that.

27th October

Oh god - *how much did I have to drink?*
Felt like crap all morning and it had to be the morning when Marc turns up ridiculously early to collect the children.

Half eight. Half eight and he turns up. He has never arrived this early before. I felt so awful. My head was pounding and I knew I needed to go back to bed. I spoke briefly to Marc and waved them all goodbye. I was actually quite relieved when the noise stopped and I crawled back up the stairs to bed.

This afternoon went better after sleep had worked its magic. I was almost walking on a high. Lee had been in touch and we were going out for a drink on Monday. I had something to look forward to and I was so happy.

The evening was spent with my mum, sister and cousin drinking in town for my sister's birthday. I drank way too much again but had a great time.

I sat in bed after saying goodnight to my cousin and I tossed and turned despite feeling exhausted. My mind was whirling with thoughts of Marc, the children and Lee. Everything merged into one and the alcohol in me made things start spinning. The room was moving round in circles in front of me and the words I was thinking were swimming between the furniture. I was reading my own thoughts, which was the most bizarre experience I had gone through and I had been through quite a few now.

I sat reading the things I was saying and questioning the ones I always did. I saw the list of unanswered questions in front of me too. It all made me want to scream out loud. I flung myself down to the bottom of the bed and pulled the covers up tight screwing up my eyes as if I was shutting out the floating words. I gasped for breath under the covers but I didn't care. I was staying there and I was not coming up for air. I waited for sleep to take me so the thoughts, the floating words and the nauseous feelings would vanish.

28th October

Another great night out last night. Got slightly drunk again - really need to curb it now. Put weight on - not good - need to sort that too!

Seb told Sue about last Friday and me staying over. It did not go down too well as you can imagine. She went mad at him - oops! He is in a bit of a mess, worrying about what she will do and say. He thinks she will call it off, she says she has had enough as it has just been one thing after another with him. I feel quite sorry for her. She has been lied to by him and I know what that feels like. It's a horrible uncertainty that nestles into you and makes you feel so bad with everything and you spend ages questioning what he has said/ done/is doing. Poor thing.

I don't feel sorry for him at all. He shouldn't tell so many lies should he. If he had just been honest with her from the start, it would never have come to this.

Felt so sick waiting for the children to come home, wondering if his mood had affected them and their weekend. They seemed ok.

They talked a little about it and Seb said he had told him he could not go any more. Arsehole.

Was relieved to have them home and I just held them for most of the first couple of hours they were back. I wanted them to feel safe.

Wonder what is being said tonight?

I had received the phone call this afternoon and was quite dumbfounded. I hadn't known what to say as I had no sympathy with him at all. He was so stressed with what had just happened and he was angry. I could hear the strain in his voice and I was worried about the children and how he was treating them and the effect it had had on their day with daddy and Sue.

He told me how they had been sitting in McDonalds and had had a lovely day out up to that point in time. Marc had gone back to the counter to fetch something and Seb and Fiona had blurted out about the weekend they had spent with mummy and daddy at the flat a couple of weeks ago. I am not quite sure how it had come up and who had said the final words 'mummy stayed at the flat' but in a way it didn't matter. She had then got very cross and was obviously upset and cold towards him. I totally understood. If I was her I would have been devastated too. No one wants the ex sleeping at their boyfriends flat.

He had phoned me as soon as he could. He came running to me with the attitude of 'Seb is intent on ruining my life.' His attitude made me angry but I still had no sympathy. I had asked to meet with her and had suggested he tell her I was staying. He had ranted about neither of those ideas were good ones and dismissed them.

I spent the afternoon desperately wanting my babies back. I was worried he was taking his stress and anger out on them and wondered whether they were being made upset by all of this.

I tried to watch TV to ignore my worries but that didn't work. I tried occupying myself with housework and other little jobs around the house but that didn't work either. I became even more agitated as the need to have my babies home became stronger and that was made worse by his phone being switched off when I tried to contact him.

When the children finally walked through the door I was so relieved, I just hugged them. They seemed ok and were not too upset and that made me feel so much better. They spoke a little about what they had said and how they hadn't meant to get daddy in trouble and upset Sue. I tried to explain to them that daddy should have been honest with her and it wasn't their fault. I tried to explain why Sue was upset and that they were not the ones who caused it, daddy was. I think they thought she was upset with them too. They seemed to understand a little more when I had finished.

I had just put them to bed and sat down on the settee breathing a huge sigh of relief. I had known I was stressed but now it was all over I could really tell how stressed I had been. I looked up to see Seb creeping down the stairs looking a little sad and forlorn. He sat down next to me and said that he was upset because of the day and that it was entirely his fault. He looked at me with tears in his eyes and said,

"Daddy said I couldn't go with him anymore."

I stared blankly at him. I could feel this heat churning up from my stomach and I asked him to repeat what he had just said. He did and with the second time of hearing, the heat turned to anger and swam through my veins with ease.

I was furious. How dare he say that to him? I told Seb not to worry and that daddy was angry and sometimes we say things we don't mean when we are angry. He just looked at me not buying it at all. I made him a hot drink, slamming the cupboards and cups around, explaining the whole time that daddy was wrong to say such a horrible thing and mummy would sort it out. He took his drink to bed a little happier and managed to fall asleep quite quickly considering.

I sat on the bench with this steam pouring in huge chunks out of my ears. Okay, the man was upset and shocked about what had just happened and he had a girlfriend to explain to as she was angry and rightly so, but you do not take it all out on your son. He felt guilty enough.

I was irate by this time but knew that there was no point in calling to try and sort it out. His phone would still be off and he would never talk to me anyway while he was trying to patch things over with her.

I stormed about in the kitchen not quite knowing what to do with myself. I paced up and down, got on and off the bench so many times I made myself sick with the motions and every now and then would say what I was thinking out loud to listen to it.

I managed to calm down and thought about what they were doing now. I wondered what Sue was saying. What lies would Marc come up with this time? He would never say it was his suggestion that I stayed at the flat. What excuse would he give? I almost giggled to myself thinking about the trouble there would be tonight.

My children had been great. They had spilled the beans quite innocently and in a way I was pleased with them for doing so. A smile crept on my face. It felt quite good actually knowing he was stressed and she was upset. I had felt sorry for her, now I just smiled at the thought of her being such a fool like I had been.

I leant back on the tiles on my kitchen wall and wished I could be a fly on their wall right now. I would love to be listening to the conversation. The anger faded as I basked in the enjoyment of causing trouble between the two of them. I was enjoying it more than I thought I would have done. I wouldn't mind doing this again.

Dating.

29th October

Went out with Lee tonight. I met him at Smiths last Friday night. We sat in the pub and drank and chatted. He is really not my usual type. He is loud, cocky and acts the fool. He swears a lot and seems so common. But I had such a good night. I haven't laughed so much in ages. He has a great smile and seems really cheeky. I had fun. I felt relaxed and not on edge at all. I didn't have to pretend with him. It was an open, honest evening and I thoroughly enjoyed myself. I think we will meet up again - I hope so.

Lee was great. We sat in a pub in town and chatted really easily. I was quite nervous at first. Waiting for him to pick me up was a little scary. I hadn't done this for so long, it felt quite strange. I could remember him a little from Friday night but the details were not quite right, probably due to the amount I had drunk.

He arrived in his car and we set off. Chatting in the car he explained how he had not put his clocks back last night and had got up an hour early for work. He hadn't realised until the time was said on the radio as he was driving down the A12. I laughed at his anecdote and the ice was broken.

He kept me laughing most of the evening. He asked a few questions about my ex and my children and I answered them honestly. I felt so relaxed and comfortable being with him that I could be quite open in my explanations.

I watched him as I listened to his recounts of him at school. A typical boy always in trouble and not willing to be there, I even felt for his teachers having to cope with him. He was so happy though in a way. He didn't seem stressed and uptight. It was such a welcome change.

He was quite rough. Had a little twinkle in his eye and I thought that he would probably be the type of guy I would keep my girls away from. I watched his smile take over his whole face and his laugh was quite an addictive, dirty one too.

At the end of a great evening he dropped me off and I gave him a kiss on the cheek. He said he would see me soon and if I couldn't get out on Friday he would sit in with me and watch a DVD when the children were in bed. It was really sweet to hear and I felt he was acting quite mature for his age.

Lying in bed my thoughts were of him and whether there was scope for seeing him for a while. I knew he would never be a long term one. He wouldn't be the type for anything too serious and he had been open about that. I didn't want anything like that at the moment anyway.

I was a little confused how he had made me consider this when he really was not the type of guy I would have ever considered before. Maybe that was what was intriguing about him now. He was a sod I could tell. Dangerous ground if you were looking for something more permanent.

What was I looking for? Did I know yet?

I sat up in bed and wondered why I had bothered to come. I knew I wasn't going to be able to sleep as I had all these thoughts swirling round and round. Mum had just turned her light off in her room and I had to go to work tomorrow so the alarm would go off incredibly early. I lay back down and discussed getting up with myself. Deciding this was definitely another sign of madness I got up and went downstairs.

I lit a cigarette and sat up on the bench. I looked down at the floor this time as I decided that looking at darkness was not a positive outlook and I shouldn't be doing it.

What do I need right now? What do I want?

I had been happy that I had met someone. I had looked forward to the date and enjoyed it thoroughly. I would like to meet him again. Am I just using him though to have someone? That wouldn't be a nice thing to do. Would he really care? I was unsure.

Thinking about all of this was beginning to make my head ache. I yawned and let out a huge sigh of yet more frustration.

I finished my cigarette and leant back against the wall.

I had enjoyed myself tonight. If we went out again and I had fun why would I not continue seeing him?

All I want is someone to help me switch off for a bit. Do I want anything too heavy? No. Do I want someone involved with the children? No. Do I want someone to have fun with? Yes. Do I want someone to meet up with every now and then and feel like I am more than just a mum and an ex? Yes. Do I want someone to make me smile again? Yes.

I sat up as if I had just been hit with a bolt of lightening.

"What is your problem then you silly cow?" I said out loud. I smiled at myself for spending more time analysing and getting nowhere. I swore I wouldn't do this again.

I climbed off my bench and walked back up the stairs to bed. Go with the flow my girl, go with the flow. Have a little fun in your life for a little while. Have a toy boy for a bit. Enjoy yourself. You certainly deserve to smile for a while.

I snuggled under the duvet much happier after sorting that out with myself. Now it was time to get some sleep.

31st October

My first 2 days at work after the half term. Feel so tired. The stress is keeping me awake at the beginning of the night. I became so angry tonight. I was winding myself up about the fact that he won't have these children. I felt a little selfish but then my mum pointed out that if I am not happy, it will rub off on the children and also that I need a life too.

Lee had said he would like to meet me again. The problem is I have to wait another week and that may well put him off. I will never know when I am free and whether he will turn up and get the children when he says he will and I think it is a little unfair. He is having his life and yet I am deprived of mine by that fact. It is really getting to me.

I text Sue last night. Asked her to get in touch again, just said we needed to talk. I would love to make her see the lies he has been telling and how he is playing the pair of us.

Have worked out he has seen the children for seven days out of the last 40. That is ridiculous. He is really pissing me off. He refused to take a day off in the half term but is taking a day off the week after to go to Glasgow with her. He dumps the children on his mum so he can go back to London. He told lies about me to Sue which is making me more and more mad.

He is one big joke. *What can I do about it though?* I'll think of something.

I am so angry with Marc right now it is making me sick. I have spent yet another day stressing out about him not having his children. So many men are fighting to get access to their children and he can't be bothered. It makes me so mad and upset.

I appreciate the fact that now I have met Lee it is even worse for me. I want to see him again and I have no way of doing that because he is such an arse and won't come and look after his children. He is giving them none of his time and that also means I am getting no time for myself.

He has said he isn't coming on Friday night again. I didn't even listen to the excuse this time; it is usually something to do with his skank and I don't want to hear it.

He has spent these last few days trying to smooth over the problems that had unfolded with her over last weekend. The fury rose in me again as I thought about what he had told her. Apparently I phoned him up when I was incredibly drunk that night and said I needed to see the children. He had let me in and then I had passed out on the bed with the girls.

A few questions that should have been asked by Sue. If she was drunk how did she manage to get to a flat she has never been to by train? Did she wear the same thing the next morning? Why did you let her in? And why didn't you tell me about it the next day?

Open and honest are two words that do not go with the name Marcus.

I am angry enough that he has portrayed me in such a way. He has made me out to be some drunk that pesters her ex and that is so far from the truth it is ridiculous.

Now he has made me angrier again. He has chosen to stay in London with her instead of spending time with his children. He has deserted them again and not made them top priority, does he not realise how much they need to see him? Does he not realise that these choices will have an impact on them?

I then became angry with what his choices are doing to my social life. I have now met someone who wants to see me, take me out, spend some time with me and I can't go because of my ex. I can't expect other people to have them and I certainly can't expect my mum to have them over and over again. They are our children not hers and he should be pulling his weight in terms of seeing them and looking after them.

I am now stuck in again.

Naturally after that statement and those thoughts about myself and my life, I tortured myself with feelings of guilt for being so bloody selfish. I shouldn't be down about being indoors. I should spend the time with the children playing and such. Maybe I am thinking of myself way too much?

I sat on my bench seething with anger and frustration and torturing myself with the thoughts of my social life and whether I was right or wrong to want one. Will this ever end? Will there ever be a time when I know that he will have the children regularly? Will there ever be a routine?

Sick of feeling like this and with anger that I couldn't let out I found myself crying again. Everything has become so stressful and confusing and going round and round in circles is driving me crazy. I am exhausted with it all and so fed up now.

I cried for a while and let myself wallow in my drama. I had to. It was just one of those nights.

Cheering up?

2nd November

Had a positive day today. Yesterday was not so good, felt awful all day.

Spent the day chatting to Nicky. She came over for the whole day. It was good to have her back after so long. We gossiped about men, children, relationships, life, and sex - all the usual girl stuff. It was nice to have the company of someone who understood.

I text Alexander all day today again. He is really starting to get to me. I am thinking about him all the time. Waiting for him to text and getting disappointed when he doesn't. All this with a guy I haven't even met. It seems so bizarre. I feel as if I know him. We have been texting and emailing and chatting for 7 weeks now and yet we haven't met once. We arranged to meet next Friday and I am already so excited. I am really hoping that we hit it off and all goes well. Not sure where to go. I know though if we go round here, I will end up doing something stupid and I need to avoid that at all costs.

Thinking of planning a night out nearer to London and staying over at my aunt Violet's house. Can't stop thinking about it. Can't wait.

Spoke to Marc this morning. We had a chat about me meeting Sue and talking to her. He still thinks I am out to destroy their relationship. I am not, well not right now. That would be shooting myself in the foot. The children are so attached to her that I can use her help with them. They are happier when they go to see her and stay with her than when they go with just their dad. They trust her and know her quite well now. I have to utilise that to my advantage. I want to make her understand what the children are going through. Talk to her about the support they need from her and Marc so she will hopefully understand why I keep nagging and arguing with him.

I feel as if we need to develop a civil relationship, however weird and uncomfortable for the both of us, as she is their second maternal figure now. We cannot go on with the tension. There is no point. Life is too short. I just hope he understands to make her understand.

It's all a little confusing - hating her and yet wanting to meet her and ask for her help. He says he is coming down on Monday to talk about it all but I am never sure whether he will turn up. I hope he does or I will get angry again and that's when the trouble starts and that is not nice for anyone. Fingers crossed it runs smoothly.

Fiona is looking forward to her day with Nanny Choc-Choc. They are walking into town and shopping and then going back to hers for the afternoon. She says she will spoil her with some attention. It's just what she needs right now. It will be so good for her.

So tired tonight, I will sleep well. Want the days to pass quickly so I can get to Friday. Big smile on my face tonight.

I sat on my bench with a smuggish look on my face. I had just had a great day. I was with people all day and it went by quickly. I text Alexander and daydreamed about meeting him. I played with the children and cooked their dinner and bathed them and they went to bed at a reasonable hour. All of which were great.

I enjoyed today.

Me and Nicky spent the whole day chatting. I told her all about Alexander and how we were planning on meeting up. I was so excited about this. It feels weird to have texts and pictures of him on my phone and yet I don't know what he looks like face to face.

We spoke about her relationship with her man and how she was fairly happy with everything. She is lucky to have that and she is lucky he helps out so much with the children. I hope to have that one day, but not for a while.

After I had analysed the day and how it was such a good feeling to not sit here and feel miserable again, I began to think about Marc and Sue. Their unhappiness and uncertainties were actually bringing me pleasure and I felt a little bad about it. I had caused their troubles and got dragged into it when I really could have done without it. It hadn't bothered me too much but not feeling guilty was a little unsettling for me. I stressed the words a little.

I had been angry that he had lied to her about the reason why I had stayed. I hadn't really expected him to do anything but tell a load of lies, so why I didn't steel myself for the story I didn't know. I blew smoke at the dark window pane and thought about what I had suggested.

I had spoken to Marc earlier on today and we discussed the way to put things right between the three way relationship. It amazes me how he can speak to me as if this is a normal, mutual split and there is nothing going on every time. He must convince himself that there are two different lives for him to lead and they never mingle even though they do so considerably.

I can hear in his voice each time that he has pushed the fact that we are having an affair to the back of his mind. I know it is not much and it is not too regular but we are still having an affair. I laughed at myself for being able to say that I was having an affair with my own husband. How pathetic it sounded.

I jumped down off the bench and sat on the settee in the living room. The voices inside my head having their conversation and the speech on the TV were mingling too much and I turned it off to calm the noise.

I had suggested to Marc that Sue and I meet. To me it seems the thing to do. She needs to understand that I am not after stealing him back. I do not want to live with that man again under any circumstances and she needs that reassurance, so he says. The other reasons are what I outlined before. She is the other maternal figure in my children's lives at the moment. I am still in effect leaving them with a stranger and I do not feel it is fair of them to continue letting me do so. She should be there to support me in getting Marc to see his children, not keep dragging him away from them. Maybe if I can make her see that they are so unsettled and missing him she would help. She seems to adore my children which is one thing I do like about her. I never have to worry too much when they are with her. I know they will be happy and as much as that knowledge hurts, it also reassures me. It's weird, but in a way, I feel more comfortable knowing they are going to be looked after by her than I do when he takes them on his own. They come back happier and more excited when they have been with her. I screwed my face up as I listened to those thoughts. How dare she have any redeeming features?

I then leant back harder against the cushion and realised that this would never happen. It is way too weird for one thing and for another, Marc would not want it, as there is always the possibility of me telling her we are still sleeping together. I also realised that I had to bear in mind the fact that he is probably telling her something totally different about having the children. There is no reason why he would not be saying to her that I was not letting him have the children. He could say anything like that. She wants them tonight. She won't let me see them. She is taking them out. Anything at all. She would have no reason to doubt him and probably thinks I am being so mean to him over them.

I could feel the anger rising and I fought it back down. I was not going to have my lovely day ruined. Not by the two of them again.

I switched off the lights and stood hovering in the darkness for a while. I breathed in the silence and the calm. I had actually come quite far when I looked back on things. I would never have been able to stand here enjoying the dark silence and the empty room would have made my skin crawl previously. There were no faceless creatures at the bottom of the stairs and there were no flying claws of depression either. Okay things were not perfect. I was still down but things were better.

With another good part of today over I climbed into bed. I pulled the duvet up close around me and cuddled my upside down girl tightly, feeling her warmth with gratitude.

"And the curtains are always shut," I whispered to myself smiling.

Oh how I love these good days!

5th November

Well after a slow weekend came a busy start to the week. I made arrangements to meet Lee today. We had lunch at the harvester in Stanway. It was lovely. We sat there for ages just chatting. He really makes me laugh. He is fun to be with and I enjoy my time with him.

The problem is I am meeting Alexander tomorrow night and I feel quite bad about it. I am really looking forward to meeting Alex and have butterflies in my stomach every time I think about it. He has become a good text friend and if we don't hit it off, then I have lost that. I don't want to have that taken away from me at all. I think about him all the time. The problem is he is so far away. Lee is round the corner. In time when I am having a lonely night in, I would be able to call him and he would probably pop over. That's what I wanted. But he is still not the type I am used to and it isn't quite right between us. God I'm confused. Will have to wait for tomorrow.

Sat and chatted to mum tonight and packed bag for tomorrow to take along to work. Really tired still and don't want to get up in the morning. I am becoming quite lazy.

The children were very settled this week. I think it is where they didn't go to Marc's this weekend. It's amazing how much that affects them. They are much happier in some ways. In others they are so upset. Fiona seems more concerned than ever with the fact that when daddy is not here, he is spending time with Sue and she is getting so jealous. I can see it in her face. She screws her nose up when she says the name Sue. She purses her lips and frowns. It's quite funny to see.

Pheobe is fine. She does not care whether she is with him or not. She is quite chilled out by the fact that he hardly comes home, though she does care because she refuses to talk to him. Upset Pheobe and you just get the silent treatment!

Seb is just Seb. He is not that bothered. He takes it or leaves it. Doesn't really seem to care.

Marc came round tonight and was very on edge about being here. We kissed and hugged in the kitchen and he told me he had said to Sue that he would be round his mums watching fireworks. Another lie that will come out eventually. He will never learn. He decided to go back to London instead of staying at his mums. So he left at 9, though he did put the children to bed first. That was really nice to see.

Not quite sure how I feel about him. I ended up kissing him and I'm not sure whether it was me or him that started it. It didn't bother me as much when he left. It used to. Things are so different now.

Was angry with him too though. He has already backed out of the next 2 Fridays, not having the children on either, and he didn't have them the last 2. It's really bugging me that he is always saying no to them and he gets away with it. I can't make him see it though, no matter how much I try.

Lee makes me see things in a different light. This was only our second time going out together and he made me feel as if I had known him for ages. He would be a really good friend if nothing else. I enjoyed my time with him today and in a way I didn't want it to end. I was happy.

I lay in bed thinking things over. It made a change to analyse the day in my bedroom rather than at the kitchen sink. I laid there looking at the ceiling, listening to Pheobe's deep breathing beside me and watching the light from the lamppost outside move with the wind. It seemed so calming.

I was nervous about meeting Alex. If I didn't like him I would lose a text friend and if I did I would have a decision to make. I couldn't have both Lee and Alex as I am not like that. My thoughts turned to Lee at that point and I smiled. See, he made me smile.

I sighed a huge sigh and turned over. Pheobe screwed up her face as if I disturbed her and I watched her rub her nose and tut her lips, ending with them pursing and her eyes screwed up tight. I watched her chest rise and fall to her breathing pattern and I wondered whether she would face all these decisions and all the heartache through her life.

I turned back over again and faced the door. I could see mums bedroom light was still on. It came under the door opposite and into my room, lighting up the bottom of the wardrobe. She was doing her crosswords before sleeping. I wondered how she was really feeling about all this. Was she ok with all the extra pressure on her? Was she ok with looking after the children? After all, she was supposed to be building her life down here not helping me out so much. I sighed as I worried about her and the feeling of guilt dropped in.

I felt so bad that I had to lean on her as much as I did. She had said so many times that she didn't mind and that she was happy to help but I still felt bad. I looked back at Pheobe. I would do the same for her and my other two. As a mum you drop everything to go to their aid, don't you? That was what my mum was doing for me. That didn't work either - still felt guilty. I decided not to think about it anymore. There was no point I couldn't change that. I huffed as I realised that was added to a huge list of things that I couldn't change.

Marc was the major one. He wasn't coming again. He couldn't come for one reason or another, both involving Sue, for the next two Fridays. I was supposed to be ok with that. I was supposed to say, oh well I understand. But I didn't. It had made me angry. Again.

I turned over and faced Pheobe again. The hurt kicked in as I thought of Marc out there enjoying himself and not wanting to spend a whole weekend with them. I looked at her sleeping and tears of anger stung my eyes.

I turned over again and just as before the guilt of my mum hit me as I looked at the light coming through. No way to turn. Which feeling was I supposed to face? Which feeling was I supposed to try and deal with? Neither.

I turned over onto my back and faced the ceiling. I stared at it intensely. I had done that before always expecting the answers to all my problems to be written up there. I continued staring upwards so I didn't have to face either direction. I felt a warm tear fall slowly down the side of my face and onto the pillow. There they were again. Those tears of pain and sorrow and also confusion. There they were again. Falling softly again. I closed my eyes as they fell and waited for sleep to relieve me.

6th November

I stood in the shopping centre almost shaking when I got Alex's call. He was trying to find where I was and my heart was beating so fast I had to sit down. I saw him walking towards me and this big smile crept across my face. He was lovely. We had a meal and then drove to the local shopping centre for a drink in the bar at the top. We snuggled on the sofa and I felt so happy to be there. We chatted about everything and nothing. We watched the football game and didn't leave there until quite late. Sitting in his car when we got back to where we had left mine, we kissed and hugged. I was sorry the evening ended.

I drove home, tired but happy and was relieved that it had gone so well. At least, I knew that even if he didn't want to see me again in that way, I had a good friend.

The feeling was that teenage feeling. The stomach turning over, the heart beating fast and the slight feeling of nausea. I looked around the shopping centre waiting for him to appear. He was on the phone. I could hear his voice but I wanted it to be attached to a face. I wanted to finally see this person in front of me. I waited for what seemed like ages and then all of a sudden, there he was.

We ate dinner, we chatted about anything and everything. We sat just smiling at each other. We watched the football and watched the people around us too. We laughed and joked and had a good time. We kissed in the car at the end of the evening.

I drove home with this huge smile on my face. I was trying to picture it now. I would have looked like the Cheshire cat if anyone had been able to see me. I arrived home without knowing how I had got there. One of those journeys.

I sat on my bench. Mum had listened to my account of the evening. She was in bed now. I had gone up but had sneaked back down. I was enjoying my cigarette at the sink again, watching the wisps of smoke curl their way to the ceiling. I took in the peace and quiet. I watched the wind blow the bushes outside and let the cold tiles send the shiver down my back as I had done so many times before.

I thought about Alex and then about Lee. I had been pleased that I liked Alex. Relieved even. It was nice to know that the man behind the texts that had made me smile for the last few weeks was as nice as his pictures. I felt bad though. I had seen him tonight when I had just started seeing Lee. There was nothing going on between either of them though was there.

I decided to let life decide. Life has this way of sorting things out for you. If I was meant to see Alex again, I would. If I was meant to be with Lee instead, I would be. Time will tell.

I blew the smoke up to the ceiling making it mingle with the curling wisp. I watched it travel freely. I looked out of the window and sighed. Not a fed up sigh, an almost happy sigh. Almost happy. That was the closest I had been to happy in a long while. I was almost there.

7th November

Talked about my date with Alex to Marie. She is so happy for me. She has been there for me through this whole mess and has listened to me moan and groan. She has supported me and I am pleased to have her as a friend. I know I can tell her anything. She never judges, just listens.

Worked through the day, thinking about the men I had in my life. There were pros and cons for both of them and I confused myself going round and round. *What do I do?*

Became tired and irritable tonight. Was fed up with everything and just wanted to climb into bed and sleep. I became angry with Marc. He had ignored us all night. He always did when he was with her. She always took over his whole evening and his phone call to the children is always so short. He said that she has told him he isn't allowed to talk to me anymore either. I have this feeling she hates me. He says she sees me as a threat and she is not happy. Oh well. She needs to learn the truth about her relationship and I think if I was in her shoes I would be meeting the ex to find out. They usually love to tell the truth to the other woman. I'm no different.

I sent a few choice texts to Marc. Threatened to tell her the truth about us and everything else if he didn't have the children one of the next Fridays. He didn't respond. I could tell his phone was off but I still text and said I would contact her in the next couple of weeks. If I can't have a life, *why the hell should he?*

I realised tonight that it didn't actually matter whether I was with Lee or Alex. The reason? Because whoever I was with I wouldn't have any time for because Marc would never have the children. What would be the point in starting something with either of them? I would only be able to meet up with them when Marc let me. It is amazing how when he was here with me, he controlled my life and now that he has left he is still controlling it. How does that work?

The bitterness and anger set in again. The majority of it, I admit, was because I am alone tonight. I hated it when mum went home. I felt a little lost again. Having her with me takes away the loneliness and the lost feeling. When she goes it bites back hard.

I could feel the anger whirling around in my stomach. It takes over your whole body until you are consumed by its power and overwhelmed with the need to release it. The trouble is I had no way of releasing it. There is nothing I can do.

I sent him a couple of text messages. Just said I was not happy and was angry with him. I also told him that I was not going to sit back and let him have his life if he wouldn't let me have mine. A life for a life.

I never got a response and that made it worse. The release of anger hadn't happened and all I could do was wander around the house in the hope that the constant movement would ease the feeling. I walked in and out of the kitchen. I kept the TV off so the noise didn't disturb the children. I walked in and out of the study.

I smoked a cigarette and thought about a glass of vodka. No, I hadn't done that for ages so I was not going to do that now. I sat on the bench and then got off. I sent him another text even though I knew it wasn't going to be received and responded to.

I hated the frustration that these moods caused. The feeling of helplessness. Nothing I could do to change it. Nothing I could do to ease it. I sighed and held my head in my hands. I pushed my hair behind my ears and turned round so I was leaning against the kitchen cupboard. I threw my cigarette into the washing up bowl and then just slid down onto the floor. I sat there with my knees up against my chest trying to squeeze away the anger.

He was out wasn't he? He was having a great time? He could see her whenever he wanted to. He could go out whenever he felt like it. He was free wasn't he? He wasn't alone and trapped inside a life that wasn't supposed to have happened.

I let out a huge breath and straightened my legs. I shrugged my shoulders at my thoughts, knowing there was absolutely nothing I could do.

Stomping up the stairs to bed, I checked on the children and sat on the bed watching them sleep. Snoring came from both Seb and Fiona's room and it made me smile a little. I looked at myself in the mirror on the landing and studied my face.

"You can't change it girl. You just have to live through it. Now go to bed and face tomorrow when it comes."

I laughed at myself for talking to myself again and did as I had been told.

11th November

I have just had a lovely weekend. I spent most of the time with Lee. We spent both Friday and Saturday evening together and had breakfast in town on Sunday morning. I am beginning to like him more and more. I feel like I can trust him. He is calming down now we are getting to know each other a little more and there is nothing to prove. He no longer seems as rough as he did to me before. He makes me laugh. He gives just enough closeness to feel like a couple but not too much so as to keep it light. He gives me compliments all the time and I am beginning to feel more confident and relaxed with him.

For a younger man there is this sense of maturity that he lets shine through every now and then, enough for me to see the serious side and then he snatches it back just in case he is showing too much. We have no expectations of each other. There is no serious side to us as a couple. I think we both know this is a bit of fun. I intend to enjoy it. I am already itching to see him again.

For the first time in ages, I feel happy. That warm feeling inside, where the stress is no longer and your insides are wearing a smile. It's not just about having someone; it is a sense of achievement. A sense of realisation. Happiness can be found in the things you have around you. My life is going well. I have a man to spend time with. I have a number of new friends. I have my children. I have my family to support and understand. I no longer feel that there is a hole. That something is missing. I feel confident that I will be ok. *What more do you need?*

I sat in my usual position looking out of the window into the garden. It was nice to see the difference in the outlook. The garden seemed much calmer. Almost still. There was hardly any wind blowing and the bushes didn't move. The scene itself was clearer. There were no smudges or blurry outlines. I could see everything that was in the garden. I don't know whether the image was different or whether I hadn't actually been looking before.

I turned to look across to the right of the window. I could see this huge patch of moonlight which shone across a large portion of the garden. It illuminated this section in its peaceful brightness and the light made me smile. Strange the things you notice.

I had been so solemn when looking out on this previously. It was my escape from facing the empty holes that seemed to be growing in my life. I could stare out of the window for hours, perched high on the bench, going off into this dreamy place that I couldn't see. I forgot everything and just seemed to stare at nothing at all. I didn't recognise what I was looking at. I didn't acknowledge any shapes and I certainly didn't focus.

Tonight was different. I could see things as if my eyes were finally open. I could see the images before me and there was no fuzziness, there were no escape routes planned and there were no daydreams.

A smile crept across my face as I slowly lowered myself to the floor.

I began clearing up after the last minute rush of demands from my babies as they stalled going to bed. I put away the hot chocolate and the cups and the toys, all in slow motion. It was all ok.

I sat and flicked through the TV channels hoping to find something but nothing grabbed my attention. At this point I would have got up and looked for an alternative method of occupying myself but tonight I could sit and be content with the silence. I lay on the settee and soaked in the silence. The once haunting, horrifying silence that had become almost a blessing that needed to be enjoyed.

I stared at the ceiling in a calm, content manner and I smiled. Lee was there in my head and I smiled.

I felt almost peaceful inside. Again in my usual style, I tried to analyse why. Was it because I had Lee? Was it because I had somebody? Was it because I finally felt that I could still find someone attracted to me?

I knew that Lee and I were not the most suited couple and I knew that this would probably be a bit of fun for a while. I didn't mind that. So then it couldn't be that I had found someone. If I knew it wouldn't last and would eventually end, it wouldn't be that that had made me so happy.

Was it because the guilt wasn't there? Was it because I was happy to be in his arms and not Marc's? Maybe. I was happy being in his arms. I felt almost safe.

Was it because I could finally see that I could move on? Yes. That definitely had a place in it. I was feeling more content as I realised that moving on and being with somebody else was possible.

I decided I was thinking about that too much. Stop analysing everything, I told myself. How many times have I said that now?

I closed my eyes and let my body relax. I had missed that feeling. That relaxed feeling. There was still a lot of stress ahead I am sure, but relaxing now was good. I let my whole body become heavy and I started to feel like I was sinking into the sofa. The cushions began to swallow me and I listened to the nothing. I concentrated on my breathing and it suddenly dawned on me that I felt normal. Normal. A strange sort of word to choose to describe myself but I knew what I meant.

I laid there for a while enjoying the quiet relaxation. As I opened my eyes again, I looked around me. I looked at my lovely house. I thought about my wonderful children. I thought about feeling like this. And I smiled.

14th November

Marc visited this evening. He came round at 6.30. He was very solemn and did not seem happy at all. I had told him about Lee and said I liked him and wanted to see him more. I explained that I would not be able to continue our affair as I was now with Lee and I was not a cheat like he was. He did not seem to want me to. I discussed the fact that this was what he wanted me to do - find someone else and move on from him. He said he was not sure that it was what he wanted anymore.

In my eyes he is feeling an attachment to me purely because she is pushing him away. She seems to want to be with her friends more than with him and I am sure that is the reason he wants more weekends off. He thinks if he is around during the weekend she will see him then. That is not always the case. He had last Friday off when he asked his mum and dad to look after the children and she was down the pub till late and didn't really see him at all. She did not even come down to see him and the children on the Sunday which he was most upset about. He is not getting what he needs from her and so is now worried about his feelings for me. I think he needs to have somebody and where I have always been there for him he feels like he is losing both of us now.

I do feel sorry for him in a way as I know what that pain feels like from when he met her but at the same time I hope he will have more sympathy about what I went through. He probably won't though. A man that selfish will never relate his feelings to others and how they have felt in the past. He is the type of man that wants everything his way.

It was very confusing for me. I had wanted him back for so long and now there is a light that I could have worked on and tried to win him back completely, I don't think I want to. I am happy with my new life. I am happy with Lee and I am happy finding myself. I don't feel as if I need him anymore.

He actually had the audacity to say he wasn't happy with me finding someone else. He said it hurt that I would be with some other guy and that he had to picture what we were up to. I would be going out with him and his hands would be touching me and he didn't feel comfortable with that. I couldn't believe it.

I had had to cope with those feelings too. I had pictured the two of them together over and over again. I had been told how Sue had made him feel so much happier. How she had made him smile more, laugh more. How he had fancied her from the moment he saw her. I had even been told stories of their sex life and what went on behind their closed doors which caused many nightmares over the nights that followed.

Why had I listened to that? Morbid curiosity? Nosiness? Wanting to? Yuk.

Now I was supposed to be concerned that he was having trouble accepting the fact I was with another man.

My problem is I think about things after the moment has passed. My brain doesn't seem to work quick enough to acknowledge what is being said at the time. So there I was once again growing angry with him that he had said these things when he was gone. I was angry with myself for this.

I sat on the bench. I wasn't sad or solemn because I was unhappy with my life as I had been previously. Alright it still wasn't the way I had planned and it still hadn't reached the point I had hoped it would, but I was more angry than anything.

The man was a joke. He was unbelievable. He had replaced me fully 10 days after we split. That's assuming he is telling the truth that nothing went on beforehand, which I don't believe and never will. And yet there he was telling me how hurt he was now I wanted to spend time with another man.

I churned the words around in my head and it didn't matter how I said them or which order I put them in; the feelings were still the same. I was amazed at the nerve. How dare he. How dare he say that to me after everything he has put me through?

I knew what it was. He doubted her. He didn't think that she was feeling the same for him as he was for her. He didn't think she wanted the relationship as serious as he wanted it. So he thought he would have me sitting on the sidelines. Keep her sweet and I can go home when it falls apart. Really?

I took a few deep breaths and tried to straighten things out. I calmed myself down and banished the feeling of understanding what he meant as I had been there. So what? That doesn't make a difference. I know it hurts. I have lived through that pain for the last 8 months. I understood but did that mean I had to understand why he was saying it.

Why was he saying it? Was he saying that he still wanted me? I knew he did as we wouldn't have slept together all those times if he didn't. Stupid question. Was he saying it to try to make me stop seeing Lee? That wouldn't happen.

I shifted my thoughts to do I really care? The answer was no. It didn't matter why he was saying it did it? I didn't actually care that he was hurting because of it. I was actually quite pleased he was feeling a tiny bit of what I had felt. I was genuinely pleased.

A little smile crept on my face for just a few seconds.

I stared out the window a while longer and then wandered into the front room. I flicked the TV channels over and settled on a programme I usually enjoyed. I couldn't focus on it though. Part of my mind was on Lee and part of it on Marc.

Oh, the confusions of life. Why can't it be simple?

17th November

I had a really good night out last night. At first it looked like I was not going anywhere. I was sitting at home. Hayley was ill and Lee had arranged to go out with his mates as I had supposed to have been.

Michelle saved the day…well the night! She was out with her mates and called to tell me rather bluntly to go and meet up with them. So I did. I was a little sheepish. I sat back and watched them all together. There was quite a big group of girls out. All bubbly and pretty and confident. The birthday girl was dancing around without a care in the world with a huge smile across her face. There was another girl that joined in too. They were so at ease with themselves and each other. I had never had that with friends.

They were all so friendly and welcomed me into their group. They chatted and drank and made me feel relaxed with them which was really nice to feel. I was asked a few questions. Michelle had obviously mentioned a few things to them about what has been going on. I didn't mind. I was willing to answer questions but was conscious about saying too much. They really made an effort to make sure I was ok and happy in their company. They were great to be around.

In O'Neill's I could see their togetherness more and I was envious. I didn't have friends like that. I wasn't like they are and will probably never be. I can't let myself go. I always watch over my shoulder. I hate the fact people can see your every move.

Still, had a great time. I met up with Lee and some of his mates afterwards. He made sure I got home ok as I was incredibly drunk by then. I felt awful and was pleased to climb into my bed at the end of the night. Feel really rough today. The heavy head, the nausea etc. A good night but not such a good day after.

Sat around tonight as I had done all day. Every move hurt my head though thankfully the nausea had stopped quickly.

The thoughts that had been churning round my head all day were beginning to irritate me. It was me thinking them and it was me that couldn't stop thinking them. Why is that?

I had enjoyed my night out. I was so happy when Michelle had asked me to come out. Well, more demanded. She has such a blunt way with words. It made me laugh and I daren't have said no.

I met up with them and was aware straight away that I needed a few drinks to catch up. I watched as they danced around in the middle of the pub. I stood with some of the other girls and just watched. They seemed so happy. They laughed and talked and danced. They didn't care who was in their way or who was watching them. None of that mattered as it shouldn't. I was envious in a way.

I remember reading as a teenager about the groups of girls that would go out together and I had always wondered what that was like. I had never had a group of friends. More just the one or two. I was not that type of person. I had never missed it before. Always had Marc and then the children. Never needed anyone else. Now, I realised I wanted that.

A few tears pricked at my eyes a couple of times throughout the evening. I drank more to try to stop them from falling but as I drank more it became increasingly harder. I watched Michelle and the others chatting away. I watched them talking even though I couldn't hear a word they were saying. They smiled regularly and laughed with each other.

I began to question what was wrong with me. Why couldn't I hold conversations like that? Why couldn't I be that happy? Why did I worry about dancing around and enjoying myself? Why did I find it so bloody hard to have a good time? Why do I care what other people see and think?

I put out my cigarette so hard on the side of my sink that it burnt my fingers. I was getting angry with myself again. I just need to accept what I am and get on with life. I don't have that ability. I am not that type of person. Get over it.

I leant against the sink and my head fell to rest on my hands. I turned my head to the side and I felt the first tear fall. I knew if I let that second one fall too, I would be sobbing again. I straightened myself up and took a deep breath. I could feel the tears hovering on the edge of my eyelids and I brushed them away quickly.

No more tears. No more.

Tension.

19th November

What a day!

Stress, tension, a little more stress and then just a tad more tension thrown in for good measure.

Marc called this morning. I was upset and angry with him at first and then after he had started talking, I ended up seeing his point of view - again - and giving in - again. God that gets me mad when I look back on it.

The problem came when speaking to mum. She gave me this long lecture about how he should have the children and how he should be pulling his weight. I know all of that, but *how do I make him? How do I make sure he comes down and sees them? If he says no, what do I say?* It doesn't matter how much I scream and shout and it doesn't matter how many times I explain the scenario from my point of view, his answer is still the same. *But what about me?*

Aaarrrggghhhh!

He can't see her during the week because she does this and that. He can't go out in the week because the social scene isn't there. He can't have them on Friday because he doesn't finish work till late, she has something planned for them, he has nowhere to take them etc etc. So I am supposed to go without a weekend out again. I am supposed to play babysitter again. I can sit indoors and have the children while he goes out and sees her.

I'm not supposed to get angry though. I'm not supposed to lose my temper. I am supposed to see it from his point of view, agree with him and then say nothing more. God the man is an arse!

Part of me wants to ruin everything. Part of me wants to destroy their bloody relationship so I don't have to listen to the crap. I don't really know why I don't do it. I have no idea. The fear of him. The fear of her. The fear they will patch it up and be ok anyway. The worry that he will have this huge mental breakdown. I don't know. I really don't know.

Wandered around the house in a daze, knowing I have been defeated and nothing I do or say will change the situation. I am gutted. Just gutted. I hate him for having this hold over me. Especially when I can't figure out what it is.

I shouldn't care but I do. Sitting here thinking for around two hours and that was the only answer that I could come up with. Pathetic.

I sat on the bench with my feet flat so my knees were high up near my chest. My hands sat between my legs and dangled there limp. That feeling of helplessness was there. What the hell can I do? What can I say? Why doesn't he want to be a father?

I shouldn't care.

I shouldn't care that I am not going out. That I haven't got a full weekend yet again. I shouldn't need it. I have the children here. They need me. I can spend time with them. I can play games and watch TV or DVD's with them. I should be content with that. Guilt. In comes the guilt. It swoops in there and takes over. I felt guilty that I wasn't content just to be with them. I wasn't happy to sit indoors. I wanted to be out. I wanted to be with Lee. I wanted to spend time away from them. I wanted the break. That was wrong. I am their mum. Guilty.

I rubbed my face with my hands and sighed. I looked up at the ceiling and tried to change my thoughts.

I shouldn't care.

I shouldn't care that he is having problems with her. I have the wish that it all blows up in his face that is true. But I think that feeling to be a natural one and any woman in my situation would feel the same I am sure. Why do I listen then? I do. I sit there and listen to his problems and how he doesn't get to see her much. He doesn't get to spend the amount of time with her as he would like to. He doesn't see her in the week and wants the Friday night to be with her. I listen so I must care. I shouldn't. I bloody shouldn't.

The guilt ebbs away and is replaced quickly by the bitterness. I am so bitter towards this man. I am his bloody babysitter. I have to be at home, putting my life on hold, while he goes out and builds his. So selfish. He doesn't want to have the children because it is too difficult. He doesn't want to miss out on whatever is happening or miss time with her.

The bitterness turns to anger as it has always done. The two emotions seem to go hand in hand and I had never realised before. I could feel myself getting quite hot and bothered by it all. It all built up.

Why can't I just call her? Just ring her and tell her he has been lying to her, he has been in my bed and he refuses to have the children because of her. Why can't I? I don't want to hurt him - really, why? I don't want to deal with the repercussions? Again - why? I don't want to hurt her maybe? No, that's not it. I don't want him to get nasty. He would I am sure.

I could feel the bottom of my back aching where I had been sitting in the same position going over and over the same thing yet again. I moved slowly, wincing at the pain. Turning the lights off and climbing the stairs, the same questions kept going through my head.

How can I make him have the children? How can I change this situation?

Lying in bed awake everything was going through my head with such force I could almost hear it whirring as it sped. I couldn't switch off. I couldn't rest and relax.

No sleep for me again.

23rd November 2007

Mum came to the rescue tonight - again! She took the children to Aunt Alice's party and then had them at hers overnight. Lee stayed over. I was really unsure as to whether this was a good idea when I thought about it too much. It was pretty amazing though.

We had watched a DVD and chilled out with a couple of glasses of wine. We snuggled up on the settee and I felt so safe and warm. I had thought that I was going to change my mind. I had thought about nothing but this, as I knew we were getting closer to this happening. I'm not sure what I was scared of. But I was scared. I was worried about everything. Being with someone else. Being naked with someone else. I wonder whether any other women have the same fears.

Still, the snuggling up close turned to kissing on the settee. It was all so slow. Not like I was used to.

I curled up in his arms afterwards and actually felt happy. There was a warm glow about me and it felt good. The guilt did try to kick in - the mind wandered for a few seconds - but the happiness and the security I felt blew that all out of the way. We were up most of the night. Not a lot of sleep.

The next morning I was a little on edge again. Lee noticed that I was not right and was great about it. He just held me and didn't pry which meant all the bad feelings just went away again. We had breakfast in bed and stayed in each others arms until he had to go to work.

The weekend was one of those that you wish would never end and here I sat now on my usual perch looking out of the window with a smile on my face. I had been so worried about the relationship developing with Lee and yet it all seemed so natural after all.

I sat there going over the thoughts and fears that I had had and they seemed so silly now. I giggled a little at some of them.

I had been worried that I would not be attractive to another man in the first place and the excitement of Lee actually wanting to be with me in any way at all was enough to cheer my days up. I had visions of him getting fed up with me as Marc had done. Brad and John too. They hadn't even got far past the first date so it was no wonder I felt the way I did. Lee had made it this far and I was pleased at that on its own.

The fears had set in more when we had been kissing the week before. His hands had begun to wander and at the back of my mind I was thinking if he doesn't leave after this, what am I going to do? I had visions of the state of my body.

I had always believed the perfect body was necessary for happiness in myself. Everyone sees faults with themselves. Everyone sees their scars and their imperfections. Everyone has a wish list of things they would change about themselves. I was no exception.

So there I was with the picture of me. The scars on my face. The scars on my back. The stretch marks I had been left with from having my babies. All of these were an issue to me and I was concerned that they would be an issue for him too. In my eyes, Marc had rejected me because of these imperfections as well as all the other reasons.

The rejection I had faced from Marc and the other two had also played a part in my fears. I believed it was going to happen again and I could see no other outcome. I thought that if I slept with Lee, he would then leave. The mental scars were eating away at my confidence and I was so scared.

At the same time I wanted it to happen. I liked Lee a lot and I felt comfortable with him. The issues were all in my head. I couldn't let them prevent me from having a relationship with him, however difficult it would be. I had talked to myself a lot about these thoughts during the last week and I had come to no conclusion. I didn't raise my concerns with Lee though. Too shy. Felt too silly.

When it happened though, it was so different. I forgot all about the fears. I forgot about what my body looked like. I forgot my thoughts and my concerns. It just happened. How it should. How it was meant to.

Tonight I was sitting here a different person to what I had been the week before. I had none of those issues anymore. I felt good about myself. The rejection from Marc had not been because of this. The issues were now a stupid memory and I was happier with myself. I was happier with my body. Yes the list of things to change about me was still long. Yes there were still the dislikes. But I realised they were just mine. They were imperfections that only I could see. Just me.

I sat back and remembered the nights of the weekend. I thought about curling up in his arms. I remembered the safe feeling, the warmth. It didn't matter how long it would last. It didn't matter if it never happened again - with Lee. I had overcome a big hurdle that I had created myself. I smiled.

I closed my eyes and pictured myself lying in his arms right now. I relaxed and felt this unfamiliar feeling. I'm not sure what it was but I felt it.

I smiled. I just smiled. On the inside as well as the outside.

26th November.

A very lazy day. Pheobe attended her introductory session at school and was fine when I left her. I am so proud of her and the way she seems to be handling it. I am expecting a few hiccups when she finally starts, but I feel more relaxed than I did before.

I hate letting her go but I am trying to be strong. It's my baby. My last child. I want her to stay with me really. I don't want her to grow up and leave me. At the same time I am looking forward to the freedom and the routine. Confusing emotional time.

This evening was awful. Seb had been sent home from school and mum went up to talk to him about why that had happened again when there was clearly nothing wrong with him. He broke down. My boy was a mess of tears. He said about how Christmas was not going to be the same without daddy. That he just wanted his dad to come home. He was reminiscing about decorating the tree with him last year. It killed me. A knife to the heart and I crumbled. I didn't cry. I text Marc and told him what had happened. He didn't bother to get back to me. So I rang and rang until he answered. Hearing his matter of fact tone - 'well I don't know where that came from, he was fine over the last couple of days' - made me hate him more. I hate him so much. He has hurt me and my babies. He doesn't even seem to care!

I feel so frustrated that there is nothing I can do. I can't make it better. I can't get him to help. I can't make the pain go away. Helpless.

I sat here on the bench crying. My usual place every night for crying. It was far enough away from the living room door for my babies not to hear me sob.

The tears fell slowly but they were so hot they stung at my skin. The red marks were there as soon as they had crept out of my eyes from the heat of them. I wiped them from my cheeks and tried desperately to stop them falling at all.

The feeling of total helplessness consumed me. The happiness I had felt just a day or two ago had been swamped by the sadness and despair of not getting through to him yet again. He had destroyed my Seb by behaving like this and the attitude he showed me more or less said he didn't care.

Christmas had been such a good time for me before now. I loved the whole family side of it. We had always decorated the tree together. Filmed it too. The sneaking around, hiding presents, preparing everything for the children. Baking the cookies for Santa and leaving them out. The excitement on their faces for at least a week before. Their little eyes wide with amazement as yet again he had come into their home and left them presents without waking them.

For Seb these memories were so painful. We had always known that Christmas was going to be hard this year but I didn't realise how hard. Marcus had told us a few weeks ago he was going to Glasgow with her over the Christmas period. He said he didn't want to be part of our dysfunctional family. He wanted to be with her instead. She had asked him to spend Christmas day with her and her family and he thought that that was the better idea. How dare she? How dare she take him away from his children? I had hoped he would listen to me and change his mind. He had ignored my tears and my pain though. Now he was ignoring the pain he was putting his children through.

I stared out of the window and thought about last Christmas. Our first Christmas in this house. I pictured us decorating the tree as we did and hiding the presents. The tears fell hotter and faster. Then I pictured my son's face this evening. The pain struck my chest like a bullet. Then I heard his matter of fact tone again and his "well I don't know where that came from" response. Does he not realise that these things will affect his children?

I looked up at the ceiling in despair. Right at that moment I hated him with a passion that blew me over. How could he do this to him? To them? To me? How does he not feel bad about it?

I let my head fall down and held it in my hands rubbing my forehead to try and relieve some of the tension. Like it would make it better. Maybe if I rubbed hard enough it would rub out the feelings too.

I sat there for hours. Just picturing my Seb's little face and the hurt that was on it. I sat there staring and went over and over what I could do to stop the pain. I searched for an answer to fill the hole that he had made in our hearts. I wanted to find a way of replacing the sadness with happiness. Bring back the excitement of Christmas for my babies and myself.

The answers were not to be found. There were none. Nothing.

Just nothing.

27th November.

Couldn't really concentrate too much at work. Marc phoned in the morning and I ended up crying my eyes out in the office. He just seems so selfish. I want him to say I'm sorry. I want him to say he will help Seb. I want him to say he will take him for a while to reassure him. No I get nothing.

Such a crap day. Went to my nephew Oscar's birthday and Marc phoned Seb. He told him that he will be having two Christmases, decorating his tree with him. *Does he think that that makes him feel better?* Seb was ok on the phone to him. I took the phone to speak to him and looked at Seb in the bathroom and he was in tears. That was it for me then. I cried my eyes out. I sat on the bed and cried. I just felt so lost. There was nothing I could do to change this and I hate feeling so helpless. Carly - Marc's cousin - was there and she helped to pick up the pieces. She listened to me moan and groan.

I confessed I had been used by him and that we had been kissing and more. She couldn't believe it. I felt bad about it afterwards but I just want people to know what I am feeling so they don't think everything is ok. It's not. Not at all. *Where do I go from here though? What do I do?*

The feelings of despair weighed me down all day and now after the drive home from the family birthday, where I had been crying again, I felt like my whole body was dragging behind me.

The sadness tinged the air everywhere I went. My sister's house brought back memories. Oscar's birthday was also the anniversary of my Nan's death. She had died on his 1st birthday. The sadness was always there though each year got better. Now today I had been sitting crying again for another loss.

It felt like I was mourning a loss. That of my husband but also that of my family. There was nothing like the run up to Christmas to remind you it was a family time and it was like everyone was pointing at you and rubbing it in your face that you were alone. I knew I had my babies and that they were my family but without him here, it would be incomplete.

I stood in the kitchen again feeling down and stressed. The family had tried to console myself and Seb. The girls had just looked a little bewildered by our red eyes and then carried on playing.

It was obviously on Seb's mind more than I had thought. Marc said to him he would have 2 Christmases. One here with me over Christmas and one with him and Sue afterwards. He thought that would make him feel better. It didn't. He still cried.

I confided in his cousin. I don't know whether that was a good idea or not but it just came out. She had shown such concern and knew I was torn apart by the thought of Christmas. It all came out. I confessed it all. I told her what he had been doing and she was surprised. I think she thought I was weak. I am.

I drove home in a bit of a daze and with all the thoughts, feelings and the words that had been said by everyone whizzing around at top speed. I tried now to remember the drive home but I couldn't. I hated doing that, it always worried me afterwards. How I don't crash when that happens I shall never know. My mind obviously wasn't on the road properly.

That familiar feeling of helplessness overwhelmed me once more. The frustration kicked in and I searched desperately for something I could do to change that feeling. I must be able to do something. I couldn't seem to accept that there was nothing I could do.

I leant back against the kitchen cupboards and threw my head back in despair. I had thought that by this time in the year all this would have been sorted and these feelings would not keep re-appearing. Last weekend I had thought that Lee would have changed the unhappy feelings in my life. He couldn't change this though could he? - Only Marc could.

I slid down the cupboards and sat on the floor. I hugged myself tightly and laid my head on my knees. I wanted to get up and go to bed as I was feeling tired, but I didn't want to face tomorrow. The pain and sorrow wasn't going to go away and each day that it hangs over you, each day that you search for answers that you cannot find, it gets worse.

I didn't want to have another tomorrow yet. I hugged myself and just sat there. I didn't cry. I didn't move. I listened to mum go to bed and watched the lights go out. I still sat there. My mind racing at top speed and my body motionless. Drained of all energy. At a low point once more. Feeling sick from the sheer drop from high at the weekend to the depth at which I sat now. That bloody rollercoaster. I wish I could blow it up.

I sat there, still, with my head facing the study door and I held on to my body tight. I let the darkness seep through my skin until I felt dark inside. I let the voices scream at me in my head. I let them tell me I was a useless mother that couldn't get through to the useless father and stop the pain my son was feeling.

I sat there. Still. Dark. Heavy. Helpless.

Power switch?

28th November

Marc phoned in the middle of a lesson. Left a message saying my mum had just had a go at him on the phone. A smile crept on my face. I was quite pleased. I want someone else to tell him what they think. I want people to say to him that they think he is being a git to the children. I don't care whether they agree with the fact that he left me. I don't care if they think that he started the relationship with Sue for good reason. I just want somebody to help me with this fight for my children.

I called him back when I had a break and listened to him going on about not being able to make Friday now and how he has to work. The rest of it just went blank. I ended up asking him to leave me alone and put the phone down. I cried in Marie's arms and felt useless again. I hate the way he can make me feel like that without really trying.

I could not get him to understand when I spoke to him again at lunchtime. He just prattled on about how my mum had said it was time to finalise it so we can both move on. He had sought legal advice and they said that he was seeing the children more than he had to. I couldn't believe I was listening to that crap. I didn't care what someone who knew nothing about what he had done, how he was behaving, what my life and the children's lives were like now etc was thinking about my children and them seeing their daddy.

Got home and decided it was time to do something about it. Time to make a change. Time to regain some power. I talked to him on the phone that evening and told him how I was annoyed and confused with the fact he still acted as if he wanted me back. He still seemed to need me. He had still slept with me those times. I got him talking about all of that. And I taped every word of it. *Now who holds the power?* What I will do with it I don't know. Whether I will use it ever I don't know. But I feel better for having it.

Feel better.

I was right. This tomorrow was as crap as the yesterday. It will continue to be so until Christmas is over I suppose. There is nothing I can do about it and there is no way of changing it. I just have to live through it.

The lost feeling followed me to work today and that is not allowed. I shouldn't let it. His voice and the words that he had said knocked me for six so much I couldn't go back to class for a while. Marie just held me and let me cry. She was great.

He spoke so horribly to me. I knew he would as soon as I had heard the first message. My mum telling him what she thought. Thank you. Someone else had stepped in. He can ignore me but he can't ignore anyone else. He hates it if he thinks people think badly of him. He hates it when there is more than one person thinking the same thing. He feels as if he has to listen then. I knew he would take it out on me. He wouldn't have fought back against my mum, so he would save the anger and frustration for me.

He did.

I heard the words....finalise things....divorce... legal advice... lose the house...seeing the children too much. Too much! Too much! Less than 24 hours a week is not too much. Lose the house - kick your children out would you! Everything he said added to all the thoughts of the past few days merged together in my head and it felt like it had just exploded.

I threw the phone on the table and cried. I sobbed into Marie's arms and couldn't control it. I felt stupid, but I couldn't control it.

Marie went and took my class and I pulled myself together in the office. I took deep breaths and thought about things logically. I needed to shift the power for myself. I needed to lose this helplessness. I needed to lose this uselessness. I needed to regain control of myself, so I felt better.

With mum gone home and the children asleep I shut myself in the study and thought of all the things that were annoying me. The lies that had been told. The lies that were being told. The threats. The not being here at Christmas. The tears my son had cried. The tears that I had cried. The constant feelings of sadness and the weight of the depression.

I needed to pick myself up somehow and I needed to feel like I had regained even a little part of the control within. To steady the see saw I was riding at the moment. Just a bit.

As I spoke to him that night about the way he had been treating me, about the way he was treating his children and all of the things I mentioned above, I held my mobile close and recorded the whole conversation. My hands were shaking. Would he realise what I was doing? Would he know there was something happening?

At the end of it, I clicked the off switch on the voice recorder and I smiled. I looked at the phone and frowned. What now? What do I do with it? I didn't know - yet. But it felt good. I had him admitting everything. He had acknowledged playing the two of us. He had acknowledged sleeping with both of us. He had acknowledged the lies. All in one phone call.

I smiled again. A tiny piece of power had been restored. It was small. It may never be used. It was still there. In my hand. Waiting. Waiting to be listened to by the right person at the right time. Whenever that may be.

I looked down at the phone and I smiled. That tiny piece of power helped a huge amount. I just smiled.

30th November

Didn't turn up for the children again. Some excuse about getting stranded because of the trains. It was end of month and there was lots happening at work. It sounds mean but I believe he had to work late but I don't believe the story about being stranded and I think he was just getting himself another night with her.

Children went to his mums and she is taking them to London in the morning. He is supposedly picking them up from there. We will see. Lee is coming over tonight. Can't wait!

I got so mad with him as yet again he couldn't make it on a Friday night. Those poor children. I thought that as it was his dad's birthday today he would be most likely to be down here with him so I thought that at least this would be one Friday when he actually turned up. Wrong again. Stupid me.

The children went off with his mum a little begrudgingly. Pheobe really didn't want to go at first but she went off with them all the same. Fiona was hurt that her daddy wouldn't be there. It hurts when this happens time and time again and I could feel the hatred surfacing.

I had felt so much better once Lee arrived. I had waited all week to see him though he makes it seem like it hasn't really bothered him. I knew he was staying the night but I couldn't settle with him in my bed. It felt weird to be sharing it again.

With him asleep I crept downstairs. I stood in the kitchen in the dark and felt as if something was wrong with me. I had been anticipating Lee's arrival and was looking forward to it. Yet I wasn't settled with him here. I sat on my bench and had a cigarette.

Looking out in the garden I began to question myself. What was my problem? As if I had the answers. I just didn't know. Couldn't begin to try to understand myself these days. I was back to feeling like a different person again. I sighed one of those huge sighs and just felt awful. Confused. Unsure. Even a little lost.

I sat upright and pulled my legs in closer. I hugged them tight and rested my chin on my knees as I had done so many times before. It was a comfort thing. I still needed comforting. Nothing else worked.

I sat there for a while just staring at my kitchen wall and thought about everything. I wondered if my children were ok. I wondered if Lee was still asleep or whether he was wondering where I was. I wondered what he was feeling at having such a strange relationship and whether he would be off soon to find another. I wondered how I would feel if he did do that. I also wondered what Marc was up too. Was he in bed with her right now? Was he sleeping soundly cuddled up close to her?

I threw my legs down and rolled my eyes to the ceiling in a huff. Again he was there in my thoughts. Can't he just go away and leave me alone? Can't I just forget him? Can't I just sleep?

I stood up and began to climb the stairs. I stood outside my room for a bit listening to the sound of Lee sleeping. He was such a heavy breather. I walked into the room and watched him for a bit. I climbed into bed beside him at the same time he turned over. I looked at him sleeping and thought about how we had curled up together. We had made love for hours and had just fallen into each others arms afterwards. It was only when he had turned over after falling asleep that I had begun to feel unsettled.

I laid my head on the pillow and closed my eyes. Stop thinking about everything so much I told myself. Have fun and stop trying to answer questions that you obviously cannot answer. I pulled myself closer to Lee and lay on his shoulder. He opened one eye, smiled and cuddled me closer.

I let the warmth and the safe feeling engulf me. You are alright girl. You are alright.

1st December

Had another lovely evening with Lee. Snuggled up on the settee until 2am. I was so happy. I feel so safe in his arms and enjoy every moment with him. I just wish there was longer for me to feel like this.

I am convinced one day I will never hear from him again. I don't know whether that is because it has happened twice before or whether it's because I think he is too young to cope with all of this. I just hope he proves me wrong.

The children seemed fine about being with Marc's mum and dad. I was very grateful to them for having them. They took them to London to see Nan and then Sue and Marcus picked them up from there. I was gutted. *Why does it hurt so much?* She is there with what used to be my family and it hurts like crazy. I plummeted down like mad. I felt low again. Walked round the corner and felt better by the time I got home. At least those down moments don't last as long as they used to. And I'm sure that if I was surer of Luke and the way we were going I wouldn't have them at all. I can never see him meeting the children/family etc. It's not something either of us would want.

Going to Aunt Alice's party tonight. Should be fun. At least I'm not stuck indoors. Dad is driving so I can have a drink as well.

Arrived home from the party quite late and waved mum and dad off. I had spent the evening texting Lee. Spoke to some of the family I hadn't seen for a while. Felt ok really. Aunt Violet gave me another speech about how I will be happier without him and that time would arrive quicker than I think. I hear the words but the whole time I am saying in my head, whatever you say. I don't believe them I suppose.

Sat up on my bench and listened to the peace and quiet. Listening to the quiet. I had been petrified of the silence before and now I love listening to it. When it is silent you can hear yourself thinking so clearly it is a little unnerving, but at the same time everything is so calm and still that it has an influence on you. My head was just making a whirring sound really. Nothing much else. It was like my brain was thinking so many things so quickly they merged together to just sound like a machine going rather than words.

I closed my eyes and let my head rest on the tiles behind me. I did feel tired. Really tired in fact. I quite liked that feeling and relished it as I didn't feel it too often. I opened my eyes and yawned. Stretched my arms in the air and my legs out to the front.

The whirring stopped and the words appeared. I heard a few. Christmas... Lee... Marc...children....Sue....Nan's flat. That wrench pulled me towards that one. That had hurt today. He said they were both there to pick up the children. She had now met all the family. Nice. It gutted me again. She had moved in on them now too. I screwed up my face in response to that remark and the image of her on Nan's settee flashed before me for a second or two.

I shrugged my shoulders and looked out of the window. Oh well. Move on love.

I slid off the bench slowly and climbed the stairs so wearily. By the time I got to the top of the stairs I could hear the whirring again. Good, no words. No noise at all would be even better though. I fell into bed and undressed while lying down. Couldn't be bothered to stand anymore. Too much effort. I pulled the covers up tight under my chin and snuggled down waiting for it to get warm. The bed smelt of Lee. That man smell.

I closed my eyes and tried to ignore the smell. It was nice in one way. A little comforting. At the same time I liked my nice, clean smelling bed. I tossed and turned for a bit and then opened my eyes with a start. Nope, can't stand it. I will have to change it. I got up and pulled the covers off as quickly as I could. I delved under the bed and pulled out the new ones. Made up the bed and dived back in it leaving everything where it had fallen on the floor.

I snuggled down again. No smell. No words. No whirring. Just sleep.

2nd December

Had a nice time last night. Lee text me a couple of times and made me feel better. He said he would have come to get me but he felt so rough. It was nice enough to hear. There would have been no way he would have found the place though and I could never have managed to direct him. I missed being with him. I wished I stayed at home but, as he was ill, I would probably not have seen him anyway.

I drank a lot and giggled with mum. The family were all supportive. My aunt's boyfriend Bernie said some really nice things to me and made me smile and want to continue the fight. I really want to try and get down there for the weekend soon. Aunt Violet knows how I'm feeling. She would probably make a good listener.

Rushed down to London after not getting up until 12.30! I wrapped presents and then got stuck in traffic because of the rain and wind. Got to little Caleb's party about 4.30. Watched the children playing and laughing. They made me smile. Half way through I went outside the gym to take Pheobe to the toilet and Seb was outside. He had been crying and looked so lost. He said he had a headache but I knew it was the feeling that I had. It felt strange. Marc was not there. It was his family and yet he couldn't be bothered to take his children to the party - Christmas shopping with Sue was far more important of course. My sister's friend Jenny was there. She was great. She made it clear that she was not happy with what Marcus had done and that made me feel better. Somebody is willing to commit to an opinion rather than sitting on the fence like so many others.

Took the children home and felt exhausted. Pheobe slept in the car on the way home and so was wide awake when we got back. She watched TV for a while and came to bed with me. Something else that needs to stop.

Sue was shopping for my children's Christmas presents. Could he not choose them himself? Why did he have to take her? That grated on me all day. Again, she was more important.

I had been fine until Seb started crying at the party. He said he had a headache but I knew he was feeling that feeling I was. A weird feeling hovered. Looking around at his family and knowing that he should have been here was so strange. It wasn't like we didn't belong there, it just felt odd.

I watched my girls running around the gym like crazy and knew they would fall asleep in the car. The thoughts of me carrying them in crossed my mind. Who do you take in first? Which one do you leave in the car? How do I move them without waking them?

I rested my elbows on my knees and my chin on my hands. I watched the people. It's amazing how you notice everyone's happiness when you are down and fed up. You watch their smiles and listen to their laughter and you question how it is fair that everybody else is happy and you are not. I watched the couples and I watched the new parents. We were like them once. Smiles. Looking lovingly at the children. All gone.

I thought back to what Jenny had said. She was disgusted with him and didn't mind saying so. It made me smile to hear it. You get so fed up with people listening to you and not commenting. They are either too scared of what you might say, too scared of what he might say if he found out or too willing to sit on the fence. Everybody has an opinion whether it is one that I would want to hear or not and yet there are so many people that pretend they don't have one. It just gets stupid.

It's also amazing how your own opinions change. I thought Jenny was mad when she took her boyfriend back after he was awful to her and yet now I totally understand. The pain becomes so unbearable that you would give anything for it to stop. When the chance is handed to you, of course you take it. The problem is that the pain might stop but the feelings don't. They are back but the ache for the truth and understanding is still there. And deep down so is the misery really.

I started to wonder what I would do if Marc suddenly said he wanted to try again. Could I? Would I? It had just begun to confuse me when I decided that as the chance would never arise; there was no point in me doing this to myself. So I stopped.

I walked around the house in a daze while Pheobe watched TV. She had gone to sleep in the car and had woken up when I moved her. The others were asleep. This behaviour really interfered with my evenings. She wouldn't go to bed by herself. She wouldn't sleep by herself. She wouldn't sleep full stop technically.

I sat beside her and she curled up on my lap. She reached up and stroked the side of my face. 'Mama good girl' she said in her best baby voice. She said that a lot. I just smiled and looked at her. She had the bluest eyes and this beautiful blond hair. Not like the others at all. I bent down and kissed her on the forehead.

'You should be in bed,' I said.

'Hmmm,' she replied with a smile.

I lay down and curled myself around her. She had her head on my thighs and my arms were wrapped round her legs.

'I love you baby girl.'

'Love you more Mama.'

I smiled and laid there watching the reflection of the TV dance in her eyes. I was mesmerised. You are missing this Marc. You stupid fool.

3rd December

It is 9.30 on a Monday morning and Marc has already called to say he may have a problem with Friday night again! He says he might have to go to Dublin on Thursday and will be late back on Friday. It's more likely that he wants to see her before she goes to Glasgow on Saturday morning. He wants to spend the time with her instead. He has the following weekend off for his works do so why can he not just do one weekend like he said he would. Turn up like a decent father does and spend some quality time with his children. He is unreal. I hate him for being such a useless daddy. Sorry children - *I made a bad choice didn't I?*

I stomped over to my usual sitting place later than I had wished to be there. I sat there, cigarette in between my fingers staring at the smoke and sighed one of those huge angry sighs where the breath you are exhaling comes out with a groan.

I had been in that mood all day and nothing I did had made it any better. I was so annoyed and fed up and stressed and let down. Again.

I couldn't believe he had phoned that early. He thought he would let me know the problem early enough in the week so I could make alternative arrangements for the children. How can he keep doing this?

I slumped my body over as if I was attempting to touch my toes and rested my head on my hands. I dragged them down my face, threw my head back and rolled my eyes to the ceiling. I rubbed the side of my forehead to try to relieve the tension that was making my head ready to explode. The skin covering those points was now so tight as if it was being stretched by everything inside my head and would have to split soon to let some of it come out.

If my life was a cartoon, that would have happened alongside the smoke and the top half of my head popping up in the air and twirling around. I giggled as I pictured the cartoon version of myself going through that and inhaled my cigarette deeply.

So, he wasn't coming again. I knew that. She was going to Glasgow on Saturday; he wanted to be with her before she went. I was expecting it. I had told mum that would be what happened. And yet I was still angry when he told me. Why?

He is off to his Christmas party next weekend. That will be hard for me and I am dreading it. I just hoped he would think of that and give me this weekend to compensate. No.

Why did I expect a little empathy and thought from a man who had never given any? Everyone does though don't they. Everyone expects others to understand what they are feeling and what they are going through and react to that. Does anyone actually do that? Does anyone take into account other peoples thoughts and feelings before they do something that will affect them? Probably not. I am probably just as guilty as anyone.

I thought about the early conversation again. I might be in Ireland. That means he will be. I might be back late in the evening. That means he will be back later than he would like to leave to pick up the children so therefore will stay in London. I bet he isn't back too late to meet up with her. I bet he has a nice Friday night out with his girlfriend. God I hate that.

I thought about my poor babies. They would not be seeing their dad for a full weekend again. They would have him for 24 hours but that would be it and then they wouldn't see him for two weeks as he has other things to do. I felt sad for them. I knew they missed him and they asked for him a lot and yet he couldn't be the father they needed or wanted. I never thought he would be like this. I never thought anything like this would ever happen to us. I didn't think he would desert them as he had done me.

Just after the point where the anger kicks in, the bitterness follows. I wanted to shout and scream at him. I wanted to talk to somebody to work off the anger. I wanted to explode so I might be left calmer. There is no point though. He wouldn't care. He would defend himself, making me angrier and then he would point out that there is nothing he can do about it. Except come down late and be with them of course. No, he couldn't possibly do that.

I rested my head against the cold tiles and the shivers ran through me. I hugged my knees in closer and switched the kettle on to build up the warmth. These days always left me so shattered. I felt completely exhausted. Anger raging through you and the stress and frustration of not being able to reduce it wears you out. I yawned and found it so difficult to open my eyes afterwards. So tired.

The problem is even if you feel this tired and worn out, when you go to bed everything starts rushing round your head again and you can't sleep. I knew I would do exactly that if I didn't relax properly first. I slid down off the bench and made a cup of tea. I hugged the cup tightly feeling the heat seep through my hands until it became unbearable.

I curled up in the chair in the conservatory, pulling my legs up so I could rest the cup on them. The heat burnt through my jeans and my top, warming my legs and stomach nicely. I stared out of the window at the dark garden and closed my eyes. I yawned again and sat there rocking in my chair. I waited for the relaxed feeling to hit me. I waited for the tension to fade. I waited for my mind to stop racing. I waited for the anger to subside. I waited.

Things get tougher - again.

4th December

Tough day at work. No real reason just lots of computer work which tends to make you tired. Journey home was not too bad though.

Fiona's Christmas show was tonight. I was the proudest mum in the church. I was beaming and when she stood up and sang in the choir of just 8 of them, I had tears pouring down my cheeks. It was partly from the thought of - that's my daughter - and partly of the thought that he should be here for her.

Pheobe had upset me before the concert had started. She had spotted her friend from nursery sitting on her daddy's shoulders and with a few tears nestling in the corners of her eyes told me and then added "my daddy's not here is he?"

It broke my heart. *Why is he not here?* We have our issues granted, but they are not supposed to get in the way of the children and the fact that as a dad he should go out of his way to be there for nights like this. The problem is work comes first.

I enjoyed watching my first nativity play with the children singing in between scenes and it amazed me at how emotional it was. I hugged Fiona so tightly when it had finished. Marc phoned later that evening from Ireland where he was on business. He hadn't even remembered it was tonight. So wrapped up in himself. I told him how hard it was but he did not seem that interested and so I left it.

Mum and I shared our feelings towards him. The major problem we have is the fact that he seems so cold hearted when it comes to the children and it is upsetting. They are picking up on it too. The anger gets greater then.

I was shattered again.

This time it wasn't the stress that was making me tired, it was the sadness. Crying makes your eyes feel so hot and tired. They were sore too. I had been sitting down here crying for the last hour. I sat in my corner of the bench in the pitch black with tears streaming down my cheeks. The reasons why I was crying were so mixed up; I couldn't really straighten them out. It was too hard to separate them and explain each one and the emotions had tangled up into a knot again. That knot had wedged itself in the middle of my chest and it made it hard to breathe and to swallow. I just felt so uncomfortable.

I sat there sniffing quietly. I didn't want to wake the children or mum and I certainly didn't want to upset them. I hadn't dared move. The darkness comforted me in a way. It gave me a shelter from them. It hid me in the tiny kitchen corner.

I sat on the floor with my back to the radiator. If anybody could see me they would just see this pathetic, weak person. That's how I feel and I torture myself with that the whole time I am like this.

It's hard enough when it is just you in pain and upset but when I see it in my babies' eyes, it all becomes unbearable.

I had looked around that hall this evening. I had looked at all the couples sitting there together chatting while they waited for the concert to begin. I had watched them arriving and taking their seats. I could see the proud looks as they searched the stage for their child. I sat alone, to the side of the stage. There was Pheobe on one side and an empty seat on the other. An empty seat - how significant?

I watched with pride as Fiona beamed on stage. She was smiling as she sang and I could hear her over all the others.

Seb was playing the role of camera man, but kept moving it so he could get a better look at her. Pheobe kept fiddling in her seat and fidgeting away. She spotted one of her friends. She had pointed her out to me. Her eyes were filled with tears as her friend's dad lifted her onto her shoulders. She looked at me and her voice was all croaky as she made her comments.

The pain shot through me at the look on her face and my eyes stung so much I couldn't stop the tears falling. I watched Fiona and the tears fell harder. I wondered if she was thinking about her daddy and the fact that he wasn't here or whether she had just accepted it.

The tears began again as I thought about it all. Pheobe's face. Fiona's proud smile. The empty seat. No one to share it with. No one to exchange proud glances with. No one to smile at.

I sat there hunched up in a ball and let my tears fall. They slowed down a little and I began to get that all cried out feeling. I just sniffed. I could picture it all so clearly.

Hearing his voice on the phone that evening had added to my sadness. He hadn't even remembered. He said I hadn't told him but I had. I had reminded him too. It seemed like nothing I told him affected him in any way. I couldn't understand how that didn't. I would feel dreadful if I had missed out on something like that. If it was the other way round I would have said no to work and made sure I was at home for it. I know it doesn't always work out that way but I would have tried. He didn't even try. He didn't even remember.

I rubbed my sticky, damp face with the bottom of my nightdress and stood up slowly. I stretched out and lifted my arms over my head. I felt weak and washed out now and so very tired. There had been that need to cry all night and it had to come out. I felt like I had got rid of some of the sadness and cried myself into a state where I could cope again.

I climbed the stairs slowly as if my legs couldn't carry me properly. They seemed so steep and there seemed so many steps when I felt like this. I fell into bed next to Pheobe and watched her breathing. Everything was in slow motion as I pulled up the covers and curled up closer to her. I breathed deeply and tried to stop the image of her little face tonight coming back into my head.

Concentrate on the pride you felt for Fiona. Concentrate on the warm, loving feeling you had as a parent I told myself. Don't think of anything else that you felt.

I kept repeating those lines over and over again. All I had to do was concentrate on the positive side of tonight to keep the negatives at bay. I had to keep them at bay long enough to go to sleep so I would forget. Concentrate. Concentrate.

5th December

Another day at work but it seemed somewhat easier. Wednesdays always do. I think it is because I know I am going home after that for the next week.

Seb's parents evening was tonight and yet again I faced it alone. It didn't bother me too much tonight. If I am honest it doesn't bother me that much when I am there. It is the thought of doing it and the build up to it that causes the ill feelings. I listened to Seb's teachers telling me what a great boy he was and how he behaves well and is polite and well mannered and again the tears bit at my eyes. I was so proud. It made me feel like I was doing a good job at being a mum after all. I know my mum has been around an awful lot and her influence will be there too, but it still made me feel like I was a capable mum. I left feeling happy and contented with what was happening in my life at the moment and content to throw all my effort into the children. If these are the rewards then I will make the extra effort.

Met Amelia after one of the meetings. She is pregnant. She said she was a little shocked but is happy. She looked blooming. I looked at her bump and wondered if I would ever do that again. I think not but I wonder if circumstances might change. She said she would get in touch soon. I hope she does.

Spoke to Marc and told him how well he had done at school and how we should be very proud. We then got into a discussion about the fact he was not having them on Friday night and I said I was never going to give up the fight for my children to see their dad for a decent amount of time and that I intended to give him a hard time every time he let them down. He got angry and couldn't see the problem with organising someone else to have them instead of him. He does not seem to understand that the children need their dad at the moment and that they should have a stable routine of seeing him when he plans to see them. I told him that I think he should do a couple of weeks down here with them doing the school routine and mornings so he understands how difficult it is. He did not seem too keen.

I get so frustrated with him at times. I just wish he could see what him not being there is doing to my babies. I just wish he would make more of an effort to see them. I wish he would move mountains for them and tell work to be mindful of the fact that he has responsibilities and that they should consider events like this which he should add to his calendar. I do appreciate that work is important but at the end of the day hearing him say he tried, instead of the 'I have a bit of a problem with Friday' sentence would be reassuring to me. Right now, I believe he puts everything else first, his work, his social life and of course that skank, and then come the children and I don't like the way that makes my babies feel.

Mum had left and the house was quiet. Everything was still. All the feelings from today had worn me out completely. I sat on my bench motionless staring out the window with my mind racing away again. It's hard enough coping with one feeling let alone loads of them.

They were all different but all powerful. They all rattled around and made so much noise my head was hurting. I rubbed my forehead at the recognition of the pain.

I was so uptight, so tense. I felt like I had been exercising for hours and hours and my body felt heavy and the aches were everywhere. The emotions ran riot through me and my head couldn't get the thoughts straight so they came out tangled up together. There were the proud thoughts of Seb and what he was achieving at school. Followed by the proud thoughts of how they were down to me in some way. There were the sad thoughts that his dad hadn't remembered and booked a day off so he could be there. There were the upsetting thoughts of last night that hadn't gone away yet. Then the anger and frustration that he didn't ensure that he was taking part in their life. Then the thoughts of Christmas.

If things were this intense now, what would they be like then?

At that thought I let out a terrified gasp and threw my head back. It was these moments when I wanted to get on the phone and act like a demented maniac at him, screaming and shouting down it until his ears hurt. It was never because I thought he would listen and try to take these things on board because that would never happen. It was more to let out some of what was inside.

There is no other way to let it out. It builds up and builds up and I feel like I will burst at any second if I don't say something. Whatever I do, the feelings are still there rising and falling like the tide. One feeling being replaced by another as if they are on a roundabout and jumping off one at a time until they are all standing on top of one another. Eventually the top of that tower reaches your mouth and they need to jump out and spill everywhere.

There is no point though, not when the person that they are aimed at isn't there. So they stay bottled up and they get heavier and heavier until I feel like I am sinking. Sinking in a hole that has no grips to hang on to and no bottom to steady me. No matter how much my brain wriggles and tries to calm them they just keep rattling.

I tried to focus on the positive and just enjoy those feelings as they don't come around too often. It didn't work. I smiled for the few seconds they crossed my head and then came the but....and the smile faded.

There was no point in trying to relax and sleep when I felt like this so there I stayed. There on my bench with my reflection for company trying to drown out the noise in my head with the silence around me. The totally impossible.

6th December.

What an eventful day today. First thing I went into Fiona's school and spoke to the head teacher. She was very understanding and concerned about the situation and how it affects Fiona. She suggested we try therapeutic art work with her. It is a way of allowing Fiona to express herself through her creativity and then discuss what is going on in the artwork she has created and hopefully then give an insight into what she is feeling and thinking. It's worth a try and I hope it helps her feel more at ease with her feelings and get them off her chest.

One of the mums at the school, Louise, came round this morning for coffee. She listened to me tell her what had been going on. She asked a few questions but was careful not to delve too deeply. She was very easy to talk to and every time somebody agrees with what I am saying it reassures me that I am doing the right thing.

This afternoon was spent at the solicitors. I have made the decision to file for divorce. I know it is going to cost me a fortune and I understand I will end up in debt because of it. I have decided that none of that matters and instead of denying the inevitable and hiding from it, I need to know where I stand with my new life and move on and start again in any way I have to. It was hard to hear how

I will probably have to sell the house and give him his percentage but why delay it. I do not want to be part of his life anymore and I certainly do not want to be his wife anymore. I need to start afresh. Starting now. I'm ready.

Amelia text me too. It was nice to hear from her so quickly. Hopefully I can catch up with her in the holidays.

This evening I had Hayley over. It was great to see her again. She is so easy going. I asked her to start reading the book I am writing and to tell me honestly what she thinks of it. She seemed to enjoy reading it and said I should continue because she wanted to know what happens at the end. That is surely a good sign.

I also heard from my Lee tonight. He was fine about not coming tomorrow. He is going to come over on Saturday after his works do. I asked him not to rush off on Sunday. I want him for as long as possible and I intend to enjoy my time with him this weekend as I know it may be the last before Christmas. Hopefully it won't be but just in case.

Today was a lot to take in in some ways. Nothing major had happened but there were little things that had been done and it seemed to be positive to me. This day had uplifted me a little. The relief at having the last few days over with was there too and I felt better.

I sat in the study tonight. I fancied a change of scenery. I sat on the chair with my feet on the seat too, hunched up like a ball. I had tried to write but it hadn't happened. I stared at the screen with the words there in front of me, willing myself to add to them, but nothing. So I gave up.

I looked out of the window into the street. It was fairly quiet outside. I pulled the chair closer to the window and looked out. The thoughts that were running through my head were much quieter tonight. It was late and dark outside and the lights from the houses were lighting the street up a fair bit.

I looked over at the houses opposite and the one next to me. I didn't want to lose this place. I wondered if the people in those houses were happy. I watched the man from the house opposite come out and get in his car. I wondered whether he was going anywhere nice or whether it was work.

I pulled away from the window. Are other people happier than me? Are there any other people that can say they are happy with their life and what they have? I looked over again at the closed doors opposite. What really goes on in their houses?

I slumped back into my chair and threw my head back so it flopped over the back of the chair. I stared at the ceiling. The thoughts of today began rattling. Why is it as soon as you recognise the silence around you, you start thinking? Even if you didn't want to think, you do.

I began to think about my Fiona. She seemed so sad all of the time. I know she was the daddy's girl. Maybe she misses him more than the others. Maybe she is too intent on understanding what has happened between me and him and it is that that causes her sadness. She is too sensitive. Too emotional. Too young to be going through this.

I stared at the ceiling some more and I could tell I was frowning. I started thinking didn't I? Stupid idea. I pulled my feet out from under me and put them on the table. I pushed forward and back, letting the chairs wheels glide on the floor. The lights from a car outside filled the room and my shadow moved across the walls and ceiling.

I thought about what the solicitor had said. How I would have to sell the house and give him his money if he wants it. That made me frown more. I thought about her saying that he would still get a fair percentage of money from it and I huffed. Why should he still get a lot when he walked away from it?

Life just seems so unfair at the moment. I know it has its good and bad times but right now the bad things won't stop turning up on my doorstep. I rocked some more on my chair pushing and pulling harder with my feet. I could feel the anger at the unfairness burn inside me and I hoisted myself to my feet with such a force that the chair rolled backwards at speed and crashed into the wall behind me leaving a black mark.

I walked into the kitchen slowly swinging my arms and stretching my legs out in front of me. I looked for something to do to remove the empty feeling hovering within me. Nothing leapt out of me so I just lit a cigarette instead. I inhaled deeply and closed my eyes. The tears welled up so I squeezed them shut harder. What was I going to cry for? Today was an ok day.

I let out a huge sigh and rubbed my face with my hands. I just wanted to scream and shout and yet I had nothing to say. Nothing that hadn't been heard before.

I leant over the bench almost laying on it. I had to remember the positive things in life. I had my health. I had my children. These things mean the world to me, so why are they just not quite enough?

8th December

Had a rough day today.

I had felt a little fed up when the morning had gone by and the children still were not with Marc. He had gone into town late. So much for missing his children and getting away early. He had asked on the phone if I was still going down to London on Boxing Day. This Christmas thing is doing my head in right now. It is hard enough to cope with without him trying to ruin the little things I had planned. He wants me to cancel. I booked the dinner because I wanted to go. *Why would I cancel?* He was not supposed to have been going anyway, he had changed his plans and now was expecting me to change mine to suit his. I phoned his Aunt Sally and explained his views. She said they were not supposed to have been going as they were away for Christmas, he had told her that when she asked about booking his dinner. She said she had invited me because they had wanted me to be there and I had more right to be there than she did - Aunt Sally had not even invited Sue there, he had informed her Sue was coming - which made me feel so much better. I feel bad that there is tension within the family but I am not missing out just because of him. I think he has taken enough away from me without taking Boxing Day away. Just because Sue wants to see the children that evening. Just because he wants to show off his new girlfriend. I'm not changing my mind for her or him. They can shove that, I am still going.

I mentioned it to his sister Lucy when she came to collect the children. She said you have to do what you have got to do. I took that as she was on his side and that I was not welcome there. That hurt a lot too. *How come I am being punished like this?* I was upset but it didn't last too long.

The afternoon saw him pick Seb up after he had been at my mum's. Seb sat in the study while we talked again going round and round in circles. I told him how I was fed up with the lies and that I was giving up on him. I was not going to nag him about seeing the children anymore. I was going to sit back and let him decide when he will see them. He said it would be better that way and that we had been more concerned with our social life than the children. Bloody cheek. He had been.

Lee said he wasn't coming over which really got me down. It was the only bit of the weekend I was truly looking forward to. Still never mind. I am not really expecting anything else from him now as I think he has made his feelings pretty clear over the last few days. Best to forget it instead of being hurt again.

Lazed the evening away and enjoyed the peace. It's nice having some time to myself. I am beginning to appreciate it. Shame it will soon end.

Each day is getting longer and longer because of the weight I am dragging along with me. I seem to be having the same conversations day in and day out and nothing is getting any easier because of them.

I feel completely listless. I didn't want to do anything. I had a Saturday night free and I was content with sitting indoors doing nothing. I felt so tired all of the time. I haven't been able to sleep. I haven't been able to eat. All I have thought about is what Marc is doing or isn't doing and of course Christmas, which is hanging over me waiting to crash down on me smothering the little bit of life I have left. It's hard to describe this dragged down feeling. I picture the ghost in the Scrooge film. The one with all the chains, heavy metal balls and locks. The one that is yanked down to hell to serve his punishment. I laughed at this image. But that is how I felt.

I stared at the floor from my hunched up position on the settee. I felt the tears prick at my eyes and the familiar burn of them as they boiled under my eyelids. I sighed deeply within though no sound came out. I was just so low. I felt so run down.

I looked up at the blank television screen before me and there she stood again just in front of me. Sue. I just stared at her.

'Why are you doing this?' I whispered to her.

What was she doing? Why was I blaming her here? I frowned but continued to stare. She was the one that made him stay away. She was the one that plans the time they spend together so he cannot see the children. She was the one who asked him to be with her this Christmas and have his time with the children later so she could be there too. Most of all she was the one who held some sort of power over him making it impossible for him to say no to her, to be away from her, to live or breathe without her. I shook my head. She must be really amazing for her to have had that affect on him. What made her so enchanting? Her sparkling eyes, her sweet Scottish accent, her feisty ways, her bedroom antics? With that last addition to the question I shivered with disgust. I did not need to think about that right now. Weirdly though, I needed an answer to my first question at the same time, I needed to know and understand.

I closed my eyes and willed her to be gone when I opened them. Peeking out of one eye I realised my will was not strong enough as she still stood there, staring straight back at me wearing this smug smile. I screwed up my face at her. She just stood there, in the darkness, like she used to do at the beginning of all this. In some ways I felt like I was back at the beginning again and that all the fight and the positive bits that had happened over the last few months had just been a waste of time.

I looked around the room, ignoring her. I pictured the Christmas decorations and the Christmas tree in the corner. How can I have those up this year? I didn't want to celebrate Christmas. The time for families when mine was broken.

Marc came into my thoughts, "we have concentrated too much on our social lives." We have. We. How dare he? I haven't had a social life to speak of really. He is the one with the new life. He is the one going out and about with his new love and his new friends enjoying himself. I threw my legs down jolting myself. I hoped it would disturb my train of thought but it didn't really.

I wandered into the kitchen. Everywhere was nice and quiet. I enjoyed my time alone. I lit a cigarette and wandered upstairs. Something I don't normally do but as the children were not here…. My children. There they were in the forefront of my mind. An image of them playing happily with their daddy and his skank appeared immediately afterwards. "Yuk!" I said out loud and then giggled. I walked into the bathroom and started the bath running. A hot bath. Something I never get the time for with the children around.

I watched the water flowing with a glaze over my eyes. I had a habit of staring into space lately. An escape from reality. I was mesmerised by the way the water ran out of the taps. It was so free. Sounds so silly I know.

I looked around the bathroom spotting all the things that were out of place. I couldn't be bothered to put them away.

Yet again, Christmas came into my thoughts. Why is it the one thing that you don't want to think about always materialises? His Aunt Sally had made me feel so much better today when she said I was welcome more than the skank was. I feel like she is the only one on my side.

All I want is a little slice of normality. That's all. Christmas has changed so much over the last few years. Losing Nan was the main reason. There used to be so many of us crammed into one small room at Christmas. The noise would be amazing and the mess even more so. Nan and Grandad had all of us over to open the presents. A big family get together. The Christmas after she died just wasn't the same. Grandad tried hard. It just wasn't right. And then when Grandad died there was nothing but a huge hole. Christmas changed again when we moved down here. Just us. Family exchanging presents before the day. Not the same. It was nice to have just us and we had a good time overall. And now again it has changed. Just me and the children and mum and dad. No Marc. I have lost someone each year.

All I want is some stability again. Some normality to life. The ones I love around me like I used to have. I became aware that I was crying quite heavily now. The tears were falling as free as the water. I went downstairs and poured myself a vodka. Didn't drink it though. I hated these feelings. Why won't they just go away and leave me alone?

I slumped into the chair in the conservatory. The black night filled the house as well as the garden and the faceless creatures were clawing at the glass to get in. They were back but at least they were outside. I cradled my head in my hands as I played with the cigarette stub between my fingers. I looked up at the sky and looked at the stars shining.

I huffed and stood up. I would have this bath and then go to bed. Locked the doors and slowly climbed the mountain of a staircase. Everything I did was in slow motion. Everything I thought was at a fast pace. I wanted the noise to stop. I wanted the images to stop flying around in front of me. I wanted the sadness to end. I wanted the weight to lift. I wanted to feel better. Please.

9th December

Lee did come over last night. I met him in town gone midnight and I was pleased to meet his mate from work. He then stayed with me until the early afternoon which was lovely. I felt much better after that.

Marc came round this evening. He had come to help the children with the tree. He suggested it so I took him up on his offer. I watched them doing it. I listened to him moaning about everything while he was doing it. He was in a bad mood anyway with Sue and the lack of communication while she was away. He hates being without her and turns into this pathetic boy who just can't cope. It was annoying.

He snapped at Seb so many times it was unbelievable. He moaned that they were not helping and yet he was not engaging them. He didn't speak to them. He kept drinking alcohol and going on and on that she hadn't rang or text him. Watching him drove me mad but it also gave me that feeling where I knew there was no way I could ever have him back in the house. He would drive me nuts and when he behaves how he used to; I wonder how I put up with him for so long. I'm quite amazed at myself really.

I was actually pleased when he left me to finish the tree. He had said he would stay at his mums to make up for not seeing the children Friday again but that didn't happen did it? Not that I was surprised.

He walked out of the door and Pheobe threw a number of tantrums. She screamed and cried. All I had to do to calm her down was hold her. I held her so tightly and she squeezed me back even tighter. She laid her head on my shoulder and stayed there for about 15 minutes. After that she was fine.

He phoned me again at 10.15pm. He was going on and on about Sue again. I didn't want to hear it. I had just watched my children get upset that their dad had walked out the door and would not be coming back for what seems like ages to them. I didn't care he was upset. I didn't care that he was struggling with his need for her. I just didn't care.

I wish she would just text him and put us all out of our misery. Does she realise what a mess he becomes without her? He is seeing her all week and yet he cannot manage a night without her. I just wanted to scream at him. In actual fact I had done quite a few times.

It's amazing how your feelings change so quickly. Last night I was so down and depressed. Then I was happy because I had Lee. I was happy this morning too because I had Lee. Then came the anger with Marc. I was angry that he had been so snappy with the children this evening. Now I was frustrated that she had been the reason behind another difficult time with him.

All those feelings inside 24 hours. No wonder I felt so sick.

I sat on my bench trying to fight the urge to have another cigarette. The stress from having him here was to blame. Listening to him going on and on.... ' she hasn't text me..... she hasn't rang me.....she is having such a good time without me......she doesn't need me......she has just forgotten all about me.......she clearly doesn't want me..' Aaaarrrggghhh!!! I nearly phoned her to tell her to call him myself.

Watching him was even worse. Snapping at Seb and making him cry. Shouting so much that the girls became really upset. I didn't want the stupid tree up in the first place and I found myself tearing it down and redoing it when he left. The children enjoyed decorating it with me though. They said so.

Holding Pheobe was hard. I knew she was hurting over everything. She didn't understand the shouting and screaming. She didn't understand why her daddy was being so horrible. She didn't understand why things were so tense. They pick up on everything and I felt so guilty that I had contributed to her distress. Only a little from shouting at him. It was his fault mainly but I was the one feeling guilty. I rolled my eyes at myself.

I got off the bench and walked over to the kitchen door. I peeked round it so I could just see the Christmas tree. The lights twinkled and it looked so nice standing there. I used to be so proud of my tree. I loved it. Now, it just broke my heart. I turned away and went back into the kitchen.

How can he be without his children at Christmas? How can he not be there to watch them open their presents?

"Stop thinking about it!" I shouted at myself.

Excellent. Now I was angry at myself.

I opened the cupboard door and pulled out the cigarettes. I couldn't hold off much longer. I planted myself on the bench and inhaled the smoke. I pulled my feet up and hugged my knees, burying my face between them. There I sat. Forcing the thoughts away. Fighting the sadness. Controlling the anger. Calming the stress. Hiding from the Christmas tree.

There I sat. Wanting to scream. Wanting to shout. Wanting to kick up a fuss. Wanting to explode.

There I sat. Waiting for tiredness to creep up on me and end yet another awful day. I just sat and waited.

11th December

Came home from work early tonight. Everything was calm. Listened to Fiona read and then did a spelling test with her. 120 out of 126. She did so well.

Towards the end she burst into tears. No trigger. No reason. She kept saying nothing when asked what was wrong. Then she whimpered 'I miss daddy.' My heart twisted. I could feel the knots in it forming. I managed to calm her down and then when she had stopped crying I asked if she wanted to phone daddy. I phoned and it went straight to voicemail. I hung up and dialled again. 5 times she watched me call and then I let her leave a message. Amazingly enough he phoned her straight back. Apparently the phone was on silent. *He just happened to notice the voicemail then did he?*

She spoke to him briefly. He didn't really know what to say. He didn't know what to ask her or how to make her feel better.

I asked if Sue was with him tonight. She was. That's why he didn't answer the calls then, because she won't allow him too. It's ok to bug me when she isn't giving him the attention he needs but as soon as she is there he doesn't need us. He doesn't call or answer my calls.

When I put the children to bed it was Seb's turn to cry. He got upset about the way his daddy behaved when he was putting the tree up with them. He was worried about his operation he supposedly has to have. He was worried that he was drinking when he was not supposed to. My poor babies. I text him and told him he had screwed his children up. No response.

It makes me so angry that he has the nerve to call and moan about his life to me and then when I need him for them he just isn't there. I don't know how to help my children anymore than he does really but he should at least try. Not if Sue is around though clearly. I have become so bitter and angry now and these times make it even harder.

I can't wait for him to receive the letter from my solicitor then he might realise just how angry he has made me. I can't wait for his relationship to break down. I can't wait for him to have no-one. I don't intend to be there for him. I will treat him as he treats his children. As nothing special.

The children were finally settled down for the night. I had already been up and down the stairs to check on them so many times my legs ached from the journey. I hated it when any one of them was so upset. It is ridiculously hard to watch your child crying and there isn't anything you can do or say to make it better. As a parent you are supposed to make all their worries and pain disappear and I couldn't do that. I tried, but I just couldn't.

The thought of Fiona's face and the tears that ran down it made me want to cry again. My eyes were red enough as it was. I walked back up the stairs to check on them yet again. I crept into each of their rooms and watched their chests rise and fall slowly as they breathed deeply. Pheobe was doing her usual tossing and turning and her mouth kept moving as if she was about to say something. I smiled. Seb was snoring. He was laid sprawled out across his bed with the covers entwined around his legs and back. It looked quite uncomfortable and I shook my head as I wondered how he could possibly sleep like that.

I paused for a while outside Fiona's room. I could hear her breathing from outside so I knew she was ok. I took a step forward and glanced round the door. She was the one that showed her pain. She was the one that made the days so hard as I knew she was suffering. I walked in a little further. She was lying with her head on her hands curled up on her side. She looked like a little angel lying there so still. She was a little angel.

Tears pricked at my eyes. I walked over to the side of her bed and knelt down. I laid my head on her mattress and just watched her. I felt the warm trickle of a few tears fall onto the sheets and I sat up again pulling back, trying not to sob.

She had been so hurt today and it came from nowhere. She was fine one minute and then she was in tears. I heard her croaky little voice saying 'I miss daddy' in my head and the tears fell faster. I felt so helpless. I hated the way she was feeling and I just wanted to make it right again. I wanted her to be happy and to smile and giggle at everything like she used to.

I stood up slowly and wrapped my arms around myself as I walked back down to the empty kitchen. The clock ticked so loudly. The TV was off. Everywhere was dark. I hugged the cup of tea which I had made earlier and I curled up on my bench at the window. I hung my head as I thought of my little girl. The tears stopped and I just stared into my cup motionless.

On the realisation that my tea was now cold, I snapped out of my thinking mode. Enough of that. I took a deep breath and sat back against the tiles, the coldness of them reaching my skin through my clothes.

His reaction on the phone came to my mind. He hadn't known what to say. He was just quiet on the phone, listening to her crying. He was pathetic. How could he not be hurting when he hears things like that?

I could feel this burning sensation at the pit of my stomach and I looked down towards it. There was the anger bubbling away under my skin. It was trying to grab my attention and take over the sadness. The constant war my emotions have inside me to try and be the one that gets to take control of me.

He hadn't picked up that phone at first. He had ignored my calls. Sue was there and she doesn't want him talking to me. Not when she is with him. I can understand that as I feel the same. This was his daughter though. He should at least pick up the phone to see why I am calling shouldn't he?

I remembered Fiona's little face when I had said 5 times it was the answer phone. She had become more and more agitated every time I said it. Her voice when she left him a message was broken and weak. She could hardly speak through her tears. She misses him so much. He didn't help her though. He couldn't help her.

The anger really kicked in now and I became frustrated that yet again there was no way to let this out of me. It would be locked in now for the rest of the night, stopping me relaxing and stopping me sleeping. I let out a huge sigh again.

The conversation started in my head. You are there for him too much. When Sue doesn't want to be with him. When she isn't there. When she has upset him. Who picks up the phone and listens? You do. When you need him. When your children need him. When you need some help with something and she is there with him, who ignores your calls? He does.

I jumped down from the bench. I knew all of this and yet I still had the urge to keep telling myself how I was being treated. I lit a cigarette and turned the radio on hoping that the songs would drown out the conversation in my head. It did. It stopped.

I sat back and tried to calm the fire of anger down. It just burnt brighter and became stronger. I stood in the kitchen and sung along to the music. I would be here for a while. Angry. Frustrated. Stressed. Sad. Mixed up and confused with no way of helping myself.

And singing of course. Singing.

13th December

Had a hectic day. Ignored his calls as I could not face talking to him when I was trying to Christmas shop on a budget. So fed up he hasn't given me any money towards the children's sacks. I know he pays the mortgage and his rent but that was the choice he made wasn't it. He should still contribute to his children's Christmas.

Marilyn came over tonight and we had a nice catch up. We have both been so busy lately that we haven't seemed to have the time to see each other. It was nice to chat again.

I feel so positive in a way but I am now beginning to wonder when I will crash back down again. I must do. I hope not but going by the past I will.

Enjoyed myself spending the money on the children and I am nearly finished. Received the draft letter from the solicitor today too. I need a cheque for £300 to proceed. Part of me is dreading him receiving that letter because of the fall out from it but the other part just can't wait. See what he says then.

Sue cancelled a concert with him tonight. He didn't say what for. He seemed a little fed up. She had been moaning that his whole world revolves around her and she doesn't like it. She said he should have friends to ask to take her place instead of not going. He has never had that. He never will do that. Maybe she sees what will happen to him if she leaves him - *is that why she keeps on at him to go out without her? Or is she just feeling suffocated?* Personally I hope she is wondering what he will do when she dumps him. I'm hoping that will be soon! Mean cow I am!

The anger had turned to determination almost overnight and I had spent the last two days deciding what I was going to do with my life and how I was going to sort out the problems I have in it. I hadn't really reached much of a conclusion but the divorce seemed the ideal first step. It was a hard decision to make. I argued with myself over whether it was the right time, whether I should let my mum help me pay it for now and then pay her back and whether I had actually wanted to do it. The signs are all there for wanting it naturally. I wanted an end to this chapter. He had cheated on me, he has another woman now and he is not a part of my life as he had been. In other ways though, it is like I am giving up. I have admitted defeat and that will be the piece of paper confirming I have lost my marriage and my life and that it is over. I shook my head at myself for thinking that and then shrugged. These silent conversations with myself need to stop.

I finished the washing up and stared out of the window, letting my hands drip dry in the sink. I let out a huge sigh. I imagined his face when he received the papers. I know he doesn't want a divorce, he said so. That puzzled me too. He wants to hang onto me. He still wants to be my husband, even though he doesn't want to be here with me. So strange. I shook my hands and walked away from the sink in the hope that I would leave the thoughts there too.

The house seemed even quieter than it was before. Having been so busy this evening with people in and out of it, I suppose it would. It was nice though. I sunk into my chair in the conservatory. I looked out on the peaceful night garden and smiled. I listed the things I had bought for the children in my head and listed the things that I wanted to buy. At that point I frowned as I tried to work out a way to afford to buy them those extra things.

I wondered what he was buying them. He was earning all that money now. Thousands of pounds in his last pay packet. I huffed angrily as I remembered that he hadn't given me a penny towards the Father Christmas sacks. I was the one earning little and I was the one paying for everything. I still had to find the money for the extra food treats that you buy in at Christmas. Where it was all going to come from I didn't know. Somewhere I suppose.

I leant back in the chair and erased the thought of Christmas from my head. I didn't want to think about it anymore. Out of the corner of my eye I spotted the soft glow of the twinkling fairy lights on the tree reflecting on the window. I stared at them for a few seconds and then got up and unplugged them. I said I didn't want to think about Christmas I thought as I pulled the plug.

I felt tired tonight. The positive days always left me feeling tired. The stress and the anger is what keep me awake. I have managed to shut it off for a bit and that is why tiredness seeped through me. I have figured that one out now.

The darkness looked so appealing outside. The silence it creates. Night times are always peaceful. I rocked in my chair making it bounce. I could feel my whole body begin to relax and I closed my eyes to help the feeling spread. I was settled there and comfortable. I liked it. I liked these days.

As I sat there my mind began to wander over to her. Sue had been so horrible to him. She had cancelled a concert that he had booked and paid for. She had moaned at him for making her his world. Most women would love that devotion. It is suffocating though I reminded myself. When we first got together I had been his world. Now look at me.

I wondered whether she was pushing him away for a reason. I wondered whether she was getting bored with their relationship, whether it was coming to an end. I wondered what he would do then. He wouldn't be able to cope. It would really hurt him if they split. I smiled. I smiled at the thought of her being out of his life. I smiled at the thought of him being hurt. I smiled at the thought of her breaking his heart.

I rocked and smiled and relaxed. What a good thought to end the day.

Sinking lower.

14th December

Feeling really low today. Was not too bad this morning but as the day went on and the thoughts of Christmas really sank in, I plummeted. There is that cloud hovering over me. There is no particular reason. A few things have happened that have just got me down and once you feel low you just seem to continue to do so.

First I was up for most of the night with Fiona. She was coughing like mad. She was sick three times before half 12. Then she started complaining that her ear was hurting her. I gave her medicine which helped but she was still very restless for the rest of the night. Took her to the doctors before school. He gave her antibiotics. She went into school because it was her party and she did not want to miss out.

Pheobe was really difficult as she had been disturbed by Fiona's coughing. She moaned and groaned and threw a couple of tantrums. She was not as bad as she can be but she was just hard work. Everything was a battle, from putting her coat on to getting her to nursery. She was against me the whole time.

I spent the afternoon cleaning the bathroom and Pheobe's room. It took the whole time I was without children. Only the two rooms!

I then got a text message from Nancy. It read that she felt that she couldn't talk to me anymore as it was making everyone feel uncomfortable. *Who is everyone?* She was really helpful in the beginning and now nothing. Straight away I wondered what had been said. I knew it was expected as she was really their friends through work rather than mine but she had suddenly changed. I wondered if it was something to do with him. Oh well.

I am now feeling terrible. It is only 20 past 4 and I just want to curl up in bed and ignore the rest of the day. I also want to destroy that man. On Monday I will visit the solicitor and get the ball rolling by agreeing to that letter and giving in the cheque. I wish I could do it now.

I have lost so much throughout this year and now yet another person has turned their back on me. Alright, I expected it, I knew it was coming but I could have done without it right now. It's hard enough to cope with Christmas being round the corner without having someone say they have chosen him over you like the others. Crappy timing.

The weight had returned. A few good days and now I am back to the low days. I hated them. The feeling of dragging my body around was back. The frowning was back. The wanting to cry was back. All because of Christmas which will only be two days out of the next couple of weeks but feels like it has been going on too long already.

I hauled myself onto the bench which seemed like too much effort this evening. There was no strength left in me for anything. I lit my cigarette and leant back on the tiles with my legs swinging in front of me.

I felt so low. I had sunk into a deep hole of quick sand and there was no way I had the energy to pull myself up and out of it. It was not going to happen. So I let myself sink.

Christmas. Christmas is crap. That is my decision. I used to love it and now I hated it. I wanted to curl up in the safety of my bed and get up in the New Year when it was all over. I sighed and looked up above me half expecting to see a dark rain cloud over me. I looked around the kitchen trying to avoid looking at the window. When I was in a mood like this, the window played images I didn't want to see, so if I didn't look at it, I wouldn't have to face them.

I hated him so much today. I had had a go at him when I received the text from Nancy. I had told him I hated him and the effect he has had and continues to have on my life. He had phoned me constantly after that and I had ignored it except for once when I answered and spat down the phone 'leave me alone.' He chose to ignore my request though and kept ringing and ringing.

I leant forward again and dropped my cigarette stub into the sink, still avoiding the window. I looked down at my feet and watched them swinging. I felt like a lost little girl. A little girl who had been forgotten about by almost everyone. It caused this huge hole to form inside me and I felt like so much was missing. I was missing something and yet no matter how hard I could search for it, I wouldn't find it. It was gone.

The emptiness was driving me mad. I felt like I was losing my grip. Depression maybe. I was just so low and sad. Where was my knight in shining armour to whisk me away? Where was the call from a friend to cheer me up? Where was the company I longed for? Where were the arms to hold me and make me feel better? Not here, that's for sure.

Yet another night of feeling sorry for myself. Yet another night of wondering how I will survive Christmas. Yet another night of feeling neglected. The more I thought like that, the lower I stooped. As if the weight from each one of those feelings was pushing me further and further down towards the floor.

I slid off the bench and walked through the rooms on my way to bed. I wanted to feel comfort and I hoped it would be there. I climbed the stairs. Lonely. Empty. Lost. Sad. Unloved.

I named a feeling for each one I climbed until there were no more stairs left.

I lay on the bed and stared at the clock. I laid there and waited for the comfort to take hold. I laid there and waited for me to stop thinking and start sleeping. I just laid there. Alone. Again.

16th December

Woke up crying this morning. I haven't done that in a while and it shocked me into questioning what the problem was. I'm not sure whether it is just Christmas approaching that has sent me flying downwards or whether this weekend was the route of it all. I let myself cry and it didn't last long. It never turned into the huge sobs either which is a good sign. I then picked myself up pretty quickly and had a shower to feel better.

The house seemed extra empty. I couldn't bear to have the Christmas tree lights on. The thought of it makes my heart sink. That numb feeling across your chest. I am really looking forward to it being over with.

The family get together was last night and I just couldn't bring myself to go. Mum took the children with her. I feel as if I should have gone but I couldn't get the strength up. I didn't want to play happy families exchanging Christmas gifts when I didn't believe that is what I am part of. Everything seems too hard to face. Everything seems so difficult. I can't separate the things that are a big deal from those that are not at the moment.

I realise looking back on this diary that I am not where I was at the beginning of this. I realise that I could not go back to the way things were. I realise that we were not happy but people believe that it is cut and dry and I realise that it is not.

I think of Marc and I hate him. I hate everything he is doing and everything he is not doing. At the same time, I can't help but miss him. I am split in half. Half of me is the woman that has lost the man she loves. *Or is it loved?* - I'm not quite sure. That woman is grieving for him. That woman wants to rewind and change the past. That woman wants to have him beside her again as her husband. The other half is the mother and woman who remembers what he is really like. She remembers the way he was with her children. She remembers the arguments, the stress and the pressure she was constantly living with. She knows she is better without him. And she knows that even if he was on his knees and dripping with diamonds she could never take him back and return to the misery of before. The battle within is so hard. The battle is still there all these months later. Perhaps her inner battle will never end.

The problem is I don't think I allow the first woman to grieve enough. I bottle her up and suffocate her feelings too much in order to stay strong. Then, when at my weakest she rears her ugly head and takes over. Perhaps I need to allow her to take over for a bit and work her out of my system. Perhaps I need to suffocate her harder and push her down to the depths of myself so that she can never climb back up. Whatever path I take over the next few days, weeks, months or years I need to address the feelings of the two women beneath. I need to give each the time to regain their composure and knit back together to form one. One strong person who knows where they are aiming to reach. And gets to that destination.

Today was a really long day. I had been unable to sleep properly last night and I felt it this morning. I hate waking up more tired than when I went to bed. The crying had made it worse. Maybe it would be better if I just stayed up all night when I felt like this.

Last night had been quite hard. Marc had been at his Christmas do. I was there last year and I would have been there again this year if we were still together. They were our only nights out in the year. Our night to be a couple. We had never done that enough. Looking back we never did that. It was all too complicated.

It had also been the family get together. They had all met up around my aunt's house and exchanged the gifts they had bought for each other. I couldn't go there. Too sad. Too down.

Too false. I would have been pretending I was someone I wasn't. I didn't want to do that.

I had stayed indoors and felt sorry for myself. I had cried and talked to myself about everything. I had let the pathetic woman back to the surface as I had no fight in me to suppress her.

It was hard being two women. I suppose everybody is two people. A strong one and a weak one. We all let our emotions rule the kind of person we are at one stage in our lives. I was analysing it again and maybe I was thinking too much. The last few days had seen me sink lower and lower and I felt more and more depressed as each day passed. It just seemed too hard to fight it and I had given up.

I had tried to encourage the stronger woman in me to the surface. I had tried to make her take control but it hadn't worked. Christmas and the 'lets play happy families' events it brings had been too overwhelming. It was all too much. Christmas is a time of year where everyone gets together. Work parties. Family parties. Friend parties. I didn't belong in any of them.

The lost feeling ran through me and my skin prickled with goose bumps. I shivered. I sat on the settee and stared at the TV screen. The children would be home in a few hours. They would be bouncing with excitement and showing me the presents they got last night. I smiled at the thought of their bright, happy faces. At least my depression and their daddy's absence hadn't stopped them feeling excited about it all. I had to buck up my ideas for their sakes.

At least I could cross off another day I didn't want to live through. That weekend was over and done with. Just Christmas Eve, Christmas day and Boxing Day to get through now and then it's all finished. Three days left. The waiting and the run up to them is often worse than the days themselves though. Maybe it won't be as bad as I am expecting. Maybe it won't hurt as much as I am predicting.

I curled up in a tighter ball. I hugged my knees and squeezed myself. I willed the strong woman to stop hiding. I willed the weak, pathetic woman to go away and take the sadness with her. I spoke to them both. I know I am upset but this is crazy. I need to find some strength to pull myself together. I need to find some strength or I am going to crumble with the weight of it all and I might not get back up.

I became angry with myself. I know I can't live with him again. I know I wasn't happy. I don't want him back. I don't want to go back to the life I had. So why sit and grieve for something I don't want?

I huffed.

The still of the house reminded me I was alone. Recognising I was alone reminded me I was sad. Recognising I was sad reminded me I was going to feel worse before I felt better. Realising that made everything seem even worse still. Round and round I went feeling awful like a never ending circle of emotion.

Too much thinking. Too much silence. Too much.

Overwhelmed I crawled back to bed and sank into it. I will get up when the children get here I decided. Otherwise I am not facing today. I am just not facing it. I refuse.

20th December

A strange week. Each day was spent rushing around getting things done at work and at home and also sitting in traffic. Was supposed to meet up with Alex at the shopping centre. He couldn't get there because of traffic and we ended up giving up. I then had to sit in traffic jams because there were accidents and closures all over the place and it was so difficult to drive. Wednesday the same thing happened. Left work at 3.35 but once I got to Goodmayes found out the A12 was closed due to an accident. Didn't get home until 7.30. So boring.

As for Marc he has been avoiding me. He has not called me or spoken to me lately. He has not said what time he will be picking the children up on Friday and I have a feeling that is because yet again he will not be coming. It is so difficult to stay calm. He had the weekend off last week. I was hoping for my weekend this week. Not going to happen again. All my plans gone again! Oh well I have to get used to it. This is the way it is going to be from now on.

I am getting a little stressed as I still don't have my wages in my account and I have not bought anything for my parents or my in-laws. The children's presents are not quite finished either. I have managed to get together a nice bundle of presents but it has not been easy as finances are not great and Marc has not given me anything up till now. I suppose he has spent all his money on the skank and his new friends.

I have been avoiding writing all week. I have avoided the diary and the book. At times it can be helpful. I can offload everything onto a piece of paper and it all seems better somehow. There are times when I am positive that it seems impossible to write and those where I have been so busy I haven't found the time to sit down for those few minutes. Then there are these times. Where if I write my feelings down for each individual day it would make such depressing reading and I would feel like nothing was getting any better.

Things have been hard this week. I have sat back tonight and thought about the events and the worries and the stresses and the thoughts that I have had over the last few days and realised that they are not going to go away until it is all over.

I tried to keep busy to forget the problems and the concerns. That didn't happen. Time in traffic jams, gave me time to think. Time waiting for people to meet up with, gave me time to think. Everything I tried to do gave me time to think. Waiting for these days to pass seems to take longer than anything. I long for this to be over and yet each day has had more hours added to it which makes the wait for it to be over even longer.

I sat staring out of the kitchen window churning the thoughts round and round in my head. I hadn't been crying lately and I wasn't now but I could have cried easily if I wasn't fighting the tears back. That zapped me of all my strength. I was so tired. So, so tired. All day long I felt like I wanted to go back to bed and then when night time falls I am almost too scared to go and lie down. Scared because I know that as soon as my head hits the pillow the thoughts of Christmas would rear their ugly head and then I would be wide awake.

I sat there thinking how stupid I was to believe I could get through this. I thought about laying out the goodies for Santa with the children without him beside me. I thought of watching them open their presents without him beside me. I thought about eating Christmas dinner without him at the table. I thought about my babies telling him what they got from Santa on the phone because he wasn't there with us. All these things hurt. To finish the pain I thought about sitting in the same room with her. I shouldn't be going. I wanted to change my mind and run and yet at the same time I wasn't going to back down and be forced to stay away.

His Aunt Sally has been so supportive. She knows this is going to be hard for me and when I talked to her about it I felt more positive. At least someone would be there to protect me. To help me get through it. Even that doesn't help that much though. I still have to do it. I'm going to do it. I'm going to face her. I'm going to be with my children and the family

420

that I have been part of for years. She is not stealing that from me too.

Motionless, I sat there and watched the night outside my window. I rubbed my eyes as they ached with tiredness. I just sat there.

Marc hadn't phoned me for days. I already know he won't make Friday night. I could just feel it. I wondered what the excuse would be this time. It seemed weird not hearing his voice for so long. I missed it in some way and yet in others it made me feel better. I didn't have to listen to any stories about what he had been up to while I was indoors with his children. I didn't have to hear her name. I didn't have to hear the excuses for being a rubbish father. I smiled very faintly as I realised I was quite happy without his contact.

I jumped down off the bench as if I had a purpose to move. I didn't have one obviously and as it became clear to me that I had just moved for nothing, I stood still and wondered what to do. Every action I made seemed so aimless and pointless lately. I frowned at myself for that.

I scoured the room for a meaningless job to do. I walked into the lounge and listened up the stairs for movement or noise of some sort. If the children were awake I was occupied and when I was occupied I stopped thinking. I didn't have the energy to do anything much though. I just needed to have something little to do.

The low feeling crept back over me and brought me down again and I sank into my settee. My head was hurting from everything. From the tiredness, from the thinking and from the stress. Christmas was hard financially as well as emotionally. It was all too much to deal with. The thoughts mingled and the voices in my head talked over each other which meant I couldn't straighten out the thoughts within myself. It made my head hurt more.

I yawned and my eyes watered. I sank lower into the settee and laid my head on the arm of it. I was uncomfortable but I couldn't be bothered to move. I just lay there, wishing I had the energy to climb the stairs to bed. Wishing I had the nerve to climb the stairs to bed instead of being too scared to try to sleep.

I wished. I wished began so many of my sentences lately. If only wishing came true. If only.

22nd December

Another blow to the fire this morning. I have just spoken to Marc after wondering whether he was with the children or not. He isn't with them and it is now almost midday. I can't believe he still isn't with his children and he hasn't seen them for the last two weeks and he won't be seeing them over Xmas either. This is just too depressing for me right now. It is me who coped with Pheobe's tantrum last night because she didn't want to go to her Nan and Granddad's as she wanted to see her daddy. She cried her heart out for about half an hour. She went off with them for the night in the end but *that isn't the same is it?* Now he informs me that as he has done so well on his sales he will be going to the USA on the 5th of January which is the Saturday before Pheobe's first day at school, which he will be missing and he doesn't return until the Monday of the following week. Then on the following weekend he will be having his operation. In other words he will not be seeing them for the majority of January. I am not surprised by this really, just wondering how the hell I will cope through it all. The children become really affected through all of this shitty routine of seeing them and not seeing them. They don't have a father anymore. I know he has to work and I do wonder whether I am not being understanding enough but that to me is a joke. *How can he survive not seeing his children for that whole time?* I couldn't do it.

I feel very sad now. Sad that my children are going to hurt so badly throughout the next few weeks. Sad that Pheobe will not be seeing her daddy for weeks after starting school so will not be able to share with him one of the most important periods of her life. Sad he will not be there to support her in the big change. Sad because I am doing this alone.

I sat there and this time the smoke wasn't just coming out of my cigarette, it was coming out of my ears too. I had been angry all day with him and I had just about had enough of it all. He makes me so furious at times. He just discards his children's feelings and gets on with his life as if he is only supposed to care about himself.

Today had seen a change in mood. It had seen the low, down feelings shift into fire and fury. I was fuming. I phoned him at lunchtime to see if he had met up with the children ok. They had been looking forward to seeing him after two weeks of not being with him. He wasn't there. He wasn't there yet!

I had stomped about all afternoon. I had had a go at him on the phone but as normal my words had fallen onto deaf ears. There was nothing I could do about it. That made it worse. I thought about last night. Pheobe had thrown an amazing tantrum when I said she would be staying at Nan and Granddad's house and then they would take her down to see daddy in the morning. She couldn't understand why she couldn't see her daddy now. He had promised them he would be there on the Friday night but as I predicted he hadn't shown up. Another let down for them to deal with.

I paced up and down my kitchen. I couldn't seem to calm down. I couldn't seem to release some of the anger and I felt so hot I was sure steam was seeping through every crevice. I stood still and threw my head back. Why do I bother? Why do I get so upset about losing him when he does this to my children time and time again? Why? I didn't know who I was talking to or whether I should try and answer my own questions, I just knew I had to ask them.

I sat back down and tried deep breathing exercises to see if they would release some of the stress. They didn't really, though they did calm me down a little in some way. I felt a little better and shrugged my shoulders.

I just didn't understand how he could go for so long without seeing his children. Why wasn't he rushing down to meet them? Why didn't he want to be with them early? Why didn't he move mountains for them or at least try to?

I felt disappointed then. Disappointed at what sort of father I had chosen for my children. Yes there are worse, granted. But there are also better. There are so many men that haven't been able to have children for one reason or another. And here was a man with three wonderful children and he couldn't spend quality time with them as it interfered with his life. His new life. The one that doesn't involve them.

The anger began to fade as I realised how sad it is that it has all come to this. How sad he is making all of us and the only winners out of this mess is him and her. I put my head in my hands and pushed them back dragging my hair along with them.

He is going away for Christmas and going away after Christmas. He will be busy throughout January. He won't be seeing the children for weeks. I have to get them through the Christmas scene, Boxing Day, New Year and starting school. And I have to do it alone. Alright mum will be here. She will be helping out and holding my hand. Yet I will still be alone. That's sad isn't it?

It's finally here.

24th December

Been so ill today. It came on yesterday. It feels like flu. I am shivering and yet my temperature is high. My chest is so sore and all I can do is cough and splutter. My throat is killing me. I went to the doctors this morning and was told it was a virus so there is nothing I can do. Last year it was Fiona who was ill. We had sat for almost 5 hours down the walk in centre with an ear infection. This year it's me.

Felt very low today. I'm not sure how much of it is the cold making me feel down and how much is what is going on in general. I think I am all set and ready for tomorrow. Marc has not even phoned them today. He phoned me for all of five minutes early this afternoon and then had to go because he was meeting people from work. He never called back. Didn't seem to want to talk to them. I'm not too sure if they noticed but I certainly did. It makes me feel so awful whenever he doesn't do what I expect him to do. It doesn't seem right. If I was leaving my children for Christmas Eve, I would miss them so much I would be on the phone as much as possible. Not him though.

Tonight just got harder. The children had gone to bed and we were sitting up waiting for them to fall asleep. All of a sudden we could hear Seb sobbing. He was crying loudly. We rushed up the stairs and into his room. He was holding his phone and staring at the text message that his dad had sent him. Seb had said he missed him and wanted him here. I tried to phone Marcus so he could talk to him but yet again it took around 8 times of constant calling before he picked it up. Seb started to talk to him. He tried to palm him off with how he will phone back tomorrow. Seb said he needed to talk now. We gave him his privacy but before long there was silence. 6

425

minutes he managed to stay on the phone when his son was crying. 6 minutes.

He eventually went off to sleep and we all went off to bed. I couldn't sleep. I tossed and turned and tried to settle but I couldn't. It was a long horrible night.

The hours dragged by today. I felt awful. Couldn't breathe, couldn't eat and didn't want to get up off the settee. Being ill is horrible. Being ill with children running round is even more horrible. Being ill with children running round on Christmas eve is even more horrible and hard to get through.

I plodded around today. Partly because the feeling of the virus dragged me down and partly because the days I had been dreading for so long had finally arrived. My body ached and it felt so heavy I almost developed a stoop. I felt low but the emotions that had rattled me before had actually numbed and I felt nothing. No pain, no depression, which was good but there was no excitement and no happiness either and that wasn't so good.

I had hoped that when I reached this day I would feel strong and plough through it as if there were no obstacles in my way. I hoped I would spend the day playing with the children, setting up the house for Santa's visit and enjoying the family Christmas feeling. It didn't work out that way though.

After all, what kind of family did I have? I had my children and I had mum and dad with me, I knew that. They were a substitute for my missing husband. A substitute for the missing parent. He had been my family for so many years. He was all that I had and now she had him. I closed my eyes at the thought of the two of them together. I wondered what they were doing now. What were they up to together on Christmas Eve while I sat alone? I hated her so much. She had him and he should be with me. Why wasn't he with me?

The tears started falling thick and fast. I was struggling so much. The house was still and quiet and I could feel my heart beating hard against my chest. Slow and hard, like it just didn't want to carry on. What was the point? A family Christmas? Who was I kidding?

I heard a noise from upstairs and I held my breath. Maybe it was mum sensing something was wrong. I listened for a bit. Nothing more. I exhaled and threw my head back. Mum and dad were probably exhausted themselves. The trauma of Seb tonight was enough to wear us all out. His little screwed up face, his bright red cheeks. I closed my eyes again as the tears stung and I hung my head. My poor boy. My poor little boy.

Seb had cried for hours. I had gone up with mum when we heard him crying and listened with anger and hatred boiling up inside. He wanted his dad. He wanted to talk to him. He had text him and his dad had text back but there was no phone call. I had rung and rung until he finally answered. He spoke to him briefly, a few minutes. He was too busy to console him. He was too busy with her to comfort him. How could he be there? How could she have him there? He should be with these children.

I went upstairs and stood outside Seb's room. I could feel my damp nightdress sticking to my chest where so many tears had fallen. They were still falling. I peeked round the door. He looked so grown up. He was still breathing hard from all the sobbing. He was still sniffing. I could see the image from tonight in front of me. His head buried in his pillow and his whole body convulsing as he wept. I hadn't known what to do. I hadn't known how to deal with that. It was too painful. I pictured my mum kneeling down beside him as she had done. She had laid her head on his and rubbed his back, her tears falling onto his neck. Mum had had to sit with Seb for a couple of hours. He had eventually cried himself to sleep.

I threw back my head and ran downstairs. I knew the sobs were going to be loud and I couldn't wake anyone up. I went into the kitchen and let the pain out. I placed my hands on the bench and my knees gave way. Kneeling on the kitchen floor with my arms hanging from the bench I sobbed into the cupboard door. It made it so hard to breathe and I gasped for air. How is it right for a child to spend their Christmas Eve in that state? Children should be laying awake because of their excitement at Father Christmas coming, not because they are sobbing with the pain of not having their daddy with them. I was feeling the pain like he did. I couldn't handle it, how could he?

I hauled myself up on the bench and lit a cigarette. I tried so hard to enjoy it. I leant back against the cold tiles and for once it felt nice. For a few seconds I cooled down a little. I just stared out of the window. I wondered what he was doing now and how he was. I wondered whether he would be in the state I was in as he wasn't with his children at Christmas. Probably not, he chose to go away with her instead. He obviously didn't want to be with us. On that realisation, a searing hot pain ran across my chest bringing tears to my eyes. I could do without additional pain, I had enough already.

It all just seemed too difficult. I just sat there, staring into nothing, into darkness. The tears were falling slowly and silently down my cheeks now and I just felt so lost. I felt so small sitting in this huge house. Abandoned, I suppose.

I thought about him. I thought about last year. I thought about how the children would be up soon. I thought about facing another day of feeling like this. The tears fell faster. Still silent. I kept watching the door to the kitchen, looking through the stairs to see if anyone had heard me cry. I wasn't sure whether I wanted them to have heard or not. I wasn't sure whether I wanted any company or not. I wasn't sure whether I could face anyone or not. I just sat there, numb and alone.

I made myself get up after an hour or so and go back to bed. I lay there, staring at the ceiling and every now and then at Pheobe who was lying in my bed yet again. Maybe she would be a permanent fixture. I looked down at the bottom of the bed where Pheobe's sack of presents from Father Christmas stood awkwardly balanced against the end of the bed. I bought all those. I made this the best I could. For a few seconds or so, the numbness was replaced by pride. I was proud that I had achieved that. That probably would have sounded daft if I had said that to anyone, but to me, it wasn't silly.

I looked back at the ceiling and rubbed away a few stray tears which had fallen again. I wanted all this to be over. It nearly was. I was nearly there. It was nearly finished. But Christmas was only a small piece of the whole. I still had lots to get through. I had to find the strength from somewhere to battle the rest of the obstacles.

I turned to face Pheobe and watched her little face as she slept. She was sound asleep, hardly moving for a change. The excitement must have worn her out. I smiled at the sight of her. She was so beautiful. Her bright blond hair spread out over the pillow, her pink lips pursed in thought and her fingers twitched every few seconds.

Once again, I let the tears fall. I didn't like the place I was in right now but there was nothing I could do to change it at this moment in time. I have to let it all out of my system somehow. I had to accept the way I felt and carry on.

I laid there and let the tears fall.

25th December

It is now 11.22am and he still hasn't called his children. It is Christmas day and his son has text him once and yet he still hasn't called. They have opened all their presents but not even that could make Seb smile. He just seems really down and nothing seems to help him. I feel so sorry for him. My pain is bad enough. I know how low he is feeling right now and I wouldn't wish it on anyone. If only Marc would do things right, then these things wouldn't happen. I am so upset with him. I have text him and told him so. He isn't bothered. Still hasn't rang.

The day went so slowly really. The dinner was burnt though the children were not complaining, they ate lots. They were a little down but in general they were ok. There were no smiles from the adults though. We did the best we could when the children were around us but there is only so much you can give.

I felt terrible all day. I know I was ill but that was only part of it. All I thought about was the fact that he wasn't here for them. He should have been. He finally phoned and spoke to them a couple of times in the afternoon though Pheobe was not that chatty.

The girls played for ages with their dolls houses. They played lovely too. I stayed in my made up bed on the settee. I didn't get out of it. I just felt so low. I thought about what he was doing a couple of times but I tried not to dwell on it. I thought about last Christmas and how it was such a nice day, and then I tried to ignore that memory too.

Seb flew his dragonfly toy round and round the house. He picked up a little over the course of the day and seemed to relax and enjoy it. We watched their new DVDs after dinner and tried to sit for the last part of the evening with a family atmosphere. The children went to bed after mum and dad left and when the house was quiet and still, I cried and realised I had just got through the Christmas day from hell.

Today was the day I didn't want to do. Today was the day I didn't want to arrive. Today was the day I needed him to give as much as he could and yet he gave nothing. Why was I surprised at that?

The whole day was quiet really. A weird eerie silence ran throughout the house. The children had opened their presents calmly and fairly quietly. They loved all of them and seemed really happy. The girls were really pleased with their dolls houses. I watched them play happily together. Every now and then they would look up at me and their faces would fall a little until I forced a smile back. It took all my effort to smile and fight back the tears. It didn't help being ill I know, but I think it would have been that way anyway. There was an atmosphere that hung over all of us too. No one wanted to acknowledge it and no one wanted to deal with it. We just wanted to get through it.

There was an emptiness that hung in the air. It sat there heavy and dark and hovered over us all, getting heavier and thicker as the day went on. Nothing could lift the feeling that had swallowed us all. We were buried deep among its layers and I am sure we all felt as if we were suffocating. I certainly did. My parents and I sat in silence. Every now and then one of us sighed or made that face you make when you don't know what to say or do. Mum did everything. I just couldn't move. I felt numb. It was like I weighed a ton and I didn't want to drag myself around. Mum seemed to understand. The TV was on in the background but no one was watching or even listening to it. We were snappy and irritable and the children played around us, checking regularly to see if we were still the same. We tried to lift our spirits for them but we couldn't do it. What was the point in acting? It only came over as false anyway.

Seb was affected the most. He sat with a down look on his face and that made the pain I was feeling worsen. It became deeper. Any parent who sees their child suffering in any way must feel the same. The pain and the heartache goes deeper within you and you would give anything for it to stop. Watching Seb hurt like crazy. He didn't smile. He was off in a day dream most of the time. He kept checking the clock and then his phone. Waiting for his daddy to call and wish him a merry Christmas. I remember catching his eye a couple of times and it was like he just stared through me. Like he wasn't really there. He was lost like I was.

I sat there this afternoon trying to block out the memories. The memories of all the past Christmases. The rushing around, the people to visit, the madness of it all. That was all gone. We had no one now. I had looked over at the door, half expecting someone to turn up unannounced. Maybe the family would realise what a hard time we would be having and come to help. No. If they had realised that they would have asked us to theirs. Would we have gone? I don't know but the thought wasn't even there. I had never felt I was thought of at all and today just proved I was right. No phone calls, no text messages. We were just forgotten.

The cloud continued to darken as I had thought of last Christmas. We had had such a lovely day last year. We had unwrapped presents, eaten dinner and played games altogether. Mum and dad had been round. Marcus had cleared up after dinner, made conversation and had even made us cocktails. He had been so happy. We had laughed and joked together and he had joined in. He had enjoyed himself. I remembered his face. I remembered his laughter. I remembered the kisses in the kitchen as he hugged me. I remembered the family Christmas feeling. The happy atmosphere. That had all been there. Then the hole appeared. The missing piece of me. I had realised then that I was merely sticking the knife further into myself with those memories, but I couldn't get rid of them. I tried to ignore them but they still replayed over and over in my head and I couldn't switch them off.

I thought he would phone as early as possible this morning. He didn't. Was clearly too busy with her to remember his three children, who were confused by the atmosphere in the room and the fact that their daddy was not around. Selfish arse. The more the day went on, the more I hated him.

We sat round the table for Christmas dinner. Last year we had needed an extra chair and had squeezed on. There was enough room now he was not there. The emptiness bit at me again. I had looked across and imagined him there for a few seconds. He stood behind the end chair where he would have sat and stared at me. A smile had crept on his face at the same time as the image of her walking over to him appeared. It was her that had made him smile. It was her that had him now. The pain reached me at that point and I couldn't eat my dinner. It was burnt anyway. We couldn't even get that right.

Life was so unfair. It was so wrong. That was all that went through my head today. It was still there now. It was still being said over and over again. We had lost so much. The effect cannot be imagined. It cannot be understood. Other people were enjoying Christmas. She was one of them. She was happy with her boyfriend, my husband, and her family around her. She had helped to destroy my life but she was ok. Other people were laughing and playing games and watching rubbish Christmas television. We were sitting in silence with nothing to say and looking as if we were going to burst into tears at any minute.

During the evening, Seb had periods when he was ok. He had smiled towards the end of the afternoon and the girls seemed to be alright. They whined and moaned and groaned but otherwise they were ok. They had drowned in the suffocating cloud of emptiness a couple of times in the day but as children, they had clambered out of it as there was always something to take their mind off it. They could escape into the world of make believe. The world of play. I wished I could have followed them there.

I lay in my bed, where I had stayed all day and just cried. The tears were partly for the day and what had been going on but they were also due to relief. I had made it through. Only just. I had made it though. Christmas day without him, the first and most painful one, was now over and done with and I was so relieved it was indescribable. I knew I had to face tomorrow but today was over and I was pleased it was.

I had begun to cry as soon as the children went to bed. Mum and dad had left and the children went straight upstairs. They hadn't moaned about going to bed and they hadn't asked to stay up a little longer like they always did. Maybe they were happy for the day to be over like I was. Maybe they were happy to escape upstairs, away from the sad state that had replaced their mum today.

As the last pair of feet ran out of view at the top of the stairs, I just crumbled in a heap on the settee. I had tried so hard to not cry too much in front of my babies today and I just couldn't hold it in any longer. I had curled up in a ball and let the tears fall freely. I sobbed and sobbed. I cried for him again. All I had wanted was him to be here for some of the day. He hadn't and what made it worse was that he hadn't even seemed sorry he wasn't here.

I was still in the same position, hours later.

Eventually I managed to sit myself up and take a few deep breaths to stop the sobbing. I had to pull myself together now. Getting through the day was a good thing and I needed to use that thought to build my strength up for tomorrow. I had to face her tomorrow. I had to watch her. The red hot pain seared through my chest again and I gasped for breath at its force.

I stood up and went into the kitchen, lighting my cigarette on the way to get the medicine to numb the illness. I wished there was a medicine to numb emotional pain. To numb all emotions. Feelings wouldn't exist then and these situations would be fine instead of difficult and painful.

I watched the kettle boil, daydreaming the whole time. I imagined my reaction to her. Would I be able to look at her? Would I be able to face her? Would I cry in front of her? Would I shout and scream and show myself up? I pictured the moment she walked into that room. I saw her face and I saw her smile. The pain rose in me once more. I closed my eyes and tried to imagine what I would do. Would I just freeze? Would I react? I was so scared. Scared because I didn't want to see her and scared because of the pain I knew I would have to deal with. More pain. More agony. More tears to come.

Too many questions again. I can't answer those and I wouldn't know how I will react until I am there, faced with it all. I made my drink and moved to the conservatory. Furniture from the dolls houses were strewn all over the floor and I smiled to myself as I trod over them all to get to the chair. At least they were happy with their presents.

I sat back in my chair and wondered whether my mum's comments had done any damage. Had it affected her at all? Marc was quite angry on the phone afterwards. He didn't raise his voice at all but he used the tone that I am so familiar with. My mum had decided to text her. I hadn't known about it until she had done it. She showed me. It wasn't too nasty. She didn't really run her down. She just asked how she could live with herself for taking away a husband and father from a family who loved him. She told her she thought she was a cold hearted woman. Mum had had enough of feeling like it was all unfair and unjust like I had done but she was braver than me and had reacted to her feelings. I wondered how I would have felt if I had received that text. If I was the other woman. I wouldn't be though. I wouldn't have done what she did.

How could she do it? How could she be there with him now, knowing that he has three children he should have been with at Christmas? I decided he had probably told her that I wouldn't let him be here and that's why she asked him to go with her. Yet another lie. I frowned at the thought that yet again I was taking the blame away from her. I had been doing that the whole time. It was probably because I knew what he was like. He could lie and manipulate people into believing what he wanted them to believe, that's probably what he has done with her. I couldn't blame her for falling for his lies could I?

I leant back in the chair feeling a little better. The day over and the crying stopped, things seemed a little brighter. I stared out into the darkness. I still felt a bit lonely and lost. I was still empty and hurting in many ways. I still missed him and hated sitting here on my own, feeling so low. I should be used to that though after all this time. I rocked gently and stared into the darkness.

"One more day," I told myself. "One more day."

Get off my babies!

26th December

I woke up crying this morning. I just sobbed and sobbed in bed not wanting to get up even though I knew I had to. I was unsure that I could face her today and whether I wanted to. I knew she was going to be there and I was unsure as to how she would react, how she would behave, whether she would say anything at all. The girls sat with me and fussed over me while I cried. Pheobe held me and said "don't worry mum." Fiona asked what was wrong and I explained the best I could. She nodded her head as if she understood.

Eventually I sorted myself out and made myself get up and get ready. We left, hit traffic and got there late. His cousin Carly met me at the door and we walked through to the table. They were all sat around it. I looked at them as I walked past. I sat next to Nan and opposite his Aunt Sally and Carly. We chatted about Christmas and the children and anything else that came up. I felt better though I couldn't eat a thing. I don't know why I booked a dinner; I should have known I wasn't going to eat it. The children all piled into his uncle Ian's cab when they got to the car park, not wanting to come home with me, so I took Sally and Carly back. It was in the car when we were talking that I realised that my mother and father and sister in law had not spoken to me at all yet. I was definitely being pushed out. They clearly did not want me there and I was really feeling it. I was appreciative that Sally and Carly were being so welcoming and friendly.

Back at the house, the children ran round wanting their presents. They behaved well and played nicely together. My cousin Jack spoke to me briefly. I'm not sure whether he was just unsure of how to act, what to say or whether he had the same beliefs as Marc's parents,

Jane and Colin, and his sister Lucy. It would be so much easier if they were just honest and said what they were thinking and feeling.

While we were opening presents they walked in together. I didn't see her as she stood behind the archway beside the door, though I felt her enter because the mood shifted. I did see them greet her better than they have ever greeted me. They walked over, hugged her and kissed her on the cheek. It was unbelievable. It hurt like hell. The knife was being turned a little more. They had ignored me and yet there they were welcoming her to the family. I was gutted. Yes everyone gave her a present. Yes everyone was nice to her. But, his parents and sister made a point of sitting up that end of the room with her. They made a point of making sure she felt safe and welcome in the house. Fine. As long as they remember that if I get pushed out then my children come with me.

I had suddenly felt very sick. As if I was going to throw up. I stood up to go outside and Pheobe held my hand to follow. He followed me through to the corridor asking if she was ok. I replied that she was fine and walked outside. He followed me out there too. Kept asking what I was doing etc. *Shouldn't he have been with his girlfriend?*

I had a cigarette and hid out at Christine's for a bit until my mum got there. I then went back and went into the kitchen as there was nowhere for me to sit. He followed me out there. For about 15 minutes he grilled me about what I was going to do. I had promised to do nothing and therefore nothing was what I was going to do. I would not have known what to do anyway. I didn't want to hear her voice talking to me; I didn't want to get too close to the woman who had stolen my husband from me. I didn't need to do or say anything. I took the children back over to Christine's house so they could see her. After a few minutes there I went out with my sister Charlie to get the presents. Mum came too and took her presents into Sally and to congratulate Jack on expecting his baby. Marcus followed her out and asked what the hell was going on. My mum and sister told him that they were friends before he and I got together and just because he and I were split they were not going to stop going. He ended up hugging them both and kissing them on the cheek wishing them a happy new year. My mum even said to him that they missed him too. It was a sweet, touching scene. I was behind the car crying my heart out. I composed myself and went back again. I sat with Charlie on the sofa and ignored the rest of what was going on. I fussed over Oscar. He even gave me a cuddle. I sat there wishing I could just get up and go. No way was I giving in now, I had come too far.

At the end of the evening, I had shown that I was upset, hurt and angry and I had been suitably ignored by the people who used to be my in laws. The toys were collected. The cab to take them to the station had arrived and they were making their way out. Pheobe refused to go. I went and collected the bags from my car and by the time I had returned over the road, Seb and Fiona had got into the cab with Sue. I couldn't believe I was not even going to get a kiss or hug goodbye from them. The pain boiled over at that point and the anger fired up inside and when Marc uttered the words "well I don't know why they have done that" I yelled "I do... because they are with the fucking skank who stole you from me" and I turned and went back to the house. I hugged them and thanked them for having me and I apologised for making everything so awkward. They hugged me back and said it was fine and I had nothing to apologise for. I loaded up the car and went to get my mum. Carly was outside and I talked to her for a while. She could see I was hurting and was ready with some words of advice. I just crumbled. I said I didn't want to do this anymore, that I wasn't sure I could keep taking the pain. I wasn't a proper mum when I was like this and that was true. I said maybe I should give the children to them and start again somewhere new. My mum came out and we all talked. I walked through into the garden and sobbed my heart out. Pheobe was there though. She hadn't left me. She was still here to hold me. I didn't get in until 12.30 that night. We were exhausted and yet knew there was no point in going to bed just yet as we wouldn't sleep. What a long day. What a stressful day. The hardest thing I had ever done in my life. But I had done it though hadn't I. I hadn't let him push me out. I had been there with my children in my old family.

All I had wanted was a little normality at Christmas. I had wanted my children to feel that they had had a family Christmas even though their father didn't want to be with them. All I had wanted was to feel ordinary for that one day.

That one day. He couldn't even give me that, no matter how many times I had explained.

I looked straight ahead of me and there stood Sue. There she was. Right in front of me. I had been home, away from her, for hours and yet there she was. Sitting on a chair with my children sitting on her lap. Hugging them. Talking to them. Laughing with them. The pain was indescribable and even though I was away from that now and it was now in the past, I could still feel the effects of the huge gash it had left behind. I could smell the raw flesh from inside me, as if there was an open wound.

I sat there on my bench having a cigarette staring out of the window. On the dark glass, images of scenes from tonight appeared and then faded as if a slide show was playing. The moment I had walked in. The moment she had walked in. The touching scene of Fiona sitting on her lap. The moment they greeted her. The awkwardness that surrounded the evening and their faces that had showed it all.

It was an indescribable feeling. I knew that that was no longer my family. I had lost them too. I would never be there again. I would never sit in that environment again. Another rejection. Another loss. More pain. I couldn't believe that it had happened. I hadn't expected the day to run smoothly and I hadn't expected it to be easy. I was under no false illusions. I hadn't expected them to turn on me though. I hadn't expected them to reject me too.

The tears were running down my cheeks and I wiped some of them away with my hands. I wasn't too sure why I was crying. There were so many reasons I could have picked but if someone had asked me, I wouldn't have been able to pinpoint anything to give them an answer. I found that so strange.

Emotionally, I was exhausted. The anger and the heartache from today and all the things that had happened had drained me completely. Yet my head was rattling so much and had so many things running through it, it kept me awake. The questions, the wondering why, the images and the rejection filled my head so much and the noise was so loud. The noise. I just wanted it to shut up.

I took a deep breath and closed my eyes. Focus. Focus on one thing at a time. Quieten the sounds. Slow everything down. I opened my eyes and was grateful that it had worked a little.

I sat there, motionless, wondering which bit had upset me the most. There were many realisations that had occurred to me tonight. So many. I had realised that he really loved her. I could see it in his eyes. The smile that came on his face as he watched her. Despite our close relationship and the moans he had about her and the things he had said to me over the last few months, he really loved her. He had wanted to show her off tonight. He had wanted to introduce her to the family so she was part of it. He had wanted that even though he knew that it would rip me apart.

No, that wasn't the worst. The hardest bit was seeing her with him. Seeing them as a couple. The slight brush of his hand down her arm. The way he looked at her. That hurt so much. He used to look at me like that. He used to smile at me like that. Now I wasn't good enough and yet that thing was. My mum seemed genuinely shocked when she came out of there. She had seen photographs of her but they are never the same as seeing the actual person. She had said, "So that's what it looks like." Subtle, huh? I giggled as I remembered her telling me she had said it. I smiled as I pictured Sue's face when faced with my mum, wondering what was going on. That was probably a highlight of the evening. Sue didn't look that great tonight. Nothing like I remembered her. She had changed, even just since the car incident in September. She looked solemn and tired. Her sparkle was not there. She was not the typical husband stealer. I always pictured the other woman as younger, taller and a bit of a Barbie look-a-like. Don't know why. Sue was pretty. She was younger and she was a few inches taller but she wasn't a blonde Barbie bombshell. She was not the image of perfection I had had before. But then that was my opinion. Obviously not my husbands!

I giggled at myself.

No, that wasn't the worst either. Being ignored completely. Feeling unwelcome in a familiar environment, with people around me that had been called my family. That was hard. I had realised that things would never be the same again. They had turned on me too. I wanted an escape route the whole evening. I didn't understand what I had done to warrant that treatment. He had had the affair. He had left behind a wife and three children who loved him dearly. He was always making excuses as to why he couldn't be a proper father anymore and couldn't see his children. He was the one who had broken the family up. Yet I was the one being punished. I was now an outsider. I was pushed out and not considered as part of the family. I didn't understand.

No, that wasn't the worst. Marc's constant nagging was hard too. He had gone on and on, trapping me in the kitchen. "What are you going to do?" he had asked. "What are you going to do?" He just kept asking me. Over and over. I wasn't going to create a scene. I wasn't going to try to start a fight with her or abuse her when my babies were there and this day was for them as well as for me. I wasn't going to do anything when his aunt had been so kind to include me in their Christmas, in their house. Why would I? He didn't believe me. He thought I was going to do or say something. He drove me mad. I knew what he was thinking though. There was nothing to stop me talking to her. There was nothing to stop me telling her how we were still sleeping together. How he told me he thought he had made a mistake. That was the real reason why he didn't want me there.

No, that wasn't the worst. I had hated the part where I had lost control. Where I had shouted at her in the street with his parents present too. I didn't behave like that. I would never have done that. It was the anger. The little devil sitting on my shoulder nagging at me because she was there right in front of me and I had done nothing. She had hurt me in ways that no one should hurt someone and I was sitting there doing nothing about it. The frustration at not being able to get to my babies was overwhelming. All I wanted was to give them a kiss goodbye. Instead she was there in my way. They had forgotten me. Just got into the car. She was there and they were happy and all that rolled into one made me explode. The door and the boot of the car were open. Did she hear me? "...because they are with the fucking skank who stole you from me," I had yelled. I bit my lip and shook my head. I was ashamed by that in some ways. At the same time a smile crept on my face too. Maybe not too ashamed then.

No, that wasn't the worst. The worst bit was the bit I was trying to ignore. The bit where my heart had stopped beating for a few seconds due to the rush of sheer agony that had cascaded through it. The moment it broke and shattered. The worst bit was watching my babies with her. Watching the delight on their faces when they saw her there. Watching her cuddle them as they sat on her lap. The pain had risen through me and left me winded and shocked. I remembered how I gasped for breath quite a few times. I had sat there on that settee willing my legs to stand up and run but I was frozen. I remembered the tears biting at my eyes as I heard them say her name. As I heard her voice talking to my babies. The nausea had churned my stomach. My head throbbed. Suddenly, the image of her was there before me once more. There she stood in front of me. She reached into my chest and ripped out my heart. She stood there with her arm outstretched and her fist clenched tightly around my heart so that it stopped beating in her crushing fingers. And she was laughing. She was laughing. I gasped for breath and closed my eyes to get rid of her. She was gone when I opened them but the pain was still there. Still gasping for breath I jumped down and ran over to light another cigarette. The tears were biting harder and they were hotter than ever before. I bent forward with my hands on my knees trying to calm the winded feeling and ease the suffocating strain on my chest.

Yes. That was definitely the worst bit.

I stood up straight and regulated my breathing. I took long, hard, deep breaths and calmed down. The effect of those scenes were still there. I bet they never leave me. I wished that I could have my memory erased because I never wanted to relive that moment again. I raised a hand to my chest as if I was checking that there wasn't a gaping hole in it and rubbed the place the pain seemed strongest.

I walked back over to the bench and checked the window for any images. My imagination was so vivid tonight I expected them to jump out at me. Hallucinations at their scariest.

I hauled myself up on the bench and shook my head. All this stress is clearly making me crazy. I laughed at myself. What a mess you are woman. What a mess you are.

Right. Last bit to deal with. What are you going to do now?

I cleared my head. Everything from tonight was now in the past. It was over, finished, all done and dusted. Talk to yourself girl, talk to yourself.

A new start. A new start that's what I needed. New Year was coming up. A new time. A new life. Divorce papers were going through. I knew where I stood in terms of the family. I never had to see them again. Would I take the children with me on that decision? Yes I would. So they wouldn't see any of us again. Fine. Wash my hands of Marc. Everything he had said was crap. He was using me and playing both of us. Get rid. Ok. I can do that. I can. Can't I?

I sat up straighter as if I had a little sense of determination. I can do it. If I survived today and stood up to him and his attempt to drive me out and make me back down, I can do anything. I don't want him anyway really. I wanted the man he used to be, I had already figured that out. I wanted him to be a father, but he wasn't prepared to be. If I wiped him out of our lives, the stress would be over. I would be sacrificing my own life for the children but didn't they deserve it?

I sat up, turned my head and stared straight at the window. There were no images. There was no Sue. There were no tears. Things were clear and straight. Determination. Determination was all I needed.

I poured water on my cigarette and walked over to the door, throwing it in the bin on my way through. I walked up the stairs to my room where my baby girl was snoring. She hadn't left me. She never would. Nor would the others. Unconditional love is what you get from children. Unconditional and constant.

I smiled at my baby girl. As long as I had them, I didn't need anything else. I got in to bed and curled up next to her. I would take the next week to finalise the plans but by New Year, there will be a new me. I will make this coming year, my year.

I will move on. I will.

The sadness lifted and the noise in my head silenced. I closed my eyes and yawned. I pulled Pheobe closer to me and kissed her forehead. I smiled. I had survived the hardest period of my life. I had survived the hardest day of my life. I had got through it. I did it.

I smiled.

27th December

Couldn't really sleep. Tossed and turned all night. Went to bed about 1am and just laid there churning everything over and over in my head. Once you start doing that there is no way you will sleep. It gets too hard. I watched my Pheobe sleep. The fact that Seb and Fiona had not said goodbye, had not seemed too bothered to leave me as they had her, was hard to deal with and it hurt like crazy. I know they didn't mean it intentionally, they got swept up in the race for the cab, but it still grated on me. Pheobe hadn't left me though. About 7am Pheobe woke up and gave me a big smile. I looked at her and said "Thanks for staying with me baby girl", to which she replied "Well you didn't want to be on your own did you?" How sensitive for a 4 and a half year old. She can act so grown up at times it's hard to see her as the young girl she is. I curled up in her arms and tried to go back to sleep. I couldn't do it but she did.

Later that morning I get a phone call from Marc. He laid into me about my behaviour last night. Apparently she has said she has had enough of all the troubles that go alongside their relationship and she needs time to sit and think about what she is going to do and whether she can handle it. If she loves him she will. I did not do anything to make her feel like I was threatening her. I didn't even make eye contact with the woman. I didn't say anything. I didn't do anything. It's not my fault. Anyway she does this to him time and time again. He is always on the phone telling me she has got fed up with him and needs her space. They will be ok again in a few days. It should technically bring them closer together.

When the children came back, Seb explained that Sue had asked him how his Christmas was. He told her the truth. That he had cried for his dad. That he had wanted him there, needed him there and that he had missed him. He said he couldn't sleep and we all had to try to calm him down. Maybe, just maybe, it is that news as well that has knocked her for six. Maybe she is wondering now that if all was mutual and we had all wanted this then how come I was acting so hurt and upset that night and then hearing that Seb was so upset and she had his daddy when he wanted him. Maybe she was questioning the split a little more. She needs to. I would have been had I been in her shoes. She needs to realise that he is lying to her. I wish I could tell her what he is doing but she would never believe me anyway.

This afternoon he had another go at me for breaking up his relationship and ruining his life and the fact that he will be resigning and that would not be beneficial to me (threats in my opinion) He had said that he would not talk to me anymore. He said he would start divorce proceedings too. About 2 hours later he was on the phone asking if the children were ok. He then called in the evening to say he had received and read through the divorce papers and he was now really angry with me. He went on about how he had wanted to wait 2 years so it was easier. How all the debts would be passed over to him - they were his! How I would take the few things he had from him. He doesn't seem to understand how it works. I just want it over as he no longer wants me. He can be free then just how he wants.

The divorce is on the grounds of adultery. My solicitor said that that was the way to go as it was obvious that he was having a relationship before the split. How come everyone else thinks it and yet him, his parents and sister can't. I don't understand. I didn't want to believe it but to me it's true. I think I expected him to say that it was not what he wanted at all because he was not sure about how he felt about me. He says he misses me, he says he still has feelings for me and he still kisses and cuddles me. *Why if he doesn't love me? Why if he loves her?* I felt a little lost tonight. A little lonely. A little empty.

I have lost him totally now and nothing will help me get over the pain and heartache. I just need to regain my thoughts and build my strength back up. Then I will be up to the challenge of facing him again - on the phone or otherwise.

I went over and over yesterday in my head. I went through my actions and the way I behaved. I hold my hands up to behaving angrily. I stomped around, I threw presents into the sack and I wasn't particularly kind to him. I admitted all of that. Otherwise I thought I had done quite well. How many other women would sit in a room with their ex husband and the woman who he had had an affair with and who eventually enticed him away and not do or say anything to her?

None is the likely answer. I must be mad or stupid for doing that.

I shook my head as I thought. My chest was still sore from where it had been exposed to such agony yesterday and my head was pounding from lack of sleep. I had tossed and turned all night. Hardly slept. Every now and then there was a glimpse of that stronger woman. That one who likes to come up fighting sometimes, but even then I couldn't settle. The stress from the day must have been just a little too much.

I rubbed my head and yawned.

I had felt a little better today. I hadn't made any great leaps or anything and I hadn't come to any major conclusions or changed the way I felt. I hadn't just stopped loving him. I still felt a little better. Getting through the day had given me a little pick me up. I felt a little more positive.

He had been so angry with me twice today. He shouted at me down the phone. Blamed me for their split. Blamed me for her questioning their relationship and whether she could continue with it. How was that my fault? Shouldn't have done what he did. If he had just let me go there yesterday and then picked the children up and met up with Sue later, none of it would have happened.

My thoughts actually turned to her. I had done my best to block her out of my head for obvious reasons but I couldn't keep her out. Not now.

I wondered how she had felt when she had received my mum's text on Christmas day. Had she said anything to him? Had she questioned him? What was he saying to her? I wondered how she had felt when he told her I would probably be there yesterday. I wondered how she had felt about the way I behaved. I didn't care what she was saying about me. I didn't care whether she felt I was wrong in any way. I just wondered what she was feeling.

I tried to put myself in her shoes. If I was her. If I was her I wouldn't have had an affair with a married man. If I was her I would have questioned the ex when offered. Putting that aside, if I was her right now with all that had happened, what would I be thinking? Surely she has to be questioning my behaviour. Not just yesterday but the last few months. If I was ok with the split, why would I have called her a skank and all the other names? Why did I stay at the flat? Why did Fiona say daddy had two girlfriends? Why did my mum send her that text? Was she still believing everything he was saying?

I hoped she was questioning everything. Mum and I had spoken of nothing but her and the last few days today. We had gone over and over everything. We had tried to see it from her point of view and we had guessed what her opinion

449

was. We had guessed the questions she was now asking herself. No way of knowing though.

I sat back in my chair and yawned again. I needed sleep so badly. There was still a lot rattling inside my head. I probably wouldn't sleep again tonight.

He had shouted at me too for the divorce papers. I knew he would. He had said before that he hadn't wanted a divorce yet. What did he expect me to do? Hadn't he had enough of getting what he wanted recently? Everything revolved around what he wanted. I had had enough of that cycle. He didn't want to divorce on the grounds of adultery either. He told me I was not allowed to name her. I wanted to do just that originally. Don't know what stopped me. I agreed not to. He doesn't realise my solicitor has all her details though, her name, address, phone number, workplace. All in his file. I smiled. Her name might not be on the papers but it is everywhere else.

I wanted to be free of him. I wanted to divorce him. I didn't want to be his wife anymore. That was something I didn't think I would ever feel. I really didn't.

I tutted under my breath. And who does he think he is saying that I would take everything and give him all the debts? They were his debts anyway. He is the one with the credit cards at ridiculous amounts. Not me. I have a small amount granted but I am paying that. That is my responsibility not his. Stupid man. He has no idea.

There is a huge mess again now. Things seem to jog along for a bit and then bang, in an instant there is a mess. I yawned again. So tired.

I willed myself to get up and finish the jobs that needed doing before bed but I couldn't do it. I sat for a bit longer before finally managing to move. Walking around the kitchen

I went over yesterday again. I really didn't do anything. I didn't care what the rest of them were saying. I had behaved well considering.

I wished I could stop thinking about it. Too many other things to think about. Getting so difficult. I yawned again. I knew if I lay down in bed, the thoughts would still go round and round. I yawned again. I would have to hope I went off to sleep because this is ridiculous. At least I would be lying down. There is hope for sleep.

There is hope.

28th December

A bad night. My cold kicked back. I tossed and turned and was sweating like a pig all night. I couldn't breathe and had to keep getting up to blow my nose or get a drink as my mouth was so dry. Felt ill all day and the children really played up. Seb gave me so much attitude and didn't listen to a word I said. Pheobe fought me with everything I needed to do. They fought with each other and shouted, screamed and cried so many times I thought my head would burst. It didn't seem to matter what I did or said I was not getting anywhere. I was tired though so perhaps they were not being as bad as what they seemed. They had periods where they played nicely. They were quiet for half an hour here and there. They are probably just up in the air with him being so down yesterday and me being ill and upset too. They pick up on it all and in some ways you have to allow for that to affect their behaviour.

I just wish I could feel better.

What a rough day. I sat there tonight, trying to breathe through my nose as if I expected it all to have disappeared in the ten minutes since I last tried. I coughed and spluttered pathetically.

Where did it come from again? Why did it kick back? Stupid cold.

I slung my head back against the settee. The children had driven me mad today with their constant noise and the way they had to defy everything I said. The silence was a welcoming noise. I fell downwards onto the settee so I was laying down, sliding down on the cushions so I didn't have to use any energy to move, hoping to ease my ill feeling. I laid there wondering how I was going to get back up.

I had become so angry with him in the last 24 hours. Everything he had said to me yesterday had wound me up. I hated that. The conversation is gone. The moment is over. It's only then that you think of what you should have said. I hated that so much.

I coughed and spluttered again. Who cares? I'm too ill to be bothered. I can't care tonight. I sat up again, using a cushion to prop my head up against the back of the seat. I just wanted to be comfy. How is that asking too much? I slammed my fists down on the arm of the chair in a fed up with this cold kind of way. I was frustrated enough about the last week or so, I didn't need anything else to deal with.

I raised my eyes to the ceiling. The silence was beginning to annoy me. It made my thoughts louder. I turned the TV on and flicked through the channels. The noise was too much. My head was pounding harder. I turned it off and threw the remote to the other side of the settee. I couldn't do that either. I laid down again, this time on a cushion. Coughed and spluttered once more. I felt awful again, but I still had an hour until I could take more medication.

I hugged the cushion; turning onto my stomach to see if that was more comfortable. No. I buried my face in the cushion and before I knew it I was in tears again. It just seemed too much. It was all too much and now everything had got on top of me and there I was again crying my eyes out.

The crying made it harder to breathe. "I can't do anything can I?" I said loudly to myself. I felt so sorry for myself. I let the tears fall for a little longer. I rolled myself over so I landed on the floor on all fours and then used the settee to push myself to standing.

I shrugged my shoulders. I couldn't even have a cigarette as that hurt my chest. That pain was still there. It was twice as bad now though as it hurt from the illness too.

"He doesn't have to do this...........He hasn't got to keep going to this time of night because he had to see to the children when he was ill........He can just tuck himself up in bed can't he?"

Talking to myself out loud again now. Great. I have had an awful Christmas, a stressful Boxing day, been blamed for his break up and his debts, been shouted at because I decided to send divorce papers at a time that wasn't convenient to him, felt more ill than I had done in ages, had a tough time with the children when all I had wanted to do was tuck myself up in bed and now I was going crazy on top of it all and talking to myself....again!

That was just what I needed.

29th December

He phoned this morning to say that he would not be coming. He has a chest infection and a cold and feels terrible. I have been like that for almost a week now. I still had to get through Christmas and I still had to cook dinners and care for the children. I had the tantrums to deal with and the outbursts too. There is no escape for me and no way that I can rest and get better. And he wonders why I am bitter.

I told the children he was not coming. They seemed to be used to me saying that. Seb said "I'm supposed to be getting my other present from dad" I replied that I knew that but daddy wasn't well and he wasn't coming. Seb replied "you are not well either mum". He then looked at me with tears in his eyes and shouted "What's the bloody point!" He threw the game he was playing on the settee, grabbed the garage key and stormed out. I felt so bad for him. He knew that he would not be seeing his dad for at least another three weeks and he was so upset that he wasn't coming today. Poor thing.

It is now 22.11pm and my wonderful mum and dad have just left with the children. They offered to have them tonight so I could get some rest and hopefully shake off this rotten cold. The cough has got slightly worse today and my head feels like it will explode any minute. I am going hot and cold. He has just phoned them saying that he maybe coming to see them on Wednesday as he is going away next Saturday for two weeks. If he knew that he was going away for ages in January why has he not made more time for them this holiday. Ok, so he is ill today but then I have been ill every day since last Sunday and guess what, I have had the children to look after. My mum was around for most of it I do not deny that and without her I would have been awful. Wish I knew what to do to thank her properly for what she has done. There is nothing I can give her that will say it enough really. Maybe just sorting my life out and proving that I am better off without him will do it. I will aim to do that for her as well as my children.

She has spoken to his Aunt Sally and Uncle Ian today. She took Sally and his cousin Carly some flowers to say thank you for looking after me the other day. They seemed to think that I handled it brilliantly. That I did well not to attack her especially when she was cuddling my babies. I had thought I would explode then. I had to keep walking away. They are fantastic. They said they would do the same thing next year too. I felt safe with them there. Like I had the support to get through it. I knew they were behind me and I am so grateful to them for that. I'm pleased they understand me.

I am not feeling such an outcast today. If his mum and sister want to be like that I will let them. I will also make more of a point of going to see Sally, Ian and his Nan more often. I will make them my family still. They have not pushed me away and for as long as I am welcome in their lives, I will be there.

Still ill. Still feeling rough.

Sat on top of the bench, staring at my reflection in the dark window. I realised I looked as rough as I felt.

My thoughts hadn't switched off from him all day and even at this hour they were still going. He was ill, poor thing. A chest infection. Felt so ill he had to crawl back to bed instead of spending the last available weekend he had with his children. He flies off to America for almost two weeks next Saturday. The children won't be staying with him before he goes.

Unbelievable. Here I am fighting to keep going as I felt so ill and he is able to rest up and get better. Can't be there for the children. Can't be there to help me out too. Such a bastard. I hate him.

I coughed and spluttered as I tried to enjoy a cigarette and then immediately put it out. No way of relaxing with this illness. All too much.

The house was quiet without the children. I wouldn't always notice that as I often went out when they were not here. Mum and dad had taken them to their house for the weekend. The house was still. Silence was bliss. I shivered suddenly and jumped down off the cold bench and made my way to the comfort of the settee bed I had created. I curled up under the duvet and laid there trembling until the warmth finally got to me. The TV was boring me so I had switched it off. There I was curled up in the peace and quiet that surrounded me with just my thoughts for company. And they were not good thoughts either.

I turned onto my back and faced the ceiling.

Again, he popped up in my head. He had made me so angry today. Should I have had more sympathy with him being sick? No, I answered. I smiled. Having another conversation with myself. I had been so ill and still coped with the children. Just shows you the difference between that expected from a woman and that expected from a man. Even his mum said he couldn't have the children as he was too ill and he should just stay in bed. She didn't think that of me though did she?

Life was unfair and didn't I know it.

I thought about the children. I hoped they were happy with my parents and they were having a fun time over there. They would have been. They always loved staying over. They had packed their bags with enthusiasm and couldn't wait to get out of the door. I smiled again.

My thoughts then turned to Sally and Ian. They had made me feel so much better saying that they had thought I did really well the other day. They hadn't thought I was behaving badly. Sally said she thought I was great to have been able to stand that without going for her. I suppose I thought so too in a way.

I yawned and sniffed. I felt dreadful. I couldn't continue thinking about anything. So tired now and so fed up with feeling ill and with feeling sick of him.

I grabbed the pillow and quilt and wrapping it round me plodded up the stairs to my bed. I curled up underneath the covers and shivered with the cold from the mattress. I laid there, sniffing and coughing, wishing that I would wake up tomorrow feeling more like myself.

30th December 2007.

Today was a nothing day. I hardly thought about Marc. I thought about Lee more and wondered what he was up to on holiday. I smiled to myself. Having a great time I bet.

I was occupied all day. Ok I slept for half of it. I didn't get out of bed until 11.30. That did me good. My cold feels a little better. I feel a little stronger.

I weighed myself this morning. 8st 4lbs. The lightest I have been in years. I am so happy. I hope it doesn't go back on too easily though.

I spent the whole day writing. I had the urge. It's amazing how some days I cannot write a thing and then another day it all pours out so easily. I felt a little calmer today. The children came home and my mum stayed for a bit. She pinned up some of my tops that are too big now so she can sew them up for me. Can't afford new ones you see.

It didn't even bother me when Marc phoned Seb's mobile and spoke to the children. He clearly didn't want to speak to me. He was fine yesterday but not today. Ok then fine. I wasn't too bothered. I have decided it's about time I moved on anyway. I want to ignore him. I want to hurt him. And if they are back together after the stress of Boxing Day then I will ruin them. I just need to divorce him first. I have planned my revenge. I know what I have to do and now I have the strength to do it. I feel so much better now. I hope the good feeling stays.

It was a good day today. I hadn't done much at all really, except write for hours, but it had made me feel much happier. Feeling better had done so too. It was nice to be able to almost breathe.

I sat in the study and read through some of what I had written. It was hard to read what had happened to you. I hadn't enjoyed any of it the first time; I wasn't going to enjoy reliving it. At the same time there was a sense of satisfaction too. And pride. I had done that. I had written that. I was quite impressed with myself as I scrolled through the pages.

I sat back in the chair and stretched and yawned. I hadn't realised I was still tired. I turned the computer off and switched off the lights. None of the other lights were on downstairs and the house was in complete darkness. I decided I liked it that way and made my way through to the conservatory which was alight from the moon and the little lights that ran down my flower bed. They looked so pretty.

I sat back in the chair, pulling my legs up beside me and rocked. Thoughts of Marc and how he hadn't wanted to talk to me crossed my mind. I had decided earlier that I didn't care and I still felt that way too. He thinks I am out to ruin his life and I understood what that felt like, as he had done it to me. I didn't care though.

I closed my eyes and allowed the darkness and the silence to relax me. It made me feel peaceful. I felt quite calm. I really noticed the calm days. With stress and anger in your life so much, its absence is so obvious.

I smiled. I liked these calm days. I used to hate them. They had made me think too much before. They had made me cry with the upset of those thoughts. They had made me ask questions and become irritable. Now though, it was ok. I was calm and quiet and I enjoyed it.

I yawned again.

I opened my eyes to get up to go off to bed and then closed them again. I would soak up a little more peace first. I would relax a little longer. I sat there enjoying it all. Enjoying the darkness. Enjoying the silent still of the house. Enjoying the calm.

Happy New Year.

1am - 1st January 2008

Thank goodness, 2007 is finally over. The year from hell has finished and there is surely no way that 2008 could possibly be any worse than 2007.

I have just seen in the New Year in a subdued fashion. Me, mum, dad, the children, my friend Marilyn and her son Jamie sat around chatting and drinking all evening. We watched the fireworks and listened to the New Year song. At midnight we wished each other a happy new year. We sent text messages doing the same to friends we were not with.

Jamie's dad phoned him within minutes. Seb watched his phone and waited. Marc had phoned earlier in the night and had said he would call back later. Clearly something else came up. Seb checked his phone and he tried to ring him. He waited a little longer and checked his phone again. He then tried on my phone. It rang a couple of times and then rang off. The next time it went straight to answer phone. His sad little eyes that looked down at the screen. He closed the phone. The third time he rang he left a message. He was upset he didn't get to speak to his dad and wish him a happy new year.

What a good start to the year from daddy. I am hurt and angry. Hurt because my son was hurt and angry because yet again the children were not at the forefront of his mind. Saving his relationship was. A parent should be there whenever and wherever the children need them. They should be the first thing on your mind when you wake up and the last thing on your mind when you go to bed. I don't understand why they are not to him. I don't get it. He did not think to phone his son at midnight and wish him a happy new year. He did not think to pick up that phone and send a text even. *How wrong is that?*

459

I once told him that he could hurt me as much as he liked. I said he can rip my heart out and destroy me if he likes. He can stab me and twist the knife on more than one occasion as he has done over the last 9 months. I promised him that if he continued to hurt my babies I would hurt him back. I would take that pain and send it straight back to him tenfold. He is still hurting them. Now it's time to hurt him back. Now it's time to destroy the pain free life he is living and give him the pain right back. And I will. I owe my children. I made a promise and I will stick to it. Divorce first and get as much as I can. His relationship second.

2008 will be my year. I will make sure that I improve my mood. I will make sure I enjoy life with my children. I will make sure my children are happy. I will make sure I do all the things I want to do no matter how small. Most of all I will make sure that I keep fighting him. I will find the strength to ensure that I get a new start to life. This is my year and no one will take that away from me. No one.

Determination is not a feeling that is in my life very often. It is not one that stays with me for long when it does appear. All in all, determination is something I felt I lacked. It was something I needed though and tonight I felt it.

I had been living the last week trying to be rid of the year 2007. I still didn't know what I had expected from the first few hours of 2008, but I had already felt the lift in me. I had begun to feel better once Boxing Day was finished and over with. I had become a little stronger and a little more assured of my decisions as the week progressed but now, with 2008 finally beginning, I felt uplifted.

I felt as if I knew what I had to do. I felt I was finally there, in that right place and the sense of determination filled me to the brim. This year was going to be my year. It was going to see me change the mood that had suppressed me in 2007. I would get a new job closer to home, I would have more fun with the children, I would feel settled in my new life and I would divorce him and become single again. Those were my plans and I liked them.

They had been fuelled with the look on my Seb's face. The way he checked his mobile constantly from the time his mate's phone rang out with his dad's phone call. He heard him say 'happy new year dad' and he just looked down. Every 30 seconds he flipped his phone up to see if he had missed the call. It never came. I could see he was gutted.

I looked down at the floor as I pictured his face staring at the phone. No smile. Tears in his eyes. A shrug of the shoulders. How could he not think of his children? I know the phone lines get jammed at midnight but half an hour later, there was still no sign.

I had been angry at Marc anyway. He was out again tonight. He got Christmas Eve and New Years Eve. I wouldn't have had any plans but he annoyed me the way he assumed I wouldn't be going out. He didn't even ask to have the children. He had wanted his freedom. When Seb was upset, it fired the anger in me once more. I calmed myself down by converting it into the determination to survive this well.

I looked back at my reflection in the window. I sat in my usual place. This was now my chair rather than a kitchen bench. I just smiled at myself. For once I could sit there and smile. Marc hadn't bothered me enough to have brought me down. He was staying away and that made me happier. It didn't mean I didn't miss him still. It just meant I knew I could live without him. I just hope my children won't have to learn to do the same.

3rd January 2008

He turned up finally to see his children. He phoned and asked me to pick him up from the station and seemed surprised when I

461

said no. Bloody cheek. Hardly talk to me and be as mean as anything and then expect me to drag the children out in the cold going out of my way to collect him.

Spoke briefly to him. He didn't seem to be listening. He went on and on about her and how she isn't giving him the time of day at the moment. She needs space to think. He is also paranoid about the man she is texting regularly. He says he believes that it is him every time her phone goes off. I stood there watching him talking wondering what he expected me to say to this. *Did he expect me to care? Was I supposed to tell him what to do? Was I supposed to be upset that she has distanced herself from him?* I didn't feel any of that. I just wanted him to shut up and go and play with his children. He managed to play a game on the play station with Seb and that was about it.

He annoyed me the whole time he was here. I sat there wishing he would leave. I was feeling quite angry about having to have him here. Partly because he didn't really want to be here, otherwise he would have come when he had originally said instead of fitting it in tonight. Partly because I was still angry with the way he was chatting away about the difficulties in his life. I had been through all of that myself and he hadn't cared a less what I was going through.

At one point he said, "I can't bear to work with her. Seeing the woman I love and watching her get on with her life without me close to her hurts like crazy."

Really? I hadn't realised that that hurt. It's not like I have ever been through anything like that. I couldn't care a less what he was going through. He had been playing a game the whole time and now it was him upset and hurting I was supposed to feel something.

It was weird spending time with him. He tried tickling me and asked to buy me dinner. He was nice and kind to me. It just made me feel uneasy. I didn't want him here.

It was a strange feeling. I feel quite strong at the moment and maybe I was worried he would take that away from me.

I was pleased when he left. I knew I was not going to have to face him for a while now. About 3 weeks in fact, which is great for me. I will be able to cut him out more, the less I see him. Seeing him tonight did reinforce one important feeling. No matter how hard my life is right now and no matter how hard it is going to get, I do not want him back. I do not want to step back into that life I had with him before. I do not want to listen to the moans and groans of how fat he has got and how awful he looks. I was not pining for him anymore. I hit rock bottom over Christmas and that is the last time I will ever do that. The only way is up.

That feeling of strength is still here with me. It is still firing me and fuelling the determination which is fuelling the strength right back. Does that actually make sense?

I had had him over today. I watched him walk around. I watched him try to interact with the children and then not really know what to do. I watched him play the game with Seb and then walk away again as if that was enough. I watched him flirt with me a little. It all felt quite odd.

I had looked at him as if I didn't want him here. He had asked to see the children tonight because he said it would be the only time he could fit it in. Fit it in. A nice way of putting it.

The children had welcomed him and hugged him when he first walked through that door. Within a few minutes they were back to chilling in front of the TV and ignoring the fact he was here. They had never really played with him or sat with him so they didn't nag him to do those sorts of things now.

He annoyed me with his constant talking about her. She needed time and space to think. So leave her alone then. He couldn't though and I knew that. He can never leave you alone. He has to know what you are thinking/doing/saying when he is not there. He checked his phone hundreds of times for her text or call. It never came and he looked so sad every time his phone was blank. I enjoyed his sadness immensely. He said she said she needs to decide whether she can continue to see him anymore. She has clearly had enough. Maybe she will call it all off. He hopes she doesn't because he said he could not survive without her. I on the other hand hope she does end it and disappears afterwards too.

He also went on and on about this man he thinks she is trying to start some sort of relationship with. He says the man was someone from her past, someone that she knew and he thinks that as she isn't entirely happy with him, this man will seem a great idea to her. He said she was constantly on the phone to him, texting him and talking to him at all hours of the day and night. He said that she smiled whenever she said his name. It had made me think of what is was like between Marcus and Sue at the beginning and a cold shiver had ran through me. So is this man the next one on her list? I wonder whether he has a family for her to ruin too? I smirked as that last question ran through my head.

What I didn't understand is how he thinks I care. Does he? He seems to. He seemed to think today that I would be sympathetic to his worries and his troubles. I just kept saying that I knew what that felt like or that I had been down to the same sad, gloomy place. I kept saying that it is a hard climb back up to the surface but it is possible. He didn't seem to take the hints that I was talking about us. He seemed to pass over that quite quickly.

I tried to escape away from him every now and then. I went out into the kitchen and sat in the conservatory. Wherever he wasn't really. He just ended up materialising again. I wished he could take them out rather than sit in here.

I sat back in my settee and watched the TV. I hadn't been able to do that recently and I smiled enjoying catching up with the programmes. I felt so different. Life felt so different. It was hard to explain. I felt like I could see again. I could see the path that would lead me to being happy. I could see the way I had to turn. I knew it wasn't going to be obstacle free but I was ready to face them. I could see a life with me and the children. I hadn't really done that before. I could see a life without him. Without a husband. I was comfortable with what I saw and it felt good, I felt warm inside.

Life had always seemed so cloudy to me. For a long while I couldn't see a future at all, it seemed non existent and I felt that everything was always going to be this hard. Now I saw the sun shining. The clouds had cleared and the future was there. It might be rocky and it might be quite a long way off and I might be pushed off the road on the journey through. But, there is a sign in the distance which reads 'to happiness.' I intend to follow the paths and find it.

I just felt so good.

5th January 2008

Had a quiet day today. Spent the whole morning in bed and chilled out for the rest of the day. Caught up on some housework and listened to the children playing. They seemed to enjoy the relaxed atmosphere too. They played all day and amused themselves well. Seb even asked to have a bath!

Had Marilyn over for the evening. We chatted about our feelings and thoughts and talked about what changes we should make. It was a nice way to pass the time. Didn't really miss being out though I had wished I was free when Lee text asking to see me. Still feeling a little rough anyway - probably would have coughed more than I kissed if I had seen him! Just hope he is free next Saturday when I am.

Very tired tonight, think I will sleep well. Hope so. Need to.

I could do with a few more calm days like this. Looking forward to having my old friend Jason over tomorrow.

I am getting used to this calm feeling. I am already used to feeling happier. It doesn't take long. Every now and then I do expect something to come along and upset my intentions but I suppose that is normal.

The atmosphere was lovely today. We all relaxed and sat around together. The children played happily, ran up and down the stairs and I could hear them laughing wherever they were. The girls marched around in my shoes making the heels clomp against the hard floors. Seb sat and played his guitar game all day completing lots of the stages. I sat in front of the TV and enjoyed the inner peace.

My Lee text me earlier and I wished he could have come round. I had thought he wasn't home until tomorrow and if I had realised I might have asked mum to have the children. It didn't bother me too much that I hadn't though. I knew he wasn't entirely happy with us and I knew he didn't see anything long term with us, anymore than I did. I had resigned myself to lose him eventually. Him on holiday and then not being able to see him tonight didn't matter too much because of that. Saying that, I would have jumped at the chance to see him if I could have. I thought about him and I smiled to myself.

Marilyn sat round here tonight. She had come down to keep me company after deciding she was too broke to go out. There was no point in both of us sitting alone. We chatted about everything. We talked about my men and my problems and then we chatted about her worries and what was happening with her. It just seems that life is hard for everyone at the moment and it is a case of getting used to living with it. Which is not nice for anyone.

My thoughts then turned to Jason. He was coming down tomorrow afternoon and staying until the following day. I was so happy to be seeing him again. I had missed him so much when he first went, but recently more than ever. Jason was my very best friend. He was such a great bloke. I was quite lost without him.

The children knew he was coming and they were excited as well. Pheobe jumped all over the kitchen shouting,' Jason is coming, hooray, Jason is coming.' She then stopped and looked at me and asked, 'Mum, who is Jason anyway?' I laughed at her and kissed her forehead. I adored the way she was. Jump straight in with a celebratory dance and then not know what she was celebrating really. I looked over to the place she had danced and it made me smile again.

I snuggled myself up a little more so I was almost cuddling myself. I looked over to the seat that Marc used to sit in. I stared at it for a bit. It used to hurt so much seeing that empty space. I pictured him sitting there now and controlling the TV. I shivered and then giggled to myself. It didn't hurt like that now. It had felt odd having him here throughout the evening yesterday. I don't think I could ever cope with evenings the way they used to be. I smiled. That was a good thought to have. Another good one.

I snuggled back down on the settee and felt warm and cosy. Tomorrow my Jason will be here and I could snuggle up next to him. Next to my best friend.

I smiled…. yet again.

7th January 2008

Had such a great time with Jason the last 2 days. I watched him play with my children and listened to the way he talked to them. That's how a dad should be. He watched Barbie, while playing sound snap and didn't moan when they climbed all over him. He was great.

We had our time together when the children had gone to bed. We stayed up until 3 o clock in the morning. We were engrossed in TV programmes and also conversation. We chatted a lot about the things that had happened and how I was coping. How the children were coping was his main concern, especially Seb. He wanted to help him out and he seemed genuinely upset with the way Marc was treating him. He couldn't understand how he could just walk away from his children and not see them. He didn't see the reasoning behind it. I think lots of people I know feel the same.

We chatted about the good old days and being at school and the lack of worry and stress. We chatted about his job and when he would be coming home. We chatted about me missing him and him wishing he was here. Part of me stayed up so late so I could hang onto him for as long as I could. I would have stayed up all night to have those few extra hours with him.

He read through my book and said he enjoyed what he had read. The part about himself and how I felt so close to him and adored him left him a little taken aback. We hugged and I was so pleased to have him here. He apologised for not being at the end of the phone. It wasn't his fault. That's the way life goes.

All of us were so sad when he left. Watching him walk away knowing it would be months before I had him here with me again was so hard. Seb felt it too. He had had that male friendship that he was craving and he was sad that it had gone. I think they are as close as we are.

If I had had him here with me at the beginning, I believe I would have been stronger. I miss him already. The house is quiet again.

As for Marc. He phoned the children. His mum phoned Pheobe. Did not talk to the other two. He said he was flying off to Charleston. Lucky you. Well done. I was polite. The call was short.

Called in sick to work and felt guilty. Feel tired and run down after being so ill and drained from the stresses of Christmas. Need to rest. Just hope they understand. I feel ready to start a new job now. I will keep looking but will only leave for the right one. It will be hard but I know I am ready now.

The sense of determination is quite overwhelming. The strength within me is different from before. Tomorrow my baby starts school. It is the first day of a new life for me. It will be hard letting my baby go. Knowing she is at school and will be full time by Easter is hard. I am not too sure how I will cope without her being here with me. I know it is the same as nursery in a way but at the same time it isn't. It is school and there is no escaping it. This is the final stretch.

She was so sweet earlier. She drew a picture for her teacher in the booklet they had sent to us. She drew herself and her family. There was no daddy. She didn't mention him or include him in her family. She drew me and then looked up and said, "And you are the best one of anyone. I love you Mummy." Yes the tears came and welled up as my heart went to mush.

My baby is growing up. She is a little girl now. I will be so proud tomorrow.

I sat perched on the end of Pheobe's bed. I had felt this overwhelming urge to be with her. I was so worried about her starting school. To me she didn't seem old enough to be at this point of her life. She was my baby, not a school girl. I laughed at myself and then sat very still as she turned over in her sleep. My little upside down girl. Never still for long.

I sighed one of those deep meaningful sighs. I hadn't stopped to think about this moment over the last few days. I had talked about it before then but as the time came closer and closer I had shut it out as I didn't want to deal with it really.

It was hard to imagine my life without her. I didn't want her to grow up and leave me. I suppose that is a selfish thing to say. She had been the one that had been beside me through all the ups and downs of the last year. She was with me at all times, whether shopping, crying or cuddling watching TV. I felt like I was losing her. Tears bit at my eyes as I thought over that. I should be concentrating on how this will affect my life positively for the future. I knew all of that. I knew how proud I was going to be. I knew she would still be around in the afternoons for a term. I knew I wasn't really losing her. It didn't make letting go any easier though.

I leant forward and lay down next to her. I wrapped my arm around her and kissed her cheek. Her school uniform hung on the wardrobe door in her room. I imagined getting her dressed in it tomorrow morning and I smiled. I will be so proud. I will be so nervous for her too but the pride will surely take over. I am thinking into this too much. As a mum I am entitled to though. I am. She is my youngest and she is starting school. I am entitled to miss her. It has been a long time since I have been without a child at home. What will I do with myself?

With that question I smiled and giggled once more and rolled off the bed. Walking down the stairs I felt the cool, chill of silence hit me and I shivered. There was no one here tonight. Last night I had Jason and I was happy. Tonight I am back to being alone again. I wasn't upset though. I was quite happy. I didn't mind being alone so much these days, not like I did before.

I lit a cigarette and made my way to my seat at the window. I sat there with thoughts of my year ahead. The determination to make it a great one was still there. The will to succeed and become more of a fighter was still there. I smiled as it felt good.

I imagined Pheobe starting school full time, my new job that I was going to look for at some point this year and my freedom to live my life how I wanted to. It seemed such a nice outlook and I was pleased I was finally seeing it that way. For once, there was a slither of positivity about a life that had at first seemed too dark and lonely to venture into.

I leant back on the tiles and looked up at the ceiling. I felt so calm considering my fears of tomorrow. I thought about how he will be missing out on that special day. He had missed Fiona's first day at school too. He was in America funnily enough, with this company too. They have been responsible for calling him away from days like this. I hated that.

He didn't seem to care though so why should I? I didn't really. I would enjoy having this moment to myself. I am the one that has worked the hardest to get Pheobe ready for this so I should be the one to enjoy it. I nodded as if I was agreeing with myself and then rolled my eyes at having a conversation in my head yet again.

I sat there with these thoughts running round my head. It wasn't a tangled web at the moment. There was no noise or rattling and the thoughts were not all jumbled up together or being thought over the top of one another. There was a cool, calm fashion about my mind now. Everything was well thought out and said in an orderly way.

Was I becoming organised here? Surely not.

8th January 2008

Well today has been a strange day.

Pheobe threw numerous tantrums this morning either because she wanted to wear her uniform or because she didn't. She didn't want to walk to school and she hated it. Yet she skipped all the way there. She enjoyed nursery too. She came out smiling. Fiona said she had cried when she left her to go back to her friends. Fiona had ended up in tears too.

Pheobe looked so sweet in her uniform. She still doesn't seem old enough to go to school to me. I suppose that is because she is my baby. I was so proud though. So proud.

I joined the friends committee at the school. I can do as much or as little as I want to. It was nice to talk to a few people at the school anyway. Spoke to the headmistress about the fact that I am thinking of leaving London and working closer to home and I hope that she will now let me know if she hears of anyone wanting a part time teacher.

This evening mum phoned with the sad news that Marc's sister Lucy had lost her baby. My heart goes out to her as I can think of nothing worse. It looks like Mum and I have got the blame though. Stressed her out over Christmas apparently. Our family are hard to understand. They should be sitting on the fence. I know everyone likes to hear about what is going on in other people's lives so I expect them to ask questions but there shouldn't be any side taking. They seem to have chosen Lucy and Jack over me and mum. I feel sorry for the children that they will lose others now as well as those they have already lost.

My thoughts tonight consisted of nothing but sad ones. I thought about Lucy losing the baby and the devastation she must be going through. I can only imagine as I have been lucky enough to never have experienced that. I just felt so bad for her. Yet I didn't feel like I could pick up the phone and say so. I thought about it. After the way they behaved on Boxing Day, they had made their standpoint perfectly clear. They probably wouldn't have wanted to hear my voice anyway.

My thoughts then turned to the family. They were behaving so oddly. They hadn't called us since Boxing Day and they didn't seem to want to know us anymore. Mum and I were angry with them for siding with Lucy and Jack. They would probably say that isn't how it is but that's what it feels like to us. It feels like because we said they had ignored me and they said they hadn't, they had decided to believe them. It didn't matter really. That was done and over with and all that mattered was the future and moving on.

My shoulders drooped though at the thought of losing yet more from my old life. That was how I referred to it now. My old life. That in itself is quite sad. It was true though. Everything I had known, the people, the family, the friends, everything had been taken away bit by bit. It was quite hard going. I knew I would be alright but I felt sorry for my children. My family were so close when I was young and they will not have the same.

I shrugged and leant back against the tiles. Nothing I can do about it. I have other things to deal with. Bigger obstacles to get through. I smiled as I realised that although the thoughts were sad, they hadn't got me down. I wasn't low and upset. I just felt a little sad.

Suddenly the image of Pheobe skipping into school with her uniform on appeared before me. I smiled a little more broadly. I had been so proud of her. She had stressed me out this morning with her tantrums and her crying. Nothing was ever easy with Pheobe though and as her mother I knew that better than anyone. I had let her get it out of her system, allowing for her nerves. It had worked. She skipped off and I left her fairly happy, though a little bewildered, in her classroom.

Pride is a great feeling. It becomes absorbed in your body and the only way out is through a smile. My baby is growing up. It's not as bad as I thought.

11th January 2008

Today was a good day overall. Sat with Nicky all morning writing her application form and chatting about men and how they are a pain when you do have one and then when you don't have one you want it. Hmmm funny thing that.

Lee met someone on holiday. Felt a little weird but wasn't upset. I just wished him well and said we should remain friends. He agreed but only time will tell. It wasn't the right relationship so I don't see the point in getting too upset about it. I could have done with this weekend first though!

Mum had children tonight. Was excited to get out and was looking forward to it. Was getting their bags packed and then the phone rings. It was Marc. The children put it on speakerphone. The next thing I hear is her voice. I couldn't go near the phone for fear of saying something awful. I just had to put up with it. If she wants to be stupid enough to get back with a lying, cheating arse then I should let her.

The voice grated on me. The accent even more so. She asked my children how their days at school had gone and whether they had had a nice time. That bugged me. Don't pretend to be interested in my children when you won't encourage their father to have them like he should.

Took the children to mums but forgot their games and things. Felt really bad. Should have took them straight back.

Enjoyed town. Had a little to drink but not much. Marilyn has just left (2am) after coffee and slagging off the exes. Feel tired but also really missing the children. It's only one night and I hate the fact they are not here. I should be sleeping with Pheobe now after checking on each of them. Instead they are at mum's house. She has had her time bringing up children and should not be looking after mine. I feel bad that she is doing so much. I just feel I should be giving them more of my time so she can do less. Then I wonder if there is something wrong with me for feeling like that.

I have made some decisions over the past few days. To ignore all men, including Marcus, for the minute and focus on settling the children into a new routine. Homework and reading need to be done far more regularly than they were before. Bedtime needs sorting with all of them going to sleep when they are supposed to. Getting up for school on time and healthy eating with better dinners are all on the list. I need to make them my world now.

The other decision I have made is to destroy Marc bit by bit. I will make sure I mention that I am looking after his children on a regular basis. I will make sure he knows I think he is a crap father. I will make sure he knows I do not want him back. Lastly, I will divorce him and then tell her the truth about us sleeping together. I never had the real urge to ruin his life before. The anger in me has made that happen. I now wish the day of ruin hurries up and gets here. I plan to enjoy it immensely.

It's amazing how I can feel so many emotions at one time. I jump around from one to another. This used to drive me crazy but I just seem to accept it now. Maybe I am used to it all.

I still felt good tonight. I was still quite calm and relaxed and I still felt like I could cope with everything. I had a couple of knock backs but I got up and brushed myself off quite quickly. It doesn't seem to bring me down with a thump anymore. Whatever Christmas did for me, I have to say thank you.

The pain came back tonight. That bloody speakerphone, I hate it. The children always put it on the loud speaker and wander round with it as they are talking. The accent hit me first as always and I froze. I just stood there. I had to force a smile for Fiona as I heard Sue asking her questions about school and what she had done there today. I walked out into the kitchen but not out of range. Some little part of me wanted to hear what the skank was saying. She spoke to Pheobe. I looked through into the room, peeking around the door... I could see the delight on their faces as they whispered to each other 'It's Sue...I am talking to Sue.' The tears bit at my eyes and they burnt like mad. They were so hot and fierce. I hated that excitement. Most of all I hated the love they showed for her.

Sue seemed so interested in how they were and what they had done. She had this upbeat tone as she was so happy, lucky her. I didn't see it as her being happy with what she was doing and where she was, I just saw it as being happy there with my husband. Hearing the two voices talking together was even worse. The right happy couple. I wondered what he had said to her to convince her to spend more time together. I wondered if he had used her obvious love for the children to bring her closer to him again. I bet they come back from there as a couple again and everything would be forgotten.

It still hurt, why did it still have to hurt?

The phone call finished and within a few minutes I was back to organising things. The pain and hurt had gone and the tears had faded. That didn't take long. I would have sat and cried a few weeks ago.

The anger kicked in and I thought about ways I could ruin his happiness. I didn't want him happy. If he couldn't help me to have a life, then why should I let his run smoothly? No chance. I thought about the divorce and the different scenarios it could bring. Then I thought about telling her everything. I know it would make me feel so much better. I hated living with these lies. Living with the pretence that there had been nothing between me and Marcus this whole time. Maybe I was being too selfish in that though.

I pictured her face when I told her. How would she react? She would probably blame me totally, as I had done her because that is what women do. We attack each other. Probably because we expect that behaviour from men but not from women. I don't know. Part of me smiled at the thought of hurting them both and then part of me was unsure. I don't like to deliberately hurt people, I am not like that. Would I really enjoy it? Don't know. I will have to wait and see as that doubt would not be enough to stop me.

Finally the sense of determination came back. I was going out tonight and I was looking forward to it. Mum was having the children. Marilyn and I were hitting the town. We would probably have a drink and then run down our exes. That always made us feel better. I shook my head and smiled at the thought.

Men cause so many of the problems in life. How do they manage that? At the thought of men, I pictured my Lee. He had met someone else. I hadn't cried. I hadn't even felt too upset. I hadn't wanted him to leave of course, but it was inevitable and I knew he would do so one day. I had kept my distance from him due to that very realisation. I genuinely hoped he would stay in touch and be happy with his new woman.

I smiled at the memories of our time together. I had had so much fun with him and he had helped me a lot. He had made me feel I could have a man in my life, when I was ready. He made me feel attractive again. He made me feel good about myself and most importantly he made me smile and laugh. I hadn't felt the way I felt when I was with him for such a long time. I was grateful for what he had helped me to realise, though I knew he would never know.

I left for my night out, with Lee on my mind, and kept that smile on my face the whole time. In some ways I would miss what he gave me more than what I had had over the last few years with Marc.

Bloody cheek!

13th January 2008

Had another night out last night. Mum is really spoiling me this weekend and I am so grateful for it. I took some games and things to her house so the children would be more occupied. Stayed for lunch and then headed home. Did the usual. Caught up on housework and then got ready to go out. Had a good night. Saw Lee with his new girlfriend. It didn't really hurt, just felt a little weird. I didn't chat to him as we were walking through to the back of the bar in order to go on somewhere else. Marilyn was upset as she had just seen the man she had a date with a couple of weeks ago with someone else. She was a little angry. She was ok though. Until the argument at the end of the evening between her, her friend and his son. It was hard going for a while and she never left till 4am hence the fact I didn't get up until 12!

Marc phoned this afternoon. He told me about his nice time out and about and wondered why I was acting bitter towards him. I told him I was pleased he was happy again and they were back together again. He said he wasn't sorted yet. It will take a lot of work. Excellent. Work at that relationship when you didn't work at your marriage. Fine. I just got angry. He frustrated me. I told him about Pheobe leaving him out of the picture of the family she drew for school. I didn't care it was hurting him to hear. He deserved to know. I told him he had a lot of work to do to rebuild his relationship with Pheobe and probably the other two as well. He just went quiet on the phone. He will work at the relationship with her but I bet he won't work on the ones with his children.

I had visitors this afternoon. My Aunt Alice and Uncle Michael came to see us. We chatted for a while about the problems within the family and how it was difficult to understand. How there was nothing anyone can do. I don't want them to get involved. I don't want them to do anything. The problems are in my life not theirs and they will get sorted out in the end. Things will never be the same again but things have to get better over time. They were really nice to have around. I enjoyed the company. I enjoyed the chat. And I felt supported by them even if they didn't understand everything that had happened and whether they agreed with the way I acted or the things I have said. I don't judge people anymore. Everyone has a reason that they justify themselves with. I don't want my situation to cause a rift in the family because that is not fair. Keep it as my rift. Keep it between the people involved. Not the rest.

The quiet house was enjoyable tonight. It was peaceful and serene. The children are in bed as they are worn out from being at nanny's house. They had a great time. I have tucked them in and kissed them goodnight. I am quite tired myself now too. Looking forward to sleep.

"It will take a lot of work," he said.

Those words had stirred up the anger in me until it came bubbling to the surface like flames, spitting out sparks with my words. He would work at that relationship, but his marriage wasn't worth it. No way. Walk out on the relationship that had lasted 14 years but work hard to repair the one that had only lasted 10 months so far.

He had asked why I was being so hostile towards him. I wonder. What on earth could be making me so cross? How does he not even know why I am angry? Why is he so bewildered about it all?

I had discussed this with my mum too. I had stomped around shouting about it and wondering why he didn't seem to understand. As normal, I switched it and wondered whether I was reading too much into it and I was the one who was making a big deal about something simple. I wasn't though was I? How dare he say that?

I threw my cigarette packet onto the bench and reached for the lighter. I knew there would be a few cigarettes needed to help me de-stress after that remark. I felt so upset and hurt too. Hadn't he thought we were worth fighting for as he so obviously did think they were?

There was no point in getting so fired up and frustrated about this I knew that. There was no way for my anger to escape and I only end up more and more frustrated. I couldn't allow that. I couldn't keep doing that. I inhaled deeply and watched the smoke flow upwards. I sighed and tried to relax a little. I closed my eyes and allowed my shoulders to sink down and my arms hang by my side. For a few seconds my mind was quiet.

I opened my eyes and looked at the wall in front of me. A blank canvass. What images had danced before me on there as well as the window for all those months, the darkness and the silence eating me up time after time. I was glad that that had all stopped. Now I just had to deal with the stress and anger he caused. There was no way to let that out though, I had found that out over the course of the last year. It still hurt and I needed to accept that and then move on to something else.

I hauled myself up onto the bench and continued smoking my cigarette. I felt the tiredness gnaw at me from within. I had had a good weekend overall and I needed to focus on that rather than anything else. A good night out, except for the row at the end of the evening. Marilyn had been really concerned about that. It wasn't a nice experience I have to admit. It was over though.

I went upstairs and checked on the children. Upside down girl was upside down of course, Fiona was peacefully sleeping like an angel and my Seb was sprawled out. All fast asleep and quiet. They had been so tired when they returned from mums. They hadn't moaned about going to bed. They had had a good weekend too clearly. I smiled as I walked out.

Walking into my room, my bed looked quite inviting. I looked at it for a few seconds and debated curling up to sleep. The voices started nagging though, ever so quietly I admit, but they were still there.

"It will take a lot of work," they said.

No, those thoughts wouldn't let me sleep just yet. What would be the point in trying? I went downstairs, collecting the ashtray en route to the kitchen sink and pulled my tired body up to its position on the bench.

I inhaled my second cigarette of the night deeply and blew the smoke directly at my reflection in the glass.

"It will take a lot of work," I said out loud. "It will take a lot of work."

15th January 2008

First day back at work and it was hard going. It was tough to get up and tough to get through. Pheobe had a bad start to the day and cried her heart out at school this morning. She said she hated school and it was really upsetting to know she was so far away. I could not be there for her. It made me angry and I text him from work telling him what had happened. He didn't reply.

I was pleased to get home and was pleased to hold her again. She had been ok at both school and nursery. She said she stopped crying. I wish you could be a fly on the wall in situations like that one. See her playing and working. See her happier than when you left. I suppose all mums feel like that.

Sat and answered the forms for the solicitors. I managed to collect all the information for most of it. Just need to fill in the rest now. It seems such a hard task really. It changes all the time - all the financial needs of me and the children. It's hard to predict them though and think about covering all of them.

Sat and had vodka with mum and tried to feel a little more positive all round. That was hard to do too. Didn't feel down as such, just a little low. Mainly from Pheobe and the fact that I am not too sure what she is thinking or feeling. She is too young to express those sorts of things. She is too young to put all that into words and probably too young to know what it is she is feeling. It's too hard for a 4 year old to get their head round. It's hard enough for me.

The day had been such a long one and I had dragged myself through it. I had hated the day from the start of it. Once the day begins on a negative, it's really hard to pick everything up to be positive.

I had sat with Pheobe this evening and spoke to her a little. She doesn't want to have to go to school all the time she had said. I wondered what she will be like when she started full time. She wants to be at home. She is still so young in her ways and that worries me a little. She seems to need to be with me and my mum at the moment and she is so uncomfortable with going off to school every day. She said she had to be there for too long. Bless her.

Too many changes. Too many different things to get used to. There have been so many it is hard enough for me to keep up and adjust to them myself. Now she was trying to get used to them.

I sat in my usual position with my back against the tiles. I was so worried about the way she was handling things. She seemed so upset and fed up and there was nothing I could do about it. There was nothing I could do or say that would ease her worries and frustrations. I felt so helpless - yet again.

It was a strange feeling tonight. I felt a little low but in comparison to other days it was nothing. I just felt sad again. It was alright to feel this way wasn't it? I was confused now. I hadn't realised there were so many different degrees of sadness. There was the despair and devastation and there was the mood where I cried all the time and then there was this mood that I was experiencing now. All different variants. I just saw emotions as sad and happy. Nothing inbetween or worse or better. Looking back I realised I had learnt so much.

I sat back and thought of Pheobe. She would be ok again soon. She would settle in her new routine and be fine. She would go off to school as Fiona did and she would wave goodbye at the door. It would all be ok.

Changes happen but children bounce back. I had learnt that lesson well.

16th January 2008

He came to see the children this evening. He spent some time with them but not a great deal. He read them a story and then put them to bed. We had a bit of a chat about the children and money etc. He left a cheque for the nursery bill which I was grateful for. He started moaning about her. I began to tell him to shut up but then became a little nosy really. I listened to some of it but couldn't take much. He said she was acting strange now they were back from America. She was pulling away from him and needing her space. I said she had him dangling from a string. I said I had been taking notes and that I was going to use them to mimic her if ever I was in a relationship. I took the piss out of her by mimicking the things he had said about her. "I need my own space so go away. Be there waiting if I come round later though." He laughed at me for doing it. He agreed that she was crabby and hard work and he moaned again about her drinking too much - two bottles of wine a night apparently, *how does she do it?* He also told me she was drink driving in America and at one point she was driving on the wrong side of the road. He then told me he had driven her mad last night by calling her lots. He had called me when he was doing it and asked for my advice. I had thought about saying he should leave her alone but then doing the exact opposite seemed far too tempting. I advised him to keep trying as she needed to know how much he wanted to talk to her. I then came up with the idea that he should phone whoever she was with. He then called her friend Samantha to find out where she was and why she wasn't answering her phone. Bad move! She was not impressed at all. Said he was acting weird. I had to agree with her to be honest though I did giggle at him actually listening to what I had said. I then decided that I had heard enough about the skank now and could we change the subject. I don't think I could have heard her name again without screaming. He apologised for talking about her too much. He also said he wished I hadn't kicked him out. I had said I wished things had been better and that it hadn't come to this. Said it still felt weird as when he came back it kind of felt normal and he agreed. I didn't expect him to say that though and it threw me a little. Maybe there was some feeling in the cold hearted git after all. I always felt he didn't feel anything having left us like he did. Maybe I was wrong but I wouldn't stake my life on it or anything. He then hugged me and bent down to kiss me. For a minute I stood there frozen and felt the brush of his lips against mine. I then pulled away and said that it was wrong to start that again. I asked him why he did this and said if he was happy and in love with her he wouldn't be doing this. He said he was going to take his stay in hospital to think about it.

Anyway the evening went ok and I waved him goodbye without that heavy feeling in my heart like there used to be. I really feel like a different person at the moment and I am a little scared it will go at some point. I like feeling positive. I like feeling stronger.

Sitting here on my own I am soaking up the peace and quiet. It's nice to have my house back. It's nice to know he isn't staying around to control the TV again or annoy me in some way. The house is still and calm. I am writing this with a little smile on my face.

Such a strange man that man. Is everybody's break up like this?

I don't know whether he knows what he has done or even why he did it anymore? I am confused by his actions but at the same time a little smug that things havent quite worked out as simple as he would have liked them. He thought he had met this woman who was going to take him away from all the stresses and strains of his previous life and live happily ever after. I laughed at that point and realised that I was smiling.

I sighed a sigh of disbelief at the thought that he had actually followed my so called advice last night. I couldn't believe he had listened to me. He had called me and said that she was ignoring him and that she hadn't replied to his text messages. I remember saying she was obviously busy and that he should give her a break. He had said that he was so used to my devotion and the fact that I was always there for him her behaviour was difficult to handle. I listened to him going on and on and when he said she was out with sly Samantha I seized the opportunity. I had asked if he had Samantha's number through working with her. He said yes so I suggested he called her to make sure that his skank was ok. He had hung up the phone and never called back. I hadn't actually thought for one minute that he had taken my ridiculous advice. I laughed at the absurdity. Knowing Sue she would not have been impressed at all.

"Well done Stephanie," I said out loud.

I enjoyed listening to the way she was behaving. She was pushing him away really. She clearly didn't want him hanging around her and driving her crazy. She needed her space. She needed to be able to do her own thing. I could understand where the woman was coming from. I still remembered the feelings of suffocation myself. I liked the fact that she was unhappy with him around and that her behaviour was upsetting him. I could actually say that for that reason, I liked her right now. I began to mimic her again as I washed out the sink. I looked up at the window and my reflection and just smiled.

Behind my reflection on the glass was the image of him bending down to kiss me like he did this afternoon. Why did he do that? I know there are some men that like the attention of two women and I know from experience that he is one of them. What I didn't understand is why he treats me like his enemy every now and then, his friend sometimes and then suggests he wants more. I suppose he is confused. So am I?

I shook the questions off as the thoughts of it all were beginning to make me feel insane. I shrugged my shoulders and flicked the switch on the kettle. The children were asleep and the house was quiet. I had checked on my babies lots already. Didn't know what to do next. I watched the steam from the kettle flow up the tiles, evaporate and then watched the water trickle back down them. Each droplet collected more water along its way and then flowed faster. That was how the questions happened in my head. Ask one and it grabs hold of a dozen others that flow round and round.

I giggled as I thought that I actually was insane and continued to make my drink. Hugging the hot cup I plodded into the front room and curled up on the settee. Looking at the remote I switched the channels over until I found something slightly interesting. I sat back and tucked my feet underneath me and absorbed myself in the programme.

It was great to be able to do this. As that thought ran through my head I sat up at its recognition. I was actually sitting down and relaxing in front of the TV. I wasn't sitting on my bench staring at the blank window watching images flash before me. I wasn't wandering round the house aimlessly. I wasn't pacing up and down and fidgetting as the frustration and anger bubbled violently inside me.

I leant back into the settee stuffing a cushion behind my head with a silly, smirk on my face. A silly smirk with a small glow of pride.

Oh!

17th January 2008

Marc phoned from the hospital. The MRI scan picked up a tumour on his liver. He believes it is cancer, the doctors said it was quite likely too.

Numb. Feels odd. Want to be there but I can't be. Not sure what to do.

I have wandered round the house trying to do all the bits of housework I wanted to do today. I have picked things up but just put them in different places. Just moved them around.

Need to do so much more here but I just can't.

Keep thinking about him and what he is going through and how I should be there to support him. I don't know why I am feeling like this. He is the one who destroyed my life and broke my heart. Now look at me. I want to run to be with him. I would nurse him through this if he needed me too. I would be there every step of the way. I don't know if he would want or need me to but I would. I feel so helpless that I can't be there. This is horrible.

So numb.

I should have known my spell of happiness and relaxation and knowing where I was going in life wouldn't last. Something else to add into the mix now. Something else.

He had phoned from the hospital this morning to tell me the news. He cried on the phone and said how scared he was. He said he needed to talk to me about it before anyone else. I had just frozen to the spot. I remembered the moment.

I was sat in the study on the floor wrapping parcels. I had just sat there not knowing what to say or what to think.

The shock of the news felt like a punch to the chest. I struggled to regulate my breathing and my body seemed to go limp and I couldn't move. Everything shut down. Everything stopped.

After I had put the phone down I had not been able to continue with what I was doing. I hadn't been able to do anything in fact. I sat there going over what had been said as if I was checking I had heard properly.

I had stayed in that same frame of mind the whole day. I hadn't been able to snap out of it. I wandered round in a daze and the thought of him just sat there in my head. It weighed me down like a stone.

I wanted to go to him. I had had this urge to just go straight to him. I shouldn't have felt like that should I? After everything he had put me through, why did I feel like that? I had told mum as soon as I heard and she was as dumbfounded as me. Crashed to earth and gone straight through the floor.

I felt numb. I felt at a loss because there was nothing I could do. I felt lost again. That horrid helpless feeling that had ground me down so many times before was back gnawing at me again. I hated feeling so useless. I liked control. Not this.

I sat there and I could feel the heat of anger gurgling away in my stomach. It had been churning away all day but now the warmth was becoming quite intense. I was angry. So angry. With what? Myself, for feeling so useless. With him? For telling me such awful news. With her? With her?

I sat back against the tiles and lit my cigarette. I was puzzled. Why was I angry at her? My mind was working so hard that I could hear the clicking and the words tumbling around at top speed in order to provide me with an answer.

I could feel the frown on my face at that point and realised I was staring into space.

I bent down with my head in my hands and rubbed my head. Straighten these thoughts out. Explain yourself. I knew I had to figure it out or it would eat me up and keep me awake and that was not what I needed to happen right now.

I was angry at her because she was there with him. She was the one holding his hand and supporting him through this. She was the one who could do what I couldn't do. I had had 14 years with him and then the time I wanted to help him the most I couldn't because he had chosen to leave me for her.

Well at least I knew now. It didn't seem a rational point really. A little twisted if anything. It was an explanation though. I had to deal with that. I could still be there for him. I would be there for him if he wanted me to. I would nurse him through all of this. After all she has her job to consider. I am here most days. I would be better than her.

"What?!" I suddenly screamed out loud.

"Why are you thinking that?"

The silent thoughts and conversations had changed to outspoken anger. Not a good sign. I laughed at myself and threw my head back.

All that he has done and all that he has put me through and I was talking about helping him out and nursing him through this. What was I thinking of? I didn't understand my feelings. My head and my heart were yet again in conflict over this. I wiped my face with my hands and just sighed.

Positive. That scenario is not going to happen. It will be fine and he will be well again soon. There will be no worries with this at all. Those thoughts were all very well but there were these nagging doubts pulling at me and the two words "What if?" were swimming round and round my head.

The confusion was back in my life once more and I realised that this could turn out to be another huge obstacle that blocked my road to happiness. Yet another one. It would sit there like a large brick wall that never ended. Too tall to climb over. Too deep to tunnel under. Too wide to walk round. Too hard to break through. I closed my eyes at the thought and the tears of frustration and uncertainty welled under my eyelids.

Please let this wall crumble away. Please let it turn to dust so I could sweep it up and throw it aside. Please I pleaded.

18th January 2008

It is obvious to me that Marc has no need for me today. The more hours that go by the angrier I get for letting myself be used once again. Yesterday he had only needed me to talk to and pick up the phone because she wasn't around. She was at work and he didn't want to disturb her so he used me instead. I am even doubting more and more whether he is telling the truth as he has asked me not to tell anyone about it. If it was me I would be telling everyone I knew to help me get through it.

Anyway, no phone call, no text messages, not a word. He has her with him today so does not need me. I just feel fed up. If I wanted to talk to him I would have contacted him myself so it is not that that I am annoyed at. It is his blatant use of me as he had no-one. Fine. As long as he does not expect it again.

I jumped up on the bench and sat down with a thump. The children had just gone to bed, I had switched the TV off - again - and I lit a cigarette and poured myself a glass of vodka and blackcurrant.

I was angry today. Oh so angry.

He had needed me yesterday. He had phoned me over and over again. She had been at work so I would do. How stupid was I? Yesterday I had sat there and worried about him. I had sat there frustrated that I couldn't be with him. Worried that I would not be able to look after him as she would be in the way. Today, nothing. So stupid.

The anger lurched inside me and I had wanted to scream at myself.

I had spent this afternoon worrying about the future. Worrying what I would do if this was the worst scenario. Concerned for the future of me and my children. Upset for Marc and what he was going through.

No phone call. Nothing. He had her, no need for me.

I inhaled deeply on my cigarette. The emotion I was feeling was pure anger. There was nothing else mixed in with it. I was angry with him for treating me like that and I was angry with myself for letting him. There used to be sadness mixed in with this anger, like when I had felt like this over the children or Christmas or anything else that he had done. Now there was no sadness. This was pure anger.

I fell back against the tiles not taking in how much it hurt. I was numb to anything else.

I felt used as well as stupid. I was used because she wasn't available. I felt second best. I hated that.

I took a few deep breaths. Fighting with myself would only make matters worse. I needed to calm down and get over it. I needed to do something. I didn't know what it was I needed to do though.

I jumped down and checked on the children. Each one lay peacefully though not quite asleep. Each one opened their eyes when I peeked round the door and smiled at me. I smiled back. I hovered outside their doors and then returned to check on each of them again.

"Are you alright mum?" asked Fiona sleepily. She pulled her head and shoulders up off the bed to see more clearly

I sat on her bed. "I'm fine baby girl. I just wanted to see if you were sleeping. I didn't mean to disturb you."

I leant forward and kissed her on the cheek, laying her back down as I did so. I stroked her hair back and watched her eyes flicker then close. I pulled the covers around her and stood up to leave.

"Are you sure?" she said, without opening her eyes this time.

"Yes, angel. I'm sure."

Creeping out of her room and into Pheobe's I felt calmer. The effect of my babies was amazing. I kissed Pheobe and pulled the covers over her. She immediately kicked them back off and I giggled and shook my head.

Seb was listening to his ipod. I peeked round the door. "What?" was all he said. "Night mate," I replied. He wouldn't have appreciated a kiss I knew that. He nodded and carried on nodding his head to the music. I shook my head and giggled once more.

Back in the kitchen I swallowed a large gulp of my drink. I felt better. I sat in the conservatory which was alight with the moon and looked up at the stars. I let my eyes wander over the garden, watching the movement of the bushes and trees in the wind. I rocked in my chair.

Life was so hard sometimes. Every time though, somehow, my children made it better for me. I was so lucky. I smiled.

19th January 2008

What a day. Talk about get out of bed the wrong side. I have been so grumpy, snappy and angry at everyone and everything all day. It started this morning when the children woke up around 6.30.

They hadn't gone to bed until gone 10pm as Marilyn popped round with Jamie. I have had to fight them all week to get out of bed for school and yet on a Saturday morning when they can lay in and let us all get some sleep, they get up at a ridiculous hour. I was angry at them at first and I sent them to Seb's room and lay back down. Then that was it my mind was off. I got angry at Marc. He didn't have to put up with this. He didn't have to get up early. He didn't have them climbing all over him at this time of the morning. He wasn't exhausted because they hadn't let him sleep. He was fine as he never bloody has them. I got angrier and angrier. I was almost crying. I made myself get up and get ready so I could say goodbye to Seb. He was being picked up for a friend's birthday treat and it took about an hour and a half before I could drag myself off the settee and start the day. I organised the present and Fiona made the card for her friend's birthday party. I was a little stressed as I didn't really know where I was going. The village it was in is alien to me and I hate driving where I don't know especially in the pouring rain. I left early and hit traffic. Sitting in it fired the anger again. Supposed to have dropped her off, grab McDonalds for Pheobe and get back to Seb who would be home alone by then. I got angrier and angrier and shouted at every idiot who blocked my path when they shouldn't have. Dropped Fiona off and sat in the traffic again to get home to pick up Seb. Sat in traffic again to get to McDonalds. Got stressed in McDonalds as the queue was horrendous and the children went missing for ages in the toilets. Then Seb made me angry by saying he didn't want anything to eat as he had eaten at his friend's and then changed his mind after I had been served when I had to leave to pick Fiona up. Sat in traffic again all the way to the station where it cleared. Ate my McDonalds at the wheel otherwise it would have been cold and almost dared the policeman who was watching me, tutting and shaking his head, to pull me over and say one word. I was fuming by the time I got back to ours. Went to the shop and bought packets of chocolate. Going to have a hot shower and then plant myself in front of the TV, under a duvet and watch a DVD with the children. Not moving off there for the rest of the evening.

Finally, there was peace and quiet. I had been longing for this all day. I sat back with my cigarette in hand and breathed a huge sigh of relief that the day was over.

I shook my head as the day replayed inside it. It had been one of those days when you wished you hadn't got up. I hadn't wanted to so why didn't I just stay in bed?

I rubbed my eyes with my fist and then let it hang loosely by my side. I stared down at the floor. I knew everybody had days like this but I still hated them. I was so pleased it was finished. Maybe tomorrow would be better. Probably not was my immediate answer to myself. I shrugged and smiled.

The mood had started from the time I had been woken up by the children. I hadn't gone to bed until late so technically it was my own fault. As soon as the familiar feeling of complete exhaustion hit me the tears threatened. They burnt at my eyes and my head began to retaliate as I tried to fight them back.

I was probably only crying through tiredness but for some reason I felt the need to justify myself. The thoughts of him and the unfairness of it all came to the surface and hit me so hard I felt the full force of their power. I laid there staring at the ceiling getting angrier and angrier. The children came in and said they were sorry which made me angrier as I was making them feel bad.

I sat up and pulled my feet to balance on the bench. I breathed deeply and closed my eyes. I had felt that same burning anger just thinking about this morning and I need to settle it so it didn't keep me awake. I needed my sleep.

I remembered standing in the shower and letting the tears fall. All the time thinking. He gets as much sleep as he needs, always had done. He gets the peace and quiet and can relax. He doesn't have to cater for their every need

495

because he never has them. It all ran round and round. He chose to have these children with me, yet he can walk away. It got worse and worse. I had sat down in the shower as I feared my legs couldn't keep me upright. I cried and cried. It was awful.

I opened my eyes to the tears welling in them again. This was just a bad day I told myself. It was all over now and none of it mattered anymore. I knew there was no way I would change places. I would always give up anything for my children, including sleep. There are just times when you collapse under the strain. Only superwoman wouldn't.

I let my feet fall off the bench and I slid myself back to being propped up against the tiles. I had had these feelings so many times before and each time they managed to hit me with the same force, never easing up at all. Life was unfair. It was totally unfair. I had to get used to it because nothing could change it. Nothing could alter the balance and make it all alright again.

I looked down at my hands resting on my lap. I looked at my ring finger where I had once worn his engagement and wedding ring. I rubbed the empty space where they had sat with the other hand. It looked so bare and I still wasn't used to it. After all this time, I still wasn't used to not seeing those two rings side by side. I sighed another deep sigh.

I leant back against the tiles and swallowed hard. I shoved all the pain and anger to the pit of my stomach. I needed sleep so badly my eyes were slowly closing now and there was nothing that could stand in my way.

The emotional rollercoaster that was now inside me stopped moving. I stalled it. I knew it would be back but for tonight at least it could stand motionless instead.

Haunt me another day I told it. Haunt me another day.

21st January 2008

Bad news.
Marc says he has cancer.
Not sure how I feel. Not sure what to say.
This is awful.
And I can't be with him.

A hole had formed through me. I could feel it. There was this large piece of me missing. It was numb and transparent and the feeling of togetherness had gone.

That phone call had changed so much. I never thought I would ever have experienced a phone call like that. I was lost and empty again.

I had blocked it out all day. I saw the children eat their dinner, I completed homework and I put them to bed, kissing each of them goodnight at least three times.

Now though, now in the silence of the house as usual, the emotions grabbed hold of me and dragged me under the surface so I was struggling to survive again. They held me down and made me suffer. I hadn't put up a fight as it had never worked before. I just let the creatures within me take over and make me sink.

The hole I felt was due to the feeling that something was missing. It formed when I was most hurt and couldn't take the pain of what was going on. It was a mental blockout of where the pain was sited. My chest was the vacuum.

I was surprised I hadn't cried by now. I hadn't felt the urge to sob my heart out. I was just stunned by what I had heard. I lay back on the bench with my head to the side just staring out the window. I couldn't have said what I was thinking as I am sure there were no thoughts running through my head.

I had been in that position, just staring, for the last hour at least. Unable to move.

The pain had arrived in layers. Each part laid made the pain more and more unbearable until I had shut it down. I had blocked it out because it had hurt so much and it was hindering my every move. I had formed the hole when I couldn't take anymore.

The first set of pain came when he told me. I had hated him for so long and then the determination to move on without him and the news just knocked me for six. I had gone quiet on the phone. Hadn't known what to say. What could I have said?

The next bit of pain was for my children. What do I tell them? The worst case scenario is that they won't see their daddy again. How do I say that? How do I break that news? In my head I fast forwarded life to the wedding days of my girls and there was an empty seat beside me where he should have been sitting and it was Seb giving the girls away at the aisle. I closed my eyes at this point. In those few seconds of being told the news I had formed that awful image in my head even though that may never happen. Was it a natural reaction?

The next layer of pain was laid when I thought about myself. I had spent the last few weeks hating him. I had made plans to move on with my life and be without him. Facing the possibility of not having him at all was not on the agenda. I wasn't sure I could live without him in my life in any capacity. I couldn't live without him.

The next layer was built with the thought of my mum and what she had been through. She had had cancer years ago and I had shut that out of my head as it was too painful. I said it was a bad habit of mine didn't I. Now though, parts of that were running through my head and it was hurting all over again. I couldn't face it. The feelings were so clear and crisp still and they had forced the pain and fear I had felt then to return just as if I was in the past and reliving it all again.

The next layer was laid with the fact that I couldn't be with him. She was there. She was in my place. I thought I was over that but clearly I wasn't. Clearly that was still so devastating for me. She was there and I couldn't be. I wanted so much to be with him. We should be going through this together. I should be supporting him, holding him and reassuring him. Instead it was her because I had been cast aside.

I closed my eyes as a tear stung and fell silently down my cheek. It was followed by a few more. Yet still I didn't move. I didn't look away from the point I was staring at. I didn't get up or wriggle to get comfy. I just laid there with my thoughts whirring, hoping that that missing part of me would come back soon.

The numbness was set in for the night. The helplessness hovered above me ready to swoop down and conquer and the sadness tinged at the outline of my body. It was all there. The despair and the uncertainty. At least the pain was quashed though. At least I couldn't feel that.

22nd January 2008

Spoke to Marc a little more today. He is coming down to tell his mum and dad tomorrow and wants to pop over and see the children. Whatever.

They have said his tumour is inoperable. It is too deep within the liver. He will need drugs and radiotherapy and someone to look after him. I hope he doesn't shut me out. I want to be there. *Does that sound weird?*

I feel as if I should be ignoring that and not wanting to be there. Like I should let him and Sue get on with it and stay on the outside. His mum would be there too. I just wanted to hold him the other night. I wanted to be there with him sitting in the silence and exchanging those looks you exchange when you are never sure of what to say. I felt so useless being so far away. It felt wrong. He is my husband and I have loved him and looked after him all these years and now when we should be working through this together I am out of the way.

Then I think about my poor children. Going through all of this has been hard enough. To see their daddy so ill and possibly worse would be too much for them to cope with. It's not fair.

There is so much to talk about and think about and sort out and we have no time to begin. No way of getting started. No way of getting together. It all has to be planned and booked in, like an appointment in his diary.

What can I do though? What can I do?

Still the same empty feelings as yesterday. Today has also brought the helplessness to the surface and that is harder to deal with in some ways.

I watched my children tonight as I carried out the daily routine. I had this urge to keep them so close to me and I watched their every move with the same wonder and awe as always with a little sadness on the side too. I listened to them talk about their high and low points of the day and all the time I was having a conversation with myself in my head. I have developed the ability to carry out these mental conversations alongside everything else I am doing. I can continue them in my head at the same time as talking to someone else, playing with the children, cooking and cleaning. Does that mean madness has well and truly set in?

I smiled a little smile.

The silence was petrifying tonight. I hadn't wanted it to be around at all and I had delayed it as much as I could. I had the radio on in the kitchen, the computer on in the study and the TV on in the lounge. All the sounds mingled together and there was a constant buzz. But no silence.

I sat on my bench and leant backwards, inhaling on my cigarette deeply as I did so. I had had this constant whirr of thoughts twirling around in my head as if they were all seated on a roundabout. It made me feel sick and dizzy. I couldn't eat anything. I couldn't settle too easily either.

There seems to be so many questions I want to ask him and so many things we need to get sorted together and yet there is no time. I have been blocked from him. By her. I wanted to be there. I wanted to see him. At the same time I imagined his reaction to all of this. He would go over and over it again and again, saying the same things constantly. Did I really want to be there for that? He had driven me mad when he was ill in the past. I could only imagine what he was like now.

I felt guilty for thinking that. Hooray, another feeling added to the pile. I rolled my eyes and looked up at the ceiling. Now the noise was driving me mad and I switched everything off. I waited in the kitchen for the silence to catch up with me. I sat there waiting for it to hit me and make me plummet to the depths of despair.

I sat there in the dreaded silence and waited nervously. The thoughts would start soon. I closed my eyes and waited.

23rd January 2008

Met Marc after work and drove him back to tell his parents about the tumour. It was a hard journey home. I listened to him talk about how he is feeling. He said he was going to take the worst scenario and hope to be pleased that it doesn't happen. Said optimism only means you get disappointed. I can understand the way he feels really but I can't think like that. I'm not sure how I would survive without him. It's hard enough to keep going now without him in my life the way he was, let alone without being there at all. I can't possibly consider that scenario.

He came back to mine to see the children for an hour before going back to London. We talked some more and I got angry that he wants to leave £20,000 to Sue from his insurance money. *Why should the woman who split up my marriage get anything?* She has enough money. That should be extra for his children. The children will get a large sum of money for their future. But no dad.

We hugged and kissed in the kitchen. We just held each other both afraid to talk too much. Probably both having some questions we couldn't ask. We just held each other tightly and let the moment continue.

I said that when this sort of thing used to happen before, I had felt like his mistress. The way we behaved with each other. The sleeping together and the sneaking around. I said I didn't want that feeling to return. I then moaned that I didn't get any of the perks anyway and laughed. He said he would see what he could do!

I feel so mixed up and so confused. I can't straighten out my feelings. I want to block it out and not deal with it but obviously that isn't going to happen. I want to do something to help him and that isn't going to happen either.

So hard to get my emotions across here as I just can't feel them.

I had been pleased to have him here with me this evening. I hadn't been pleased the whole time though. Now he had left and I was sad again.

The house felt empty like it used to do when he had first left. I had been through so much and there was no sign of it letting up. He had treated me so badly and continued to do so and yet here I was upset that he had gone home. I didn't understand myself at all. I was so confused.

I sat in my usual position and thought about the things he had said. I had hated him talking so negatively. He had always been a pessimist. He used to worry about things going wrong before they had even happened and yet there were only a few times in his life where his pessimism had been right.

I felt sorry for him going through this. Yet it seemed that he needed to talk to me about it. I had asked if he had spoken to her and he said he couldn't talk to her as he could me. That touched me a little and I smiled remembering it.

I leant back against the tiles and recognised the lost feeling biting at me. I was low and fed up but the lost feeling was worse.

Suddenly the hot gnawing sensation in the pit of my stomach grew stronger and stronger until it was bubbling away like hot lava. The anger had hit me. She was getting her skanky hands on my money. The children's money. What?

I sat bolt upright on this realisation as I had done when he had first told me. He said she would be caring for him a lot and he wanted to thank her. Stuff that! I had taken care of him for years now. I would do it now too because that is what I am like. What about the children? They would get a large sum of money from him I knew that but if he changed that one, would he change the other? Would I be able to finance the home ok? Would I be able to keep up the payments to run this place? Would the children be left with huge trust funds but nowhere to live?

Was I wrong to be angry about this? Were these the wrong questions to be asking? Did asking them make me a bad person?

I threw myself back against the tiles and frowned. There was too much to take in. I couldn't stand it.

The feelings were so mixed up and so was my head. I didn't know which way I should be turning. I lit a cigarette and blew the smoke at the window. The darkness outside just about summed up my mood at that moment.

There was no point in trying to understand each emotion I went through; I had learned that from the last ten months. I had to wait patiently until I was ready to attempt to separate them. If I ever became ready.

24th January 2008

He phoned this morning and we had a brief chat. Said he was on his way to work. Said she was really ill. Nothing too interesting. I wish he would stop talking about her. I don't care. I don't want to know. It hurts every time I hear her name.

Had a busy day with visitors but nothing else. I didn't want to do anything. There were lots I should have been doing. Didn't want to though so didn't move off the settee unless I had to.

Spent the evening on the phone. So many things rattling around my head now. So tired and yet with all this I bet I wouldn't sleep.

My cousin Sophia phoned first. She wanted to try and sort things out within the family. She said it shouldn't be like this. His sister Lucy is apparently upset she hasn't seen the children for a while. She hasn't phoned them. She hasn't spoken to them. If she doesn't want to speak to me she has Seb's mobile and could call him. I don't want anything to do with them at all. Lucy has made her position perfectly clear. She didn't think I should have been there on Boxing Day as I am no longer part of the family. That's always nice to hear. I have no inclination to be part of that side of the family any longer. Her and her parents are out of my life now. That is what they have chosen and I am merely granting them their wish.

After Sophia was mum. Spoke to her about what was said. She then decided to phone Sophia and give her version. Explain her feelings and thoughts and opinions on all of it. Aunt Violet then phoned me because mum did not answer the phone to her. I tried to explain but it is so hard to do so. They don't understand. No one does. No one was there.

Then Marc. He had nothing to say on the matter. He said he tried to explain why I was so angry with them on Boxing Day but they just said I shouldn't have been there. Fine. Fair enough. We then spoke again about his illness. He said he had been transferred from his original hospital to one in London. That is better for him. He said he would need me there when he is going through it. I hope he does. I want to be there for him.

The family situation is not bothering me as much as you would think it should. Jack had said he does not want anything to do with my mum again and Lucy and I will never be able to patch things up again. That means we can never be part of them again. We cannot be in the same room as each other again. Therefore we cannot be part of that family again.

I feel like they do not understand how hard it is for me. I know that is because they have not been a single mum and I know that you can never really appreciate what people are going through unless you have been there. But they have. They have been there. They have watched my aunt Violet and cousin Cathe go through this. They have seen the problems and they have seen the heartache and the misery. *There should be a higher level of compassion then shouldn't there?* Jack has been there before. *Why has he not taken Seb aside and spoke to him?* Everybody keeps saying that Jack is not like that. Marc's mum is not like that. *Why can't the same rule apply to me? Why does it have to be me that is in the wrong?*

They couldn't approach me and I couldn't approach them. Therefore it's stalemate and no matter how much talking isn't going to change it. Therefore accept it and move on. Like I have to do. I have lost an awful lot of people over the last 10 months and I have become used to not talking to them ever again.

I cannot get over the pain that Jack and Lucy have been out with Sue. I cannot get over the hurt and the betrayal I feel from Marc and his family. I have to forget it and move on. I wish them well but accept they are no longer part of the lives of me and my children. Subject closed there really.

People can not see other people's points of view. It is a natural thing. No one understands thoughts and feelings on a situation unless they have actually been through it. They can try to understand but the connection isn't there.

Family are supposed to understand. They are supposed to relate to each other and support each other. I feel that that hasn't happened. I have lost my family.

I knew the split would take its toll on the relationship between me and his family. That is obvious really. There isn't that closeness between in laws. Sometimes there is and there is the support and understanding needed, but most of the time that doesn't happen. Fine. I didn't expect to lose my cousins and aunt because one of them is engaged to my sister in law.

The phone calls tonight were to try to sort it out. Sophia tried. She conveyed their side of the story and I conveyed mine. Neither of us agreed with the other. That is what happens. It was a sad situation to be in. It really was.

I had been gutted when Marc said that his family firmly believed that I shouldn't have been there on Boxing Day because I am obviously no longer part of the family. The problem is I am not going to allow them to make the children part of it as they are with me. They haven't been here to help me with them so they are not going to get the enjoyable bits. I will stick to that decision as much as I can only allowing it to break when I have no control over it.

I sat back and thought how sad it was that I didn't feel any upset over cutting out the family. How I would never have been able to do such a thing in the past and yet now it really doesn't bother me. I feel bad that my children won't have that network but they have us and we will more than make up for it. It is hard to think that I have become so used to people walking out of my life for good over the last year. I have lost so many friends and now members of my family too. At first it was so difficult. I can remember at the beginning of my diary it was clear that I struggled to think about those people, how it upset me when he was with them and I was alone. I remembered how lonely I felt. I smiled as I realised how I had become stronger now.

The journey I have been forced to make will help me become a stronger, better person in the end.

The anger was present a little tonight. I had been frustrated at not being able to get people to understand how I was feeling and how I couldn't get my point of view across adequately. I had become annoyed with them for allowing him to manipulate them all when they clearly had only his point of view and didn't seem to want to listen to mine.

A feeling of calm had washed through me after that initial burst of anger. I realised that I didn't actually care anymore. It was a relief. I didn't care that they wouldn't listen. I didn't care that they had made their mind up and had seemingly taken his side. Lucy's side. Whichever. It didn't matter to me. All that mattered was me and my children, my parents and sister. They were all I cared about now. I realised they were all I needed.

I sat back, shrugged and breathed a huge sigh. A smile crept on my face as I had dealt with yet another obstacle that had popped up in my way.

I jumped down off the bench and checked on the children. All asleep. All sound asleep. I kissed each one of them and ran my hand over their heads. A smile for each one too as they turned over at my touch.

I crept out and stood in the darkness of the hallway. I looked across to the mirror and stared to make out my reflection. For the first time in a long while, I smiled back at myself.

25th January 2008

Had a nice day today. Spent the afternoon at a friend's house so Pheobe and her friend could play. It was a lovely relaxing afternoon chatting about nothing in particular and laughing too. I had a great time. Pheobe showed off when it was time to leave because she wanted to stay and continue playing. It was nice to know she was happy with her new little friend.

Had mum to stay tonight. We shared a bottle of wine and chatted till fairly late, discussing any topic which came up no matter how bizarre. We went from the ridiculous to the profound in easy swoops and didn't bat an eyelid.

Marcus had said he wasn't going to make it as he would be at the hospital till late. He stayed there to have more tests done as he has just been transferred. It is probably a better place for him to be anyway. I told him again that I would not be allowing the children to travel back and forth to London within the 24 hours as they had been doing, because they are too tired and run down and also with Pheobe at school she would be too tired on Monday morning. He seemed to understand.

When I lay down to sleep my thoughts were of him as normal. They are becoming more and more so as the time goes on. I worry about how he is feeling, what he is thinking and how is coping. I worry about the future and how it could be that the last couple of years we would have had together have been snatched away by her. I worry about how I will cope without him if anything happened to him.

I worry how I would cope if I never had him in my life at all.

I lay down in bed and could see the stream of light coming through the curtains. I had had a nice evening with mum and now I was doing my best to sleep. It just wasn't happening.

I tossed and turned but the constant whirr of thoughts kept my mind awake no matter how much my body begged and pleaded for sleep. I huffed and kicked the covers back as the heat got to me. I was fed up with just laying here. I had done this so many times and I knew that there was nothing I could do.

I looked up at the ceiling, following the light as it moved across it from the car outside. I looked at each of the corners of the room, though what I was expecting to see I don't know. I turned my head and looked over at the wardrobe. I could see the dust shimmering in the dark light and realised how I hadn't cleaned up here for so long.

As that was the least of my problems, I turned my head back the other way to find Pheobe's face right in mine. I smiled at her little button nose and her pale pink lips. She looked even more beautiful in this light, if that was possible.

There he was again. An image of him behind Pheobe where he used to lay. I even sat myself up on my elbows to make sure it was just an image. He had been on my mind constantly lately. I fell back down onto my pillow. I wondered what he was doing right now. Probably with her. He always was. Another weekend goes by without my children seeing their daddy. That made me so frustrated. Again.

I pulled the pillow out from under my head and placed it over my face. I lay there in the pitch black, wishing the conversation I appeared to be having in my head without realising it would stop now so I could sleep. I pulled the pillow off and placed it on my waist, laying my hands on top of it so it was sandwiched between my arms and stomach. Snug and warm.

I turned over and laid on it next. I seemed to be so uncomfortable at the moment. I couldn't relax and stay in one position. Pheobe seemed to mimic me and I smiled to myself.

Again my thoughts wandered to him and my smile faded. What would I do if I never saw him again? Would I be able to cope without him? I didn't know and I shut my eyes tight as if that would stop me thinking about it. I opened them again, pulled the pillow out from underneath me and placed my head back on it. I just wanted to sleep. I didn't want to think about him anymore.

My legs ached so much that I had to keep moving them to try and ease the pain. I placed the duvet between them and rolled over, pulling the covers with me. He used to do that and I used to get so mad when he had pinched all the cover. I smiled again. I didn't have to share anymore. That was definitely a plus.

I turned my head to the side again and faced Pheobe. She was breathing so deeply, she was almost snoring. I lifted my head up, folded my arms on the pillow and placed my chin on top. Was he alright? I rolled my eyes at the recognition that I had gone back to thinking of him and promptly rolled over and placed my hands over my eyes. Stop thinking I yelled to myself. Stop thinking.

I threw my hands down by my side and laid still. I stared up at the ceiling again. Where is the sandman when I need him? I need to sleep.

1st February 2008

It has been almost a week since I wrote last and what a week it has been.

On Saturday Marc decided that he couldn't come down to be with the children and stayed in London. He phoned at 8.30am to say he would be at the station for 10.30 so could I be there with the children so he could get them back quickly. He said he had bought tickets to go somewhere with Sue and a couple of others and wanted them to go, but he was unsure as to whether Sue wanted them there till Sunday so he may have to bring them back in the evening. I repeated what I had said to him yesterday about them not travelling there for the few hours they get there. I said he could come here and have them. I said he could stay overnight and be with them the whole weekend. He said as he had already made plans with her that he couldn't get out of and as I would not let them do the trip to London for possibly just a few hours, he would stay in London instead.

I was a little angry that he wouldn't give up his time with her to see them but understood that as I had said no to them going that was the way he would play it. I didn't understand why he couldn't change his plans but I never understand anything like that.

Me and mum took the children into town and then onto the zoo. They had a nice time but halfway round the zoo I started to feel ill. My stomach was so painful and I felt quite sick and very cold. I curled up on the settee and could have cried with the pain. Mum took Seb to hers and the girls played and went to bed early allowing me to do the same. Eventually in the early hours of the morning I was throwing up time and time again. I still had the pains and tossed and turned so much I ended up getting up. I asked Marc to come and help me but as he was meeting his sister he couldn't. Seb came home from mums late morning and took over. He was an angel. He cooked the dinner, brought me anything I needed and bathed the girls and put them to bed. He was great. A few moans and groans but I figured he was entitled to that.

Still no better the next day so mum came over to fetch Pheobe and help me out. I couldn't work Tuesday as I was so ill and planned to go in on Wednesday. Wednesday morning brought more complications though. Pheobe woke up with an astonishing fever and I had to phone in sick and take her to the doctors. A throat infection - antibiotics, nurofen and calpol. Fiona was then sent home that afternoon with a temperature and was also fed nurofen and calpol which meant the invention of a rota to watch the times carefully. Kept them at home Thursday and Friday.

Spoke to Marc Thursday night, the tumour has grown and they have confirmed that it is inoperable. Tried to help him but wasn't sure what to say. Was fairly tough but in a nice way. He listened anyway and agreed with most of it. He hadn't stayed in hospital when they had wanted him to. I told him he was wrong and that he came out for the wrong reasons. I also said that it was about time he got his priorities straightened out. First his health and then his children. I'm hoping he will listen as Seb seems to be getting quite angry and confused as to why he hasn't been to his dad's flat recently. I felt really sorry for him.

Then tonight, Seb sets fire to paper in his room burning his carpet. He said he didn't know why he did it but knew it was a stupid thing to do. I lectured him though I tried not to scream at him. I was so shocked by it all it was hard to find the right words. I texted Marc and asked him to phone as soon as he could as I needed him to talk to Seb and wanted him to know what had happened but I didn't get any response. He is probably still in hospital so I have to understand. Felt quite alone.

Another difficult week had finished and another month had begun. I am pleased January is over - never liked that month. Don't ask me why because I don't know.

I had been so ill. I was then a little hurt that he wouldn't help me out when I was throwing up and in agony although I knew when I was asking for his help that I wouldn't get it. I don't know why I bothered really. That thought came with the roll of the eyes and the shaking of the head that thoughts of him often carried these days.

I had been worried all week about his illness. Each night brought a broken night's sleep and even when I felt sorry for myself for being so ill I was thinking that I wasn't as bad as him and I should count myself lucky. I had told him that if he didn't feel up to having the children then I would understand and I knew that this weekend would not be an exception.

He had said that he was in hospital after feeling in pain and being sick. He said they wanted to keep him in longer but he just wanted to be at home. I felt sorry for him. I hung my head and looked down at the floor. The familiar wave of sadness washed over me and my eyes were filled with tears almost instantly.

Seb had scared me tonight. I had found him with burning paper on his carpet after smelling burning. I could see the fear in his eyes at what he had just done. He was confused. Said he didn't know why he had done that and I didn't push the issue. I lectured him on the dangers of doing something so stupid but left it at that. I was frightened by the whole thing. Not just the fire. Not just the stupidity. Not just the 'what if it had been worse' questions. The fact that he had done it scared me. Really scared me.

I leant back against my settee cushions and hauled my hands up over my eyes. I had text him saying that I felt useless and that Seb had set fire to books in his room. I had hoped for a response. The tears fell between my fingers. Then the guilt hit me. I had disturbed him while he was resting in hospital. If he hadn't received it now he would do tomorrow. How would that make him feel?

The feelings became so strong they overwhelmed me and I immediately got up and went for a cigarette in the kitchen. The tears still fell. I hauled myself up on the bench and tried to fight back against the guilt and sadness demons but it was no use. They were stronger than me.

I sat there for a while, inhaling deeply every now and then and just staring out of the window. Weeks like this were hard. My babies ill, me ill, Seb acting oddly and my husband in hospital with cancer. When I listed it I realised why it had knocked me down and I felt so low.

Tonight was a bad night I could sense that. I needed to feel sorry for myself. I needed to cry. I just felt so alone. Again. Loneliness was the one feeling I couldn't handle. Loneliness brought on the sadness and the emptiness and when all three demons attacked it was impossible to save yourself.

The darkness swept in swiftly and the silence clawed at my ears. I sat there like a frightened rabbit who didn't know which way to turn when the bright headlights had appeared. I didn't know where to find the comfort that I needed. I didn't know how to numb the pain of the demons claws ripping at my insides.

I just cried.

2nd February 2008

Chilled out with the children all day today. Sat around and read magazines and completed crosswords. It was nice to not have to do anything. Mum and Dad came round to baby sit and I went out on the town with Marilyn. It was quite a nice evening though I was ready to come home about midnight. I chatted to a few people in the last bar but by that time I was ready to go home. I had had my fill of adult conversation and I did not want to drink anymore. We went for cheesy chips and then called dad to pick us up. Was home and in bed by 2.30am. A nice escape though.

A better day today. The demons were controlled and I had won. I had relaxed all day and had done absolutely nothing. I had occupied myself with mundane activities and read stories in magazines about other people and their pain so I didn't have to realise my own.

Mum and Dad had gone home and Marilyn had left after her cigarette and cup of tea. I walked up the stairs and checked on my babies. They were all sound asleep. Pheobe was taking up most of the space in my bed and I wasn't sure how I was to fit in. It was amazing how a small child could take over a double bed. I just smiled down at her watching her purse her lips and sigh deeply.

The silence of the house was deafening me and the darkness was uneasy. I couldn't understand why. I had felt ok today. I squeezed in next to Pheobe and hoped that I

514

would soon be in the world of dreams. I turned the radio next to my bed around so that the light from it shone onto my face and my pillow. The glow was quite comforting. I laid there looking at the bright light and watched the minutes changing. Every now and then I felt Pheobe turn over and shuffle further down the bed. The covers followed her each time and with that came the cold air against my skin which sent chills through me.

I was so cold.

The shivers continued to keep me awake. I lay on my back with my arm under my head, propping me up. I thought about some of the faces I had seen that night. Those people seemed quite happy in their little lives and a little pang of jealousy hit me. I sighed deeply. It wasn't that I was unhappy. I was just overloaded. Other people must feel it too at some point in their lives surely.

I pulled out my arm and slammed it down by my side. Pheobe moved again and I clung to the covers tightly so they didn't move yet again. I didn't want the cold to get me. I hauled the covers up under my chin and tightened my grip on the inside of them. I turned my head to the side and watched for another movement from Pheobe as she snored quite loudly.

I smiled at her. A broad, proud smile.

I turned my head back to the centre and looked over at the window. The curtains closed and no light peeking in. The lamppost still visible through them. I turned onto my side. Facing the door I could see the outline of the dressing gown that hung there. I got up and reached over for it tugging at it to make it fall down. I wrapped it round me and pulled the covers back over the top. I was still shivering.

I curled up in a ball and laid there listening to the silence around me. I snuggled up next to my baby girl and stayed there waiting. Another night spent waiting for sleep to arrive. Just waiting.

4th February 2008

Ran around today doing nothing much. Ironing. Taking children to and from school. Had to be there for 2.45pm today for the school workshop I was doing with the girls. We dug trenches and set logs in to make seats for the children and we made badges and dens too. Apart from being freezing cold, the children seemed to enjoy it. We came back exhausted, had a quick dinner and went to bed fairly early. Mum came over for the night with a headache. We chatted a little about Marc and his illness. The confusion is making me feel sick now. He was crying on the phone again yesterday and I feel quite bad for him. Then on days like today when I haven't heard from him because he has her, I just get angry with him and with myself. It becomes very frustrating.

I yawned as I sat staring out of my window. My usual spot. Cold tiles on my back and the darkness trying to get in through the glass. My reflection staring back at me.

I yawned again. I was tired from not sleeping and from the work I had done today. So tired. Didn't want to go to bed yet though. Mum was already upstairs. She was ill with a headache. She had felt awful. Looked pretty rough too. I hated seeing her ill. My mum was wonder woman; she wasn't allowed to be ill. I giggled at that comparison and smiled at the image of myself before me.

I had become quite angry this evening. Nothing from him today. I sat waiting for his call and I hated the fact that I did that. He must have her there tonight. No need for me. I sighed deeply. I hated feeling so unwanted again. I had just been rid of that feeling. I felt it so much when he left me for her and I hated the fact it was back.

I sighed again, puffing out my cheeks as I exhaled. I lit my cigarette and sat there staring at the window. I tried to block out the image of me there but in some ways I was grateful it was me instead of the haunting pictures of her that used to play on the glass.

I rubbed my eyes and yawned again. I reached for the phone and checked that I hadn't missed a call or text from him. Yesterday he had been so upset. He was crying on the phone saying he didn't know what to do and wasn't sure he could cope. He had turned to me then. He needed me then. Was that just because she wasn't there?

The image of her sprang to my mind again. She was there right in front of me. Her. That woman. She was with him now so I was shut out. God, I hated her for that. Even now. After all this time she was still affecting our relationship. Couldn't she see he needed me? I answered 'no, of course he wouldn't let her see that,' straight away and burst the floating image of her and sat back again.

Another conversation with myself. Great.

I was so frustrated. I was frustrated with him for treating me like that and using me the way he does. I was frustrated with her for being in the way and not letting me care for my ill husband. I was frustrated with myself for letting him pick me up and use me when he wanted to and then dropping me as soon as she was around.

I let out an angry sigh and shook my head.

I rubbed my face with both hands and yawned again. I need sleep. I need my bed.

I checked the phone one last time, just to make sure. I jumped down off the bench and headed upstairs. As soon as I got to the top I made my way back down to collect my phone.

'Just in case,' I said to myself. 'Just in case.'

That bloody woman.

5th February 2008

Went out after work to meet Alex. Got to the shopping centre and had missed Marc's calls all day as I was teaching. I phoned him when I first arrived and he sounded terrible. I talked to him for a while and felt so sorry for him. She had gone out to a works do and left him home alone. He cannot be alone. He never has been able to and now he is going through this he is even worse. He cried a little and said he didn't feel he could carry on with all of the treatment. I tried to encourage him but it's hard. I can't even contemplate what he is going through at the moment so how am I supposed to make him feel better. I went shopping and then met Alex. We sat in pizza hut enjoying our meal and talking away about everything. He is such a nice guy. He makes me smile and feel better. He will be a great friend if nothing else. We went for coffee afterwards and Marc kept ringing. I took the call and listened to him rambling. I knew he had been drinking and eventually he admitted it. I spoke to him while Alex was ordering and I tried again to help him. I was tempted to ring her and tell her what he sounded like and that he had been drinking. I felt she should do something about it being his girlfriend. I couldn't though. I told him I couldn't talk any longer to a man that was drinking when he was so ill and that he needed to stop now, drink some water and then get some rest. After I left Alex I rang him again. He seemed better. I didn't hear from him again after that.

"How could she leave him like that?" I had said loudly. "How could she leave him?"

Driving along the A12 at ten o clock at night was not the best time to have a conversation with yourself. I had been driving for about a quarter of an hour after listening to him on the phone. He had been in such a state because she had gone out and left him.

"How could she?" I had said again.

The music was blaring and I talked to myself the whole time. All I had thought about was Marc indoors alone going through what he was going through. I felt so bad for him. It was awful. I was angry with her too. Putting a drinking session with her mates before looking after her sick boyfriend, my sick husband. My emotions were running riot tonight.

I had turned the volume up to try to drown out my thinking but it hadn't worked. I had just got louder when I was talking to myself and that was why I think I had started talking aloud. I needed to be heard.

"That bloody woman cannot even give up one night out for him," I screeched.

I had sat in the car park that evening and listened to him crying. He had said over and over again that he couldn't be alone when he was healthy but to be alone now was worse. He had felt like she had deserted him and I felt angry with her. I knew she needed her nights out but honestly, could she not give up just one. He said he had told her that he was feeling so down and needed her and yet she still went out and left him. Apparently this was not the first time she had done so either. I didn't know that before now and I was fuming. All this time I thought she was looking after him and she wasn't.

"How could she walk away from him knowing he felt like that," I shouted.

The selfishness of the woman struck me. To go out on the town with your friends when your sick boyfriend had practically begged you to stay in with him must have taken some nerve. Leaving him home alone to cope with the fear of everything.

"How could she?" I shouted as I slammed the car door.

I sat on the bench, wondering how I had made it home in one piece and flicked up my phone. The light went on and it shone around me. I scrolled down the numbers until I came to hers. I wanted to phone her and tell her what I was thinking. I wanted to say to her that she had driven a sick man to drink tonight and that she should be there with him instead of being out with her mates drinking herself into a stupor. I know she has this need to be drunk constantly but surely she can give it up if her boyfriend needs her so desperately? Selfish cow. I stared at the number for a few more seconds and then slammed the phone closed.

I couldn't do it. I couldn't hear her voice.

He was so drunk when I spoke to him the second time. He had been drinking vodka neat. That would be good for him. He was such a weak man. How could he get into that state just because he was alone? Other people don't do that. Other people don't get so unhappy.

I shrugged my shoulders.

I made myself a drink with the full intention of going to bed. Thoughts of him entered my head again and I picked up my phone. Maybe I should call him. I stared at it again for a few seconds. She was probably back with him now though. She had probably stumbled home to pass out there. He wouldn't talk to me.

Then a realisation hit me like a bolt of lightning. I had done it again. I had been there for him when she wasn't there. She had probably gone back to him and that was why he hadn't phoned again. I threw my phone onto the bench shaking my head with disbelief. Every single time I fall for it. Every single time.

I perched myself back on my bench and sat back against the tiles. Too angry to sleep. Too worried to relax. Too annoyed with myself.

What would be the point in trying?

6th February 2008

Marc tried to phone me a few times this morning. I knew it was the day of his treatment and he probably needed support but I was teaching and couldn't answer. I felt bad that I couldn't help him. I can't be there all the time and he doesn't necessarily want me with him anyway. He only needs me when she is unavailable. Again I became frustrated about last night.

Went to see his Aunt Sally and cousin Carly after work and told them what had been going on. They listened to me and were very supportive. I felt bad about going round there but they seemed to understand why I had. They agreed to play it carefully so I didn't look the bad guy who told people when he didn't want anyone to know.

Marc phoned the children tonight and spoke to them for a short time. Fiona seemed aware that something was wrong with him and I said he had a stomach bug. I will try to keep this from them for as long as I possibly can. He spent all of 2 minutes talking to me. I asked if she was there with him tonight to which the answer was of course yes. He couldn't speak to me then. I hung up feeling quite annoyed again. *Who was the one he ran to last night? Who interrupted her date to answer his call? Now who gets pushed to the sidelines? How stupid am I?*

Anger kept me company today. I didn't feel lonely when anger was by my side. I felt so stupid. So used. So foolish. But not lonely.

My breathing was faster than normal and my heart was racing a little too. Anger had this effect on me and I knew the signs well. I knew there would be no point in trying to do anything about it. I just had to control the feeling long enough for it to go away. At times like these I wanted to smash around the house. I wanted to pace up and down and shout and scream. I wanted to throw things across the room. I couldn't do any of that and I couldn't let the fire in me be released. There was nothing I could do to extinguish it and feel calmer. I had to let it burn itself out.

I hauled myself up onto my bench and stared at the wall ahead of me. I was biting the inside of my cheek out of sheer frustration and I could feel the level of pain I was inflicting on myself getting worse. I shook my legs constantly as if that was going to relieve me. I couldn't seem to sit still.

Thoughts of him came and went followed by thoughts of her. He has somebody to jump in and help him whenever he needs it. He uses me to help when she is out getting drunk and then drops me as soon as she is back. I hated her for that as well as him though I probably couldn't explain why if I was asked to.

I threw myself back against the tiles banging my head quite hard as I did so. It hurt lots but the anger numbed it for me. The ticking of the clock broke the silence as I sat there staring at the wall with my mind racing. I had been in this position so many times before and yet I still hadn't figured out a way of calming myself down in these situations.

I had picked the phone up to call him back so many times tonight but I knew he would ignore me. It made it worse when I realised that and I could have hit myself. I let him do this to me. I was so stupid. I had come to his aid again last night and now I was the one abandoned because someone else had come along. No need for me, cast me aside.

My muscles clenched as I felt the wave of anger being fuelled by my thoughts. I had to stop this. I had to stop all of it. I wouldn't though. I knew I wouldn't. Next time she left him and he phoned me I would be there as I had done last night and all the times before.

I was so stupid. I knew that. I actually knew it.

What is going on here?

9th February 2008

Marc arrived mid afternoon. He looked tired and run down and I felt sorry for him. He was staying here tonight and I was a little concerned as to how I would get through it. I knew it would be weird. I took him into town in the afternoon as he wanted to treat himself to a Wii. He bought the children one too but it quickly became apparent that he was overdoing it. He could hardly walk and became so breathless. After the children had eaten I brought them all home and made sure he got some rest. He drove me mad in the evening by checking his phone. Sue was in Paris with her friends. It was a 30th birthday. She had been a little down the night before as she had wanted to go out instead of sitting in with Marc. He was quite hurt by this. She had said that she still needed her space despite the illness and needed to have some time to herself. He was upset. He checked his phone constantly to see if she had got in touch which she hadn't. He became more and more anxious as the evening went on.

We snuggled up on the settee watching Eddie Izzard. We cuddled up and kissed a little. He said how he wanted me and pulled me in so close for most of the show. At the end we went to bed. He stayed in my bed as I had put Pheobe in hers. It was a little weird at first. Cuddling up again after all this time knowing he was here for the night. It was strange. I had wanted that all that time ago and now I had it I didn't want to share my bed. He kept me warm though. He held me close probably just as confused as I was. We made love once again but this time it was not as passionate as it had been before. I laid beside him feeling terrible, holding him while he laid awake waiting for the text from his girlfriend. Oh so weird. Oh so wrong.

I sat in my usual position. My house was still and quiet. The children were asleep and he was restlessly asleep in my bed. In my bed. I hated sharing it with him. I had hated laying there awake and seeing him there. That was why I was up at this hour.

I inhaled deeply on my cigarette and blew the smoke slowly up to the ceiling.

I felt used again and things were not like they used to be. When we had first started sleeping together, it was great. It was taboo and not supposed to be happening. We were caught up in it and in some ways I liked him going back to her again. I didn't have to live with him and I didn't have to put up with his moods and his moaning. I didn't like that he hadn't gone tonight.

I sat back and thought about how I had craved this in the beginning. Was I just sleeping with him so I could get at her? Was I merely doing it out of the feeling of rejection and wanting him away from her? Was I doing it for some power over him?

The thoughts and questions confused me. I sighed and held my head in my hands. It had felt wrong tonight. It wasn't the usual passionate affair that we had been having. It was strange. Maybe I was changing. Maybe he was not what I wanted at all. I didn't really have him though did I so how could I say that?

So confused.

The evening had been fine. We had spent it watching TV and cuddling on the settee. Even that had been a little annoying for me. I smiled as I thought back to him pulling me over for a cuddle and I had become agitated as I used to before we split. I hated being pulled around. He dictated what we watched and that was annoying too, I had had nearly a year of doing my own thing in the evening and now I had to cater for him. But wasn't that what I wanted back?

I just wanted to scream at the confused state I was in. I pushed my head back against the tiles and raised my face to the ceiling. What did I want?

I slumped back down pressing my chin to my chest and huffed. I didn't have a clue. I hated analysing things and I hated making decisions I didn't want to make. I thought I had been happy to have him around. I had thought I wanted to look after him. I hadn't known I was going to feel like this when he was here. Maybe it was just because she wasn't out of the picture?

I groaned to myself as the thought of her entered my head. The image of her face and her smile and the memory of her voice with that bloody accent, that now grated on me so much, was back inside my head and I knew when she was there, there was no way to remove her.

'Great. Well done girl,' I muttered to myself.

She hadn't text him tonight. He had got up and down so many times to check his phone. He was charging it over on the sideboard. He would push my head off his lap to get up and then, while moaning that there was still no word from her, return to his seat, pulling me back over to him. I huffed at that now. I had let him though hadn't I?

She was still in my head. I closed my eyes and willed her to go away but she didn't. 'Stubborn cow,' I muttered to myself again and then giggled at the craziness.

The searching for her contact had continued when we had gone to bed. He had really hurt me. He had checked his phone when we first laying there. He had looked over at me, said there was no word from her and then leant over to kiss me. It felt wrong. I had laid there thinking, 'I don't actually want to do this.' A few minutes passed and I had felt better. I got caught up in the whole thing and had forgotten my initial thoughts. While we were making love, he stopped. He looked down at me and kissed me. Then, to my horror, he reached over to check his phone once more. I just stared at him, my mouth open in disbelief. I was subdued by the shock but was relieved that it was over quickly after that. He pulled me close to him and I tried to search for the words to convey what I was feeling about what he had just done but the shock still kept me silent. I was lying on his chest and every now and then he would reach over and his phone would light up as he checked for her message again. It made me feel awful. I didn't understand why it didn't make me feel angry. Where was the anger?

I had this sunken feeling. This weight was pulling me down and I didn't understand why. Had I got in over my head here? Had I not actually wanted this? Had I just been upset because he had wanted her? Was this just supposed to be about revenge?

I hadn't felt angry. I hadn't felt upset. Him constantly looking for her response while in my bed hadn't cut me apart like it would have done. Why not? It just felt weird and wrong. It all felt weird and wrong. This whole scenario. What was going on here?

I let out a deep sigh and jumped off my bench. I couldn't stay up and think about this any longer. Besides, if I went to sleep that might get rid of this woman's image inside my head.

'You are still here,' I muttered to her under my breath and smiled, shaking my head.

I climbed the stairs and then stopped at the top. I looked across to the two rooms that were opposite each other. In one room slept my husband in my bed who was waiting for contact with his girlfriend. In the other was Pheobe. In her single bed with hardly any room where I would be so hot and squashed all night. I looked between the two. I walked into my room and looked at the bed. He was asleep still. He shuffled around in the bed and I just looked at him. I didn't want him there.

I walked out of the room, still confused and walked into Pheobe's room. I looked at the small space that was beside her. I glanced over at the door to my room and stood there for a few seconds. I didn't move.

No contest, I thought, as I climbed in beside Pheobe. No contest at all.

10th February

What a stressful day!

It started when we woke up. Marc didn't want the children to see him in my bed as they would tell Sue and cause world war 3. He threw the covers over his head as Fiona came in. He then went out the front door when we went to fix breakfast and rang the doorbell to make it look like he had just come in. I'm not sure whether they realised or not.

After we were all ready the nagging started. First about Sue and the "still nothing from her" and then because I would not allow him to take the children to see his mum and sister Lucy. Why should I? They haven't bothered up till now. They haven't approached me. They were never here for them. They didn't want them before now. They treated me like shit on Boxing Day, had no contact with the children since then and expect me to say they can have the pleasure of my babies now. Not bloody likely.

It was hard to keep saying no though. He kept on and on. Eventually he did admit that he saw my point of view and gave up. We took the children to the indoor play area and sat around drinking tea. He kept checking his phone over and over and became really agitated. She had called in the car on the drive over to the place but he hadn't spoken to her for long. He was hurt that she hadn't phoned sooner to see how he was feeling. I could understand that but the stress now I couldn't understand. He said at one point that he was going to end it with her as he couldn't take this. I didn't understand that either. He had the ump the whole time we were there. We went to Mcdonalds afterwards and he cheered up a little although I then went down as he was talking about his plans for Valentines Day with her and I really didn't want to hear them. I would be doing nothing. I dropped him off at his mums and went to visit mine. I sat round there for a while then came home to play games on the Wii with the children. I got a phone call from Aunt Violet. She was asking why I wasn't letting his parents and Lucy see the children and how that was unfair and I would be cutting off my nose despite my face. How exactly? What am I missing? They had the children for Marc, never any other time. They never popped in to see how we were. They never picked the children up from school and took them round theirs for tea. They never came to sit with me when I was lonely and sad. How was I going to miss them? More to the point the children hadn't even asked for them. They haven't mentioned them at all. I began to wonder why she was trying to help. I couldn't see what she would be gaining from this. I couldn't work it out.

Jack then text me and asked to meet up and talk about it. I hope that comes about.

I went to bed a little stressed from it all and couldn't sleep. Hope I am not back to this for too long.

Two o clock in the morning and I was sat on my bench staring at the window drinking a steaming cup of tea that was burning the roof of my mouth. Insomnia returns again - great!

I had so many things running through my head it was driving me insane. The more I tried to untangle the mess and understand them, the more I tossed and turned. The more I tossed and turned, the more I couldn't sleep. Now here I was sat on my bench waiting to be tired enough to return to bed.

I hated nights like these. They were awful. They lasted so long too as I knew from experience and that made me hate them more. I was so fed up with this. When would all this end?

I had had him nagging at me all day for one reason or another. I had felt that if I had heard her name mentioned just one more time I would phone her my bloody self. Sue hasn't bothered. Still no contact from Sue. Sue doesn't care. Sue, Sue, bloody Sue. She didn't care. She was having a good time. She was with her friends. She wasn't thinking of you. Get over it man.

I smiled as I pictured his face if I had actually said that. Him standing in the car park after telling her he was in a cab taking the children out. Liar. Him talking to her as if her lack of contact hadn't really affected him. Liar. Him saying that she was angry with him now. Probably lying about that too. Probably trying to make me feel better once he had seen me getting so angry with him.

He had sat in a terrible mood while the children played. They ran around but kept coming back to the table and he snapped at them loads. "I think I will just end it when she comes back," he had said. Yeah right. Like you could ever manage that I had thought. He was so hung up on her. He was obsessed and needy and he expected me to believe he wanted that all to end.

After the nagging about his mum and Lucy seeing the children I had felt so fed up. I wasn't low or too upset, just fed up. No one saw my point of view. That was enforced with my aunt's phone call. They had never bothered with me and yet I was supposed to worry about their feelings. Why the hell should I? I couldn't be bothered to explain. There was no point in explaining. No one really cared. Everyone stands up for Lucy. Everyone worries about her and how upset she is. I am nothing to them. They couldn't care a less about me and how their actions affected me. Cutting my nose off despite my face. How? I would miss......nothing.

I sat back with a huff as I realised that I was winding myself up all over again and I knew it had to stop. If it didn't there would be no sleep at all.

My only wish was for all this to stop. All the tension. All the upset. All the nagging. All the moaning. The talking about her. The thoughts of the two of them. The infatuation he had with her. My family and their not caring. I huffed again. It had to stop.

Where was my fairy godmother? Where was she?

I raised my eyes to the ceiling as if I was looking for her. As if I would see her waving at me, taunting me with her sparkly wand. Insanity was closing in on me, I could feel it.

I rolled my eyes at myself. Now I felt even worse. Well done. You brought it on yourself, woman. Now you will be sitting up all night. Well done.

12th February

Took all my frustrations out at work today which wasn't a very nice thing to do. Had to cover year 6 all day and have meetings at lunchtime and do some work for science booster. No rest for the wicked. I know I only work 2 days a week but I don't want to feel overloaded when I am there. Still I wouldn't have been as bad if things were ok at home. I discussed some of my problems with the headmistress. She was great about it all and understood what I was going through. She made me feel so much better. Calmer in the afternoon and fine driving home.

Spoke to Marc briefly. He was meeting friends for a drink after work even though he shouldn't be drinking at all.

Sat talking to mum again tonight and once again did not come to any conclusions. Went to bed fairly early but was still awake at 2am. I hate not being able to sleep.

I sat on the bench rubbing the back of my neck with one hand, while a cigarette smoked itself in the other. I pressed my fingers deep into my shoulders and I could feel the muscle throbbing underneath them.

I had been particularly tense all day. I had knots in muscles all over me and I felt exhausted, both physically and mentally. I had tried to relax and switch off to everything that was troubling me, but my problems and concerns seemed to have this hold over me and they were not going to be loosening their grip any time soon.

It was a weird feeling. Before when I was angry and frustrated with whatever life was throwing at me, I would churn things round and the thoughts would be shouted loudly at me in my head. This time, they were quieter. They were almost a whisper and I could hardly hear them. This meant that I couldn't talk them through because I didn't know where they began. It meant that I couldn't try to lift the weight of them or break them down to be easier to handle. I had to carry them around with me. Maybe I had buried them too much and they were taking longer to come to the surface.

I rubbed my face and threw the burnt out end of my cigarette into the sink. I hadn't even smoked any of it. I had just sat staring out of the window. I felt strange tonight. I could feel the weight dragging me down but I wasn't sure how much of that was sheer tiredness as opposed to the troubles I had.

Marc was the main one of course. He was off out tonight. He said he was going for a drink. Surely he shouldn't be drinking at all. Surely she wouldn't be letting him. Surely his friends were not letting him either. I didn't understand. I sat back on the bench and tried to get comfortable. I was obviously in for the long haul tonight and I wanted to make sure I was settled. It still seemed odd how every night was spent here in this spot.

I thought back to the weekend. My feelings were still questionable towards that. I was still asking myself why I had felt that way. Why had I not wanted him here? I had fought so hard to have him here with me. I had wanted to look after him. I hated him being with her, I was still upset they were together tonight. Why had the weekend felt so wrong?

I hung my head a little. I was beginning to realise that I really didn't want him back after all the fighting I had done for him. After everything I had been through. After all the lies and the deceit and the cheating. I didn't want him back really. I would have relished that weekend if I still wanted my husband back, wouldn't I?

I brought my knees up to my chest and rested my forehead on the top of them. I turned my head from side to side and then stopped in the middle. The darkness surrounded me. What was I thinking? What was I feeling?

It all felt so strange and I couldn't make sense of it. It had so many questions as I had had previously, but this time they were all for me. They were all directed at me and my actions. I had never felt like that before. I had never questioned myself to such a degree.

I had talked and talked with mum. We had gone over and over everything. The family situation, him, her, the children and then we had tried to address them all. The problem though, for me, is quite clear. Until I understand what it is that I am feeling towards him and the future and what I want to achieve, I am never going to be able to reach any conclusions about the rest of the issues.

I threw my head back. Tears welled in my eyes out of the confusion and the frustration. I folded my arms and pulled my feet closer towards me so I was as snuggled up as I could get. I felt comforted by that. Just a little.

The silence let me relax and think at the same time. I sat there with an empty feeling and a confused mind and I watched the darkness grow stronger as I felt I was growing weaker.

13th February

Work was much better today. The teacher I usually cover in the afternoon was out on a trip so I had the afternoon to catch up on some assessment work. Didn't realise I was so far behind. The little jobs I did do, took ages. Marc phoned in the middle of it all and spoke about the fact that Lucy had text again and asked to have Fiona. She shouldn't single them out. They need to see all of them or none. She isn't asking to talk to me to sort out the mess and she isn't asking to see the others. Just Fiona. That isn't fair on the other two. Marc seemed to be understanding and said we would talk it through that evening. When he called though he was with her and some others and couldn't talk. I sent him a text saying how upset I was with that and how I felt I was always there when he needed me whereas he isn't. I must be a mug. A complete fool. Became quite annoyed with myself once again and then spent the next few hours trying to calm myself down so I would sleep. Didn't work.

I had plodded through the day today. That was the only way I could describe it. Plodded. Everything I did was slow. Slow movements, slow walking, and slow talking. Just got on with it and got through it. It was hard work. I felt drained. Physically, emotionally and mentally drained.

I had received no text back from him. Again I had waited for him to see that something was important to me to sort out and yet again that hadn't happened. I was annoyed and stressed at how he couldn't look past his own life. He was alright and that was the end of the conversation.

He spoke to me this afternoon so soothingly. He had said he understood my point of view over Lucy just wanting to take Fiona and he said that he would help me by talking about it all tonight, so we could see if we could come up with a solution between us. I felt that at last he was going to be by my side. At last he would be supportive to me as I had been to him. No. That wasn't the case. As usual something better had come up. His new life, his new girlfriend or his new friends were always going to be first. I would always be second.

It was all beginning to have much more of an effect than it used to but in a different way. I used to get so angry and needed to slam things around and pace up and down or just do something. Now though, I was much calmer. Again I was questioning myself. Why did I let him do this to me? Why do I continue to be there for him and yet accept that I get nothing in return? Again, I didn't understand.

I sat on the settee tonight. I had chosen not to move. I couldn't be bothered. I didn't want to stand up. I kept looking at my phone and not concentrating on the TV. I still hadn't received a reply. I was so fed up of being pushed aside. I really had had enough.

I still wanted it though clearly. I wouldn't be this upset that I hadn't heard from him or that he was treating me like second best, if I didn't still need that contact with him. 'But when he was here I didn't want him' was my immediate retort to that thought. I bowed my head in confusion. What was it I wanted from him?

The TV lit up the room and I could see myself looking so forlorn sitting alone on the sofa. I had been reduced to this once more. This empty feeling. This lost feeling. The sounds from the TV being made but not registering. The urge to text or phone him again and say something but not knowing what it would be. The darkness around the house seeping through my skin and making me dull and lifeless.

It was back. It was a silent shift of mood and it had crept up on me, but it was back. All those feelings were there again. I just couldn't understand why.

14th February

Valentines Day is a crap day for singles.

Cards everywhere, tacky gifts, movies about falling in love and love songs on the radio all day.

I wasn't too bad actually. I had never thought much of the day anyway. If you only spoilt the one you love once a year then that was pretty crap. We never made too big a deal about it so it didn't really affect me.

Went shopping and to the library with the children. They were so bored walking round Asdas but they behave so well now I didn't need to worry. I'm quite proud of those little differences that I have made.

Marc text me a few times throughout the evening to make sure I was ok. And the children obviously. I was quite intrigued by it as he had already spoken to me 3 times this afternoon. Told me he had just bought her card - a teddy bear one - and he was pleased as he didn't have to think about it too hard like he had to with mine. I liked the cards with words in rather than cute little pictures. He text me up until quite late.

Went to bed late again and again couldn't settle despite being tired out and wanting to sleep. I tossed and turned and went up and down the stairs so many times I got the exercise for the day and tomorrow in about half an hour.

Each time he had phoned this afternoon, I had rolled my eyes. One of the calls was him choosing the card. Why did he do that? Was that to hurt? He said he was pleased as he didn't have to think too hard when picking one for her. Was that good? For him, her or me? It was like he was checking on me. He asked how I was. Fine was my only answer. What did he expect me to say? Did he want me to be in tears? Did he want to find me hurting because he wasn't here? I wasn't.

I had been quite intrigued by his texting this evening. He was spending the evening with his girlfriend, the one he loved supposedly on Valentines Day and he was texting me. That didn't make much sense and only added to my confused state.

I sat back against the cushions feeling tired. I always felt tired. Insomnia does that to you. I snuggled up on the settee in the peace and quiet and held my phone in my hand. There was no urge to return his messages. There was no need to hear his voice. I looked down at the phone and wondered whether she knew he was contacting me. What were they doing if he had the time to get in touch with me?

He had made me laugh when talking about her wishes for Valentines Day. I had blocked out most of that conversation, but I had heard the part where she had said that he was not allowed to cook for her. He had cooked for me. It was the only day of the year that he ever cooked me dinner. We never really went out anywhere. He had offered but we still never went. We stayed in and he cooked. She had remembered that apparently and said that she didn't want the same as what he gave me. I smiled at that again and could understand her point of view.

I rolled onto my back letting my phone fall underneath me. I felt it vibrate as another text message from him came through. 'Thinking of you xx' was all it said.

I closed the phone and placed it on the arm of the sofa. I looked back up to the ceiling. A romantic movie was on the TV and it was making me feel sick. I am not much of a romantic. I don't believe in doing things differently just to prove your love. If you are happy with the one you are with, then you don't try to prove it in any way. Especially not with teddy bears and heart shaped chocolates. I just smiled.

I began wondering what we were doing last year. I think his mum had had the children for the evening so we could have dinner alone. Thai red curry. That was it. It was delicious I remembered that. It was amazing how I could think of these things now and not be hurt by them. I smiled again and then yawned.

I rolled back on my side and flicked through the TV channels. All mushy, lovey dovey shit. They obviously don't think of the single people on this day much. Thanks for that.

I pulled the cushion underneath my head and closed my eyes. I couldn't be bothered to think anymore. I just needed to sleep. I lay there, staring at nothing. I wondered what he and Sue were doing but I didn't dwell on it for long. I didn't care.

I jumped up and checked on the children. They were settled and sleeping and I longed to be like they were right now. I had been to bed twice already but had got up again. I went back downstairs, smoked a cigarette and then went back upstairs. I had laid down in bed, stayed there for a while and then got up to check on the children. Then back downstairs. Up and down. Up and down. In and out.

This unsettled routine of the evening was annoying. But I had come to know it ever so well.

15th February

Boring day today. Made the boring phone calls I had to make. Arranged insurances and claims on other insurances. Tidied up a little and caught up on the ironing. The children played happily. The girls together and Seb out with his mates. Mum came to lunch and we chatted about my sister Charlie and the fact that we think she will leave her boyfriend Danny. He has been texting and meeting another woman just like Marc had done. And just like Marc he has said that nothing had happened between them. Don't believe him either.

He has said sorry but we don't think Charlie can forgive him. It will eat her up as it did me. She will never trust him again. Charlie is thinking of coming to live with me. I don't mind. It will be company and we can share the evenings with the children and the school pick ups etc. I think she will be happier here. She needs to make her decision though. Mum and I said we would make sure she knew that she would be welcome but we agreed to not influence her decision in any way.

I am not sure whether I will be able to be civil to Danny when I next see him. I am so angry with him. He watched me go through all that pain and heartache with Marc twice. Now he has done the same to my little sister. I think I might just hit him if I see him again.

Have spent the evening trying to get the children to sleep and updating this diary. I haven't had any time for the book lately and I am missing it. I am hoping to get some time to do what I want to do next week while I am on holiday and the children are at school.

Not sure whether Marc is coming down tomorrow as planned. He has said he is ill again and needed to go to hospital again today to get something for his sickness. He went to his flat to rest though and said she would not be sitting with him. I reckon he will use this excuse for not coming tomorrow. He has already said he would not be seeing them next weekend despite it being my birthday weekend so that will be another two weeks go by. It is getting beyond a joke now. If he is this ill why does he not want to spend every minute he can with his children just in case? I don't understand.

539

Another woman to add to the list. Yet another one. What is it with men? I am so angry with Danny for doing this. I have always been protective of my little sister. Always. No one is allowed to hurt her. I can be as horrible as I like to her, for as her sister that is part of my role in her life. I can say what I like about her when I am annoyed with her and I can become frustrated. No one else is allowed to do any of those things. Especially not a man.

I wondered how she was. I knew exactly what she was going through which meant I knew the pain she was feeling and that was really hard for me. I hated the thought of her being alone with that. She would be feeling lost and empty and would be hurting so much. Confused by what things she had heard were the truth and what were the lies.

I had spoken to mum about it all. We had chatted and we both agreed that it would eat her up as it had done me. She was more of a believer in monogamy than I was. It would probably be hurting her even more. I couldn't stand that thought either.

I sat in the study tonight writing. I needed to let it out of my system and writing was a way I could do that. I hadn't much time for it but the urge was quite compelling tonight. I sat back in the study chair and rolled backwards and forwards.

Marc had upset me again today. He had said he wasn't able to have the children this weekend even though I had already planned things for Friday and Saturday. He knew it was my birthday weekend and he knew that I was looking forward to it. Selfish man.

He was ill again today. It seems a little convenient that he is always ill when he has said he will do something with the children. That was an awful thought and I tutted at myself. I twirled around on my chair and faced the wall opposite the computer. A blank white wall. It made it so cold in here. I turned my head to face his CD collection. It was still here. He didn't have the room for it and the people on eBay didn't seem to want it either. I always thought it was crap. I giggled.

Why didn't he want to see the children though? If he was ill like he said and he was really worried about dying like he said, why wasn't he spending as much time with his children as possible? That was something else that didn't make sense to me. Add that to the long list in my head.

I twirled back round on the chair and got up. I headed for the kitchen and grabbed a cigarette. I hauled myself up on the bench and stretched my arms and back. I was cramped from sitting in one position for so long. I released my muscles from the stretch and sat hunched up looking out into the garden. It was dark out there and it made the room seem colder somehow. I shivered with the thought of what it was like outside.

I leant back against the tiles and closed my eyes.

My poor children would not be seeing their dad again. He hadn't been around for the last few weeks. He wasn't coming next weekend and he wasn't coming the weekend after because it was her birthday and he needed to be with her. She gets to celebrate. Sensible woman for not having children.

I opened my eyes and rolled them. I hated it when I had thoughts like that. I didn't mean them. Not really. I loved my babies and I wouldn't swap them for the world. I certainly wouldn't swap them for a career. Even if I did miss mine.

I sat forward and inhaled deeply on the cigarette. I blew the smoke slowly out and up into the air. I had given up trying to understand everything and I didn't seem to care that the list of unanswered questions was getting longer and longer instead of shorter. I didn't seem to care that I was fed up. Maybe I had just accepted all these things. Maybe it was what I deemed to be normal now.

Was anything normal? Would I feel normal again? Would it be soon? I laughed at myself. More unanswered questions for the list.

16th February

It is now midday and I have briefly spoken to him. He has said he was in hospital overnight again as he was bleeding. He started to tell me about it and then said he would have to call me back. He text me to say that Sue was there so he would have to call me back later. This made me so angry as I was being pushed aside yet again. He needed me last weekend because otherwise he would have been on his own. That is the only reason he uses me to fill the gap of her when she is no longer there. I am so fed up with this situation now. I feel used in so many ways and I hate myself for getting into this mess. I wish I could have just got really angry at the beginning and switched off from him. I wish I had never started the 'affair' between us and I wish I could end it all now. I could then grieve and get it out of my system and stop the constant up and down feeling. The rollercoaster is calmer now but I am still riding it. I don't think I can hold on much longer. The problem is if I do let him go then I will have to tell her everything. I'm not sure I could do that to him. Not yet. If ever.

I spent most of the night on the phone. I called friends and I called my mum. I needed to vent my anger and frustration. He was the one who called me to start with. He had phoned from the hospital and said that he had been there all night. He said he was ill. He was mid flow when he said he would have to call me back.

The text message came within a few minutes. Sue had just picked him up and now he couldn't talk to me. He would get back to me later. Unbelievable.

I had been so angry I had thrown the phone across the room. How dare he do that to me? He must have needed me at that point and then as soon as she came into view he had changed his mind. Thanks a lot. Again it made me feel that I was just the one who had filled some time. I came in second to her again.

This was beginning to get beyond a joke. It had happened a lot of times before and each time I got angrier and angrier. Before this it had just made me sad. I was always upset by it but now the anger boiled in me and I churned it all up inside me. I had thought at first I was getting used to it. Now it seemed I was getting annoyed with it.

I slumped back in my chair in the conservatory and let out a huge sigh. I was so fed up with being second. Second to her. Second to his lifestyle. Second to his new friends. Second to his social life. In one breath he was talking to me and saying he needed me and my support and in the next breath I was being told I would be called back later.

I had thought this situation through time and time again. Each time I had reached the same conclusion. I had had enough. I felt like the other woman only I didn't get as much attention as one would. I felt used and not good enough and I needed to stop these feelings otherwise I would be trapped like this forever.

That dawning shook me to the core. How long was I supposed to play this role for? How long could I take the rejection over and over again? I couldn't do this much longer. I really couldn't. It was time to stop it all. I sat bolt upright as if

I had finally reached a conclusion and I was ready and strong enough to face it.

I slumped back in my chair within a few seconds knowing that that wasn't the case. If he was so seriously ill and I didn't get the last few meetings, however rare they were, I could never live with that. I would feel terrible. I couldn't do it.

I had always said that if I let him go and give up the tiny piece of him that I had, I would have to tell her everything. I didn't know why I felt that way but it seemed fair to me. I would need to let go of him completely and to do that I had to release the truth. I would need to do that. The dishonesty of it all was driving me crazy as it was. It hurt to think that I was capable of such deception. I was sleeping with another womans boyfriend. I know he was my husband but did that make it right?

I was tormenting myself again. I was blaming myself for all of this again and it wasn't really my fault was it. Was it? I didn't know. I pulled my legs up on the chair and hugged them. I buried my face in my lap and bit my lip to stop the scream.

This rollercoaster of emotions was such a nightmare. I want to get off now. Please let me get off.

17th February

I have been really hurt today in so many ways. He never got back to me last night. He was obviously too busy. He spent the night at Sue's as he was not well. It makes me so sad that she is looking after him. He is my husband after all. I picked him up from the station at 11.20am. He had got up and come to see the children. Feeling better today clearly. He was so angry with me as if I didn't have the right to be mad or upset that he ignores me when she is there. I am feeling so used by it all that I am angry at myself as well as him. In the kitchen he grabbed me and kissed me. Like that would somehow make me feel better. It didn't really; in fact afterwards it made me feel worse.

He told me all about the Valentines night he spent with her. I stayed in alone. He likes to think of me suffering I'm sure.

He then said he was coming down next weekend but not staying. Excellent. On the Friday he will be in Glasgow with her and then the Saturday he will be here for a few hours and then go round his mums. I won't get out either night then. Again I was upset. He then said he wouldn't be down at all the next weekend as it is her birthday on the Saturday night. Another weekend gone. I was hurt again.

His sister Lucy turns up next. He allowed her to come. I told her how I was feeling which made me feel a little better but not much. She doesn't understand where I am coming from. No one does.

As he was leaving he said he was going for his next treatment with his mum on Tuesday. I was supposed to have been going with him as it is my half term and probably the only one I will be able to do.

I was quite overwhelmed by the whole day and how my emotions were affecting me and I just cried. I cried and cried in the study and the children found me. They were great as always. They hugged me and kissed me and told me it would be ok. Pheobe told the other two I was crying because I miss daddy. Bless her.

I am sitting here now feeling very lost again. I know what I need to do. I need to break free of him completely. I need to walk away now and not let him do this to me anymore. If I do that it will hurt me like crazy. If I don't, it will still hurt. What a great situation I am in.

I didn't want the children to go to bed tonight. I was now sat on the bench feeling so very lost and alone. They had hugged me and made me feel so much better and I had clung to them all night. I had let them stay up till late too. And now it was just me.

I sat with my arm across my legs and my other arm was rubbing it trying to make myself feel better. It's horrible when you just want a hug and there is no one there. No one to tell you it will all be alright. No one to pick you up. No one to talk to. I knew mum was at the end of the phone but that didn't seem to help me right now. I was lost in emotions and I felt drained as the constant flow of feelings seemed to stop me from going forward.

It had been such a tough day. I seemed to have been forced into doing something I didn't want to do. I didn't want to see Lucy and talk. Not right now. Yet he had got his own way and arranged for her to come without telling me, backing me into a corner. I couldn't take it. I had enough thoughts floating around my head and it was driving me crazy and then I had another one to add to them. One that I didn't want to do.

The tears fell silently down my cheeks and hit my arm. I looked down at the small, watery pool that was forming just above my wrist. I lifted my head slowly and stared at the wall in front of me. Nothing was there and I felt as if nothing was inside.

I longed for the comfort of my children again. I jumped off the bench and went upstairs. My legs ached as I climbed them. They felt like they weighed a tonne. So heavy. I made them carry me into Seb's room and then into Fiona's. Both were sleeping soundly and I smiled as I watched them. They had been so good tonight. Seb had made me a cup of tea and Fiona had hugged me. They had seen me like this before and knew just what to do.

I dragged myself into my room. Pheobe was sound asleep in my bed as normal. I fell into bed next to her and curled up beside her. She shuffled around and then laid her head on my shoulder. I laid my head on hers and wrapped my arms around her, pulling her close. I felt safe again at last.

Safe and warm and loved.

18th February

Spent the whole day today thinking it was Sunday. It didn't really register my children are back at school until this evening when I suddenly panicked about whether I had everything ready.

Went to mums for dinner this afternoon and stayed there later than planned. I get so comfy round there and the children were happy to be there too so I didn't want to get up and move. Enjoyed having a dinner cooked for me though. It was nice. Talked to mum about the Marc situation. She understands that I am upset about being pushed to last on the list and seems to feel for me. I looked through her catalogue for a new bed. I am planning to get a four poster if it fits in ok. It would be great.

I chilled out this evening after getting the children to bed. The girls wanted to sleep together tonight and they did go off pretty easily. They had been extra close all day and clung to each other. They played really nicely with hardly any arguments at all. It was so nice to watch them like that.

Spoke to Marc really briefly today. I know I need to have the conversation with him. I need to broach it but there never seems to be a good time. The first time he called he was on his way to a meeting. He was in the street and it was noisy and I was about to leave for mums. He said that when he arrived at his flat last night his flatmate had his children there. He has them there for the week as it is half term and he is a dad that puts them first. Marc just got angry with me for saying that. He said the people in the office were mad that his flatmate had taken time off this week as there were things he hadn't finished and lots going on. I just said that that meant he didn't care about work and he put his children before everything else and that was a good thing. Marc got umpy and said goodbye. I couldn't help it, that is how I feel and I commend the bloke for doing it.

The second time Fiona needed to call him. She had become so upset in the car by a song that spoke about missing the person you love. She was listening to the words on the drive home and had burst into tears. She phoned him and spoke to him but there is never much you can say to her when she is so upset. It was hard for a while. Seb wrapped his arms round her and took her upstairs. It was a lovely display of how they care for each other so much. Marc phoned again when he had finished dinner with his cousin Carly.

She had met him to talk about his illness and he was a little pissed off at me for letting them know he was ill. I knew he would be. I knew he would moan at me. He was walking back to his flat so didn't have much time to speak to me.

All three times were not the right times for me to talk to him. I feel as if I need to get this off my chest sometime soon but the situation doesn't arise. He will now be too ill tomorrow and the next day and he is in Glasgow with her Thursday and Friday and so will not be able to talk to me. No time will come up for a while then.

Not feeling tired tonight. I think the stress and the upset of it all is keeping me awake. I bet I don't feel awake when the school alarm goes off tomorrow morning.

I sat back marvelling at how yet again the day could be so mixed up and have emotional changes that made me catch my breath and pause for thought. The emotions come in waves and the tides sweep in and out of you rising and falling.

The day had started so relaxed and for the most part was a happy day. All of a sudden things changed and there I had been again feeling dreadful with this chunk of me boiling with the temperature of anger raging inside me.

It was so disorientating in a way. I wandered aimlessly around trying to get my bearings and remember what it was I was going to do. My mind had started racing with the words of today and the tears of Fiona had brought a sad lump to my throat. The helplessness raised its ugly head again.

I sat back against the tiles and sipped on my hot tea. I had become quite cold. I am sure it was the fire of anger that kept me warm and when I started to calm down, my temperature dropped and I spent the rest of the time shivering until I had adapted to that change.

His flatmate had his children this week. I had asked Marc to have them for their half term. I had to work last week as our holidays were at different times and I had thought it wasn't fair that I couldn't organise much for them to do because of my work days. He hadn't bothered. He said he couldn't get time off. For him to tell me that his flatmate had managed it yet again was like rubbing salt in my wounds. He had them for one holiday, when they went with her, but that has been it. I would have worried about them but at least I would have felt like he was putting his children first. He hasn't had them since Christmas.

I hung my head at that thought. It angered me in some ways but mostly it just brought sadness. I felt so upset that he had become like this. I was annoyed with him. Every time I looked at the children I would think about him and then the fact that he hadn't had them for ages would pop into my head and upset me more. It was so frustrating.

I sighed a huge sigh and leant forward to reach for my cigarettes. They were just too far out of my reach so I sat back as I couldn't quite be bothered. I huffed as I realised the drain of energy I had experienced yet again. All down to him yet again.

I sipped on my tea and held the cup to my lips for a few seconds. It was now barely warm but I didn't care. I stared out of the window and thought about my poor Fiona. She had cried so much. I remembered her little face and the tears streaming down it and the tears bit at my eyes. One single tear fell down my cheek and dripped onto the handle of my cup. He hadn't even known what to say to her. He seemed distracted. I wondered whether she was there. Did she know my baby was crying for her daddy?

I turned my head away and placed the cup on the bench. I wiped the sticky track the tear had left and lowered myself slowly to the floor. I leant over, reached my cigarettes and lit one, inhaling deeply and slowly, closing my eyes as I did so.

I hated the come down from the anger. The rage inside fuels your body into acting at top speed and then when it leaves the extra energy vanishes, leaving the body drained and tired. Not mentally, just physically.

He had been so angry with me about telling Carly. She was his cousin and I needed to talk to someone. I sighed and leant back against the bench. Why didn't he want people to know? That seemed so strange to me. It isn't something to be ashamed of. It is something people can help you with. It didn't make sense. I shrugged my shoulders. I hadn't understood my husband for quite some time, why would I understand now? I smiled.

My mind jumped back to him and how I had wanted to talk to him. I had wanted to explain how I was feeling. I needed to talk things through. No time for me. The Glasgow trip would be coming up this week. He is off for a couple of days and won't be back in time for the children on Friday as usual. He will only have time for her then. Not us. Not me. Not his children.

I leant forward onto the sink and propped my chin up with my fists, elbows on the bench. He is so wrapped up in that woman it made me feel sick. What has she got over him? I didn't understand. I smiled. The same sentence I just said a few minutes ago. How surprising.

I threw my cigarette in the sink, even though it wasn't finished and stretched up to the ceiling. I was worn out from all the emotional upset of the evening and I wanted my mind to shut up now. I hauled myself back onto the bench and curled up as tight as I could, resting my head against the hard wall. I stared ahead motionless. Too much upset for one day let alone just a few hours.

Just too much.

Stress!

19th February 2008

Oh what a day!

Felt awful this morning when the alarm went off. I remember texting Marc at 1.30 this morning. I said something like I wanted him to know that I was too stressed and too upset to sleep again and that he had made me feel worthless and unimportant. I didn't hear back from him but he said on the phone that he was woken up by it. Felt a little bad for a few minutes and then that ebbed away. He has done worse to me.

Spent the day with mum feeling on edge the whole time. Talked to Carly about meeting him last night. She said he seemed quite together about his illness and that he was positive. *So is it only me that he puts it on with? Or is it only me that he can show his true feelings too?* I don't know which way to look at it.

Mum said I needed to be stronger and find it inside me to fight back. I have come to the conclusion that after this week, which my intention is to talk to him about the way I feel, I am going to cut all contact with him. That is my aim. I am even thinking about changing my phone numbers to sever the contact completely. She agreed that it might be the only way to move on. I have to accept that he no longer needs me or loves me and although it is the hardest thing to do for me it must be better than feeling so used and unwanted all the time.

I picked the children up from school and was freezing cold by the time I got home. Pheobe lost her book bag which meant we were delayed by 5 minutes looking for it and then I needed bread from the shop. I didn't have any cash so I had to spend a fiver to buy it on the card. I don't have the money to do that.

I made my phone calls. One to the insurance company to fix my toilet and one to the other insurance company to pay the vet bill from November as they want their money and I don't have three pounds to give let alone three hundred. Stress again. Again things out of my control.

I put the children in the bath this evening and then there was screaming. Fiona appeared pale white and frantic as Pheobe had put a small bead from my pot pourri up her nose. I couldn't believe it. She was screaming saying it was hurting and to get it out. I was trying to stop her from putting her finger up her nose to get it out as that would have pushed it up further. She was almost hysterical so I called my mum to come over while I took her to hospital. I got her dried and dressed and tried to calm her down. Marc called and I told him. Pheobe was screaming for him but she wouldn't listen to him to calm her down. She just kept crying and shouting I want my daddy. He became upset and I told him I would keep him posted. I then phoned Michelle. I wasn't sure whether to or not - thought it was a little too cheeky - but I decided to hear her say it was a common thing and that it would be easy to get out probably would be better than waiting here alone. I called her and I could have cried when she said she would be round in 5 minutes. She turned up with her little bag and coaxed Pheobe into letting her have a look. As soon as she said she could see it Pheobe let her try to get it out. It took a few goes but Pheobe just laid back and let her do it. She didn't moan or groan and she was so good. I'm sure she wouldn't have been that good at the hospital. Anyway Michelle managed to get it out before my mum arrived. Mum got here within 2 minutes of removing it and was relieved herself. Michelle gave me a hug and left. Me and mum sat and had tea and couldn't help but laugh at the day of stress that was today. If tomorrow isn't better I think I will declare myself mentally insane and go to hospital myself just for the break!

As I sat and thought about today I realised that I was in one of those horrible situations. The kind that you know you have come up with a solution to things and yet you know that that solution is going to cause more problems and more upset before it works out.

I knew I was fed up. I was fed up. I had had enough of the treatment I was receiving from him. I had had enough of giving him support and help and understanding and then receiving nothing back. I was tired of being used as a stand in. The seconder. The next in line. I huffed at all those feelings. He couldn't do this to me anymore. I didn't want this anymore.

I knew I had to break all contact. Mum had said that that was the best way to do it. She knew what had been happening between me and him and she knew how I was feeling. I had told her everything and she could see quite well that I was beginning to change in my attitude towards it all. I had needed it at first. I had needed the little pieces of contact that he had given. Now I didn't seem to need that anymore. I needed a normal, quiet life. A normal split to be honest.

The trouble was I knew that severing all contact with him would be one of the hardest things I had ever done. I knew it would hurt. Would I be able to cope with it? Would I be able to stick to it? I was unsure of the answers to that too. I just knew I had to get through to him that it needed to stop now. It was becoming too much for me. I wanted out.

I could feel myself shaking. I wasn't cold so it must have been from the tiredness and the stress of the day. Talking about all this with mum gets me stressed. I know she is great and she understands my feelings and in some ways my actions, but I was admitting that I couldn't cope with things right now and that is hard for me. I liked coping or seeming like I was coping. It made me feel stronger. Sounds stupid huh?

I held my hands to try to stop the trembles. It didn't work. Looking at my hands, they seemed to look old. They were quite thin now from the weight loss and they were pale with the veins showing more than ever. I watched them shaking as I held tighter. I dropped them in my lap, sighing and looking up at the ceiling. Yet again, I think I expected to see the answers to all of this written up there. Instead there were just cobwebs, so I looked away again.

The thoughts of Pheobe screaming were still there. I had seen that sort of thing happen on the TV. Seb had done it too but he had put a plastic light bulb from some game he had up there and as it was thin and small I had hooked it out with my fingernail. She had placed something quite large up there. I had been so pleased that Michelle had come to help. She had popped straight round. It had made me feel quite safe and supported which again probably sounds really stupid to others. I shrugged that thought off as I didn't care what others thought anymore.

I stretched my arms and legs out in front of me. They felt like large weights hanging off me. My thoughts went back to him. He was making me so stressed and fed up. It was all down to him as it had been so many times in the past. I was so sick of this.

It had to be done. I would talk to him. I would back away. I had to. For my own sanity. If I didn't I could see the men in white coats coming for me really soon. If they didn't I would run and find them. Give me a bed in a padded cell for some peace and quiet please. I laughed at myself. I was going crazy I was sure.

I was worried though. Could I withstand another period of pain? Could I really separate from him now when I hadn't been able to so far?

I held my hands over my ears tightly as if it was somebody in the room asking me these questions instead of my own head. I couldn't stand this anymore. No more thinking. No more thinking.

I stood up, with my hands still over my head and walked into the kitchen. I grabbed my cigarettes and my lighter and my ipod. I would drown out the voices with music and smoke the night away. That was the way I would deal with it.

Excellent plan!

21st February

A very busy day. Had Nicky pop over for a couple of hours this morning. Sorted out a lot more stuff to sell on eBay. Marilyn popped in this afternoon and then I went back to hers for coffee for half an hour. Spent an hour writing the book before the cycle of school run, homework, dinner and bath began.

Felt like I got swept up into a whirlwind this evening but at least the time went quickly.

Marc spoke to the children briefly and then me for a second or two. I indicated that I was still unhappy and he said he would call me tomorrow to talk a little more. I really need to get all this off my chest. I came off the phone to him thinking about what I would say and how I would start it. The thoughts were going round and round while I sat in the study. I felt a little down and decided to put the children to bed so I could sit in the peace and quiet for a bit.

First, I said goodnight to Pheobe. I lay over the top of her wrapping myself around her so I could lie on her chest. She spoke a little about her daddy. I can't remember how he came up but he did. She said she wasn't missing him. She moaned about sleeping in his bed when she went to his flat. She said he took up all the room and he smelt funny! That cheered me up a little. She looked straight at me and said - you will never leave me like daddy has will you mummy. No I said. She said you go to work though to get money. Yes I said. We need money so we can buy food. She studied this a little and then commented on how that was a good idea because we needed food and she didn't want to be hungry. I left her giggling and walked down to Fiona's room. I cuddled up to her and asked her about her day. She said she had a great day but that she had missed daddy today. She said she didn't know why she had thought about him, she just did in the playground. She asked when she would see him again. I explained that we were having Auntie Charlie over instead this weekend and then daddy was staying with Sue the next weekend as it was her birthday. She screwed up her nose. I explained that mummy was a bit angry with daddy as he will not have them from Friday to Sunday like other dads do. She said then he isn't a proper daddy. I said no not really and told her it made mummy upset because it made her upset. She said "don't get upset about it mummy - you can't fix it. Only daddy can fix it." Tears welled in my eyes at this point and I felt as if I would cry at any minute. I couldn't believe this 6 year old girl had such an old head on her shoulders. She then looked at me and said that I got too upset about things. I said yes things with daddy still make me upset. She said "that is why you need to stop thinking about him mummy. You should stop thinking about him and start thinking about yourself. You need to be happy again mum."

With that I had to kiss her goodnight telling her how amazing she was and I promised I would be happy again just for her. I walked down the stairs and the tears fell. She was so wise for someone so young and I felt a little guilty that I wasn't her happy mummy. She seemed to understand why though.

I am sitting here now feeling a little bit better about things. I know that it doesn't matter if I am lonely sometimes and it doesn't matter that I get a bit fed up, because I have the most wonderful children. They are absolutely amazing and I love them so much. At the end of the day they are all I need. They are all I need in my life and I am so pleased they are here bringing such joy to me. My babies are my life. They are my world.

I sat back against the tiles. For the first time in a while I was smiling. I was crying still from Fiona's words, but I was smiling too. There was a warm feeling inside of me. A sense of pride and amazement. My girls were so amazing. I felt guilty that I hadn't said goodnight properly to Seb but I couldn't let him see me crying as I wouldn't have been able to explain anything.

Fiona's words made so much sense to me. She was so bright for her age. So empathetic too. She amazed me with the things she thought about and the words she said. I was so proud of her I thought I would burst.

I composed myself and rang my mum to tell her. She was the same as me. Tears caught the back of her throat too and we marvelled at her understanding and how grown up she was for her age.

I sat back after the conversation and I just smiled. My babies were so fantastic and I had done that. I had brought them up, with a little help from him of course, but mainly me. I had done it. I had made her take other peoples feelings into account and this little girl was my creation.

I walked up the stairs with a little bounce in my step. I had a reason to be happy. I walked in and out of their rooms all night. I watched them toss and turn. I listened to their moans and groans. I kissed their foreheads while they slept.

I sat outside their rooms on the landing and sighed. Not the deep, meaningful, emotional sighs that had been coming out of me lately, but a light, happy sigh. As darkness swept through the house I sat there still. I didn't want to move.

I got up and checked on them all one more time, adjusting covers and pulling curtains closer together. I crawled into bed hours later and felt my body relax as my head hit the pillow.

I didn't need anything else. I had everything I wanted right here. I had love, kindness, warmth and understanding. What else would be on the list?

My little sister.

23rd February 2008

Woke up this morning feeling like I had slept for hours in the same position. I was so stiff and I was hurting all over. My phone was vibrating and I was confused who would be texting me so early on a Saturday morning. But when I picked it up the shock really set in. It was Lee asking what I was doing. The text was sent at 1.10am. He must have been drunk I decided. I text back that I had been sleeping and we text for a while during the morning. He was still with his girlfriend but wanted a chat - though he jokingly hinted it was a little more he wanted.

Took Seb to his bowling party and waited for my sister Charlie and nephew Oscar to arrive. The children played well. We took them shopping and bought dinner. We hung about chatting and playing the Wii until the children went to bed. She seemed upset about what her boyfriend Danny had been up to. She spoke about it a little and I empathised with her naturally. I could feel a hatred for him developing as she spoke and the hurt on her face made it bite at me harder. I kept having flashbacks about what had happened between me and Marc that was similar to what she was going through now. It was hard to listen. I wanted to grab hold of him and throttle him. All the respect I had for him has gone. He was so supportive and understanding with all of the things that I went through with Marc and now here he was making my little sister hurt the way I was. *How could he?* If she does forgive him and keep battling to save her relationship then I will have to tell him that if he ever hurts her like that again, I will ruin him.

We stayed up till late talking about everything and I noticed she was doing exactly the same as I had. Going round and round in circles. I advised her the best I could and I tried to help her form a plan of action and get herself a focus but I know that all is fruitless at the moment because nothing she does will take her mind off the hurt for a while yet. Crikey I have been going through this almost a year now and the hurt is still there. I know she has a long way to go and wish there was something I could do.

The rush of excitement at the sight of Lee's name on my phone had kept me on a high for the morning and the afternoon. It was a nice buzz that had been given to me and I had been thankful for it. I wondered why he had thought of me. I was an ex and he never kept his exes numbers. He had kept mine though and I questioned why. We had got on well and had fun together. I had missed him. I had missed him a lot actually. Not just as a lover but as a friend. I could have that couldn't I?

I spent the afternoon with the girls watching them playing happily. I had relaxed back in my chair and waited for Charlie to arrive. It was to be the first time I had seen her since the problems she was having and I was a little concerned about her. I knew what she was feeling. I remembered it so well and I hated the fact that she had to go through that. I wouldn't wish that pain on anyone. Well, anyone except Sue. I sniggered. She can have all the pain she deserves in my opinion.

We had gone to bed after spending hours talking but I couldn't sleep. Charlie and I had chatted away about everything and I had felt the pain return to me. She was talking about Danny and how he had made her feel and I was there picturing Marc and how I had felt when he had done the same to me. Everything she said to me made perfect sense.

Images of myself all those months ago hit me quite hard. They had still been there when I had laid down and I was sure they were my reason for sitting up now. I sat back in the chair in the conservatory, watching the dark night outside. I had been angry at Marc for not having the children this weekend so I could go out but now I was feeling quite grateful as it had given me that time with Charlie. I pictured myself lying on the settee crying. I remembered the torture of trying to find the truth in what had been said. I remembered the difficulty of trying to piece together the puzzle of what had happened, when it had happened and why.

I hung my head. I felt useless. Useless because I knew what she was thinking and feeling and yet I couldn't help her. There was nothing I could say or do to help take the pain away from her. I wanted to rid her of it, to carry it around with me for a while, to relieve her stress and heartache and yet, I knew I couldn't. No one can do anything when you feel that way.

I got up and walked into the kitchen. I pinched one of her cigarettes as I couldn't be bothered to get mine. She wouldn't mind I was sure. I smoked it beside the sink all the time going round and round in circles. Thoughts of Marc and then Danny. Thoughts of why they would behave that way. Wondering why men had to seek attention from females they had met. Thoughts of Charlie. Thoughts of what she was going through.

The pain I had felt seemed far away to me these days. My own confusions over Marc and how I felt about him now had taken over and things had changed for me. Yet now that I was standing here thinking of my little sister and her situation, it had come back so raw. It had hit me hard and I had gasped for breath quite a few times over the course of the evening.

I put the cigarette out and went upstairs. I needed to sleep I knew that, even if I wasn't sure how I was going to achieve that. I checked on the children, they were sleeping fine now. They had taken so long to go off. I pushed open the door to the room Charlie was sleeping in. At least she was able to sleep. She lay on her side and was breathing deeply. I could still see the tear stains on her cheeks and my eyes welled up looking at them.

I knelt down beside her making sure I didn't disturb Oscar. I just watched her sleeping as I had done with my children. I felt so protective of her. She was my little sister. I had watched her grow up. I had watched her make mistakes and had fought with her lots. Despite all of the difficulties between us over the years, I felt as if I was the only one in the world that was allowed to hurt her in any way. No one else could. He had and I hated him for it. That wasn't allowed. I should have been there to protect her from him. I smiled at myself. I would help her feel better.

I got up and went back to my bed where Pheobe was sprawled across it. Time to sleep or at least try. Tomorrow will be better. Tomorrow would be brighter. Charlie and I deserved that.

I laid there with all the thoughts swimming round and round my head. The images coming and going in front of me. I laid there and waited for tomorrow.

24th February 2008

Took the children to an indoor play area for a couple of hours this afternoon. We let them run riot and fed them and sat about watching the people and the children. We then came back and they left after a couple of hours. Chatted to mum on the phone, sorted the children out for the school week and sat about really doing nothing. The weekend had gone quickly and I was pleased that there was another one over with. The weekends are still the hardest. I'm not sure why. Part of it is knowing that he should be having the children. Part of it is knowing that I would have been out if he was having them and part of it is knowing that we would have had time together. I do remember the nightmare that weekends were and I know I don't miss all that too much but it still seems the longest days and the worst parts of the week. I still live each week waiting for them though so they can't be that bad can they.

Mum came over this evening and sat with me. The night before my birthday and all was quiet. I didn't feel anything about tomorrow except old as I would then be 32. I know it isn't that old but it is closer to 40 than I was and it is further away from being young!

I chatted to mum all evening. We talked about Charlie and as I spoke about her I could see her face as she sat in the play area. She looked so sad the whole time. She stared into space quite a lot and every now and then she would realise and try to seem upbeat and chatty. I kept the conversation going as long as I could but I also knew that she needed to sit and think and that was fine with me.

It didn't feel like the day before my birthday. There was a sombre air to the house tonight. I was never one for celebrating getting older but the disappointment of not having a night out at all had hung over me more than I realised.

I thought back to last year and how he had spoilt me. He had bought me an ipod and I had been worried as to where the money had come from. We couldn't really afford things like that, though I didn't show him that was what I was thinking. This year he wouldn't be around and while that didn't bother me too much at all, it still brought a sad, heavy feeling to my heart. It seemed strange to be feeling that way when I hadn't wanted him around much recently.

I was more upset with the fact that he hadn't organised the time to let the children get something for me. I suppose in a way that isn't his job anymore but it would still have been nice for them. Fiona had said that she didn't have a present for me and had been upset. Mum had to take over. She asked them what they wanted to get me and she went and bought their gifts. They had written their cards with her tonight. They were so excited.

It had dawned on me that I was going to be 32. It didn't sound that old. I felt a lot older than that though and a lot more tired too. I had planned a nice quiet day with mum. We were going for breakfast in town and then shopping. I was really looking forward to it.

I sat back and wondered what the heaviness within me was about tonight. Was it because I was sad he wasn't here? Was it because I was upset he hadn't remembered to organise anything for the children? Was it because I didn't want another birthday? Was it just the feelings I had had over the weekend with my sister bringing me down? I just wasn't sure.

I inhaled my cigarette and looked at the clock. It was getting late now and I was aware that I would probably be jumped on early tomorrow morning by the children in their excitement. They would be wanting to open my cards and presents for me. I smiled.

Switching off the lights, I climbed the stairs wearily. Another weekend over. Another day finished. Tomorrow will be fine.

Happy Birthday.

25th February 2008

Happy birthday to me!

I woke up feeling crap today. I hadn't slept at all really. I couldn't. Not sure why. Was still awake at 1am and sat downstairs drinking hot milk. Pheobe then got up at 2.30 and phoned Marc's mobile when she used my phone as a torch to go to the toilet. I just hung up. I couldn't be bothered to explain. I then laid in bed for a while trying to get back to sleep and before I knew it Seb was standing in my room at 6.15 telling me he had a stomach ache and was almost sick. I then tossed and turned for the next hour listening to my mum and Seb discussing this and the girls walking about. I ended up crying even though I tried so hard not to. I couldn't believe my day could be ruined again. The girls opened my presents and cards for me and I got ready. Seb finally got ready saying he would be alright at school but he had forgotten to remind me about his food tech stuff again so I had to go to the shop and buy it and then drop it off at his school.

Me and mum then went for breakfast in town and sat in the Café enjoying the time together. We shopped and she bought me a new jacket for going out for my birthday. She also bought a new sim card for my phone and I organised Fiona's friend's birthday present. We picked Pheobe up from school and went to Sainsbury's to buy chocolate cake (Pheobe's orders).

Pheobe and I went to forest school while Fiona went to her birthday party. Pheobe did very well in the school workshop and really got into it which was more than she did last time. We went back home, picked up Fiona from the party and got a takeaway. My aunt Alice and Uncle Michael visited for an hour or so and the children enjoyed blowing out my candles of which there were not 32!

I went to bed pleased that it was all over and also with the thought that when that day comes round again, maybe I will be even better than I was this year.

Even my birthday had to be stressful at first. I couldn't believe it when Seb came into me saying he was ill. I was exhausted from not sleeping again and as soon as he said it I felt deflated even further. My mood plummeted downhill at such speed I felt so sick and before I knew it I was crying. I hadn't wanted to do that on my birthday. I hadn't wanted that sinking feeling to raise its ugly head at all today and yet there I was wallowing in it.

I shook my head at myself as I thought back to that. It had all turned out alright in the end but I had let things get to me. It's the lack of sleep I am sure. I yawned and stretched at that point.

I looked across the room to my birthday cards. On the fireplace sat a beautiful cream vase with cream roses in it. The card read 'Happy Birthday love Marcus xx' I wondered why he had sent that. I found it odd to think that he felt the need to send me a bunch of flowers through interflora for my birthday when he hadn't really acknowledged me at all in his life lately. I turned my head away from them to stop myself thinking about it.

The house was quiet again and I sat in the darkness. I wasn't really thinking about anything. I didn't have lots of thoughts running through my head. I had had a fairly nice day with just a few hiccups. I smiled. What day didn't have those?

I rubbed my hands up my arms as I felt a chill in the air. I heard the children moaning in their sleep and I raised my head to look up the stairs towards the noise. I rested my head on the side of the settee and laid there.

This time last year I didn't know the hardship that had laid ahead of me. I wondered what laid ahead of me for this year. Would it be a great year or another set of struggles and obstacles to clamber over? Would there be more emotional distress and heartache or would things get easier?

I closed my eyes and relaxed into the chair more. Where do I want to be this time next year? When I am 33. I couldn't think of anything in particular really. I pictured my children another year down the line. A bit older. Maybe even a bit easier. Settled properly in school. Happy. Seeing their daddy more. I would like him to be healthy again. I would like him to be happy to be a daddy. I huffed. I wasn't sure that was ever going to happen.

Most of all I wanted to be happier with life itself. I wanted to smile often and laugh lots. I wanted to walk down the road with a spring in my step and my head held high. I wanted to confront any difficulties with a laid back attitude and let life carry me through it all. That was where I wanted to be. In that happy place, right there.

27th February 2008

Had a hard morning teaching yr 1 nets of shapes. Was pleasantly surprised at lunchtime when I got a text message from Lee asking if he could pop over tonight. Happily I said yes. I enjoyed spending time with him before and it would be nice to have his friendship back again.

We chilled out on the settee. He had split from his girlfriend and was quite down about it. She had been quite hard work by what he said. She didn't want to see him all the time, made him shave off his beard, stopped him smoking and seemed to want to change him. He said their relationship was a little argumentative and he found it too hard to be treated that way. I saw his point. It did make me question myself a little. I wondered whether I was like that at all. I know I am hard work when in a relationship as most of us are but I was still thinking back to figure out how much.

He stayed until midnight. He seemed to be ok with being here. It was nice to have someone to talk to, though I wasn't too impressed with his choice of film. Werewolves and vampires are not my thing!

I sat back down on the settee. I had just seen Lee out and locked the doors as he told me to. I had had a good evening with him. It was nice to have him round and being part of my life again in friendship. He made me smile again and his stories about what he had been up to made me laugh. I had missed that so much.

We had watched a scary film and I had to keep burying my head in his shoulder as I hated the gory scenes of vampires and werewolves. They made me shiver and I didn't want to look. He did enjoy teasing me for being such a coward.

He had gone now and I had realised how much I had missed having that closeness with someone. I had missed sharing those moments with friends and I was pleased that I could do that again. Whether tonight was a one off or not, I had enjoyed it immensely.

I could feel myself smiling. It amazes me how I never realise I am doing it. I just feel it across my face as if somebody had come along and stuck it there. I felt happy. I hadn't felt this warmth for a few months now and it was a welcome return.

I yawned and rolled my eyes at myself for getting so excited about having another friend to spend time with. I suppose after not having any, collecting them was a great change that I appreciated. Again I laughed at myself. Just go to bed woman. Just go to bed.

28th February 2008

Spent the whole day so angry at Marc. His credit card statement had come through. It showed transactions abroad on the weekend of the 1st of February which as this diary told me he had said he was in hospital. I couldn't believe he had done it again. I was so angry I did nearly text her a couple of times but ended up yet again thinking what would be the bloody point! She wouldn't care anyway. As far as I was concerned she was as bad as him.

I shopped in the morning, sorted things out at the bank and then visited a friend for an hour. It was nice to sit and chat and have somebody else agreeing with me. She couldn't believe he was there either. I think he amazes everybody with his lies.

Naturally when I confronted him with it, after he had helped the children write their cards to her in my house, he denied it all. He said he was not there that weekend. He said he went towards the end of the week and was back at the weekend. He said he would never do that to his children. I just couldn't believe him. I looked at him as if he was someone I didn't even know standing there. He could see how angry and upset I was and seemed stressed about what I was going to do. I had wanted to get in touch with her and he knew it. I think he is expecting me to do that one day. Maybe. I threw him out at 9 saying that I had Lee coming over. He was a little surprised. Warned me to be careful as he was on the rebound and only after one thing.

Lee popped over after he had gone. We watched another crap film on TV. At least it wasn't too scary this time. We cuddled up on the settee and I realised how much I had missed the closeness. Just a cuddle and it makes you feel better. He listened to me rant on about Marc and how much of an arse he was and of course he agreed. We fell asleep for a while cuddled up on the settee. It's nice to feel so comfortable with someone. I enjoy having him here and I hope he isn't doing what Marc said.

I couldn't believe what he had done. More lies. I was so sick of them. That one had really got to me. To say he was really ill and that was why he hadn't been able to have the children. He had had me so worried about him. I had felt guilty about texting him. I went through my diary for that day. How I shouldn't have been bothering him when he was in hospital. How I had felt so alone that night when Seb had acted so strange.

The anger was running through my veins like a car on a racing track. The fumes from the car was the steam coming out of my ears as I tried to soothe the feelings I had. The screech of the tyres was the voice in my head yelling at me. How had I fallen for it yet again?

My thoughts turned to the children writing her cards. He hadn't even bought one for me from them. He had come into my house and sat them down at the table and gave them my craft box to make cards for her.

'It's Sue's birthday on Saturday. I thought you could make her some lovely cards for me to give to her.'

How dare he? How could he do that in his ex wife's house? I was hurt and angry that he had done that. It hurt that the children were so happy to do it too. They adored her and they were excited to be making something for her. I didn't have the heart to stop them like I had wanted to. They looked up at me and smiled.

'Do you think she will like this mum?' Fiona had asked me.

'Of course she will baby girl' I replied, 'she will love it'

I had slipped off into the kitchen at that point and lit a cigarette while they were busy. I didn't want to watch my children organising her birthday cards with their daddy in my house. I felt my body tense up again as I recalled the scene. I remembered the children asking if they would be able to see her on her birthday and him explaining that he was taking her out so they couldn't. I took a deep breath as I tried to calm down again.

He had come into the kitchen and asked if I was ok. That grated on me more than ever. I knew he had lied to me and I wasn't going to confront him in front of the children. I gritted my teeth and said I was fine but I would talk to him later. He didn't like that reply and stormed off.

I looked over to my left where I had had the conversation about that weekend with him. I could picture the scene as if it was replaying to me before my eyes. He had stood there defending himself, saying I had the wrong end of the stick. He had said he would never do that to his children and I shouldn't be getting so angry. He said he had gone abroad for a break with a couple of friends on the Thursday.

I could see myself glaring at him and the hatred I had for him was written all over my face.

'You told me you were really ill in hospital.'

'I was. I wasn't lying to you.'

'Were you with her?' I had spat. 'She come before your children again did she?'

'No of course not. She wasn't even there.'

He expected me to swallow that crap. I turned my head away as if I had seen enough. I hadn't wanted to hear anymore when it was happening let alone hear it all over again. It was then that he had given me the divorce paper he had signed to return to the solicitor. He had left it for me to post though why he couldn't do it himself I didn't know.

I shook my head at that too. The anger inside me was at boiling point now. I picked up my phone. I scrolled down to her number. Had she been away with him? Had she known that he was neglecting his children for her? I wanted so much to call her but then her voice came into my head and I knew

I couldn't do it. I couldn't call. I didn't want to hear that soft, Scottish accent of hers on the end of my phone. I threw it back down on the bench. I had no way of knowing anything if I didn't get in touch with her. I should be doing it. I should confront her. I knew I couldn't do it though so why try.

I hung my head in shame and held my face in my hands. I wished I had the guts to do that. Other women would have done it ages ago. Why was I so scared of her? Why couldn't I face her? What was wrong with me?

I needed Lee back. He had calmed me down. He had held me for as long as I needed it. He had cuddled me and made me feel safe and stronger. I hadn't wanted him to go home and I needed him to come back now to take me away from it all like he had done for those few hours.

I raised my head again and looked out of the window. Will all this ever end? Will I get to the end of this mess at any time soon? I didn't feel like I could take anymore.

29th February 2008

Was looking forward to going out tonight but it wasn't to be. Hayley had to call off again due to emergency dental treatment. She had to be knocked out and was in pain too. I was upset but understood.

I was due to take the children to mums anyway and was planning to spend at least an hour of my evening in the bath and having a long lay in in the morning. That wasn't to be either. Some stupid idiot went through a main cable near her and caused a huge power cut. They had no lights, heating or cooker. They came round here and cooked dinner and then waited for the call to say the power was back on. At 8.30 I gave up and put the children to bed. They were upset and so was I. The children were really disappointed but the girls managed to get to sleep pretty quickly so I was lucky.

Mum and dad left at 9 and Lee said he would pop over anyway. I got a phone call from mum to say that all power was back on when they arrived there and we were all incredibly frustrated. I wonder how long it had been back on for. Stupid electric people.

Lee came over; we had Chinese and watched a Jackie Chan film. It was quite funny actually. Again we ended up cuddling up on the settee and this time inevitably we ended up kissing. Not sure what is going on here but hey I'm not going to complain too much. I just wonder whether he had planned this all along. I would be so hurt if that was the case. I hope he wants to retain the friendship as much as possible. I don't want him flitting in and out as he pleases and then vanishing. Maybe I worry about things too much. I should just enjoy myself. Yet again not sure.

Lee had been on my mind ever since he left. I lay in bed staring at the ceiling with the thoughts from tonight rattling around. The day had not gone as planned which seemed to be a theme of days recently. Stupid people always get in the way. Never plan anything is the moral of the story here.

I closed my eyes and the picture of me and Lee kissing on the settee came into my head so I opened them again. I bit the inside of my cheek as I thought over it. Why was it such a big deal? Why was I worrying about it like I was?

We had already discussed the fact that he couldn't have a relationship with me as we were too different. We didn't want that but we liked each others company. I had heard that men and women cannot be just friends. I never believed it as I had managed it with other men. I seemed to be struggling here though.

I sighed a huge sigh and stretched my arms up to the ceiling as if I was reaching for the answer book. I let my arms fall onto the bed. I looked around the room and noted all the bits I didn't like about it. I really wanted to decorate my house.

Realising I was straying from the worries I had and also that therefore these worries would yet again keep me awake, I threw the covers back and got up. I huffed at myself as I walked slowly and heavily down the stairs. I went into the kitchen where the darkness seemed to be less deep and lit a cigarette. I placed myself next to the kettle on the bench and pulled my knees up to my chest as I felt the cold air and shivered.

I leant my head back on the tiles and blew the smoke to the ceiling. I thought back to the kiss and smiled. It wasn't that I didn't enjoy being with him in that way, it was just it wouldn't work and I wanted his friendship more than anything else. I didn't want to lose him because we made a mistake.

I had answered my own questions. I didn't want Lee in that way but I did want him as a friend. That is probably the same from his point of view too. There we are, sorted. I huffed again. I didn't feel tired anymore. I just stared out the window and watched the rain fall down the glass. The realisation that it was probably incredibly cold out there made me shiver even more. I hugged myself, cursing myself for getting up.

I looked around the kitchen as if I was searching for something to do. It seemed to be so boring at the moment and yet I never did any housework or any of the little jobs I could do. I just smiled at my own laziness.

The minute I stopped thinking, Sue popped into my head. The image of her made my heart sink and my face fall.

'So that is what is really keeping you up,' I said to myself.

I sniggered and sat upright. Bringing my hands to my face I rubbed them down it and then let them fall into my lap. Why did I get so fed up with things like this? She shouldn't affect me in this way? I didn't understand my own feelings, but then that was nothing new was it.

I looked over to the window again and as so many times before she seemed to be there outside. The image of her was clear. There she was with him opening the birthday present he had bought her for her bithday tomorrow. He was there for hers. Not mine. Mine didn't matter anymore. I shrugged my shoulders at the lack of pain at that thought. Normally, something like that would cause that huge, crushing rush of pain that knocked me over. It hadn't though. I frowned.

He is with her instead of the children. Couldn't have them again because they have some great night out planned. There it was - there was the pain. I fell backwards against the tiles as the wave of heartache ran through me. That was it, there it was. It hadn't bothered me when I was thinking in terms of myself. I had never thought that would happen.

I folded my arms across my chest as I slipped down further off the bench. As my feet hit the floor, I felt my legs crumble and I slid all the way down. It used to be at this point that I burst into tears, but I just felt fed up now. So fed up. I huffed again.

I yawned and looked up at the window. That was weird, she was gone. She usually stuck around for ages. I stood back up and looked out as if I was looking to see where she had gone. She had gone. The image was over. So quick.

I turned to walk back to bed. I stopped. I wasn't fed up anymore either. I just felt tired. I frowned. These feelings were all new to me. I liked them though. I was happy they were over so quickly. I knew I could cope with feeling a little fed up, a little down even and a little confused, if they left that quickly.

I smiled. I laughed at myself too.

Happy Birthday Sue.

1st March

Happy birthday skank.

No phone call from Marc yesterday made me so angry. The children didn't get the chance to talk to him and yet again I ended up fed up. It bugs me that he can't find any time for them at all.

The children went with mum for the day and I caught up on housework and this diary. He phoned early evening and told me he was in hospital. He hadn't even seen her. He had cried off from seeing the children this weekend because of her birthday and he hadn't even been with her. Such a joke. He told me about their little get together tonight and how it was mainly girls and him. It just pissed me off to be honest. All I could think about was them out having fun while I am in with the children yet again. I must be a mug. I got bored with the conversation and said goodbye. I told him to phone back later if he wanted to speak to the children. It's alright for her having a birthday celebration with him when I was denied one by the same man. The hatred is pretty intense today and I'm not sure how I will use it yet. Off to mums now to meet up with the children and prepare for Mother's day. The last of the firsts. Such a good feeling. I am nearly there.

There they were dragging me down a little yet again. I should be used to this. I should be used to feeling a bit fed up, a bit upset, a bit angry, a bit blah. I was not though. I was not used to it and every time it happened I felt annoyed with myself as well as them.

I was having a nice night. I was at my mums for the night. We would spend Mother's day together. We had a drink and a chat and we were fine. I was smiling and not thinking about them and what they were doing and I was not jealous of what she had and I didn't.

I laid down in bed and the smile faded away and it was forgotten. It was gone. The silence in the house deafened me. The weirdness of not being in my house made me uncomfortable. The emptiness engulfed me and I felt like I was alone.

I huffed and looked over to the window. The thoughts of them together tonight caused tears to bite at my eyes. It was ok for them. They were free, having a great time, celebrating her birthday. He had probably spoilt her with lovely gifts and now they were laughing and smiling with their friends. I wouldn't have gone out tonight as it is Mother's day tomorrow. I would never have left my children tonight so why did I feel like this? Why did I feel so low at the thought that it was her birthday and she was out enjoying herself?

'It's just because you didn't get to do it,' the voice in my head cried.

That was probably true. I didn't get a birthday weekend like I had planned and I was angry with that more than anything else. I nodded my head in agreement. Yes that was what was playing on my mind. That has to be my problem.

I smiled briefly and then it turned to a frown again. I knew he wouldn't come though so why had it affected me. It can't be the reason as I am used to the let down.

'It's because she is with him for her birthday and you were not,' another voice piped up.

Maybe. Maybe that was it. I could feel the puzzled look on my face. That didn't feel right either. I had had so much confusion with not wanting him around anymore over the last few weeks. I had enjoyed my birthday with my mum and the children. I hadn't missed him at the time, why would I miss that now? I sighed at myself at the frustration of trying to figure things out too much. I shouldn't do this. Especially not when I wanted to sleep.

I rubbed my legs against the sheets and turned over to face the girls. They were sound asleep laying on each other, squashed together as if they didn't have the room to move. They looked so sweet curled up that close.

I placed my arms underneath the pillow and pulled it in tighter, hugging it under my chin. I propped my head up on my wrists. I was wide awake now. I laid my head back down and closed my eyes. I had to at least try to get some sleep.

As my eyes searched for images in the darkness I prayed that they wouldn't appear. I closed my eyes and within a few minutes there they were. I could see her laughing with her friends. She was holding a glass of wine and she was dancing. There were her two friends around her and they were giggling. I opened my eyes quick. I didn't want to see that. I sighed and hugged the pillow even tighter.

Suddenly, I realised that I had not seen him. He had not been part of that image. I closed my eyes again quickly, to see the image again. To check if I was right. I scoured the picture I was seeing. Nope. He wasn't there. I opened my eyes and I could feel my face fall into a frown. He wasn't there.

I rolled over onto my back and stared at the ceiling. With my mouth open I realised that I was jealous of her. All this time I had been jealous of her. At first because she had my husband. Then because she had my children. Now I was jealous that she had her life. It wasn't so much she had him.

It wasn't that she was out with him. It was that she was out. She had her life. She had helped him deprive me of mine over the last year; he had deprived me of mine for longer.

I sat up in the bed, propping the pillow behind me. I pulled my knees up to my chest, keeping the cover over them and rubbed my eyes as if I was disbelieving everything I was thinking. I was jealous. I wanted the life she had. The freedom. The birthday celebration. The friends. I huffed and shrugged my shoulders.

I looked down at my girls lying beside me. I didn't really want it. I wanted a taster that was all. I wanted a little of that life. I wanted to build my social life and be able to do what I wanted to do without him ruining my plans and making me change them.

The guilt washed over me. I shouldn't be jealous when I have my children. I shouldn't feel deprived of life when I have an amazing family with me every step of the way. I felt awful and I hung my head in shame.

I felt so confused by the thoughts of tonight. I sat, in a morose silence, motionless, just staring at the clock on the video that lit up that section of the room. Every now and then I would raise my hand and push my hair back. Every now and then I threw my head back in disbelief at my own thoughts. Every now and then I sighed a large sigh and shrugged at myself. Every now and then I looked down at my girls and said sorry for feeling like that for those few seconds.

Every now and then, I wanted to cry.

Goodbye Sue?

2nd March 2008

Mother's day.

My mum took the children out yesterday and bought presents from them to me. It was a little upsetting to think of her doing that as it is not her job. He should have done it. He couldn't even think of me in his plans to ensure that the children had all they needed. They were a little anxious before my mum told them they would be going out with her. They thought they wouldn't be able to get me anything. I felt sorry for them. They shouldn't have been having their doubts.

The morning was weird. I was a little tearful though I couldn't really explain why. I was quite pleased that all my firsts would be over and there would now only be seconds. They should be much easier thankfully. I was very tired. It was a little hard to get to sleep in a strange house but I was tired from sitting up with Lee the last few nights and I did eventually drop off. I felt as if I hadn't slept at all when the children woke me up. That makes you feel weepy in itself. Maybe I am trying to find excuses again.

Seb bought me some earrings and Fiona bought me a gorgeous dragonfly bottle for my chest of drawers. Pheobe was great. She bought me chocolates that I didn't like and was very happy to tuck into them. She had known I didn't like them because we had tried them last week. Cheeky moo.

Lee phoned me while I was at mums and I spent 40 mins on the phone to him. He was worried as he was picking up the stuff from his ex girlfriends place. We arranged to meet up later.

Then Marc phoned. He was upset. Sue had just dumped him. He had been behaving like an idiot again last night. He was not enjoying himself at her birthday evening and he showed it which upset her. He said he was coming over to see me and the children as he needed us. He did get a little angry when I said I would not change my plans with Lee. He was not too impressed. Tough.

He came in and sobbed his heart out to me. He seemed devastated and yet in the same breath asked if he could stay here. No. He said he needed to be with me. No. He then asked if my offer of him moving back home, which I had said he could all those months ago, was still open. No. I felt mean. I hate hurting anyone but I knew in that moment that I couldn't do it. Of course I still loved him, in some way, but he was making me feel like I was second best. Sue has gone, so let's go back to Stephanie. No chance mate.

He apologised for making me feel so bad and for hurting me so much but it didn't seem to be real to me. I just felt as if he was acting out of his fear of being alone. I laid with Lee watching a film and I knew I was happy with him. *We are just mates but if I feel that comfy with another man then I cannot need Marc as much as I thought can I?*

Went to bed confused.

Flaming cheek!

Couldn't be bothered to organise anything for Mother's day. Hasn't been bothered to see the children, some nights not even calling. Couldn't be bothered to be there for me when I asked him to or when I needed him. Gets dumped by the skank and then within four hours asks if he can come home.

I couldn't believe the audacity of the man. Really? I pinched myself a couple of times when stood in the kitchen. While he was asking me and saying that he wanted and needed me right now and could he move back home and be together, I actually pinched myself to check that it was for real. Was I dreaming? No.

I looked over to the spot where he had stood. He had cried and cried for ages when he was telling me how she had dumped him. She had said she had had enough. She had said that she wanted to end it before and that last night with him was the last straw. He had behaved weirdly. He was upset that she hadn't been upset. He said she sat stony faced without shedding a tear and just told him to leave. He said there was no feeling in her at all.

I had stood there listening and watching him as he was talking about it. I felt sorry for him but, knowing my husband as I do, I knew that he probably did act strangely and I knew how difficult he could be. I frowned at how I understood what she was saying.

At the same time as I was listening to him, I was talking to him in my head. It hurts being dumped doesn't it? I felt like that when you left me, did you care then? I cried like this over you, were you there? Did you think of me when I was going through this?

With each of the thoughts, I chewed my lips hard and I could feel my heart racing as I got more and more angry. Angry at him for being there. Angry at her for hurting him. Angry at myself for listening.

I looked down at the floor for some of it. I couldn't bear to lift my head to see this pathetic man in front of me crying like a baby because he had lost her. I realised then that I didn't really care. I wasn't happy that he was hurting. I wasn't happy that she had dumped him. I just didn't care.

I lifted my head when he started to say those words.

'You said a few months ago that if I asked to come home...' he had begun. Remembering that made me feel the shock all over again and I shuddered.

'...you would take me back,' he had continued. I pictured myself standing against the bench with my mouth opening wider in disbelief that the man was asking me this already.

'Can I come home? Can we work things out?' he had asked.

I had turned away from him as I needed to smile. I wasn't sure, even now, whether the smile was at him being so low to ask me that question. Or from the disbelief he had asked it. Or from the smugness at him being so hurt and in pain at that moment.

A flash of her crossed my mind. She had stolen him from me for all of a year. Just 12 months. I had gone through all that pain for her to dump him after such a short amount of time. I smiled again.

I had turned back to him and said no. I actually said it. No. You cannot move back in. No. You cannot stay here tonight. No. I don't want you here anymore. I said it. I actually said it.

He had asked me to change my plans. He asked whether Lee could come over another night so he could stay here instead because he needed to be with me. I said no to that too. No.

My thoughts turned to Lee. I had had another night, curled up in his arms on the settee. I felt safe and secure. I was comfortable with having him in my house and with him laying beside me. We were just friends. There was nothing in it. I was happy with him there though. That had to mean something.

I stared out the window. I was so confused. For months I had waited for this day. For months I had waited for him to come home and be with me again. For months I had waited for him to realise that she was no better than me and what he had here with me and the children was far better than what he had with her. Now it was here, I didn't want it.

I sighed a huge sigh. Life is so strange.

I looked out of the window. I wondered how he was. Was he ok? Was he crying or sleeping? Was she ok? Was she upset? Would she think that she had made a mistake and ask him back? Was she crying? I found it odd that I was thinking of her and how she was.

I looked over again to where I had stood. I could see the moment when he had asked me. I could see my face. My mouth had dropped open at the shock. I looked a little closer. I could see panic. I could see the panic in my eyes. The racing heartbeat. The sweaty hands. That wasn't disbelief, that was panic. I hadn't expected that. The last few weeks I had made my mind up that I didn't want that man anymore and now I had to tell him.

I held my head in my hands and took a deep breath. Would I stay feeling that way? Would I remain the same determined woman who said no and meant it? I shook my head. What if he backed me down? What if he ground me down like he had done so many times before?

I wanted to scream. I hadn't wanted any more confusion or stress. I thought it was all over. Now it seemed, there was so much more to come.

3rd March 2008

Was woken up at 5am. I was sleeping light so I was not surprised to hear my phone buzzing when he was phoning. Marc on the phone. I picked it up and started to say what the hell do you think you are doing calling me now but before I had finished the sentence he just said I am on your doorstep. Let me in when you can. I laid there for a couple of minutes and then went downstairs and opened the door. I crawled back to bed and tried to ignore him moving around downstairs. I must have dozed off because the next thing I knew the bed was moving and it was because of him getting in it. I glared at him and he just said I need to be close to you. I replied you are not doing this and picked Pheobe up and went into her room. I curled back up in her bed and we both went off to sleep.

Getting up for school the next hour felt awful. I was so tired and on edge because I knew he was there. I got them ready and woke him up. He said goodbye to Seb and he walked the girls to school with me where he was introduced to Pheobe's teacher so he could pick her up from school. He was deemed a stranger otherwise. How sad.

He came to Asda with me and ended up in tears when I played Leona Lewis' Better In Time to him. I told him I would buy it for him and he just cried all the way there. We shopped like the old times and he paid for it all which I was incredibly grateful for. It meant I had saved a little money this week. We talked a little more. I reminded him of all the things he had done and said to me over the last 11 months. He realised how hurt I was and that things would be hard graft. He was thinking along the lines of us getting back together so easily. *How can he think that he can just waltz back into my life when he walked out of it so readily?* He never looked back either which was something else I brought to his attention. He kept apologising.

He left for the afternoon when a friend came over and returned later. He was leaving and said he didn't want to go. He was talking like he wanted to see her again and seemed happy that she had contacted him and seemed concerned for him. He can't really want me then. He needs to stop giving out mixed messages and decide what he wants. The problem is I don't think I want him back. I have my reservations. *Would he be coming back because she has left him? Would he be coming back because he had no one else? Would he do what he has done again? Would there be yet another woman? Would things get too stressful again? Would he run again? What about his debts? What about all the little things that we rowed about? What about the way he treated the children?*

There were also the questions for myself. *Do I want him back now? Would I ever be able to trust him again? Am I prepared to give up the life I have now to go back to the one I had before?*

I don't want to give that up. I want to see Lee and Alexander which he would not let me continue to do. I enjoy my life on the whole. I hate it when I can't do the things I want to do but who doesn't. I hate knowing he is free while I am here looking after the children he walked out on. I hate it when he doesn't have the children at all. But overall. With the way my life is going now I am happy. *Would I really want to change all of that?* I don't think I do.

So many flaming questions!

It felt that all I had done all day was ask myself questions.

I rubbed my head. I was so confused and I could feel the stress in every muscle of my body. I was weighed down by everything that had happened. The thoughts swam around and every few minutes one would jump up to try and grab my attention completely, like it was demanding to be answered and quietened. It all felt like such hard work. It was so difficult.

I thought back to the feelings I had had through the day. The sadness at the father of my children not being known at the school. The anger at the way he thought he could come back now and make a go of a marriage he walked out on. The frustration at how he couldn't see why I didn't jump at the chance even when I listed the reasons. The disbelief at him not realising he had hurt me so much. The sinking feeling when I realised I was right after his face lit up when she contacted him.

I knew I was right in having those concerns. If she asked him to come back and try again he would go. She had responded to his texts, whatever they were, and so he left for London to be with her. Even though I didn't think I wanted him I was still upset by that. I was still gutted. I didn't understand that.

I looked at the blank TV screen in front of me and I hoped that the answers to everything would suddenly appear before me. No such luck. I walked out into the kitchen, scouring the place for something I wanted to do and then feeling the disappointment as I found nothing.

All that kept going through my mind was Marc. Did he really want that? Did I really not want that? Would I be able to trust him again? Then in came the image of Lee. Would I have to give him up as a friend? Marc would see to it I am sure. I couldn't just have him round when I wanted. I would miss that and I wasn't prepared to lose him. Then there was Alexander. I wouldn't be able to meet him either. I wouldn't be able to have dinner with him when I wanted to. I didn't want to give him up either.

I huffed a loud sigh and groaned at the end of it. I laid my arms on the bench in the kitchen and placed my head on them. This wasn't what was supposed to happen. There wasn't supposed to be any more confusion. Things were supposed to get easier. I rocked my head from side to side trying to ease the throbbing.

I stood up straight and got a cigarette down from the cupboard. I walked over to the sink, lighting it along the way, and hauled myself up onto the bench. I flicked the kettle on and reached for the T bags and cup. I looked at them on the bench beside me and then looked out of the window.

'That's not going to do it!' I said loudly.

I jumped down and went to the cupboard on the other side of the kitchen. I reached in and pulled out a bottle of whisky.

'That's more like it,' I said aloud and then smiled.

I poured myself a large glass of whisky and added ice cubes and a splash of cola. I hauled myself back onto the bench and leant back against the tiles, sipping my drink. I could feel the heat of it all the way down my throat and I pulled a strange face at the taste. I wasn't sure I liked it but that didn't stop me continuing to drink it.

I inhaled deeply on my cigarette and blew the smoke across the room.

'You wouldn't be able to trust him would you?'

Again I was talking to myself. Again I was going crazy. I sipped at my drink again as I thought. There would probably be some other woman one day. I might have to go through all this again. I wouldn't be able to believe a word he was saying. I don't even know the real truth about Sue. There are probably more lies there than I thought. Maybe.

'Everything he hated about living here is still here.'

He had been stressed with the children, the travel, the house and work. All of those things would still be in his life if he moved back. He would still be stressed and he would still be snappy and difficult to live with. What if he decided after a few months he couldn't take it again and walked out again? I couldn't handle going through any of this again.

'He has so many debts.'

I was struggling myself financially. He would bring extra money back again granted but he would also bring a lot of debt back too. I would have to work so hard to clear it all. I didn't want to do that again. And what if he added to it still? What would I do then?

'He did all those things.'

That was a big one. I knew that. He had hurt me and the children. He had left us behind completely. He hadn't been there for us. He hadn't had his children regularly. He hadn't been the father I needed or wanted for them and he hadn't made them his world like they should have been. He cannot change that can he? The pain from all those things hit me. I choked as I tried to swallow. I rubbed my chest as it felt sore now. My heart was still bruised. I held my hand on my chest and I felt my heart beating. It had been damaged by him and it had fought hard to heal itself. There had been so many tiny pieces to put back together. It couldn't take another battering like that. I was sure it wouldn't mend again.

'I don't want to give up my life now to take a chance on the man that destroyed it in the first place.'

So significant. I stopped still. My glass was at my lips but I didn't move. That was it. That was it. I couldn't take the chance. I liked my life. It was hard and it was stressful and it was confusing and sometimes it was downright sad and depressing. But I liked it. It was mine. I slowly lifted my glass to fill my mouth with the drink. I didn't take my eyes off the spot ahead that they were fixed to. I didn't want to let go of me.

I thought back to that first day. I thought back to that woman I was. I wasn't her anymore. I was a different person. I wanted different things. I was me now, I was me. I was going to stay that way. Wasn't I?

5th March

Felt better once I had received the call from Marc to say he had gone for his treatment. He was scared. He also told me he was wearing his wedding ring again. Thought it might give him strength. It felt weird to hear that. I was shocked. It was great to hear something like that and I hoped it did install strength in him to get through it. It was still weird to hear. I never thought the day would come when he said he wanted to come home. Never thought I would have the decision to make and so had blocked it out of my head and forgotten about it. Yet after hearing those words and talking to him it suddenly dawned on me that I would have to decide after all. I knew it would be so difficult. Not sure what to do. Began to feel quite sick on the drive home trying to work it out and talked myself round in circles.

Lee came and sat with me tonight. We just watched the TV and had a cuddle on the settee. I feel so safe when he holds me as if none of the problems in my life are there. He is my escape. I can hide in his arms and know that none of that can touch me. I could easily fall asleep lying with him. Warm and secure. I know there is nothing in it but it is nice to have those few hours when I am protected from my life.

I had blocked it all out. I never for one minute thought I would need to decide whether or not I would want to take the man back. Never. He was gone for good as far as I was concerned. I had even worried about what I would do if he ever told me they were going to get married or she was having his baby. I laughed at myself. It amazed me how I saw them that happy and with such a future together.

Here I was now though faced with a decision to make that I really didn't want to acknowledge.

He was wearing his wedding ring again. Was that supposed to instil some happiness in me? Was that supposed to make me believe he was telling me the truth after everything? He could be with her now begging her to go back to him for all I knew.

The confusion from everything was starting to make me feel nauseous. I had spent the evening snuggled up to Lee on the settee, feeling safe and warm and now I was cold and insecure. I hated the vast change that had happened so quickly.

I lit a cigarette and stood by the window. The night was closing in and the chill in the air radiated off the glass. I shivered. I thought back to the decision.

It would be so nice to have a family back. It would be great for the children to have their daddy back. I just didn't know whether I still wanted that enough. I didn't think I did. The problem with these decisions is that the one you make could be the one you regret. Would I regret not giving him another chance?

I sighed deeply and bowed my head. It ached so much from all the thinking. The thoughts had churned round and round all day and I rubbed the tension hoping it would go away. I felt so tired too. I yawned as if to confirm this. So tired.

I stretched out my arms and then let them fall to my sides. I stared ahead of me. What do I really want? What do I do? Any other woman would probably know. Any other woman would have told him to leave her alone months ago. Not me though. No. I stay in touch, I end up sleeping with him while he is with his girlfriend, and I listen and support him. What did I do that for? If I hadn't done that, I wouldn't be in this predicament now.

I laughed at myself as I realised that I was blaming myself for the situation. He used to do this to me all the time and now here he was doing it again. Unbelievable. I was taking the blame when really it was him that started it. I was doing it again.

Back to that already. No chance.

6th March

Spent the day shopping in town. Mum said I was miserable and miles away half the time. I was not myself apparently. My mind must be racing without me realising it. Marc text me this morning. He didn't come down as originally thought and in some ways I was relieved. I wanted Lee to come round again and give me that warm, safe feeling once more. I like being in that place more than this one. There is no pressure and no fighting him off. He doesn't moan about everything and he makes me laugh. It is great to have him here with me.

I felt bad then. Wishing I was in another mans arms instead of my husbands was still wrong in some ways. *Or was it?* I don't know anymore.

Everything confuses me right now. I dread to think what would happen if anything else comes into the mix. Simple decisions are difficult right now. What to have for dinner. What to buy at the shops. Remembering what I needed to get today was hard. I couldn't think and yet my mind was quite calm considering. I wasn't daydreaming every now and then like I had done in the past.

The girls parents evening cheered me up. Both of them are doing so well in school and I was so proud of them. They were well behaved, they listened to their teacher and they worked hard. All good news. Fiona is now on the gifted and talented register and she is blooming. She is making good progress and her teacher is pleased with her. Pheobe is calm in school and I am pleased her anger doesn't go with her. They behaved really well while they were waiting for me too. Chose their books from the fair for me to buy them tomorrow. Was a little sad that Marc hadn't made it again. Understandable though. He is in too much pain.

Spoke to him a little and he seemed to cheer up a bit. He is still wearing the wedding ring and he talked to me like he was just away for a bit.

Lee came round again and we cuddled in front of the TV. He left fairly late but it was nice still.

I was such a proud mum tonight. I was beaming from the time I came out of their school and I was still beaming now. It was so lovely to hear all the things that their teachers said. I had been so worried that everything they were going through would influence their schooling in some way and I was relieved when it hadn't.

Everything was calm for tonight. I had laid in Lee's arms and relaxed. I had felt that safe feeling once again and once again it felt as if nothing could touch me. That my life had stopped for a bit and I was ok right then.

I huffed at the thought that that was gone now.

I lay in bed staring up at the ceiling and all the thoughts and feelings mixed up together again. Mum had said that I hadn't been myself while shopping today. I didn't feel weighed down by any of it and it didn't feel as if there were things on my mind. It felt calm and collected and I was happy. It hadn't showed though which meant that things were being buried again. Maybe if I hid it all well and forgot about it, it would go away.

I rubbed my eyes. I could feel the tiredness sweeping over me and it felt as if I needed to sleep forever. My whole body was heavy and I could hardly move. I couldn't be bothered to move. My legs ached and my head was spinning.

I yawned. I still felt so confused. Everything had been hard. I had wandered around town trying so hard to remember what I needed to buy but I hadn't managed it. I didn't know what to do for dinner and I didn't know what I was supposed to be doing half the time as my mind would wander and I would wake up in a daydream.

I sighed and rolled over to the side. I could see the light coming in from Pheobe's room through the gap in the door. I couldn't even be bothered to get up and switch it off. I sighed again and rolled back onto my back.

What did I want to do with all this rattling round my head? What was I going to do with it? I wished somebody would come and open my head up and remove everything that was in it. I wouldn't have to think anymore then.

7th March

Hooray it's Friday! That was my first thought. I was planning to have a quite morning indoors and sorting out eBay parcels etc, housework. Then got a phone call from Marc to say he was coming.

He arrived at 9am. Met me on the route home from the school run. Had a nice morning. Got him to eat something. We talked about how he was feeling and how I was. Tried to explain that I wanted him to have the children and enjoy them and their closeness. He didn't seem to understand. He just kept saying that I didn't want him round me. That wasn't the case. I wanted a quiet weekend to chill out and have some time to do what I wanted to do. I wanted to see he was serious about our routine and have him enjoy being with the children.

It became very tense in the afternoon after Seb and Fiona came home from school. They wanted to go and then they didn't. He kept asking me to cancel Lee coming over and let him come round after he was gone. He wanted to stay here and then take the children in the morning when I had already been over and over why that wasn't a good idea. It took all of my strength to fight back and stand my ground.

Sue phoned him a couple of times. He didn't answer. He didn't want her to know where he was. He didn't want her to know he was with me. That hurt. Lots.

I got really angry with him and threw things around and ended up shouting at him and demanding to take him back. I drove him to a station just outside London and even though I knew it was near his sister Lucy, I didn't care. I just wanted him away from me and I wanted to make sure the children had a weekend with him and also that my mum didn't need to have them again. I feel under so much pressure to stand my ground and not compromise and make sure that everyone is happy. The stress is amazing and I ended up with palpitations on the way home. I had to pull over as it made me feel so awful. After a few deep breaths it was gone and I felt better again.

Got home and Lee came over straight away. I couldn't wait for a hug and he lay behind me on the settee. I held his arms. I had forgotten how he was quite muscly and I found myself wanting more than friendship tonight. He also picked up on it and we ended up kissing on the settee. We kept saying we shouldn't be doing this and we never took it any further but both of us needed it. Aaaggghhh!!! How confusing. One minute I have no one and then I am confused as I have feelings for two men. Life changes so quick. Lee left late and I was shattered from the stressful day. I was pleased to fall into bed. I spread out in my bed making the most of having it to myself.

He tried to convince me he had changed and then she pops up and that is all over. He couldn't let her know that he was with me because it might hurt her. What did that matter? She hurt him. She had hurt me. She hadn't cared. Now we had to be considerate of her.

I found it hard to believe that he wouldn't pick the phone up to tell her that he was here and he would call again later. Was he thinking that if he had said that there would be no chance of sorting things out with her? Was there a chance?

I threw the tea towel I was holding on the bench. I didn't know anything anymore and it felt like I was losing my grip. I was shattered from everything and the stress had been amazing. It still gripped me even now.

I remembered the look on his face as I asked him to answer her call. It was almost a scowl. He stared straight at me. I had looked at the phone, her name alight in front of me and waited. He just said no. It had knifed me again. Why couldn't she know he was here? What was he playing at?

I shrugged it off. I didn't care really. She was gone hopefully. Gone. Hopefully.

I reached up for a cigarette. He had driven me mad today. I never needed to smoke when Lee was here. I could just sit with him and I was happy. With Marc here, I had smoked lots. He made me so uptight I had to.

I lifted the hair off the back of my neck as I stretched my arms upwards and twisted my back. I caught sight of the time on the microwave - 1.15am - and rolled my eyes. I was up late again. I needed to straighten my routine out.

I had thrown the children's stuff together so quickly. I had driven all the way down the A12 to drop them at a station on the underground and then I had turned and driven all the way home again. In the car, my mind was racing with the frustrations of the day. Him in general, him coming home, him not understanding why I was upset or why I wouldn't let him stay, Sue and her bloody phone calls and then having to throw a tantrum to get my own way and drive for miles when I didn't want to.

I huffed as I fell back against the bench. I slid down it until I was sitting on the floor. Why did life have to be so hard? Why did it have to be an uphill struggle? I was so bored with fighting him all the time. I had always just given in last time but this time was different. I wasn't giving in. It was my way or none.

I closed my eyes and thought of Lee. He had held me again as soon as he walked in through the door. He could sense I needed a hug and just came over. I immediately felt safe. It is that feeling that is quite dangerous though. We lay on the settee watching the TV. Feeling his arms around me made me sink into them. I could feel his grip tightening and I placed my hands on them. I could feel the muscle underneath. I remembered turning to just smile at him and before we knew it we were kissing. It didn't feel weird or wrong as such. It was great even. Just not what we wanted. We both agreed to that. We stopped with both of us aching for more.

I sighed and rolled my eyes. Why did I stop? I laughed at myself.

I placed my head back against the cupboard. I hated confusion, I was sick of it. Did I want Marc back? Did I want Lee? Did I have feelings for both of them, either of them or neither of them? Did I want the stress back? Is Sue out of the picture for good?

I rolled my eyes. Enough already. Enough.

Is she back?

9th March

Woke up about 10ish and refused to get up. The night out with Frances had been such a late one. Eventually we got up around 11 and sat downstairs chatting again. We had breakfast and tea and then forced ourselves up to shower and get ready. We lazed about talking until I had to leave for the children. She decided to go then as well and drove off saying she would come again soon. It was such a good weekend, I was sad it had ended so quickly.

Picked up Marc and the children at the station. He had brought his clothes to stay the night but he got called away to meet with someone about a new job. *How can he contemplate starting a new job when he is so ill?* I was a little worried about him leaving. He had sat around and said that when he moves back in we should knock through into the garage and gain another room. I found that thought a little scary. He is assuming he will be back and I was a bit unnerved by that.

We chatted about her too. She had been around at the weekend and the children had seen her for a few hours. I still believe that if she asks him to start again he will. I am a little worried that he is with her tonight. Just can't believe him anymore. This is how it would be if I did ever take him back. I don't think I could live like this. It's too hard.

Are they together right now? Are they making it all up now? Had he gone to her instead of whoever it was he had said he was seeing?

I sighed. This is what I would feel all the time. When he went to work I would know he was with her. When he went out with his friends from work, I would know he was with her. I couldn't handle this anymore than I could the first time. I would never believe him and I couldn't trust him anymore. That was a sad thing to admit.

I inhaled deeply on my cigarette and sighed again. I felt so fed up with everything. I held my head in my hands and just stared out of the window. Frances and I had sat around all weekend talking about men and how horrible they are. We had both had our hearts broken. We were both miserable and fed up. I smiled. Most women are aren't they?

The assumption he had made about moving back in was on my mind. The way he had said that "when I move back in" rather than "if" really had made me feel uneasy. It was like he planned to get his own way no matter what. As if he had made his mind up and I would have to accept it eventually. It felt odd listening to it and it had angered me.

He had planned to stay tonight. I had said yes after plenty of persuasion. Now though, despite coming all the way down here, he was going all the way back again to meet somebody about a new job. Huh? Why would he leave this job when he was ill? How could he start a new job when he was ill? Surely that would be too difficult for him.

I didn't understand at all. It seemed too weird for him not to worry about the illness and just head off for a new start. He had told me that he needed to leave because he couldn't face her. I know that it is hard but I am sure it is just as hard for her. She is not running away and I didn't run away when I had to face him knowing he was with her. Is he a man at all?

I laughed at the thought of whether classifying Marc as a man was possible. I came to the conclusion that no it wasn't.

My thoughts still strayed back to the same question that was nagging at me. Had he gone back to Sue? Had that woman got in the way again?

Why did I feel like this when I didn't want him anyway?

12th March

Marc met me at work. He came down to see all of us and to talk to me. He kept saying "when I come home we can….." He was assuming that I was going to take him back now. That made me angry. He started talking about her and how much she had hurt him and how he was crying all the time over her and how there were so many things he couldn't do now she had left. I just looked at him and said

"If that is how you feel about her, you can't want me." I explained to him that he wanted to come home for all the wrong reasons. He needed someone. He thought it was me but it wasn't. He was still in love with her and he had to accept that. He needed support through his illness and the difficult times. I told him I would be there for him as much as I could. I said I would help him cope through the pain of losing her and that I would try to help him rebuild his life. I would be there for him for the reasons he needed someone but I couldn't take him back. Partly because I would be setting myself up to be hurt again. Partly because I have worked hard to achieve this life I have and I am not prepared to give it up and partly because I know he doesn't really want me. He doesn't love me. He loves her. I have been through hell this last year and he has been the cause of it. I can't forgive and forget. I'm not sure whether this is a decision I may end up regretting. I'm not sure whether I have made the right one. But I am happy with this decision at the moment and I am going to stick to it. This is my life and I am keeping it just how it is.

I listened to him again today. I listened to him telling me how much he missed her. He said he couldn't stop crying and that he couldn't do some things now she was not with him. He couldn't watch certain TV programmes and he couldn't

listen to certain songs as they all reminded him of her and when they were together. In the next breath he said, when I come home...

I shook my head again at the man. How could he have even thought about playing that game with me? Did he think that because we had still been together while he was with her I would take him back and put up with the fact he still loved her. He did. He did still love her. I knew that.

I sighed. I had said I would help him. I looked out of the window into the garden. Was I mad? Did I mean that? Can I help him? I shook my head again and looked down at the floor.

The darkness in the house was very apparent tonight. It was overwhelming in fact. It was probably just my mood. I felt a little low in some ways. It was hard saying all the things I had said to him. It was hard watching his face twist and change at my words. It's difficult telling someone you once loved that you no longer want them in your life.

I hung my head even lower. I hoped I wouldn't regret that decision. I hoped I had done the right thing. I hoped that it was all over now.

I looked up at the stars through the window. The night sky looked so calm and peaceful. I smiled at the sight of it. I leant back against the tiles and sighed. My life can be so difficult sometimes but when given the chance, I just couldn't change it.

14th March

Hooray it's Friday. I have been looking forward to this day all week. Nicky came round earlier. We had a chat but then I had to leave to pick up Pheobe's glasses. Nicky came back after school. She stayed for dinner and the children played so well we carried on chatting not really thinking about the time. We opened the bottle of Whisky and drank and danced in the kitchen. It was good fun. We put the world to rights and ran down the male race as women usually ended up doing. Then the phone calls started. Marc had left the pub as he couldn't handle it. He said it was too upsetting. He was going home to his empty flat to sit on his own. I did feel sorry for him. He said that her friend, sly Samantha, had given him nothing but grief. She had sent evil glares across the table and spoke nastily to him. He never explained what she had said but that didn't seem relevant to me anyway. He told me that Sue had then text him and called him pathetic because he couldn't stay in that pub with his friends. That's when I became angry. She was really getting to me now. She was upsetting him a lot lately, her and Samantha made a nasty little couple too. She had destroyed my marriage, she had stolen my husband, taken a father away from his children, caused so much pain and hatred in our lives and now she had broken his heart and cast him aside. *That was worth it love wasn't it?* How dare she.

I listened to him for a bit and then he went. He phoned back about 10 minutes later anxious as I hadn't answered his call to my mobile. I was sorting children out and hadn't heard it. To him it was on purpose. I listened again and tried to advise him. He hung up. Another phone call a few minutes later and all he said was I just phoned to say goodbye. He said he had taken some tablets and alcohol as he couldn't take the pain. Something inside me snapped. I tried to phone him back again and again and no answer. I was worried but at the same time I thought - *why am I dealing with this?* Straight away I picked up the phone and rang his sister. I told her what he had said and done and asked her to call him. She phoned back shortly afterwards and said that he wasn't answering her call either. She was now frantic and they were going to call the police. I tried once more while on the phone to her. He answered. I had a go at him for being such a fool and for worrying us all. He didn't like it but it was tough. I then phoned Lucy back and told her what he had said. She said she hated it when he did things like that. I agreed. She said he was attention seeking. Again I agreed. I said how he had said that he had nobody and that his mum wasn't going to be there for him. She said that was a lie. That didn't surprise me at all. I knew it had to be. It doesn't matter what type of woman you are, you are always there for your children. Of course she would be there for him.

I put the phone down and Nicky and I carried on drinking and dancing. Her daughter stayed at mine and Nicky left with the boys asleep about 12.30. I collapsed into bed with the thoughts of today churning around and around.

Two o'clock in the morning and I still couldn't sleep. I was exhausted too and had hoped that I would have crashed out quickly but that wasn't to be.

I sat back on the bench and sighed a huge sigh. Yet again I had had a stressful day. Yet again this stress was down to him. I was so fed up with having to constantly deal with his threats and his moans and groans. Yes I felt sorry for him but he hadn't been here when I was going through the same. He left and let me get on with it.

I sighed again, rubbed my face with my hands and then inhaled deeply on the cigarette and sipped my whisky before I had exhaled it. Drinking and smoking again, that was the answer wasn't it?

Thoughts of her came into my head. She had called him pathetic. Did she really do that? Did she really expect him to be ok with everything and not find things difficult? I was beginning to doubt what Marc was saying and I felt unnerved by this. That meant that I was beginning to believe that her actions were not true and that meant I was siding with her. How could I do that? It didn't feel right when I looked at it like that.

Sly Samantha got involved too. Why would she? Again I was doubting that too. My friends hate him more than I have hated him throughout this whole time and never yet has one of them said or done anything to him. Why would Samantha?

Unless there was more to it. What was he doing? How was he behaving?

Had any of it actually happened?

I caught sight of my puzzled expression in the window and just smiled at myself.

Had I done the right thing tonight? Should I have phoned his sister and passed the buck onto her? I hadn't been able to deal with it. No that wasn't true actually; I hadn't wanted to deal with it. He has to get over her and move on and if he wants to behave like an idiot then I had to let him.

The memories hit me at that point. The memories of what he had done to me all those months ago. I remembered feeling so hurt and upset. I remembered the low feelings that swam around. He was feeling all that now and he was ill on top of everything. I had to feel sorry for him. Didn't I?

I took another sip of whisky and frowned. His behaviour is so irrational. Why would you attempt suicide or pretend to or whatever it was he actually did, just because you had been dumped. Did he really love her that much? Was that it? Why did he then come running to me the same day and ask to come home? He cannot be alone. I had answered my own question.

I laughed momentarily. I wasn't sure I could handle looking after him. He was too needy and too weak. He could cry for a bit but he was supposed to be a man for crying out loud. He didn't have to act that way.

At that point I felt sorry for his sister. I shouldn't have phoned. I had panicked her and that was all for nothing. At the same time though, she needed to know. There was no point in me suffering in silence and trying to cope alone. I had had a busy night, why should I have let him spoil it?

I shrugged. It didn't really matter what I should or shouldn't have done, I had done it and that was the end of it really wasn't it. I couldn't change it now so why feel sorry. I shrugged again and then nodded, taking a sip of whisky. I looked in the glass at the small bit that was left. I raised my glass as if there was someone with me to respond and say cheers and then I downed the rest of the alcohol. The strength of it hit me and I scowled. Why was I drinking this stuff? It was vile.

I jumped down off the bench and stared at my mobile. Should I ring him and make sure he was ok? Should I leave it so he doesn't get the attention? I slid the phone up and down while I tried to make up my mind what to do. At the same time, thoughts of ringing her and finding out the real truth crossed my mind. I wanted to know. Should I?

I dropped it back on the bench deciding that it would probably be best if I left it all alone.

15th March 08

I took Nicky's daughter back home this afternoon and sat round there for a bit. I felt really down and fed up and it probably showed. It's probably from last night but I just didn't feel myself. I went into town and got the stuff for the spring day at the girls' school. Also looked for shoes for the girls but there were none in the cheap shops and I didn't have the money for the decent ones which made me feel bad.

Marc phoned and asked me to go down to his flat tomorrow. He said he didn't want to be alone and I felt sorry for him. As I was ill I said I would think about it and see how I felt in the morning. He said 'please don't say no babe.' Talk about try to make me feel guilty. It nearly worked.

I just kept repeating to myself, if she was around he wouldn't want you. Which of course we all know is true.

Spoke to mum this evening. My cousin Sophia had phoned her and asked if she would be prepared to meet aunt Violet. She is unsure. Some of what was said was nice to hear. How most of what had happened is actually Marc's fault and we shouldn't let him ruin our family. There was still no recognition of what they had done though and that angered us both. They chose to believe him over us and it still hurts no matter how they say they didn't do that. They did to us.

It's been a weird day and I was glad to fall into bed.

I dragged this weight around with me all day today. I knew that some of it was tiredness at the lack of sleep but I also knew that there was more to it than that. I felt down today. Down and confused with everything. I had sat in Nicky's staring into nothing and I was doing the same thing now. Staring at nothing. The gloom of the day still with me and still making me feel awful.

I turned my head to try to find something worth staring at but there was nothing there. I huffed and looked down at the floor.

The confusion was coming from lots of different things. Obviously I had the stresses and difficulties that were in my life all of the time, like the financial ones and the raising of the children etc. The rest was the confusion over the Marcus and Sue situation. I had thought about it a lot and I was still considering the fact that she wouldn't have done what she did out of spite. She must have thought about it for a long time. Surely no woman would be heartless enough to dump their boyfriend when he was ill.

I huffed and wondered why I cared. I didn't know, but maybe if he was exaggerating that about her, then he was exaggerating the rest. I was beginning to hate her more and more with the things she was doing and saying and I was automatically blaming her. If that wasn't the truth then my feelings towards her were unjustified.

I felt my teeth clench together and my muscles tighten. I wanted to scream. What the hell did it matter? She was gone and he was heartbroken. End of. Not my business and nothing I could do about it. I kicked my legs against the cupboard door and threw my head back.

I was the one dealing with him and helping him though and I needed to know what I was helping with. I needed to know the circumstances because it would change the way I viewed things, the way I viewed him and the way I viewed the woman that had caused all my suffering. That was an unfair thing to say. It wasn't really her if she didn't know. Did she? That was the other thing see. If he had said all those things about her to me that had been lies or exaggerations then had he done the same to her about me?

I decided that all these thoughts were confusing me and I would never know unless I contacted her and as she was the last person I wanted to speak to that would never happen and so I should leave it there. The nagging didn't leave it there though, it carried on.

I went into the study and turned on the music to drown everything out and to try to escape from the reality that was making the evening drag so slowly.

16th March 08

I stayed in bed for as long as I could. Everything was hurting this morning and I didn't want to get up but I couldn't stay in bed either. It was horrible. Marc phoned early and I told him I couldn't make it. He was disappointed but then he said that as I was ill, he would come down and help out with the children so I could rest. I was really pleased to hear that.

The afternoon went quite well. He ordered pizza and looked after me a little and then helped get the children ready for school. They were pleased he was here.

He cuddled up to me on the settee and mentioned again about coming back. He said he still wanted to be home. He knew what I had said but he wasn't going to give up. That was what I had wanted to hear ages ago. There was still part of me that didn't believe him though, if she comes back to him, he would go. He just needs someone. Not me.

I am stuck with this in some ways. I would love to have my family back. I would love for it to work out and everything settle back down and there be a mum and a dad for my children. That won't happen though. He would come back and the stress would be there again. It was there slightly today. He snapped a couple of times at the children and moaned about the noise. He took over the TV which made me annoyed and he kept moaning about the mess. I have become used to living without that and I enjoy being without that.

It is a mixed up mess. If it was just me to consider then maybe I would have took him back. Maybe. Not sure though. With the children the way they are when he is around, which is awful, and after what he has done to them, I would never consider it. I will not let him put them through that again. It would trample them to pieces.

Decisions that you have to make in life are so hard and always complicated. I have to decide whether I want my family back or not and to be honest it was really getting me down. It hung round my neck from the time I woke up to the time I laid down and tried to sleep.

I wanted to have a loving family as everybody does but that isn't what I had or would have. He would be annoyed by the children again, he would moan all the time again. I had lived without that for so long now and my life was adjusted to being without him. I couldn't go back to what I had, I just couldn't.

I felt guilty though. Guilty, that when I had finally reached the point that I had wanted for so long, I said no. I said no. Why? Was that not what I really wanted then? Had I changed in my hopes and dreams? Had I made too many adjustments? Had I been hurt too much?

I didn't know any of the answers and the confusion made me dizzy and the guilt weighed me down so the dragging my body behind me feeling was back. I took a deep breath as I tried once again to face things. He had looked after me today when I needed it. He had come round and taken over and dealt with the children. He had sorted out their dinner and bathed them and put them to bed. He was being nice to me, though he moaned about their noise and their behaviour a fair few times.

When I looked at him though, I didn't see that. I saw the man that had put me through so much heartache. I saw him saying the words 'I don't love you anymore' all those months ago. I pictured him with her and the pain hit me again as if I was back there facing it for a second time. I didn't understand why it was like that and I didn't understand that it couldn't be different. I knew it couldn't though. So strange.

I staggered back to my bed on the settee and fell into it. I was in so much pain still and the tablets I had taken hadn't worked. I curled up under the blanket and allowed myself to feel sorry for myself. I gave myself the permission. I smiled as I said those words in my head.

I pulled the cushion under my head and hid my face under the covers. The children, and him, were in bed and the house was quiet. The TV was on so low that I could barely hear it. I thought back over the day and all the nice words he had said. The nice words didn't change the horrid actions of the past though.

I thought back even further. The day he had walked out on me and left me crying. The days he broke my heart with his callous words. The evenings that had dragged by due to the sheer emptiness and loneliness that my life contained. The lack of trust. The day I found out about her and their relationship. The day she met my children. They came back in a different order. They were not in chronological order and they were not from most painful to least. They came in waves and no matter how tight I closed my eyes I couldn't stop them.

I curled myself into a tighter ball. As the pain throbbed all over my body and the thoughts continued on the path of painful memories, the tears started to fall. I stayed hidden under the blanket as I sobbed. I didn't want the children to see if they came down. I hugged my arms round myself trying to gain some comfort. I hated this uneasy feeling. I hated reminiscing on the past especially such a bad one and I hated feeling so low and confused all the time.

I began to struggle for breath under my blanket and I lowered them so my face was exposed. I stared at the TV screen and watched the people there moving around it without sound coming from their mouths. The tears fell still.

After a few minutes of this, I wiped my cheeks with the corner of the blanket. It immediately became soaking wet. I had been crying that much. I sat up. The cushion had a large wet patch and I huffed at the sight of it. I hadn't done this for a while. I hadn't felt so sick from it all for a while either.

I sat back against the settee and held the cushion in my lap. I pulled my knees up to my chest and cuddled the cushion tighter. I rested my chin on the top of it. Yet again he popped up in my head. His face. Just his face. I could see him. I could hear the words he said to me.

'I won't give up. I know you said you didn't want me but I won't give up'

I didn't want that. It was nice to hear and I was glad that he felt I was worth fighting for. It just seemed too late. It was all too late. I buried my face in my pillow. I buried it tight as the tears fell faster and faster.

I just wanted it all to stop now. I really couldn't take any more.

17th March 08

This was supposed to have been my busy day but I had to cancel everything as I felt so crap. I was exhausted and felt rough. All I did was sit in front of the TV. He irritated me this morning. He didn't even make sure he was ready to take the children to school. He could have been as he was here. He slept in my bed again last night. I couldn't sleep with him there but he didn't move. He slept soundly most of the night. He had said he felt comfortable there. I watched him sleep as I did for the few nights before he had left. Almost a year ago I was doing the same thing. I kept asking myself the question 'should I have said yes?' Every time I replied no. I must have made the right decision. I don't know why I keep going over it. I suppose I just don't want to make the wrong choice.

He spent the day talking about what he would do if he came back and where I want to go when we go away for the weekend. He was talking as if I would eventually change my mind and that angered me slightly. He then spent some time on the phone to his mates and arranged 2 nights out this week. Straight after he turned round and told me he couldn't have them this weekend. Well he said it was possible that he might not be able to have them. That means he wont. He says he may have to have an operation. Easter weekend - really?

I began to get quite tired of the crap. You don't tell me you are not having the children and list the social events you have going on during the week. It just wound me up. I felt bitter towards him again. I tried to suppress it but I couldn't and it just made me angry. He has had his time to have fun, now I want mine. I felt like saying to him as you have made your mind up that you want this life and not the alternative, you move back in with the children and let me go out and see if I want the alternative. I didn't say it because I knew I didn't mean it. I would never want a life that didn't involve my babies. That was already set for me.

He left shortly after the children came home and I didn't hear from him again. Mum came over and so did Marilyn. She stayed for a while and cut the children's hair. When Dad left, Mum and I had a chat as normal. She was going over what had been said to Sophia and how she didn't feel ready to see Violet yet. I don't see why she should. Violet was too nasty to her and if that was Charlie to me, I wouldn't forgive her. I totally understand her. She shouldn't go unless she is completely ready. And she isn't. So forget it.

I had watched him sleep last night. He had slept fine. I remember trying to sleep. I just hadn't managed it. I couldn't. I had laid there for hours just listening to him breathing and thinking that he shouldn't be there.

He didn't get up with the children this morning. He didn't bother. He was here and I was ill and yet he wasn't ready to take them so I had to. It annoyed me like it used to. He was never ready on time. He could get up and out the door for work when he lived here but he couldn't be ready to leave with the children on time.

I had been tired all day and that had put me in a bad mood. The pains were a little better and I had begun to feel a bit more normal but I couldn't escape the feelings. The frustration at this morning was added to throughtout the day on a regular basis.

He said he couldn't have the children again this weekend. Something about an operation. I didn't believe it. I had had my doubts for a while and now more and more of the things he was saying didn't make sense. This one was the worst. No way would they do an operation on Easter weekend. Or would they?

Confused again I had to say it would be ok and that was the end of it. He spent a fair bit of time on the phone to his mates outside in the garden. He always hid his conversations from me. I tried to listen but he saw me and kept walking away. When he came in he told me about his plans to go out with them a couple of times this week. Too ill to have the children but not too ill to go out and socialise. Another thing that didn't make any sense.

Confused even more, I had stormed about the house for the rest of the day. I was so fed up and again it was all down to him. He kept asking if I was ok. Every time I turned around he was there behind me and I trod on him. Every time I got up to move he asked where I was going. Every thing I said I wanted to do he asked when, why and who with. It began to drive me crazy.

I sat back against the tiles and stared into space. I had cleared my mind and stopped questioning everything for the last half an hour and I was enjoying the blankness of my mind. I was aware of the silence creeping up on me and that meant that the thoughts would follow shortly. That raised a fear inside me and I tried to shake it off.

I breathed deeply and closed my eyes. 'Just give me one night off please,' I asked myself. Just one night with a clear head and no thoughts or worries or doubts creeping in would be bliss. It was all I could think about.

I opened my eyes. I had to fight to open them as if I would see something so nasty and horrid standing in front of me. I was so tired of all this. I was so tired.

18th March 08

Went to work today and had a nice day. I wasn't covering at all and spent the day catching up on the assessment forms I had started weeks ago. I enjoyed shutting myself away; it was a bit of a break for me really, which probably sounds strange to most people.

Drove home and ended up in tears when the song - I know I'll never love this way again by Dionne Warwick came on. I didn't want to turn it off so ended up trying to sing along - how sad - and cried all the way through it. It was immediately followed by Lily Allen's Smile and that cheered me up straight away. I love that song. Spent the night gossiping with mum. Sue had gone round to Marc's flat to look after him. I felt a little uneasy but at the same time not over bothered. I have this feeling they will end up back together. If that happens, I want nothing more to do with him. He is not going to treat me like that.

She was with him tonight. That revelation from him had made me sit up and think for a bit. He had said on the phone that it could mean that she still cared for him and he seemed happy that she hadn't walked away completely.

My immediate reaction was to think 'Oh no, she is back.' This confused me a little as I had spent the last few weeks not wanting him back. Now all of a sudden, because she was there, I felt hurt and disappointed. Why?

I sipped my tea as I sat back against the settee. Mum had gone to bed and I felt lost in this big, empty living room. The silence had engulfed me and my mind had begun whirring again as it always did.

I looked up at the TV screen. It was switched off and the glass was black with a tiny glimpse of light reflecting on it from the conservatory doors. That is what my life looks like I thought. Dark with a glimpse of light that he kept turning on and off as he wished. I looked down at the cup feeling a little sorry for myself.

Why had she gone there anyway? To make herself feel better? To look after him as a friend? What were they doing now? Was she fighting him off? Were they kissing and cuddling on the settee? At that thought a repulsed look appeared on my face and I scrunched my eyes closed tightly so I would stop picturing that image.

I leant forward and put my cup on the floor. I had drunk so much tea now that I had started to feel sick. I sighed. Had he really made me believe that it was me he was interested in again? Had I really fallen for it again? I shook my head. I didn't want him, what was my problem? I just needed to know the truth about everything that was all. I needed to know when the affair started, what he had been saying about our relationship, how she could take my husband from me, how ill he was. There were so many things I needed to know. With her back in the picture, I wouldn't be close enough to him to find out.

I huffed at myself again.

I thought back to the drive home. The first song making me cry and the second cheering me up. I was obviously mixed up right now. I felt it too. I was so confused. It showed in my lack of organisation and my lack of willingness to sort things out and get jobs done. This whole situation was beginning to take over my life. My every thought was of him and what he was saying about coming home and her turning up tonight had created another twist.

I didn't want her to have him. I didn't want her anywhere near him. I didn't want them together. I couldn't figure out whether that was because I still wanted him or I just wanted to get to the bottom of everything.

I sighed again and stood up quickly. I walked into the kitchen, lit a cigarette and jumped up onto the bench. The words of the Lily Allen song ran through my head again and I smiled.

I wondered what he was saying to her now. Was he giving her the same spiel that he had given me over the last few days? Had he been giving it to both of us at the same time? That thought knocked me sideways for a bit. He probably had the lying piece of crap!

In some ways she and I had more in common than we thought. We were both listening to and believing his lies. I wondered whether she knew the truth about the illness. She would be able to answer my questions on the other issues, but would she on that one? Would she give me any of the answers? I sat forward, straightening myself so I was perfectly upright as if I was guarding myself from something. Of course she would I thought. She would know it would hurt me and she wouldn't be able to resist that.

I yawned; I was too tired for all this. That song was in my head again and I smiled. I put out my cigarette and climbed the stairs, singing and smiling all the way.

Is she back this time?

19th March

Work was ok. It went quick. Wednesdays are always ok as they are the last day for me.

Spoke to Marc on the journey up. He said that things went ok last night and she ended up staying the night. She spoke about their trip to Glasgow which was supposed to have been the weekend he is going out with me. She said how she had missed him and that the space he had given her was a good thing. But she also said that it wasn't fixed yet. She was still not sure she wanted to go any further than friends. *What the hell is she playing at?*

I made sure I told him that if he went back to her or blew me out when it came to the scan, his birthday or the weekend we were supposed to be spending together, I would cut him off completely. I told him that I would not let him use me the way he has been. There would be no phone calls, no texts and all communication regarding the children would have to go through Seb. He said that that was a threat and I replied that I was just letting him know where he stood so he was well informed when he makes his decision. I know what his decision will be. He will blow me out for at least one of them if not all. I will blow his whole world apart. I will have nothing to lose this time.

I still couldn't believe what he had said to me this morning. She had stayed there the night. Nothing had happened - yeah right, like I believed that. They had just talked. They had just chatted away about what they were feeling and thinking but nothing else.

After that phone call I had driven like a crazy woman with road rage. I had been so angry. Or was it jealousy? Aaarrgghh!! So confusing, I hated it all.

I threw myself up on the bench. The anger was still raging away inside of me desperately trying to find an escape route. I felt hot and bothered and I couldn't settle. What was she playing at? Why tell him that she didn't want to be with him anymore and then begin to go back on it? Just stay away woman.

I slouched back against the tiles, aware that I was incredibly uncomfortable but not willing to move again. I blew the smoke out of my mouth really hard and after every sip of my drink, I slammed the glass down on the bench, expecting it to break every time.

I looked out of the window at the night sky and wished I was on that aeroplane flying over me. I didn't care where it was going; I just wanted to transport myself onto it. Mind you, knowing my luck, it would be going to bloody Glasgow. I laughed out loud at this thought and shook my head.

I sat forward, swinging my legs and wondered why I was getting so wound up. The raging fire was burning the pit of my stomach. I hugged it tightly to try to get it to stop, but there was no relief. I slouched back again, feeling unable to do anything to help myself.

Doubt crept into my mind. Had she really said all those things? Would she really be thinking about getting back with him after everything she said? If she didn't though, why stay the night?

I knew what he was like. He only ever heard what he wanted to hear. He never took on board anything you said.

He always thought he could manipulate the other person into thinking what he wanted them to think. Maybe he was telling me what he was hoping he had heard.

My thoughts turned back to them together last night. I didn't believe nothing had happened. You don't stay with your ex overnight if you didn't want to be with him. I shrugged my shoulders. It didn't matter really.

I took a deep breath and closed my eyes.

'What would you do if they did get back together?' I asked myself.

I would definitely freak out I replied. I would change all contact numbers, so I didn't ever have to speak to him again. He had needed me this whole time so he would be affected by that. I would have to contact her and make sure she knew everything. I would be as nasty as I could be. He wouldn't have anyone then would he?

I smiled an evil smile. I would love to do all of that. Am I really that kind of person though, someone who takes pleasure out of the pain and misery of another. No. I would have done it by now if I was, wouldn't I?

21st March

Good Friday! No school. No lay in either. Was feeling quite rough again and Pheobe woke everybody up at 6 this morning. Got ready and wasted no time getting stuck in to some housework. Enjoyed it too. Shot up to town and bought some drawers for Pheobe's wardrobe. Nicky and the children came round and helped me turf out all the rubbish and unwanted toys. She took most of them which was great. Spoke to Marc eventually. He said he was in hospital again and felt awful and couldn't come for the children. He said he was coming tomorrow morning. I had this sick feeling that it had something to do with her again. I felt awful and didn't know what to do. I was just so angry. He had done it again. Dropped me for her. She had obviously made him think that something could be sorted out and he wanted to be with her. So he dropped the children. They were upset at first but then began to enjoy their time with Nicky's children. I took Nicky and the toys back home about 7. Dropped them off, said my thank yous and came home. Put children to bed and had one of those nights where I couldn't settle. I couldn't stop thinking about him and her and what they were doing. He had said nothing but, as it was at the beginning of all this, in my head they were together. *What if they do decide to work things out? What if he does go with her? What if I don't get to go to the scan on Friday?* I will still be sitting on the unknowing side of the fence.

Not knowing the real truth is killing me. I just keep going over and over all the times he had lied to me over the last year and beyond. All the times he said he was ill, working, busy with her so he couldn't have the children and then that was proved to be not true.

People had said to me in the past that they wondered whether he was telling the truth about the illness. I was beginning to doubt it now too. I felt awful though and I still defended him completely. He would never put me, her or his friends and family through that. Would he?

He was ill again supposedly. It amazed me how he was always ill when he was supposed to come and have the children. When he was working or with her or going out with his mates, it never happened. I was doubting this excuse and I really believed he was with her.

I had also been asked about his treatment. I knew nothing. I had been asked about his medication. I knew nothing of it. I had been asked about the way he was when he was here. He was fine. Could he really be lying?

I brushed off that thought and felt the wave of guilt wash over me. I had become used to that in some ways but it still made me nauseous. I clutched my stomach as it gurgled. I felt so bad. Had I really reached that point where I doubted my husband that much and believed he would be that evil? That was such an awful thought.

I sat back in my chair and rocked gently so it bounced. It usually made me feel quite relaxed but tonight I just felt sea sick. I grimaced. I sat forward and rested my elbows on my knees and then my chin on my hands.

What if? What if? Those two words had haunted me so much today. I had asked myself so many 'what if....' questions, my head was still spinning. I hadn't managed to answer them either. That made it worse.

I sat back again. I couldn't get comfortable here either. I had sat on nearly every seat in the house, on the bench and even laid down in bed, but nothing was comfy. I was fed up now.

I looked over towards the garden door and saw Pheobe's little pink slippers sitting beside it. I smiled. My little baby. Well, girl now. My poor children had been deserted again. He had said to them he would probably be coming. He had said he would spend the weekend with them as it was a long weekend. They had even packed their bags. Had she been the one he had dropped them for again?

'Of course she was,' came a reply in a firm voice in my head.

I stood up and picked up the slippers. Slinging them in the porch, I thought of how they must be feeling. They had been sad when I said that daddy wasn't coming. I said he didn't feel well. That's what he told me after all. Their faces had dropped when they heard that news. Fiona said that she would have looked after him. I had smiled at her and felt so proud. She was such a sweetie.

My thoughts turned to him. Was he really tucked up in bed and feeling ill? Was I being too harsh on him? Was I expecting too much? I shook my head. No actually I wasn't. I wasn't expecting too much by thinking my children deserved their father to spend time with them. What were they doing that was so important? Drinking down the pub probably. That's where they usually were.

I screwed up my face as I realised that yet again getting drunk with her was more appealing than having his children. He is such a selfish man. He is obviously intent on patching things up with her and that means that my children are on the back burner again. I should be used to that after everything.

I fell back onto the settee, landing on my back with my legs over the arm. I stared up at the ceiling. If only there was a way to make her see what an arse he was. If only I could be brave enough to approach her and ask her what was going on. If only I could get rid of the nagging questions.

I sighed and decided it was time to switch off my brain. There was absolutely nothing I could do about it. I had to sit back and see what happened. He would call to tell me tomorrow so I didn't have that long to wait.

At the end of the day, what will be will be and there is nothing I can do to change it.

22nd March

He turned up and left with the children inside 15 minutes. He had booked cinema tickets for them to see the Dr Seuss film. They were so excited. He was happy in himself and I told him again that I knew she was back and giving him hope and that I was angry that he had dumped me yet again. I text him a couple of times and asked him whether I would still be going with him on our weekend. He said that she was insinuating that she wanted to still go to Glasgow with him. She was thinking about it. I was gutted. Gutted that I was being dropped again. I was ill too and felt terrible anyway and that news just made things worse.

I threw myself into decorating. I painted my porch and went into town to buy more hooks for it. I knew I needed lots. I bought the paint for my room too. I thought I might as well make a start there also.

He phoned a couple of times while I was painting and moaned on about her and how she had been thinking about getting back with him. I told him that if he blew me out that would be it. I also said that if they did get back together I would take out an injunction preventing her from seeing the children as it was an unstable relationship and she would be gone again in a few weeks. He didn't take kindly to that. He said it was unfair to say that. *Huh?*

About 8pm he called to say there had been an accident. Pheobe had fallen over on the way back from the shops and landed in a pile of glass. He said there was blood everywhere and that she had wet herself from being so scared. I said I would come up but he kept saying no. Sue was due to be there tomorrow and I would need to stay if I went. He called back about an hour later and said that Pheobe was ok. I asked him to take her to hospital to get it checked but he refused. I spoke to her and even though she asked me to come so she could come home she seemed ok in herself. I finished painting my room late and by the time I tidied everything up I was exhausted.

Went to bed after dosing up on lemsip which did nothing and I still couldn't breathe.

The frustration was immense. I had woken up with that feeling of not wanting to face him. I didn't want to see him knowing he was off to have a lovely day or two with that skank again. I felt low as soon as I opened my eyes. I was ill again too. Again. A nasty cold. I could hardly breathe. At least I didn't notice the paint fumes.

I had decided to paint the porch and my bedroom this weekend. I had been meaning to do it for weeks and never had the time because the children were always here. This weekend I wouldn't be going out as I was feeling too rough so I could stay in and paint.

I huffed around this morning trying to pack for the children's stay with their daddy. I slung the clothes in their cases and got stressed when they couldn't make their minds up what to take. I was in a bad mood from the start and I knew it was all down to the fact that he was coming. I bit my tongue to stop myself from constantly shouting at the children, the poor things. I had locked myself in the kitchen and had a cigarette out the window. He text me to say he was nearly here and my stress levels had rocketed at that point. I took lots of deep breaths to stabilise myself but ended up needing the nicotine desperately.

He breezed in and out of here as if he was the happiest man in the world. She was going to be there. Apparently, she was thinking of trying again with him and he was blissfully happy now. I bet she didn't know he had been trying to move back in here the whole time they had been split. I scowled at the thought of her and how yet again, she would have my family for the weekend. I thought that was over.

I had asked about our weekend away that we had planned. It was next weekend so I wanted to know. He said she wanted him to go to Glasgow with her. He would go too. Drop me again without thought.

'I thought you wanted us to try again,' I had said.

'I didn't think she was coming back then though, did I?' he had replied. 'Sorry.'

Sorry. Sorry. That would be enough would it. I don't know how I stopped myself from hitting him. I don't know why I stopped myself from hitting him.

He left with the children and as soon as he had got in that cab I turned and screamed as loudly as I could. The man was a joke. How dare he play me like that? How dare he think I was there to be picked up when no other option was available? How dare he...?

I stormed into the kitchen where I had picked up my phone and text him. I said something like I wanted to go for that weekend away as I wanted to see if we could work. I said that if he was going to get back with her then he has gutted me once more and that as I couldn't cope with that I would have to get in touch with her.

He didn't reply.

When he did reply he said that he didn't know whether he would be free or whether he would be going with her and could I wait and see what happened.

'No, I fucking can't,' I had screamed out loud as I dragged on my fag.

The nicotine wasn't doing its usual calming thing on me. Either I had been too wound up by it all or the cold had hampered its effects. I tried to calm down and breathe deeply but it didn't work. That was when I decided to walk it off and went into town to escape for a bit.

He phoned in the afternoon and said that she had gone but she would be back tomorrow. Nice. Glad you two are spending so much time together was my immediate response. I explained that if he dared blow me out for any of the plans we had made, I would make sure that she never saw the children again. I said I would start the divorce up again and he would lose me completely. I was unfair I was told.

I had spent the rest of the day fuming that he could be such an arse. I was angry with him at treating me, and her in a way, so nastily and had played the game again. I was angry with myself too for doubting my original decision and I was angry that I might be missing out on going to his scan and also the relaxing time away which I really needed right now.

I took more deep breaths.

The phone call after that was worse. Pheobe had fallen over in a broken bottle and sliced her hand. He said there was no glass in there but she was screaming in the background. He was panicking and shouting at her and I was shouting back at him to stop. I pleaded with him to go to the hospital. I said that I would come and take her. He said no because Sue was coming in the morning and I couldn't be there when she was. He was stopping me from being with her. She was stopping me being with her. She needed her mum.

I was still worried about her now. I was sitting feeling very ill on my bench. I hadn't bothered to light a cigarette as it hadn't helped me today and made me feel even more ill. I sat hugging my lemsip in my dressing gown. I looked so pathetic, I could tell that and I couldn't even see myself.

I could feel the tears trickling down my cheeks. I constantly nag him to have these children and then when he gets them I cannot handle it. I cannot handle them being away from me. The tears fell into my drink and I lifted my head slightly. My tissue was so wet it couldn't possibly absorb any more tears but I couldn't be bothered to go and get another.

I just sat and cried. I cried for Pheobe. I wanted to be with her when she was scared and hurt. I cried for the lies he had told yet again. I cried for the fact that I would still not know the truth now she was back on the scene. I just cried and cried. I was entitled to, I told myself.

Goodbye again, Sue?

23rd March

Woke up early, not being able to breathe and began painting again. Painted my room with the second coat and then cleaned it up from top to bottom, replacing the furniture. He called this morning and said she was planning to go round there to sit with the children and had had a go at him for not planning anything for them to do in terms of Easter. She was right and I was pleased she had said something. I drilled the holes for the hooks, mucking up one or two of them and hoping that Lee would help me sort them out this week. I tidied up again and sat back on the sofa feeling ill and fed up. I was so tired too. I laid down thinking about going to bed but not having the energy to get up and go. Marc sent me a text saying - "can you get here tonight? I need you x" my answer was of course no. Didn't go well with her then no was my immediate thought. *How can he expect me to drop everything and run to him when he needs me?* He called and asked if I would go. I said no and said I was ill and that he needed her a few minutes ago. I couldn't believe the audacity of the man. I asked if she had left him then and he replied she was in the other room at the moment. Cheeky git! If only she knew. She had obviously told him he was barking up the wrong tree and so he had turned his attention to me again. No, not falling for it. I am not jumping when he says so. I hung up and then he phoned back. He said he was so upset and I could hear him crying on the phone. My thoughts straight away turned to the children. He shouldn't be crying in front of them and I became angry when I couldn't get him to realise that. I then became angry with her as she could have waited for him to be alone before she told him. It was so frustrating. I was worried for them and what they were thinking and what he was doing. He said he could see no other way out but to take his own

626

life. Again, I was going through that. Again, he was threatening that. My immediate attention was turned to the children. They were with him. *He wouldn't do anything stupid would he?* I sat talking to him until I had calmed him down a little and got him to put the children to bed. I was so concerned for them. They shouldn't be seeing all of this. They shouldn't be hearing it all either. I felt better then and went to bed thinking that tomorrow would be a long day.

I sat back on the bench, cigarette in one hand while biting my nails on the other. He seemed so irrational tonight. I was so scared for my babies. They were there with him in this awful state. What would he do? Would they suffer at all? I couldn't bear to think about what they were going through. Mind you, they were sleeping now surely. I calmed myself down a little with that thought.

I took a deep breath. This was all down to the fact that he hadn't got what he wanted. He had thrown his toys out of his pram, yet again, as part of a major tantrum because she said no. It made me question again his comments from the other day. Had he just been hopeful? Was what he had said she said all figments of his imagination?

I snubbed that last question out of my head as to think that would mean that I doubted whether she would have played the games that I had thought and I couldn't cope with that right now. To believe that would mean that I had a certain level of understanding towards her and I didn't want that at all. Not with that woman.

I sat there chewing my lip as it took some time to force those thoughts out of my head. I needed to concentrate on what was going on while my children were so far away. I shook my head and pulled my hands to my face, rubbing them down my cheeks. I huffed again. I hated it when he made things so hard for me.

His stupid little tantrum. She doesn't want me so I have nothing. You wanted me last week you idiot. I pictured me and her standing in a room both asking him to get back together and sort things out. I wondered who he would choose. I huffed a laugh and shook my head again. He would have no idea.

His audacity came back to bite me. It made the anger flare up inside again and I scrunched my eyes up tight as my body tensed. I jumped down off the bench and reached for another cigarette. He had asked me to go to him while she was still there. She hadn't even left yet. She hadn't quite walked out on him and he had already been calling in the back up lover. Unbelievable.

I thought back to my children. I pictured them in bed sleeping soundly, oblivious to their father's crying sobs of heartache in the other room. I hoped it was like that, I really did. I couldn't handle the thought of them trying to console him. He wouldn't, would he?

What did she have to do that for anyway? Why couldn't she have waited for the children to be gone? Why couldn't she have waited for one more day, that was all, one more bloody day? She had been so good to the children. She had had a go at him for not organising anything for them to do when it was Easter weekend. I smiled. I liked that. I'm glad she did it, though he wasn't when he told me. I smiled again. That was immediately followed by a frown as I realised that it meant that there was a part of her I liked. I shook my head as the words, 'I don't like anything about her, I can't like anything about her,' ran through my head at top speed.

I leant back against the tiles and inhaled deeply on my cigarette. I blew the smoke slowly out in the hope that that would increase the effect it had on me. I needed to de-stress and calm down as he had really got to me. It was hard having my children so far away.

'Should I have gone to him,' I thought.

'NO!!' I screamed back at myself.

Another smile crept on my face as I realised that yet again I was showing the signs of complete insanity. I looked around the kitchen. In just 24 hours, the children would be running through here, shouting and demanding anything and everything and I would be tearing my hair out with them. My smile faded as I realised that that wasn't what was happening now. I wanted them back safe and sound. I wanted them back now.

I looked up at the ceiling and then back down to the floor. I swung my legs back and forth like a child sitting waiting for their treats. I just wanted them back.

Within a few minutes of sitting quietly, the anger in me started raging once more. It was her fault. It was her fault I was going through this. Her and her I want you, no I don't, yes I do routine. Her telling him that she had wanted him back and spending the weekend with him and the children and then changing her mind, upsetting him in front of them.

'Was that what really happened though?' that little voice inside my head asked.

"AARRGGHH!!" I screamed loudly. I took a deep breath and inhaled the last drags that I could get out of my cigarette and threw it in the sink. I jumped off the bench and walked into the front room, throwing myself on the settee. I curled up in a ball and laid on the arm of the chair. I could feel the stress clawing at my insides as it tried to settle in for the night. I felt the soaring temperature of my body as the anger raised its flame that laughed as I grappled to suppress it.

I turned and hid my face in the settee as if I could block it all out that way. I closed my eyes tight and as I raised my hand to rub them I realised that my temperature was sky high. I immediately coughed and spluttered at that feeling and turned onto my back.

My heart rate slowed down and the laughing flame stopped laughing. The muscles in my body relaxed as the tiredness hit me hard. My legs turned to lead and my arms hung limply by my sides. I looked up at the ceiling. I was really feeling sorry for myself now.

I yawned and wiped the tear from my eye. I held my hand on my head in an attempt to stop it spinning. I closed my eyes and once again pictured my babies. My girls huddled together in their bed sleeping soundly and my Seb sprawled across the other bed, snoring his head off. I smiled. That is what they are doing right now.

I laid there with that image just in front of me. I dared not open my eyes, just in case it went away. Just in case.

24th March

He brought them back about 3 this afternoon. He looked terrible. They had had an argument in front of the children. I was fuming. It's bad enough when you are the parents arguing, let alone the girlfriend. He cried a little and said that he just wanted to be with me. He said he didn't want her and what she was offering and that he had chosen to walk away from her. I didn't believe it for a second. She had said she didn't want him more like. After listening to his pathetic story and letting the children do their Easter egg hunt that I had set up for them, I decided to wash Pheobe's hand again to check it out for myself. As soon as I looked at it I knew there was something wrong. It didn't look right, I couldn't explain why. I left him with the other two and took her to the walk in centre and waited for an hour and a half. The nurse cleaned it but advised me to take her to A & E to get an x-ray to check there was no glass in there. I did so straight away. It was packed. She happily played and I felt as if I had just wasted my day off. We went to see the doctor and then had an x ray. When we went back in we all got a shock as there on the film was this sparkling piece of glass. She would need an operation and I needed to stay overnight. I phoned mum straight away and she came down, collecting a few bits along the way. We were admitted to children's ward and I was petrified by the whole thing. Mum stayed with Pheobe while I shot home to get pyjamas and a change of clothes for her as well as my medicine. I broke down in tears on the drive home and smoked a cigarette in-between sobs. I arrived home and I was so angry with him. *How could he have left it? Why didn't he take her?* I collected my things, composed myself and drove back. Mum left a few minutes after and I laid down next to Pheobe just watching her sleep.

I lay in the hard hospital bed shivering. I looked over at Pheobe sleeping soundly in the bed next to me. Her little hand was bandaged with a paper clip beside it so they knew where the glass was. I could see it poking out from the sheets. She was so peaceful laying there and I couldn't take my eyes off of her. Every now and then I would get up and go over to her. I would adjust her covers or stroke her fingers. Sometimes I would bend down and gently kiss her forehead.

It was so horrible. The whole day and now I was here. It had all happened in a blur. It had gone so quickly and I felt ill from the speed at which it had gone downhill. I blinked back the tears as I watched her turn over. I heard the cries from the babies down the corridor. That must be even worse.

I hugged the pillow, pulling it underneath me. I curled up in a ball to try to get warmer and I dragged my coat over the top of the blankets. I was trembling beneath them. I couldn't stop myself shaking. I felt the tears begin to fall and was grateful for the warmth they brought with them.

I lay there, motionless, watching Pheobe and thinking about the day. This was all his fault. I had already told him that. I had felt a little bad when his face fell but at that point, and in some ways still at this point, I had blamed him. He was looking after her when she fell. He was with her. He hadn't been holding her hand. He hadn't taken her straight to hospital. I lowered my head as if the guilt was straining my neck with its weight. My eyes slowly closed, tired from the tears and I forced them back open.

'This could be my last night with my baby girl,' I had said to him through my tears.

'Don't be silly,' he had said as he tried to hug me.

I had pushed him away. I knew that it was a bit of an extreme thought but it was what I was truly feeling. I had directed my anger at him. I rolled my eyes as the guilty feeling washed over me once more. I pushed my hair back and sat up. I pulled the covers over me tighter, aware that I was still shaking.

He had sat there this afternoon and gave me the whole sob story. Sue had led him on. She had made him believe that there could be something between them again. She had then broke his heart again apparently. In the next breath, he had said, ' I don't want that life she is offering though, I want you.'

She didn't want you more like I had laughed. You cannot be crying your eyes out over one woman one minute and then saying you didn't want her and you want to be with someone else. I huffed as the words echoed through my head. I looked over at Pheobe. She had kicked her covers off again. How was she not cold?

As I looked at her I could feel the surge of love ploughing through me. That was our baby lying there. Our baby girl. Shouldn't I consider them in my decision? If he wanted to be there, shouldn't I let him? I shouldn't deny them a father. The tears fell as the confusion pricked at my eyes, like burning hot needles.

I sat up in my bed and stared straight ahead of me. There was only one person in the ward and she was up the other end. I just stared ahead and let the tears fall. I wiped the tears away with the edge of the sheet. I hauled my knees even closer to my chest and wrapped my arms around them tight so that I could barely breathe. I turned my head to the side so I could see Pheobe laying in the bed and I watched her as I cried.

A shadow formed to the side of me. There stood a nurse holding a cup of tea. He handed it to me and rubbed my back. 'Everything will be fine you know,' he said. 'It will all work out just fine.'

All I could manage was a faint smile and a very pathetic thank you. I held the tea close to me so the warmth radiated through the layers wrapped round me and into my skin. I let it seep into me, closing my eyes as I warmed up slowly. I leant back. It had to be alright. I could never ever survive without one of my babies, never. She had to be alright.

I hauled all the covers up so they untucked around the edges and I went and sat on the end of Pheobe's bed. I rearranged the blankets and huddled round my cup, wishing I could fit my whole body in that tiny space. The tears dried up and I stared at the most beautiful girl I had ever seen. My baby. I smiled a faint smile. I wished someone was there to hold me right then. Yet again I was facing this on my own.

Yet again, I was alone. Lost, confused, scared and alone.

'Everything will be fine you know,' I repeated the nurse's words in my head.

'Everything will be fine, you know.'

Will it? I asked myself. Will it really?

25th March

I had no sleep last night. I was worried about Pheobe, stressed beyond belief. I was freezing cold, the bed was rock hard, I felt so ill and all I could hear was these poor little babies crying. It was an awful experience and I felt for all the people who have to do that on a regular basis. There is no way I could cope with anything like they do.

Pheobe seemed pleased when Marc arrived at 7. I still didn't leave her. They explained again what they were going to do and put the numbing cream on her hand and feet. She skipped up and down and played in the playroom for the next couple of hours until we had to take her up. I took her in the room and held her while they put the IV in and knocked her out. The minute she went floppy in my arms, I fell to pieces. She was in such a vulnerable, fragile state and I was handing her over to complete strangers. It was so hard to walk away from her. I went downstairs and the tears just kept falling. I felt sick at the sight of food and could just about hold my cup of tea. Marc kept telling me it would be ok but I knew I wouldn't believe it until she was back safe with me. She came down after what seemed like an eternity and she was just crying for me. She wanted a cuddle, a drink and then a plaster. When we said no to the plaster she kicked off. She was hitting out and screaming and nothing I could do or say made her calm down. I had to lay her on the bed for fear I would drop her. I couldn't comfort her and it broke my heart all over again. I walked out and she stopped crying. I peered round the doorway and saw her cuddling her dad as he walked her round the ward looking at the pictures. I went downstairs broken hearted as she didn't need me. I had tea with sugar and spoke to mum. I went back and she still pushed me away. I felt lost. Without her wanting me, *what was I doing?* Nothing.

I bought her a teddy from the shop - a nurse teddy - and took it to her. She frowned at me when I gave it to her. I sat beside her and curled up, placing my head on her shoulder. She shrugged me off. I looked at her and asked if she was ok. She studied my red cheeks and wiped them with her hand. She laid her head on mine and then said "I want a cookie!"

I burst out laughing. She smiled a huge smile. I was allowed back again.

She played and watched TV all afternoon as we waited to be discharged. We didn't get out until 7 after I had said I had to go home regardless. The medicine appeared and we were free to go. She hugged everyone so tightly when she walked through the door. It was so sweet.

Mum left and I fell into bed so early after checking on her again and again. I watched her sleep for about half an hour. I cried a little as I watched her. I was so pleased to have her home. Thank goodness she is safe.

I laid in bed waiting to fall asleep. At least I was warm tonight. Today was over. Finally the nightmare was over. I felt awful. So tired. I had watched Pheobe sleep in her bed for quite some time tonight. She looked cosy and warm and comfy. Not like last night.

I shuddered as I pictured her in that hospital bed. I hugged the covers tighter under my chin to feel their security. I looked over my shoulder. It hadn't seemed to have affected him. Him laying there beside me, sound asleep already. He hadn't checked her over and over again and he seemed preoccupied in the hospital. He read his papers and sat about eating and drinking as if it was just a normal day. Had he just been strong for me?

I turned and laid on my back. I scanned the ceiling and watched the light from the car outside pass across it. Again, I had the urge to get up and check on her. I perched myself at the foot of her bed and stroked her feet. Her little toes curled as I did so and she turned over. In some ways I had hoped that she would wake up so I could have taken her in with me. I smiled. I had wanted her in her own bed for so long and now I missed the closeness like crazy.

I stroked her leg again and yawning went back to bed. I lay down next to my husband and sighed a huge sigh. I glanced at him again. I didn't want him there. This was my bed now. I huffed at myself and snuggled under the covers. He turned over and I gripped the covers tight and pulled against him. I hadn't missed that at all. I pulled harder and managed to free them again and wrapped them round me, lying on the ends.

My thoughts turned to Pheobe again. Back to that awful moment when she lay in my arms, floppy from the anaesthetic. I closed my eyes and bit back the tears. That moment will haunt me forever. I took a deep breath.

'She is home now - she is fine,' I told myself.

She had felt so lifeless. She was like a rag doll. Her head had rolled back and her arms and legs dangled over my lap and my arms. I had laid her down ever so gently. As they took her away, my legs buckled. I wanted her back. I watched the trolley move into the theatre and the doors closed behind it. My heart was thumping and I just sobbed on the chair, unable to stand. The nurse put her arms round me, just smiling as if to say she will be ok but knowing I wouldn't believe her if she bothered to actually say it.

That walk down the corridor seemed so lonely. So long. So slow and so empty. I couldn't see anyone around me, though I had seen so many people as I walked through. My body dragged behind me and it felt as if I was in pieces. I had looked up and seen Marc standing there waiting for me. Half of me had wanted to run to him so he could hold me and the other wanted him to vanish as I was still blaming him.

I turned over to face him. The tears were falling again now and I felt lost and alone once more. The powerful effect of a memory. Again, I watched him, part of me hoping he would wake up and console me and the other part wishing he wasn't even there.

I turned back over. I pictured Pheobe proudly showing her brother and sister and grandparents her bandage as she ran through the door. It was huge and looked like a boxing glove. She was quite proud of what she had done. She had showed off her princess certificate that she had received from the surgeons.

The tears slowed up a little and I took another deep breath. I hadn't meant to blame him for all of that. I hadn't meant to feel so bad about him. He had stayed with us and supported me. He had been great. He had said the right things and had calmed Pheobe down. He had taken over when he needed to and he had treated us well. I had been so harsh on him. I felt awful and I closed my eyes as that dawned on me. I turned back to him, 'Sorry' I whispered.

I lay on my back placing my arms behind my head and under the pillow. I was so tired; I didn't know how I could possibly be awake.

'I want a cookie!' said a little voice inside my head.

I giggled at that memory.

I breathed a huge sigh of relief. All that was just a memory. Just a memory now. It was all over and my baby girl was back where she belonged. I was so grateful.

Unforgivable lies!

26th March

What a day. Marcus stayed over last night and it was like he had never left. He didn't get up in the morning with the children and it was me doing all the work. I was the one that was exhausted from the lack of sleep with Pheobe in hospital and yet he was the one having the lie in. *How on earth does that work?* I was so tired walking around, making packed lunches and walking to school. Pheobe couldn't wait to show off her bandage. She took great pride in showing her teacher and the headmistress and her friends. She beamed when they all said "Wow!"

Sat around all day not really doing anything. The evening came and we went shopping and then he treated us to some Indian food while the children were in bed. It was me that cooked it though. And it was me that put the children to bed. And it was me that made the drinks.

Anyway, the weird things started happening while all that was going on. I heard my phone vibrating on the bench and was surprised when I saw there was a text message from her. Sue. She had asked if she could have his parents' number so she could find out about Marcus. I thought this was a bit strange, asked why she needed it first of all. I was confused as she hates him. She doesn't care about him anymore, she told him that. I couldn't make out what she would need it for. She wanted nothing more to do with him and said she hoped he would rot in hell. *Why was she now texting me?* She wouldn't text when Pheobe wanted her when she was in hospital despite him pleading with her to get in touch. I was still angry with her for that. She replied that she was waiting for news on Marcus and she was worried about him. I forwarded the number and asked what news she was waiting for but I got no reply. I hated that, I wanted to know. After dinner, Marcus came in from the kitchen looking very pale and turned the TV off. He said he had a problem. That somehow Sue had got hold of his parents' number and phoned there asking his dad if he was in hospital. Naturally, his dad replied that he had seen him this morning and that he was fine. I didn't understand the problem. I was confused.

Then it all became clear as he unravelled his lies to her. He had told Sue that he was in hospital. Him. He had told her that he had taken a turn for the worse in order to make her feel guilty. Now it had all backfired as she had found out it was a lie. Deep down I blamed myself for giving her the number and felt bad. That was over in a few seconds when the reality of what he had done hit me full force. The anger was amazing but all I could be was stunned. I didn't know what to say to him. I just looked at him and wondered how anyone could do such a thing to someone else.

I sent him out as I said I didn't want to even look at him right now. While he was out I tried to phone her but she didn't answer. I text her and said that I had done this as I thought we needed to talk. She needed to know he was a liar and that I had caught him out before. She replied that she hadn't heard the phone and asked if he was ok. She said that was all she cared about. *What? Really?* Even more confused now. I replied he was fine. I said I had calmed him down and stopped him doing something stupid. I said I would look after him. She had asked if he was with me and said she wasn't aware of any lies he had told me. I told her that he had lied and that he was here with me now.

The texting stopped.

He and I spoke a lot. He kept saying that she didn't want him and that she had hurt him and he was trying to get her attention and make her realise what she had done to him. I made sure he knew that I didn't understand. I didn't.

She called him and he ignored her. She kept ringing. I persuaded him to talk to her. I said it was wrong to leave her without an explanation even if it was a crap one. Eventually, he phoned her and they talked while sitting in my conservatory. She said she couldn't believe what he had done and didn't buy his bullshit explanation. Said it was the worst example of attention seeking she had ever come across. She seemed quite understanding in a way. Said she wouldn't tell anyone. Said she would cover for him. I was angry. *How can she react like that?* I thought she was feisty and would shout it from the rooftops like he said. Now she was sitting there saying she would keep quiet - oh my word, *what is this woman like?* She asked if he was with me. Said she didn't care. He admitted he was. They talked a little longer going over and over the same thing and then they hung up.

We went to bed and he held me. I didn't hold him back. I couldn't. I was numb from all of this and didn't know quite what I was feeling. The shivers were still there from realising that it was a year to the day that I had been going through the pain and heartache of discovering he was with her.

After an hour of laying there, both not sleeping, he remembered his phone was downstairs. He came rushing back up and began to get dressed. She had left messages saying that she was upset. He said she was crying and beside herself and he needed to help her. He went downstairs and tried to talk to her outside. I followed and said that he had made things worse with me by getting out of my bed to talk to her.

I listened to their conversation as they spoke in the study. She was angry that he was with me still. She asked how long he had been there. *Why he was still here at midnight, why was he here at all?* She said that he had broken her heart so many times tonight and she couldn't believe he had done it. He told her there was nothing going on between us. He said there wasn't a me and him. I stood by my cupboard and felt a mixture of emotions. I was pleased she was hurting. That is what she had done to me a year ago. That was where I was this time last year exactly! At the same time to hear him saying there was nothing between us hurt like crazy.

He kept ringing her back as she kept hanging up on him and rejecting his calls. At one point I sat on his lap to hear what was being said, the rest of the time I was standing beside the cupboard listening to his lies. They talked to almost 1 am. She eventually told him I had given her his parents' number. Thanks for that love! Cow. I must admit that I didn't care too much at that point. It didn't seem to matter too much to him either. He asked what I had said to her, told me I had probably made it worse but I just kept saying it was between me and her. Eventually he stopped questioning me and left it there.

We went back to bed but I couldn't sleep. I had this small smile on my face. I was happy she was upset.

Comeuppance is what they call it isn't it?

What the hell just happened?

The shock of the whole evening had just set in properly. I looked at the clock - 1.54am. I was still awake going over and over everything. It all seemed a blur and I was desperately trying to search for a logical explanation but I just couldn't find one. There wasn't one.

There were lots of emotions running riot for me tonight. They scrambled over each other and ran round in circles. They were like monsters crowding round their prey. I felt so weird. I was uptight and the adrenalin was pumping furiously around me. I didn't want to be in bed and I certainly didn't want to be next to him right now. I threw the covers back and marched downstairs.

I walked straight into the kitchen and lit a cigarette, slamming the drawer shut behind me. I walked over to the kitchen sink and leant forward on my elbows, fists clenched against my face, dragging my cheeks down as if that would relieve some of the tension.

I laughed and shook my head. Had I just dreamt all of that? Was I really living this?

I shook my head again and turned round to face the study door.

Heartbroken? She had said she was heartbroken. Why? You only have your heart broken by someone you love and she had said in no uncertain terms that she didn't love him. She had told him that weeks ago and said she hadn't loved him for months.

641

A smug smile crept on my face. She was hurt and confused and crying. Good. I was there a year ago exactly because of you, woman. You had done that to me. I had cried my eyes out that night when I found out they were together. The two of them. The picture of them going into that concert together came into my head and the smile faded.

I remembered the pain. It was awful and she was feeling that now. I felt so sorry for her at the same time. Was that why I had made him pick up the phone to her? She had rung and rung him over and over again. The phone had sat in between the two of us. Pick it up I had told him. She deserves an explanation. Part of me had needed to hear it as well. She must have been hurting so much the poor thing. I felt so bad for her. I shook my head again but more viciously this time. No way was I feeling that. No way could I feel sorry for her. No way could I feel bad that he had hurt the skank he left me for. Stop it woman, stop it now.

I turned back to the sink and looked out of the window.

'There is nothing going on between us,' he had said to her.

'You need to get it out of your head, baby, get it out of your head,' he had told her.

'We are not back together' he had stated clearly.

Technically, no we were not but I had thought that we might have been. Why couldn't he say that to her? I had been standing there listening. My mouth was hanging open catching flies. In my head I had had a massive sign above me with flurescent light bulbs which read 'stupid cow' and an arrow pointing down at me flashing away. I huffed at myself and shook my head again.

I inhaled deeply and turned back round to face the study again.

I pictured him sitting on that chair trying to console her. He was so worried about her, how touching. I had sat on his lap and tried to listen but she had been talking so fast that I hadn't understood a word she had said. Bloody accent didn't help either.

'Who do you think gave me your parents' number?' she had said.

He had looked straight at me at that question. I had shrugged my shoulders and smiled at him. I gave it and I didn't care. I didn't care that she was upset and crying on the phone to him. I didn't care that his lies had finally caught up with him. I didn't care. He didn't seem to either. He just stared at me.

He told her he wasn't with me. Liar.

He had said he wasn't sleeping here. Liar.

He had said our relationship wasn't like that. Liar.

Oh so many lies. How easy they tripped off his tongue. I turned back round to face the window again and dropped my cigarette in the sink. With straight arms I leant on the sink, rocking slightly. I looked up in the air and took a deep breath.

How could he have said he was in hospital? Why? To make her feel bad he had said. That was a bit of a long way to go to make her feel guilty about dumping him. That wasn't the way to get her back was it? She had hardly come running to hold his hand had she? I hated him for what he had done. Stooped so low.

I took another deep breath. I walked over to the kitchen door. I couldn't go back up to him. I just couldn't. I took another cigarette out and walked back to the sink.

I chewed the inside of my cheek.

I had caused the whole thing. I had been saying I would blow his world apart one day and I had. I smiled. I smiled and inhaled deeply looking into the distance like you see people doing in films. I giggled.

If I had ignored her text, none of this would have come out. If I had told him she had text me, none of this would have come out. If I hadn't forwarded the number, none of this would have come out. I smiled again.

Did it make me wicked that I had enjoyed every second of that? Did it mean I was evil and was really the psycho ex wife that I had tried so hard not to be?

No, he had done it all. He had told the lies. He had made up such an awful story. He was the one that had hurt her.

I turned back towards the study door.

'You have broken my heart so many times tonight,' she had said.

Mine wasn't much better when you stole my husband love, I retorted in my head.

I smiled. I hung my head and smiled.

I turned back round to face the window. My mood was lighter again now.

I looked over at my phone that was on the bench. I flicked it open and read her text messages again. 'Is he with you now?' I closed the phone. I had been honest and truthful the whole time. It was not my fault I was the only one with the knowledge.

I pictured her in my head. Sobbing on the phone to him. Asking how he could do that to her. Asking him why. A year ago it was the reverse. A year ago to the day. A shiver ran down my spine as I thought that again.

I climbed back up the stairs, picturing her crying the whole time. She was hurting and I was quite pleased. I had finally had my revenge. I could do a lot more if I wanted to but for now I was happy to have done that. I was happy to have helped 'break her heart so many times tonight.'

As I laid down to finally get some sleep, a smug smile sat on my face. I'm sure it wouldn't have left me all night.

27th March

Marc's birthday. I felt a little bad that I hadn't bought him anything but then I was in the mind of *why should I?* I wasn't going to get him anything from the children as he hadn't for my birthday; my mum had to do it. Also I know he had got me the flowers but I didn't know what to get and I didn't have the time or the money to go shopping. I felt mean at first. But I just couldn't do it.

It was weird having him here on his birthday and remembering what a hard time I was having exactly a year ago. If you had told me then that this year was going to be the hardest thing I have ever had to get through I would never have believed you. It is a good job we can't see into the future in circumstances like these.

The children all went to school and me and him spent the morning chatting. It was tough going. She had text him again to say that she still couldn't believe what he had put her through and I could see how bad he felt. The feelings for her were so apparent. He still thinks the world of her. It hurt still. I would have thought I would have been used to it by now.

He left mid morning to go to his mums. He was upset as we had been discussing us getting back together and I had said that I didn't think we should keep talking about it as if it was certain to happen. He didn't like it.

I kept thinking back to last year and how I had had to go to work that morning as if nothing had happened and how I had locked myself in the office and not come out. It had been so hard talking to him after the night before. That was when our marriage ended and he no longer needed me and now he was here asking me to take him back.

I spent the day writing and wandering around the house trying to get my head round the situation. Trying to think about what I was going to do and at the same time trying to block it out of my head. It was a mixed day. Up and down the white knuckle ride.

He came back and said that the scan tomorrow had been cancelled and I was dubious about him telling the truth. *Was he just trying to put me off going? Was he intending to cancel the weekend? Would he go back to try to make amends with her?*

After a brief chat with mum I decided to go anyway and I fed the children, packed the bag and planned the weekend with a hint of excitement. A couple of times I stopped what I was doing and hovered hearing that little voice in my head saying "What are you doing?"

I left with him feeling a little excited, a little relieved of a break from reality and a little apprehensive. Sue had told Tobias how he had lied about being so ill and all he spoke about on the journey was what to say and how stupid he felt. There didn't seem to be a sorry bit about the conversation. He was just scared. The hotel room was amazing and tranquil and I relaxed in the bath straight away while he spoke to Tobias, handing out more lies to back up his poor me story. We ordered room service and chilled out in bed watching the TV. Would love a TV in my room - future requirement I think.

I had found it so hard to look at him this morning. He hadn't got up again for the children and again didn't take them to school with me. I did it all. I was exhausted too. I had been through it all yesterday too.

It didn't dawn on me at first that it was his birthday. I hadn't remembered until late when I sent the children up to wish him a happy one. I didn't. It felt too hypocritical to say that, I didn't wish he was happy.

We talked all morning. He had tried to explain his behaviour towards her. He had been honest about when she was texting him too. He told me each time. She just kept saying she didn't understand why he did that. Why he would have hurt her. Why he lied so awfully and took everything to the extreme.

No one would understand, not her, not me, not anyone. There was no point in trying. I listened to him and his pathetic ways. All the time I was thinking how I was going to go away with this man. I wanted so much to be at that scan tomorrow, I would have done anything. But, to be alone with a man like this, after his lies last night, I didn't know if I could do it.

His voice was so pathetic and every now and then he would cry. I pictured myself on this day last year. I had shut myself away in the office at work and cried. I had felt so numb. I had felt awful. I had just sat there and avoided everyone. I couldn't take everything in. It had been so hard. I just kept looking at him thinking, you did that to me, you.

I had had discussions with my mum about us getting back together. She said she didn't like it but that she would support me as I had the children to think about and of course the fact I still loved him. Did I still love him? I had never questioned that more. I think I did. I just didn't know for sure.

How could I go away for the weekend with him, to talk about making a go of our marriage and trying again? How could I?

I felt so low. I listened to him going on about poor him and poor Sue and I wanted to scream at him. Did he worry this much about me when he left me last year? No.

I looked straight at him and it dawned on me. He was still so in love with her. He adored her. He was so worried that he had lost her completely because of what he had done. He didn't think they could even be friends now and he was so upset and didn't know how he could survive without her in his life. I remembered that pain so well. It was him I had felt all that for. It was him I didn't think I could survive without.

Could I go away with him knowing he was still madly in love with her and was just using me still? I know he had been in love with her the whole year. I had been with him the whole time and I accepted that. Him coming home made it all different. I wasn't sure I could be with a man who really loved someone else as much as he loved her. Of course I couldn't.

I bowed my head and asked him to leave. He seemed shocked by it all and asked what I meant by that. I said I didn't know if I could go away with him now and I just needed some time alone to think about it. I said I didn't know if I could take him back. He sat and cried and then left to go to his mums.

I sat in silence for ages. I didn't know what to think or feel. I was confused. I was lost and I was alone. The loneliness so apparent again. I needed someone to turn to and yet I needed to be alone. So confusing.

I wandered round the house in a daze asking myself the same questions over and over again and every time I came back to the fact that he still loved her and therefore couldn't possibly want me. I fell onto the settee and cried. I wasn't sure whether I was crying for the fact that I would never have him completely if I had him back in my life or whether the tears were out of the confusion and stress I was feeling trying to make a decision.

I phoned mum and had a lengthy discussion. I wanted her to make a decision for me. I wanted her to say I should or shouldn't go so I didn't have to worry anymore. We talked for a while and I decided I would regret not going more than I would going.

He was overjoyed when he came back but I didn't have the same level of enthusiasm. There were hints of excitement and part of me was looking forward to it, but every now and then the voice in my head would say 'What the hell are you doing?' and I had stopped dead in my tracks with second thoughts.

The cab ride to the station was hard. The train journey was harder. He kept going on and on about us working it out and how happy we would be. He would then switch the conversation back to her, wondered what she was doing and spoke about what he would say to Tobias when he rang. I just stared out of the window the whole time.

Inside the hotel room everything was peaceful. There was no reminder of what had happened. I had the hottest bath I could get into and I ignored the lies he was telling Tobias on the phone. Nothing was going to spoil this. I was going to spend my last weekend with my husband, pretending everything was normal. My last weekend. Those words echoed.

The scan was cancelled. We were going into London tomorrow. He promised to spoil me. I just wanted his love for now. That was all. But she had that didn't she.

I curled up in bed beside him after dinner. We watched TV and spoke about nothing in particular. He looked me straight in the eye and told me he loved me. He said he had never really wanted her. He said he needed me to live. My heart melted. I had wanted to hear that for so long. My head was screaming at me to not be so stupid and that it was all lies but I blocked it all out as he kissed me.

I succumbed to my heart and the feelings of wanting to be loved again. I was weak and he played on it as he knew me. We made love and as I laid there in his arms I thought that it all would work. She was out of the picture now. She was gone. With a bit of luck she would never speak to him again and I would be the love of his life. I would have my family back again.

As I lay in his arms, feeling so relaxed and happy, I dared to picture a future. We would sort out his financial problems. We would move house again. We would go out more as a couple. We would go on holiday. We would have more breaks like this.

I dared to dream that all those things would come true. I dared to believe, for that would bring happiness.

Could I go back?

28th March 2008

Woke up wondering where I was. Seb had text me and the phone kept vibrating. Got up, got ready and went out. Sat on a number 15 bus to London. Saw the tower of London which I had never seen before and saw his office across the river. Hit Oxford Street in the rain and headed for Selfridges. Never been there before either and easily got lost. Everything was so expensive. He didn't seem to care what the price tag was. He just bought what he liked. Spent around £200 on a jumper, t - shirt and nose trimmer! Wandered round the store looking at all the different things and he bought me a pair of designer shoes for a bargain £19. I was very happy. Went in and out other shops and talked the whole time about what had happened and also about her. She sent him a dodgy message thanking him for telling her his scan had been cancelled. *Huh?* You said you didn't want to talk to him again. *Why would he tell you?* I was getting quite agitated with her getting in touch every now and then as it knocked him for six. He treated me to a new outfit and bikini and we headed back. Tired and curled up on the front seat of the DLR I felt happy. Just he and I makes such a difference. No stress. No children. No housework. No worries. We were fine.

Back at the hotel we had an hour in the sauna and steam room and also a massage. We relaxed on hot chairs and took ice showers. It was fun. There was no one else in the rooms so we talked the whole time. We spoke about her. Each time he referred back to her I ticked the list in my head. Dozens of times. Can't really want me then so I was right. I was having a conversation in my head at the same time and bits of what I was saying in my head were being said out loud.

Got ready and went to O2. The old Millennium dome. Looked so different to how it was. Restaurants, bars and a cinema all inside. Strange atmosphere though. Lots of young people.

Went to build a burger place. Sat there eating away. She text him asking what he was doing. He never said he was with me. That hurt even though I could kind of understand. We spoke about the last year. Not sure how it came up. That's when the memories really hit home. I thought about the date and realised that at this point last year I was holding the phone curled up on the settee wanting him to call. I had cried so much and the pain was so intense. The memory of the pain hit me and I nearly choked on my food. I looked at him and remembered. I told him that he hadn't wanted me then. How he had left me in such a mess. How I had tears permanently falling and my chest had felt like it was going to explode. He just said he was sorry. I looked at him and I had to bite back the tears as I remembered everything that had happened. "I thought you would come home," I said. "But you didn't."

He just said sorry. That memory was a powerful one. Yesterday I had dared to dream we could be together again. Today had been so nice and we were getting on great and enjoying each others company, but in that split second the heartache came back. I could see myself that night, I was looking down on this woman who was in so much pain and I could still feel it. He had done that. He had left me like that. He hadn't cared. He had just gone. I don't think I can forgive him. I certainly can't forget. It still seems so real. It is so clear in my head. He did it, him.

Thoughts were then turned to the night I found out about her and we discussed the pain of that too. She had been with him that night. She had heard me crying. She had heard me sobbing and shouting down the phone at him. She had stayed with him anyway. Said she didn't care and had laughed at how pathetic I was. *How could she do that? How could she have stayed?* He must have talked to her about it. He knew I was hurting that much but he still continued to want her. He had ignored that. He had ignored my suffering. He had ignored me loving him. He had gone off and stayed away anyway. *How could he?*

I couldn't eat anymore as I was starting to feel sick. Memories are so powerful. They can switch the mind so quickly. I'm not sure how I love this man. I do. In some way. Maybe not enough. I know I can't picture him with anyone else without feeling as if I am stabbing myself in the chest and I know he says the same thing about me. Yet, I was right the first time I made the decision. I can't take the chance - I don't want to take the chance. I can't decide to try again and risk that pain re-entering my life. Sorry doesn't heal wounds; it's just a plaster to cover them.

Tomorrow I will go back to the children. Back to my house. Back to my life. The one I have spent so long rebuilding after it was shattered into tiny shards of glass. Tiny pieces that I am painstakingly sticking back together, though there are still so many left. I have become a different person. A stronger person. A happier person and in a strange, twisted way I have him and her to thank. I am going back alone. Not with him.

If I ask myself whether I have made the right choice. The only answer I can give is at this point in my life, yes I have. Ask me that same question at some point in the future; the answer just might be different.

It was strange waking up. A weird place. A weird bed. A weird noise. A weird feeling. Like I had been dreaming. I turned to face him. He was awake. He said good morning and kissed me on the nose like he had done so many years ago. I forced a smile.

I had stood in the shower, not moving. I had been dreaming. I had dreamt we had been back together. I had dreamt we had picked up from a better point than we had left. It wasn't real. None of this was. None of it was real.

The trip to London was nice. I had never spent much time there and I realised that I had not seen so much of it. Parts of it were brand new to me.

'There is my office,' he had said pointing across the river. I looked over. All I could see was a large image of her sitting at a desk, looking at a laptop. Other images of her flashed before me. Her in her pink scarf in the original photo, her at the Christmas do, her in the holiday pictures with my children, her on the front screen of his phone where his children used to be, her sitting in the car when I had approached her and her on Boxing day. I turned away and smiled at him.

He spent so much money that afternoon. We had got lost in Selfridges. I was gob smacked by the size of the store and all the different things in it with their amazing price tags. This world was so unknown to me and will probably always be.

The texts from her interfered with our day. Would she ever be gone? She was annoyed he hadn't told her about his scan being cancelled. Whatever. I didn't care; this was supposed to be about me not her I huffed. His sister text too asking about his scan. Why hadn't he told everyone? Was he telling them it had been cancelled? The questions again.

The sauna and steam room was great and my massage was even better. I felt so relaxed and I happily got ready in my new outfit he had bought me. I looked at myself in the mirror. He had chosen it for me. Was it something she usually wore? What kind of question was that to ask myself?

Eating dinner, she text him again. I had wanted him to say he was with me. He didn't. I understood why, a little anyway. It felt wrong though. The whole day had taken a turn. From the time I got up, it had all felt so wrong.

The memories were the straw that broke the camels back. They were the deciding factor. I had had enough of her and her texts, I had had enough of her name being mentioned hundreds of times, and I had had enough of her being on his mind the whole time. I could live with bits of that, if I had really wanted to. If I really loved him as much as I thought, I would get past that because I would still want us to be together. I didn't want to get over it though. I didn't want to come to terms with it.

My mind was racing the whole time he was talking. We sat in the build a burger bar. He had already said he had been to one with her before. That had hurt. I began to play with my food as my thoughts straightened out.

I looked at him solemnly. I couldn't forgive this man before me. I couldn't forget what he had done. I looked at him. I could see his mouth moving but there was no sound. There was no voice and no words, just his face moving. When he nodded, I nodded, when he smiled, I smiled. Still no sound. I looked around the room. There were lots of people sitting round the tables. I could see the faces laughing and their mouths moving. I could see feet walking on the tiles and I could see hands drumming on the tables. No sound at all. Just silence, this eerie, weird silence.

I looked towards the other side of the room and the people vanished. There was my front room. There was my settee. There was this pathetic woman crying with the pain and agony of a broken heart as she laid waiting for her husband to call. She was holding the phone in her hand and her cheeks were bright red. Everything around her was black and so was the hole that had taken up her chest. I could see right through it. Her heart and her soul had been removed by a man she had loved.

Suddenly I was gasping for breath. I was coughing and spluttering as a wave of immense pain coursed through my body in a split second. I dropped my fork on the floor and spat the food in a napkin. The sound was suddenly back on.

'Are you ok babe?' he had asked.

"You didn't come back," I replied. "I waited for you," I said pointing towards the scene that was still playing to me in the corner, "you didn't come back."

He glanced over his shoulder and then stared back at me blankly. He reached out and held my hand. "I made a mistake that I regret so much."

"You didn't want me. You didn't love me. You left me." I said meekly.

The tears began to bite at my eyes. I looked over at the image that was still there in my mind. It was so clear to me. The tears faded. The pain stopped running through me.

I looked at him again. He was saying he was sorry, so, so sorry. He was saying he didn't meant to hurt me and that he didn't know what he wanted at that time. He was saying again that she was a mistake. It was all a mistake and he wanted to prove it to me.

I looked once more at the image in front of me. I looked once more at the crying, desperate woman who had been broken. Broken.

I took a deep breath as it faded. That wasn't me. That was not who I was now. This was me and this me knew what she wanted. She didn't want to become that woman again and she would if she took him back. She would if she took that chance.

I took another deep breath and pushed my food away. I looked up at him.

"I want to go now," I said. "Take me back."

My mind was clear as I walked back. I knew I had made a decision. I couldn't take that chance. I couldn't allow the pain to be brought back into my life. I wasn't the same person anymore. I was stronger now and I was running my own life. Look how far I had come. Look at me now. I was different. I didn't need to accept situations. I wanted total devotion and a man in love with Sue wouldn't be able to give me what I wanted.

He wouldn't be able to give me anything I wanted. He couldn't give me a trusting relationship. He couldn't give me security, emotional or financial. He couldn't give me a fantastic father for my children. He couldn't give me the independence I needed to thrive. He couldn't give me love. Therefore, he couldn't give me happiness.

He had said sorry and I had forgiven him I suppose. But not entirely. Not completely. I certainly hadn't forgotten. I would never.

I held my head high as I walked out of the arena to the cab. I held it high and a smile spread across my face. I knew the answer. I knew what I wanted. I knew where I needed to be. At home with my babies. At home by myself. At home finishing the final touches to my life. My life as me. Not Marcus's wife. Not the mother of Marcus's children. As me. My life.

I looked at him in the hotel room.

'I don't want to be your wife anymore,' I said. 'I don't want any of this anymore as it isn't who I am anymore.'

He looked at me shocked.

'I'm not saying I don't love you because that would be a lie. I do love you. I just don't think I love you enough.'

He still stared at me. He walked over and he kissed me.

'One more night,' he said.

'Then it's goodbye and its friends.' I said.

'Its friends' he replied.

Did those words get said out loud? I didn't know.

As we made love that night, the feelings were intense. It was the last time we would do this. It was the last time we would be lovers. It was like we both put in that extra bit of effort. We both tried to show what love was left. We poured it out of us as much as we could. The passion faded as the night wore on, like I was actually letting go. I didn't need this anymore. I didn't need him and I finally knew it.

There was a sense of uncertainty I don't deny. I asked myself if I was making the right decision. I felt the fear. I felt the anguish. I also felt the freedom. I also felt the security in myself and the knowledge that I was so much stronger without him.

I had been so petrified of silence and yet it was that that had made me listen to myself. I had hated my thoughts haunting me. I had hated the images that had appeared in front of me and I hated the fact that I couldn't forget them. I hated that I remembered every inch of pain that had wracked my body all those days and nights. I had hated the clarity of every memory that I had of those months I had spent longing for him to come back. And yet, it was exactly those things that had helped me in the end.

I was still on my journey to discover the real me and I was going to finish it. I would return to it tomorrow. I would go back to the reality of my life tomorrow. I would return to being me tomorrow.

The strength was in me to carry on. The strength was in me to continue to change myself for the better, to continue down the path that I had been forced to take. I had taken charge of my life. I had picked myself up. I had repaired most of the damage he had done. I had pieced myself back together, painstakingly rebuilding the shattered woman that had been left behind. I had mended her broken heart and

I had addressed the wrongs in her life and I had changed it all. I had become a different person, I had become me. I had Sue to thank for that. If she hadn't come into his life, he wouldn't have gone out of mine and I wouldn't have altered things so drastically. She had done this for me.

Sue..... thank you.

future questions

Would I break down eventually? Would I succumb to the temptation of being a family again? Would I listen to him in the future and change my mind? Would I wake up tomorrow and feel completely different? Would he prove he really loves me and rebuild the trust between us? Would I be renewing my vows in twelve months time and making a fresh start with my husband? Would I be nursing him when the cancer grips hold completely? Would I be a widow at some point in the near future?

Who knows? You never can tell the difference a year will make.

Lightning Source UK Ltd.
Milton Keynes UK
04 November 2009

145777UK00001B/1/P